IRISH TIGER

ALSO BY ANDREW M. GREELEY

BISHOP BLACKIE RYAN MYSTERIES

**The Bishop and the Missing L Train
The Bishop and the Beggar Girl of St. Germain
The Bishop in the West Wing
The Bishop Goes to The University
The Bishop at the Lake**

NUALA ANNE McGRAIL NOVELS

Irish Gold	**Irish Love**
Irish Lace	**Irish Stew!**
Irish Whiskey	**Irish Cream**
Irish Mist	**Irish Crystal**
Irish Eyes	**Irish Linen**

THE O'MALLEYS IN THE TWENTIETH CENTURY

A Midwinter's Tale	**September Song**
Younger Than Springtime	**Second Spring**
A Christmas Wedding	**Golden Years**

**All About Women
Angel Fire
Angel Light
Contract with an Angel
Faithful Attraction
The Final Planet**

Furthermore!: Memories of a Parish Priest
God Game
Jesus: A Meditation on His Stories and His
Relationships with Women
Star Bright!
Summer at the Lake
White Smoke
Sacred Visions (editor with Michael Cassutt)
The Book of Love (editor with Mary G. Durkin)
Emerald Magic (editor)

IRISH TIGER

A Nuala Anne McGrail Novel

ANDREW M. GREELEY

**Doubleday Large Print
Home Library Edition**

A TOM DOHERTY ASSOCIATES BOOK
NEW YORK

This Large Print Book carries the Seal of Approval of N.A.V.H.

— Cast of Characters —

NUALA ANNE MCGRAIL (née Moire Phioulaigh Ain Mac Griel),
singer, accountant, fey, Irish Tiger
DERMOT MICHAEL COYNE, husband to Nuala Anne

Their children
MARY ANNE (Nelliecoyne), age eight
MICHEAL DIRMUID (the Mick), age six and a half
SOCRA MARIE, age five
JOSEF PORRIG, age two and a half

Their hounds
FIONA
MAEVE

Cops
MIKE CASEY
JOHN CULHANE

TERRY GLEN
NIKOS MASHEK

Clerics
CARDINAL SEAN CRONIN
COADJUTOR ARCHBISHOP JOHN BLACKWOOD RYAN
REV. GEORGE COYNE ("Prester George"), brother to Dermot Michael

Clients
JOHN PATRICK DONLAN
MARIA ANGELICA CONNORS

Persons of interest
LOUIS GARNER, classmate to John Patrick
JOSEPH MCMAHON, staff to John Patrick
CONGRESSMAN STERLING SILVER STAFFORD, onetime suitor to Maria Angelica
BROTHERS SABATTINI, brothers to Maria Angelica

Friend (and friend of friends)
DOMINIC

IRISH TIGER

— Prologue —

(Excerpts from the columns of the
Chicago Herald)

Observed by Eyes and Ears
of Chicago

The Eyes observed two of Chicago's most beautiful of beautiful people huddling at Ambria. John Donlan, CEO of Donlan Assets Management, and Maria A. Connors, CEO of Elegant Homes (and cover girl in a recent issue of *Chicago Market*). Were the handsome couple discussing corporate mergers or perhaps more intimate mergers?

. . .

The Ears hear that talk of a romance between John Donlan (Donlan Assets Management) and the gorgeous Maria Angelica Connors (Elegant Homes) reported a couple of weeks ago have caused a tsunami. In both families. "If he wants a fling with a woman like her only two years after his wife died, that's up to him. But he can't expect us to accept her," said an angry Donlan woman.

Eyes and Ears on Channel 3

ANCHORPERSON: What's happening in the controversial marriage of John Donlan and Maria Angelica Connors?

EYES AND EARS: It looks like it's not happening. The Donlans have their skirts in a twist because Donlan Assets Management has invested a ton of money in Elegant Homes. Ears hears that none of the Donlans will be in the wedding party or come to the ceremony in St. Frederick's Church. One of their nicer words they use for the gorgeous Ms. Connors is "shameless gold digger."

ANCHORPERSON: They're both grandparents aren't they?

EYES AND EARS: That's part of the problem.

Channel 3 News on Saturday Night

ANCHORPERSON: There were Catholic fireworks at St. Frederick's Church this afternoon. Father Michael Hennessy, the pastor of St. Freddy's canceled the Gold Coast wedding of John Patrick Donlan to Maria Connors. In a surprise announcement just before the service began, the pastor informed the stunned congregation that he had evidence that there had been a previous marriage of Ms. Connors in a Catholic church. Our Mary Alice Quinn was there.

QUINN: That's right, Clarice. It was supposed to be the most fashionable wedding in the autumn season here in the marvelous old German church. Father Hennessy spoiled all the fun.

(Interior shot of priest in a high German-style pulpit overlooking the congregation. Bride is radiant in a light blue gown.)

HENNESSY (*a smart and overweight young punk in a biretta*): I'm afraid that the bride has not been completely honest with the church. She was married at St. Lawrence parish in Oakdale, Illinois, by Father Thomas Hartnett while she was still a student at a non-Catholic university. This marriage was before her alleged marriage to her late husband, in which she lived in sin for many years. Her attempt to marry again here today makes her liable of the punishment of canon law.

(Quick shot of the shocked bride and groom. Cries of outrage from the congregation.)

QUINN: Ms. Connors made a statement as the bridal party left the church.

(Dissolve to exterior shot of bride and groom emerging from church, she wearing a mink coat over her gown. Both are ashen. Media swarm around them with microphones.)

MEDIA: Maria Angelica, why didn't you tell the priest about your prior marriage?

MEDIA: Did she tell you about it, John?

MS. CONNORS (*stony-faced but in control*): My only previous marriage was to my late husband, Peter James Connors, God be good to him. We will talk to our attorneys to seek relief from this defamation . . . Now if you'll excuse us we have a wedding dinner to attend.

QUINN: A young woman, presumably from the groom's family who would not give her name, had a different view.

YOUNG WOMAN: She's a whore! Serves Jack Donlan right!

QUINN: So there you have it, Clarice, a controversial wedding becomes a controversial banned wedding. We haven't heard the end of this story. The next scene will probably be in a courtroom.

ANCHORPERSON: A modern Romeo and Juliet in Old Town, Mary Alice?

QUINN: Romeo and Juliet as grandparents, Clarice. Very attractive grandparents.

Channel 3 5:00 News on Sunday Night

ANCHORPERSON: The Catholic church has apparently lifted the ban on the marriage of two high-powered Chicago executives. Our Mary Alice Quinn is at Holy Name Cathedral interviewing Coadjutor Archbishop John B. Ryan.

(Cut to steps of cathedral. Blackie does not look like a coadjutor archbishop. He is wearing black jeans and a Chicago Bears jacket.)

QUINN: That's right, Clarice. Archbishop Ryan has just told me that Sean Cardinal Cronin has administered the sacrament of matrimony to John Donlan and Maria Angelica Connors in a private ceremony in the cathedral. And the cardinal is now having supper with them in the rectory. How can he do that?

BLACKIE (*blinks behind thick glasses*): As we all know, Mary Alice, a cardinal prince of the Catholic church can do just about anything he wants. In this case he determined that there was indeed no evidence to support the claim of a prior marriage. Therefore he apologized to the couple and offered to bless their marriage which the bride and groom administer to one another in a Catholic church. They accepted the offer, if I may say so, with considerable joy.

QUINN: Is that a rebuke to Father Hennessy?

BLACKIE (*sighs loudly*): One could suggest that due diligence in such matters might have led one to determine whether there is or ever was a parish named after St. Lawrence anywhere near Oakdale, Illinois, or whether there was in the last four decades a priest in the Rockford Diocese named Thomas Hartnett. It might have required as much as two minutes to make such a determination.

Channel 3 5:00 News on Monday

ANCHORPERSON: The controversy about the wedding between Chicago tycoons John Donlan and Maria A. Connors continues, as one would expect these days in the courts. Our Mary Alice Quinn has been following the story.

(Cut to Daley Center Plaza.)

QUINN: Clarice, Tony Cuneen, the husband of Evie Donlan, filed a suit this afternoon asking that he be appointed conservator of the trust funds for his wife and her two sisters. The funds which are currently under the control of Donlan Assets Management. He also asked the court's authority to remove all stock in Elegant Homes Inc. from these trust funds.

CUNEEN (*combative and nervous*): My wife and my sisters-in-law are anxious that the trusts which will provide college tuition money for their children not be diverted to purposes which might endanger their solvency. None of us in the family have any idea of how the monies in the three trusts are invested. We would like to have some accountability, especially in view of the current controversies in the family.

EVIE: We don't want that strumpet to have any control over our children's future. We don't want her near any of them. She might be contagious.

QUINN: So, Clarice, the fight gets dirtier. No comments on the suit yet from either Donlan Assets Management or Elegant Homes Inc. Back to you, Clarice.

Channel 3 5:00 News on Tuesday

ANCHORPERSON: Another chapter tonight in the battle of the Donlans and the Connors. Our Mary Alice Quinn is in the offices of Meyer, Meier, Major, and Suarez.

QUINN: Jaime Suarez, who is acting for John Patrick Donlan, made a brief announcement this afternoon.

SUAREZ (*tall and handsome, thick black hair edged with grey*): I'm Jimmy Suarez and am acting today as Mr. John Patrick Donlan's attorney. I feel called upon to make a statement with regard to the suit filed yesterday against Mr. Donlan by his son-in-law. He is, as you might suspect, on his honeymoon and in any case would not want to make any public comment. As to the three trust funds for his daughters.

Each of them received certified quarterly statements since reaching their majority which list both the contents of the funds and the gains and losses and provide charts of the net gains since the funds began. If they can find any copies of these reports, they will note that consistently over the last two decades, the trusts have grown at a rate exceeding the Dow. They will also note that there is not and never has been any admixture of the common stock of Elegant Homes Inc. in their trusts. I have sent copies of the quarterly reports for the last four years to Mr. Cuneen's office. But that there may be no confusion in the future, Mr. Donlan has ordered me to hand the trusts over to the appropriate officials at the Chase Bank. We will move tomorrow to quash the suit.

QUINN: What about the mixing of Elegant stock with the trust funds?

SUAREZ (*charming smile*): That will be a matter for Mr. Cuneen to discuss with the trustees at Chase. I should probably say that anyone who has studied Mr. Donlan's methods knows that he has several different investment products, the most famous of which is his Frodo Fund. He shifts investments in and out of that fund with great care. Other securities that he might acquire go into other products. On some occasions he also acquires other securities which he invests in his other products. Some time ago he acquired stock in Elegant Homes for one of his real estate funds. A review of *The Wall Street Journal* pages of the last several months would show ELG, as it is called, has done very well. Whether it will ever be added to the securities in Frodo is an open question. I would add by the way that as someone who was involved in the acquisition of ELG stock I can testify that he made the decision to acquire those securities before he met Ms. Connors.

QUINN: Do you think, Jimmy, that your clients have been defamed?

SUAREZ: In my opinion they certainly have. We have yet to decide whether to seek relief.

— Dermot —

THE COUPLE walking up the stairs to our house on Sheffield Avenue reminded me of Lladro statues— handsome, perfectly shaped, well dressed, flawless. And so fragile that a sweep of my hand might shatter them. A Lexus limo waited for them in front of the house. At the wheel sat Sergeant Gabrielle Lopez, of the Chicago Police Department, in her off-hours with Reliable Security. If Gaby was on the job, then someone thought the couple was in danger. The dark sky glowered at all of us who were stupid enough to be in Chicago after the middle of November.

"Jack Donlan," said the man, poised, urbane, wavy black hair with just a touch of white—an ad for a men's magazine of a decade and a half ago. "My wife, Maria."

"Archbishop Ryan sent us," said the tall, slim woman in a mink coat. "He said you didn't want nobody that nobody sent."

The light of an imp flashed quickly across her face as she repeated the old Chicago political cliché.

"Dermot Coyne," I said shaking hands. "Come in, as my good wife would say, before you catch your death of cold."

It was my good wife they wanted to see, the legendary singer and puzzle solver, and not her loyal and brave spear-carrier.

Earlier as I had entered our master bedroom and discovered herself in red and green lace lingerie in honor of the coming holidays, I gulped as I always do when I see her, especially if she is partially dressed.

"Well, didn't I tell you that they would call us?"

I had been running the dogs and my two older children at the dog park. Even the elderly Fiona had better wind than I did. They had bounded up the stairs to the second-floor entrance and down to the playroom on the ground floor where my niece and our nanny, Ellie, would preside over them and their two smaller siblings.

"Who would call us?" I demanded putting my hand on her bare shoulder.

"Och, Dermot Michael Coyne, give over," she replied, leaning against me. "We have business to do. The lollygagging can come later."

"Promise?"

"If I don't, it doesn't matter, does it?" She returned to arranging her long and formidable black hair in a bun on the top of her head. She was putting on her business mode. "And meself telling you that them poor folks would call us and I not needing any more of me hormones chasing around in me bloodstream."

"What poor folks?"

She smelled of soap and perfume and promise. I didn't remove my hand from her shoulder, but I refrained from attempting further progress. My wife is easy to seduce, but I had grown skilled through our years together at reading the proper times and places.

"Them poor folks that German shitehawk over at St. Freddy's wouldn't let marry and the poor woman so lovely in her blue gown and her gorgeous boobs."

My wife had an Irish woman's fury at injustice, especially when a woman was a victim.

"Jack and Maria Donlan . . . Blackie must have thought it was a case for a fey Irish woman."

"Doesn't your man say I'm the second-best detective in the whole city of Chicago?"

"As I heard him, he said best."

I kissed the back of her neck and slipped away. Her black pants suit was on the hanger. Over a white blouse with silver jewelry, she'd be ready for heavy lifting, an Irish professional woman. Indeed, a veritable Celtic Tiger. The Donlans would find a major ally against their enemies. And poor Dermot would have to find his spear and sally forth to battle.

You knew what you were getting into. And not a moment's hesitation either.

"And yourself leaving without hooking me bra?"

"I thought you'd never ask."

Me wife and herself looking like an Irish goddess and blue eyes which could skin the flesh off your face if she were angry at you

and a voice that hinted at distant bells ringing across the bogs was in high dudgeon
these days—indeed stratospheric. The new
president of the TV network which had
presented her Christmas specials every
year—hereinafter known as "that frigging
gobshite"—had canceled this year's production and terminated her contract. "Many people," the said gobshite had observed, "think it
is not correct to have so much religious
music at Christmastime. Such songs ruin the
holiday season for those people who have
no religious belief and resent having such
music imposed on them. Moreover, popular
reaction to the series has been slipping over
recent years."

This was frigging bullshite, my woman
insisted. The ratings were higher than ever
last year, indeed higher than all other Christmas specials. He also canceled the concert
without consulting Nuala's agent or without
negotiating payment for a cancellation fee.
Then when another network tried to pick up
the performance, he said that as he read the
contract, Nuala Anne couldn't perform for
anyone else but he didn't have to pay her.
She didn't give a friggin' damn about the pay,

but she had prepared twelve numbers from six different religions so that *Lullaby and Good Night* would be politically correct.

So the matter went to court. In Chicago, much to the dismay of the media lawyers from Los Angeles.

When my Nuala is in dudgeon, she becomes an Irish Tiger, though we in the family are not targets but audience. We try not to laugh. The Donlans had come at a good time. Her aroused fury would be aimed at their enemies too.

In the parlor I took our guests' coats and hung them in a closet, barely covering my gasp at the sight of Maria's lovely body pressed against a maroon knit dress. Without her mink coat she looked like a timeless Sophia Loren. I must not gape too much when my wife joined us. Her husband was wearing a three-piece black suit of Italian make, no casual for him. Both of them looked like models in a high-class magazine picture of Milanese fashions. Surely they exercised and dieted and went to spas, but their striking beauty was almost certainly genetic luck. I knew enough about human nature that those not so fortunate would envy and resent them, especially Maria. No woman over fifty had any right at all to look that timeless.

My wife, given to running down the stairs when she was in a hurry, descended with regal grace. I introduced her to both of them. She and Maria sized each other up quickly and bonded immediately as women sometimes do.

"Would you ever like a wee drop of something to banish the cold or maybe a small drop of Barolo?"

"There's enough Northern Italian in me," Maria said with another flash of her impish grin, "for that to have some appeal, but I'll settle for a drop of tea . . . black." Jack nodded with a smile, not nearly so exuberant as his wife's smile.

Her dark skin and flashing brown eyes suggested the Levant, wherever the hell that is, probably some place just outside of Palermo.

Stop undressing her before Nuala notices.

"My husband has cured me of the terrible Irish habit of polluting tea with milk! I'll put the kettle on and I'll be right back." She left with the same dignity with which she had descended the stairs, though, knowing her as I did, I was sure she wanted to bound. Left to her own desires, my Nuala Anne bounds rather than walks.

"We've seen her on television of course," Jack Donlan said softly, his normal tone of voice. "But she's even lovelier in person."

"And herself with four kids and a career and a house to manage and a laggard husband to be given instructions!"

"Fey too?" Maria Donlan said, asking a question.

"When she comes back, she'll have slices of Irish bread and jam which she made earlier because she knew you'd ask for tea. She predicts the gender of children even before they are conceived. You get used to such things after a while. Archbishop Ryan calls it a neo-Neanderthal vestige."

A small laugh around the room in honor of Blackie.

"He is a most unusual man."

"A very holy man."

"And a very smart man, according to my brother the priest."

The couple were patently, as Blackie would say, in love. They could not take their eyes off each other. Sitting on our antique couch their hands frequently touched.

Somehow this infatuation did not seem inappropriate, even if they were over fifty. Age had nothing to do with it, nor their physical perfection. A man and a woman had every right to fall in love again or for the first time. As a sixty-five-year-old colleague on the Exchange said, "I get on the elevator with her, my legs turn to water, and I forget she's my wife."

Don't pretend you don't know the experience, boyo.

Nuala reappeared with the tea tray, distributed the cups, saucers, and the plates with the soda bread and jam, and placed the cozy on the Galway teapot, all these rituals performed with maximum West of Ireland ceremony.

"We'll let it steep for just a minute longer. We Irish know just how long it takes tea to steep."

She poured it and we all sampled it.

"The soda bread is excellent."

"Thank you, sir, and didn't I make it meself."

"Her mother always says," I added, "that the best Irish bread is made in the house where it's served."

Then, just as we were about to turn the

conversation to the reason for their visit, a strange apparition took place. Two large, snow-white animals, bronze age remnants, pushed their way out of the door leading to the ground floor, and without looking at Nuala who had forbidden such intrusions into the parlor, walked to Maria Donlan's feet, sat on their haunches, and raised their right paws.

"Maria Donlan," my wife said, "may I present our two resident doggies, Fiona and Maeve. They are absolutely not supposed to be here, but I presume they know what they're doing."

She lifted an eyebrow in my direction, as though I were somehow responsible for their violation.

The dogs shook hands with their new friend. She hugged them and told them they were wonderful, which of course they knew but were glad to hear again. Thereupon they lay down, definitively in charge, both with their huge muzzles at her feet.

"You'll think I'm crazy, Jack, but I've always wanted one of these creatures."

"No reason why you shouldn't," he said quietly.

"This is all very serious," my good wife said grimly. "Very serious indeed."

"How so?" Jack Donlan asked.

"Fiona, our matriarch here, was a police dog in her youth. She sometimes has an instinct that someone is in danger."

"And you have Reliable Security looking after you? I noticed that one of their operatives was driving your limo."

"Sweet child," Maria said softly.

"And a crack shot," I added.

"We've had some threats. . . ." Jack said, his voice trailing off. "Very serious threats. Filled with hatred . . ."

"I agree with Archbishop Blackie," Nuala said. "There is serious evil at work here."

Then, as if the tension were not already turning creepy, Fiona stirred herself, rose from the floor, and began to howl. Maeve, not to be outdone by her mother, joined in the cry. The hounds of hell were loose.

— Dermot —

I GLANCED out the window. An old Chevy had pulled up in front of our house. Three men in black overcoats and grey fedoras emerged, each of them holding a big club of salami. It looked like a scene from the Capone era, called up from the nineteen twenties by an evil wizard. They strode toward our stairs, undaunted by the howling hounds. But then, someone threw open the door of our house and the great white monsters, howling with rage, emerged and rushed down the stairs followed by a banshee—a woman spirit, also howling and waving a club of her own.

That's my wife. She shouldn't be doing that.

A smaller woman spirit followed, aiming a small camera at the invaders.

That's my daughter. She shouldn't be doing that either.

I punched in Mike Casey's number on my cell phone.

"Casey . . ."

"Mike, tell Gaby to drive the car back around our corner. We have visitors from the nineteen twenties. Tell Culhane to get his people over here too."

I realized that I should play some kind of subsidiary role. I grabbed the snow shovel on the porch and dashed down the two flights of stairs, almost slipping near the top. My personal seraph intervened.

Just as I regained my balance, the invaders scurried back into their car. Their movements were frantic and clumsy. Two of the three fedoras were lost in the rush as well as all the salami clubs. The bad guys made it in the nick of time. They slammed their doors shut just as the white monsters arrived. The woman spirit pounded on the windows of their car with her camogie stick, a weapon used in the woman's version of hurling. Hadn't my wife been all-Ireland when she was in high school?

The weapon smashed the back window of the car just as it began to move. Nuala got a jab at one of the thugs. The hounds circled the car yowling and yipping, snarling and screaming. Nuala called them off, lest the terrified invaders might hit one of them. Obediently they sat next to her and continued to howl.

Some one of these days our neighbors would complain.

I should remonstrate with my wife about taking chances. She would argue that with her doggies and her camogie stick there were no chances involved.

"What are you doing here?" she demanded of her elder daughter.

"Taking pictures of them and their car. I got the license number," our eight-year-old said proudly.

Gaby's Lexus sped around the corner, police siren crying out in dismay.

"The rest of the flying squad is ready for action," I said, pointing up the stairs. The three younger children, commanded by Ellie, stood on the porch, each of them holding some kind of weapon or would-be weapon.

"Nelliecoyne," Nuala said, suddenly sounding very weary, "go upstairs and help Ellie get your brothers and sister back downstairs."

"Yes, Ma!"

"Dermot love, I know what you're thinking. I'm a terrible eejit altogether. . . . Would you ever calm down our guests and tell them that I'm not always that crazy."

"Only when someone attacks your house."

The dogs sniffed at the salami clubs and turned up their noses in disdain. Not their kind of food.

Several squads from the Sixth District arrived on the scene. Their cars are doubtless programmed to come to our block automatically.

Captain Cindasue L. McLeod of the United States Coast Guard materialized from down the street in a USCG sweat suit, her forty-five service revolver, bigger almost than she is, at the ready.

"What in tarnation you uns a doin' down hyar on a quiet Sunday afernoon?"

"Jest, a stirrin' up the shite, Cap'n ma'am."

Our two guests, eyes wide, were watching us as we climbed the steps.

"It's part of our campaign to force the

people of the neighborhood to put us under peace bond."

"Anyone want a small splash of the creature? . . . Ellie, would you wet the kettle again?"

"They were going to attack us with those sausages?" Jack Donlan asked.

"Old Capone gambit . . . clumsy . . ."

I poured splasheens for the guests and filled the jar tumbler for my wife and me.

"I'll never eat salami again," his wife murmured. "I see why the archbishop sent us to see you. You have a formidable team."

"Who were those men?" Jack said as he accepted the jar I gave him (a Waterford tumbler, but still a "jar" when the creature is poured into it).

"Lowlife thugs for hire. Very amateurish. Those who are out to make trouble for you are clumsy and stupid. But not undangerous."

My virtuous wife was calm and serene when she came from her conversations with the cops.

"Sorry for the interruption. . . . Please pay attention to the hounds. They are very proud of themselves. . . . Dermot, you have treats?"

I gave her the treats and she rewarded

the dogs who were then assigned to the backyard to run off some of their energy. Of course, they expected embraces and praise from our guests.

"You don't have to persuade us, Jack and Maria, that you have enemies out there. Maybe you could tell us something about yourselves and your lives."

— **John Patrick** —

COMING HOME from my wife's burial at All Saints Cemetery, I realized that an oppressive burden had been lifted. I was choked with painful grief. I had loved her. I had failed her. I would miss her always. Yet I was finally free of her mean miserable family. I could move out of their neighborhood, buy a co-op somewhere along the Gold Coast, one with a swimming pool, and relax into a solitary, almost monastic life. It would be a struggle to keep Faith's grieving family at bay, but I hated them so much that it would be easy. My eldest daughter, Evie, was already married, my second daughter, Irene, was engaged, and my youngest daughter, Mary Fran, was in first year at Loyola Medical School and living out in Forest Park, near the campus. I had protected them as best I could from the family. They would be on their own now. I was getting out.

My in-laws are mean, miserable, overweight drunks. Faith was the only one who was an alcoholic, but her unmarried sisters—Hope and Charity—her mother, Eulalia (aka Lallie), and her father, Guy, and her grandmother Evangeline were all drunks, woozy from drink at the end of the day.

I found myself furious at them once again. Their behavior at the wake and the funeral was one long boozy, hysterical bash in which the principal theme was that I had killed Faith. As expressed by the enormous Evangeline, if I had not persuaded the "poor kid" that she was an alcoholic, she would not have drunk so much and would not have piled up her Lincoln Town Car on Magnolia Street returning from her mother's birthday party while I was away in Washington.

"You never gave a damn about her," Lallie, her mother, screamed at me as she fell on her daughter's body at the funeral home.

Her father, in addition to being an enormous fall-down drunk, was a pious fraud. A huge man, he was a crooked lawyer who interfaced between the more corrupt elements of real estate trade and the local governments. The Feds had questioned him often and the media had labeled him "Mister Fixer." But none of the many United States Attorneys for the Northern District of Illinois had found enough to indict him, much less to persuade him to testify—or wear a wire—against some of his "business associates." Despite his reputation for adroit maneuvering on LaSalle Street, he was without influence in his own family. Like me he simply avoided conflict with his daffy, and half-tuned, women. He had an office somewhere near the county building, but did his business in a string of bars and restaurants in the heart of the Loop, none of them places where he and I might encounter one another and be embarrassed by our inability to find appropriate small talk. For my part I usually hung out at the Chicago Club or the University Club, just off Michigan Avenue. Though he was well known in the parish as a shady operator, as well as a perennial officer in the Holy Name Society, a trusted head usher, and chairman of the parish finance committee. When he lumbered down the aisle with the collection basket, I thought to myself that I wouldn't trust him as far as I could throw him.

My three daughters were loyal to me at the wake and funeral, protecting me as best they could from the family and easing me into the head of the procession into church.

Evie even whispered into my ear as I drove her and Tony, her husband, home from the final explosive night of the wake, "The next time you marry, Dad, choose a different kind of family." Given what subsequently happened that was a strange comment indeed.

"I'm sure I'll never marry again, hon."

Marriage seemed so easy in the early nineteen seventies. One went to Notre Dame to study economics, met young women either there or from St. Mary's across the road or from Barat in Lake Forest, danced with them, fooled around with them (the meaning of which was expanding even then but not nearly so far as it has now), fell in love with them, decided to marry while we were still in graduate school (MBA at Loyola for both of us because it was right around the corner), and settled down for a life of happiness together. Faith was a lovely, affectionate young woman, brimming with energy and enthusiasm. Her family was a little strange, but most families are. At least they knew how to have fun, which is more than I could say for my own careful, responsible parents.

Neither of my parents drank. They were both only children born late in the lives of their own parents. I had no experience of drunks when I was growing up save at teenage beer bashes. I was not sensitive to the signals that a person had moved from jollity to intoxication. I did not realize that Faith's parents and grandparents as well as her older sisters were "tuned" at the end of almost every day. They were, after all, capable of getting up the next morning and going off to work in their offices in the city or county bureaucracy. Faith hardly drank at all when we were dating and then courting during our last years at Notre Dame and Barat. Yet she became an alcoholic and they were merely lushes. I could have protected her from her fate. I should have protected her. Ignorance is not an excuse. Or maybe it is. I don't know. She seemed a cheerful, charming, and pretty young woman. Her family were all vulgar. She was not and I was marrying her, not them. We didn't have to live with them.

Again in my ignorance and inexperience I didn't know that very few young people are able to exclude their families from their lives.

Nor did I have any knowledge about what we would later call postpartum depression and what it can do to a woman's body and soul, especially if a woman has three children and an interlude of PPD—postpartum depression—after each birth. I didn't realize that the other women in her family would close in on her like a swarm of worker bees around an ill queen and exclude me as for all practical purposes a drone. Nor did I understand that they would try to "cheer her up" with a steady diet of booze.

Finally I didn't understand how different women are from men. I still can't claim any comprehension of that matter. One autumn evening while my daughters and I were having supper at an Italian restaurant on Walton Street after we had witnessed a disastrous defeat of Notre Dame by Michigan I tentatively raised the question. "Daddy," one of them said, "how can you be so totally chauvinist? Women and men are basically the same. The argument that we are different is just an excuse for patriarchy."

"When it comes to enjoying sex, there is no difference between us and guys. We both want all we can get."

Mary Fran, who usually avoids arguments with her sisters, blew up. "You guys are full of shit. That stuff is just hardcore feminist propaganda. In our profession we know that men and women have endocrine systems that are radically different. Men don't go into postpartum depression after a baby is born."

The argument turned into an attack on Mary Fran because it was alleged that all doctors, even women doctors, were ideological chauvinists. Mary Fran won easily because she had the facts. She explained why the hormone oxytocin made young women easy targets for predatory males.

I phoned her the next day and asked about postpartum depression. She explained it clearly and concisely. I was silent.

"Mom have it?" she asked softly.

"Three times."

"Dear God! The poor woman! . . . Is that why . . . ?"

"She became an alcoholic? Her family

tried to cheer her up with booze. It seemed to work. . . . Perhaps I should have stopped them."

"No way, Daddy, no way. Stop blaming yourself."

"This oxytocin stuff . . ."

"I call it the crush hormone. Gets activated when we form a crush on someone and reinforces the crush. It's a bonding chemical in most vertebrates. Generates desire and trust, sometimes dangerous."

"Disappears after marriage?"

"Stimulates mother's milk too, ingenious and untrustworthy. Probably helps in renewal of married love in humans, like you and Mom often did."

If Faith's family had only left her alone. . . .

"I knew so little then. . . ."

"Nobody knows anything much when they're young."

Mary Fran wanted to be a psychiatrist and apparently was already working on it.

"I'm surprised that you noticed."

"I was probably the only one that did. . . . Daddy, stop blaming yourself. They were determined to get her. She was the only one of the three that was beautiful. The other two put on weight to take them out of the mating game. Mom broke the rules, she broke ranks, she didn't care what she was doing to her older sisters, damn them all."

"That's too simple, hon."

My daughter was not a certified psychiatrist yet. She shouldn't even be thinking such thoughts about her family.

"Sometimes, Daddy, reality is simple, tragically simple. . . . You're not getting any oxytocin jolts are you?"

"I'm too old for a crush, Mary Fran."

"No one is ever too old to fall in love."

I went back to a report from one of my researchers on a new stock. They thought it might be a good bet. Oxytocin would surely distract me from making investment decisions for my clients. I did not want to fall in love again. It was too dangerous. Marriage was dangerous too. I'm good at calculating odds and hence a good gambler and a good asset manager (as we call investment managers these days—I would not even consider the title "wealth manager"). I was not going to gamble on marriage again. I would go through life alone from now on. That would mean a certain amount of loneliness and also a freedom from the problem of sharing my life intimately again with a woman. Even in the best possible circumstances that was a risky business. One had to negotiate personal differences, learn to read the other's mind (not what she said, but what she meant), strive to be sensitive to her moods, read the complexities of her sexual needs, and the anxieties and fears which plague her life. Then if one had been modestly successful at acquiring these intricate skills, one could still fail miserably at the crucial times in her life.

There was no reason in the world to think I would not fail miserably again. I had made my contribution to the continuation of the species. I had fallen into the tender trap once. I need not do it again.

There were costs to this monastic style, especially loneliness at the end of the day when there was no one to talk to. Maybe I should be a monk. Or join the Jesuits . . . I'd be eighty before they ordained me. . . .

Nor could I pretend that I was so disillusioned with marriage that I did not find women attractive. That was the wound that might be original sin. With all my wisdom and all my determination, I would have to maintain an iron discipline against their appeal, especially because my money and power might make me attractive to them.

Faith and I began to work immediately after our honeymoon, which was fun, but somehow disappointing. Neither of us knew much about sex, to say nothing of marital sex; nobody does, it turned out. I went to work for my father, who had just changed from an investment broker to an investment adviser.

"Whatever we call it, Jackie, it's the same game. We bet and our clients bet with us that over the years we will keep their profits anywhere between five and ten percent over the Dow."

"And their losses," I said.

He laughed that quiet little laugh that meant I had made the point.

"We won't talk about those, Jackie, no gambler does. But there's not going to be another Great Depression, not for a long time."

Dad was an interesting man. His own father had been a Pullman conductor on the Chicago-to-New Orleans line. Dad had been born in 1914 and went to St. Ignatius College as it was called in those days to study accounting. He began to work as a messenger on the Chicago Board of Trade when he was eighteen, in the depths of the Depression. He joined the Army on December 8, 1941, and rose to the rank of lieutenant colonel. He never talked about the war or explained why he had won the Distinguished Service Cross at Bastogne during the Battle of the Bulge, the last desperate charge of the German army in about the same place that the Kaiser's army had launched its final attack in 1918.

He came back to Chicago with his secrets and the money he had made in poker games and opened his broker's office in the old Conway building across the street from what is now the Daley Plaza. He never bothered to get a seat on any of the exchanges but would call his orders into brokers on the floor.

"You didn't have to be very smart in those days to know that all the money people made during the war would flood into the economy like a levee break in the Ole Miss."

A lot of returning GIs, having money to invest for the first time in their lives, heard rumors about the brilliant poker player colonel. He made a lot of money for them and for himself.

He also went to night school at Loyola up at Lewis Towers and got himself an AB in accounting and then a law degree.

"When you have enough money you can buy your own lawyer, Jackie," he told me. "Until then a man has to do it himself."

Did I seduce Faith or did she seduce me? We used to argue about that and laugh at the rituals of the springtime of love. Those were sweet times, nonetheless. Almost thirty years of marriage. If we had another thirty years . . . Even twenty . . . Even ten . . . We might have made something out of it.

But that was nonsense.

I was adjusting to being alone. Indeed I had been alone much of the time when she was still alive. Lust would diminish through the years, would it not? I compared my own marriage with my father's. In 1950, when the war in Korea had just begun, he married an Army nurse whom he'd met in Germany after the war. I would learn later that they had written daily letters to one another for six years. I was born three years later, right in the middle of the Baby Boom, the only child they were able to have. They were quiet, gentle people. In their own undemonstrative way they were deeply in love with one another and that love spilled over to absorb me. Nothing in our big house on Balmoral Street prepared me for the conflicts and the agonies and the failures of my own marriage. I presume they had to adjust to each other as every husband and wife must, though maybe not. For them simple goodness and affection might have been enough. Were they just lucky? Or did they learn somewhere wisdom that I had never acquired?

While I was finishing my MBA, I worked in my father's office, studying companies in what we would now call research. He nodded in appreciation at my summaries. "You have the green thumb, Jackie. Good instincts. Beware of them. They'll usually be right, but when they turn wrong, you can get yourself into real trouble. Never trust an instinct completely."

I didn't know what he meant then. Now I do.

My parents met her family only at the rehearsal dinner at the Lakeshore Athletic Club. They were too polite to say anything, but I could tell by their eyes that they were horrified.

"Faith doesn't drink at all," I said.

"And she is not in the least vulgar," my mom said.

They lived long enough to know and adore all three of their grandchildren. They never left our neighborhood for Florida and did not buy a summer home in the Dunes, much less Door County, like many of our neighbors.

"We're a half a block from the Lake," my father explained to their friends, "and we have all our books and records here in the house."

He drove a Chevy all his life and rode the Howard Street L down to his LaSalle Street office every morning. I was pretty much in charge of the office when Mary Fran—my mother's name—was born. (My in-laws were furious at the choice and whispered loudly about their displeasure.) Dad would read the papers, glance at the ticker (which he called the screen), mutter a few suggestions, and then ride back home to spend the day with Mom, maybe to go to the "movies."

"Old gambler knows when to back down," he said with a laugh. "Let the young gunslingers take the chances."

He died in 1986 of a stroke. Mom died five months later of a heart attack. They died as they lived, quietly, gracefully.

I was on my own with three daughters and

an alcoholic wife who had been fired by Lilly, Smith because of her drinking. Her increasingly eccentric sisters blamed me. If I had not forced her to work and if I had left her alone (by which they meant not slept with her) she would never have become a heavy drinker.

When she began to work Faith was hired at a much larger brokerage—Lilly, Smith—doing the same thing I was doing.

"They're pretty high over there on your young woman," Dad said to me one day. "They tell me she's as bright as they come and they generally don't like women around their shop."

It was the middle nineteen seventies, however, and even a stuffed shirt firm like Lilly, Smith had to hire some women. When she told them that she was pregnant, they took counsel with one another and decided to tell her that they wanted her back after the baby was born. I was proud of her but uneasy. Yet she was one of the generation of young women who believed they could have everything and I had enough sense not to argue against her choice. I would have lost anyway.

Faith's first pregnancy was a nightmare, sickness almost every day. Childbirth was long and agonizing, then depression and a long struggle back to health afterward. Her family blamed me for making her go back to work, though I had done my best to talk her out of it. I wanted to move out to a suburb like Hubbard Woods or even River Forest to escape from them, but she argued that she had to live near them to prevent them from killing themselves.

"I'm the only sane one in the family," she insisted. "I can take care of them and watch poor little Evie at the same time."

"And hold down a job too?"

"I'm supermom," she laughed. "I can do anything."

In principle she could have done a lot of things easily, but the PPD, as we would call it now, came back after her next two pregnancies. She wanted a son the worst way. Her doctors were skeptical, but she insisted.

"God is playing tricks on me," she insisted. "I have to produce a son. I grew up in a house with two sisters and it was hell on earth. Women are mean to one another."

She began to drink heavily during the

depression after Irene's birth. Stubbornly she went back to work before she felt better. They fired her after the first month.

"She needs help," the senior partner at Lilly, Smith confided to me in the pompous tones which are essential to a man in his position. "A long vacation, a good therapist, and maybe some AA."

She did go to a psychiatrist and we did take a vacation. She came back from the Caymans pregnant with Mary Fran. Same scenario—depression and alcohol. She fired her therapist, quit AA, and sank into an emotional swamp. I persuaded her to try a mental hospital in Evanston where they helped women out of such messes which were not their own fault, as I put it. Invariably she followed my advice, indeed enthusiastically, and praised my patience and kindness. I was such a wonderful man. She didn't deserve a husband like me.

Her family turned to obscene phone calls when they found out that I had barred them from visiting her. Looking back on those days in the early eighties when the Reagan Revolution was transforming American life and repudiating us Boomers and we ourselves were buying the gospel of greed, I realized that the country was in revolt against the intensity of the sixties radicals. It was also turning to a vision of human life which preached that happiness came from wealth and possessions. My daughters laughed at all the funny clothes and the stupid demonstrations of my era (even though I never wore funky garments or protested against anything). But their laughs were affectionate. They were convinced that their mother and I were "cool." And were on their side. Their bonding with Faith was intense and inviolable. They were the ones who talked me into suggesting the Betty Ford Center.

Why not?

By then she had slipped into what the doctors had been calling a "manic depressive syndrome" and later be called "a bipolar disorder." She spent six months at Betty Ford. I would leave my office at noon on Friday and fly to California to visit her and return on the Sunday night red-eye. I did my best to be both mom and dad to the kids and they tolerated that, but none of us fooled ourselves, I was no mom, at least not a mom like their mom. But I was still "cute" and "cool" and sometimes even "adorable."

She came home a "new woman" as she proclaimed herself. She went to AA every week and begged me to permit her to revive her old work skills. She also went to all the kids' activities at Sacred Heart parish.

"You don't have to hire me," she explained. "I'll just sit in my office here at home and explore companies for you."

"Fine," I said. It seemed like a good idea. She soon proved herself as good a researcher as her bosses at Lilly, Smith claimed she was. It was the era of the dot-com bubble and a legion of madcap start-ups. Faith thought it was all nonsense.

"A lot of people are going to get hurt," she said, "and you and your friend Frodo are not going to be among them."

By that time Frodo had achieved a certain fame, which my father's son that I was, I did not like. I told myself that I would not believe the good things *The Wall Street Journal* said about me. However, I rented the office next to mine in the Conway building, fixed up the two offices so they looked mildly prosperous, and hired a couple of assistants.

Faith prospered at her desk, recommending several new stocks for my increasing variety of products. She went home early in the afternoon to be with the kids, though her family leaned on her the way they could that she should be home with them all the time, just as their mother had. By definition, any idea I had for my wife was wrong. However, those months when we shared both home and office were the happiest time in my life.

The Frodo Managed Fund (FMF) was my pride and joy; some of the stocks in it I had inherited from my father, so Frodo spanned the generations. It became a legend in wealth management. Some years it ran a full ten percent above the Dow. It was of course an instrument in gambling. My investors bet that they could trust me to deliver a presentable profit every year. And I bet that my instinct and sense of the markets could achieve that goal. The riverboat gambler in me loved the contest and the instincts, both of which I had inherited from my father. If the instincts started to fade I could go into the business of being a floating corporate trustee, not that I didn't have some personal money protected in the safest of safe havens.

The so called "dot-com bubble" was a merry time for us three-piece-suit bettors. I sensed it was a bubble and protected my friend Frodo from most of the trolls lurking in the bushes and the alleys. When the bubble burst my clients and I felt that we had been kicked in the stomach by an NFL field goal kicker. But, because I had taken a good hard look at the cards, we survived and bounced back quickly.

Unfortunately for Faith the bottom fell out of one of the stocks she had persuaded me to take on. It was the only truly devastating loss for Frodo, my fault rather than hers. I had very little doubt about it when I decided that Internet food markets would certainly prosper. Dumb! I told Faith not to worry about it. She had warned me of some of the possible downsides of the stock. The buck at Donlan Assets stopped at my desk. I never blamed a researcher who sold me a lemon.

My reassurance was not enough for poor Faith. She had to blame herself. When I arrived home (riding the L as my father had) I found the three daughters crying in the parlor. Mommy was sick in the bedroom and grandma was taking care of her.

"Well, I hope you're proud of yourself," Lallie shouted at me. "Look what you've done to her."

I ordered Lallie to leave the house

immediately and never come back again. She called the wrath of God down on me as I forced her out the door. My daughters swarmed around me and hugged me.

"She's a terrible woman," Evelyn informed me. "Thank God you came home."

"Any time she tries to get in here when I'm not around, call me at the office. . . . Also if Mommy comes home sick again."

They solemnly promised.

She went to an AA meeting the next night but it didn't help much. I told her the job would always be waiting for her at my office. She replied with a bitter self-hating laugh. A week later she whispered to me one night, "I think I'd better try Betty Ford again." This time the effect of that splendid institution lasted only a couple of months.

I tried to persuade her to help me set up a new Nasdaq fund (I called it DOT), which was for the high rollers among my clients, including myself. Faith had read *The Wall Street Journal* every day at the Betty Ford. I never consciously gambled for high stakes with clients' money unless they wanted me to. But I had no scruples about gambling with my own. In truth I was much more of a high roller than my father would have tolerated.

So I made a bundle for all us high rollers with DOT, including Faith, for whom I put a bundle in our joint investments. "We'll make a killing on it," she said to me confidently and she was right. We went to Ambria in the Belden-Stratford Hotel on New Year's Eve to celebrate that we had made enough money to pay for the college education of our kids. She refused to appear again in the office, but continued to provide me with first-rate research. Our interludes of happiness lasted longer, but they were never permanent. The final one ended when she attended her mother's birthday while I was in D.C. I felt certain that they invited her to the party just so they could prove to her once again that she was not an alcoholic.

The light went out of my life. She was a lovely, brilliant woman and good bed partner. I would miss her forever. As I have said, I was glad to be rid of her family, but I would have gladly put up with them and with her problems, if only she had survived.

I was paralyzed by grief and guilt for the year after her death. Her daughters insisted that it was not my fault.

Two years later, firm in my informal vow of celibacy, I was looking over the research on

Elegant Homes, feeling very dubious about a start-up corporation from Oakdale, Illinois, formed by a woman real estate person. The prospectus looked good, however, and Jim Leavy, my most brilliant research guru, suggested we ought to think it over for DOT. I do three sessions with my staff about each research suggestion. Then I do one thought session by myself in which for the first time I look over all the papers.

Joe McMahon, my research director who keeps his eye on start-up stories, brought the project to me from a lawyer in Rockford. While I trust Joe's good sense, Rockford is downstate—which is to say any part of Illinois beyond Cook, Lake, and DuPage counties. Rockford is in fact north of Chicago but it still is downstate and good Chicago Democrat that I am I don't trust downstate. I had never heard of Oakdale and have rarely been west of the DesPlaines River. The ELG project had a lot going against it, i.e. Rockford, downstate, luxury homes, a real estate woman, all of which raised warning flags.

Joe is a rotund little leprechaun of a man who went to work for my father fresh out of high school. He is an absolute genius at separating good buys from bad buys and is a pleasant if eager man with whom to work. He cannot make decisions or even recommendations. My father paid him well for a man who had not attended college (just as he had not), but not what he is worth. When I took over I gave him a big raise to what he was worth and continued raises and bonuses through the years. He always seemed grateful but hardly surprised. He's in his middle seventies and may or may not want to retire. I know nothing of his personal life, but he has two sons about my age, both of them MDs of whom he is very proud. His wife died (of cancer) I think ten years ago. I was surprised when I went to the wake and funeral in Bridgeport by the crowd and the grief. She must have been a remarkable woman. I regret that I never met her. Somehow I had gained the impression that he did not want me to meet her. As far as I can tell he is very devoted to me.

The proposal was that instead of the firm going to a bank to float the IPO, DAM would undertake to acquire a large block of stock at the IPO asking price. Since the stock would presumably shoot up in the first week, we would make a tidy sum of money. The company would be protected from underwriters' fees. And everyone would be happy.

It is not the sort of venture that I would normally make. The bubble of the late nineties became a bubble precisely because too many people engaged in such crapshoots. ELG properly belonged in a hedge fund in which the truly high rollers played with chips worth millions of dollars. I don't do hedge funds because there is too much money involved, too much uncertainty, and too many ruthless investors. Joe McMahon has been pushing me for years to edge in that direction. Each time I decline with thanks.

I wouldn't let ELG within a light-year of Frodo. The loyal fans of Frodo would think I had lost my mind. Jim argued that because much of the strength of the concept of designing boutique homes was dependent on specialized software that enabled clients to design splendid homes online before a single spade of dirt was displaced, it might well belong in the DOT fund, which I had renamed Samwise. Besides there were so many odd stocks in Samwise the customers wouldn't notice one more madcap toss of the dice.

I didn't like the proposal, however. Real estate markets are notoriously volatile. The data from ELG made a persuasive case that luxury and quasi-luxury markets were more stable. People with lots of money or moderate amounts of money consistently bought special homes. ELG's contribution to this market so far had been to provide a range of choices in such homes that would be environment-friendly, attractive to men and women of good taste, and easy on the purchasers' time. ELG was not for those who wanted to spend most of their time for a year or more agonizing over the details. Rather it was for those who were in a hurry but wanted a home that would have their own imprint on it and confirm the discrimination of their owners. Moreover because ELG had market power in the areas where it had offices, they could virtually guarantee that builders would finish their work on time. In an afternoon or two you could design your house and decorate it on a computer, make your down payment, and move in a year later.

An appealing idea perhaps for those in a hurry, but also a comment on our speed-crazy culture. So too, however, to be fair, were asset management services like mine. Yet could any good come out of Oakdale, a

suburb of Rockford out in the prairies? Moreover it was a start-up created by a woman
real estate agent, albeit one with a good
technical team. The prospectus was well
done and had cleared my technical team. I
couldn't base my decision on my residual
sexism, could I?

I turned over the last paper in the file. The
woman stared up at me—Maria Angelica
Sabattini Connors. I gulped. It was a color
photo cover of a magazine called *Chicago
Markets* that did puff pieces on local entre-
preneurs. Ms. Sabattini was unquestionably
beautiful—dark skin that suggested the
Mediterranean, perhaps Lebanon or North
Africa, brown, smoldering, and intelligent
eyes, a hint of a smile which implied mystery
and perhaps romance, and a delicately
carved face that could haunt a man for the
rest of his life, especially if loneliness made
him susceptible to haunting by such a one.

I sighed and turned the magazine over. It
would be most unwise of a man in my situation to become involved even in a business
relationship with one like that. I was overcome by the temptation to read the article.

Nonetheless I had to know more about
her. There was little in the article to support

my romantic fantasies—how could there be romance in Oakdale? The youngest daughter of an Italian immigrant from Tuscany and an Irish American GI who worked as a mechanic at a garage in Oakdale. Homecoming queen at Oakdale High School, Miss Kishwaukee County, a year at Northern Illinois University, married high school star quarterback who had attended Notre Dame. Like any Catholic kid in Chicago I knew the names of all the Notre Dame quarterbacks for the last two generations. Peter Connors wasn't one of them. Rabbit in an Updike novel?

Went to work for the Connors family real estate and development company at nineteen. Mother of two daughters and two sons. Named president of firm when she was thirty. Won a national award for a high-scale development along the Rock River. Involved in civic and artistic activity in Oakdale; led committee which rejuvenated the town. She and her husband inherited the firm, renamed it Elegant Homes. Has been refining the concept for years and expanding it beyond Illinois. May go public soon with a listing in Standard and Poors. Vivacious, charming, witty. Rebounded from her husband's death three years ago with the usual clichés about how much she missed him. After her children were raised went back to school in computer science at NIU. Earned a master's degree. Has designed much of the software for the new Elegant.

A lot of shallow stuff about the firm, covering some of the material that was in my file.

And pictures. Maria Angelica as a sumptuous Miss Kishwaukee County. Maria Angelica with her four kids. A still sumptuous Maria Angelica at a benefit ball in Chicago in a black gown that showed just enough to be provocative and not enough to be immodest. Did she look fragile in that picture? I glanced again at the cover. Yes, there was a hint of vulnerability, or at least my brain, now perturbed by racing hormones, thought so.

I threw the magazine in my wastebasket and closed the file. Then I realized that my secretary, Elfrida, would check to make sure that I had looked at it. Better not to give that woman any hint of my reaction. I retrieved the *Chicago Markets* issue, placed it in its proper place at the end of the file, and put it in my out-box.

I had to leave in ten minutes for my weekly tennis match at the Racket Club. Still I sat motionless at my desk, thoroughly ashamed of my adolescent reactions to the woman. My reactions, however, remained the same. Was I so hungry for womanly flesh that innocent pictures could fill my imagination with a stew of lubricious fantasies? No way could I enter into a business relationship with that woman. My team had set up a meeting to discuss our purchase of their stock for Samwise. I would cancel the meeting.

For a couple of decades four of us Loyola grads had played tennis every Thursday—two matches of two sets each. We purported to be equally skilled. In fact, over the long haul, I had won more matches than anyone else, though I was the only one who counted, and that secretly. My competitiveness in the assets management game marked, perhaps blighted, my whole life. The day I had fixated on Maria Angelica Sabattini my need to win, now driven by my male hormones, was fearsome. My friends suggested that I was about to make a "killing" in the market.

After our showers, I went into the dining room for a salad and a glass of iced tea with Lou Garner, a financial adviser on the North Shore. Neither the cold water nor the frugal meal calmed me down.

Lou, moderately successful in a tough market, was an incorrigible gossip. He kept up with all the rumors in the financial services world, especially the scandalous ones.

"Are you really going to hop into bed with Maria Connors?" He demanded.

"I gave up that behavior when my wife died," I said primly.

He was unembarrassed.

"Didn't mean it literally but with her it usually comes to the same thing. She sleeps with anybody that can promote her career and then dumps them when she's got what she wants out of them."

"That's her reputation?"

"Everyone knows it's true. . . . Hey, one year at DeKalb and the daughter of Sicilian immigrants and from Oakdale? Gimme a break. . . . She's really vicious, but so far it's worked."

"One would think the reputation would catch up with her."

"It will eventually, I suppose. . . . But stay away from her."

"I am forewarned."

My team does excellent due diligence work. They do not screen, however, for Jezebels.

Back in my office I phoned Mike Casey, a former police commissioner.

"We're involved with a project that would imply a relationship with one Maria Sabattini Connors from Oakdale, Illinois, a firm called Elegant Homes Incorporated. We would in effect be taking a long position on her firm. Would you be able to run a screen on her . . . ?"

"Reputation, trouble with the Feds, record, that sort of thing?"

"Yes . . . She has a reputation of being promiscuous in her business dealings. I mean that in the strict sense of the word."

"That you don't need. . . . I'll be back to you in a couple of days."

I was relieved. I could tell my staff, all very eager on a project they thought was right down our alley, certain confidential matters had arisen that made our taking a position in ELG inappropriate at the present time. They would not press me on the point.

Mike Casey called me back on the following Tuesday.

"The woman is a chaste and modest matron, Jackie. There are rumors in the financial services community in Chicago, based on envy. But out in Oakdale, a place everyone knows everything about everybody and they don't particularly like beautiful and successful Sicilians, they'll tolerate no criticism of her. The sheriff out there in Kishwaukee County, a shrewd old bird, told me Chicagoans had dirty minds. Which may be true. 'Chaste and modest matron' are his words."

I thanked him and went into another fantasy tailspin. A chaste matron was even more of a potential delight than a woman out of an Eric Ambler novel.

"Eric Ambler" dated me.

Nothing would happen at our meeting or at any other event as we added her to Samwise. I would certainly decline to accept a position on her board of trustees.

— Maria Angelica —

I DRESSED very carefully for my meeting with John Patrick Donlan—competent, professional businesswoman—somber grey dress, loosely fitting, longish skirt, one turquoise pin, hair severely combed back, hardly visible makeup. My due diligence had revealed that Jack Donlan was generally thought to be a "gentleman," not known for hitting on women. However, widowers in their early fifties are often a problem, especially for a widow in the same age range. I have had enough experience with men hitting on me to cope with them, though it's always distasteful—an occupational hazard for a woman who is thought to be attractive.

There had been one love in my life, my high school sweetheart and husband, God be good to him. The sex in that relationship left a lot to be desired because poor Peter Connors knew very little about women. However, I had learned that most men know very little about women. Real orgasms, as opposed to fake ones, are few and far between. It doesn't take very many to produce four kids. As our marriage went on, sex became unimportant, for me because it wasn't much fun and for Pete because it required too much of him as had everything else in life.

I was very frank about sex with my sons while they were growing up, about how a man should love a woman. They were surprised and grateful. Peter Junior told me how important my lecture was in their marriage. Vicki, his wife, told me in an awed whisper that my son was a great lover. That made me very proud.

I don't recommend the celibate life to anyone, except a priest or a nun. I tell the latter that they don't know how lucky they are. They laugh at me. Uneasily.

My husband was a loser. Is it possible to love a loser? Not to pity him, but actually to love him?

I fell in love with Peter in a high school crush on a hero. I learned early on that he was not much of a hero. He threw the passes that brought the championship to Oakdale. But he was terrified before every game that he might blow it. In fact, he went through high school and all his life afraid of personal failure—as well he might have been. His father, Michael Reed Connors, was a great bear of a man, all-American tackle at Notre Dame. He didn't like me at first because I was a Sicilian but he came through the years to respect me and be grateful for my love and care of Peter. His mother, Violet Egan, was a nervous timid little woman who had, I'm afraid, shaped Peter's soul. She resented me all her life because I cared for that soul much more skillfully than she could.

Peter needed to be cosseted, propped up, sustained. I knew that the summer before he went to Notre Dame with expectations that he would be another Paul Horning or Angelo Bertelli. I hoped and prayed that he live up to his own skills. It would have eased his path through life. Alas for all of us, that goal, while within his athletic skills, was not within his personality skills. He never stopped being homesick. "I don't like it here," he said to me often on the phone. He couldn't face personal conversation with me or write letters. Everything was on the phone.

Against my parents' wishes, I had enrolled at NIU as a day student, riding back and forth on a bus. I did well enough my first semester to earn a scholarship, which didn't make them happy. I should be earning money for the education of the rest of the family—that is, the boys in the family. The spring football practice at the Dome (as my kids call it) was a disaster. Peter was cut from the team. He came home a broken man.

NIU signed him up. He was second string during his sophomore year and did pretty well. We dated often. Peter was proud of me and the reaction of his athlete friends who were not bad guys. Old Michael Reed Connors was smart enough to comprehend that I was responsible for his son's improvement.

"I used to think you were the problem with him, Maria," he said in a tone which for him would pass for gentle. "Now I see you are his only hope."

I thanked him.

I began to work in their real estate office after school and bought a car with which I could commute over to DeKalb. Mike, as I now called him, was proud of me.

I also was making enough money to pay for my brothers' education. Still I didn't please my parents and understood that I never would. They had not wanted a daughter people thought was beautiful. That was not good for a young woman.

Peter tore cartilage in his knee during a game in which he threw five touchdown passes for the Huskies, a record which still stands. It was a career-ending injury. The coach lamented the loss of such a promising player. I realized that Pete's career ended in the nick of time.

We were married in the parish church the following autumn by the bishop of Rockford. It was a big wedding with a huge reception at the country club for which I paid with money that Big Mike had slipped to me. My parents were embarrassed by the whole event. We went to Europe for two weeks on our honeymoon and then on return we both went to work for the firm.

Sex between us was not much, though we

managed to produce four adorable kids, two boys, two girls. They tell me that on balance I was not a bad mom—always with wicked grins, which have become their trademark when dealing with me. We sent them to the Catholic school in Oakdale and Oakdale High, then on to what they now call the Dome. I was never much of a Catholic and they are Catholic fanatics in a laid-back, comic way. The oldest three are involved in the ACE program from Notre Dame in which they teach in Catholic schools in impoverished neighborhoods after graduation and Clara, the youngest, intends to go the same route. I've become a much better Catholic because of them.

My husband had little aptitude for the family business. Big Mike made him president of the firm and me the vice president—inside and outside persons. He would sit in the front office of our storefront and chat with those who would drop by, take customers or influential folk or cronies to lunch at the country club, pick up all the local gossip which might affect our business, maybe even scare up some rich customers. I would do all the work and create our new ideas. I never resented this division of labor. Both roles were important. I liked running things and he liked talking. He never pretended that he was in charge and on the contrary praised me to his buddies as a genius at our game.

Oakdale had been a camp for Chief Black Hawk on the Kishwaukee River when Illinois troops, including young Abe Lincoln, were driving the Fox and Saux out of their Illinois homeland. Then it became a trail post on the road between Chicago and Rock Island, and later a station on the Rock Island Railroad and a commercial center for the surrounding farms, prospering as the farms prospered and suffering when the farms suffered. When the Rock Island ended its passenger service after the Second War, the town went into eclipse, the parks declined, and the storefronts on Chicago Avenue, as we called our main street, turned shabby and almost derelict. Donlan Development was a happy exception.

My premise through the years was that Oakdale, even almost halfway across the state, was a satellite of Chicago, only an hour by expressway from the Oak Brook complex and maybe an hour and ten minutes at the most from O'Hare. Our future lay in being a desirable exurb, "boonie," for Chicago. So we developed a plan for sprucing up downtown and building high-quality homes in the empty spaces and elegant developments outside of town along the Rock and Kishwaukee rivers. There was some opposition from the local establishment, which had never quite adjusted to the end of the Great Depression. Big Mike won them over—after I won him over, which was easy because he approved of me. We had Chicago Avenue declared a historic district and pried loose some state money to refurbish it. We built a four-star hotel downtown with an inside/outside pool and a courtesy link to O'Hare—a quiet rural Illinois setting, we alleged, for weary travelers. We opened two excellent restaurants, one in the old railroad station, and persuaded the country club to permit visitors to play golf for an appropriately exorbitant fee. My husband organized a campaign to improve the course and we made a large contribution to the fund. I became president of Oakdale Civic Association and a member of the revived Kishwaukee County Democratic Organization. There were nice articles in the travel magazines and in one airline magazine. I loved the image of travelers reading it as they circled over O'Hare.

Urged on by my zealous Catholic children I also became chair of the St. Cyril's financial council, which approved an expansion to the Catholic school which I had never attended.

My brothers, Jimmie and Paulie, were a problem. They had founded a construction company which might have done a lot of work for us. Unfortunately their bids were sloppy and unreliable and their work was often shoddy. My parents were furious at me because I wasn't willing to "help your brothers out." I had sold out, they shouted, to old man Connors.

"I'll be eager to help them," I replied curtly, "when they submit proper bids and do professional work."

"You're not loyal."

"And this is not Sicily."

Actually we were not Sicilians. But we were very poor Tuscan dirt farmers, which may be almost the same thing, though my mother and sister and I looked like aristocrats born on the wrong side of the bed.

Instead they built a new riverboat gambling complex outside of Rockford with ties to the Chicago outfit. My brothers, overweight bodies stuffed into expensive Italian suits, seemed to fit right in. Then the Chicago mob made them an offer they couldn't refuse. They would continue to manage the casino and take a percentage from the profits, but the "boys" owned it.

My sister, Gina, moved to Chicago, got a job as a nurse at Northwestern, and married a rich doctor. We drifted apart, though the last couple of years after I had opened an office in Chicago, we'd have lunch occasionally and became if not quite friends, at least pleasant siblings.

"I don't want either of those guys in the store," I told my husband and father-in-law, "and I don't want either of you to associate with them at the club. They're bad news. We're Caesar's wife."

They didn't argue. They never argued with me when I laid down the law, which I did rarely. I also told my kids to stay away from their cousins.

"Get real, Moms," my elder daughter, Marissa, admonished me with the required crooked grin. "We're Florentines, not Sicilians."

"Sienese," I insisted.

"Whatever!"

The idea for Elegant Homes slowly developed through the years—designer homes that you could create for yourself with our software. It caught on quickly. My instinct seemed correct that some of the newly affluent Boomers would want their own tasteful and environment-friendly home that they designed and furnished themselves on the Net. We provided the alternatives and the builders and the decorators, who dared not be tardy or go over estimates.

"You gotta go ahead with this," Big Mike insisted. "It will make a lot of money and a lot of people happy."

"Fersure," my husband agreed.

I noticed that I didn't age much through the years. I had managed to slide through menopause rather easily. My children told me that I embarrassed them by being a "dish."

"I can drink three malts every day if you want."

"Won't do any good," Clara replied. "It's in your genes, like your mother. Only you're not a wicked witch."

My husband got along fine with the kids. They figured he was another kid like themselves. They were not far from wrong.

He deteriorated slowly through the decades, so slowly that I would notice only when I'd recall the difference between birthdays. A hint that his world was disintegrating came five years ago when he withdrew from the annual country club golf tournament, which he had won twice when he was in his twenties.

"Just too tired," he sighed. "Mar, you go out and defend the family honor."

I had never played in the tournament because I did not want to humiliate him. It was silly because he knew how good I had become while I was working on the golf course modernization. I've won it twice since then, but only after he had died.

Peter began to go to Mass every morning. Clara or I would drive him down the street to St. Cyril's. Usually we both would go with him. My children had made me a good Catholic. My husband made me a devout Catholic.

I refused to think about his death, though deep down I knew he would be lucky to live to be sixty. Big Mike once said to me in a choked voice, "I'll outlive my own son. It's all my fault."

"The doctors say that his depression is genetic, not psychological."

"I didn't help matters by pushing him so hard in high school and college."

"That's what fathers do. You weren't worse than anyone else in this town."

You'll have to take care of him when Peter dies, I told myself with Italian fatalism. But I didn't think it would happen so soon. . . . Nor that Big Mike would die a year after.

I awoke a couple of nights after our thirtieth wedding anniversary. Beside me in bed—better a sexless bed, I often told myself than an empty bed—Peter was twisting and turning restlessly. Then he doubled over and cried out in pain.

"I'm dying, Maria! Call the ambulance! Oh, please call the ambulance! Now!"

I had made a deal with Ladislas, the director of our town ambulance service, that I would call him on his top secret number when we had an emergency, and just tell him my name. He would come immediately. I had precoded his number in all my phones.

"Laddy, it's Maria."

Then the rectory, "Father Matt. It's Maria."

"I'll be right over, Maria."

"Hold my hand, Maria, PLEASE!"

"I love you, Peter. I always have. I always will."

"Best wife a loser like me ever had."

"You're not a loser, Peter. You never were."

Then Big Mike.

His whiny wife answered.

"Do you know what time it is, Maria . . . ? We both need our sleep."

"We're taking Peter to the hospital."

"Can't it wait till the morning?"

Miserable little bitch.

"Put him on!" I shouted into the phone.

She whimpered but put Mike on.

"We're taking him to the hospital, Mike. He may have had a heart attack."

"I'll meet you there . . . ! How bad is it?"

I hesitated.

"Pretty bad?"

"I think so."

The ambulance wailed outside. I put on a sweatshirt and jeans and grabbed a raincoat. Then back to my husband. I held his hand with all the passion I possessed.

"I love you, Peter. I love you with all my heart and soul."

"I didn't deserve you, Maria. But I'm happy you've been with me. You have to get yourself another husband."

"Don't be silly. . . . I better open the door."

The paramedics eased him out of the bed

and carried him gently down the stairs. I
trailed behind, cell phone in hand. Pete's
young wife, Vicki, whom he met during their
term in ACE, halfway through her first pregnancy, answered the phone.

"We're taking Dad to the hospital, hon."

"Oh, Mom, how awful!"

"How bad is it, Mom?" Pete was on the
phone.

"Pretty bad. We're putting him in the
ambulance. Father Matt is here and is riding
down the street with us."

"We'll be right there."

"Let Vicki drive. You call the kids. Tell them
not to be reckless driving home, especially
Clara."

"I'll tell her to wait till morning. She usually
does what I say."

"You must marry again," Peter pleaded
with me, clinging to my hand.

Father Matt performed the Last Rites with
sincerity and grace as we rolled down the
street to St. Angela's Hospital. Big Mike and
Pete and Vicki arrived at the same time. Just
inside the entrance of the hospital thunder
growled above us and lightning danced
across the sky, my husband sat up on the
stretcher, his face glowing, his eyes bright.

"I'm here, Jesus," he said with a strange laugh. "Please take me home."

Then he fell back on the stretcher, closed his eyes, and died.

None of us said anything. In fact it would be months before we allowed ourselves to speak about that last half minute of his life.

I was numb through the wake and funeral, unable to weep, hardly able to speak. I thought I had prepared mentally for his death, but I knew nothing about grief.

The wake and funeral were overwhelmed by strangers, men and women I had never met and did not know, but who worshipped the legend of Peter Connors. My brothers and parents did not appear. Gina and her handsome doctor drove in from Chicago. My kids steered me around and whispered instructions in my ear. After the burial in Oakdale Memorial, they urged me to go away for a couple of weeks. Instead I went back to the office the following Monday morning. Life went on and so did the firm. So too did Elegant Homes, my firm.

Denial and grief continued for a year. Mourning will never end. I was finally able to ask myself whether I had been happy, whether I would do it all again if I had the chance, whether I had any regrets. I didn't know the answers and I still don't. I do know that I had been a shallow and naïve young woman who knew nothing about life or marriage and who was unaware that she had other choices. I also concluded, after several conversations with Father Matt, that I had been a good wife and a good mother, a conclusion on which Big Mike and my kids vigorously insisted. I had not failed completely in these responsibilities. In that hardly dramatic and minimal conviction, I found solace.

I also decided that I would not try marriage again, it was far too demanding a venture to attempt more than once. After my required year of mourning, I put away my widow's clothes (always fashionable, mind you) and began to act like a responsible aging grandmother. "Men are going to start hitting on you, Mom," my adorable Vicki informed me.

"Vick, men have hit on me all my life. They didn't pause for more than a moment or two when I had a husband or when I was wearing black. The only problem is that none of them are the kind of men I wouldn't mind hitting on me."

She and my son both laughed, as did my

grandchild, who laughed all the time. They didn't realize that I was speaking the literal truth. I had had it with men.

Or so I thought.

— Maria Angelica —

WE HAD, I told myself, nothing to lose by going public with Elegant Homes. We needed more money to spread our software and offices around the country. If the shares went up, my children and I would make a tidy sum of money, enough maybe for my grandchildren's college education and for me to retire to my native Sienna some day. Actually I don't think we are Tuscans, more likely Lombards or Goths or some other barbarian crowd.

Nor did I resist the idea of offering a large block of our stock to Donlan Assets Management. I had some money in Frodo, which had paid for my kids' long residence at the Dome. Jack Donlan apparently knew what he was doing. His accountants and lawyers swarmed over our offices both in Oakdale and Sears Tower.

"Very smart people," my son, Pete, who ran the Oakdale office now, observed. "If they think we are a good investment, a lot of other people will too."

"He makes mistakes like all of them."

"Not very many."

"His Frodo fund paid for your education."

"I told them that. . . . I don't know whether he knows you're a client."

"I'm sure that wouldn't affect his decision."

Finally the day came when he and I would meet. Apparently we had passed all but the final test—his meeting with me. Was I the kind of person who could be trusted to protect the stockholders' wealth he had put in Samwise, his more speculative fund. I didn't like the idea of the test. I wore a conservative navy blue suit with a single oak pin. I had not removed my wedding ring for two years. I solemnly resolved that I would choke all my wisecracks.

So my lead-off remark was, "It doesn't seem to be a level playing field—three Irish speculators and one Sicilian widow."

"Tuscan, as I remember."

"You read the article? I hope you didn't take any of it seriously. Actually we are Sienese, to be honest, from a little farm on a hill outside of Siena. Probably Goths or Lombardi or some other primitive Bronze Age tribe."

"Some of the genetic research suggests that the Etruscans were a Celtic tribe."

"Then you have one female Celt against three male Celts. Be forewarned that you're outnumbered."

"My late mother, a lieutenant colonel in the United States Army, would have agreed completely."

"Smart woman. Presumably you inherited her intelligence."

Our colleagues around the room laughed nervously at the banter. I was an idiot.

John Patrick Donlan was what my daughters called totally cute. Slender, maybe five foot eleven, pale baby blue eyes, curly blond hair with a faint touch of white, a quick, heart-melting smile, a three-piece dark grey Armani suit, gleaming white shirt, and a blue tie with a thin pattern that sort of matched his eyes. I warned myself that I should keep my mouth shut and that I should not let myself drift into a crush on this man. Those baby blue eyes had a veneer of cold steel.

He was a strong man with a tough, disciplined body and an aura of integrity that suggested moral strength. I would not fool him. Indeed every time his eyes focused on me, I felt vulnerable, even naked.

A handsome African-American woman drifted into the room with tea and coffee and Belleek cups and saucers.

"This my assistant, Elfrida Jones, Ms. Connors. Elfrida, this is Ms. Maria Connors."

"Hi, Elfrida."

"Hi, Maria."

I had an ally in the room.

"You take tea, I believe, Maria."

"Black as midnight on a moonless night."

"Elfrida is the one who put the relevant issue of *Chicago Markets* in my file."

"We used models for the swimsuit pictures," I blurted, feeling my face flame.

"I very much doubt that, Ms. Connors," he said with a matching blush.

Stop, you fool. Shut your big mouth. And banish all those errant thoughts.

"Now tell me a little about Oakdale. I'm afraid I don't know much of Illinois west of the DesPlaines River."

"So we took down the rusty old statue of General Atkinson who led the American forces and put up a monument to Black Hawk. Almost no one knew who General Atkinson was."

"That would doubtless please the faculty from NIU—Northern Illinois—who live in town."

"The symbolism would be lost on them. They think a Black Hawk is a hockey player."

"You always have the last word, don't you, Ms. Connors?"

Those steel blue eyes probed me, body and soul.

"Only when I'm awake."

He smiled faintly, as though impressed.

"Now could you tell me three good reasons why I should not become involved with your enterprise?"

Ah, now was the real test.

"The first reason is that Elegant Homes depends on a sufficient level of prosperity in our society and a management class that wants homes that honor what the art critics and the environmentalists say, but do not have the time, and perhaps the talent, to build such homes. If our economy should collapse, then we would certainly go down with it."

"As would all of us."

"A second reason is that there might be something inappropriate about earning a living off such homes while there are still homeless people on our streets, minorities living in slums, and young couples who cannot afford homes of their own. We must vote for reforms that diminish or eliminate such injustice. When we do that in fact, we strengthen the economy instead of weakening it."

"Spoken like a good Democrat."

I permitted myself a first taste of the tea. Spiced.

"The third reason is that you might want to consider serious doubts about whether you want a babbling woman like me deciding the fate of your investment."

"I would never dare to think that, Ms. Connors. You must excuse me for declining to serve on your board for the present. I have a marriage coming up in my family and that will consume a lot of time. Later perhaps . . . However, I would urge you to assemble a good group of outside board members."

"May I ask you in another year?"

He considered carefully.

"Of course," he said with a slight nod of his head.

He signed the document in front of him on the desk and passed it across to me.

I raised an eyebrow to my lawyer, who smiled.

"I've vetted it. If you want to read it . . ."

"Too excited."

I pushed the document across the desk. Both lawyers applauded. We shook hands all around, thanked one another, and departed. There was no offer of lunch, thanks be to God. As we were walking out of his tastefully antique office—I must get some slides of it for our repertory—he followed me.

"I have a check here, Maria, for the agreed price. Do you want to accept it and sign a receipt?"

"You better give it to my lawyer. I'd spend it all in one place."

I left the building, my heart beating, my head throbbing. I called Pete on my cell phone.

Vicki answered.

"Tell your husband I passed."

"Hooray! . . . Was he cute?"

"In a button-down way. No big deal."

But it was a big deal.

— John Patrick —

MARIA SABATTINI had invaded my imagination and refused to depart. I would get over her, I told myself, it will just take time.

Why get over her? Because if I did not I would fall in love with her and have to marry her. I was determined that would not happen.

She was not only beautiful but she was intelligent and funny and admirable. She was still wearing her wedding ring, which meant she was not available, did it not?

It had been my intention to take them all to lunch at the Chicago Club. The lawyers both expected the invitation. Had either of them told her? I had also told them that I would be ready to serve on the board of Elegant Homes where I could keep an eye on the efficiency of the staff. Yet I had changed my mind. They would want to know why.

Would she want to know why?

Because I was scared of her? That would be the behavior of a coward. Could I say that I was afraid of her? She had not tried to "hit" on me, a word the origin of which my daughter had to explain to me. Rather she had dismissed the meeting and my role as the Grand Inquisitor as silly and acted as if money and success were not at stake. She had decided to be her normal self, intelligent, fearless, and funny.

Was she not a woman to be pursued? Did I want to pursue her?

She was not the fetish woman I had made of her after reading the article. Rather she was the kind of woman you had to respect as well as desire. I was not at the age of life to take on such a task. I was not ready for the challenges of matrimony. And marriage to Maria Sabattini Connors would be all challenge, despite the obvious advantages it would involve.

My first wife would have said that God had seen fit to proffer me a great opportunity in addition to the gains that would arise from having part ownership of Elegant Homes. God would be upset with me if I waived such an opportunity.

Was God telling me, "Bed the woman while there's still time. Don't let her get away"?

I will not marry again, I insisted. Been there, done that.

I reached for my phone to call someone, I knew not whom.

I picked up the phone and there was Joe McMahon.

"What did you think?" he asked.

"I think you were right, we made a very good deal."

"I know that. . . . What did you think of her?"

"Apparently a very intelligent woman."

"Is that all?"

"Clearly attractive."

"And just a little crazy?"

"I wouldn't say that. She was obviously nervous and covered it up with wit."

"We should keep an eye on her."

"Not I."

Joe, I told myself, was not a matchmaker.
Or was he.

I did not want to share my life with a woman, any woman. Certainly not one larger than life.

That's where I left it. On the day of the public offering the shares opened twenty percent above the floor. They fell fifteen percent the second day and ten percent more the third day. The *Journal* had a heavy-handed article about frivolous corporations. By the end of the second week, the share price was thirty percent above the initial offering and stayed there. The *Times* weighed in with a feature article about Maria Angelica, as she now claimed was her name. "Rural Woman Reads the Signs of the Time" was the headline. "Claims to Be a Lombard or a Goth. Build Your Dream House Online."

That kind of publicity you can't buy. I was not worried about my investment. Neither article mentioned my involvement. Publicity I don't need. Then, however, I began to suspect that God was conniving against me. It was a moderately hot Chicago day in August. It had been a listless summer for me. None of the other acquisitions we looked at seemed interesting. My funds were doing well, Samwise was prospering in great part because of ELG. When I was a kid I loved summer. I would run down to the beach at Montrose, swim, read, and then swim again. I'd buy an ice cream bar on the way home, joke with my parents at supper, and then read some more. I bought a little beach house in the Dunes where we would go on some of the weekends and for a week in August. After we married and before my wife's serious problems appeared, we'd spend two weeks over there with our daughters, much to the resentment of her family. They wondered why they were never invited to visit while we were at the beach. The answer was that there was just enough room for two adults and a child or two. There was no room for a bunch of overweight people who would be drunk by one in the afternoon. My wife begged me to keep them away.

Later I took up sailing because my doctor urged me to find recreation that was more relaxing than my tennis obsession. I bought a thirty-two-foot sailboat, berthed it at Montrose Harbor, and took sailing lessons. My teenage daughters thought it was cool and wanted to take lessons too. We had a lot of fun, especially during the summers Faith was away at the Betty Ford Center. The *Mary Fran,* named after my mother and my youngest daughter, was a kind of a hangout for the kids and their friends. My mom absolutely refused to board it even at the dock.

"That's no boat for you to be driving around," she warned me. "It looks as unreliable as the old woman after whom it's named."

Nonetheless she and my father would walk down to the edge of the park to watch us sail by.

"She's a pretty boat, Grams, once you get to know her."

"Well, your pa is a rich speculator so he's entitled to a pretty boat."

Her problem was that the boat would give a "bad example" to others.

Since Faith died, I used neither the boat nor the cottage, though I had paid to maintain both and had remodeled the cottage so that my daughters and eventually their families could use it. I felt not the slightest desire either to sail or drive to the other side of the Lake.

I was acting like a worn-out old man.

Grief, I told myself, maybe I'll just have to live with it.

I remembered fondly the summer days when my father and I would walk over to the Italian Village on Monroe, eat pasta Bolognese, and drink a bottle of Barolo—in memory of his days in Italy after hostilities had ended.

"They're a strange, wonderful people," he remarked. "Just the opposite of the Irish. We are generally pretty happy but pretend we are morose. They are very sad but do a wonderful imitation of happiness."

Why not?

I turned right at Clark and walked two blocks to Monroe.

Did Maria, or Maria Angelica as I must call her, fit that model?

Suddenly, as I thought of her, she appeared in front of me, in green sundress, and carrying a matching bag, strolling down Monroe Street like she was on the Champs Elysées—which I'm sure she had never seen—and totally unaware of the admiring glances that trailed after the sundress that outlined the shapes of her body.

"Maria Angelica," I murmured, as we almost collided, "green goddess of summer."

"Jac— uh, Mr. Donlan . . . What are you doing here?"

"Walking down Monroe Street to the Italian Village, a right I have by virtue of my voter registration in this city, which is more than I might say for you."

I had taken her completely by surprise.

"What Italian Village?"

I pointed at the sign down the street.

"My late father, God be good to him, and I had the custom occasionally on a hot summer day to eat a bowl of pasta there and drink a bottle of Barolo."

"I never knew it was there. . . . I must have walked by it a hundred times."

"Every Chicagoan knows about the Italian Village. You must learn these essentials or you'll earn the reputation of being a hick."

"Exurbanite . . ."

"Congratulations on the wonderful publicity in the name of all those who have invested in Samwise. . . ." I took her arm. "Surely you will join me in disposing of a bottle of Barolo in celebration of the good fortune of Samwise?"

"Jac— Mr. Donlan . . . This isn't a good idea!"

She was breathless, but she did not resist my directing her across the street.

"It's Jack, or if you wish, Jackie, and yes it is."

"No, it's not."

"On some occasions there is an obligation to test something that seems not to be a good idea, but which in fact may well be."

We were at the door of the Italian Village. I released her arm to give her a chance to decline my invitation.

She took a deep breath, sighed, and murmured, "I just love Barolo," and recaptured my arm.

This is your idea, I said to God. I hope you know what I'm doing. I warn you that I will pursue this woman and learn all I can about her. I doubt that anything I learn will dissuade me. Okay?

There were no signals from heaven that the deity demurred from this game plan.

I will, however, pursue her slowly and gently and with all due respect.

"I was surprised that the *Times* didn't have a picture of you."

"They wanted one the worst way. I refused. I am not a sex object."

"You certainly are not, Maria Angelica. You are a very beautiful woman and for that you should be thankful to God and not intimidated by either envious women or lecherous men."

I am certainly invoking God often. I should also plead with Him to help me. This is an art that I never learned.

"You are leering at me now, Jackie."

"I am not, Maria Angelica. I wouldn't dream of leering at you."

"You're fantasizing about taking off my sundress."

"Guilty as charged, but only respectfully and reverently."

"Sometimes the fantasy is much better than the reality."

"I'll take my chances."

She relaxed and grinned.

"You're winning all the exchanges today, Jackie. I warn you, it won't last."

"I'm duly warned and I'm sure it won't last."

"Do you miss your father?" she asked cautiously as we arranged ourselves at the table and I ordered the Barolo.

"He was not just a father, but a teacher, a mentor, and good friend and never tried to run my life."

"You've been very fortunate. My parents and my two brothers won't speak to me, haven't for years. My sister, Gina, and I are friends, but we don't see each other often. My brothers have a construction firm. They are sloppy in their proposals and sloppier in their work. Everyone thinks that because they are family, I owe them business."

"Ethnic standards."

"I couldn't do it. . . . I wouldn't do it. My father-in-law and his father had created a reputation for integrity that I could not violate."

We ate our pasta and consumed our Barolo and toasted each other every couple of minutes. She told me her life story, candidly and without any show of emotion or occasional flashes of wit. I realized then how vulnerable she was and promised the deity that I would always protect her—but only when she wanted to be protected. Her romance with Peter Connors was the stuff out of which Verdi operas were made—beautiful and bittersweet.

"Now you know all there is to know about me, Jackie. Not much of a story really. I tell myself that I was a good wife and a good mother, not perfect, but I tried hard. I probably saved the family business."

"And remade Oakdale and created Elegant Homes."

"I guess so." She was close to tears.

"There is always a sense at a certain time in life that the youthful dreams, especially the romantic ones didn't come true, but for all the heartbreak something was accomplished. That is consoling, but it does not justify acceptance."

Who was I of all people to say that?

"That's an improper comment, Jackie. It presumes an intimacy between us that does not exist."

Strike one.

"I don't presume any intimacy, Maria. I was not reflecting on your experience but on mine."

"I'm sorry. . . ." Her shoulders slumped. "Too much Barolo. I feel too vulnerable . . . a little scared too."

"I'm not hitting on you, Maria. And, when I'm thinking seriously about that, I'll give you warning so you can exercise due diligence."

"If I want to . . . I've told my story, now do you want to tell me yours?"

"Fair is fair."

So I told her my story. She had the right to know it anyway. Moreover, shared memoirs strengthened bonds. As I told her about Faith's family, her lovely face tightened with rage.

"Those bitches! Evil people! They killed that poor girl because she found a husband and her sisters didn't. . . ."

"I don't make that charge."

"That's up to you! I make it. Small, passive-aggressive, mean-spirited people like that make me want to puke!"

"I tell myself I should have done more to protect her. . . ."

"She knew that you did all you could. . . . I wonder that you would never become involved with a woman ever again. We are such nasty, petty, miserable people. . . ."

"Not all of you! . . . And I'm not sure that I'll ever marry again."

She just grinned.

"Walk me back to Sears Tower, Jackie. I'm so tuned that I'll get lost. . . . Never should drink a half bottle of wine at lunch."

She took my arm and we walked slowly back to Wacker Drive and Sears Tower.

"It was good to talk to you," she said.

"Likewise."

"Would you be interested in another adventure that we probably shouldn't do?"

"In for an inch, in for a mile."

I wasn't quite sure what that meant.

"I don't suppose that out there in the prairies, you ever did any sailing?"

"We have lakes in the prairies."

"Lakes with a small *l*."

"What other kind are there?"

"Here in Chicago we have the Lake with a capital *L*."

"So I'm told."

"You never crewed on a lake with a small *l*?"

"I certainly did and on a twenty-two-foot boat that our firm owns."

"I have a boat on Lake Michigan. I haven't used it in a while."

"How big?"

"Thirty-two feet."

"That's a yacht."

"It has three staterooms and a head and will sleep twelve, though it never has. It can do the race to Mackinac though it also never has."

"You want me to crew on that monster thing?"

"I'm inviting you to come for a ride tomorrow. I bet you never saw the skyline from the Lake."

"We really shouldn't do it, Jackie. It's a workday."

There are other and better reasons for not sailing the *Mary Fran*.

"The winds are forecast to be light and we can have a nice leisurely sail, perhaps drop anchor and swim."

"No Barolo?"

"I permit myself and my crew only one can of beer. . . . Your virtue will be under no assault."

"I make no promises about yours. . . . What time?"

"I'll get there early to make sure everything is in working order. I'll meet you on the deck of the yacht club about eleven?"

"I haven't said that I'll show up."

"That's true."

"Well, I guess. I'll be there. . . . I reserve the right to change my mind when I see the boat."

— Maria Angelica —

SO THE next morning at a quarter to eleven, courtesy of a taxi, I stood on the deck of the yacht club, covered with suntan cream, and stared in amazement at the busy harbor and its panorama of yachts, most of them covered up though it was August. I was early because I'm always early, an obsession I did not learn from my parents. I was wearing cutoff jeans and an NIU sweatshirt over my brand-new and very modest two-piece black swimsuit. I had purchased both swimsuit and new boat shoes late Thursday afternoon when I had recovered from the Barolo. Grandmothers, no matter how well preserved, should not wear bikinis—at least not in ordinary circumstances. I was carrying a shopping bag with a cover-up, a change of clothes, and four sandwiches, four cans of Diet Coke, and a box of oatmeal raisin cookies. I felt very much like a hick from the prairies, especially compared to the well-dressed people that strolled around the harbor. The shopping bag is the best I can do, folks, I'm a hick from the prairies. I leaned against a wall and tried to pretend I wasn't there.

Jack Donlan showed up promptly at eleven o'clock, wearing khaki shirt and slacks and a matching baseball cap with gold braid and the words *Mary Fran* on it. My heart jumped at the sight of him. He was so cute. Careful Connors, real careful. You don't want to be that way so soon.

"Good morning, Captain," I said with a salute. "Sea-person Connors reporting for duty."

"Good morning, Maria," he said, brushing my cheek with his lips. "You look gorgeous, as always."

My heart did several more leaps. This was not good.

He took the shopping bag from my hand.

"Sorry about the matched luggage, I didn't bring any of my sailing gear in from Oakdale. . . . I have some food in there. . . . I assume you have refrigeration on board. . . . This Lake is bigger than Oak Lake."

Mary Fran was a lovely boat: black hull; teak decks; polished bronze hardware; electronic winches; bulkhead dials reporting radar, wind, water temperature, and air pressure; and three comfortable cabins.

Jack helped me into the boat.

"She's beautiful!" I said.

"We had a lot of fun on it," he said, a touch of sadness in his voice.

"You haven't used it the last two years."

"Kids were busy with other things, marriage, family, courtship."

"Father Matt, our pastor in Oakdale, says it's all right to own an expensive boat, so long as you use it."

He laughed.

"Father Matt is right, but *Mary Fran* earned me money the last two years by appreciation. Paid for her upkeep."

He gave me a thin khaki life jacket and a cap, both labeled with the boat's name.

"Rule on this boat is everyone always wears a jacket. Regardless. I note that you

have already smeared suntan lotion on yourself. That's another rule."

"And you've got chains to put me in if I
disobey any rules?"

"Bread and water."

He instructed me on my duties on the
craft, easier than on the *Maria Angelica*
because of the electronic winches.

"Any questions?"

"No sir, Captain, sir."

He pushed a button on the bulkhead and
a fan cleared the hull of gas.

Then he pushed another button and the
auxiliary motor hummed confidently.

"You buy the best, don't you, Captain, sir?"

"For my wife and kids, only the best," he
said, the touch of sadness back in his voice.

If this turned into a memorial voyage, it
would be a big mistake.

"Cast off the mooring lines!"

"Yes, sir! Right away, sir."

He laughed.

I had him. You don't dare be a sourpuss
on a boat ride with me!

"Sure does beat an outboard!"

Mary Fran slipped out of her berth and
eased her way into the channel, uncrowded
on Friday morning. In a few minutes we were

out of the harbor and on the gentle waters of the enormous, scary Lake. With a very scary captain.

"Raise the foresail!"

I pushed another button and the foresail flapped in the breeze. Jackie turned off the motor. *Mary Fran* hesitated, not quite sure what to do. He eased the wheel around and the jib caught the wind.

"Raise the main!"

Another button to push and the boat surged forward, knowing now what she should do.

"Wow!" I exclaimed. "Totally cool!"

"A good boat. She does what's she told."

"Unlike most human women!"

I kept him laughing all the way down the shore beyond Navy Pier. The breeze was offshore, consistent, and moderate. Ice cream cumulus clouds were moving slowly across the sky.

"You want to take the con?"

"You mean drive this boat? Course not!"

I moved over to take his place.

Mary Fran, not at all sure about this new pilot, hesitated and I moved the wheel gently. She settled down like a trained horse. Good girl.

"You have the touch, Maria Angelica."

"It's a lot easier than doing the rudder thing."

I had been so bemused by the skyline, the boat, and captain, my captain, that I had not noticed I was hot and hungry. The thermometer said eighty-six.

"Would you excuse me for a moment, Captain, sir?"

"Certainly."

"Permission to go below."

"Of course."

I removed the sandwiches, Cokes, and cookies from the fridge, took off the life jacket, shed the Huskies sweatshirt, slathered my self with suntan lotion, put on the life jacket, and climbed back into the cockpit.

"Grandma in a bikini!" he gasped. I mean literally he gasped. This might not be a good idea either.

"It is not a bikini," I said primly. "It is merely a very modest two-piece swimsuit. Grandmothers," I repeated my own principle, "no matter how well preserved, should never wear bikinis unless for a very special occasion. Here's your sandwiches. They should distract you from staring."

"What would a special occasion be?"

"A honeymoon or something like that."

As soon as the words were out of my mouth, I regretted them. Jack, however, guffawed.

"I'll try to remember that."

It was my turn to feel a flaming face.

"Very good sandwiches," he said, saving both of us.

I wasn't trying to seduce him, not really. Only in the long run.

Back at Navy Pier, I steered us into the calm water behind the breakwaters.

We lowered the sails. He pressed another magic button and an anchor slipped into the water, gripping bottom after a long time.

"Permission to swim, sir?"

"You note the temperature of the water?"

"Sixty-four."

"That's cold."

I shrugged my shoulders.

"Do I have to wear the jacket?"

"Stay within twenty yards of the boat!"

I kicked off my jeans, tossed aside the life jacket, and dived in from the gunnel. It was a longer way down than a jump from the *Maria Angelica.* When I hit the water, I thought I would die, it was so cold. I surfaced, shivering and, I suspected, blue.

"Piece of cake," I shouted.

"I can see that."

I swam maybe a hundred yards back and forth, just to prove I could do it. My poor body adjusted reluctantly to the water temperature. Finally, it was time and past time to stop. I swam to the side of the boat. Jack tossed a rope ladder.

"I have to climb that?"

"Only way."

I tried twice and failed, took a deep breath, and clambered up to the gunnel. I was too weak to force myself over it. He took me in his arms and lifted me on to the deck. Very strong arms.

For a brief moment I was powerless in those arms. My face flamed. Then he let me go, reluctantly I thought.

"You're a tomboy, Grams," he said, throwing a huge towel around my shoulders, one that announced it was from the *Mary Fran.*

"And proud of it," I gasped, still shivering.

"The barometer is falling. We'd better get out of here."

I glanced at the western sky. A line of black clouds on the horizon was moving right toward us.

"That wasn't part of the prediction."

I pulled on my cover-up and my boat shoes.

"Sometimes on humid days weather cells blow up without warning. NOA weather radio hasn't picked it up yet."

"Let's get out of here," I announced.

We lifted the anchor, raised the sails and gave *Mary Fran* free rein. The wind continued to be offshore but picked up to sixteen knots. The harbor was three miles north of us. We were flying along at six knots an hour and were almost at the harbor mouth when the rain hit us. The lines on the main sail jammed. I climbed up to the top of the cabin and lowered it by hand, without being told. The jib went down easily. Then we turned into the harbor and a gust of wind rocked us. I clung to the mast for dear life and shouted for the joy of the contest. Jack helped me down and returned to the wheel. I collapsed on the floor of the cockpit.

"You okay?" he yelled.

"Never better!"

Then the lightning and thunder started.

"You and your big ideas, Jack Donlan!"

"Wanted to see what kind of a sailor you are."

The auxiliary motor brought us to our

berth. We covered the sails in the driving rain, secured everything that needed to be secured, and walked as quickly as we could to the clubhouse.

"Buy you a hamburger?"

"Great idea."

I went to the women's room, tidied up, put on my change of clothes, and joined him in the bar.

"You okay?" I asked captain—my captain—who was nursing a beer.

"I wouldn't want to be hit by one of those in the middle of the Lake."

"You'd need a crew like me out there to survive."

"Maria Angelica, you're too much."

"I've been told that."

"Instead of fear, you were shouting with the joy of the battle."

"I could turn out to be dangerous. We don't quite have storms like that on Oak Lake. . . . By the way, you're really good at that sort of thing."

We laughed together again, finished our beer and burgers, and he drove me back to Millennium Towers. I ached in every bone and muscle of my body. I had to get back in condition. It was now a serious issue.

"Next Friday?" he asked at the door of my apartment.

"Only if you promise more serious action."

He laughed again, kissed me with some vigor, and departed.

This was courtship?

Whatever it was, it went on till the middle of September when we sailed the *Mary Fran* to her winter storage on the river. I wanted to cry. We had great fun. I would miss her. As for her captain, I had no idea what was going on in his head.

However, I had great stories to tell my children back in Oakdale on Saturday morning.

"Has he made a move, Mom?" Clara demanded.

"Nope."

"Will he?"

"Honestly, hon, don't know."

"Do you want him to."

I hesitated and then told the truth.

"I haven't made up my mind."

Just the same, after I had waved a sad good-bye to *Mary Fran,* I paid a visit to an elite lingerie store and bought a fresh supply, in case I needed it. We had been very careful that our late summer sailings were very cautious ventures—as far as our courtship was concerned. Both of us were concerned about stirring up strong emotions too early. Too cautious? I don't know.

The next week there was an opera. My invitation came in a phone call two nights before.

"Would you like to attend *Turandot* this week?"

"Why not?" I said.

I loved to listen to opera music, but I'd never once in all my life been to a sure-enough opera.

There wasn't even enough time to find a script and read it. I had yet to learn about the supratitles they use at the Lyric.

Supper at the Graham room was lifeless at first. Then he asked the question that was on both our minds.

"What are we doing, Maria?"

"Well," I said, pretending to weigh my words carefully, "one might say that we are at the early stages of tentatively beginning something folks might call a courtship."

"How do you feel about it?"

"Interested, obviously, and scared silly."

Time for honest talk.

"Me too . . . It's happened too quickly for me to grasp. . . . It's a serious business."

"With serious risks," I added.

God knew how often I had pondered the risks in rides back and forth to Oakdale.

"I have the feeling that if we go on like this much longer, there will be no escaping. . . . Only a fool would want to escape from you, Maria. . . ."

"I understand the fear," I assured him. "The other side of the coin is the fear I might lose the opportunity of my life. . . . I kind of enjoyed those boat rides."

We both laughed. I would have to lead him into laughter for the rest of our lives. Would that be bad?

Not necessarily.

"Might we need a hiatus to be sure?"

"I'm sure that's a good idea. . . . How long, do you think?"

"Two or three weeks maybe?"

"Is that all?"

"No more, certainly."

My mind was not completely made up, but it was more made up than his. I should say something wise.

"Jackie, take as long as you want. I don't want to cause any pressure."

Well, not any unfair pressure.

"I knew that's what you'd say. Thank

you . . . That you're that kind of woman increases the pressure."

"Naturally."

And we both laughed again.

His good-night kiss was not quite violent, but it certainly was vehement. So was the touch of his fingers on my breast.

"No pressure at all," I gasped.

As I was falling asleep, I said to myself, "Maria Angelica, there is no such thing as the perfect permanent lover, but you could do a lot worse."

Like the time you almost went to bed with Chip McConnell, who was the running back on Peter's high school team. Dear God, thank you for stopping me.

I have to ask myself whether I might be slipping into a similar disaster.

— **John Patrick** —

I TORMENTED myself with worry for the next three weeks. I reminded myself that I was a speculator, a gambler, a risk taker. I firmly believed my father's dictum that certainty is not possible either in love or the stock market. You play the odds, he used to say. And how do you figure the odds in love? I would ask in return. You just know, he'd sigh. Like I knew with your mother the first time I saw her.

I was overwhelmed by Maria Angelica the first time I saw her. I continue to be. She is fun—fun to talk to, fun to banter with, fun to laugh at, and fun to yearn for. But so was

Mandy Clifford, the national TV reporter. At the last minute she dumped me because I was a Catholic and wouldn't divorce my wife who at the time had been six months at Betty Ford on her third session there. After Mandy walked out on me, I realized that it had been foolishness from the very beginning. I would have become her boy toy. Yet at the time it looked like a good risk. My daughter's oxytocin, I guess. Yet I felt about Mandy the same way I feel about Maria. How can I figure out what to do? Mandy was a nasty person. She loved to obliterate people she was interviewing. That troubled me at the time, but I paid no attention to it till she turned on me and tore me to shreds. What troubles me about Maria? Her laughter? It suggests she's never serious, but her life story shows just how serious she can be.

I agonized for three weeks, sleeping poorly and not listening as carefully as I should to my staff. They knew something was wrong, but they would never have guessed. ELG stock, in the meantime continued to climb, not wildly but steadily. Good investment. Better than I thought it would be.

Finally, on impulse, I phoned her.

"Maria Connors," she said crisply.

"Jack Donlan."

"I knew someone by that name once."

"I wonder if we could have supper at Ambria this evening. Pick you up at seven o'clock?"

She should have bawled me out for the delay.

Instead she said, "Good, I've been waiting for an occasion to wear my brand-new black lingerie!"

— Maria Angelica —

I DID not mention the subject at hand when I climbed into his Lexus. I was scared again, not that he would say that he didn't want me, but that he would say that he did. I was fully prepared to rebuff him if all he did was hit on me. That was unlike my Jackie, however. He would rather affirm his eternal love for me and then lead me off to his apartment. Unless I said, no, not yet.

I wouldn't do that to him. I loved him too much. If he told me that he loved me, that would be for the moment as good as a marriage vow. He'd been without a woman too long. The only sensible thing would be to give myself to him completely. I had never done that before. What would it be like? Scary—like clinging to the mast of *Mary Fran*.

And fun too—of a terrifying variety.

"I'm sorry I kept you waiting."

"You had less than twenty-four hours before I took out my personal phone book and drawn a big black line through your name."

"Really?"

"No, a red line!"

"I'm glad you're not angry. . . ."

"Who said not angry, 'white man'? . . . Do you realize you could have lost the best crew you'd ever get for that silly old boat of yours? A woman has her honor to consider, after all."

We kept up the banter until we left the outer drive. Then at the stop light at Lincoln Park West, he crushed me in his arms. Preview of coming attractions. Yet very gentle and very sweet.

"You plan on raping the poor chaste matron, even before she drinks half a bottle of Barolo?"

When we were shown to our table, I noted

that an uncorked bottle of Barolo was already waiting for us. Nice touch.

After we ordered, Jack Donlan began what would be for him a painful conversation. I resolved that I would not make it more difficult for him by any smart-ass remarks.

"I must begin by apologizing for taking so long. I made up my mind this morning that I was acting like an idiot. . . . How long did you ruminate?"

Mistaken word!

"I bought some Wrigley's gum so I could chew on a cud and decided the next morning that I love you very much and can accept the possibility of sleeping in the same bed with you for the rest of my life. . . . You don't snore, do you?"

"I don't believe so. . . . You would be perfectly right if you just got rid of me. . . ."

"Perfectly wrong."

He reached into an inside pocket of his brown Armani and produced a small box. Pure corn! And I was from the prairies. . . .

"Whatcha got there?"

It was the biggest diamond in all the world . . . well not quite, but certainly satisfactory.

"The standard response," I said, "is that

you shouldn't have spent so much money and I hope you didn't have to sell the *Mary Fran* to pay for it. . . . But it is beautiful. . . . Too beautiful for the likes of me, but I'll wear it anyhow."

Then, without any planning, I began to cry. How like a woman!

"Don't cry, Maria!"

"Tears of joy," I sniffled.

"I'll love you always," he said, again displaying little creativity.

"You'd better!" I replied and then broke down completely as he put the ring on my finger. It was indeed huge.

I'd better say something memorable.

"I guess we're engaged, huh?"

Maria Angelica being memorable.

"That's a fair assessment of the situation."

"I'll try to stop making my idiot remarks."

"If you do that, I'll take the ring back. I fell in love with you in the office that day because you were beautiful and you had a wonderful gift for wit."

"Oh," I said very quietly. "I hope it doesn't dry up."

"Not a chance."

I was floating toward the sky. We were a pair of happy kids.

"Second childhood," I said, "is better than first."

"Experience helps us enjoy it more."

Under the table his knee touched mine. I quickly pulled back.

"Sir, are you hitting on me?"

"Yes, ma'am, but it's all right because we're engaged."

"That's true. . . . Incidentally I reject out of hand the vulgar phrase *get engaged*, as in 'Jack and I got engaged last night.'"

"I think I can remember that."

I moved my knee back in contact with his. He rested his hand on my thigh. That was very nice.

"I want to say something serious, affianced one."

"I await your words, madam."

"I have learned through the years that if a woman is going to give herself to a man, she should be a total gift. So at this minute, halfway through the roast beef and more than half through the Barolo on this our engagement day with our knees touching and your hand pleasantly on my thigh, I give myself to you totally and completely, John Patrick Donlan. Henceforth I am yours and you can do with me whatever you want."

He gulped and his hand tightened on my thigh. Grandma in delirium.

"I will always treat you with respect and reverence, Maria Angelica Sabattini Connors."

"Naturally," I said dismissively. "Incidentally that is, though now officially permitted, a strong grip you have on my thigh."

He moved his hand up and down, as though he owned me and everything about me. I wanted to shout with pleasure.

"Strong thigh," he observed.

"All the better to squeeze you with, my dear."

We went back to my apartment and he carried me triumphantly inside.

"I have the feeling that the captive matron will be violated in this cave."

"Count on it," he said, absorbing me in a total kiss.

So we began the dance of consummation. I had expected that it would be a clumsy and awkward waltz as we began to discover one another. It was not that way at all, however.

It was an exquisite pleasure as he slowly undressed and aroused me.

"What's your fantasy now?" I demanded through lips tightly pressed together.

"I've violated the modesty of a chaste suburban matron. . . . But as I progress I see how regal and graceful she appears as I strip her, I perceive that she is perhaps a grand duchess or maybe even an empress."

"I want to be a high priestess."

"Virgin high priestess?"

"Yes but very horny . . ." I gasped.

"Who am I? A pagan high priest?"

"A desert warrior," I whispered, "who has kidnapped me from the temple and has made me his slave."

We were both laughing in this exchange, but the laughter was no more than erotic background music.

We melted together and soared, floating above the ordinary world of problems and fears into a state of body-wrenching pleasure where multicolored surprises waited with promises of wonders unimagined. I was ecstatic with victory. He was mine forever. Then we slipped back into the world we had left behind, but it was now a place of peace and tranquility where a good night's sleep was possible. I wanted to proclaim my victory but was too weary with joy to speak

"Jackie Pat," I murmured, "you're pretty good at this kind of thing, just like sailing the boat. . . . You're a keeper. Don't ever think of trying to get away."

"I wasn't," he was able to murmur.

"'Cause I'll never let you go."

That seemed to settle that.

"And you should watch some old Valentino films to see how desert warriors treat their slave women, not that you were all that bad at the game."

— John Patrick —

IN THE days and weeks to come, I had expected the ordinary stresses and strains of intimacy to rear their mean little heads as we rushed from our work to our beds, either at her apartment or mine. Yet while we bantered constantly, we did not squabble. It helped that we were both fastidious neatniks. Moreover my wife, as I had come to define her in my own mind, seemed possessed by the conviction that it was a wife's responsibility to keep her husband happy. I suggested once, very gently, that there was no such obligation in our relationship.

"I always spoil my boy kids rotten," she replied.

I wondered if I would ever grow weary of her brash "last words."

Probably not.

She enjoyed sex and seemed ready at any time I was ready and even if I were not.

However busy we were during the day, at night we lived in an indolent and luxuriant paradise. Then we visited Ambria for a second time and the news of our romance made it into the media.

"Looks like we'd better get married," I said to Maria.

"I suppose I gotta make an honest man out of you."

Then my eldest daughter, Evie, phoned me on my private line in the office, her voice tight with rage.

"Dad, what the hell are you doing to our reputation?"

"Whose reputation, Evie?"

"Our family's reputation. Why are you letting yourself be seen in public with that whore?"

"That's a harsh word, Evie."

"It's the only word to describe her. Don't you know her reputation?"

"I've looked into her reputation. There's nothing in it of which she or I should be troubled."

"Then, Daddy dear, you're an asshole."

I was in a nightmare. None of my daughters had ever spoken to me with such disrespect.

"My investigation was carried out by a highly respectable agency."

"Then they're full of bullshit. . . . Look, I've talked to the girls and they agree that if you want to have a fling with her, screw her every night, and carry on with her in public, then go ahead and do it. But if you marry her, which is what she wants, we will never accept her and you will no longer be part of our family. I will not permit that woman to be near my children."

I hung up.

A few minutes later, the phone rang again.

Irene, my second daughter, did not waste any time on preliminaries.

"Why the fuck did you hang up on Evie?"

"I don't like your language, Rene."

"We don't like your behavior, Dad. How dare you humiliate us by appearing in public with that hooker?"

Different words, same party line.

"She's not a hooker."

"You're full of shit. If you dare to marry her, we'll disown you."

"That will be your problem."

I hung up on her too.

I waited a few minutes for Mary Fran to call. Evie had a powerful influence on her sisters. She was the oldest, the most articulate, the most determined. She bitterly opposed Mary Fran's decision to be a psychiatrist. Mary Fran did not argue, but she ignored her sister, which created a permanent state of war between the two sisters.

I concluded that Evie had seen the piece in the Chicago *Herald* and jumped to a conclusion. This would mean a long and bitter conflict because, once Evie made up her mind, she was not likely to change it.

A dam burst inside me and sadness swept through me. It was all too good to be true.

It got worse that night. We went over to St. Freddy's to make arrangements with the new pastor for a wedding the week after Thanksgiving. The housekeeper informed us that Father Hennessy would not see anyone who had not made a previous appointment. I informed her briskly that I had lived in the parish since my baptism and had made major contributions to it and that I demanded to see the pastor. I wondered if my daughters had put in the fix against us.

She shrugged and left us standing in the hallway. I led my fiancée into an office. A half hour later, Father Hennessy, a large young man wearing a cassock and a biretta, stormed into the office. We stood up.

"You rich people are all alike," he said. "You assume that the priest must be at your beck and call. To talk to your parish priest is a privilege, not a right."

"We want to arrange for a wedding."

"So I am told. . . . When will this wedding take place?"

"In the week after Thanksgiving."

"Typical . . . I must inform you that it is impossible."

"Why?"

"Because the guidelines require six months' preparation for marriage, including a Pre-Cana conference."

"Father, Ms. Connors and I have both been married before and we are in our early fifties. I assure you that we do not need a Pre-Cana conference."

"Nonetheless you attend one if you wish

to be married here. . . . Are you living together?"

"I fail to see that's your business, Father."

"It is my business because I have made it
a rule that no couple who are living in sin
may be married here."

"We are not living in sin, Father," Maria
said calmly. "Are you living in sin, Father?
We will not be married by a priest who has a
partner."

"Do you live in this parish, young
woman?"

"I live in Oakdale, Father, and I am old
enough to be your mother, who clearly did
not teach you good manners."

"Then you must marry in Oakdale. That
settles the matter. I ask you to leave the rectory."

"Father Matt from our parish has agreed
to perform the wedding ceremony."

"Father Matt will in fact not preside over
the ceremony. I do all the weddings in my
parish. I bid you good evening."

He stomped out of the office.

A chill wind blew across the Lake.

"Did the Vatican Council ever happen?" I
asked.

"Only the first one . . . What do we do now?"

"I call my friend Cardinal Sean Cronin tomorrow. He will straighten that fat slob out."

"The shortage of priests must be serious if men like that are appointed pastors."

The cardinal congratulated me on my forthcoming marriage. "I met the woman at some kind of civic event. She is clearly a very special person. I'm happy, Jack, that she has found a special spouse. Now tell me what that idiot at St. Fred's said to you."

I described our visit to the rectory in careful detail.

"That young man will end up shortly as a hospital chaplain if he doesn't grow up. . . . Let me call you back."

"There are no Masses scheduled for the Saturday after Thanksgiving. . . . Can you imagine how many couples he's driven over to Old Saint Pat's? You deliver the documents to Father Lulu, a wonderful young Filipino who will shortly be the next pastor—baptism, confirmation, death. He will fill out the forms. Father Matt is authorized to preside over the wedding ceremony.

If you have any more problems let me know."

And that was that. Cardinal Cronin was one of the more liberal American bishops, but he is not afraid to use power to protect the layfolk from crazy priests.

Okay, we'd be married (*get married* was banned just as *get engaged* was) at St. Freddy's and Father Matt would be the officiant. But we'd have to fight our way through my family. That would be very unpleasant. My daughters were choosing to assume the role of my in-laws. I permitted the family's influence in my first marriage. I permitted them to kill her. I would not tolerate similar behavior from my daughters. They thought they could disown me. I would disown them first.

I called Maria on her personal line.

"Sabattini," she said with a thick Italian accent.

"Johnny Pat."

"I've slept with a lot of men who call themselves that."

"I had a phone conversation with your very good friend Sean Cronin."

"Darling man."

"The St. Freddy's problem is solved. Father Matt has the cardinal's permission to preside. . . ."

"I'll vote for him in the next conclave."

"Let's have lunch at the Chicago Club and I'll tell you the details."

"I can't go there."

"Why not?"

"I've never been there before. I won't know how to act."

"Noon, Maria Angelica."

"They'll all stare at me."

"They are too old to be the staring kind."

I then hung up, having the last word. That was the only way I'd ever have the last word.

They did stare, however.

"The cardinal did not say those things about me."

"He did so."

"He never said that I was beautiful."

"He did so. . . . But now I have something serious to talk about."

"We're in love, Jackie Pat, and we're going to make love tonight and we're going to be officially united by the Catholic Church. What could be serious?"

"My daughters."

She put down her salad fork.

"I was afraid they might not like me. Kids don't like stepmothers."

"That would be an understatement."

I recited my conversations of the morning.

"They don't know me."

"They think they do."

"Can I win them over?"

"Evie is the problem. I don't think she has changed her mind from a snap judgment in all her life."

She swallowed nervously.

"They threaten to disown you if you marry me?"

"Literally."

"That's not fair."

"Of course it's not . . . I've told you how their aunts and their grandmother and their great-grandmother define reality so it fits their suppositions. Apparently my daughters inherited that propensity."

"What will you do, Jack?" She pushed aside her salad.

"Eat your lunch, Maria Angelica. It's expensive."

She laughed and did what she was told.

"They killed my first wife. I won't let them kill you."

"I'm different." Her chin went up in defiance.

"They can't disown me, because I will disown them."

"Take away their trust funds . . . ? You wouldn't do that. It would be vindictive."

"They inherit their mother's fund. They can live off that."

"They'll hate you forever."

"They already do."

"Can I meet them? Persuade them that I'm not a whore or a hooker? . . . See, I've eaten my salad!"

"You shouldn't have to go into the lion's den."

"Lionesses . . . Are they really serious?"

"They get carried away by their rhetoric and can't admit that they've changed their mind."

"Do they believe that they can intimidate you?"

I thought about it.

"They know how much I love them. . . . Yes, they probably think they can. They're wrong."

"I know that. . . . They can make the rest of your life miserable. . . ."

"And yours too, if I let them."

"I still want my shot at them. Get it over and done with."

"You may have to adopt me into your family, Maria Angelica."

"Oh, we already have done that. . . . I even got a unanimous vote."

I had spent Labor Day weekend in Oakdale, not a little taken aback by the fact that it was a lovely little place and the people seemed very much like Americans. Her bright and handsome kids seemed to like me at once, even Clara who, her mother had warned me, was very suspicious of Chicagoans. Maria told me later that after dinner, Clara had demanded to know if her mother was sleeping with me. Maria denied the charge, which wasn't true then.

"Well," she said, "you're crazy if you don't. He's totally cute and a total keeper."

"A young woman of excellent judgment."

Conversation around the table was a tournament in which five very quick people fought desperately for the last word. They didn't know they were doing it, much less that they were imitating their mother, though Clara and Marissa knew that I was amused and competed vigorously with each other.

I explained to them all that I was not really

an investor nor even a speculator. I was a gambler. . . . A riverboat gambler who bet with other people's money as well as my own that I could earn them more money every year than the Dow Jones index could.

"Ever fail?" Pete asked.

"Sometimes, but only in the years when the index went even lower."

"Vegas?" Marissa, fresh home from her first year in ACE, Notre Dame's peace corps, and a radiant clone of her mother, asked.

"I've never been near the place. People are reckless down there. I am not a reckless gambler. I win some and I lose some, but I win a lot more than I lose."

"Timing is very important in gambling, isn't it?" Clara asked, pushing what I suspected had become her new agenda.

"It's the whole show."

She smiled in satisfaction. I had heard her message, clever little witch.

I laughed all the way home as I recalled the day in all its rich sending and receiving of messages. I promised them all a ride on the *Mary Fran* first time out in spring.

"He's a very stern captain," my love said. "Very authoritarian."

"A good captain has to be that way," Clara said, now completely on my side.

Now poor Maria would have to face a much more hostile bunch. We sat at the table in a private dining room in the Four Seasons Hotel, sipping from a glass of Barolo, waiting for my daughters who were already half an hour late.

"A couple of sips for eloquence," Maria commented.

"This is not a good idea," I said.

"No, but it is necessary."

There was a tentative knock on the door; a guest but a hesitant guest. I opened the door and my youngest, Mary Fran, came in.

"Hi, Dad, the others are downstairs, drinking and plotting against you. I couldn't take it anymore. . . ."

"Maria, this is my youngest daughter, Mary Fran. . . . Mary Fran, this is Maria Connors."

"I knew, Mary Fran, that a young woman who lent her name to such a lovely boat must be very beautiful. I know now my expectation was not wrong."

"Thanks, Maria." Tears cascaded down my daughter's face, as the two women embraced. "I wanted to tell you that I was on your side, but I'm afraid I'll have to desert the battleground."

"A wise decision, Mary Fran. We'll get to know each other at other times and other places."

The two hugged each other and Mary Fran hugged me.

"I guess you will have to make some choices, Mary Fran," I said.

"It's about time. I've already done it in my head. The choice is easy. The action won't be."

"In your own good time, hon. There's no rush," Maria said soothingly. So far she had made all the right moves. What, however, could she do against angry drunks?

"Who's down there?"

"Great-Grams, Grandma and Grandpa, the aunts, Evie, and her weasel of a husband, poor Irene and her irrelevant boyfriend—they all hate you and want to get even with you for different reasons, mostly that you're a success and that you and Mom had a happy marriage, regardless. I know I should stay and fight them, but I don't have the stomach for a drunken Irish wake."

"I walk out on Italian fights too," Maria

assured her. "Your father can take care of himself and I can take care of the two of us."

"Irene follows Evie, as always, but what is Evie so angry about?"

"Dad shouldn't marry a woman so much younger than he is."

My lover laughed.

"Hon, I'm two months older than he is."

"Yeah, but you are much more beautiful than Irene and presumably stuck up. . . . I better run before the Huns storm the gates."

"I wish we could ask her to be in the wedding party," I murmured, as Mary Fran, still weeping, left the private dining room.

We sat again at our empty table and watched men and women in their Sunday garb entering the gothic Presbyterian Church across the street.

"I'll call her at the hospital during the week and invite her to join Clara and Marissa as bridesmaids. She won't be able to do it, but after the wedding she'll come over to our side. . . . Is she right? Could your oldest daughter be jealous of me?"

"She's always been possessive. And Irene has followed her around like a little puppy."

"Hard cases, Jack. It will take a long time, but I'll win them over."

"I'd never bet against you."

No one knocked, but the door burst open and my family entered bearing with them the thick aroma, not of a cheap bar, but of an elegant lounge—a sure sign that they had signed my name to the tab. They staggered into the room, their obesity taking over all the free space.

"Maria Angelica," I began calmly, "let me introduce you to my late wife's family and my own. . . . Faith's grandmother Evangeline Clifford Fahey."

Grandma had collapsed into a chair and was busy pouring Barolo in a water tumbler.

"Why don't you leave our family alone?" Grandma Fahey demanded as she put two ice cubes into the wine. "We don't need anyone like you."

"I'm not sure that I need anyone like you either, Grandma. In any case I'm not marrying your family. I'm marrying John Donlan."

"Faith's father, Guy O'Meara . . ."

"You're all Republicans out there aren't you, Mrs. Connors?"

"In fact, Mr. O'Meara, Kishwaukee has gone Democratic in the last two elections because of the influence of NIU and Rockford. Our town has historically been Democratic and as chair of the Oakdale Democrats I intend to keep that tradition alive."

Guy was protected partially from the family nuttiness by his political obsessions.

"Not far enough away for us," Lallie snorted. "You'd better be careful of this fellow, young woman. He killed my daughter when he got tired of her and he'll do the same to you."

"My mother-in-law, Eulalia Carmody O'Meara, commonly known as Lallie."

"My sympathy, Ms. O'Meara. And I don't believe you. I have read the records of her accident. She should not have been permitted to leave your house alone in the condition she was in, especially since her husband was in Washington and could not be expected to drive her home."

So I wasn't the only one who did preliminary investigations.

"Faith's sisters, Ms. Hope O'Meara and Ms. Charity O'Meara."

The two aunts had both aged since the burial scene at All Saints Cemetery—and put on more weight. Moreover they were both on the fringe of the fall-down state of Irish intoxication.

"Fucking bastard," Charity said, her voice slurred, not a response that was in keeping with her name.

Nor was her sister's barely audible "cocksucker," an appropriate word from someone called Hope.

"It is not worth answering them, Maria. They won't remember tomorrow what you said. . . . Finally my daughters, Evelyn and her husband, Anthony Cuneen, who is an attorney at law, and Irene and her 'boyfriend' Christopher Riordan, who is an aspiring filmmaker."

And, I did not add, is alleged to be heterosexual, even though he does his best to exhibit a gay persona.

"I was hoping," my beloved said, in a dangerously meek voice, "that you young women would be part of our wedding party."

"Where did you get your boob job?" Irene asked, on a signal from her sister. I had a strong urge to strangle them both.

Maria dismissed her with an amused laugh.

"I'm afraid I have to blame my Tuscan genes for my figure. There's not much one can do about them. I've never had any cosmetic surgery. Only pretty good makeup. I could recommend it to you if you're interested, though it tends to be expensive."

Chris Riordan, who may not have had a shower for the last week, yawned. He did not realize that he should memorize the scene, which might have been drawn from one of Eugene O'Neill's plays about Irish drunks. The scene was now set for the end-of-the-act performance by my firstborn daughter, the light of my life, my pride and joy.

"We will not, Ms. Connors, accept positions in your wedding party. Nor will we appear at the ceremony itself, which is probably sacrilegious. To be candid, we don't like you. We don't want you. We will not accept you as, God forbid the word, our stepmother. You are a strumpet, a whore, a hooker, a cunt, a punch card. I would not let you near my kiddies for fear they would pick up some hideous disease from you. . . . Dad, you have shown incredibly bad taste in your choice of a woman. You disgrace and humiliate us and our mother. If you go ahead with this hideous marriage, we have no choice but to disinherit you. Permanently. From the day of your marriage you will simply not exist for us. You can try to take our trust funds away from us. My Tony says that you will not be able to do that. But fuck the trust funds and fuck you too."

"You might also have called me a drab, a blowen, or even flattered me a bit and used the word *courtesan.... Heinous* would have been a better adjective in the context, more Catholic." My bride would have the last word, would she not?

"Do you have anything to say, Dad? We are all prepared for fervent denials. We reject them out of hand."

"No response at all," I said. "I will not play Lear to your Goneril, now or ever."

"What your father means"—Maria stole the final word again—"is that you can't excommunicate him because he has already excommunicated you. I assume you have sent up the ticket for your bar amusements, a charge which excommunication does not cancel. This time."

They all exited silently.

"I suggest," she continued, "that we have our dinner sent in, and another bottle of wine and then return to your house for whatever amusements are available to us on a lonely autumn night."

— Maria Angelica —

WE DID just that. It was a memorable night of love for me. Sex with Jack was better than I imagined it could be, but the ultimate pleasure had still escaped me. However, that evening with the full moon bathing both of us with its inviting glow I plunged over the edge into abandon and the depths of pleasure. . . . So this is what it is supposed to be like. . . . Sometimes . . . I must remember the way down, so I can come back. . . .

Then Jack was speaking to me, the sound of fear in his voice.

"Are you all right Maria! Wake up, please!"

"I'm all right," I sighed, "but if it's just the same to you, I'd rather not wake up. . . ."

"What happened?"

"Abandon, I think. Sometimes women lose consciousness for a few minutes. . . . It is not serious. . . . But, oh, Jackie dear . . . It was so wonderful. . . . Thank you . . ."

"Can I get anything for you . . . ?"

Poor dear man, he was so worried about me. . . . He really does love me. . . . Like most men he is afraid of the depths of womanly orgasm.

"I just want to lay here with you, naked in the moonlight and bask in all the warmth. . . . It beats the Cayman Islands. . . ."

He wrapped his arms around me and pulled me against himself, as though he were afraid he'd lose me again. Poor dear man.

"You could bring me a large glass of iced tea, spiced kind please, heavy on the ice, a touch of lime."

When he returned I had pulled myself into a chaise and tossed a towel around me, not so much out of shame as pride. His naked body was very beautiful in the moonlight. Mine . . . all mine.

He reclined next to me and gave me the iced tea.

"Hmmm . . . Good."

"Sweet and tart . . . Just like you . . ."

I caressed him gently.

"You want more?" he asked, astonished.

"Not right away." I touched his lips gently with my own, tasting his strength and goodness against the tea.

"Those poor people," I said.

"You feel sorry for them, after the terrible things they said?"

"They are so lonely, no joy in their lives at all."

"That's certainly true. The O'Mearas are filled with pride and bitterness and drink. They'll never escape. . . . It's my daughters I worry about."

"Don't worry, Jackie Pat, I'll get them back for you."

I must have fallen asleep then. The next thing I knew it was morning and I was in bed, curled up in my lover's arms as the sun peered above the horizon to warn me that there was more to life than fun and games, though they were fine too.

You know the rest of the story. After the nonwedding banquet we walked over to the cathedral to protest to the cardinal. The sweet teen at the door whose name was Megan told me that the cardinal was not in but Archbishop Ryan would see us. A funny little man with pale blue eyes behind thick glasses, he was wearing black jeans, a clerical shirt, and a Chicago Bears Windbreaker.

"Ah," he said, "you have fallen into the hands of idiots, clerical idiots. I will make a phone call that should clarify matters. Forgive me while I don my clerical persona and call the cathedral rectory in our suffragan see to the West, Northwest in point of fact, though it is politically 'downstate.'"

The darling little man assumed an expression of mock pomposity.

"Yes, this is Archbishop Ryan calling for Cardinal Cronin. May I talk to the monsignor . . . ? Ah, good afternoon, Monsignor . . . The cardinal has directed me to call you to seek information. We have a situation here which he wishes to resolve promptly. . . ."

He grimaced at his role of the ponderous ecclesiastic.

"Yes, Monsignor, I appreciate your willingness to cooperate. . . . My first question is whether there has ever been a parish in honor of St. Lawrence in Oakdale or any-where in the adjoining communities. . . . Yes, I see . . . My second and last question is whether in the last half century or so there has ever been one Father Thomas Hartnett in your diocese. . . . Yes, I will wait till you check the necrology. . . ."

He put his hand over the phone and rolled his eyes.

"Yes, Monsignor . . . Indeed, well that resolves our little problem. . . . The cardinal directs me to thank you and to convey his fraternal greetings to your ordinarius. . . . Yes, Monsignor, but the pleasure has been mine.

"Hooray for our side . . . as I expected you have been victims of a foul and, if I may say so, sloppy plot. . . . Can you gather your wedding party together tomorrow morn-ing? . . . Good, Milord Cronin will be pleased to offer a nuptial liturgy in one of the side chapels in the cathedral tomorrow morning at nine-thirty. I would suggest that if you require an explanation of this nasty and messy plot, you contact this young woman. . . . Her name may be familiar to you. . . . She sings. . . . Yes, that one . . . she also has considerable talent at disentangling puzzles. . . . Oh, yes, I will be present for the liturgy to, uh, assist Milord Cronin and, if it pleases him to say a few words that might be appropriate for the occasion."

The next morning the cardinal said the nuptial Mass, a choir of teenagers led by a young woman named Crystal sang. The wedding party was there and Mary Fran whom Maria had seen coming out of Mass at St. Freddy's and dragged over to the dinner, where she seemed to bond quickly with Maria's kids. My Cordelia.

After he had read the Gospel, the cardinal, tall, handsome, and charming, said a few words to us about how the Church should be judged by this service instead of what happened yesterday.

"I could preach for you and maybe put our lovely choir maidens to sleep. Instead I am going to ask my helper archbishop to tell you why God made strawberries."

The nice little man was wearing a white alb. Only a gorgeous silver St. Brigid's cross around his neck suggested that he was anything more than a random deacon who had wandered in.

This is a story I first heard from a Cherokee princess. My Cherokee brogue isn't
very good, so I've changed it to a brogue
and a setting I know a little better.

Once upon a time, long, long ago, there
was Earth Maker and First Man and First
Woman. They lived in a whitewashed
stone cottage on the edge of a green field
with a silver lake and a road leaving over
the hills and out beyond. First Man and
First Woman were very much in love and
very happy together. Earth Maker was
pleased with himself because it appeared
that his experiment of creating male and
female had been a huge success. Oh,
they argued a few times a week, but never
anything serious.

Then one day they had a terrible fight.
They forgot what they were fighting about
and fought about who had started it and
then about what the fight was about.

Finally First Woman was fed up. You're
nothing but a loudmouth braggart! she
said and stormed out of the cottage and
across the green field and by the silver
lake and over the hill and out beyond.

First Man sat back in his rocking chair,
lit his pipe, and sighed happily. Well, at

last we'll have some peace and quiet around here. The woman has a terrible mouth on her.

But as the sun set and turned the silver lake rose gold, he realized he was hungry. Woman, he shouted, I want my tea. But there was no woman to make the tea. Poor First Man could not even boil water. So he had to be content with half of a cold pratie (which is what the Irish call a potato). Then as a chill came over the cottage and First Man felt lonely altogether, he sighed again, let his pipe go out, and felt he needed a good night's sleep. He didn't light the fire because, truth to tell, he wasn't very good at such things. First Woman did all the fire-lighting in their house because she could start fires in a second.

The poor fella shivered something awful when he pulled the covers over himself. Well, he told himself, she did keep the bed warm at night. He didn't sleep very well and when he woke there was a terrible hunger on him. Woman, he shouted, I want me tea! Then he realized that there was no woman and no tea. So he had to be satisfied with the other half of the cold pratie.

Well, he was sitting in front of the cold fireplace, puffing on a cold pipe, wrapped in a thin blanket, when Earth Maker appeared.

Let me see now, said Earth Maker. This is earth and I made ye male and female. And you're the male. Where's herself?

She's gone, Your Reverence.

Gone?

Gone!

Why's she gone?

We had a fight!

You never did!

We did!

And she left you?

She did, Your Reverence.

You're a pair of eejits!

Yes, Your Reverence.

Do you still love her?

Oh yes, Your Reverence, something terrible!

Well then, man, off your rocking chair and after her!

She's long gone, Your Reverence. I'll never catch up with her.

No problem. I can move as fast as thought. I'll go ahead of you and slow her down! Now get a move on!

Poor First Man, his heart breaking, trundled out of his chair and down the path across the green field and by the silver lake and out beyond.

Meanwhile Earth Maker caught up with First Woman. She was still furious at First Man. She walked down the road at top speed, muttering to herself as she went.

The woman has a temper, Earth Maker reflected. But that fella would make anyone lose their temper.

So to slow her down, said "ZAP!" and created a forest. Didn't she cut through it like a warm knife cutting through butter?

Then Earth Maker "ZAP!" created a big hill. Didn't she charge over the hill like a mountain goat?

So ZAP, Earth Maker created a big lake. That'll stop her, he said to himself.

It didn't stop her at all, at all. She charged into the lake and swam across it, Australian Crawl.

I don't know where she learned the stroke because Australia didn't exist way back then. But she knew it.

Och, said Earth Maker, there are problems in creating women athletes, aren't there now? Well, the poor thing is hungry, so she'll slow down to eat. ZAP. There appeared along the road all kinds of fruit trees—peach trees, plum trees, grapefruit trees, apricot trees (no apple trees because that's another story).

What did First Woman do? Well she just picked the fruit as she was walking and didn't slow down a bit.

Sure, said Earth Maker, won't I have to fall back on me ultimate weapon. I'll have to create strawberries!

ZAP!

First Woman stopped cold. Ah, would you look at them pretty bushes with the white flowers.

As she watched didn't the flowers turn into rich red fruit?

Ah now isn't that gorgeous fruit and itself shaped just like the human heart?

She felt the first strawberry. Sure, doesn't it feel just like the human heart, soft and yet strong and firm. I wonder what it tastes like. Sure, doesn't it have the sweetest taste in all the world, save for the taste of human love?

Well, she sighed loudly, speaking of that subject, I suppose the eejit is chasing after me, poor dear man. I'd better wait for him.

So didn't she pick a whole apron full of strawberries and sit by the strawberry bush and wait for First Man.

And finally, he came down the road, huffing and puffing and all worn out.

This is called the strawberry bush, she said, pointing at the bush. And doesn't the fruit taste wonderful? So she gave a piece of fruit to First Man, like the priest gives the Eucharist.

Oh, says First Man, isn't it the sweetest taste in all the world, save for the taste of human love. So they picked more strawberries and, arm in arm, walked home to their whitewashed cottage by the green field and the silver lake and the hill and out beyond. 'Tis said that they lived happily ever after, which meant only three or so fights a week.

Now I want all of you here, especially Maria Angelica and John Patrick to remember every time from now on when you taste strawberries, that the only thing sweeter is the taste of human love. And remember too that love is about catching up and waiting and true lovers know how to catch up and wait.

So that's our story, Nuala Anne, I hope it
didn't bore you. . . . There's people out there
that wanted to stop our marriage and now
want to ruin it and maybe kill us. I'm afraid
that both of us are not as scared as we
should be. . . . And as we saw a few minutes
ago we have hired ourselves very classy
angels. . . . I take your point, Dermot, ser-
aphs.

— Dermot —

"WELL, DERMOT Michael Coyne, what would you be after thinking about the afternoon show?"

"I thought the dogs were wonderful and weren't you smashing altogether and yourself swinging your camogie stick like you were a fifteen-year-old again!"

"Give over, Dermot Michael! That's not what I meant!"

Give over is Irish English that is more or less equivalent to *get real,* though it implies that the addressee is also a bit of an eejit.

My lovely wife and I were engaging in a new ritual we had inserted in our lives. We

were sitting on a couch in our master bedroom, wearing robes, and sipping a small
splash (a splasheen) of Baileys, though on
other nights it might be a swallow of Bush-
mills Green, and discussing the events of our
day. It was an interlude of peace and recollec-
tion marking the end of the chaos of the day
and anticipating the wonders of the night,
sleep, and perhaps love. It was supposed to
constrain us not to retire with any resentments against each other. It was herself's
idea of course and like all such, altogether
brilliant, by her own admission. She argued
that it had increased not only the frequency of
our "messing around" and the quality. We
ended the ritual with a decade of the rosary.

"And your older kids swarming up the
stairs with their softball bats and meself
swinging the snow shovel, faith we could
have repelled the whole Brit parachute regiment, couldn't we? No one pulls up in front
of the Coyne house and looks suspicious
and the dogs howling like they were audi-
tioning for *The Hound of the Baskervilles.*
We scared them shitehawks!

"And me daughter thought to bring her
camera and take a picture of their friggin' car
and get its license plate number."

One of the rhetorical rules of our happy union is that when one of the kids does something "brilliant altogether," it's her offspring and when one goofs up, the child becomes "mine."

"The whole business suggests that the plot against our new friends is clumsy."

"Reckless and possibly dangerous . . . And them poor folks just beginning a brilliant new marriage . . . And don't think, Dermot Michael, that I didn't notice all the attention you were paying to the woman."

"I was only imagining myself at that age and having such a gorgeous spouse."

"Och," she said with a sigh, the typical West of Ireland sigh which sounds like a severe asthma attack. "Doesn't she have pretty boobs? And herself experiencing full orgasm for the first time. . . ."

"Ah," I said, figuring that if my wife could predict pregnancies before they happen, she could also sense the quality of a woman's orgasm after the fact.

"Some of us never experience it at all, the trick of it, as you well know, is for the poor woman to yield to her body's demand for total abandon of which she is afraid. Sometimes she even passes out for a moment. . . . But her pleasure then is much greater than that of the eejit with the pent-up hormones who's riding her."

"So I have been told."

"Sure you don't even remember when it happened to me for the first time, do you now?"

"Woman, I do. It was in Limerick town . . . and you scared the living daylights out of me when you passed out."

I had the day marked in my calendar and gave her a present on the anniversary.

"Sometimes you see a woman on an elevator and you can tell where she's been the night before."

"And where's that?"

"In the antechamber of heaven, where else . . . And meself praying to God that her eejit lover will remember how it went . . . and that he shouldn't expect it all the time . . . So we have to protect them both, poor dear people, from those who want to destroy their love, isn't that true, Dermot Michael?"

"Woman, 'tis."

"Those gobshites in the car weren't the people behind it. Commander Culhane says that they are just thugs sent to harass them, like all the phone calls and the anonymous e-mail. But the evil people behind them are really dangerous. Sloppy maybe but that makes them only more dangerous, doesn't it now?"

"I think the real plotters—conceding for the moment that there's a plot . . ."

My contribution to the resolution of the mock attack on Sheffield Avenue was to call Mike Casey on my cell phone and tell him to tell Gaby Lopez to drive around the block before I had grabbed the snow shovel and belatedly joined our mob. They would have fled quickly enough anyway, the Devil himself would have run from the howls of our hounds.

Afterward, terribly proud of what they had done, they returned calmly to the first floor to play with the kids.

"Dermot Michael Coyne, there is a plot, haven't I told you so?"

"Woman, you have . . . They're probably playing it all by ear, taking advantage of the opportunities that come up. . . . Empiricists . . . I can't imagine what they're up to. . . ."

"They want to destroy Jack and Maria and we have to find out why."

"They both said that if their marriage

becomes a media sensation, it could destroy their businesses. . . . Is that true, Dermot?"

"His asset management funds depend on investors' confidence in him. I can't imagine Frodo or Samwise tanking but he might have to sell them, though he'd collect enough to live the rest of his life in total comfort. Her venture is new and promising, but fragile. It's on the bubble. It could come under assault from suspicious customers and disappear into the night."

"So tomorrow morning, don't you have to go out to Loyola Medical School and interview this Mary Fran person and find out where they heard all the misinformation about Maria Angelica and whether they passed on that fake letter to the gobshite at St. Freddy's?"

"Wasn't I thinking the same thing meself?"

"And we must say our decade of the rosary tonight that them gobshites and CTN (Consolidated Television Network) back down. Or that the judge gives us . . . What do they call it?"

"An emergency order. Our guys made a strong case about catastrophic harm. The judge will grant the order. They'll appeal and we'll need the Seventh District to grant their own emergency. The CTN people are dumb enough to try the Supreme Court. That will be a waste of their time and money."

"I still don't like it."

"What you don't like, good wife, is staying out of the fight."

"Och, sure, Dermot Michael, don't you have the right of it."

We said the rosary. It was her turn to lead. The tone of her voice suggested that the deity was receiving his instructions.

Then we would make the rounds of the bedrooms. Both the boys and the girls were sleeping soundly, the former under the watchful eye of Fiona and the latter snoozing under the surveillance of Maeve. Both would slip into the master bedroom in the course of the night, nudging the door open with their big snoots.

"Well," I said rising from my knees, "I don't suppose there'll be any riding tonight."

"Go long with ya, Dermot love, after the sexuality oozing around our living room today, I won't permit you to dream about that woman's boobs all night long."

"Well then." I pulled off her robe. "I'll have to find an alternative subject for my lascivious dreams, won't I now?"

— Dermot —

"EVIE CARRIES a lot of anger," Mary Fran Donlan said in the calm tone appropriate for a Freudian therapist in her middle fifties or a newly ordained priest. "She is angry at our mother whom she adored for being an alcoholic and then for dying too early in life. She is angry at the O'Mearas for killing her and at Daddy for permitting them to kill her. She is angry at me because, as she thinks, Daddy named the boat after me, when it was really his mother's name. She is also furious at me because she thinks I'm prettier than she is. She is angry at the Church because it is there, inviting anger. She's angry at her husband because he is a creep with no confidence in himself and lets her browbeat him. . . . I'm sorry, Mr. Coyne, for lecturing. . . ."

"Dermot," I insisted. "Mr. Coyne is my father."

"Actually, he's Dr. Coyne." Her brief smile would have melted an ice cap. "He's one of the nicest men in this place. And Dr. Coyne asks questions just the way you do, Mr. Coyne . . . Dermot."

We were sitting in a cubicle for students doing their clerkships at Loyola University Hospital and Medical Center in Maywood. There was room for a small metal desk on which there were two paper cups filled with coffee (black), two uncomfortable metal chairs, and us. In her shapeless green coat and without any makeup, she looked like a pretty, natural-blond teenager playing nurse and not the beautiful young woman that Maria Angelica had described.

"A deeply troubled young woman," I nodded in agreement.

She smiled slightly in acknowledgment that I was giving a therapist's response.

"Yet her fury turns her into a dynamic

leader for any cause that happens to come along. Back in the days when Daddy was young she'd have marched on the Pentagon alongside Norman Mailer. She has charisma and charm to spare, all driven by her rage at the O'Meara family and at the O'Meara inside herself. . . . Now look at me! Analyzing my sister like I'm a teaching analyst at the institute! And I'm really only a third-year med student."

The "institute" was the Chicago Institute for Psychoanalysis founded by one of Freud's pupils, Franz Alexander, and not to be confused with the Art Institute or *The* University.

"But you hope to be one some day."

"Maybe," she shrugged. "I'm not sure I buy all that Freudian stuff. . . . Anyway she's very angry at Maria because my stepmom, as she is now, is a perfect target—another O'Meara and yet a non-O'Meara."

"And too beautiful by half, as the Brits would say."

"And she has laid-back kids like Evie wishes we were. . . . Well, she doesn't know the kids yet, but wait till she does."

Before I drove out to Maywood on the Congress Expressway (as we Democrats still call it), my wife and I took our three oldest children, accompanied by the two dogs, across the street to St. Josephat school. I wondered if they might some day become a viper's tangle of conflicts that would be our fault. Nelliecoyne (aka Mary Anne) was four years short of her chronological teen years but had already become a certified, card-carrying preteen, especially in her ability to be acutely critical of her parents' inconsistencies. She and her mother argued constantly, though with little anger.

"You and Ma banter, Da, me and Ma argue. It's the way we bond."

"Ma and I," Nuala Anne corrected her.

"Yes, Ma," she said with a sigh almost as loud as her ma's.

She was also fey like her mother, "even more than I was at her age, the poor dear little thing."

So Nelliecoyne and her ma often communicated without the benefit of words, especially when I was the subject. That alliance against me would become stronger as the years went on.

The Mick, named after me Micheal Dirmuid, was all boy, soccer, baseball, Cub fan, Bear fan, Bull fan, Notre Dame fan, even

Marquette fan. He loves to play with trucks. He also loves to paint. Just as his sister carries a camera all the time, he has a sketchbook in his pocket and would translate that sketch often to a computer graphic.

Socra Marie, at the moment leading her two doggies into the little band of kindergarten children who screamed with joy every morning at the sight of the huge white beasts, was our miracle child. Impatient to get into the world, she left her mother's womb after twenty-five weeks and was so tiny I could hold her in one of my hands. She entered the world with a determination to stay with us that was barely strong enough to ensure her survival. But she made it and finally came home with us, still tiny and still filled with vitality. By the time she was two her energy made her a tiny terrorist who, with great éclat, broke or spoiled everything she could get her hands on. She also wore "gwasses," which hung askew on her little nose but never quite fell. She tried her best to be a "good little girl" but her ongoing celebration of life precluded such a transformation till she went to preschool. She charmed teachers and classmates alike and calmed down a bit because she perceived that was necessary to her charm. But the mania was still there just beneath the surface. "Teacher says I'm an adorable handful," she had told us proudly.

Last of all came two-year-old Patjo, who was described by one of my sisters as "just like his father, big, strong, good-looking, and useless."

Such comments infuriated the child's mother, but I never did dispute them. I did hope that Patrick Joseph would graduate from college at the appropriate time instead of failing at both the Dome and Marquette. But I also hoped he would never let his studies interfere with his education. Herself agreed completely.

"Haven't I been saying all the time that you're the best-educated man I know, Dermot Michael? The poor little fat punk will be blessed if he ever knows all that you know."

"I was a fat baby too."

"See, I'm always right."

"Yes, you are."

I wasn't sure about what, but it didn't matter.

So I kissed the kids good-bye and patted

the two hounds who never liked to see anyone go away, and themselves not being
sure we'd come back, and kissed Nuala
and off I went to Maywood and meself
knowing that I would think of her all the
way.

And recall the images of our love the night
before. If we were to avoid the family mess
that had overwhelmed Jack Donlan it would
be Nuala's doing not mine.

"So you believe that your sister will never
accept her new stepmother?"

"I don't think so."

"And where does that leave you?"

Mary Fran considered that question for a
moment.

"I'll have to make up my mind, won't I?
Evie was furious at me because I sneaked
into the Church for the wedding and that I
then went to the reception."

"You went to the Mass at the cathedral?"

"I didn't know about it. I'm sure the others
wouldn't attend."

"All three of you were there outside of St.
Freddy's?"

"Evie said we should see how vulgar she
looked. . . . I didn't think she looked vulgar at

all. I thought she was gorgeous . . . and that Daddy was a very lucky man."

"And to hear what the priest said when he ordered them out of the church?"

"That was as much a surprise to us as it was to everyone."

"Might Evie have received it from some-one and passed it on to the priest?"

She thought about that.

"I doubt it, Mr. Coyne, uh, Dermot. She would have lorded it over us as soon as she received it. It might have come from the same source as the original letter but not through us. Evie was ecstatic. She said it proved she had been right all along."

"And what did that original letter say?"

"You have eyes just like your father's."

"Even when I'm playing my role as a pri-vate eye?"

"Asking questions for your adorable wife."

"The last one of which you have not answered."

She opened the single drawer in her desk.

"I scribbled a copy of it when Evie wasn't watching," she said as she handed me a single sheet of computer paper. "She wouldn't let the original out of her hands. It was a scrawl on a lined page of notebook paper."

> Your new mom is a whore. Out in Oakdale everyone knows she screws every man she's working on a deal with. They keep count of her victims. There's twelve of them that are common knowledge. She didn't take over that company because of her intelligence. She's a regular punch card. The guys she fucks know her reputation, but they can't keep their fly zipped when she puts out. She takes a lot of money away from them because they can't think straight. She's already taken from your asshole father and she'll clean him out before she's finished. She'll take your inheritance if you don't watch her every move.

It was, I thought, not so much an obscene letter as a letter from someone who was trying to give the impression that she was a truck driver. I used the word *she* advisedly— a proper woman trying to sound dirty.

"Can I take this?"

"Sure."

"What do you think of it?"

"Maybe a jealous middle-age woman

pretending to be a truck driver . . . Evie should have torn it up and thrown it away. But she was looking for dirt. It was all she needed to organize the family against Ms. Connors."

I slid the paper into the pocket of my trademark yuppie navy blue blazer. I'm not a real yuppie because real yuppies don't flunk out of college, do they? But it's a helpful image when I am carrying the spear for Nuala Anne. A nice, wholesome-looking professional wouldn't be mixed up with Bronze Age superstition, would he?

I thanked her and gave her my card, which carries just my name and my e-mail address. It does NOT say "Spear Carrier."

"Working for that dangerous daughter-in-law of mine . . . Mother of my favorite grandchildren?" my father said when I stuck my head into his office to pay my respects. "Let's see—to give them their Christian names—Mary Anne, Michael, Sarah, and Patrick."

My folks have never been able to get their tongues around Socra Marie.

"Trying to earn an honest buck in the garden of good and evil."

"Well, that young woman is one of the best students we've had here in a long time."

Dad was telling me that he knew what I was doing around the Med Center.

"Maybe you should go to work for herself," I responded.

We both laughed.

The theory in the family is that Nuala Anne is the nice girl I brought home from Ireland who had forced me to grow up, though not nearly enough. They don't propose it to her anymore because those luminous blue eyes of hers turn as dark as storm clouds rushing in from the North Atlantic. The myth of shiftless Dermot will never die. Just as well. When I hear it from my sisters, I reply, "At least I taught her to wear shoes."

On my way back to East Lincoln Park (a more pretentious community name than "DePaul") I drove through my own "old neighborhood" River Forest, just to convince myself that the Italians hadn't ruined it yet.

(When I was young, the Irish in our suburban enclave were considerably upset at the migration of Italians from their "old neighborhood" on Taylor Street. They would "ruin" the neighborhood, it was whispered. In fact they were zealous in their home and landscape improvements, though their exuberant

Christmas decorations were deemed "tacky."
Which just goes to show you.)

That reminded me that I should talk to my
old friend and classmate Dominic. A man
who was clearly connected but clean. This
meant that the money for his electronics firm
may have had some shady antecedents but
Dom himself was not involved directly with
the outfit and that he used no outfit thugs to
promote his electronics firm. I have his private number in my cell phone and he
responded immediately. "Dominic."

"Hey, Dominic, it's Dermot! What's happening?"

"Hey, Dermot, what's happenin'? I hear
that your beautiful wife is gonna cream this
Triple A crook from Hollywood?"

"It's going down today, Dom. It looks like
we're going to win."

Triple A was the name the Chicago media
had assigned to Archibald Adolf Abercrombie, the president of Consolidated Television
Network who was trying to stifle the Nuala
Anne Christmas show. A tall, dynamic, and
totally bald man, he treated Chicago media
and Chicago judges and lawyers as though
they were ignorant peasants standing in the
way of progress. Not a particularly wise

stance for somebody engaging in litigation that was dubious at best.

"Hey, Dom, you hear what went down in front of my house over in Lincoln Park yesterday?"

"No, I didn't hear. What happened?"

"A couple of individuals in a stolen car pull up to the house and get out carrying what looked like baseball bats or maybe large salami sausages. You know what certain kinds of people used to do with those?"

"Dumb! Dumb! I can't believe anybody would do that in Chicago these days, much less to you and your family. I've told you often that the friends and my friends respect you and admire her greatly."

"Yeah, well, it was kind of a mess. Our wolfhounds got angry and howled and you know what it's like when wolfhounds start howling. These individuals climbed back in their car and pulled away. We got their license number but the car was stolen."

"Sincerely, Dermot, I'm sure that no one who is a friend of my friends would do that kind of thing but let me find out. Okay?"

"I sincerely believe you, but I'm just asking that you check it out to see if your friends know who was behind this caper."

"Yeah, yeah, Dermot, I understand. We'll look into it. And I sincerely assure you that whoever was doing it won't do it again. They'll be warned off. You can count on that."

"I'm happy to hear that, Dominic, and I sincerely believe what you say. Tell the friends of your friends we don't want to complicate this one. I'm on what went down at the marriage between the Sabattini woman from Oakdale and our very good friend here in Chicago John Patrick Donlan."

"He was born with the gift of laughter and the sense that the world was mad."

So Dominic had read *Scaramouche?* Strange world.

"You got it, Dom."

"Oh yeah I heard about that. Really a strange one. So you're working on that case?"

"Trying to straighten it out a little."

"Sabattini, I've heard of them. She's supposed to be totally clean and a very nice lady. Her brothers are no good, no good at all punks. . . . Yeah, and a fake letter in church? The punks have been watching too many episodes of *The Sopranos.*"

"The brothers might not be involved. . . ."

"Yeah, but they know about it. Just a few

quiet words whispered into their ears. They're such lowlifes that even a whisper from the friends of my friends will scare the shit out of them, you should excuse the expression. Pleasure to help you, Dermot."

"I sincerely trust you and believe you, Dominic. Let me know what the friends of your friends are able to unearth."

The Outfit, as we call them in Chicago (or sometimes "the boys") are a group of serious businessmen. Some of their businesses are legit and some are not and some are somewhere in between. Crime interferes with business. So they try to keep a lid on crime as best they can, other people's crime. Like Blacks and Latinos and punks from out of town. It also brings in the Feds who are not very effective in their periodic campaigns against the Outfit, but who can create inconveniences. If they discover that punks, from out of town or Chicago, are messing around without asking permission, they are extremely upset. If you have good relations with them, they'll keep you informed about what's going on and what's going down. One deals with them through intermediaries and communicates in a kind of code. They'll do favors for you without necessarily picking up a marker.

So Dominic might say to me (though he never has), "I don't think I can help you on that one, Dermot. I sincerely wish I could."

That means the wiseguys are involved and to mess around could be dangerous.

Or he might say (as he sometimes has), "My friends tell me that their friends are aware of the situation and are taking care of it."

That means exactly what it says and adds the suggestion, "you'd better stay out of it."

Or yet again, "Please tell your friends that we'll clean up the mess."

When you agree to pass on the message they will have picked up a marker.

That meant that the cops should stay out of it (or the state's attorney, or Mike Casey, or even the Feds).

The Feds pretend that they eschew such communications with sworn enemies. But they engage in them as much as anyone else. It eliminates a lot of mess.

The boys take good care of me because I saved Dominic's life when we were in high school, which gives me a kind of unlimited marker. I don't use it much, in part because the thrill could become addictive.

I turned on the car radio to pick up the noon news.

Harold Hastings was reporting, one of my favorites because he is skilled in very mild African-American English, a creative and humorous dialect that deserves more respect.

"Triple A got himself canceled this morning in the Dirksen Federal building. The National Bureau of Standards obtained a permanent injunction against the man so he could not interfere with their production of the Nuala Anne McGrail Christmas special this year. Old Triple A canceled the series, which had another year to run on its contract. NBS picked it up with considerable enthusiasm as you might imagine. The tycoon of CTN came to town to block such a switch. He didn't want Ms. McGrail on his network or anyone else's and he was not about to negotiate a termination agreement with her production company. As Federal Judge Ebenezer Brown commented in granting a permanent injunction, Mr. Abercrombie's lawyers should explain to him contract law. Even in Hollywood you cannot terminate a contract short of a termination date and still control the other party of the contract. Mr. Abercrombie announced that they would immediately appeal the decision.

'It's our show. If we decided not to present it, we will not permit anyone else to present it. *Christmas with Nuala Anne* is dead, permanently dead.'

"Gerard Mooney of the Chicago firm of Moody, Mooney, Meany, and Mularky, who represented NBS, remarked that ole Triple A must never have heard the story of the Dog in the Manger.

"Mary Anne Coyne, a spokesperson for Ms. McGrail, said that the immensely popular singer was unavailable for comment because she was practicing songs for the special."

Mary Anne Coyne was not a spokesperson for her mother.

I punched in the Heart Line Number intended for exclusive use of meself and me wife.

"Nuala Anne McGrail's line," my daughter informed me.

"Are you Ms. McGrail's spokesperson?"

"Is that you, Pa?" she said with a giggle.

"Possibly."

"I'll get Ma."

A louder giggle.

"Dermot, we beat the nine-fingered shite-hawk!"

"The shitehawk in the manger . . . Woman, you're violating the child labor law!"

"She's your daughter!"

"You hired her!"

"I have to practice me singing. Won't I be talking to you when you get home? . . . Did you like me 'dog in the manger' line?

"Wasn't it grand!"

"Love you, spear-carrier!"

She hung up.

Bitch.

Go long with ya, you're proud of her!

— **Nuala Anne** —

"I'M SORRY to disturb you on a day which is so important to you," Maria Connors began hesitantly.

"Och, don't fret your soul about it," I replied, slipping into me ma's reassurance style. "Hasn't poor Mr. Triple A dug himself into a hole which his stockholders won't like at all, at all, so we'll probably win, perhaps even with enough time to get the show together. It was supposed to be the last one anyhow. Sure, I've been thinking all year that this would be the last one anyway. We maybe need a rest from it, but NBS wants a two-year commitment. . . ."

"You must be a very busy woman, Nuala?"

She was wearing black trousers and a fluffy white blouse over the waist with a thick black belt holding the whole thing together. She was beautiful altogether and her boobs were firm and perfect underneath the blouse. But what was the point in hating her?

I was holding me youngest in me arms. He was about to fall asleep, an impulse which, like his father, he rarely resisted.

"Handsome little guy," she said.

"They say he's lazy, just like his father, but me Dermot is anything but lazy. He's just laid back, as this little punk . . . I think I'll put him down now. He won't bother us again."

I hummed me favorite lullaby, the Connemara, as I carried Patjo up to his room. . . . *Blow winds blow* . . .

Maeve had followed me upstairs. It was her turn to supervise the boys' room.

Fiona, and herself napping, was lying at Maria's feet.

"Sweet, sweet dog . . ." she said, stroking the massive head.

"And a lifesaver too sometimes . . . How's business?"

"So far, so good, down a little bit maybe,

but it's Monday morning and the holidays and our usual yuppie clients are busy on other forms of consumerism."

"Don't be a cynic, Maria, you're not one, not anymore."

"You see too much, Nuala Anne," she said, blushing. "I have a story to tell you, however, that may have an impact on the puzzle. I haven't told it to Jack yet, but I will this evening. He deserves a warning of what might happen."

Now I may be a tad fey, and I may see auras around people's heads—Maria's was a kind of dusky rose gold—but a confessor or a counselor or a spiritual director I am not and I'm not sure I want to be.

"He'll love you just as much as he did before you told him and maybe more."

"It's about my affair, fling, fall from grace whatever with Congressman Stafford of our district. He lost in the election a couple of weeks ago. Kishwaukee County, which has had a lot of war casualties, beat him into the ground. Oakdale went overwhelmingly against him, though he never won a majority from our voters."

"And yourself the precinct captain, aren't you?"

"I always campaigned against him even before our fling. Since then I have worked even harder, though I realized that it might be risky. . . . You may not have seen any pictures of him. He's a big, good-looking man, broad shoulders, long gray hair, big smile, oozes charm. I always thought the charm was a bit sinister. I should have been wary, but I wasn't."

She paused, stopped petting Fiona who protested by raising her head. Maria renewed the affection. Someday, I thought, I'm going to be as grown up as she is and won't I be about ninety?

"Anyway, one weekend five years ago, his office in D.C. called and suggested we have dinner on Saturday night at the country club. He had good news for me. I was suspicious. He was married and his wife, a smartly dressed woman about his age, had decided, unlike the current congressmen's wives, to live in Chevy Chase. Sterling Stafford nonetheless flew back to his district a couple of times a month. Maybe that ought to have made me suspicious. He had enormous power in Congress, lots of lobbyist money, and was close to Newt Gingrich when he was Speaker and a leader in the impeachment of Clinton."

"Nice man," I said.

"The news was really good. He had made a deal which would bring some major grants to his district for historic preservation and development. I needed good news. My poor husband's decline was accelerating. We were no longer making love, though we hugged and held hands. I didn't think I was any more deprived sexually than many women my age who were in unsatisfactory marriages—which seemed to me most of the women I knew. Their favorite conversational topic was how inadequate their men were in every respect. My plans and projects and big ideas and little crusades seemed useless and boring. Only my kids kept me going. They were fun and they let me have fun with them.

"I drank too much wine that evening in the club. Sterling didn't push his luck which was wise because I would have smote him with righteous anger as my evangelical friends say. His kiss good-night was too forceful but it stirred up emotions and sensations that I had not experienced in a long time and expected not to experience again. . . . That's when my adultery began."

"It began," I said firmly, "when you went to bed with him."

She was weeping now, a thin line of tears slipping down her cheeks. She hugged a delighted Fiona as though the wolfhound promised salvation.

"We drove up to Rockford in his wife's Cadillac the next week for dinner at an expensive and elegant steakhouse—probably the only one in town. I drank too much and surrendered all thoughts of resistance. Sterling pawed me all the way back to his home on the Kishwaukee, one we had built for him. I knew what would happen and I no longer cared. He had said nothing about the appropriation bill for our grants and I didn't care about that either. Nor did I care about the animal heads and the gun racks with which he had ruined our design for the parlor. No wonder, I thought, that his wife stays in D.C. He carried me upstairs to the master bedroom which was one of our standard models. He began to remove my clothes, none too gently, and to kiss me with increasing brutality. One of those kind, I thought, but it doesn't matter."

"Why did you get out?"

"How did you know that!" she exclaimed, startled.

"No way you were that drunk or lonely."

"I heard the camera running."

"Camera!"

"There was a vague sound of something whirling—even, mechanical, implacable. I was on a soundstage. Like I say, I knew the room and I looked at the corner where one might hide a camera. Sure enough! I pushed the bastard off me, dashed across the room, picked up the camera, pulled out the tape, and threw the camera at him. It hit the bastard in his head and stunned him for a moment. I grabbed my dress, ran down the stairs, and seized one of his shotguns."

I applauded.

"I hope you shot him!"

"Och, Nuala Anne McGrail Coyne, aren't you the violent one!

"He stumbled down the stairs, stark naked, and dazed. He called me a lot of names, the mildest one of which was 'tease.' I told him I would blow off his balls if he came a step nearer to me. I wouldn't of course, but I would have hit him on the head with the butt of the gun. I could see the safety was on the gun. He was still woozy. The camera was a good weapon. I picked his car keys off the mantel where he had deposited them when we had come into the house.

"He collapsed into a chair and rubbed his

head. 'You hurt me, bitch.' 'Not as much as I will if you get out of that chair. Now I'll tell you what you're going to do. You're going to take some aspirin and sleep this off. Then tomorrow morning at ten o'clock you drive into the parking lot behind our store in your Taurus. You will bring the rest of my clothes in some kind of suitcase, enter our front door, and deposit it inside the door. I will throw this key at you and you will get into your wife's car where this gun will be on the backseat, minus the bullets, and drive home. You can have one of your guys pick up the Taurus. And that's the end of it. I have the tape and I'll write up an account of the evening. I will place the tape somewhere where you won't ever find it. I won't blackmail you and you don't try to have me killed. And we'll call it even. Clear?'"

"Quick thinking," I said.

"Salespeople have to think quickly."

"He called me some more names and then groaned and held his head. I was ready for him the next morning with one of my father-in-law's guns, not loaded. 'Just put the bag down and leave.'"

"He tried to make peace?" I said.

" 'Maria, it was all a terrible mistake. I beg you, please forgive me.'

" 'It certainly was a mistake. I won't use this against you. Just get out of here and leave me alone.' He begged some more and I raised the gun and he dashed out.

"He phoned the next day to apologize again and promised that he would tell no one."

"Damn well better not," I said.

"The money actually came through for our project. I publicly thanked him for his support. We chatted amiably on the rare occasions we were together in public. He looked like a whipped little puppy dog."

At the word *dog* Fiona perked up her ears to see if she were under discussion. She rearranged herself and went back to sleep.

"And a frightened one at that!"

"Yes, he did seem scared."

" 'Tis yourself who needs a drop of the creature."

I left the room and came back with two jars of the finest. She had suspended her weeping and repaired her makeup.

I glanced out the window. A reliable limo was waiting.

"Slainte!"

"*Slainte!*" she said in return, not pronouncing the word properly at all—most Yanks can't.

We both sipped our drinks. She shuddered, but she needed something strong, didn't she?

"So," I said, "when did the adultery happen? Did you give him a second chance?"

I knew very well she hadn't.

"I drove up to Rockford to go to confession. I couldn't tell Father Matt. The priest said that I had intended to commit adultery and that was already a mortal sin of adultery. I had to say all fifteen decades of the rosary."

"Bullshite! You never really intended to do it, else why would you be looking for a way out and hearing that friggin' camera? He would have had to rape you and I suspect you would have beat him up while he was trying. . . . You never went to Catholic schools?"

"My parents said we couldn't afford it."

"Well, if you did, you'd know it was no sin at all, at all."

Nuala Anne McGrail, mother superior, confessor, and doctor of the Church.

"If you want to know what I think, you

should forget it all together . . . though it's a great story."

"I have to tell my husband."

"Why ever would you do that?"

"They say that Sterling Stafford is very bitter over his defeat and is talking about getting even with his enemies."

"If you ask me, and I know you haven't, he still regrets his lost opportunity. So you tell Jackie and won't he laugh like I did!"

"You will tell Dermot, won't you?"

"We'll find out what your man is up to. I suspect he's still terrified."

"You're a wonderful confidante, Nuala," she said, her eyes shining.

And the woman a good twenty years older than meself, even if she didn't look it. Wait till I tell Dermot!

"I don't understand why sex is so important to women my age. We're not likely to produce more kids. There is no need for us to stay married so that our kids will receive an education. I thought I was through with it till I met my husband. Now I'm like a raging inferno."

How fortunate for your man.

" 'Tis the discipline, isn't it now?"

"Discipline!"

"'Tis! Sex is great craic, but only if we can learn the discipline of being sensitive to our lover. All the time. No complaining about him to our women friends. Same for him. We learn how to respect everyone by respecting our lover. And if we're not generous to him, we won't be generous to anyone else and we'll be miserable human beings, won't we? So sex at any age civilizes us, at least if we want to keep up the craic. Lots of times it isn't easy because the other is often a friggin' amadon. But that's the way they are. Women can be eejits too, you know, friggin' onchucks."

"We have to learn how to preserve our lovers?"

"'Tis true and if we can do that we have learned how to be good in all our relationships."

"The lover is paradigmatic?"

"Isn't that what himself, the little archbishop says and doesn't he know everything about it and himself an outsider."

We drained our jars, she put on her Brit trench coat and walked down to the car, meself with her lest she fall. She hugged me again.

"I'd better go home and prepare myself to

be generous to my lover, not that it is difficult these days. . . . I must learn to understand him better. . . ."

"Ah, no, that's useful, but the trick of it is to understand yourself better."

She nodded, as if she got it. Smart woman that she was, she surely got it.

"Come on, Fiona, we've done a good day's work," I said and we walked up the stairs together.

— Dermot —

"WHAT'S HAPPENING?" I asked as I ambled into Jack Donlan's office.

He glanced up and smiled, a smile which me wife had said would break many a married woman's heart if she were Irish. Not mine of course, she had added.

He stood up briskly and shook hands.

"A cup of tea?"

"A touch of it," I said. "It's been a dry morning."

Waiting in the doorway, Elfrida said, "I'll make it, Mr. Donlan. You don't know how to do it for an Irishman."

I thought of pleading that it was me wife that was Irish.

"To answer your question, the Dow, Nasdaq, S and P are all nervous. Frodo and Samwise are no more nervous than anyone else. The lightning is still up there, but so far so good."

"You think that will continue?"

"Until the other shoe falls."

"What's the other shoe?"

"The next phase in the plot."

"You think there is a plot?"

"Dermot, as a gambler, I have to deal with probabilities. If it looks like a duck and walks like a duck and quacks like a duck, it's probably a duck—eighty-five percent probability. Maybe it's a South American pigeon which is invading our shores. This affair looks like someone—singular or plural—is out to get either Maria or me. They are hasty and clumsy but so far they have proven themselves skillful at seizing opportunities."

"You are remarkably calm about it, sir."

He shrugged, a hint of Celtic fatalism.

The good Elfrida returned with tea and buttered scones and admonished us to let it

steep for a while. I immediately captured one of the scones and swallowed it whole.

"One wins some and loses some. I won Maria, I might lose Frodo, but with enough cash to live luxuriously for the rest of our lives. As my father used to say, don't fight the Holy Ghost. I might sail a boat round the world or do something else constructive."

"Who are the plotters?"

"I don't know. I'm trusting you and your wife and Mike Casey to figure that out. I think my family is involved, but only as unwitting tools. . . . Have you managed to find any evidence about that?"

He poured tea for both of us. Perfectly steeped, as I knew it would be. Like me wife he must have a stopwatch in his head for such matters.

"This is a copy of the letter they received," I said, passing it across his desk. "The original was crudely scrawled on a lined page torn out of a notebook."

He glanced at it and shrugged again.

"I would say probably an outburst from a hysterical middle-aged person, likely a woman. Just the sort of screed that would appeal to my family."

He gave it back to me.

"They certainly made a lot out of it," I suggested. "Would you suppose that she knew how they would react?"

I sipped the tea. Delicious.

"Milk?" he asked.

"As I tell the woman of the house, I never pollute perfectly good tea."

"Or maybe the one who sent the letter had a shrewd guess about what they would think anyway of a new stepmother. . . . I never would have thought that adult women would so resent another woman in the master bedroom. . . . Shows how much I understand women, doesn't it, Dermot?"

"Me wife, who knows about such primal things, tells me that the mystery of the parental bed is both fascinating and terrifying to kids as they grow up."

"Mary Fran gave you the copy, I suppose? Where is she?"

"She understands that she must make a decision and knows that she will choose you and Maria but hesitates."

"Spirit is willing, but the flesh is weak, eh?"

"A colleague of yours made roughly the same allegations, did he not?"

"Lou Garner, a classmate at Loyola University, real estate, loves to gossip, but is not vicious, means no harm by it . . ."

"A rival?"

"On the tennis court . . . Otherwise a friend. He came to the wedding and the reception and was very gracious in his congratulations. I don't think he is capable of conspiracy, but then what do I know?"

"Either he made up the allegations or they are free-floating rumors up and down LaSalle Street."

"I thought they were the latter, the sort of remark which is made about a woman who is beautiful and successful. I asked Mike Casey to investigate."

He opened a drawer in his desk and with the unerring instinct of the man who knows where every document is, removed a file folder and handed it to me.

Three typed pages of notes, which I read quickly.

"When is her feast day?" I asked, returning the file to his desk, still opened.

He chuckled.

"'Chaste and modest matron' summarizes it all, does it not? I'll confess that I found the prospect of bedding such a one to be, how shall I say it, appealing. I hope that does not make me sound like a degenerate."

"If it does, then much of the human race is degenerate."

You think herself is a chaste and modest matron?

Among other things.

That's why you fuck her in the kitchen?

Once in a while when no one else is around.

I shook off the murmurings of my everpresent Adversary and returned to the discussion with my client.

"You might mail this report to Mary Fran. It would confirm her inclination to admire your wife."

He considered the folder and glanced up at me.

"Better you send it to her. It will then appear in a more neutral context."

"Good idea . . . Now, would you give me permission to talk to Lou Garner?"

"Why not? I would have a hard time thinking of him as a suspect."

A classmate and a foe on the tennis court who was not nearly so successful as you? Gimme a break.

I gathered together the remnants of our

morning tea, but Elfrida intervened to prevent servile work by such an important man. As I left the office I observed that John Patrick Donlan had returned to the eternal flow of stock reports on his big computer screen and rejoiced that I had withdrawn from that casino.

I hurried home in the hope that I might find me wife in some domestic situation in which she could play the role of the chaste and modest matron.

I was out of luck. There were vehicles all along Sheffield Avenue, including a Channel 3 TV truck. Several small ones were thundering up the stairs. Nuala Anne was having a party. Celebrating our victory in court.

The parlor was swarming with people, rug-rat people and grown-up people, neighbors and their kids like Peter and Cindasue Murphy, kids from school who were in Nuala's chorus, teachers from the school, the priest from the rectory, my sister Cindy and her husband Tom Hurley who was one of the lawyers for NBS and parents of Ellie, TV technicians, me wife pouring tea, me older daughter and son offering Coke or water, Ellie and Danuta serving scones, Socra Marie hugging anyone who looked like they needed a hug, and the hounds proudly sauntering around as if they were in fact the cause of all the celebration.

"All right, quiet please! . . . Are you ready, Nuala? . . . You can put the teapot down for a moment. . . ."

The ever-present Nelliecoyne removed the pot from her ma's hand. In a red and gold Marquette sweatsuit me wife looked every bit the surprised yuppy matron.

I was proud of her, like I usually am.

"Nuala," Mary Alice asked, "would you have any comment that you seemed to have won the case and your Christmas special will air again this year on NBS?"

"Winning is better than losing, as we Irish know because we've lost so often in our sad history. And isn't it NBS who had the injunction lifted, so didn't they win? And isn't the decision on appeal and no one knows what this new bunch of lawyers will do? So it's still early days, isn't it now? But it's time for a preliminary celebration anyway. . . ."

"Isn't it true, Nuala, that Ireland is now the richest country in Europe?"

"Och, 'tis, but we don't like to talk about it for fear of hurting the feelings of your poor Brits. All that proves is that the Irish win in the long run but they have to wait a thousand years. . . . And we only have a couple of more days?"

"Do you have any comment on the fact that Mr. Abercrombie will appear in all the papers tomorrow morning as the dog in the manger?"

"I'm just happy that you Yanks are all familiar with Aesop's fables."

The kids began to sing the Connemara lullaby.

The camera turned on them. They sang more loudly.

"Great!" Mary Alice gave the cut sign. "Now let's rush this, guys, so we can get down to the studios in time to get it on both five and six o'clock."

The TV folks exited loudly. The eating and drinking and talking and singing went on. In Ireland, they would have called it a comeallye, though there would be liquor on the premises.

"This wasn't me idea," Nuala assured me as she pecked at me, uh, my cheek. "It was your sister and her husband and their daughter and themselves, terrible people altogether!"

"It was worth a celebration," I said, returning the kiss.

"Did you find out anything?"

"We better talk about it later."

"Sure, don't you have the right of it, Dermot Michael, like you always do."

My cell phone rang. I walked into our library and closed the door.

"Dermot Coyne," I said tersely.

"Hey, Dermot, it's Dom, what's happening!"

"We're having a little celebration."

"I heard you won the case."

"They're appealing."

"Them appellate judges are no good, Dermot. I hope you got a good one. . . . Say, I talked to my friends. Their friends tell them that none of our people were involved in that caper that went down yesterday. The guys who put out the contract were punks. They were told to get out of town and not come back. My friends said that their friends assured them that there wouldn't be any more trouble and that I should tell you that they still have enormous respect for you and your wife."

All very neat.

"Where were these guys from?"

"Somewhere in Wisconsin. They're back there now."

"And the guys who pulled up in the stolen car?"

"Already gone, back to St. Louis."

"No one from Oakdale?"

"Like I told you, my friends' friends don't like the Sabattini bunch at all but this is not the way they operate."

I found that reply unsettling. It probably meant that the wiseguys had no evidence and had not investigated that angle with any great care. Probably however, the wiseguys would keep an eye on them. As far as I was concerned Maria Angelica's brothers were still on the suspect list.

"I assume they'll watch them."

"Dermot, the friends of my friends always watch guys like them that are crazy and are too close to Chicago. Someday they'll go too far and then it's zero for them."

"Thanks, Dom, thanks a million . . . You'll let me know if you pick up anything more."

"I promise you that sincerely, like I tell you, you are a man my friends respect."

I never have been able to figure out why they respect me. The wiseguys have no reason to be afraid of me or of Nuala Anne. But they get nervous when they get near people that seem supernatural.

I went back to the parlor. Nuala, as is her wont, was giving orders. I noted that Cindy and Tom were not looking happy.

"All right, folks, it's getting dark outside, and all the kids should be going home. We'll continue this party on another day. Mick and Nelliecoyne, will you take the doggies downstairs so everyone has protection going home?"

"Yes, Ma!"

"Now, everyone goes right straight home, understand?"

"Yes, Miz Coyne."

Only in the context of St. Josephat school is she Miz Coyne. If she's not, how can she be Nelliecoyne's mother? At other times Miz Coyne is my mother.

"We had bad luck at the Seventh Circuit," Tom Hurley reported as Nuala was ushering the kids down the stairs, lest anyone fall. "There is only one man on the circuit who might give us trouble, Rick Rowbottom. And that's who we got. Anyone else would have thrown the dog back in the manger. Rick delayed a ruling till tomorrow morning so that he could study the case and that's very bad news."

Cindy and her daughter were in the

kitchen putting together a supper. They were getting along very well, much better than they would in their own kitchen. Nuala's idea to hire her as babysitter had been, as usual, wise.

Cindy stuck her head into the dining room where her husband and I were setting the table.

"He defines narcissism. He imagines that he is the best lawyer on the circuit and that the pretentious and self-important opinions he writes are going to be cited for the ages. Now he has another chance to primp and preen and perform on a high-profile case about which there is no serious question of law at all. He'll delay a decision until the matter is moot on the grounds that there are very serious—his favorite words—matters of law at issue. He is a pimp and a prick!"

"Mother!" her daughter protested from the kitchen.

That's my sister Cindy, never one to be guilty of excessive moderation—five words beginning with a *P* leading up to prick, alliteration with a vengeance.

"What will you and Gerry do, Tom?"

"We'll go into Rowbottom's court tomorrow assuming that obviously he will sustain the injunction while he reviews the serious matters of contract law at issue. He will suspend the injunction until there is a full review of the issue. It's a matter of national importance and a full review is essential, especially because media law is extremely complicated. We will be astonished and then outraged. It is a simple matter of contract law, that every second-year student in law school could answer. He will be offended, which is good because he says stupid things. He will set a date for argument sometime after Christmas. We will yell that the issue will be moot by then because the program is scheduled for the week before Christmas. He will reply that the majesty of the legal process cannot be subservient to the television schedule, especially when that is dependent on a religious feast. He will be very proud of himself for having introduced the church/state issue. We will announce that we are appealing to the full circuit and storm out in high dudgeon, just like Nuala Anne when she's upset, to say nothing of my wife."

"Rick ought to be locked up," Cindy cried from the kitchen.

"Then we'll go down to the chief justice's

office and scream bloody murder. This kind of grandstanding is what gives appellate courts a bad name. Can you see the headlines tomorrow—'Judge keeps dog in the manger!' You can imagine what that will do. He will try to calm us down. We will repeat the argument. He will say, 'Religious feast, did that asshole really say that?' and we will say it's all on the record and he'll say we should appear before him first thing in the morning and ask for emergency relief. He'll set up a panel of justices that will have an emergency hearing and a decision by the end of the business day tomorrow."

"Are you sure that it will work out that way?"

"Not certain. Probably."

"The chief justice hates Rick's guts." Cindy arrived with salad. "There's enough problems in the circuit without his muddying the waters. . . . My daughter made this salad and it's scrumptious. . . . Where's Nuala?"

"Out with the dogs," I replied, "taking her choir kids home."

The front door opened and the white demons thundered into the house, followed by the "big kids," followed by their mother. Then the "little kids" appeared from the playroom.

Socra Marie, now always a self-designated spokesman for her little brother announced, "Patjo says he starving."

"Downstairs, doggies," she ordered. "You were wonderful!"

She had to hug both of them.

"Nelliecoyne, Mick, feed them please."

"Yes, Ma."

"Thank you . . . Dermot Michael, I need a drink!"

"Yes, Ma."

MUCH LATER, when the Hurleys (save for their daughter) had gone home and the kitchen and dining room cleaned up and the kids put to bed, and Danuta had driven off in her Honda, and Ellie was studying sociology in her room—herself and meself had settled in with a "splash" of Baileys—we sat at the window overlooking Sheffield Avenue for our end-of-day conversation.

"Dermot Michael, I may die before morning."

"Woman, you will not!"

"I am too old for days like this. . . . Anyway, tell me what happened."

"I want to go on record as claiming that I

am too old for days like this too and I'm a lot older than you."

"Five years."

"Five and a half."

We sipped our Baileys.

"You first," she said. "I have a wonderful story for you."

I recounted my conversation with Mary Fran.

"Poor child. She'd find Maria a wonderful confidante."

"I'm sure she will eventually."

"Is that something of which you are sure or that you know?"

She laughed my favorite Nuala Anne laugh, wicked, fey, impish—a leprechaun child.

"Sure would I be saying it so confident like, unless I knew it?"

"Here's the copy she made of the letter that led to the big family fight."

Nuala Anne looked at it and frowned, turned it over to look at the other side, and then frowned even more deeply.

"It's a copy of a note scribbled on a lined page torn out of a notebook."

"Hmm."

"It ain't what it pretends to be. It's very evil."

Rarely does she slip anymore and say *ain't*. It's not accepted American usage anymore, though herself insists that it is a perfectly "daycent" word.

"Oh," I said.

"It's someone pretending to be a hysterical middle-class woman, pretending to be vulgar. But that's not what it is at all, at all."

"What is it?"

"Evil."

Then I told her about my first conversation with Dom.

"I've never met the man, but I don't like them."

"He's not a Tony Soprano type."

"I hate that program," she said firmly. "I won't let me kids watch it. It's evil."

"The outfit imposes some social control here that otherwise wouldn't exist."

"So did the lads in Northern Ireland . . . Did he call back?"

"He did."

I repeated his message, almost word for word.

"Wisconsin, St. Louis. Your friends on the

West Side are not telling us the whole truth, are they?"

"They know more than they're telling, that's for sure. Their own guys are not involved. And they've warned off the out-siders. But that doesn't help us much. Our friends are safe for the moment. We'll tell Mike Casey to keep a close watch on them."

Then I told her about my visit to Jack Don-lan's office, about the nervousness of his funds and about his tennis friend Lou Gar-ner. Then I gave her Mike Casey's three-page report about Maria Sabattini Connors. She read the document carefully and grinned.

"Chaste and modest matron, fersure!"

"In my experience they are great craic in bed."

"And yourself with great experience of them kind! You're supposed to mail this to Mary Fran? Good idea. They'll all come home eventually. And before you ask, Der-mot Michael Coyne, let me say that now I know that."

How does one not know something and then know it?

Don't ask me. Am I fey?

Darn good thing for all of us!

"Dermot, since we're too tired to do anything but sleep, would you ever bring me another little splash of Baileys?"

I had been thinking the same thing.

"She came to see me this morning," Nuala informed me when I returned with two brandy snifters, her eyes twinkling mischievously.

"Who came to see you this morning?"

"The chaste and modest matron."

"Why?"

"To confess an act of adultery."

"She never did!"

"That's the way I talk."

"Did you give her absolution?"

"Dermot Michael, I did not. Wasn't there nothing to absolve?"

"Why did she tell you?"

"Because she thought we should know it."

"Are you going to tell me?"

"I might just," she grinned and yawned.

The story of Sterling Stafford was wild.

"So you see your chaste and modest matron is also a warrior queen, maybe descendant of Granne O'Malley."

"Jackie Donlan is an even more fortunate man than he realizes," I observed.

"We'll have to charge your man extra for

our fee. Doesn't the woman think that I'm her confidante now?"

We don't take fees. If people ask how much they owe us, herself always says, "Give whatever you want to the charity of your choice and don't complicate me income tax returns."

I don't know what that means, but one of the advantages of marrying a woman who is, as she says, a "chartered accountant" is that she does our tax returns, which, as she avers, "They'd never dare question."

"She'll call me in the morning to tell me whether your man has thrown"—pronounced *trun*—"her out of their apartment. . . . Well, we've made enough on Samwise, so I suppose we can't complain, can we?"

"Does he know you're a client?"

"He didn't say, but then he wouldn't."

"That's his high-risk fund! I didn't know you were a high roller, Nuala Anne McGrail!"

She yawned loudly.

"Didn't I marry you?"

"'Tis true . . ."

"Dermot love, I'm going to bed now. Tomorrow night we can say two decades of the rosary."

I tucked her in like she was a little girl. She was already asleep.

Poor kid. One moment she was sitting in O'Neil's pub off the College Green and the next moment, almost before she knew it, she had a lecherous husband, four kids, a big house, a couple of demanding careers, and a major court case.

I was tired too, but, unlike me wife, I couldn't wipe out the stimuli of the day. I walked the house for another hour trying to sort out the problems before I slipped into bed next to her. As I disappeared into the magic world of Nod, she took my hand.

Thank you, I whispered to the deity.

About time you said that.

— Nuala Anne —

I BEGAN the day peacefully enough. I brought the big kids over to school, along with the dogs. I then glanced at a picture on the front page of the *Herald,* depicting Triple A in a manger labeled "Christmas," and reading his comment, "Judge Brown is typical of the subhuman hacks that suck graft out of the city for the Daley administration." I settled down to practice my lullabies for my younger son who stopped playing with his trucks long enough to climb into my lap and grin his idiot grin, which is an imitation of his father's grin. . . . Och, me Dermot isn't an idiot and neither is Patjo.

The first call was from Cindy Hurley.

"There's bad news and good news. The bad is that Judge Rowbottom lifted the injunction this morning and scheduled a hearing after the first of the year. He's preening around the Dirksen building like he's just been named to the supreme court. The good news is that Judge Brown has held Abercrombie in contempt of court and sentenced him to a week in the Federal lockup. The marshals arrested him when he came out of the Hilton this morning. His lawyers are going crazy. So are the media. Don't miss the noonday news! Gerry and Tom are appealing this afternoon as planned. Funny thing is that George Bush the First appointed Ebenezer to the bench and he's a Republican. I'll keep you informed."

I'd spent too much time in the courtrooms of this litigious country to regret that I was not part of the scene. Cindy was a lawyer. She loved every second of it. If we lost the case, the Christmas specials were dead. I could still sing me songs to me own kids and we'd get out a record anyway.

Ellie came in about ten from her class at Loyola, all excited about how wonderful college was. She took me son from me arms.

Faithless one that he is, he deserted me without protest.

"Come on now, little punk, your ma has work to do."

"Didn't you and your ma get along well enough in the kitchen last night?"

She sighed, a bad habit that she had picked up from me.

"My mom is okay, Aunt Nuala."

"Learned a lot, has she now, since you walked out on her? Sometimes parents grow up in a hurry, don't they?"

"Like you say, Aunt Nuala, mothers and daughters bond by fighting."

Aunt Nuala was becoming an authority to be quoted.

The next interruption was a call from another one of those who had decided I was a trusted confidante.

"You were right, Nuala, as you well know. Jack was wonderful. He told me that he always knew I could take care of myself, but now he was absolutely certain!"

"Brilliant."

Me husband says that *brilliant* is the superlative of the Irish adjective *grand* and the comparative is *super.*

"He laughed at my description of my

'destruction' as he calls it of Sterling and said he wasn't sure he wanted a shotgun rack in our apartment. I felt like a fool for ever doubting his reaction. He also said to pass on the word to you and Dermot that Sterling is a bad 'un and that we should keep an eye on him."

"Me man has already passed that information on to Mike Casey."

"He made me promise not to throw a camera unless it was one of those small ones."

"And you replied . . ."

"Oh, that there were always objects around the house that you can throw at an obstreperous husband. . . ."

"And then you had a lot of fun?"

"We did that, Nuala Anne . . . I still feel like a fool for being scared of him . . . I'm a very lucky woman."

"You're not the only lucky person in the family, not even the luckiest."

I went back to my annotations of the working script for our problematic show. It had started out as fun, now it had become a heavy burden, even without the eejits in the Dirksen building.

I heard the hounds barking, their we're-going-out-now bark. Danuta was making lunch and watching the rug rats and Ellie was picking up the older kids to bring them back for lunch. No cold lunch in the school for Ms. McGrail's kids.

The phone again.

"Nuala Anne."

"I wonder if I could speak to Dermot?"

She sounded teary.

"I'm sorry, Mrs. Coyne. This is Mary Fran Donlan. We have more problems, I'm afraid."

"Och, isn't Dermot Michael out hunting the bad guys. He mailed something to you this morning. . . . I'll try to reach him on his cell phone."

"I'm afraid that my dad had Tony Cuneen, my brother-in-law, fired from his law firm, just as he was about to be named a partner. It's not fair. Tony is a good lawyer. Okay, he made a fool of himself about our trust funds. . . ."

"And on television."

"We were all upset. . . . We should have known better."

"What did they say to him?"

"They told him that the managing partners didn't think he would be comfortable in the firm. . . . They didn't throw him out on the spot. His contract doesn't expire till February first, but he can't appear in court for them again. So he's free to look for another job. . . . But who would want him?"

"You're after being sure your dad is behind this, are you now?"

"Who else might it be?"

"I don't know your father very well, dear, but wouldn't I be thinkin' that he's not the kind of man who takes revenge that way?"

"I know, but Evie is certain. . . ."

"She's always certain, isn't she now?"

"She says that woman drove Dad to fire Tony."

"Might she not have a fixation on that woman?"

Dead silence.

"You're right, Mrs. Coyne. I think I've made a fool of myself again."

"Mrs. Coyne is me mother-in-law and a grand woman altogether. I'm Nuala."

"I'm sorry, Nuala."

"Wouldn't it seem to an outsider that your poor brother-in-law disgraced the firm by his remarks on the telly and that his firm really had no choice? And that maybe your sister is the one to blame? Would you want to hire a lawyer, no matter how gifted, who behaved so foolishly?"

Silence.

"I never thought of it that way, but you're right of course."

Poor beaten little girl child. Her sister was a bitch.

"Me Dermot hasn't checked in yet, but won't I try to get him on the cell phone and tell him what's happening. I don't know what we can do about it. Probably nothing at all, at all. But we'll try."

"I'm sorry I've made a fool of myself, er, Nuala. I should have thought for a minute and realized Dad would never do anything like that."

"He seems a very decent man to me. . . . *Decent* is Irish for good and honest and kind."

"He is, oh, yes, he is."

"Well, maybe you and your sisters should try acting that way toward him."

"Maybe we should."

"I'll call me Dermot."

I tried again. No answer. He was obviously very busy. I thought about it. What the hell. If people treat me like a friggin' parish priest, maybe I should act like one. I pulled out my phone book and punched in Jack Donlan's phone number.

"Mr. Donlan's office."

I put on my professional face and the voice to go with it.

"This is Ms. McGrail calling. May I speak to Mr. Donlan."

"Certainly, Nuala Anne. Just a moment please."

Good enough for my professionalism! I switched my face.

"Wouldn't you be Elfrida now?"

"Yes, ma'am."

"Well doesn't me husband say that you make better Irish tea than I do?"

He'd never said that, but sometimes a compliment doesn't hurt.

"You know what Irish men are with their blarney!"

"'Tis true!"

"Good morning, Nuala, it's good to talk to my wife's confessor!"

Speaking of blarney!

"Ah, no! I don't have the power of absolution, only the power of listening, so wouldn't I more properly be called a spiritual director?"

"Whatever, you were a big help to her yesterday and I'm grateful."

"Won't I be after adding a charge to me fee?"

"I'm a very fortunate man, just how fortunate I keep learning."

I sighed my Connemara sigh.

"Well, I have a bit of a problem for you this morning. . . . Your son-in-law has been fired by his law firm. . . ."

It was his turn to sigh.

"I was afraid they'd go after him, poor kid. He's a good lawyer, top of the list for partnership until my daughter dragged him into court to protect their trust funds. . . ."

Danuta appeared at the door of my office with the frown she uses to indicate the food is getting cold. I raised the finger that said I'd be right there.

"And isn't she blaming you instead of herself?"

He was silent for a moment.

"And her sisters agree?"

"Not Mary Fran."

At least not after I had a quiet word with her.

"Thank God for that!"

"And yourself having no markers at all, at all at the firm?"

"You're a desperate woman, Nuala Anne McGrail!"

"And yourself picking up the Irish idiom quickly enough."

"As a matter of fact, I have several markers over there. They probably dumped him as a favor to me. So it won't hurt them to take him back, another year as an associate and a promise to never appear in a case with his wife. . . . Doubtless he'll be happy to keep it."

"Won't he have to rein in that one?"

"I've never been able to do that."

Then I thought to myself, the marriage will fall apart. Hasn't me poor Dermot saved our marriage a couple of times by shouting at me? . . . I shiver at the thought of losing him, poor dear man.

"After this escape, he may have learned a lesson."

"I'll call him now and ask what they said when they terminated him. Then I'll call them to pick up my markers. . . . I owe you a lot of favors, Nuala."

"In a whole lifetime you won't be able to pick them all up. . . . Now don't I have to eat my lunch before me housekeeper fires me."

I sighed again, with satisfaction for a good deed. That poor little bitch was asking for lifetime heartbreak.

Danuta appeared again with a plate of salad.

"Everyone watch TV," she complained.

In the kitchen all the kids, Ellie included, were watching Mary Alice Quinn on Channel 3.

"Yesterday's dog in the manger has become today's bird in the jail. This morning Judge Ebenezer Brown ordered Federal marshals from his courtroom to arrest Archibald Adolf Abercrombie and bring him to the courtroom to face charges of contempt of court."

(Pictures of three marshals trying to muscle Triple A into the Dirksen Federal building.)

"Judge Brown, a Republican appointed to the Federal bench by the first President Bush, asked Mr. Abercrombie if he had made a statement contemptuous of the court yesterday."

(Picture of Abercrombie coming out of the building yesterday.)

"Judge Brown is typical of the subhuman hacks that suck graft out of the city for the Daley Administration."

Mary Alice again.

"Under advice of his attorneys, the so-called dog in the manger refused to answer. Then Judge Brown solemnly sentenced him to a week in the Federal lockup. Mr. Abercrombie announced that he would appeal and that he was sure the appellate court would assert his right to freedom of speech about an incompetent and retarded judge. Judge Brown extended the sentence to three weeks in the lockup."

Pictures of Triple A emerging in shackles, still struggling with the marshals.

"We asked Tom Hurley, one of the lawyers representing NBS which wants to produce the Nuala Anne Christmas special what impact he thought the imprisonment of a celebrity Hollywood mogul would have on the case."

(Tom Hurley relaxed and confident with a leprechaun's twinkle in his eyes.)

"Out in Hollywood the bosses of Kosmic Entertainment might begin to wonder whether the entertainment Mr. Abercrombie is providing for us in Chicago is worth the cost."

"Didn't an appellate court judge deliver a setback to your case this morning, counselor?"

"A temporary setback, Mary Alice. Judge

Richard Rowbottom lifted the injunction we had won from Judge Brown and set a date for a hearing on our motion for January third. We intend to appeal that decision this afternoon. Obviously January third is after Christmas."

"If Mr. Abercrombie is the dog in the manger, what would that make Judge Rowbottom?"

"Well, if Judge Rowbottom is successful in his ruling—and we confidently expect a reversal—then some people, certainly not including me, might think that he wants to be the Grinch who stole Christmas."

"Mr. Hurley is well known in the Chicago area as the husband of celebrity trial lawyer Cynthia Hurley."

Then there was a commercial about a weight-loss diet. My children and my niece were exchanging high fives and I had to join in. Slapstick entertainment for Chicago.

— Dermot —

"LOU GARNER," Mike Casey told me, "is both sleazy and slippery. Jack Donlan should find himself another tennis partner. He has his fingers in lots of minor little development deals and light clout with some aldermen with whom he drinks a couple of times a week. He always has a deal in the works and usually makes some money when the big players buy him out to get rid of him. He pretends to be one of the big players, but he never will be."

"Not enough money."

"Money is not the problem in that world. Not enough smarts. He skates pretty close to the edge. The Feds have him on their radar scopes but he's too small-fry for them to bother about unless they want a slam-dunk conviction to raise their conviction rates. They'll get him eventually of course."

"Is Jackie Donlan involved?"

"No way! Much too smart. I told him that he shouldn't pay any attention to his gossip about Maria Sabattini. Garner is a bottom prowler on LaSalle Street, always trying to soak up gossip that he can use for one of his capers. I wasn't surprised that we were able to clear her."

"Chaste matron?" I said ironically.

"Absolutely."

I called Elfrida to make sure her boss, somewhat reluctant for me to corner his high school and college friend, had set up the appointment.

"I don't like that Lou Garner," she said, exercising a woman's right to criticize her employer's friends. "He's no good at all. Shy, shifty, too suave. Be careful of him, Mr. Coyne."

"Woman, who's this Mr. Coyne?"

She giggled. "Dermot!"

"That's better."

I was to meet Mr. Garner at his office in

Andersonville, a North Side neighborhood whose name reveals its Swedish past and high quality of its Swedish bakeries. His office was on Clark Street, just off Foster Avenue, near St. Gregory's Church. He would be happy to talk to me as we toured some of his North Side properties. He would reserve a parking place for me behind his storefront office and we would drive around in his "jalopy."

I'm West Side Irish—indeed River Forest Irish which is the worst kind—and I know very little about the North Side. While I am in constant verbal combat with the South Side Irish (who tend to be unenlightened White Sox fans), I usually deny that there are North Side Irish, only Germans and Swedes whose closeness to the Polish Corridor along Milwaukee Avenue is their only claim to Catholic virtue. It is not a stance that is likely to please anyone. I do believe, however, that the Italian influence on the West Side has civilized us West Siders and that those of us who do live in enclaves on the North Side are not positively affected by the dour Germans and the silent Swedes. My bedmate is baffled by all of this urban village talk and points out that she and our children are all North Side Irish. I deny this and insist that she is Connemara Irish and our children are Lincoln Park Irish. She throws up her hands in dismay and proclaims that I'm an eejit. Which in these matters is true until you've been around Chicago for a couple of generations.

I parked my ancient Benz behind the storefront with a huge "Garner" sign hanging out over the sidewalk, like it was a funeral parlor. Next to my car, looking very imperial, was a silver BMW X-5. Classy and a little boring, I told myself.

Lou Garner met me at the door. He was not what I expected, not an overweight gum-chewing, heavily scented man with razor cut white hair. Rather he looked like someone who might belong in the Racket Club with John Patrick Donlan—a little taller perhaps, sharp but handsome features, conservative and expensive dark blue, but not quite navy, suit, gleaming white shirt and a tie with stripes which suggested an obscure English regiment. His pale blue eyes did, however, look a little shifty. And his radiant geniality suggested that I would not want to buy either a secondhand car or house from him. He spoke in staccato outbursts, like an AK-47.

Me bedmate would have instantly tagged him as "a bit of a gombeen man." His office was indeed part of an old Jewish funeral parlor, spiffed up with modern Danish furniture.

"The old Mercedes yours?" he asked easing the BMW out of its parking place as it purred softly, a jungle cat eager for the chase. "Great little car, should be a classic in a couple of years, probably appreciating even now."

"My wife owns a Lincoln Navigator. She figures it will be useful, if the English should come down from Toronto and try to repeat the Fort Dearborn massacre. We'll all need tanks then."

He didn't say anything in reply.

"I figure," I went on, "that they'll try to land at Loyola Beach, like the opening shots in that flick *Flatliners*."

My loony words had stopped him cold.

"I also figure that the Jesuits will yield land till Broadway and then hold the line till the Cub fans pile out of Wrigley Park with their axes and pikes."

"The Broadway-Clark corridor," he began his spiel, "is critical for the redevelopment and expansion of the North Side. You have to view it as a funnel coming out of the loop and the Magnificent Mile and channeling all the excitement and vibrancy of Downtown right through to Howard Street and beyond into Evanston and Northwestern University. It will become the exclusive place to live and work and play and absorb art and culture. It has two critical assets—Lake Shore Drive and the elevated lines. . . ." He babbled on and on, doubtless trying to weary me and turn me away from the subject at hand. People do that, blond kid in a blazer, clearly not very bright. You overwhelm him with talk and you have no problems.

"Lake Shore Drive," I said, "is no good unless the mayor is able to extend it beyond Hollywood up to Howard Street and Calvary Cemetery, maybe even up to the Bahai Temple. Sheridan Road is a joke, always has been. So is Evanston. Prohibition started up there. Women's Christian Temperance Union. You sell all the old homes in Evanston to upwardly mobile Blacks, great market! And they're welcome to it. What you have to do is lure the Winnetka and Lake Forest folk to come down the Drive to the Loop and Michigan Avenue and Grant Park. Then they'll see all the high-rises, the old ones and the new ones you'll probably build and want to live in them when they have empty houses on their hands. Or even Balmoral or Lincoln Park, they're one step or two away from slums. Look at them in the winter when the leaves are off the trees. Your corridor is good for what it is, shops, offices, car dealers, that kind of thing. All high class of course. But face it, Lake View is finished. How long have you known Maria Angelica Sabattini?"

"For a long time, twenty years maybe," he stumbled. "Not well, but she's a hard one to miss at real estate meetings and conferences. You know what I mean?"

"Yeah, though I suppose it depends on your tastes. Nice tits, if that's what you're interested in. . . . So you were surprised when your buddy Jack Donlan invested in her company."

He had pulled off Sheridan Road and parked where the road turns left to circle around the Loyola campus. We were looking at the Lake, grey and somber on an early December afternoon. I shivered, though I wasn't cold.

"Well, she didn't seem quite his type, I don't mean physically." He stumbled again.

"They're obviously a striking couple, right out of an issue of *GQ,* people can't take their eyes off them. I mean corporately. Tell you the truth, the idea of people designing their homes on the Net and then a national office supervising the construction and decoration sounds like another dot-com bubble sort of thing, know what I mean? . . . It seems to be working out fine so far. Old Joe McMahon has done a pretty good job scouting out firms for Jackie. And to give Jackie full credit, he has an instinct for a good deal."

"But you warned him about her?"

"You hear things about her, know what I mean? You hear things about women who are successful, huh? Especially if they got looks. So there's always talk along LaSalle Street. I understood that he hadn't met her and he wouldn't until Joe McMahon and the lawyers worked out a deal. But, hell, there are pictures of her everywhere and Jack is lonely. His marriage was a mess, know what I mean, kooky family and she'd become a fall-down drunk. I always regretted not warning him about her family. He was head over heels and I didn't want to make him angry, so I kept my mouth shut. Big mistake."

"So you figured you'd not make the same mistake this time?"

"Something like that, know what I mean? He's lonely, they're together a lot on business, she's gorgeous, she's a widow looking for a guy, he's a great catch. I was right on that, wasn't I?"

"It would appear so."

"I warned him. He wasn't offended. He did an investigation and she came up clean, as clean as any woman her age can, know what I mean? So first thing I know we're getting a wedding invitation. I'm surprised and I keep my fingers crossed. Then I hear his kids are against it and I get uneasy. . . . Marriage is a tough slog, know what I mean?"

"Do I ever!"

I would not report that part of the conversation to me wife.

Better not.

"You gotta have a wife that understands you and stands by you, regardless. Sex holds people together just so long. Then you gotta have shared values and commitments, like my wife and I have, and good kids too. Poor Jackie married the first time essentially because he wanted to get laid. It didn't work. I think he'd be more careful this time, know what I mean? I'm sure he's getting a lot of action and I say good for him. More power to him, but, like I say that wears off. The kids won't come to the wedding. There's that nightmare over at St. Freddy's and all the publicity. Hell of a way to start a marriage. I met her the first time at the dinner at the Four Seasons. She knew who I was and understood what I was doing, more than poor Faith ever did. Anyway Maria was charming and gracious and I thought, well, maybe it will work out. But I notice she has a tongue on her, know what I mean. Funny, real funny, always has a final comment that makes you laugh. I tell myself that Jackie who is a very serious guy will get tired of that after a while. Then she might be just a little too much. Like I say, sex is the most important thing a couple of months before the marriage and the least important thing a couple of months after. Know what I mean?"

"Do I ever!" I lied again.

Liar.

Shut up.

You think he's abnormal. Ever think you might be?

No.

Yes you do.

"You know who the people were who warned you on LaSalle Street?"

"You know what it's like with those things, someone says something in passing and you hear it and kind of remember it, but you can't call back the face. I do remember the guy saying that one of the victims was the Congressman out in that district, what's his name . . . ?"

"Sterling Stafford?"

"Yeah, that guy . . . Well the word is that she let him screw her into the next county and then dropped him and he's never been the same since."

Threw a camcorder at him, actually.

"He's married, isn't he?"

"Yeah I saw him concede on television. She was lurking near him. Not bad for their age, but I don't know."

Bingo!

"Come on, let's have lunch, there's a great steakhouse up on Sheridan Road. I made a reservation."

I resolved firmly that I would have fish.

He couldn't let the topic go. After I had ordered my Alaskan salmon, so called, he returned to it.

"I sure hope she's nice to him, long run I

mean. Poor Jackie is a fragile guy and he's been hurt enough, know what I mean. She could destroy him, eat him alive like they say she did to Stafford. That's what a lot of women do. Can't blame them. They have to get as much as they can, before it's too late."

"Does she seem like she's the kind to do that?"

"No, but Jackie was probably the biggest catch she ever encountered, that's the way those kind of women are."

As I drove down Clark Street toward Fullerton, I decided I didn't like Louis Garner, one bit. His elegance was an expensive veneer of class for a man who was quite incapable of being anything but vulgar. He would have been suspicious of Nuala reading her world economics book that night at O'Neil's on College Green and her dismissal of me as a "focking rich Yank" when all the time she was thinking that she might have to fall in love with me. She's still embarrassed when I remind her of it.

"And yourself taking off me clothes in that dirty imagination of yours!"

Those issues were irrelevant, however, to the present case.

When I pulled up to our prefire (Chicago

Fire) house on Sheffield, the same crowd of cars were lined up, plus a network van from CTN. So we'd won the case? Well good on us.

You let that gombeen man interfere with your normal good disposition. Don't rain on their parade.

Your metaphors are worse than ever.

As I walked up the two flights of stairs—Chicago houses in those days immediately after the Civil War had their entrance on the second floor because the first floor was a sea of mud—I heard singing, not lullabies, but drinking songs and also the happy howling of wolfhounds.

My daughter Nelliecoyne emerged and waited for me on the little porch at the top of the steps. She gave me the thumbs-up sign and then shouted ecstatically when she hugged me, "We won, Da! Poor Ma is so happy and herself pretending that it was no big deal!"

In the parlor, me good wife, tears flooding her face, which in turn glowed with light, was talking to the camera.

"Well, the Grinch didn't steal Christmas, did he now, and himself, poor dear man, furious at his colleagues . . . The fight is a shame altogether. I don't like fighting at all, we Irish women are a peaceful and forgiving people. We have to be because our men require so much forgiveness. . . . Christmas should be a peaceful time. I'm sorry we had to protect our Christmas songs and themselves again from all over the world. I hope they do a little bit to bring people closer together. The children for whom lullabies are sung deserve a world where people are closer together. So we'll all pray that the people who hear the songs will feel more peaceful. . . . I'm going to ask the kids to sing our Arab lullaby."

While they sang the marvelous little number, mostly wordless exclamations of joy, Tom Hurley and I drifted into the library.

"The panel restored the ban on the injunction?"

"They did indeed do that and with withering sarcasm for the attempt to moot the issue with gobbledygook incantations—the chief justice's very words—about church and state."

"That's the end of it, I hope?"

"Not at all, Derm, not at all! After the hearing in January, we'll go back to the district court for relief from the damages done to the

show by Mr. Abercrombie's defamatory comments about it and for his gross violation of
NBS's contract. If herself wants to quit after
next year, that's fine. I don't think they're fun
for her anymore, but we can't let a raving
maniac ruin it and leave a bitter taste in
everyone's mouth."

"They'll settle, I suppose?"

"Yeah, they'll settle and they'll put a lid on
Triple A. . . . And your sister and I will be
able to buy Christmas presents for our
kids. . . ."

There was another dinner, for which
Nuala had laid in supplies of hamburgers
and hot dogs and much toasting. My heart
was not in it at all. I was worried about the
Donlans and the forces of evil I saw swilling
around them. If I could sense converging
threats, what might Nuala see. How did you
prepare a Christmas concert and protect
good people from crazies?

We said last night's decade of the rosary
before our conversation. Nuala poured a
"jar" of whiskey for each one of us. Solemn
high conversation.

"So tell me about the gombeen man who
made you come in with such a long face?"

The woman doesn't miss a thing.

You just noticed that?

So I told her about Lou Garner, Jack Donlan's great friend.

"Wouldn't he love to destroy him! All his success and fame and now Maria!"

"That about summarizes it."

"And the gobshite thinks he fooled me husband too?"

"The curly haired yuppie in the blazer!"

"And Sterling Stafford apparently is talking about Maria?"

"Maybe he was talking about her before she whupped him and then lied to cover up what really happened."

"Do you think so, Nuala Anne?"

"What do you think?"

"He sounds like the kind of man who broods about his failures in the seduction contest, especially when the woman makes a fool out of him. Then he gets drubbed in an election and he broods some more. Then he reads about a wedding and he explodes, but he's not too smooth anymore and does some clumsy things."

"He's giving a talk down at the Union League Club tonight. The subject is the 'Republican Revival.' . . . Nine-fingered shitehawks! They're properly beaten and already planning a way to sneak back in."

My wife had never paid much attention to Irish politics, save for denouncing the leadership as amadons. However, she had been strongly influenced by my mother's intense loyalty to the Democrats.

"If our man Barak wins the election," I mused, "they'll need a new senator from Illinois two years from now. Sterling is a little long in the tooth, but that would be a spectacular comeback."

"And Maria is out there with the film of his trying to rape her. She'd never use it. . . . She hasn't looked at it herself. . . . But she's still got it, in case she should ever need it."

Film is pronounced the Irish way as though there were a *u* between the *l* and the *m.*

We were both silent, nursing our jars cautiously because we knew they'd weaken our thinking.

"The problem is, Dermot Michael, that none of these things hang together yet. There's a pattern out there, but all they tell us is that someone has a grudge against Jack and Maria, but they're inept. . . . Maybe someone whom she once hit in the head with a camera. . . . I'll ask Mike Casey to go down to the Union League and listen to your man."

"Good idea . . . You've got a TV special to jump-start. . . ."

"That's what you Yanks call a slice of cake."

"Piece of cake."

"Isn't that because you eat it with your fingers! . . . When do you think they'll reinstate that gobshite Tony Cuneen?"

"Huh?"

"Och! Dermot! And meself only a tad over thirty and losing me mind altogether . . . I forgot to tell you!"

She told me about the call from Mary Fran and her conversation with Jackie and "that sweet little Elfrida kid."

"I think you should probably see a doctor or take a long rest. Yourself with four brat kids, a gobshite of a husband, and a court battle with some bad people, and you forget that you save a young man's career and marriage by a single phone call."

She was blushing and, having to decide between laughter and tears, opted for laughter.

"Would you ever fill up me jar again?"

"Woman, I would not!"

"Then you'll have to make love with me or I won't sleep at all, at all."

"Well, it's been a long, hard day, but I guess I might manage it."

I snaked my hand up her thigh. She groaned in response.

I took her in my arms and warned her, "I'll probably have to kiss you everywhere tonight."

"Isn't it what you would do to a poor woman who is losing her mind! . . . Do you think they have reinstated Tony yet?"

You weren't even thinking about screwing her tonight and now you're acting crazy.

There's a lot of sex in this case and it's festering in my head.

"Dermot Michael Coyne," she gasped. "You've taken off all me clothes and we're not in the bedroom yet. . . ."

"Who needs a bedroom!"

"Och . . . DERMOT!"

— Nuala Anne —

ME POOR husband is a heavy sleeper and after a small jar and a bit of serious loving, he sleeps like the room has fallen on his head.

I love him so much. I'm glad I decided when I came to Yank land that I wanted to spend the rest of my life in the same bed as he.

However, I have to keep one ear open at night in case there's any noise in the kids' rooms. The dogs are watching, but what's the point in having a mother unless she is listening for your sounds at night?

Me husband doesn't know all me secrets yet, but the ones he doesn't know, don't matter much. I hope he never becomes bored with me. Well, I can probably come up with some more secrets if I put what's left of my mind to it.

I was only half asleep when the phone rang. Isn't the phone ringing at night the most terrible sound altogether? You're after wondering if someone is dead. . . . Dermot was next to me in bed, the kids were in their rooms . . . me ma or dad . . .

"Nuala Anne," I said, as crisp as if I was wide awake.

"Blackie . . ."

Real trouble.

"What's wrong?"

"Our friend John Donlan is in the emergency room at St. Joseph's Hospital. He has been beaten brutally. . . ."

"Brigid, Patrick, and Colmcille! He isn't dead, is he?"

"No life-threatening injuries, concussion, maybe some internal injuries. They're doing X-rays and scans. A little concern about the concussion . . ."

"Maria is there?"

"Oh yes, she drove off the perpetrators with a golf club. . . . She is, however, somewhat stressed, as they say."

"I'll be right over."

"That would be a good work. The situation here is somewhat problematic."

I jumped out of bed, put on black jeans, a black sweatshirt, my black leather jacket, and my black boots. Granne O'Malley goes to war at night.

Well, you have to look the part, don't you?

I grabbed a sheet of computer paper and a Magic Marker.

Dermot Michael. Jack injured. Off to St. Joseph's. Call me on my cell.
The woman you slept with last night.

Maeve followed me downstairs.

"You coming with me, girl? Okay, but you have to act right, understand?"

I jumped into me Lincoln Navigator, the hound right behind me. The thing about me car is that in a crisis situation it provides a certain gravity.

I know St. Joseph's better than I'd like to. For four months we were there night and day, taking care of our little neonate, whose survival will always seem to me to be a miracle. "You sang her into life," the resident told me. Socra Marie and I still go over there a couple of times a year "to sing for the babies" as she says.

Now she even sings on key sometimes.

I pulled up to the emergency room driveway—cop cars, Reliable cars, ambulance, Blackie's cute little Smart Car, thank God no TV vans. I jumped out of my SUV—the license which announced "Nuala"—and walked in the door, my hound tagging along with me. Two young Latino attendants and a pretty African-American nurse waited at the door.

"The archbishop said you should go right in, Nuala. . . . And who is this lovely lady?"

"This is Maeve."

Mavie politely offered her hand.

"Maeve, you stay here with this nice woman. If we need help, we'll yell."

"Archbishop Ryan said that you would come in a big red SUV with a big white dog, he didn't say how pretty you are, darlin'."

The hounds love adoration and when the two attendants Juan and Rodrigo cautiously joined the group, she was ready to settle in for the night.

The corridor outside the emergency room was crowded with people—Mike Casey, John Culhane, the commander of Area Six detectives, two detectives, both women, two cops, both men, several people in hospital gowns looking serious and a screaming Evie Cuneen and her befuddled husband Tony. Neither Blackie nor Maria were present.

Naturally I walked up to the two senior police officials. In me old country I'd avoid the Guards like they were Brits and we were still under occupation.

"Mike, how is he?"

"Nuala! I didn't hear you come in! He's still unconscious, likely concussion and possible internal injuries. They are a little worried about the concussion."

I don't like hospitals at all at all. I spent too much time in this one with my darling little tiny terrorist. At night they are especially gloomy. St. Joseph's, being a Catholic hospital, was so clean that you could eat off the floor. Still these were places where life and death met under bright lights with the whole world dark outside and the smell of antiseptic dense in the air. Purgatory must be something like this—purgatory where you know for sure that things would somehow improve.

"Two thugs managed to sneak into his building and trapped him between the elevator and the door to his apartment," John Culhane said. "Gangbangers probably. It's not clear that they wanted to kill him. Amateurs, probably, though as the superintendent points out, getting into that building would have been very difficult."

Mike Casey hadn't been superintendent of police for a long time, but it's like a governor or an ambassador here in Yank land—the title is lifelong.

"His wife heard the ruckus outside, grabbed a five iron, rushed out into the corridor, and assaulted the perpetrators. They fled for their lives. She may well have saved her husband from far worse injuries. They were unsheathing knives when Maria entered the fray. Jack was covered with blood when they brought him in here, only it wasn't his blood."

"*Mulier fortis*," I remarked.

"We picked up a couple of individuals on Clark Street, one of them bleeding," Commander Culhane said. "They may be the perps. Both high on crack."

"Amateurs of a sort," Mike Casey added. "Someone else must have provided them with the means of access to the building."

"Is that hysterical woman his daughter?" Culhane asked. "She's making reckless charges against Ms. Donlan. And her kid is wailing. No one needs that here. . . ."

"It will be a pleasure to shut her up," I said.

I strode over to Evie and shook her.

"Shut up, you crazy little bitch. You almost ruined your husband's career the other day on the telly. Your poor dad bailed him out. If you don't calm down, he'll be chasing ambulances for the rest of your life."

She glared at me, hate darting from her eyes.

"That isn't true, is it, Tony?"

"Yes, it is, Evie. They told me this afternoon I'd have another year of probation. If I appeared in public with you again, I'd have fifteen minutes to leave the offices."

His face was dark with despair. His little son continued to wail.

"Why didn't you tell me?" she asked, her body caving in on itself as though she had been hit in the stomach.

"I've been trying to tell you all afternoon. I couldn't get by your hatred for your father's wife."

She leaned against the wall of the hospital corridor and slowly slipped to the floor. She curled up in a knot and began to wail. The child, in his father's arms, joined in. The little guy could have been cute under other circumstances, a clone of his grandfather.

"Get them both out of here, Tony, before she does any more harm."

Holding the child in one arm, he lifted his wife with the other.

"Thanks," he said to me as he struggled to bring his pathetic little family to the lounge at the end of the hall. The next stop, I feared, would be the divorce court.

Okay, I was a bitch on wheels, but it worked. I had cracked open her cocoon of hatred, perhaps for only a few minutes.

The door to the emergency room opened and a young woman, blond with gentle eyes and a kind smile, came out—along with the archbishop. Blackie was wearing his usual uniform—black jeans, a black turtleneck shirt, and a Chicago Bears Windbreaker. Since they made him an archbishop, he remembers more often his silver St. Brigid's pectoral cross and his New Grange silver Episcopal ring, both made by his favorite cousin Catherine Collins who does gorgeous sunbursts.

The young woman, who looked like she was sixteen, was wearing the standard green hospital clothes. A student nurse, a nurse's aide?

"Doctor Reynolds," Blackie announced, "will discuss Mr. Donlan's condition, which thanks be to God and the Blessed Mother, may not be as serious as was first thought."

The child was an MD?

"Mr. Donlan was a victim of a savage attack. He suffered a brain concusssion of moderate severity and lost consciousness for a period of time. However, he is regaining consciousness now and brain scans show no serious malfunction in his brain. He was able to recite not only the names of his own family, but of Ms. Donlan's family. There was no evidence of internal injuries in our CAT scan, but there is a chance that some may show up in the next couple of days. There may also be some bruised ribs. The assailants apparently did not know how to inflict anything more than cosmetic injuries which can readily be repaired. Mr. Donlan is a very fortunate man. I would ask the police to give five or six hours for further recovery before they attempt to interview him. I trust that his personal security protection will remain here with us. It may also be several days before he should attempt to return to work. He will awake tomorrow with aches and pain in most parts of his body. Thank you."

The crowd began to disperse.

Blackie motioned me toward the emergency room.

"We're waiting for you and your daughter to visit us again. Whenever she comes to neonatal, I go upstairs to listen."

"Thank you . . . Maybe we can sneak over in the next few days to try some of our Christmas lullabies."

Good practice for the kids from Josephat.

"Just a minute, Nuala Anne." Mike Casey, looking for all the world like Basil Rathbone playing Sherlock Holmes in the films me ma loved, though she had only seen a few of them. Holmes the savior, Holmes the powerful, Holmes the total Brit.

"I did wander over to the Union League Club with my good wife, Annie Reilly. To escape from purgatory I did listen to Sterling Stafford and did not become ill. It was, however, the same old stuff—Ronald Reagan won the cold war because he had courage. If we can be courageous we will bounce back in the next election, old-fashioned American values, no substitute for victory, keep faith with the troops, no substitute for victory, international terrorist conspiracy, if troops come home too early, terrorists will come right after them, prosperity depends on cutting taxes, Democrats are traitors etc. etc. etc."

"He's running then?"

"Oh yes he's running, said Senator Obama is a foreigner, should not be permitted to run."

"Any chance?"

"Not that I could see. He's too long in the tooth and too confused. His wife is pushing him hard. She was sitting there beaming. Democrats stole the election. We'll be back."

"Suspect?" Mike asked.

"Our client hit him with a video camera! Threw it at him!"

"He has a lot of grudges. We'll take a closer look. . . . Maybe send Dermot over to talk to him . . . Interesting politics out there in Kishwaukee County."

"I've been thinking of that. Press credentials?"

"Didn't I tell you he had signed on as a stringer at the *Herald*? Just in case you don't want to sing anymore?"

Inside the emergency room, his face black and blue, with streaks of red, a couple of teeth missing, a bandage on his head, and his chest taped, John Patrick Donlan still managed to look chic, with just a touch of a smile on his swollen lips.

"Hi, Johnny Pat," I said.

"Hi!"

"Who is she?" Maria Angelica in blue slacks and a dark blue and green sweatshirt, demanded.

Maria had endured a horrid experience. She was also very tired. Yet her verve was undiminished and her beauty as radiant as ever.

"Isn't she the McGrail woman," Jack whispered, "and herself a bit of a witch."

"Where did the Dow finish?" I asked.

"Around 12,000, near a record."

"See, Jackie," his wife said, "nothing wrong with your brain."

"He's just resting a little," the Latino nurse said with a smile, glancing at the brain scan on its monitor. "Which you should do, Mr. Donlan."

"I'm afraid that if I go to sleep again, I won't wake up."

"The effects of the concussion are wearing off, sir. You'll wake up all right."

"I know I've asked you this before, but have I had a stroke?"

"Didn't Archbishop Ryan tell you that you had not?"

"And," I added, "would himself not tell you the truth, and a holy bishop he is?"

"My dad used to say, trust everyone but always cut the cards!"

"Where's . . . Dermot?"

"Isn't he back at house with the kids and all of them such sound sleepers, they didn't hear the phone.

"The dogs heard and didn't Maeve ride over here with me?"

"You left the poor dog outside?" Maria protested.

"The poor dog is in the lobby charming everyone in sight."

"We're going to move him upstairs in the morning," Maria said, "perhaps into intensive care. He'll have aches and pains all over, but it seems that he has a high tolerance for pain. . . . He'll need some dental work. . . ."

"If this isn't heaven, I'd love to walk down LaSalle Street with a cane . . . create a sensation."

"So long as I'm on your arm, it's all right."

He shut his eyes as if about to sleep.

"Steal the show."

Someone knocked gently on the door.

I opened it—a nurse's aide who belonged in grammar school.

"Are you Mrs. McGrail?"

"That's me ma. I'm Nuala Anne."

"I've seen you on television," she said shyly. "Is that gorgeous white dog yours?"

"She's not making a nuisance of herself?"

"We should add her to the staff. . . . You remember that obnoxious woman you threw out of the corridor? Well she and her kid were back there wailing and the dog . . ."

"Maeve walked over to play with them?"

"It was incredible! In just a few minutes they were both laughing and smiling and the woman was hugging her husband. . . ."

"And me hound was strutting around like she owned the hospital?"

"She's so lovely. . . . Anyway the young woman asked if she could visit her father. She promised she'd be good."

I glanced at Maria Angelica.

"Evie?"

"Herself."

"Why not?" She lifted her arms in a magnificent Italian gesture of fatalism.

"Daddy! Daddy! Daddy!" Evie screamed and fell on her knees next to the bed. "I'm sorry, I'm sorry!" She grabbed his limp hand. "I am a spoiled brat, an ungrateful bitch. Tony says I've become my own hate and he's right! I'll regret as long as I live what I've done. Please, give me one more chance! Please!"

"Limit up!" he murmured with his wisp of a smile.

She looked up at a thunderstruck Maria.

"You too! The little good in me wanted to love you! I beg for one more chance . . ." She struggled to say the word, "Mom!"

Maria of course had the last word.

"I already have two daughters. A few more will just add to talk in the kitchen!"

Evie scampered to her feet and rushed to the door.

"I love you all! Thank you!"

At the door, she touched my arm and won me over finally.

"Great dog! Really great!"

Jack Donlan closed his eyes.

"Would you sing him a lullaby?" Maria asked.

"Won't I sing a couple?"

Actually I sang the whole repertory for the Christmas show. The smile remained on his face. Poor dear man would have a lot of pain in the next couple of days—teeth, face, ribs. He was entitled to a pleasant night's rest.

"Brava," said the young doctor standing behind me at the door. "He's sound asleep now, helped by the medication and the music. He'll be fine tomorrow, except for all the bumps and bruises. His brain looks great. We'll keep our eyes open for internal injuries. Home the day after tomorrow, please God."

"We'll have guards here all the time. If he can't walk twenty yards down a corridor without getting into a fight, we'll have to protect him all the time."

We'd better push ahead with our work. What kind of morons would beat a man as they beat Jack? Someone who hated him a lot.

Me cell phone beeped.

"Nuala," I whispered.

"Meself . . . How is he?"

"Pretty good, nothing too serious. They'll keep him around tomorrow to check for internal injuries. Sleeping peacefully. A lot of things happened."

"I didn't hear the phone."

"Good thing you married a light sleeper."

"Maeve went with you. . . . She's not around here."

"Stole the show. She's snoozing right outside of the emergency room now."

"Fiona is pacing anxiously and your elder daughter is wondering where you are."

"Tell them I'm coming home right away and that they both should go back to bed."

I suggested a decade of the rosary for Jack and led it, of course. Then I kissed poor Maria good-bye. "Call me in the morning.

"Come on, girl," I told Maeve who had managed to break the rules and sneak up to the door of the room where I was, her primary responsibility. "They're waiting for us at home. . . . And quietly!"

She restrained her impulse to bound. Nonetheless when I opened the door of me Navigator, didn't she jump in before me. The night's work was done and it was time to go home.

— **Dermot** —

NUALA ANNE had crashed completely when she returned from St. Joseph's last night.

"He'll be fine in a few days," she said as she shed her boots, jeans, and sweatshirt and tossed them in a disorderly heap on top of her black leather jacket, behavior utterly untypical of my fanatically neat wife.

"Maria and Evie made peace," she said as she snuggled beside me in her underwear. "And the puppy stole the show, as she always does."

Then she was in whatever precinct of the land of Nod to which fey mystics go when they crash out. I folded her into my arms, a place she likes to be when she returns from East of Eden. Or in her case perhaps West of Eden.

About eight o'clock I went downstairs to make her breakfast. Ellie was feeding the kids who were in a wild mood, though they were not quite at the food-throwing stage.

"Ma came home late from the hospital last night," Nelliecoyne informed me. "She was there alone."

"Except for Maeve."

"Maeve went to the hospital with her?" the Mick said. "Totally cool."

"Maeve should be chaplain at the hospital," I said.

"Maeve stays here," Socra Marie insisted as she slowly consumed her dish of fruit.

"And you, young woman, finish every bit of that delicious fruit."

"Yes, Da!" she said with a loud sigh.

There were logistic problems. Ellie had a class at ten thirty. Danuta's hours were irregular. Ellie would take the kids across the street to school, but someone had to take care of poor Patjo—who looked anything but poor as he devoured all the food in sight.

"Patrick Joseph," I commanded, "don't you dare eat Socra Marie's breakfast."

"Yes, Da."

"Your ma might come downstairs and catch you."

"Yes, Da."

"You can leave right after you dump the kids, Ellie. I'll cover for the punk."

I then brought herself's breakfast upstairs—tea (so strong you could walk on it), orange juice (a full-to-the-top glass), oatmeal (steaming hot), and three slices of toast with the crusts cut off.

I gave the crusts to Patjo who made them disappear instantly.

My wife was sitting, freshly showered and smelling of soap, at the breakfast table in the master bedroom, chin in hands and staring glumly at the gray autumn.

"Lake effect flurries," she said. . . . "Sure, Dermot Michael, aren't you a paragon of a spouse! . . . The oatmeal is hot, is it?"

"Woman, would you look at the steam coming off it?"

She touched the mess with her index finger and withdrew it quickly.

"'Tis hot!"

She then gave me a play by play account of the dramas at the hospital. Maeve appeared, stretched contentedly, and lay down for a morning snooze at my feet."

"Good dog, Maeve," I said.

The hound sniffed in contentment.

"And yourself now having two women in your cult group?"

"Och, Dermot, won't she be on the phone this morning? And meself with a Christmas show to prepare. And I have no choice about her, do I?"

"You don't! You open your big mouth and you have another dependent. . . ."

"So does poor Maria Angelica, a battered husband, and a newborn child . . . Dermot, what would you be doing on this terrible day?"

"I was planning on fantasizing about my adventure last night."

She flushed.

"Heathen."

"Well, ravishing an Irish goddess is an event to remember, isn't it now?"

"An experience you've never had be-fore . . . Aren't you going to pour me tea?"

"Yes ma'am."

"Why don't you ride down to the office of

Donlan Assets Management and see what this fella Joey McMahon is like? Didn't he start this whole friggin' mess? Besides, you can read all them silly reports on the computer and tell how DAM is really doing?"

"Yes ma'am . . . Do you think it possible that your new friend Evie might be faking her personality transformation?"

"I do not. I was there, Dermot Michael. It was all quite transparent and moving. . . . 'Course we'll have to see what happens."

"And what about former Congressman Stafford?"

"I don't like the man, Dermot love, and I wonder if it is a coincidence that poor Jackie was attacked the same night he was giving a lecture. . . . Yet from what Mr. Casey reports, he's a loser."

"Losers can be dangerous!"

"Well that's for tomorrow. Joey McMahon for today . . . Och, the friggin' phone."

Someone from CTN about today's practice. Me wife turned on her charm.

I picked up the breakfast tray.

She put her hand on the phone and kissed me, revealing a notable amount of décolletage, enough to sustain me through the day.

"You're a grand lover, sir, and a desperate husband altogether."

What more could you ask, idiot?

Energy, stamina, hormones.

Give over, you're getting a lot more of her than you deserve.

'Tis true.

— Dermot —

THE OFFICES of DAM were peaceful the morning after my ride through the North Side. Joe McMahon was presiding with a sure touch in Jack's office. He confidently assured all callers that "the boss" is fine. Highly strong guy. "He'll probably be home tomorrow. You know the Irish! We all have hard heads! We got a computer over to St. Joseph's so he can watch the indexes. Both Frodo and Samwise slipped a little in early trading, but they're doing fine now. No, this stuff isn't doing any good, but not much harm either. Yeah, I'll tell him you called."

Despite his smooth responses to the phone calls Joseph Xavier McMahon seemed woefully out of place at John Donlan's desk. A short, round man in an off-the-rack grey suit with patches of hair around a bald head, a constant frown and darting eyes, he did not look like the market wizard he was alleged to be.

"The last time this happened was when the old fella died. He had stepped back from the business and Jackie was running it with the same intelligence as the old fella and a lot more flair. He was out in California at the place where his wife went to dry out. I'm here by myself and I don't even know whether I have a job and people are calling me from all over the country. Jackie flew back of course and commuted to Los Angeles on weekends. Tough times for all of us, but things settled down and his poor wife came home all bright and shiny. I asked him whether I still had a job the first day he was back. 'Of course you do, Joey,' he says to me with a puzzled look. 'As long as you want and with a lot more money than you're getting.' That's the kind of man Jackie is."

"You've been here how long?"

"Fifty-five years come next June. I came

when I was eighteen and I'll be seventy-three next month. Old enough to retire. No reason to do that. My sainted wife is dead, my two fine sons are highly successful doctors at opposite ends of the country. I'll die in the harness."

"And you started out as an office boy and a clerk?"

"Yeah and the old man was a tough guy to work for. Demanding, ridiculed your mistakes, but a great teacher . . . I loved the old bastard."

"And when did you start making investment recommendations?"

"First year I was here. The old man made fun of me. But he wrote them down in a notebook. I kept on making them, he kept on ridiculing them, but he also followed my advice sometimes. When I was twenty-three, twenty-four, he said to me one day out of the blue, 'I've followed some of your hunches, Mac, as you've probably noticed. We made a lot of money on them. So I'm promoting you to the title of investment adviser. Your job is to find good investments. I'll pay you a hundred dollars more a week.' He was a hard man with the buck, but that's what comes of growing up during the Depression. 'Course I got raises later on, and especially when Jackie came on board. But I've been contributing highly to the success of this firm for a hell of a long time. I tell myself that they couldn't have done it without me!"

"Could you have done it without them?"

"All I needed was a college education and a little bit of class. But I went to work here straight from DeLaSalle High School, because we couldn't afford college. In our neighborhood you didn't acquire 'class,' not unless you went to college and for a lot of us even if you did go to college. That's why I sent my own kids to Yale and Princeton. That's why I'm happy they didn't marry a girl from the neighborhood or move back into it. The neighborhood girls they were dating were good kids, but not the right kind. I had to be candid with my guys about where that would end. They didn't like what I said at first, but they followed my advice. I'm sorry that I don't see them more often, but they probably had to break away from me too. I have no regrets. . . ."

His words were spoken brightly but his face was sad. We were no further removed from the immigration experience than he was, but River Forest is in another world, compared to 42nd and Wentworth. And an MD father was different from a streetcar motorman.

We were both silent for a moment.

Then Joey McMahon hastened to clarify his vision of his own impact on the firm.

"But, hey, I don't want to minimize the importance of the old man and Jackie in this firm. It's one thing to come up with the bright ideas and it's another to take full responsibility for them. I don't have to do that. . . . Every one of my bright ideas has to pass two scrutinies, mine and the boss's. If it's still a bomb the boss has ultimately to blame himself. Sometimes I'm wrong, sometimes the boss is wrong."

"No one keeps score?"

"The old fella did. Kept a chart in his office. Jackie doesn't do that, but with that memory of his he knows. They have made a lot more money by following my leads than they've lost. We all know that. I don't have my reputation as a wizard for nothing."

"What's your technique?"

"You worked on the CBOT for a time, didn't you? How did you do? Make a lot of money?"

"A ton of money, mostly by mistake. I quit

when I was ahead. Turned it over to investors I trust more than I trusted myself, including this firm."

"You were just lucky? What about the longtime players?"

"They all had theories, but it came down to instincts. I didn't and don't trust mine."

I was not cut out to be a gambler. Only one big gamble in my life and I made it that night in O'Neil's pub on College Green. I was a winner that night.

That's what you say.

That's what I know.

"Yeah, that's it all right. Instincts. I read everything I can get my hands on, pursue hunches. Poke around. Mine are still good, real good . . . I weigh the pros and cons, let them percolate around in my head and then make a recommendation—strong, not so strong, and maybe. Mostly the boss buys only the strong ones. Only once did he go for a 'maybe.' Biggest risk he's ever taken. Spam catcher on the net. Good deal so far."

"What's the history of the Oakdale company?"

"A lawyer from out there comes in to see me. Highly reputable man—Langford Greenwald. Sounds crazy to me. Yet I do due diligence and it seems to be one of those new projects that might just catch on. It has three negatives—Oakdale, real estate, and a woman CEO. Don't get me wrong, I'm no chauvinist, but you still raise your eyebrows. I poke around a lot and I bring it to the boss. His reaction is the same as mine—dubious, but let's check it out. Finally it depends on both our instincts. His are more in favor of innovation than mine. Just the opposite with the old fella. He didn't like new things, which is why we weren't hurt by the dot-com bubble as much as other guys."

"The woman was a problem?"

He hesitated.

"Not really. She's a real dish of course, but she's also highly smart and honest and works hard. Better bet than a lot of men with bright new ideas. Like a dummy I didn't think he'd fall in love with her. It would have been a good deal if he had cooled it. Now, well, you see what's happening."

"And what is happening . . . ?"

"Controversy. In our business controversy is death. If this keeps up, the boss will have to step down. Maybe even sell the business at a huge loss. A big price to pay for a bit of fluff."

"Do you mean he should have considered the bad publicity beforehand?"

"He should have considered the possibility. If he told me he would get the hots for her, I would have said, forget the deal. Highly risky. He should have figured it out himself or wait till the publicity over the deal died down."

"You told him that?"

"It wasn't my place."

"I see your point. . . . But surely you must have been aware of the danger. . . . Jackie is still a young man. His first marriage was very difficult. He is lonely and unhappy. If a smart and beautiful woman should come his way . . ."

"Maybe I should have seen it coming. I had too much respect for him to think he'd go down that path."

"I see . . ."

His ordinary dour face changed to a look of grief.

"I've learned that marriage is a sacrament, no matter how tough it might be. If you lose your spouse, the sacrament is still there and you should respect it. I loved my wife and always will, even if sex didn't mean much to us after all those years together. A

lot of women tried to land me after she died.
I didn't give them the time of day. They
wanted my money anyway. I had to be faithful to Barbara. After a while it wasn't hard.
Lot less complications. I was wrong to think
that the boss would operate the same
way. . . . He should go to Mass every morning like I do. That's a big help."

His eyes filled with tears, a loyal follower
deeply disappointed by his hero.

"Uh-huh."

"There are a lot of things more important
in life than sex, like loyalty to your family and
your colleagues and your friends. I was
really disappointed in the boss at that wedding, none of his kids there and then the
cancellation. I suppose Cronin didn't have
much choice about doing the wedding Mass
himself the next day. There's clout everywhere, even for a highly respected cardinal.
Then this business last night . . . I don't
know, I simply don't know. . . ."

"You believe the firm is in serious trouble?"

"A half a step away from it . . . You're a
serious investor, you take one look at pictures of that woman and you know something fishy is going on. . . . You figure pretty

soon she'll be running the firm. It's like Hillary Clinton . . . One more scandal and you'll hear the pitter patter of rodent's feet scurrying off the ship. . . . The boss has chosen pussy over loyalty."

Outside, in the Daley Plaza I phoned home.

"Nuala Anne."

"ET calling home."

"So?"

"He's one very creepy character. His last words, just before I fled, were, 'The boss has chosen pussy over loyalty.'"

"I suppose a lot of men will think that way. If only Maria were ugly, then women wouldn't envy her and men wouldn't demean her."

"I take your point. . . . What's happening in your life?"

"Phone calls . . . Panic from the CTN people . . . They need to panic to do their jobs. I don't."

"Ah, soul transplant!"

"Friggin' gobshite!"

"If there is enough order in the house in this new modality, I thought I might drive out to Forty-second and Parnell, find a pub, and have a bite of lunch."

"Go on, letcher, Danuta is here and Ellie

will be back from school after lunch. The punk already wants his afternoon nap, lazy loafer. I'll drive over to the soundstage for a run through. The moms will bring the kids down after school and we'll do it again."

"I'll be back in midafternoon in time for my nap."

"Isn't it meself that needs the nap?"

"The ashram on the phone this morning?"

"I've always been a little sister, Dermot love, I don't quite fit in this big sister role."

"You'll play it well though."

"I love you, Dermot Michael Coyne."

"Not as much as I love you."

"Gobshite!"

My sexy Irish Tiger was tired. She needed a vacation. In a warm place. And winter coming to Chicago. The idiot Brit poet who said that if winter comes, can spring be far behind didn't have to live in Chicago.

In fact the Christmas show would be a splendid success. The producers from CTN would quickly discover two things: the Chicago freelancers my wife used as technicians and musicians and singers were pros and Nuala Anne was the boss, especially if she wore her boots and her black leather jacket.

Still she had to worry about it in line with the ineluctable Irish conviction that if you didn't worry yourself into sleepless nights about things going wrong, they surely would. God might be good and generous and eager to smile on your parades, but the fates were something else again.

— Nuala Anne —

HARDLY HAD my beloved spear-carrier ridden off in his chariot to do battle with this Joey McMahon person, when his private line rang.

"This is Dermot Coyne's private wife. Mr. Coyne is away. You can probably leave a message with me. I usually remember them."

I had a headache, needed a couple hours more of sleep, and was in a generally foul mood.

"Hey, Nuala, it's Dominic."

"Hey, Dom, what's happening?"

I did a little acting when I was at Trinity

College Dublin—me Dermot said I'm acting all the time, which is probably true. I love to play the moll with Dom.

"Certain individuals I know want to pass on a message to Dermot about what went down last night."

"Yeah, we were expecting a call. We were upset, as I'm sure your individuals understand."

"Yeah, they want me to tell Dermot that they deplore the incident. Also the cops got the right perps."

"One feels safer when one knows the cops did a good job."

"Uh, yeah, and they say that the punks were freelancers. . . ."

"Gangbangers on crack."

"Right. They want Dermot and his friends to know they are trying to find out who the real perps are. Punks from out of town probably. Clumsy like the gangbangers."

"Clumsy punks can do a lot of harm, Dom."

"The individuals I'm in contact with know that . . . they were impressed with what Mrs. Donlan did to the punks. She's a brave woman."

"Tuscan, Sienna."

Why did I say a thing like that? Maybe me Dermot is right, I am a shite kicker.

"Brave and beautiful people . . . Well, I have to get back to work. . . . Looking forward to the Christmas concert . . ."

"Don't we have a Neapolitan lullaby this year?"

"Hey, that's great! My kids will love it."

What was the point in that conversation? I thought as I hung up. I'd pass it on to Dermot, who could probably interpret it better than I could. I was sure that Dom and his family were likable people, good neighbors, fine Catholics. But there was an aura about them of the IRA Provos at their worst. Then the phone rang again.

It was the third call as I tried to make a list of the "must-do" matters for the session at the soundstage. The most important challenge was to shut up the CTN producers who would want to mess around. The technicians and the musicians were all right, but the new folks in town from Hollywood would surely want to throw their muscle around, especially about the filming of Christmas lights at the Daley Center.

The first call was from a timid Evie.

"Mrs. McGrail . . ." she said tentatively.

"Ms. McGrail is me mother and isn't she off in Ireland enjoying the benefits of the Irish Tiger? And Ms. Coyne is me mother-in-law and herself a wonderful and sweet woman putting up with a screaming fishwife like meself . . . I'm Nuala Anne."

She gulped.

"I want to thank you for last night. . . ."

"Och, didn't me hound Maevie do all the work and herself all curled right next to me in me study?"

The good dog Maeve perked up at the sound of her name and shifted closer to me for some petting.

"You saved my marriage and maybe my life. I will always remember that. . . ."

"You saved it yourself, child."

"That's what Mary Fran says. But you and Tony and the dog woke me up. . . . Mary Fran says that I should see a shrink. She says I have a lot of hate for my mother who left us when I needed her the most and I've got to work that out of my system. So I have already called the woman she's recommended."

"'Tis good, but don't let the woman violate your common sense."

"I won't. . . . I probably need a spiritual director too. . . ."

Brigid, Patrick, and Colmcille! It was like I had hung out a shingle.

"Wouldn't that be a good idea?"

"I, uh, wonder if I might come over and see you sometime . . ."

I didn't need any more kids. I already had four.

"Wouldn't I be willing to share a drop of tea with you. . . . Though we'd better ask Maeve to join us?"

"Wonderful! There's no rush! I know you have a TV program . . ."

"Sure that's no problem at all, at all. . . ."

Liar.

Fiona ambled in and curled up next to her daughter. Often when me husband isn't around they both set up camp in my study, in case I need help or protection.

"How's your da keeping?"

"He's sore all over and wants to get back to work. Mom won't let him even think about going home till tomorrow. . . . She's such a fine woman. . . . I can't believe I hated her so much. . . ."

"Well, child, overnight you have a ma, a shrink, and a loudmouth spiritual director. . . . All ready for a new life!"

"A second chance . . ."

"Don't wait for a third one!"

"I won't, believe me, Nuala Anne, I won't."

Good on you!

The two hounds were sniffing uneasily. I reached into the drawer of my desk where I hide a box of their treats. As soon as I touched the door they were on their feet, mouths open, eyes begging. I removed four treats.

"Oldest first!"

I offered one to Fiona who took it from my hand with great delicacy and then inhaled it altogether. Maeve had not yet learned such delicacy.

"Gentle, gentle," I warned her.

Poor thing, she tried hard. But still a puppy.

I repeated the process and they both reclined again on the floor, content up to a point; well aware that I never went beyond two treats.

They were big dogs, I assured myself. I wasn't spoiling them, was I?

The phone rang again. This time Maria Angelica.

"How's your old man keeping?" I asked.

"He's edgy and uncomfortable and wants to go back to work. . . . His daughter, well, our daughter, came to visit this morning. She is a very sweet child, terribly conflicted now, but I think she'll be all right, thanks to you and that doggie of yours. . . . Remember, I have an option on her first puppy."

" 'Tis only fair," I agreed. "Mind you they are terrible nuisances altogether. Shed a lot of hair, smell terrible, make demands, eat a lot . . ."

"As bad as human children!"

"Ah, no, not that bad, at all, at all!"

"Still they become part of the family, don't they?"

"Me Dermot says that's how they domesticated us. They ensconced themselves in our families and were so cute we couldn't get rid of them. 'Tis the way of things. . . . You'll keep your fella there for another day?"

"Or two! The doctors are still cautious and he's not in any condition to go back to the office. . . . Oh, that Eyes and Ears person called and asked if it was true that there had been a reconciliation. I told them that I would not deny it."

"Good on you!"

"Well, I'm going to ride over to my office and make sure the firm still exists."

I opened my notebook, waited for the

phone to ring again, and started working on a "must-do" list.

I was uneasy, anxious. So were the hounds who were now stirring restlessly. I knew that something bad was going down. . . . What?

Nuala Anne, you frigging eejit!

I grabbed me black leather jacket and me camogie stick.

"Come on, girls, we have work to do!"

The hounds bounded up, ready for action.

We thundered down the stairs.

"Is yourself here?" I shouted at Ellie.

"I am, Aunt Nuala!"

"You're in charge. The doggies and I have to prevent a murder!"

We rushed down the stairs and jumped into me Navigator.

— **Dermot** —

IN MY venerable Benz, I exchanged my blazer and tie for my own black leather jacket, unlike Nuala's BLJ, even more venerable than the Benz. It was the perfect uniform for a pilgrimage to Back O' the Yards, which is south of the Yards as opposed to the "Royal Borough" of Bridgeport which is east of the Yards, an essential distinction, if not to all Chicagoans, and least to those who live in the eleventh and twelfth Wards.

The bar I chose—Mike's in bold green and gold letters—was an old storefront just down the street from Joey McMahon's residence. It was filled with a well-mannered, if boistrous, lunchtime crowd. It was a modern layout, if by modern you mean what was modern when aluminum and red plush were in fashion. There was even an elaborate jukebox in one corner, though it did not appear to be operational. The place was spotlessly clean which suggested to me Polish rather than Irish ownership. The only smell was disinfectant. It would have suggested a waiting room in an older hospital if the conversations were subdued. However, the talk was often loud as was the good-natured laughter. The clientele knew one another and enjoyed the constant bantering in which friends engage. The room was decorated with pictures and banners from the Chicago White Sox. Just behind the bar was a very old picture of a football team.

I walked up to the bar and gestured at the one empty place. The bartender, a red-haired, freckle-faced mick about my age but eight inches shorter with a constant smile and shrewd green eyes, said, "Why not?"

"You really have the best hamburgers on the South Side, like the sign says?"

"Wouldn't say it, if it weren't true, would he?" one of the fellows at the bar said. He was a giant of Eastern European origins with whom one would not want to argue, unless one happened to be an ex-linebacker.

"Is he Irish?" I asked.

Everyone at the bar laughed.

"Takes one to know one," my Slavic friend agreed.

I don't look like a linebacker, exactly. I quit my high school team because I didn't approve of the ethics of the coach and won a wrestling championship, which confers much less prestige. At the Golden Dome I was a walk-on because they thought I looked like a linebacker and were willing to take a chance. I walked off after the second practice. "Not vicious enough," I said to the linebacker coach. I settled in, determined to learn a lot, which I did, but not in the subjects that I was supposed to study. So I flunked out after my sophomore year to the tune of many complaints from Holy Cross Fathers that I was wasting all my talents. I did bring a lot of trophies home from intramural sports and became something of a legend because of my refusal to volunteer for any varsity teams. I then went to Marquette to study theology for the next two years and learned a lot, but did not pile up enough credits to graduate. So I appeared at the Chicago Mercantile Exchange where I lost a lot of money and then made it all back and much more on a single trade. Whereupon I retired and went on a grand tour of Europe, ending in Ireland. In O'Neil's pub on College Green, one rainy, misty night I met this gorgeous young woman and that was that, save for the novel and the books of poetry I wrote. I also became Watson to her Sherlock, Captain Hastings to her Hercule, Flambeau to her Father Brown. My wife beats me in golf, we are evenly matched in tennis, and I can beat any punk in the neighborhood in basketball.

Nonetheless, I could take the big guy that might be looking for a fight and, after a quick glance, anyone else in the room.

"I hear you don't make them medium rare on the South Side."

"Not for South Siders, but for aliens, I can try. No cheese on it. No junk, just a bun with a little bit of butter. Large, medium, or small?"

I feigned astonishment.

"Large, naturally!"

More laughter.

"Nineteen Fourty-Seven Chicago Cardinals—Trippi, Harder, Angsman, Chrisman. Only one championship, but still the greatest."

"You're not that old," said a gentleman on the other side of me, with an Italianate wave of his hand.

"Despite their present lamentable condition in the desert," I continued, "they are the oldest professional football team in America—called among other names in their South Side existence, the Morgans after Morgan Street, the Racines, after Racine Avenue, the Normals after the stadium at Chicago Normal where they played, the Cardinals after the faded University of Chicago maroon jerseys they bought, briefly the South Side Cardinals before they became the Chicago Cardinals, but that after they joined the nascent National Football League with the Green Bay Packers and the Decanter Staleys who, as we also know transmuted themselves into the Chicago Bears. While they were the South Side Cardinals they won a place in one of Jimmy Farrell's Lonigan novels."

"You play football?"

"For a couple of years in high school!"

"Where did you learn all this stuff?"

"I didn't learn much in the colleges I went to, but I did learn to read."

I also learned somewhere along the line to call up Wikepedia from my wi-fi utility in any local Starbucks and read about the Cardinals when I was venturing into an old South Side neighborhood.

"The mayor"—pronounced *mare* of course—"promised us he'd bring them back. Hasn't done it yet."

"The Mare or Mare Rich?"

"Both of them."

"I'm sure they tried."

"It all went down when Old Man Bidwell died," the retired cop said, "and those creepy sons of his got involved."

"And doesn't me wife, who is fey, predict that they won't be winners again till they come back where they belong."

"What do you?" the Slavic gentleman demanded.

"Financial services racket . . . We've got four kids and we need a new home. I'm out here looking for a home. She wants to live in a real neighborhood."

That was the only time in the conversation that I had wandered to the far edge of truth.

Herself wanted a neighborhood all right. But she had one. I did look at the homes in Back O' the Yards because the time might come when we'd have to expand our own home and I was interested in how they did it out here. Odd constructions, but functional.

The men around me joined in boosterism.

"This is a great place to live, clean, stable, peaceful."

"Integrated too . . . Look around this bar. Everyone lives here, whites, Blacks, Latinos, Russians, Armenians, Muslims . . . No sweat."

"Good schools, great parishes, near the loop on the Orange Line . . ."

"DeLaSalle, Ignatius, UIC . . . the river . . . Lots of clout with city hall."

"Everyone keeps up their places, great Christmas decorations."

"I was over looking at Bubbly Creek, pretty place. . . . Till you think about what's at the bottom of it. And while I was there, it kind of bumbled. Kind of scary!"

"Did you smell it?"

"I don't think so. I took a good deep whiff. Nothing much."

"Nothing like when the Yards were still working."

Silence, as if in memory of the Yards and all it had meant to this area before it had become a dormitory suburb inside the city, despite its legendary stench.

"We got a guy who hangs around here a lot," the bartender said, "who's in financial services and claims to be a big success. . . . Joey McMahon . . . Know him?"

Aha, it finally came up and it had taken a long time.

"Hell, yes. He's a genius. Works for Jack Donlan. Lots of people say he is the genius behind the firm."

"Well, he certainly thinks so," the retired cop observed. "I'm not sure he's all that smart. He shouldn't be coming in here all the time and talking about how dumb his boss is."

Bingo!

"That sort of thing," I said piously, "is never a good idea."

"He thinks this marriage problem the boss has will force him to sell out and Joey will be right there with his ton of money."

Bingo again.

"Those things happen," I continued in my pious mode. "Never good to talk about it."

"Joey has been waiting so long that he

can just taste it," said the bartender. . . .
"Hey you want another hamburger?"

"Don't ask . . . Best one I've ever had on
the South Side."

**Now that is a lie! You were so busy
tricking these guys that you didn't even
taste it.**

Go along with ya.

**You don't fool me when you talk like
her.**

"I figured you'd like it, the way you ate it."

He promptly set about making another.

**You blew that. You should have praised
him earlier.**

**I wouldn't make mistakes like that if
you'd shut up.**

Fortunately Mike the proprietor was still
interested in talking about Joey.

"I don't think Joey is smooth enough to
run a big-time firm like that, is he?"

"Never can tell . . . What's the scandal?"

"This woman he's married. She's supposed to be a little shady. . . . Joey takes
credit for bringing them together. You know
her?"

"Yeah, met her a couple of times. You'd
turn your head when you pass her on the
street. Italian, Sophia Loren type. But, hell,

she's a grandmother and as far as I can see a very nice person."

"Joey," the cop said, "is full of more bullshit than anyone in this neighborhood. My friends over at the precinct say they think there's some kind of plot going down. I tell Joey that he should keep his mouth shut."

"If he's had that much experience in what we do in financial services, he should have learned that long ago or he'll never learn it."

I bid my new friends "see you around" and slipped out.

"Next time you come in, bring your fey wife. Maybe she'll have some predictions about the White Sox next year."

"Yeah, I will. She might just know something."

But she'd never play that kind of game, even if she did. Wouldn't even tell me about the Bears and the Super Bowl.

Nice guys. They'd make good friends. But don't claim you're special or they'll eat you alive. Good neighbors. Too bad they're South Side Irish.

I told them that my name was Mike McDermot—close enough to the truth.

I drove over to the parking lot at Comiskey Park as we call it (not U.S. Cellular Field)

and called Nuala on her personal office
phone. No answer. Maybe she had already
left for the first "walk through" of *Lullaby and
Good Night.* I left a message. I tried her cell
phone too, though she tended to be a bit of a
Luddite about that annoying bit of machinery. No answer. I left a message there too. I
felt a little uneasy. I should have called her
before I went into Mike's bar.

— Nuala Anne —

AS I thundered down Fullerton, I decided it would be a good idea to tip off Mike the cop. My puppies and I might need some help. I pushed his button on my car phone, a machine I normally dislike.

"Mike Casey."

"Meself here. I'm driving toward St. Joseph's Hospital. Something bad is going to happen to Maria Donlan unless me and my doggies stop them. You and Commander Culhane should get some of your people over here to clean up the mess after we're finished."

"Nuala," he shouted, "don't do anything crazy!"

"Give over!" I said. "Meself crazy!"

We'd have all the advantage. The would-be perps would be terrified by the hounds. And meself with me club. I worried a little about Fiona. She was long in the tooth for a fight, but she was in good condition from all her running in the park. I went through the stoplight and turned right onto the Inner Drive. . . . People don't usually want to argue with a Navigator. The dogs knew we were going to have a fight and the memories of ancient battles encoded in their genes began to stir. One of my ancestors must have been a woman warrior, one of those who charged naked into battle with clubs and the dogs. This caper would not require such extreme measures. I hoped me camogie stick wouldn't break the first time I hit one of the perps with it.

A half block away I saw the snatch going down right in front of the main entrance to the hospital. Three thugs in ski masks, all kind of small, were dragging Maria toward a car.

"Hang on, girls," I told the dogs and rammed the car into which they were trying to pull Maria. Another thug came tumbling out of the car. I pulled back from the car and then hit it again, pushing it over the curb and turning it over on its side. I turned off the ignition and opened both doors of me battle cruiser.

"Go get em, doggies!" I ordered. Almost instantly they bounded out of the car and hit two of the guys in the ski masks, knocking them to the ground. The dogs went immediately to their throats and sunk their teeth into the flesh, just enough to terrify them. Screaming what I thought might sound like the battle cry of an enraged Irish warrior woman I charged the two guys who were trying to manhandle Maria. She was clawing, scratching, kicking them, distracting them from me assault and me cry. I swung me camogie stick and banged it against the bigger of the two of them. He released Maria and crumpled to the ground. The other one let her go and reached for a gun in his rear pocket. I hit his male organs with a mighty swipe of the hook of my stick and pulled the gun away from him as he fell to the ground. I conked him on the head just for good measure. I retrieved the gun, some fool German thing, and slid what I hoped was the safety into place.

A crowd of people were assembling at the hospital entrance to watch the fun. I noticed that I had stopped my yelling. So I began again as I turned to the dogs' two prisoners. One of them was trying to free a knife from his belt. I hit his hand with me stick and it went flying to the ground. He reached for it and I stomped on his hand. As he pulled his hand away I scooped up the knife and held it in me right hand, shifting the gun into me left hand which also held me camogie stick

I pointed the gun at the bad guy's head.

"Try something like that again and I'll blow your focking brains out. Both of youse relax real nice and me doggies won't cut out your focking throats unless I tell them to. If you mess around with us, you'll be dead in less than a minute. Me doggies love to . . ."

Almost said "kill." But that would be a signal to the doggies to kill them.

". . . drink human blood."

Tony Soprano, where are you when I really need you?

I realized that I was out of control. Nuala Anne didn't talk that way in public. Nor did she ruin her vocal cords right before a big concert.

Two big uniformed hospital guys were

disarming the first of Maria's assailants who had staggered to his feet. Two other guys were searching the other attacker, taking away his guns and knives and pulling off his ski mask as he struggled to regain consciousness.

A good thing I didn't kill either of them. It wouldn't look good before a Christmas special, would it now?

The growing crowd was cheering, had been cheering for a while. Hey, assholes, this isn't a movie.

"Step back, please, the police are coming."

I was still totally out of control. But I sounded polite, amiable, a sophisticated woman of the world who with her wolfhounds and red Navigator broke up capers and then retired for a martini before supper.

I know meself well enough to know that if I begin to have such fantasies I am really out of control.

Then a cop, not the cops, showed up, a single cop in a single patrol car.

"Ma'am," he said as he waddled toward me, his holster open, his radio in his hand, "I will have to arrest you for disorderly conduct.

Please give me your weapon and release those two individuals."

"If I release them, eejit, they'll go after your throat instead of those perps."

"Ma'am, you're under arrest for disorderly conduct. Now please give me your weapon."

The crowd, now counting nurses, doctors, and other hospital staff types, booed loudly.

Good show, Nuala Anne. You'll never live this down.

"Those frigging perps were trying to kidnap Ms. Connors," I explained.

"We can discuss that all down at the station, ma'am. I'll have to cuff you now."

I lifted my left hand with what I would learn later was a Lugar in it and pointed it at his ear. I know what a safety is on a gun and I had slid it into place.

"Back off!" I shouted. "When this is over I'll sue you for false arrest, dereliction of duty, and attempting to imitate a police officer."

"Ma'am, you're compounding a felony!"

The cheering crowd was chanting. . . . What were they saying?

"Nuala! Nuala! Nuala!"

Me reputation as a sweet and gentle singer of Christmas carols was finished.

Now I was irredeemably an Irish Tiger. Och, won't me Dermot be proud of me!

I hope.

"I said, back off, you friggin' amadon. When Commander Culhane arrives, I'll report you as a disgrace to the police uniform."

I had said the magic words. A tumultuous cheer from the audience.

"The dog is killing me," one of the perps pleaded.

"Only if you misbehave."

Oh, but the doggies, gentle peaceful souls that they are would so have loved to kill them. These stupid humans had dared to attack not one but two of their friends.

Then, thank the good Lord, before I could make even a worse fool of meself, the rest of the Chicago Police Department arrived on both sides of the Inner Drive, sirens screaming in agonized protest—squad cars, detective cars, Reliable cars, command cars, tech trucks, prisoner cars. John Culhane emerged from the first one, gun in hand. Mike Casey was in the second, his gun also in hand.

"Them two." I pointed at the two terrified perps. "Let 'em go, doggies."

Fiona and Maeve complied but stood next to them, growling dangerously. The crowd cheered wildly. The cops cuffed all four of the perps and loaded them into the prison wagon (called but never by me the paddy wagon).

"Doggies, here!" I commanded.

They ambled over to me, looking quite pleased with themselves.

"Sit!" I ordered.

They did, because they were perfectly behaved hounds of heaven. Far from being worn out, Fiona acted like she was the queen of all wolfhounds, immune to the cheers. Just like me.

But then they began to howl. In triumph. Wild cheers from the crowd. So they howled again.

"I thought it was a Christmas special," Mike Casey said. "I didn't know it was an episode of *Law and Order*. With a live audience . . . Do you want to give me the Lugar, Nuala Anne? You might hurt someone with it."

"Sure isn't the safety on it?"

"It's off," he said, flicking the switch.

"Just as well I didn't shoot that cop who was trying to arrest me for disturbing the peace."

The dogs stopped howling. They saw Maria and Jack hugging each other and himself in a wheelchair with robes and blankets.

"Go say 'hello' to them."

They bounded over to their old friends and embraced them both.

More cheers from the crowd.

"Shouldn't youse all go back to work? Isn't there a lot to be done before Christmas?"

Then they swarmed over me, demanding autographs. The hounds shook hands with everyone.

Nuala Anne can do no wrong, I thought. Even when she acts like a focking eejit, out of control altogether. However would I explain it all to me poor husband?

— **Dermot** —

I PULLED up at the soundstage on Racine and West Ontario. There was already a crowd outside. My Irish Tiger was a celebrity. Two cops stopped me at the door. I showed them my ID. That wouldn't do. Only relatives of the cast could come in. I showed them a picture in my wallet of Nelliecoyne. That was enough to get a faintly contemptuous wave from the cops.

Inside they were singing an Arab Christmas carol, a young Arab woman in long dress and veil was crooning to a baby in her arms. Nuala was singing the lullaby softly along with the mother, while the tiny choir—Socra Marie,

Katiesue Murphy, and some of their class were watching the baby and his mother in mute admiration. Then at a signal from herself, they began to hum. In the background a couple of strings joined in.

"Them thar lil polecats a'singin like to call judgment day," Katiesue's ma, Captain Cindasue McLeod of the Yewnited States Coast Guard, whispered to me.

"How's it going?"

"Hit's a goin' long tolerable well. Your woman say happen you come in, I should a telling you what she done this hyar mornin'. Hit tonishin!"

Captain McLeod, some sort of gumshoe for Homeland Security, was from Stinkin Crik, West Virginia, or so she claimed. She spoke three Mercan dialects: Federal Bureaucratese, Plain English Talk, and Mountain Talk. With her friends and "plain ole folk" like her neighbors, she reveled in Mountain Talk—"hit a-bein' talk that thar Willy Shakespeare a talkin all-ta-time."

So she pretended that we war down ta hollor in Stinkin Crik by the ole hard shell Baptist church and recounted the events that morning in front of St. Joseph's Hospital. The hounds, who had been sleeping backstage, ambled up to me and sat on their haunches, doubtless aware that their praises were being sung.

I didn't say anything at the end of the story. My wife was still alive, so were the hounds, the kids were in various spots on the soundstage. All's well that ends well.

Cindasue ended the story in Plain English Talk.

"They were going to take Ms. Connors to a whorehouse, gang rape her, and throw her out in the street."

"Who paid them?"

"Some man paid them twenty thousand dollars in cash. They didn't know his name. Cops and FBI morons investigating, but they won't find anything. This hyar place a-crawlin' with security. Ya uns be careful."

"Shunuf!"

Two large and authoritative women in pants suits a size too small elbowed their way past us and pushed out on to the soundstage.

"I'm Ethel Showalter and I'm assistant director of the Cook County CPO, Children Protective Office. I'm closing down this performance."

My wife turned on her, eyes dark with rage.

"I don't think you are. . . . Cindy, will you take care of this witch and have security eject them?"

My sister, the redoubtable Cynthia Coyne Hurley, mother to our wondrous Ellie, appeared on the floor. Though I was technically not part of security I ambled over behind her, knowing full well that my sister could more than take care of herself.

"You're guilty of harassment, Director Showalter. I will seek an injunction against you in Judge Ebenezer Brown's courtroom in the morning and ask for punitive damages against you and the County of Cook. Please leave this soundstage immediately or I will ask security to throw you out."

"Federal court has no jurisdiction over us."

"If the Federal court makes this case its own by assuming jurisdiction, then it has jurisdiction. We will ask Judge Brown to confine you in the downtown Federal lockup."

My beloved Celtic Tiger was closing in on our little conversation, the two pooches acting as escorts.

"No way he'll do that . . . This soundstage is lousy with violations."

"Your choice of language is offensive. I have here in this manila folder all the waivers, permissions, contracts, and agreements into which we have entered for this activity and a letter from the secretary of labor of the State of Illinois stating that it is his considered judgment that we are in full compliance with the laws and regulations of the State of Illinois regarding child labor. You could have ascertained this compliance by a phone call to the State of Illinois building. . . . Young man, you're in charge of security, are you not?"

"Yes ma'am, Ms. Hurley, ma'am."

"Then will you and these police officers show these two women out of the building or direct the officers to arrest them?"

My Irish Tiger grinned wickedly and walked back to her podium. The doggies followed, looking reluctantly it seemed to me over their shoulders.

"We're leaving," Director Showalter snapped. "You haven't heard the last of this."

"Nor, Director Showalter, have you! Guard!"

"This way, please, Director."

Behind me, as I walked our two unwelcome guests out of the building, the hounds howled again. They had been doing that a lot lately. Bad habits!

The media were ready for them. Ms. Showalter was prepared.

"They are out of compliance in there," she snapped. "We will ask the sheriff to close them down."

As she departed the bank of microphones I slipped in.

"Our attorneys gave her a file with all the waivers, permissions, contracts, and agreements into which we have entered for this activity and a letter from the secretary of labor of the State of Illinois stating that it is his considered judgment that we are in full compliance with the laws and regulations of the State of Illinois regarding child labor.

"Our attorney also pointed out that Director Showalter could have ascertained this compliance by a phone call to the State of Illinois building and suggested that her harassment of the production might put her in contempt of the order of the Honorable Ebenezer Brown, forbidding all further harassment of the production."

"Do you think, Dermot, that Director Showalter is another Grinch trying to spoil Christmas?"

"They might need a whole Grinch floor over at the lockup pretty soon."

"Do you have any comment, Dermot, on the incident at St. Joseph's this morning?"

"I wasn't there."

I retreated quickly to resist the additional comment that I wasn't sure that I wanted to know what had happened.

I returned to the building with the hounds in tow.

My Nelliecoyne was singing the Connemara lullaby with perfect pitch. Nuala joined her on the first refrain, and the choir joined in for the second refrain.

"That's it," my wife said. "Well done, everybody. Same time tomorrow. We'll try to go through it all without any interruption."

Applause from everyone in the theater.

"They a-cheerin' like they cheered the li'l polecat down to St. Joseph's this morning. . . . Irish Tiger, shunuff."

Then me wife dashed into my arms and sobbed.

"Dermot!" she wailed. "I'm totally out of control."

— Dermot —

 "DERMOT," SHE wailed for perhaps the fourth time that day, "I was totally out of control."

"Woman," I responded firmly, "you were not out of control. You just called up one of those personalities you stored away in your preconscious, one of those characters you know pretty well. I've seen her work several times, like that night in the alley in Dublin when those thugs came after me . . . surely you remember that?"

"Not at all, at all . . . I never did anything like that."

We were having our end of the day chat

with the usual splash of the creature, this time a very large splash for herself who was so tense that I feared she might break if the phone rang again.

The last call was from Maria Angelica, complaining that her new family—her three new daughters acquired that afternoon—would not go home.

"I'm too old for this emotion," she had said.

"A lot of anger and guilt being discharged?" me wife had replied, in her psychiatric mode.

"They are sweet young women when given half a chance, but I'm not sure I'm up to them. You wouldn't want an extra daughter or two, would you?"

"Not at all, at all. Isn't it hard enough with the two I have? . . . How you keeping, Maria Angelica?"

"A little tense . . . Yourself?"

"Feeling no pain at all, at all. Just sitting here with my man and drinking the creature like they were locking it all up tomorrow!"

I returned to my discussion of the many faces of Nuala Anne.

"I don't suppose you recall the time you came charging down our stairs with the very same camogie stick and the very same dogs when those eejits were trying to beat me up in front of our own home and Cindasue coming down the street with her forty-five?"

"I don't remember that, at all, at all."

"You're the kind of woman I'd want behind my back when the lights go off in a room. I figure that when the lights come on, a couple of my enemies will lie smote on the floor."

"Nothing like that ever happened!"

"Not yet, but face it, Nuala Anne, when your friends and family are under attack they know they can count on you. . . . and the fire engine and the hounds of heaven . . . Doesn't it make me safe altogether?"

You're talking like her again.

Go back to your hole in the wall.

"Give over, Dermot Michael! . . . And don't I need another splasheen!"

"Not at all, at all! I have some special amusements to relax you and I don't want you to be fluttered."

"Well then let's get on with your silly games!"

"Not till we talk about the case."

"Well then report on what you did today while I was fighting off the barbarians!"

So we returned to our usual modality of my reciting almost verbatim my conversations with Joey McMahon and the guys at Mike's bar. I took my sweet time.

She nodded.

"He probably knows some bosses in the drug gangs out there. He could have turned them loose . . . what did those poor men tell the cops? Some man they didn't know gave them twenty thousand dollars in cash to kidnap and rape Maria? He wouldn't have done it himself. Too risky. But a man who knows his village as well as he does, would know a discreet go-between. . . . But Dermot, isn't this savagery? Terrible, terrible savagery?"

"'Tis. The Outfit which can be brutal and its upset would never put out a contract like that. . . ."

"Did you call your friend Dominic to thank him for the tip?"

"Sure . . . His friends say that their friends are furious. The police ought to do something about it. No one is safe in Chicago anymore. They're trying to ascertain—Dom's word—who put out the contract. I suspect that the perpetrator has vanished in the mists. He or they or she or whatever are clumsy but they're vicious."

"And they're getting more vicious. . . . Dermot, whatever will we do!"

A unusual plaint from herself!

"We'll do what we always do, we'll solve the mystery."

Silence.

"And we'll be careful. We'll stay close to our security people and we'll keep the hounds a little hungry, so they're ready to fight!"

"We'll not starve my poor little puppies. . . . Och Dermot, I've lost me sense of humor altogether. . . . And, Dermot love, as you Yanks say, I haven't a clue. None of it makes sense. . . ."

I didn't like that. At all, at all. If me wife's carefully tuned fey sensitivities hadn't picked up any emanations we could be in deep trouble. She certainly was in contact with Archbishop Blackie. If neither of them could figure out what was going down, we'd better invest in some automatic weapons.

"Your sis says the insurance company has to pay for the damage to me car. Isn't that nice and it being me own fault?"

"I bet she also said that your rate would shoot up or that they might even refuse to insure you at all, at all."

"She did . . . but, Dermot love, there were only a few bumps on the front, hardly to notice. I might just leave it that way. . . . Well let's run through our suspects. . . . The first ones that come to mind are those brothers of Maria. . . ."

"Small-time punks with big-time dreams who hate their sister. But we have no evidence on them and Dom says the Outfit thinks they're clean on this one."

She nodded.

"Then there's the Donlan daughters, but they have made peace, have they not? And with much weeping and phone calls to meself."

"Most unlikely suspects but they might know something."

"Something they don't know they know, is it now? Won't we have to talk to them again?"

Which meant that I would have to talk to them again.

"The next one on the list is Lou Garner," I continued, "a four-flusher who envies Jack Donlan's success and has some shady connections in the construction world. He's nasty but not violent."

"What's a four-flusher, Dermot Michael?" she said with a yawn.

"Someone who has four cards of the same suit in a poker hand but fakes that his hidden card is also in the suit and he's hold-ing a flush which is five cards in the same suit. . . . A faker in other words."

"You must teach me that poker thing sometime, Dermot. I used to watch me classmates play when I was a young thing at Trinity College. I always knew what was in everyone's hand."

"Can you still do that?"

"I suppose so . . . I'm pretty good at pre-dicting what your Bears will do on Sun-day. . . . Why?"

"When we've solved this puzzle, we might go down to Vegas and win enough money to repair your Lincoln."

"Wouldn't that be cheating?" She yawned again. "Let's finish this conversation or won't I be too sleepy to satisfy your obscene needs?"

That would be most unlikely since she wanted lovemaking as much as I did.

"There's your man down at the office and out in the neighborhood?"

"Isn't he the prime suspect? I don't suppose you asked Dom to check him out?"

"Dom and Mike Casey both. He doesn't seem to be the kind of man that would have underworld contacts. But I'd bet he's a sneaky little guy."

"Still himself talking to people in the pub which is pretty clumsy and all this stuff being clumsy?"

"I agree that he's the prime suspect, but I want to know more about Sterling Stafford. He sounds like the kind of man who doesn't like to lose, either elections or women."

"You're not thinking of going out there by yourself, are you now Dermot Michael Coyne?"

Actually I was.

"I'll ask Mike Casey whether he can provide me a chauffeur for the ride out to Sunshine in Kishwaukee County. Tomorrow about noon."

"And meself with another rehearsal."

"It will be swarming with cops and Cindasue will be carrying her forty-five."

"It's not meself that I'd be worrying about."

"There are rumors about me kicking around in the empyrean?"

She pondered thoughtfully.

"Just wifely concern."

"Speaking of which, it is now time for an exercise of your wifely duties."

"Wifely rights . . . But not till we say our decade of the rosary and drink a toast to one another."

So we did both and what happened afterward exorcised at least temporarily whatever demons had been hounding my wife since her adventures in the morning.

— **Dermot** —

Memo
From: Michael Casey
To: Dermot Coyne
Subject: Sterling Silver Stafford
Representative Sterling Silver Stafford
(Rep. Ill.) is your classic rural Middle
Western Republican Congressman of
the Reagan era. Not very bright, not
very articulate, but very loyal to the
party and never guilty of thinking for
himself. Born in 1940, he inherited from
his father, Fair Profit Silver, his hard
shell Baptist religion, his good looks,
his populist Republican style and his

ability to go for the main chance. He also inherited his father's General Motors franchise in DeKalb and a thousand acres of prime Illinois prairie. Before running for Congress in 1984 (at the time of the second Reagan election, a Republican sweep) he had transferred his GM franchise to Rockford and transformed it into the largest Cadillac agency in Northern Illinois. He also increased his land holdings in Sunshine County to three thousand acres at the time when the American farm belt was feeding much of the world. It was easy for him to get on the Agriculture Committee and not much more difficult to take over the subcommittee responsible for farm subsidies, a position which in the heydays of the Newt Gingrich Congress and the K Street lobbies, enabled him to become a multimillionaire. He played high school football at Sunshine High School but, despite his campaign claims he was never All-State. Indeed he was a perennial second string, though as his friends say, with a touch of irony, he sure did look like a football star. He was described in journals like TIME as a leader of the Farm Block, but in fact Sterling never led anything and was more a docile member of the Agribusiness Block. He sure did look like a congressman, however—white suit, white shirt, white shoes, black string tie, silver hair, rich baritone voice which could make the most unoriginal right-wing clichés sound like Gospel truth. He was compared to the late Everett McKinley Dirksen as a speaker, a comparison he reveled in, though he was not in the same ballpark as the "Great Ooze" when it came to oleaginous and shrewd statements.

He was twenty-six when he married Vivian Whitherspoon, a nineteen-year-old former cheerleader and stenographer at the Silver Cadillac agency. Their firstborn, Ron Silver, was born five months later. Vivie was a poor white trash country girl who wanted the good life. She hated Kishwaukee County and its memories of poverty and enjoyed the District and all its ceremony. She fit in perfectly with the rich white trash environment of the Reagan and Bush years, so much so that she rarely returned home on weekends with her husband or on recesses. Nor in Washington did she attend church with him at the upper end Southern Baptist Church where he occasionally preached on Sunday.

"Ole Ster" was a perennial candidate in the area around Sunshine and Kishwaukee counties, seeking membership on county boards, the State Chamber of Deputies, the State Senate, and even for Congress in primaries which he invariably lost to a popular veteran of World War II who was a natural on television and both smart and shrewd, claims that could never be made for poor "Ster." In 1984, however, the incumbent died two weeks before "Ster" was swept into Congress from which the wiseacres in that part of Illinois said he would be routed only by the same grim reaper who defeated his predecessor. Sterling Silver Stafford was just the congressman his constituents wanted, he looked like a senator, talked like a senator, and didn't say much.

He voted to impeach Clinton and,

perhaps unwisely, gave a strong speech about morality and family values during the debate. Those who knew him both in the district and in Rockford and were aware of his constant and serial pursuit of attractive women—"don't matter none their age or sex"—thought he was skating on very thin ice and expressed the fear or the hope that the ice would sink beneath him. His reputation as a Don Juan made him attractive to a certain kind of woman who was desperate enough for one reason or another to take a chance.

His strongest opposition politically came from Oakdale Township, despite his home on the river inside the township and his membership in the Oakdale Country Club. His voting residence, however, was over in Sunshine in a palatial "family home" he had built on his vast farmland. It was an Oakdale member of the Oakdale Democratic Club (whose president was and still is one Maria Sabattini Connors) and a professor of English literature at DeKalb who finally defeated him with almost 60% of the vote in the 2006 election.

"Ole Ster," it was said, had not kept up with the times. Chicago was spreading into the prairies beyond the Fox River and Illinois was becoming a persistent "blue" state. The Iraq war, for which Congressman Stafford had voted enthusiastically, had turned sour. President Bush, whom he worshipped, had lost much of his popularity. Students from DeKalb picketed his office in Rockford every weekend. Local soccer moms were fed up with the rumors of his romantic affairs. Ordinary folk (i.e. white Protestants) didn't like the suggestions in Chicago papers that he might be indicted immediately after the election. As usual "Ole Ster's" campaign was perfunctory. Unwisely he wept at his concession speech as he said, "Ah reckon that eleven terms is a long time for any one man to live in a pressure cooker."

To the media after the concession, he denied any plans to run for the Senate.

"I reckon I could have beaten that

African fella, if I had enough time to prepare a primary run. I was too busy doing a good job on my agricultural committee."

The editorial in the Oakdale *Democrat* suggested that "Ole Ster's" seat had been a lazy monopoly one term too long.

I have tried, Dermot, to keep my Democratic biases and my Irish sense of irony out of this memo. To sum up, Sterling Silver Stafford is a political dinosaur, albeit a relatively harmless one. He does not have a character that is capable of great good or great evil. He is probably too lazy to organize a major conspiracy, but he is a very bad loser.

I closed the file as my limo eased past the exurbs of Chicago, across the Fox River and beyond into more or less open farm country, brown, flat, and dull under the slanting rays of a sun moving ever farther away from us. The sky was cloudless blue and the temperature was in the mid forties. A nice early winter day, the kind that said, "Enjoy me because you will not see my like again for a long time."

Soon the fields would turn white, though that would not improve their appearance. Would it be a white Christmas this year? I hoped not. We would have to attend the Christmas Eve kids' Eucharist at St. Josephat's and the Christmas Mass at Old St. Patrick's where my wife sang in the choir, which, by definition could not do "O Holy Night" without her. Then we would double back to the cathedral to sing at the noon Mass—where she would sing solo "for all the furriners" and pay our respects to Cardinal Sean, Archbishop Blackie, and my brother Father George who was now the pastor of the cathedral so that Blackie would have more freedom to play his coadjutor role. Then we would venture on to the Congress Expressway for the final step in our pilgrimage to River Forest and the Coyne home, where my siblings and their numerous progeny (all of whose names Nuala would remember but I would not) would gather. Noisily. My "small ones" would yield second place to no one in their exuberance. My wife was, of course, one of the kids. I would sit on the sidelines and wonder where that quintet had come from and why, when the other brats began to whine, my bunch simply fell asleep, their mother included.

If it were a white Christmas, however, she would have to lead the whole pack outside for fun in the snow. On arrival in our Republic, Nuala announced that she didn't think she'd like snow all that much.

"Don't we do without it most of the time up in Connemara? I can't see why you Yanks insist on it."

When the blizzards came, however, you'd think she invented it. Wasn't it a wonderful time to play with your husband? And the doggies, and the small ones when they came along? Frolicking in the snow was not an option, a conviction enthusiastically embraced by her offspring, leaving poor Da to mutter that he needed a jar of mulled wine or a small cup of hot chocolate.

After fun in the River Forest snow we had to drive up and down the streets and admire the madcap decorations with which our neighbors—truth to tell, especially the Italianate neighbors—had created to celebrate the joyous season of the birth of Baby Jesus, as he was familiarly known to my kids. Dermot drove the Navigator on the trip, because as me wife announced, "You hardly had a drop to drink." Under normal circumstances she would drive "because everyone says I'm a better driver than you are, Dermot love."

Then finally home to Sheffield Avenue where the sleeping small ones had to be guided to their beds and the weary hounds had to be rewarded with several treats because, sure, isn't it Christmas Day?

Beginning last year weren't we up bright and early on Boxing Day (St. Stephen's Day as the devout Nelliecoyne would insist) to pack for a quick Christmas trip to her ma and pa. Wouldn't it be brilliant altogether for them to see the small ones this time of the year? It would indeed especially since Patjo was so adorable and himself named after me great-uncle. Thus had begun what my brother Prester George would have called an immemorial custom. Interminable, I thought. We would escape from one mad round of parties with family and friends in Chicago to a similar frantic rush in Carraroe.

Last year there had been an excessively white Christmas which clogged O'Hare and gave me family (herself included) a brilliant opportunity to prove that they could be as ill-tempered international travelers as anyone else and worse than most. Poor Da was the only one who had to keep smiling.

Even without the snow, this year's proof that you too can go home again would be difficult. Life was catching up with me good wife, the struggle over her Christmas special, the growing family, the Donlan case, the now almost legendary battle of Lake Shore Drive, the Donlan girls and their new mom—there was no upper limit to the responsibilities that me Celtic Tiger had collected. And she'd weep halfway across the Atlantic at the plight of the "poor doggies" who would not come with us this time and were not consoled by her promise that "won't you be able to come home with us in the summer?"

The doggies were farmed out to the Murphys down the street.

"My polecats are goin' ta think they a dyin' and a goin' to heaven."

We had "minded" the Murphy kids while their parents had spent time in the Cayman Islands. So they owed us and we picked up their marker.

Nuala protested that this wasn't fair—four kids for two. But she didn't protest too loudly.

She needed a vacation—away from the

kids, from Mike Casey, from the Donlans, and even from Blackie Ryan. From everyone but me. I wasn't sure she'd agree and less sure that she'd relax.

When does a good husband try to draw the line? What does he do about an Irish tiger? A fragile Irish tiger?

My worrying ended when I saw a sign shaped like a large oak tree which informed me that I was "Welcome to Oakdale—Where Past and Future Meet!"

Maria Angelica's theme.

She must love Jackie Donlan a lot to shift her dwelling to Chicago, though she probably could cope with both worlds.

The town lived up to its theme. New restaurants and motels, mixed with restored homes and stores in a blend that was either miraculous or ingenious. It was not quite ready for national landmark status yet, but it was well on its way. No wonder that faculty from NIU were moving in. The newer homes may have been the first hint to Maria that there was a market for something like Elegant Homes.

The latest report on both the Donlans was that they were recovering "better than could be expected." The latest report from the forces of law and order was that they had all the perpetrators but none of them seemed to know who the contact man was other than "someone from out of town." My friend Dom reported that the friends of his friends reported that the guilty party was some "wiseguy" from Vegas who was "out of line." A message from one of the most important of the friends of Dom's friends warned him that he was so far out of line his misbehavior would be reported to the "Council" and that didn't mean the one in Rome either.

Apparently he was a person of such importance that the people on the West Side (many of whom live in places like Oak Brook or River Forest) would not consider putting him down without national authorization, unless they decided that they would lose all respect if they didn't.

This was high-level stuff. I asked Mike Casey about it.

"Your guy out there," he said, "was the one that warned you about the put-down on Maria?"

"Yeah," I said. "He has some friends who are friends to some people who are very important."

"Probably live right down the street . . . Dom is clean?"

"He's connected, but not involved in anything. . . . He thinks he owes me some favors."

"I don't like dealing with those people," he said with a sigh. "But sometimes it doesn't hurt to listen to them. They know we do some work for herself?"

"How would they not?"

"Yeah, so they figure you'll tell me. That's the way their convoluted Sicilian minds work."

"Our bunch has perfected indirection to its highest point in human history and we've done it without even trying."

Mike thought that was very funny and did not dispute the point. How could he?

"This is a neat little town," my driver, a young cop working for Mike on his day off, commented. "I bet it didn't happen by accident."

"No, Colm, it didn't."

"A smart woman with good taste?"

"You gonna go detective when you get out of law school?"

"I'll leave that stuff to your wife. I want to be a trial lawyer."

No one thought I did anything on me wife's little puzzles. That was grand with me. Grand altogether.

He was clearly from the South Side. He had two of the four characteristics required for trial lawyers in Chicago—he was short and gregarious. He had yet to put on weight and drink too much beer.

We pulled up at the congressman's "lodge," a sprawling brick house on the Kishwaukee River which despite its marvelous Native American name was a lazy and meandering creek.

"I'll wait outside," Colm told me. "Yell if you need me."

"I sure will."

I didn't expect any trouble, not from someone mulling the possibility that he could defeat Senator Obama, in the event that charismatic Chicagoan did not win a presidential election.

A security heavy with dark eyes and a high forehead met me at the door.

"Mike McDermot to see the congressman."

"He's expecting you, Mike. Have a seat in there in the trophy room."

The heavy looked me over and decided that he'd have no trouble taking care of me. He was wrong, but my glowing face and curly blond hair fool a lot of people.

The trophy room was patently, as Archbishop Blackie would say, the place where Maria Angelica had threatened to remove the congressman's genitalia with a shotgun blast, after she had knocked him daffy by throwing a camcorder so that it collided with his handsome, if outsized, head.

Good on you, Maria.

Sterling Silver Stafford appeared in the room with a certain flourish, clad in chinos, a brown corduroy jacket, and a bright red scarf wrapped around his neck. His large, classical head with its flowing white hair might well have been detached from his body and affixed to the wall where it would have fit in with the heads of somewhat lesser animals. Homo sapiens as king of the forest. However, he seemed relaxed and self-confident, quite the opposite of the grey and wounded veteran who had conceded victory to Mrs. Hallinan in the early morning after the election—not Ms. Hallinan, much less Dr. Hallinan.

"Good to meet you, Mike," he said with the usual friendly grin that had characterized his TV appearances and had created the impression that this nice man was probably a smart man too. "I don't see enough of your work, but I've been impressed by it."

The *Herald* had run a political commentary of mine once a month or so to confirm that I really was an investigative journalist. They even offered me a permanent job. I declined with thanks "for the present."

"Thank you, Congressman."

"Just Ster, Mike. Only judges, governors, and ambassadors get to keep their title after they step down."

"Some senators are trying to claim it for themselves."

"They'll never get away with it. . . ." He reclined in the very chair in which he had cowered when the shotgun was pointed at him. "I've asked for some coffee to be brought in and I thought we could talk till noon and then go over to the country club for a bite of lunch. Or are you a good Irishman, Mike, and drink tea?"

"I drink tea, Ster, though I'm not a good Irishman because I don't pollute it with milk."

A man who was either a Native American or an Asian, who had been hovering at the doorway, scurried away.

I noted a camcorder on one of the occasional shelves of books which provided décor for the room—the owner was not only a hunter but a student of primitive countries.

"Do you play golf, Mike?" he asked. "I've given up hunting for golf and would like to give all these heads away. They embarrass me."

"I swing a club occasionally," I said. "When I have the time. I don't exactly burn up the fairways."

There was a certain false modesty in that statement. My handicap at Butterfield is one and at Oak Park two. In the County Galway, I'm known colloquially as "that focking Yank who shoots even and wouldn't be permitted on the course if his wife weren't from Carraroe." I am very proud of that allegation.

"A hunter has to fight another animal, one that's inferior to him and doomed to probable defeat. A golfer, given certain minimal skills must face the worst possible enemy— himself, even one as good as Tiger Woods. . . . I suppose you want to know my view of the recent election?

"I am told that you said the other night that the election was neither a victory for liberals nor a defeat for conservatives."

"That's what I said and that's what I meant. The American people are in substantial part Christians and conservatives hence the Republicans should win almost every election. This time we were defeated by this damnable war. If the president had fired that fool Rumsfeld two weeks before he did I'd still be chair of my committee."

His face turned red in anger for a moment and then relaxed.

"I thought that you supported the war, Ster," I said as I nodded my head at the somber servant who had poured my tea. He looked like photos of Chief Sitting Bull (another head for Ster's gallery). I was willing to bet there was a gallery somewhere in his house commemorating all his sexual conquests too.

The tea was as black as midnight on a moonless night. So was the houseman's stare.

"Like every good American I was proud to see our country hitting back at the evil murderers who slaughtered so many of our fellow citizens. I felt we had to reestablish our self-respect and our power in the world, the only surviving superpower. Unfortunately we made some intolerable mistakes. The military leaders wanted us to go in with four hundred thousand men. That fool Rumsfeld thought he could do it with thirty-five thousand men plus special forces, air power, and

Iraqi allies that the CIA had won to our side. I personally think that he was right about that. Such a quick strike force could have toppled Saddam Hussein easily. As a compromise he agreed to a little over a hundred thousand—too many for a military victory, too few for an occupation that could pacify the countryside. Now, when it's probably too late, we're arguing about twenty thousand more. . . ."

"What some people would call too little and too late."

"Not the words I would choose, Mike. . . . And I don't want to be quoted in that notebook of yours. . . ."

I inclined my head at his request for confidentiality.

". . . But materially correct . . . If we're going to go to war, we should go to war with all the power we have and to win as quickly as possible. That's common sense. . . ."

"It's what they called the Powell Doctrine, isn't it?"

"I don't particularly admire the former secretary, but any soldier with common sense knows that. Yet in Korea and Vietnam we did just the opposite for fear of offending the people with the casualties. Better to have heavy casualities for a few months than to dribble away your resources and the people's goodwill over four years. I thought that from the beginning. I admit that I should have spoken out. I was being a loyal team player. I'll never excuse myself for that. It would have been hard to dissent a couple of years ago. I guess I lacked the courage to go after the defense secretary. . . . and all those Jewish intellectuals he had around him."

"And the vice president? Didn't he have his own group of intellectuals?"

"I never liked the man. . . . I couldn't stand him, to tell the truth. Never give an angry man like him a little power. . . . He also has offended a lot of good Christians out here in my district . . . well, what used to be my district"—he laughed lightly—"by publicly supporting his lesbo daughter. Privately I don't mind. But doesn't the Bible say that the sin is an abomination in his sight?"

"I'm a Catholic, Ster, I don't know much about the Bible."

I had studied the scriptures for two years at Marquette and knew a lot about what God said and didn't say. Once I had the idea of becoming a Jesuit and going off to the Biblical Institute in Rome.

"You'd flunk out there too, Dermot," my brother Prester George had said bluntly. "You're not cut out for schoolwork."

He was probably right. However, I believe that I know a lot and did a good job as an autodidact even before I met me wife—and that was a whole education in itself.

"I finally came to the conclusion as I was trying to put the rest of my life together that the president isn't a very bright man. We all kidded ourselves on that. And he's as stubborn as a German farmer out here in Sunshine County."

I was silent for a moment. No point in jotting that down.

"In other words, Mike, we had a great opportunity after we got rid of that notorious sinner. And we blew it. And I'm partly responsible. . . ."

He reclined back in his chair and sipped his coffee. He was himself a notorious sinner. Yet his reverie seemed to disclose a man who, within his own limitations, was trying to be honest with himself. Or perhaps a man who was trying to persuade himself that he was trying to be honest.

"I made a lot of mistakes locally too. . . . You just came out from Chicago. You saw how the prairie which once separated us from the city becomes smaller every year. I came back here often and hardly noticed it, even though I was heavily engaged in the local modernization effort. We rehabilitated this town, so it was true to its past and yet a place to escape from the hubbub of urban life—especially the drugs and the crime . . . and the sex. . . ."

The kids at the local high school almost certainly had similar problems as did kids in Chicago high schools.

"And a good place for someone to catch a breath of fresh air between flights at O'Hare or maybe to schedule a small private professional conference in a restful environment. Maybe play a couple of rounds of golf between sessions. I am proud of the course at Oakdale Country Club. I put a lot of work into its development. We believe it is the best golf course west of Lake Michigan and we are hoping to get a major professional tourney here in the next couple of years."

"That's quite an achievement."

"I'm facing an obvious decision now. I've been offered a senior position in an important firm. . . ."

"On K Street?"

He frowned, not appreciating my insight.

"As a matter of fact, no . . . But right around the corner. I would like it. I'd still be playing in the big game. As much as I hated life in the district, I also loved the excitement, the drama, the challenge. . . . Something like hunting . . . Well I gave up hunting and I lost the big game in the district. Viv, my wife, would be happy to stay. She's winding things down in our condo now. She'll be home for Christmas and we'll make a decision then. Man and wife should not be separated for long."

Two days away from me own high-maintenance wife and I became your prototypical melancholy Irish male wondering where he'll find his next drink.

"Well, come on, let's go over and have lunch. Your driver can follow after us, can't he? Tell him I'll wind a bit through the town so he can see what we've done with it."

As he conducted his booster's tour of Oakdale, I tried to put together my thoughts about this not very bright but not uncomplicated man. He loved the town as much as Maria did. Or did he? Was this whole story an attempt to clear himself of suspicion? Or was it on the level? In his own way, twisted surely, did he also love her and hence want to add her beauty and talent to his collection? A strange kind of love.

I'd have to see what me wife could make of it.

The clubhouse was magnificent, reminiscent of Augusta, but somehow more decent and matter-of-fact. One could admire it and not suffer the temptation to dismiss it as reaching too far.

The course itself was not the best between the Great Lakes and the Pacific Coast, as he claimed while we walked a couple of holes. But it was damned good. He carried a seven iron and a bag of balls as we walked. (My Reliable followed at a distance, watching very carefully. He would make a good lawyer.) We came to the tee for the eighth. It was a par three with a narrow fairway which was mostly rough and woods between the tee and the green save for a ring of sand traps and a tiny pond in front of the green. He teed up a ball and slammed it. It went into the water. The second burrowed deep into a sand trap and the third lost itself in rough.

"Have a shot, Mike?"

All my deep macho competitive genes

surged within me. The hormones coursed through my veins. I'd show the son of a bitch. A good investigator would have botched all the shots. But under those circumstances I was not a good investigator. I put my first shot three feet from the cup.

Ster chuckled softly. I glanced back at him. Amusement was already replacing rage on his face. Not in time.

"Great shot, Mike, you do play a little golf now and then, don't you! Can I interest you in a complimentary membership in the club. You'd be eligible for a shot at the championship tourney at the end of the summer. We'd make a great two-ball team."

I accepted the gift, but made no promises about the tourney.

"My work piles up then . . . so many of the older men are on vacation."

"Let's go in and have a drink on it."

"Only one . . . I have to take notes."

"One is my limit at lunch and only when I'm entertaining. One at supper too. Any more than that and I become dangerous."

Again I wonder whether this was true or part of an act.

At the lunch table I ordered bourbon on the rocks—Scotch is forbidden in our house and Nuala would want to know what I had to eat and drink for lunch, especially if she thought I might do some of the driving. He ordered a Caesar salad for lunch and assured me it was first-rate. It was, though I like my Caesar best when it was soaking in garlic dressing.

A symbol of the reformed Sterling Stafford? I didn't know.

"Another thing I missed out here was the importance of Northern. I remembered it as a kind of teachers' college and I didn't want to be a teacher. I got them a lot of grants and in return they gave me an honorary degree. I got them more grants and they asked me to give a graduation address that one of my staff wrote for me. Then somehow—I'll be damned if I know when—it became a great university, about where Champaign was when I was thinking about college. That was something I should have been proud of. And afraid of too. Great university means high-quality faculty. The way things are these days that means a lot of liberals. And that means a lot of Democrats. And a lot of Jews. They not only vote all the time, they campaign like Chicago precinct captains. You put them together with Oakdale and add the soccer moms and the Hispanics and you have the beginnings of a winning coalition. I was not unaware of them because they picketed my office every time I voted against something they liked—this damned global warming stuff, for instance. You add Iraq to the mix and I'm in serious trouble. There were a lot of other Republican team players in the House in the same fix. We murmured about it in private, but we still believed that the country was in a conservative mood and in favor of punishing the Islamofascists. We kept our mouths shut, confident that the president and his boy Karl Rove would pull the rabbit out of the hat again."

"They let you down?"

"Hell, yes! They didn't care much if a lot of us lost, but they thought their majority was safe. Turned out it wasn't and somehow that was our fault."

"The buck doesn't stop in the Oval Office?"

"Not for a long time."

He toyed with his salad but ate only some of it.

"So here I am, back in my district, hurting from defeat and wondering whether I should go back to the Beltway and play the game for the fun of it and not because I need the money or stay here with my farm and my country club and my national landmark little town—and it was the little town that beat me."

"Oakdale?"

He sighed again, not like the way my Nuala Anne sighs, but a sadness of real agony mixed with grief for the passing of the years.

"Not merely the voters here, they were never on my side, though this time they really turned out in force. But, you see, Mike, the president of the Oakdale Democrats was the woman behind the Oakdale plan. . . . What should I call her . . . ? The organizer and the creative genius . . . We were allies, not exactly friends, but I thought we respected each other. . . . That's the way it is in politics, I guess. . . . You won't put anything about her in the story, please?"

"Okay," I said, closing my notebook.

"We were never lovers, you see, though I often thought that would not be a bad idea, especially since Viv never came home on weekends. And my friend had a marriage problem of her own. Nothing ever came of it and I'm glad now of that. But it still hurts."

A quick flash of anger appeared in his dark eyes and then disappeared.

"I understand."

"Well, her marriage problem cleared up and she married a man in Chicago. She comes back often, but I don't see her. . . . Sometimes I wonder . . . But this defeat has brought me and Viv closer together than we've been in a long time. . . . So I suppose it's all for the best."

An expurgated version of what happened but a usable rationalization for a fractured ego.

"Maybe Junior did me a great favor when he didn't fire Rummy. Maybe I'm out of there in the knick of time. Maybe I should be proud of my achievements and let it go at that. Let the liberals run the country for a while and see how they mess it up."

At the door of the clubhouse, I introduced him to my man Colm, a student in law school.

"I always thought I might like the law," Sterling Stafford mused. "One thing led to another and I never did. I've concluded that I made a mistake. Lawyers have an edge on everyone in society."

"Only," my man Colm said, "because they make the rules where the edge is."

We all laughed.

"I'd know your friend was Irish," Ster said, "even if I didn't know his name."

I waited till we were out on I-80 before calling Nuala Anne.

"Nuala Anne," she said crisply, her artistic impresario face totally in place.

"Her husband."

"Och, Dermot Michael Coyne, aren't you a wonderful husband altogether to be calling and myself in a disaster area?"

"A frigging disaster, is it now?"

She pondered for a moment.

"I wouldn't go that far, not yet? But in all me life as a director, I've never seen a worse dress rehearsal or final run-through or whatever you want to call it."

"Did you cuss them out?"

"I'm an amadon as you know, Dermot love, but not that much of an eejit. I had a swarm of little girls, including poor Socra Marie and Katiesue. Didn't I tell them how great they were and how wonderful they'd be tomorrow night at the taping? And weren't some of the mothers angry at me for not going after them?"

"That's not your style, Nuala, except when you're straightening me out."

"Go long with you, Dermot Michael Coyne, I never give you a hard time save when it's for your own good and don't you know that?"

"What will it be like at the taping?"

"Won't they be friggin' brilliant? And if I made them cry, any more than they did, after tomorrow I'd have to be on the first plane to Shannon."

"Do you *know* this?"

"Would I be saying it if I didn't know? The small ones are winners! Now what did you learn about our gobshite friend out beyond?"

"Not what I expected at all, at all."

"'Tis interesting . . . We'll have to talk about it tonight."

"You'll be too worn and frazzled."

"Don't be an eejit. . . . How long have you been married to me?"

"A couple of eternities . . . All right we'll talk about it tonight. . . . How are the Donlans doing?"

"Doesn't poor Jackie feel like he's died and gone to heaven and his wife and his daughters and his stepdaughters treating him like he's best thing since the invention of stock markets. The dentists and the plastic people have done him so that by Christmas he'll look better than new."

"And his company?"

"Still the value of the company is falling but not too badly, considering. Frodo and Samwise are standing firm. So's the ELG thing. If we can unknot this puzzle by Christmas, they'll bounce back."

"Will we? Can we?"

"Don't ever doubt an Irish Tiger. . . . See you at supper. Tell Colm to drive carefully."

Which I did of course. With a wife from the same ethnic background he assumed such a warning and would have been disappointed if it were not delivered.

At supper it emerged that the doggies were in, you should excuse the expression, the doghouse. They had misbehaved terrible altogether at the run-through, fighting with each other, and interrupting the songs with their infernal howling and chasing imaginary rats. That was unlike them. They had been banished to the Navigator where they howled all the more.

Me wife who looked thin enough and haggard enough to be hauled off to the emergency room herself was upset with the hounds.

"The kids," she said "don't know any

better, but the puppies know they're supposed to behave."

The children were helped with their homework and put to bed as they sang songs to one another.

"You'll be brilliant tomorrow," she informed them. "Now just one more time through the Connemara lullaby and then off to the land of Nod."

Patjo and Socra Marie were most of the way there.

The hounds wandered into the songfest looking sheepish, if such a description can be applied to wolfhounds. Fiona, by reason of seniority, nudged me wife by way of apology. She embraced them both and produced a treat for both of them. The reconciliation was thereby sealed.

In our bedroom, after our showers, I recounted for herself my verbatim discussion with Sterling Silver Stafford aided by my notebook.

"Now isn't that the strangest thing!" she said, pondering my report. "What were you after thinking, Dermot Michael?"

"Wasn't I kind of thinking that he wasn't quite clever enough to make up the whole story."

"It's a story he's told himself many times and yet he can't quite believe it all. . . . He'd be happier if he filled in the blanks with the truth. . . ."

The hounds entered the room together, a rare enough event. Something was brewing.

"It's all right, puppies, I'm not angry at you anymore."

They cuddled up around her legs, and she patted them both. They were still restless.

My good wife began to shiver. She looked at me, her eyes wide with fear.

"Dermot! Someone's going to blow up my Navigator in the parking lot tomorrow night, just when people are coming out of the auditorium! Hundreds are going to die, including maybe us. We have to stop them!"

— Dermot —

WE BOTH froze. Nuala Anne has such intense warning experiences only rarely. They terrify her and frighten me as if someone is holding a gun to my skull. Something very bad was about to go down out there and we had to stop it. But we had only the faintest idea what it was and how to stop it. The warnings were vague and erractic and sometimes wrong. There was no way to be sure. Who would want to blow up her car and kill the people that would come to the taping, including, if John Culhane were to be believed, the mayor and the senator? Was it part of the Donlan puzzle which seemed to escalate every day? It had started out as a harmless item in a gossip column and now it threatened mass murder.

"Are you sure?" I asked, wrapping her trembling body in my arms.

"I'm sure the explosion is out there. . . . But sometimes it's wrong, never when it's this strong. . . . Och, Dermot love, don't I wish that I was never fey? Isn't it terrible altogether."

"Are you sure it's your Lincoln?"

"It looks like it. . . . Sure, I hope that we all of us die together, even the puppies."

"None of us are gong to die, Nuala Anne. We've beaten the bad guys before and we'll do it again."

"Ma! Ma!" Nelliecoyne rushed into the room in her Snow White and the Seven Dwarfs pajamas.

She threw her arms around her ma and sobbed.

"What's wrong, cara, what's wrong? Are them terrible Snow White dreams bothering you again?"

She had discovered an old Snow White tape and shown it to the younger kids, who loved it. Somehow it had scared her—though she was immune to nocturnal troubles after Harry Potter and the Ring books.

"The wicked dwarf is setting off a huge explosion, like a meteorite hitting our neighborhood! It blinded me for a few moments! . . . Oh, Ma, wasn't it terrible altogether! I knew I was dying! We were all dying!"

The two hounds rose on their hind legs as if to protect mother and child from impending doom. Poor Da could fend for himself.

This was the first time that the sight had affected both me wife and me oldest child. It was a major happening. I must do something. . . .

"All the dwarfs are good in the filum, darlin'. 'Tis the wicked queen who's the bad 'un."

"The queen wasn't in me dream at all, at all, Ma."

"And the dwarfs are good 'uns, aren't they?"

"Kinda dorky but they try to be good . . ."

"So it wasn't a true dream, was it?"

Nelliecoyne dried her tears on the sleeve of her pj's.

"No, Ma, it's not going to come true, but we have a lot of work to do."

"Your da and I always have a lot of work to do and we always get it done, don't we?"

"You're the greatest ma and da in the

whole world! Katiesue's ma and da are real nice too."

"Then you'll go back to bed now and get a good night's sleep because we have the show tomorrow night."

"Yes, Ma."

"Did you wake up Socra Marie?"

"Och, Ma, the end of the world could happen outside our window and that one wouldn't wake up."

"Too true."

Ma and the small one went hand in hand back to the girls' bedroom. Me wife rolled her dangerous blue eyes at me as they went.

I had to do something, so I called my friend Dominic.

"Dominic," he said, polite as always.

"Dermot, Dom. Sorry to call so late."

"No problem, Dermot. Whole family is in bed, so I'm working on my taxes. What's happening?"

"We hear there's a contract out on us. An engineer is going to blow up our car tomorrow night in the parking lot after Nuala's show. Kill us and a lot of people!"

"Holy shit, Dermot. The mayor and the senator are going to be there. We can't let this go down. My friends won't permit it.

That's all. They just won't permit it! . . . Is it part of this Donlan caper you people are involved with?"

"Probably."

"Okay, Dermot, thanks for calling me. I gotta get in touch with some of my friends right away."

"Thanks, Dom."

"You can count on us, Dermot. Tell your wife, my friends just won't let it go down. No way. Count on us."

"Thanks. We will."

"Your man?" Nuala asked.

She had come back to our bedroom, accompanied by the two hounds who had escorted her and Nelliecoyne back to the girls' room.

"Good idea," she said, filling our two Irish crystal tumblers with a large splash of the creature. "Last ones before the show wraps up tomorrow night."

"Slainte!"

"Slainte!"

My wife had rebounded. Once more she was the Irish Tiger, Granne O'Malley getting ready for a raid on the friggin' English.

"I'll call that nice Mr. Casey," she announced as she sat down at the desk to take charge. She gestured at the other phone for me to listen on.

Mike was always "that nice Mr. Casey."

"Hi, Annie, Nuala Anne here, sorry to ring so late, but you know what me husband is like. Keeps terrible late hours . . . Could I have a short word with himself.

"Hi, Mr. Casey. Sorry to trouble you, but we have reason to suspect that someone will try to blow up me little fire engine in the parking lot after the show tomorrow night."

"What kind of reason, Nuala? Ordinary or otherwise?"

He knew her well.

"Otherwise and very powerful . . . Aren't me poor doggies worried, but me poor little chile saw it in a nightmare. . . . A terrible explosion would kill all of us. . . ."

"And probably the mayor and the senator and their wives," I added.

"Hi, Dermot . . ."

My presence, of which he was certainly aware, was duly acknowledged. He could assume that I was sharpening up the spears which were what I carried in our joint operations. The spears (imaginary) would be useful should we encounter any vampires. Herself denied their existence.

They were a silly English superstition, even if your man was Irish.

"I've already talked to my friend on the West Side," I said, nodding my head toward Taylor Street and beyond, which is de rigueur if you're talking about "the boys."

"Good idea. I'll call John Culhane and we'll be there for breakfast. . . . Lots of coffee, Nuala . . ."

"Tonight," she said bluntly.

"It's that serious? Okay, I'll ask John to call Terry Glen, the deputy superintendent. He'll be skeptical, but if we win him over, we'll have all the good guys on our side as well as the guys out on the West Side. Make the coffee anyway."

"Come quietly," I said, "and park in the alley behind the house. No cop cars."

"Won't we be letting you in the back door on the ground floor? You just have to walk down the steps."

So me wife and I put on our black jeans and our black sweaters and she tied her long hair up in a businesslike knot. We carried our black leather jackets and our ski caps and the sound monitors for each of the kids' bedrooms downstairs to the ground floor. The kids' playroom was in only mild disarray.

"Let's leave it as it is," she said, "so they won't think we planned all this. I'll take the soda bread out of the freezer and heat it up. You get the balls off the floor so no one will slip on them. Would you ever, Dermot love, turn on the coffee and teapot in the archive room?"

Me woman believed as a matter of faith that soda bread should be served fresh out of the oven. Then she saw her ma heat it up in the microwave we had given them for Christmas a couple of years ago.

The archive room was an L-shaped corner on the ground floor adjoining the playroom, but separated from it by a soundproof door. When we bought the house it had been a storage for old newspapers, some very old, and documents. We saved a few of the documents and papers, installed cabinets, paneled the walls, and provided a table with easy chairs around it. There was also a police radio scanner, a TV, and maps of Chicago on the wall and a bank of phones, a wet bar, a fridge, and coffee- and tea makers. I called it "the Situation Room" because Nuala had the room of that name from *The West Wing* in mind when she furnished and decorated it. We also had a bank of monitors from which we could survey the approaches to our house. I turned them on so we would be ready for the Chicago Police Department when they appeared. For the first time I realized that snow had been falling for several hours. The alley outside the house was already covered with snow. Four to six inches possible, the weatherman had promised, though most of it would be on the South Side and the southern suburbs.

A blizzard was all we needed.

The cops arrived just as Nuala descended with a platter of steaming soda bread. I opened the door and assured them that they didn't have to worry about tracking snow on the floor. I poured the coffee and tea and herself distributed scones, clotted cream, and jams and jellies, most of them imported from Ireland. There were four cops, Mike Casey, John Culhane, Deputy Superintendent Terry Glen, and Lieutenant Nikos Mashek, head of the bomb squad. Mike Casey acted as chair.

"As some of you know, the Sixth District has worked with the Coynes for some time on various puzzles and problems that have occurred in the district. Reliable Security has also worked with them in certain matters.

We do not believe that Mrs. Coyne—
professionally known as Ms. McGrail—is
either psychic or fey. We do know, however,
that she often puts together components of
a problem in a way that escapes our skills.
We have rarely discarded her insights and
we have never been wrong in listening to
her."

And so as the wind assailed our old
wooden home and howled through the cran-
nies and the snow continued to fall in our
alley, we discussed the problem of whether
we should cancel the taping of the Lullaby
Christmas special.

"'Tis all part of the plot against the Donlans," she insisted. "It escalates each time.
First it was just a leak in a gossip column,
then it was a lie to stop a wedding, then an
assault on Jack Donlan, then an attempt to
kidnap Maria Donlan with intent to gang
rape, now a car bomb in a crowded parking
lot to kill hundreds of people. There is madness behind this escalation. The plotter
grows increasingly angry as his clumsy
schemes are foiled. He now plans mass
murder."

"We should understand," John Culhane
continued, "that Nuala's insights have never

led us astray. When she senses trouble, there is trouble brewing, as we learned in the matter of the attempted kidnap in front of St. Joseph's Hospital. I believe we have to take this insight very seriously. The risks are too great if we do not."

Deputy Superintendent Glen, a tall, solid, charging-end person, was uneasy with the prospect of police involvement with what seemed a supernatural matter, as he should be. Reliable Security was a private company. If it wanted to take seriously the uncanny, that was its right, but the Chicago Police Department could ill afford the risk of media ridicule. The soundstage was not in Area Six's jurisdiction, but it could offer the usual protection for public events, though it would be better if Reliable Security took that responsibility. Ms. McGrail would be within her rights to postpone the taping.

My wife was calm and articulate. She would inform the network of a threat to the taping and recommend that it be canceled. Doubtless they would take her advice. They would have to say that there was a threat with which the Chicago police were not prepared to deal.

Sometimes when I watch my wife, I feel

that I couldn't possibly be married to this beautiful woman and experience the evanescent desire that attacks a man's brain when he sees a beautiful young woman walking down the street. It would be nice to make love to her, but in a civilized society men don't do that kind of thing, don't even dwell on it in their imagination. Therefore I could not entertain lustful emotions in the present circumstances, whatever they might be.

No way.

The conversation was polite. Glen and Casey called each other "superintendent," though the former was only a deputy superintendent and the latter a retired superintendent.

In the repetition of the lines required in the discussion, Mike Casey played the role of the sophisticated Irish politician who sought in all disputed matters a sensible compromise.

"Reliable could always provide a security net around the soundstage and search every car that comes in. It would delay the event. It would be better if we could deploy a massive cordon of force."

"I can't see my way clear to doing that, Superintendent."

"And you're prepared to say that, Superintendent, if we should lose the mayor and the senator and their wives to a terrorist's bomb?"

"I don't think that will happen, Superintendent. . . . What's that noise?"

"It's our two Irish wolfhounds," I said. "They're retired police dogs. They've been upset all afternoon. They've been trained to sniff trouble."

Glen sighed patiently.

"You realize that you're asking me to accept the warnings of a psychic and the instincts of a couple of dogs?"

"I'm not a psychic," Nuala said. "I'm one of the dark ones."

"My wife means," I insisted, "that she's a mystic."

"Whatever!" He threw up his hands.

The dogs shut up. Nuala can tell them to shut up without speaking a word to them.

I consider that scary. She also sees the auras around their heads, halos if you will. I would consider that creepy if the halo around my head hadn't convinced her that she would have to sleep with me someday.

Or so she would later tell me.

"There is no way we can keep this out of

the media," Commander Culhane insisted. "If we go ahead with a massive security cordon, it will be news and if the network cancels the taping, then there will be tough questions asked at the news conferences tomorrow morning."

"Mike, that's not for me to decide. What I need is a better reason for that cordon than signals picked up from the supernatural."

The dogs began to howl again.

"Well, then, I suppose that we'll have to take the bombs off me motorcar won't we?"

"Now?"

Lieutenant Nikos Mashek spoke for the first time, his quiet Slavic face shining brightly.

"How do you know that the bombs are in the car?" Terry Glen demanded.

"Weren't we after telling you that the hounds are police dogs? That car makes them nervous. It has all day long."

"We can't disarm a bomb here in the middle of a snowstorm!"

"Depends on the bomb, sir. I can inspect the car and see if there is explosive material on it. Then I can activate my unit and do whatever is necessary."

"Do you mean evacuate the whole block?"

"That's what we're trained to do, sir."

"How do you know that it won't explode while we're looking it over?"

"It hasn't blown up yet. If Ms. McGrail's suspicions are correct they intended it to explode tonight."

"It didn't explode when I was driving it home from down below this afternoon, it's not likely to explode now. They put the bombs or whatever into the car so that it would blow up during the concert tonight. There'd be no point in it exploding now. . . ."

"Unless they were careless or sloppy," the lieutenant said. "There's always that possibility."

Reluctantly the cops donned their overcoats. I helped me wife on with her black leather jacket.

"Well, Dermot, we'll go to heaven with all our kids, won't we now?" she whispered.

"They'll only let me in on your say-so."

"Sure, don't they know up there, that you're a livin' saint?"

"Let me calm down the puppies. Like I said they're police dogs. They love cops and they'll know you're cops and will want to be friendly. Tell them how wonderful they are."

In the kids' playroom, the hounds stopped

howling and erupted in joy at the smell of cops. Perhaps I should say "other cops."

"Chill out!" Nuala ordered.

Reluctantly, they sat back on their haunches and awaited further instructions, troops prepared for battle. Superintendent Glen gingerly ignored them. Lieutenant Mashek patted them on their heads.

"Nice doggies," he said.

The hounds were delighted. They were working with cops again. If we were all blown up, they would go off to doggie heaven happy to the bitter end.

"You have the keys to your car, Nuala?" he asked.

Silently she handed a set of keys to him, keys to every room in our home and in a pinch a useful weapon.

"Superintendent Glen," he said at the door. "You've been on the force for how long? Twenty-eight years? How many members of my unit have we lost in that period of time?"

"None, Nikos," he said, "and we're proud of the unit's work."

"And no civilians?"

"Not a one."

"We won't break that record tonight."

"You'll be needing this floodlight." Nuala handed him a floodlight that she always kept in a closet on the ground floor. There were a few streetlights in the alley, not much use in the blizzard which was wrapping everything in a thick white blanket.

"You'd better stay in here," Nikos said to us, "until I come back from my car with my tools. In fact you can stay inside all the time. If the car should blow up, you won't be safe inside or outside."

He tried to push out the door to the alley but the wind resisted. I pushed with him.

"Thanks, Dermot," he said with a wicked grin. "I guarantee you there's no danger here, not much anyway."

"I am reassured," I said with a touch of irony in my voice.

He chuckled, a guy from the neighborhood, not this one, but a neighborhood somewhere.

The hounds gamboled out after him and leaped through the snow, ecstatic to be back on the force again and at the same time playing in the snow.

In a few moments Nikos returned carrying two small briefcases.

"Not many tools," I whispered to me wife.

"Hush, Dermot," she said to me, "isn't he a nice young man with two sons and a daughter on the way?"

She was showing off.

We walked to the Lincoln which was just a few feet away from the door.

"I've activated my night unit," he announced. "They'll be here soon. And quietly, like I told them."

Then he began to examine the car with some of his mysterious instruments, a medieval wizard plying his secret craft. Cautiously he opened the door of the Navigator and opened the hood. I was fingering my rosary. Me wife was peering over his shoulder. I stood next to her.

"Where are the explosives?" I whispered.

"Isn't it obvious? Aren't they in the boot? The puppies are letting him do his work and then they'll tell us all."

He examined the motor and the ignition and the gas tank with great care, moving an instrument like a long thermometer in and out of the innards of the car's machinery. Then he crawled under the huge vehicle and explored its underbelly.

My sweater and leather jacket were poor protection against the winds and the whirling snow. I was shaking with the cold. The snow assaulted the skin of my face. My feet were wet from the slush and the wind shook me from head to toe. My wife of course wasn't shivering at all, at all.

Finally, covered with snow and grease and looking like a circus clown, Lieutenant Mashek crawled out from under the Navigator.

"Sir," he said to the superintendent, "there are no explosives linked to the ignition and none in any of the usual places in the motor or under the car where they are usually placed. . . ."

The hounds bounded to the back of the car and growled at the fender. Then they howled.

"The boot," Nuala shouted above the wind and the wailing hounds.

In Dante's inferno, hell is a frozen place. I felt that I was in its antechamber.

We huddled over the trunk, Nuala, Nikos, Glen, and myself. I was hoping that I was in the state of grace as we used to call it and realized once again that the God of Jesus was not a hanging judge. The father of four children should not be out in a blizzard and himself watching a nerveless cop try to open the trunk of a car which, if the snarling hounds were to be believed, was filled with high explosive.

Nikos had put on thick gloves and was wearing the standard police armor, neither one of which would be much protection against a car bomb, one that might demolish our whole block on Sheffield Avenue. He inserted the key into the lock and turned it. But the key was somehow jammed in the lock and wouldn't turn.

"It worked yesterday," Nuala protested.

"Someone messed with it after you closed it," Nikos said softly. "Probably pried it open so they could put in the explosives."

"There'd be no reason for the explosion to happen before the taping this evening," Nuala said confidently. "Why waste all that effort on a block on Sheffield Avenue."

My Nuala Anne didn't seem at all frightened. But then maybe she could see things that I couldn't.

Nikos tried again. The lock wouldn't budge.

"Let me give it a try," my wife ordered. "I'm pretty good with contentious locks. . . . Just like contentious husbands."

We all laughed nervously, meself louder than anyone else.

The door, knowing as I did who was the boss, promptly sprung open. I peered inside cautiously, as if looking at the explosives would set them off. A piece of tarpaulin covered a shapeless mass.

Nikos ran one of his little magic tools over the mass.

"As I expected there is no indication of an ignition device which would cause an explosion at this time. Everyone can relax."

"I'm shaking because of the blizzard," I protested.

Everyone laughed again.

Nuala clutched my arm. We would die together just as the ancient warriors, male and female alike, died together.

With a gentle and delicate movement, Nikos pulled back the tarp.

"Just kids' schoolbags," Superintendent Glen said, as though he were disappointed.

"Madrid," Nikos and I said together.

"When the jihadists destroyed the commuter trains in Madrid," Nikos explained, "they put the explosives in backpacks which did not seem to have any traditional ignition mechanism. They did not want them to explode before the proper time. Instead they used the insides of cell phones. When someone called the number, a simple device connecting the phone to the bomb ignited the explosive material. All the bombs went off at the same moment. With these pastel-colored backpacks, intended for little girls like my own, you need to ignite only one of the packs. When it explodes it will ignite all the others. You would have quite literally a blockbuster."

The hounds howled again, just for the record I suppose.

"This device—" he produced from his kit of surprises a slender instrument, about a foot long, with a scale running its full length. "—will measure each of the backpacks for the presence of metal, like a mobile phone mechanism. I will assume that like all crazy people, these morons had a sense of symmetry and that they chose the center bag." He touched the far left bag first and then the next one. He skipped the center and touched the final two. In each case, the instrument flashed on and off.

Then he touched the central backpack. His magic wand went crazy, flashing red lights and howling. The hounds not to be outdone howled in response.

"That's the bag with the ignition mechanism. Now, my last bit of magic, this camera is no ordinary camera. Rather it photographs the inside of the bag, penetrating the fabric around it. Moreover it produces a picture in thirty seconds."

He flicked a switch, the camera made whirling and swirling sounds like a small waterfall. Then it spat out a three-by-five picture. Nikos considered it carefully.

"You were right, Dermot. It is the same kind of mechanism used in the mass murders in Madrid. Note the lumpish material that fills the bag. That's the plastique, the plastic explosive. The bright red object as you can see is the innards of a cell phone. Someone dials the number, the ringer is activated and with it a current that flows into this blob of explosive and ignites it. The result is an exploding car bomb, or in this case an exploding truck bomb. In a crowded parking lot many, perhaps most of the gasoline tanks would explode almost at once. Instant mass murder. I am going to disconnect the ignition and remove it. In that way the truck bomb is permanently defused. . . . I presume, Nuala Anne, that during the rehearsal yesterday, they pried open the trunk, quickly dumped these bags into the car, and departed. It was a chance, but they are people used to taking chances. Fortunately for us, Fiona and Maeve knew that something was wrong and alerted us to the problem."

He patted the large heads of the great white dogs and they tried to lick his face.

"Chill out!" Nuala ordered. The dogs settled down on their haunches, panting happily.

"They were also taking the chance that you would not notice the bags and that your security resources here"—he patted both dogs again—"would not sniff something wrong. Their scheme was to mine the car when there was no one around, you would drive it home, and not activate the bombs. Then you would drive it into the parking lot this evening. They would be located somewhere in the vicinity. Once they saw this distinguishable vehicle, they would know that they could activate the bomb at their leisure and with a simple phone call kill hundreds of people."

"Well done, Captain," Superintendent Glen said.

"Lieutenant, sir."

"Not anymore."

"Thank you, sir . . . I will now remove the ignition device. I assure you that there is nothing at all dangerous in this exercise."

He removed a sharp knife from his bag of tricks, cut open the center bag, lifted the remains of a mobile phone, snapped the wire that fed into the plastique, removed the mobile carefully, and placed it in a transparent evidence bag.

Me wife loosened her compulsive grip on my right arm.

"If I may make a recommendation, Nuala and gentlemen." He began to assemble the tools of his trade. "When our bomb truck arrives, we will transfer the explosive material and bring it to our headquarters. I will drive this impressive vehicle to the appropriate lab and demand that it be swept for all available evidence. I would suggest that forensic teams finish their work in early afternoon and return the car to its present location. Then Nuala and Dermot could drive it over to the soundstage. In the meantime the force could search the neighborhood for the observation post of the perpetrators."

"I personally will direct the search," Terry Glen said. "Moreover we will throw a cordon of cops all around the soundstage and its environs. We will also search every car entering the parking lot—even the mayor's car."

"Having informed him earlier in the day of the situation," Mike Casey said with a laugh.

Terry Glen echoed the laugh.

"I'll tell him the whole story. He'll love it."

The police brass left us, their cars slipping and squirming down the alley. The big bomb squad truck arrived, lurching into the alley like a clumsy dinosaur. Some young cops examined the Lincoln repeating the steps that Nikos Mashek had taken. Then they loaded the backpacks into the truck. Nikos shook hands with us and the dogs, climbed into Nuala's car, and turned over the ignition. The Navigator started smoothly and followed the dinosaur down the alley and out on the street. Suddenly our alley was quiet. The wind subsided but the snow continued to fall, like your man said, on the living and the dead.

— Nuala Anne —

WHEN I woke up, I wondered what day it was. The sun was shining and there was kid noise outside and a couple dogs were barking enthusiastically. My dogs and my kids? I reached over to ask me husband what was happening. He wasn't there. Where was my friggin' husband?

We had slept in each other's arms all night, too weary to do anything more exciting. What day was it? If the kids were playing outside at this hour—my alarm claimed it was ten o'clock—it must be Saturday. Something important was supposed to happen on Saturday. What was it? Something very important. Nothing in court. Some test at TCD? No, I had four kids outside playing in the snow. I hadn't attended Trinity in ages. . . . What was it?

Then I remembered—the Christmas special . . . *Lullaby and Good Night* . . . I had a terrible nightmare about it. . . . A big explosion . . . Then I remembered it all and bounced out of bed. Had someone really tried to plant a bomb in my battered Lincoln Navigator?!

I put on me robe, stumbled over to the window, and peeked through the blinds. There was me friggin' husband out there rolling in the snow with me kids. Didn't he know we had a concert. The kids should be resting their voices.

Then the phone rang—the private line.

" 'Tis meself."

"Who else would it be?"

Familiar voice.

"It might be me friggin' husband and himself outside in the snow playing with me kids."

"You sound like you had a terrible night. . . . Or was it a bad run-through yesterday?"

"We were up terrible late altogether."

My memory started operating again.

The blizzard had been real. The bombs in the boot of me car had been real. The dinosaur truck had been real. I wanted to cry.

"Everything's all right?" Maria asked.

"Everything is brilliant," I said, crossing me fingers.

"My family," she said tentatively, "would like to come to the concert. By that I mean my five daughters and my poor, dear husband."

"And how is that good man keeping?"

"Much better . . . They've fixed him up so he's not reluctant to go outside. . . . You can get us tickets?"

"It's me own concert. Of course I can get you the tickets. Why don't you come over to our house."

"I'll be right over."

I hung up and thought about jumping into the shower. But the phone rang again. It was Dermot's private. We have a rule in our house—well, didn't I make it—that he can't answer me private line, but I can answer his.

'Tis only fair.

"Nuala Anne."

"It's Dominic, Nuala."

"Hey, Dom, what's happening? . . . Me Dermot is outside playing in the snow."

"My friends tell me that their friends have cornered the bad guys in a house on Ohio Street, Nine Eighty-seven West, right near your concert place. They don't know my friends are on to them. But my friends want to know whether they should put them down or leave it to the cops."

"I think me husband would say that it's better to leave it to the cops. Let me have Dermot call you back in five minutes, okay, Dom?"

"That's beautiful. But no more than fifteen minutes."

I put on me sweater and me jeans and me playing-in-snow boots and rushed downstairs, Dermot's mobile phone in me hand.

It was bitter cold, but the sun was shining brightly.

"Dermot Michael Coyne!" I shouted, instantly regretting the possible damage to me voice.

He knew after all the years of marriage that was a command.

It was bitter cold, so I stood at the top of our stairs staring down to the ground, waiting impatiently.

"Wasn't I thinking all along that I was sleeping in your arms, and yourself outside playing in the snow and ruining the voices of me talent."

And then, before we could get into an argument, I told him about Dom's call and gave him his phone.

"I'll see what Mike Casey says."

As he punched in Mike's number, I whistled me letcha-come-in whistle. The kids and the dogs froze in their tracks and then disconsolately gathered their snow things and trudged up the stairs.

"Youse can play all day tomorrow," I told them, "after church, but won't you be needing your singing voices tonight? Take off your boots and then inside with youse."

I always feel guilty when I use my boss voice with the small 'uns. They should not be afraid of their mother, should they?

The two puppies were the last ones up the stairs. They paused hoping for some sign of approval, as if they were saying, they weren't singing tonight, were they? I patted both of them and they charged happily into the house, doubtless working havoc with the parlor rugs. I followed them in.

"Downstairs with the lot of youse!"

"Ma," Nelliecoyne pleaded with me, "Da wouldn't let us shout."

"I know that, dear."

"You just wanted to remind us?"

"Just wanted to remind you."

Diplomatic little bitch, wasn't she?

Dermot was talking to his friend Dominic.

"My contacts at the department tell me that they'll collect the bad guys in early afternoon, so they'd appreciate it if your friends keep an eye on them until the contacts get all their players in place. They also direct me to say that they're very grateful for the cooperation of your friends. If anything happens over on Ohio Street, you might give me a ring. . . . Uzbekistan, that's an interesting innovation. I'll pass that on. . . . Our cars are clean now. . . . I appreciate your concern. . . . Once again thanks for all the help."

He smiled at me, the same smile which has melted me heart since the first night at O'Neil's pub. He pushed another button on his mobile phone.

"Mike? Dermot . . . The boys apparently have the bad guys under surveillance on the West Side. They say they're commandos from Uzbekistan. My feeling is that you good guys should proceed with caution but get them all out of there, one way or another, by four this afternoon at the latest. . . . Mike, don't give me that. Those Soviet-trained commando units traditionally bring mortars with them. It's an easy shot from where they are to the parking lot or to the soundstage itself. There'll be some activity there among the cops when the mayor's car shows up. . . . Or the senator's . . . Doesn't the Chicago Police Department have tear gas anymore? And what if the bad guys have gas masks? . . . You remember the Powell Doctrine? Right, maximum force! . . . Helicopters overhead . . . We're certainly not coming over in the red tank and we're not coming at all until that place is cleaned out."

"Trouble?" I said meekly.

"The friggin' cops don't get it. I've told them where the commandos are and they have to take them out now or they'll spread through the neighborhood shooting at anything in sight. . . ."

"Dominic's friends might be willing if the cops are not?" I asked.

Me Dermot's face brightened.

"Why didn't I think of that?"

He punched in Mike's button.

"Busy signal . . . I'll call Culhane. . . .

"John . . . What the fuck is going on with you assholes?"

I looked around to see if any of the kids were present to hear Da engage in cop talk.

"Don't they understand that they're black berets from Uzbekistan. They're tough, resourceful, and just a little crazy. If you're not going to use maximum force then don't bother. . . . I don't care what anyone says. . . . Look, my friends on the West Side are perfectly willing to take them out. . . . They will if I say so. . . . I want to hear in fifteen minutes or it will be St. Valentine's Day Massacre all over again. . . . What will they do? I don't know and I don't care. . . . Maybe they'll drive a truck bomb into the two-flat. . . . Fifteen minutes . . . Have your friend Terry give me a ring. . . . Or I'll call the mayor and tell him that the taping is canceled and why. . . .

"Woman," he said, as he hung up, "I want me breakfast. . . . No, wrong line . . . Woman, come down to the kitchen and I'll make you some breakfast. . . ."

Who was the Irish Tiger now, I wondered. Poor dear Dermot said I was. But I was frazzled and scarcely coherent and wasn't he giving out something fierce altogether. Normally I make breakfast because I'm up a little bit earlier, though Ellie does it often these days because she does her best studying in the morning or so she says. Danuta comes in around breakfast time and insists on making something healthy. But today Ellie is finishing a paper and Danuta doesn't come in on weekends. So I let Dermot make me favorite breakfast, oatmeal with brown sugar, apple juice, and toast with marmalade. He hates the very sight of marmalade which he says pollutes perfectly good toast. But this morning wasn't he slathering it all over.

"You didn't feed yourself, did you?"

This in the tone of voice that suggests that of course he had.

"Woman, I did and the chiles too."

"Aren't you a perfect whirlwind of a Celtic Tiger?"

"Woman, I am."

His mobile rang.

"Dermot Coyne . . . And the best of the day to you, Terry Glen . . . Ah, you want to thank me for the support. . . . I scared the big brass did I? . . . Well, good enough for them . . . Look, Terry, there may be only a handful of them and they may not feel like dying quite yet, but the CPD can't afford to be too little and too late. . . . Your very point? Lots of fingerprints on the bags? That will help. . . . Hey, sure enough, the tank is back in the alley where it belongs. . . . You'll excuse me, but our family will come over in one of Superintendent Casey's limos. . . . We're retiring the M1A1 tank until we find the time to fix the grille. . . . Me wife likes her cars to look sharp. . . . Yeah, she sure is . . . becomes more beautiful every day . . ."

"Dermot Michael Coyne, you are totally full of bullshite!" I said, blushing at the exchange of compliments. . . . "I have put some of that awful raspberry stuff on a couple of slices of toast for yourself."

"God bless you and keep you!" he says to me. He likes to talk like he's a mick when he's nothing but a friggin' rich Yank.

"And aren't you acting like you've become the Irish Tiger and meself a shattered wreck!"

"Well, you're going to have a nice long nap this afternoon and won't Ellie and I get the clan ready for the concert."

"'Tis yourself who deserves the nap. . . ."

"I won't hear a word of it. You have to be your smiling self tonight!"

"I don't deserve a husband as good as you, Dermot Michael Coyne."

"As Archbishop Blackie would say, arguably."

Our eldest appeared, camera in hand.

"That cute Ms. Connors is here, Ma. She said you had tickets for her."

"Thanks, cara. Did you get a good picture of her?"

"Wouldn't it be impossible, Ma, not to get a good picture of her!"

"She won't stay long, Dermot love, and then I'll be off to the land of Nod."

"And not a minute too soon."

Maria Angelica was sitting in the parlor, in slacks and NIU sweatshirt, drinking a cup of tea and eating some of our remaining soda bread.

"That little imp of yours is a wonder," she said. "I have too many daughters of my own these days, but I'd be willing to trade any two of them for one of her. She did a wonderful portrait of me without my even noticing it."

"Better than the one in that real estate magazine?"

"No cleavage but sexier. I ordered a half dozen copies at five dollars each—a real bargain!"

"No trade! Won't she be supporting me in me old age . . . How's the old fella keeping?"

"He's fine, though the companies are slipping. Not too much yet . . . We can make love again which is nice. I lived thirty years or so without much sex and was none the worse for it. Now in sunset years I find a man I love and I can't get enough of him."

"Which he enjoys?"

"He's astonished. Can't understand why he's a sex object. I wonder if it will last."

"Why shouldn't it?"

"I've not been lucky with men."

"That's your old story. Now you have a new one. As long as you're good to him, you'll have a very happy marriage, even if he's occasionally an eejit."

"Such a sweet eejit," she said with a weak sigh.

Why should I laugh to myself at that? I had whispered the same words to meself about my poor, dear Dermot.

"And the daughters?"

"A lot of strong emotions trying to focus. It's working out, but like I tell them, I'm not a referee or an appellate judge, only a dorm mother."

"So you'll be needing seven tickets for tonight?"

"I will, if you have them."

"Sure, why wouldn't I have them? It's my show isn't it now? And won't I be glad when it's over!"

"It will be brilliant altogether, to use your terms."

"There will be a small party afterward backstage. Nothing stronger than a splash of Baileys . . . All you need is the tickets. Not long because we must get the small ones home."

"One more thing. My son tells me that my brothers are acting strange . . . laughing at the incident in front of St. Joseph's. They say that I'm finally getting what I deserve."

A light flashed in the back of my head. There was no time to investigate it, but it would stay there and I'd return to it tomorrow.

"Sweethearts, aren't they? Nothing will happen to you, Maria Angelica, as long as you have one of the Reliables around. It will all be over soon anyway."

I said that with more confidence than I should have. I knew, however, that it would be over by Christmas.

"Why do your brothers hate you so much?"

"Gina and I were popular in school, they weren't. I had good grades, they didn't. They're clumsy, I'm an athlete of sorts. I made it in the town's elite, they never had a chance. They're ugly and I'm not. My mother hated me and she loved the boys, she turned them against me. I was a traitor to the family. They were always loyal. It went on and on and on. They could do nothing wrong. I did nothing right. She spoiled them rotten. They've always been little boys who never had to grow up. When someone or something frustrates them, they react with rage. The mob in Chicago almost killed them."

"Not nice people?"

"I'm sorry, Nuala, you touched a sensitive spot in my memory. I try not to be angry at them. . . . I try to forgive them. I think I have and then someone asks about them and my fury comes back. . . . I don't think they're killers. Don't have the courage for that."

Somehow that information calmed me. I would have a good nap this afternoon.

I stopped at the door of Nelliecoyne's

darkroom. The red light was off, so I knocked.

"Come in, Ma!"

"Ms. Connors said you took a real sexy picture of her and sold her a half dozen copies."

"Should I have? She insisted."

"Congratulations . . . We'll have to start charging you room and board."

"You'd never let Da do that," she said with one of her big grins. She showed me her first print. It was indeed very sexy. No way it wouldn't be at this time in Maria's life.

"Very sexy."

"She has beautiful boobs, Ma. Just like you."

"Are the other kids napping?"

"Not the Mick. He's drawing pictures. Aren't the young 'uns dead to the world, as I will be in a few moments."

"It will be wonderful tonight, cara."

"Of course it will, Ma."

So I went up to the master bedroom where me poor dear Dermot was waiting for me. I thought he might want to make love, but he took off my clothes and put me to bed with a promise.

"I'll wake you up in two hours, woman. We can't have you groggy tonight. Then we'll have our showers and engage in a little light focking."

"With you, Dermot Michael Coyne, there is no such thing as light focking."

Then before I knew it I was sound asleep.

— Dermot —

AFTER PUTTING herself to bed, I went back to the Situation Room and turned on the TV monitor of the CPD, which we weren't supposed to have, but we managed to obtain nonetheless. It picks up the same feed which goes into the superintendent's office. We didn't watch it much because the fare was usually pretty dull. I had no doubt that the top cop would be watching with great interest. Terry Glen's career was at stake. If he carried this caper off, then he'd be the next man. From what cops told me that would please the present boss and most of the force.

The monitor showed a quiet street in a very old neighborhood on the near West Side, some abandoned buildings, some vacant lots, some ancient brick two-flats, once superior housing for the emergent middle class, maybe a century and a quarter ago, back when the Cubs were winning championships a mile or so away at the old Playing Fields.

We were a half mile away in an unmarked van, probably an unprepossessing near wreck. Cars went by, looming large for a moment and then disappearing off camera.

My mobile rang.

"Dermot."

"Dominic . . . I hear from my friends in the neighborhood that they're pulling back out of sight. They'll see what happens and let me know. I'll be in touch with you."

"Stay out of there, Dom."

He laughed.

"Derm, you're the crazy one, not me."

As we talked a large, grey buslike thing lumbered down the street toward the camera. It stopped in front of what had to be the house where the commandos had established their command center. Instead of windows it had gun ports out of which automatic weapons protruded. No one fired from inside the house or from the armored bus. In case there was any doubt the blue letters on the side of the bus spelled out "Chicago Police Department—Tactical Unit 1."

Then a second and similar vehicle pulled into the alley behind the two-flat and clumped behind it. The gun ports opened and more automatic weapons appeared.

At the far end of the street, out of the line of fire, scores of police cars and other vehicles appeared and cops set up street barricades. Only a few cops left their cars. This was perhaps the combat infantry who would clean up the remnants after the battle was over. I had heard that the department had purchased some vehicles (pronounced always as *vee HIK ils*), but I was not prepared for the next grotesque monster—a broad, squat thing which looked like a heavily armored tank, with a squat pillar on top, a large artillery piece jutting from its front and two lighter weapons, looking like the Gatling guns from the Civil War or the Philippine Insurrection, poking out of recesses in the front. At the end of the pillar a radarlike device with a red light spun nervously. I was a couple of miles away, but the scene scared me.

The tank featured on its front a mammoth shovel which looked like a huge front loader. It wheeled around in front of the house and paused. The spinner on the tank spun furiously.

Then a man appeared in an open window on the second floor of the flat with one of those grenade launchers that we see on TV in the hands of Middle Eastern "militants." A puff of smoke appeared in the window and the grenade leaped out of its launcher. Suddenly the tank threw up what looked like a large steel hand, deflected the grenade, and hurled it back at the two-flat.

An incomplete forward pass. An agile cornerback like Mike Brown of the Bears.

Then a barrage of small-weapons fire erupted from the house, pinging noisily like hail on a tin roof against the sides of the armored bus.

"We're taking fire, sir," said a voice presumably from the bus.

"Well," said Terry Glen, "return the fire."

The Gatling guns on the tank rose from their recesses and began to eat into the bricks of the house. Then the automatic weapons in the gun ports on the buses opened up. The windows disappeared, some of the walls disintegrated, the front door vanished. Smoke poured from the house.

"Try the tear gas!"

A long arm appeared at the top of the tank, leaned over toward the disintegrating structure and, casually almost negligently, distributed several tear gas canisters through the available openings.

A white sheet appeared from one of the windows. Surrender.

"We know there are four of you in there. Come out of the house without your weapons and your hands in the air. If there are any missteps you will all die."

Then the command was repeated in a Slavic language. Russian. Best we could do.

"Ten seconds and we will begin firing again."

Four battered men, two of them wounded, staggered out of the remnants of the two-flat, hands over their heads.

"Get them in the bus and get out of there. The residence is filled with explosives."

A door opened in the side of the bus and a set of stairs unfolded. Four men in grey armor appeared and helped the prisoners into the bus and the stairs folded. The bus inched away from the wrecked two-flat and trudged down the street toward the camera. Suddenly there was a loud *whuf* as the building turned into a red and black fireball. The camera shook, the bus heaved to the side, and the strange tank thing rocked back and forth in alarm, its antenna quivering in the blast. Then a nozzle appeared from the top of the machine, spun toward the flaming two-flat, and emitted a thick stream of heavy liquid which turned into foam as it encountered the flames. The tank was prepared for absolutely any eventuality. A brilliant contraption altogether.

The fire was quickly snuffed out. No noisy Chicago Fire Department required. Then, as if offended by the temerity of the two-flat, the tank lowered its front-loader shovel and attacked the smoking ruins, reducing them in short order to a mass of rubble. Finally, it swept the remains into a neat pile, doused it again with foam, and then harrumphed back on Erie Street and, as if wiping off its hands in satisfaction lumbered toward the camera and then out of sight.

My mobile phone rang again.

"In case you're wondering, Dermot," Mike Casey said, "that monster, appropriately named Godzilla, operates completely on remote control. Tactical has been waiting eagerly for a chance to try it."

"And no media there to observe and record."

"Precisely . . . The only problem is that there were just a few terrorists. We don't know for sure what would happen if we had forty or so holed up in that building and they were real terrorists instead of out-of-work commandos."

"Either they would have surrendered or that monster—"

"We call it Godzilla."

"—would have stacked them up in neat little piles . . . I suppose your good friend Terry Glen will have a press conference on Monday and let the media take pictures of Godzilla from a safe distance, let it inundate them with foam."

"It does have a mind of its own. See you tonight. The boys in the blue uniforms will swarm on the ruins and dig out whatever they can. We'll have a thick cordon of them all around the soundstage tonight. Enjoy!"

I turned off the monitor just as a swarm of "civilians" tried to push against the police barriers to inspect the modestly withdrawing

Godzilla. I checked my recording to make sure I could show it to Nuala before I destroyed it.

The word *modestly* reminded me of another Saturday afternoon responsibility I had.

Outside in the playroom, the kids, up from their naps and still in their pj's, were playing with their various amusements, the TV was playing *My Fair Lady,* and Ellie was teaching Patjo to read, an exercise he seemed to enjoy.

"Hi, Uncle Derm! Did you have a horror movie playing in there?"

"Godzilla!"

"I just love *Godzilla,*" Socra Marie announced.

Nelliecoyne was working on a scrapbook of her pictures.

"Will Mr. Donlan and Ms. Connors be at the show tonight, Da?"

"They wouldn't miss it for the world."

"Good! I'll give her the copies of my picture. Ma says she looks real sexy."

"Ma would know."

Upstairs in our master bedroom, Ma was sleeping peacefully, looking like an innocent teen. Once again I found it difficult to believe that this beautiful woman was my wife and indeed the mother of my four rug rats. My desire for her surged as though she were a new conquest. Yet I felt sorry for the enormous burdens that had intruded into her life, mostly because of me. She shouldn't have to assume all the Christmas responsibilities that would weary her next week and then fly "home" on the day after Christmas. But then she wouldn't be Nuala Anne, the Irish Tiger.

She opened her eyes and saw me standing above her. Her face eased into a smile of adoration, which broke my heart every time I saw it. I didn't deserve that kind of love. However, since it was there, I might just as well take advantage of it.

"You're late for our tryst, Dermot Michael Coyne."

"Only two minutes."

"Sure, wasn't there a time when you'd be five minutes early."

"I didn't want to cheat you out of an extra minute of sleep."

"Well, make yourself useful and turn on the shower to just the right temperature and yourself knowing how much I hate a shower that's too cold or too hot."

— Dermot —

NUALA ANNE was radiant and relaxed as we drove in the Reliable Lexus from Sheffield Avenue over to West Ohio Street. She glanced at me occasionally and winked, sharing the joy of our marital love. She led the gossons and the colleens in singing some of their favorite lullabies which they would sing later in the evening. First the "Castle of Dromore":

The October winds lament
Around the castle of Dromore
Yet peace lies in her lofty halls
My loving treasure store

Though autumn leaves may
   droop and die
A bud of spring are you
Lullaby, lullaby,
Sweet little baby,
Don't you cry
I'd rock my own little child to
   rest
In a cradle of gold on the
   bough of a willow
To the shoheen ho of the wind
   of the west
And the lulla low of the soft
   see billow
Sleep baby dear
Sleep without fear
Mother is here beside your
   pillow.

Then they turned to their absolute favorite, the Connemara lullaby which all the mothers of Carraroe had sung to their daughters for generations and which according to family legend had kept Socra Marie alive in the hospital when she was too small to come home.

The childish voices were a pleasant background to my delicious memories of the amusements of our tryst in the shower and afterward. It had been a dangerous gamble on God's part to permit such pleasure to humans. It did bind husband and wife together but the bond was a two-edge sword which could so easily tear itself apart. Well, there was no point in being philosophical at the present moment, sometime in the next couple of days I must start the poem that had been hiding in my head, not quite ready to emerge fully blown like the mythical Venus on the seashell.

The car, even with its Reliable sticker, was searched thoroughly by apologetic but competent cops. Then we had to go through a door frame like the kind they keep at the Federal building and the county courthouse.

The rest of my family would go backstage. I hugged each one of them and told them that they were wonderful. Me wife hugged me and whispered, "Well, Dermot Michael Coyne, won't you do as a lover until someone better comes along?"

"See you later," I said.

"She didn't seem nervous at all," Maria Donlan murmured to me as I found my seat in the row in front of theirs.

"She's chilled out," I explained. "She

refuses to worry on the day of a performance. 'Tis a waste of energy altogether."

I was nonetheless uneasy. We had done lullabies before and that special had been enormously popular. Now we were stretching for politically correct Arab lullabies, Sea Island lullabies, Russian lullabies, Chinese lullabies, African-American lullabies as well as Irish lullabies and the ones that everyone knew and loved. This did not mean that Nuala sang less but that she sang translations (that she had made) after the native singer and then the two joined together in a final chorus. It would be a tour de force if it worked. Moreover the kids and the Old St. Patrick's choir would background almost all the numbers. The choir was flawless of course. The kids were problematic. Not problematic, however, was Nuala. When she put on her Christmas special persona, she became the smooth, sleek, Irish Tiger whose rare mistakes carried on the performance. Her daimon at the Christmas special was flawless and carried the performers, the technicians, and the audience.

She left behind the barefoot lass from Galway and talked Trinity College Irish, patently Irish to the uninitiated, but all the wonderful diction of the West and its slang, not to say its vulgarity, left far behind.

"Good evening! It is good of you to permit me to visit your home again this year to sing my songs and help you to get in the mood for Christmas or whatever your mid-winter festival may be. I promise you that I will intrude on your peace and quiet for only a little less than an hour and that my children won't be disruptive. This year we're doing lullabies again, singing some of the old ones and adding some new ones from all over the world. We'll begin with the favorite American Christmas carol, a blues carol written by Irving Berlin and sung famously by that great Irish American jazz singer Bing Crosby. I'm asking the kids from our Sheffield Avenue neighborhood and everyone in the audience here and at home to join in."

My Nuala can sing a song in its proper color no matter what's going on around her. She has the knack of carrying an audience, just as easily as she waves a hand at the Sheffield Avenue chorus. We sang "White Christmas" the way it ought to be sung—a blues carol. I was weeping at the end as was the mayor on one side of me and the senator on the other side—and most of the Donlan-Connors crowd behind me.

I relaxed. It would be the best special yet.

She glided from scene to scene and from performer to performer like a benign fairy godmother or perhaps a friendly local seraph. Her gracefulness permeated the performances, the soundstage, and I'm sure the millions watching.

And this was the same wanton woman with whom I had romped earlier in the day. Grace is indeed everywhere.

"I should tell you that the young mother and child are Arab Christians, Assyrian Catholics but their lullaby, I am told, has been sung by Arab mothers to their children, regardless of their religion, for thousands of years. Mary may have sung a lullaby like that to Jesus.

"Now as some of you might expect I'm an Irish-American and proud of both heritages. I'm from a place so far out in the West of Ireland that the next parish west is on Long Island. Out there in the town of Carraroe many of us speak the ancient Irish language, which was made to be sung. So I'm going to sing our own favorite carol in Irish and then in English. And I'm going to sing it to my youngest Patrick Joseph Coyne. . . ."

Applause for the little blond brat.

"We call him Patjo and everyone says that he's just like his father, big, blond, handsome, and laid back."

She sat on a chair and accompanied herself on the harp. Patjo, the little scamp, rested his head on her thigh just like he was going to sleep.

"Now we're going to sing it in English with his brother and sisters and some of the kids on the block. . . ."

On the wings of the wind, o'er
**   the dark, rolling deep**
Angels are coming to watch o'er
**   your sleep**
Angels are coming to watch over
**   you**
So list to the wind coming over the
**   sea**

Hear the wind blow, hear the wind
**   blow**
Lean your head over, hear the wind
**   blow.**

The kids sang as though they really liked the little monster (which they did) and blew like the wind with enthusiasm and, for them, wondrous restraint. And so it went, the show did not drag, her voice did not falter. Her grace did not fade, her charm did not wane. She was getting better every year. And not just in her songs either.

There was a brief five-minute break halfway through which Nuala used to talk about her own family.

"I'm delighted that for the first time people in my other country are watching this program on Irish television and that my mom and dad, me ma and me da, as we'd say over there, are watching it out in my home town of Carraroe, which is the most beautiful little village in the west of Ireland. *Nollaig Shona Duit* to everyone in Ireland and especially to everyone in Carraroe and especially my mother and father."

A panoramic slide of that lovely little village appeared.

"Now we're going to start the rest of the program with the second and last Irish lullaby—the 'Castle of Dromore.'" The kids rushed out, lined up smartly, and let their mother lead them. Socra Marie was off-key as always and won everybody's heart.

The program moved along briskly, not losing a beat in its tempo as it wound down.

"We have one last lullaby, maybe the most
famous of them all, written by the great German composer Johannes Brahms. It's the
theme of tonight's program. My daughter
Mary Anne and I will sing in the original German and then in English and I want everyone to sing the English along with us."

Nelliecoyne appeared carrying her
mother's small harp. She was dressed in
Christmas red and green appropriate for an
eight-year-old. Great applause and a nod of
her head in return. She had a junior version
of her mother's stage presence and a lovely
little voice to which her mother deferred in
the German version. Then "Lullaby and
Good Night."

"Now that we're in German, let's end the
program with the greatest of all Christian
carols. Let us imagine that we are in Bethlehem honoring the Baby Jesus or our own
most favorite new baby . . . but not so loud to
wake him up."

The Sheffield Avenue choir, led by Socra
Marie and Katiesue, scurried into position.
Shaped by Nuala's restrained singing the

program eased into a conclusion. Nuala turned to face the millions all around the world.

"Thank you for letting us sing in your homes again this year. Good night, Happy Christmas, and with the help of God till we meet again."

The ovation from the listeners rocked the building. Then they began to clap and demand an encore. Nuala hesitated, shrugged her shoulders, and took the small harp out of her daughter's hand.

"I'll sing one more song and that'll be the last one. . . . One cold rainy night a long time ago I was sipping a pint in O'Neil's pub just off College Green, minding my own business and studying my world economics book. An obnoxious Yank sat down at my table and tried to chat me up. He was kind of cute, but not very perceptive. So when the people in the pub started to shout for a song, I figured that was an excuse to dump this Yank. So I sang this song. The Yank, who obviously had no manners, just sat there at my table and stared at me. I haven't been able to get rid of him ever since."

So she sang "Molly Malone." After all these years it still makes me cry.

As the crowd left the hall and passed through the line of police guards, a few of us drifted back in to the bowels of the studio for a small splash of Baileys. The mayor walked next to me.

"How did you like our Godzilla?"

"She's totally cool and adorable," I replied. "I was disappointed that she didn't get to show off all her little tricks."

"It's nice to know she works," he replied.

My radiant wife greeted me at the door to the party room, with a plastic cordial glass containing a generous splash of Baileys and a broad smile, just short of a grin—still in control of the event with her grace and charm.

"Not bad," I said hugging her cautiously so as not to spill either of our jars. "Not bad at all, at all . . . You improve with age Nuala Anne McGrail."

"So do you, Dermot Michael Coyne, so do you!"

Her one arm hug became more insistent.

The Sheffield Avenue rug rats did not run wild. On the contrary, they behaved decorously as they accepted congratulations from their admirers, quite unfazed by the praise of the mayor and the senator and the various functionaries of NBS and Kosmic Entertainment. The president of the latter, a nervous but exuberant little man, was especially lavish in his praise of everyone.

"You're her husband, aren't you? . . . She's a delightful young woman. . . . Her performance was reviewproof. . . . Most of them will be good anyway. . . . We'll have DVDs out by the middle of next week. . . . I think we ought to make a film about her. . . . There'd be a tremendous market. . . ."

"You'll have to talk to her about that. . . . I'm not her agent, you know. . . . She acts for herself. . . . She's a tough one. All those West of Ireland women are tough. . . ."

"Still you're a very lucky man!"

"Tell me about it."

"You look good for yourself," I told Jackie Donlan a few moments later.

"My wife has had a lot of experience as a caregiver. . . . Also at managing a high-energy group of young women!"

"That project goes well?"

"It will take a little time for them to under-stand and adjust to one another, but they seem to genuinely like one another. They're going home tomorrow so we won't be running a sorority house anymore. . . . And my wife and I are going back to work on Monday. Maybe our lives will settle down. Christmas dinner in Oakdale next Saturday."

"Business is okay?"

"It would seem so. My eager little gnome, Joey, worries a lot, but nothing much will happen in the markets till after New Year's. Then the world will know I'm in charge again and we'll be okay. It will take some time, but we'll bounce back fine."

Only if we—well Nuala—can sort out the puzzle.

"Not an easy transition, Jack."

"Nonetheless, as you can imagine," he blushed, "a very welcome one . . . And we still have a honeymoon ahead of us, maybe in February."

"Best time to get away from Chicago."

In our family there were no vacations, save for trips to Grand Beach and Connemara and they weren't vacations. I'd have to work on that.

"Dermot love, I think we should get the chiles home. They're beginning to fade and we have a big week ahead of us. And Mass in the morning."

Only two Masses.

Indeed yes. A big week. Christmas shopping. Gift wrapping, tree decorating, carol singing, Aer Lignus to Shannon. Mad rush there. I'd get my annual cold. Then back to Chicago and back to school.

Ugh. I needed a honeymoon too.

We took the kids home and put them to bed and then staggered in our own room for a last little jar to calm our nerves then to bed for a quiet night.

"You're the best husband in all the world," Nuala whispered as she sank into sleep.

"Till you find a more resilient one."

She was, however, sound asleep as I was a few minutes later.

Still we have a puzzle to solve.

— Dermot —

THE KIDS were irritable, Nuala was snappish, and I was glum—not exactly a band of cheerful Christians on the fourth Sunday of Advent. Why do we have to go to Mass twice? None of the other kids do. Why can't we play in the snow before it melts. Mass at St. Josephat is dull. Mass at Old St. Partick's is dull. Didn't we sing enough last night?

You're nothing but a bunch of heathens. You're lucky you can go to Mass in two churches. Stop fighting and pay attention to the priest. It is *not* boring. Dermot why don't you do something about your children?

I think it's *boring* too.

You should be ashamed of them.

It's not their fault. We're all worn out. It's just a letdown.

Da's right. We're all let down. It's natural after a big victory. Just like after a big volleyball game.

You're a little pagan and yourself with the use of reason.

I've given up the use of reason. Besides Da's right.

He is not!

He is so.

All of youse be quiet. I have a terrible headache.

That stopped them cold. The very thought that poor Da might be sick always silences the murmuring. What would happen to the family if poor Da were sick? I didn't use this tack of poor sick Da very often. It always worked.

But then we were back in the kitchen for our Sunday brunch which we all make together—blueberry pancakes, scrambled eggs, piles of bacon, Quaker Oats for Ma, soda bread, and maple syrup over everything and everybody. And lots of treats for the doggies who had been left alone last night. It is a family myth that we all make it together because Da presides over the effort, does most of the work, and prevents the younger kids from throwing syrup-drenched pancakes at each other.

Then the kids went to the playroom and Ma and Da to her study. (I have an office and she has a study, which is not to be confused with her music room where she has a piano. The next thing she'll be wanting is a "meditation" room. She also has an exercise room which I can use when she's not.)

"We may have to cancel the reservations to Shannon," herself said as she sank into her thinking couch. As always she approched a problem from the perspective of the consequences of not solving it.

"We have a whole week before we'd leave."

"The week before Christmas is not a time to solve puzzles."

"'Tis true," I admitted.

"And ourselves knowing not much more than we did at the beginning."

I had been idly glancing through the Sunday papers. My article on Congressman Stafford had yet to appear. I saw a heading in "Eyes and Ears."

Peace on Earth for Donlans?

It would appear that the divided Donlan clan has decided to kiss and make up. The daughters of stock tycoon John Patrick Donlan (Donlan Assets Management) are now praising their new step-mother, Maria Angelica Connors (Elegant Homes). "We were not fair to Maria and we feel terrible about it. She's a wonderful woman, very sensitive and sympathetic and very, very witty. She and her kids are welcome additions to our family and they don't seem to mind us in their family. We're all going out there to Oakdale for Christmas." The combined families were in town for the taping of the newest Christmas special of singer Nuala Anne McGrail. Ears hears that all the reviews will be ecstatic.

I read the item for me wife.

"Just asking for trouble," she fumed. "They need a convoy of armored cars to get out there unless we can untangle this mess. . . . Well, what do we know about it, Dermot?"

"If we assume that from the false allegation at the wedding, to the bomb plot last night were the work of the same perpetrator, that person is a clumsy amateur who has access to some dangerous people, not approved by our friends out on the West Side, that he becomes more reckless each time he tries something, and that he knows how to cover his tracks."

"And why is he doing these terrible things?"

"He seems to want to destroy both their businesses, especially Jackie's."

"Why?"

"For some reason he hates him or maybe both of them. He's obsessed by his hatred. He started low key when he tried to ruin the wedding. Then when that didn't work he escalated."

"Mad?"

"One would think so."

"Does he have anything personally to gain by it?"

"Other than personal satisfaction, probably not. Unless it is Joey McMahon. He thinks that he could buy out the company and make more money on it than Jack. He's probably wrong. I suspect that someone else would buy it out first if it came to that. Someone with deeper pockets than Joey."

"Disgusting little rodent."

"True enough. But where does he get his troops? Even if there may be wiseguys in his neighborhood, they'd be afraid of offending the boys to say nothing of the political organization."

"He's been out to Oakdale, hasn't he?"

"To do some of the preliminary work on the deal."

"He might have heard about Maria's brothers and talked to them. Maybe a deal to get rid of both Jack and Maria . . . Drive them out of business and then do physical harm to them."

My Nuala would think of something like that.

"We don't have any proof of that. Ster Stafford might have used them as a go-between."

"Give over, Dermot Michael. Your version of the congressman tells me that he never recovered from being hit in the head by the camera our friend Maria Angelica threw at him."

"Yet he clearly worships her."

"He had a terrible way of showing it."

"For which I think he is genuinely sorry . . . In any case he is not smart enough to fake his admiration and regret. In a strange way, he seemed almost glad she defeated him in the election."

"Fair play to you, Dermot love, sometimes you're wrong about women, but never about men. I'd just as soon not leave him out of the game, though if you don't mind, I'd also like to call him tomorrow morning."

"Be my guest."

"Still. That leaves us with the possibility that the rodent, and Lou Garner and the brothers Sabattini might have entered a conspiracy against our clients, doesn't it now?"

"It does, though Garner is too clever a small-time gombeen man to mix himself up with anything as crazy as the assaults on our clients and then the attempted murder of our family and perhaps our neighborhood."

She considered this for a moment.

"So in this perspective we are considering, without any evidence, save for the characters of the people involved, the possibility that Joseph McMahon in conspiracy with Maria's brothers, is the solution to our case?"

"An eminently plausible thesis, love of my life. All we lack is proof."

"And also any conviction on my insight that this theory is correct."

"Alas, 'tis true."

"We should ask that nice Mr. Casey if he knows of any evidence at all at all of any link between them recently."

Mike the cop is always that "nice Mr. Casey" when I'm expected to call him. So, loyal spear-carrier that I am, I called him and it being Sunday morning.

"Casey."

"Coyne."

"Wasn't herself brilliant last night, dead friggin' brilliant!"

Mike likes a phony Irish brogue.

"Brilliant altogether . . . We have some matters on which we need your input."

"Why does that not surprise me?"

"Is there any reason to think that Joe McMahon has had recent contact with the Sabattini brothers out in Oakdale and secondly has he had recent contact with Lou Garner, a gombeen man who went to school with Jack Donlan?"

Nuala scribbled on a piece of paper. "Tell him about the Christmas plans."

"So that's the way herself is thinking? You're right about Lou being a gombeen man. Joey and the brothers out in Oakdale?

That's an interesting idea. It will be a little difficult, but I'll see what we can find out."

"If you haven't risked your Sunday peace by reading the papers, you'll be pleased to know that Eyes and Ears reports reconciliation in the Donlan family and a planned Christmas dinner in Oakdale."

"Isn't that nice now!"

"An invitation to the bad guys. And they'll probably be quiet all week to lull us into thinking they have the Christmas spirit. . . . Joey would figure that he'd take over DAM, eh?"

"Wrongly, I think, though that would depend on how much money he has socked away. More likely it would be a target for a hedge fund or private company like Blackstone . . . Anyway we'll get on it first thing in the morning. . . . Don't forget to watch the Bears."

"Game doesn't matter. They're in the playoffs anyway."

"Anytime they play, the game matters."

"I figure that without Tommy Harris and Mike Brown they'll never win the Super Bowl."

There was a faint smile on me wife's face when I hung up.

"Don't bother watching them today," she said. "They'll lose."

"You don't have to be fey to figure that out."

"I don't know why I didn't think of an alliance between Joey and the brothers, Dermot Michael," Nuala said. "It fits perfectly. Crazy and sloppy."

"They'll probably do something crazy on Christmas, blow up the house maybe."

"Och, Dermot, this time won't they be more subtle?"

"What will they do?"

"Poison!"

"Poison?"

"Slip something deadly into what everyone will eat, something that might not show up in an autopsy."

"We'll have to stop them?"

"Faith, Dermot, of course we'll stop them, but this time we'll have to get the evidence against them."

The "dark" one was back. I shivered a little. That persona scares me a little anytime she sneaks into the house.

"Why don't you call your poor da, and himself knowing everything there is about medicine and everything else besides."

Poor in this case meant "long-suffering." He was the instant pediatrics consultant for all his children, though in his career he'd been a cardiac surgeon.

I called him.

"Doctor Coyne."

"Nuala's husband."

He loved all his children and their spouses, but he had a special soft spot for his own mother, Mary Anne or Nellie as she was always called. Hence our Nellie was the super favorite.

"I see by the papers that she will get great reviews for her special."

"Probably on Wednesday morning. It was the best yet. She improves with age."

"That doesn't surprise me."

"She wanted me to ask you a question."

"Something about a nefarious way to commit murder?"

"Just so . . . Imagine that she wanted to wipe out a whole family with poison at Christmas dinner. What would be a convenient and safe way of doing it?"

"Well, she might introduce a very powerful dose of E. coli into the dressing. We've had a lot of E. coli poisoning going around lately. It would be lamented as a tragic accident."

"Where would they get it?"

"Your local hospitals keep cultures around, for comparative purposes. They're watched pretty carefully. Still . . ."

"If someone wanted it bad enough . . ."

"That would be a simple way to do it. I hope you're able to catch them before they do any harm."

"Count on it."

Nuala, who had been listening on the other phone, looked glum.

"Didn't herself tell me that one of her nieces works at Kishwaukee Community Hospital, just down the river from Oakdale?"

"And I'd bet that a niece or a nephew works at the supermarket where the Connors do all their shopping?"

"This is too easy altogether, Dermot."

"Easy to know what they're doing, hard to stop them."

— Nuala Anne —

THE NEXT morning was another bad 'un for me. At my age in life I should know meself well enough to understand that after a successful show I would experience a deep letdown. But I always forget until it happens again. If the special didn't do all that well, I'd bounce back immediately, but when it is a huge success, as *Lullaby and Good Night* was, I go into a tailspin. This is very Irish of me, but as I've learned here in Yank land, I am very Irish—cheerful and brave in defeat, melancholy and depressed in victory. My poor dear husband has figured out through the years to put up with moods and bring me back to the real world. He let me sleep in this morning, made breakfast for the small ones, and then took them over to school. Then he's meeting with his publisher about the contract for the new novel which will be about me, like they all are and are very flattering, though no one recognizes me because the character in the story has such a stable disposition. I didn't even wake up to wish him good luck, not that he needs it because they are so desperate for a new story.

Poor Dermot needs a vacation away from this house, away from the kids, and away from me too. Except that would never work. So I would have to go with him. His parents would love to have the kids to themselves for a couple of weeks. I'll just have to talk poor Dermot into it.

Anyway thank you for sending me such a wonderful husband. Help me to be a better wife to him and help us solve this puzzle so Jack and Maria can have happiness together while there is still time. And themselves with at least thirty more years of life. We can't go to the Cayman Islands until we solve it. Now make me get out of bed and have some soda bread and a cup of tea and get to work. I love you and thanks again for me poor dear overworked husband.

The first thing I did after my breakfast was call that nice Mr. Casey. I chatted with his wife Annie Reilly for a couple of minutes. She's so sweet to me, though she thinks I'm round the bend altogether.

"Mr. Casey," I says to him, "I presume that me husband told you that I think there will be another assault on the Donlans on Christmas out beyond in Oakdale?"

"Woman, he did!"

"And he told you that I think there is a conspiracy between the Sabattinis and this rodent Joey McMahon?"

"Woman, he told me that you *knew* this to be true!"

He likes to imitate Dermot Michael when me poor husband tries to imitate me.

"So you'll be after monitoring his phone calls to the Sabattinis out beyond?"

"Haven't we started that already and doesn't it confirm what you *know*?"

Me heart jumped just a bit. So I was right after all.

"Sure was there ever a doubt?"

"Not at Reliable . . . He's making most of the calls from his office, which shows how reckless he is. Haven't I been talking to the sheriff out there who has no love for the Sabattini boys? Won't we be keeping an eye on them?"

"Good on you, Mr. Casey . . . You'll keep us informed?"

"Is the Pope Catholic?"

I hoped that I would be as lively as Mike and Annie when I'm that old and that me poor husband still loves me as much then as he does now. There's no good reason why he should and meself being such a nag. How much longer will I be a good lay? . . . Now that isn't fair to me poor dear Dermot at all, at all!

I thought about it all and decided I'd better chat with Maria Angelica again. I called her at her office.

"How are both of youse keeping?"

"I'm keeping fine, my spouse still hurts all over, but that doesn't interfere with his love-making."

"Still. And your company is doing well?"

"As good as ever, given the present state of the housing market. It's DAM we're worried about, but we'll know how much all this scandal stuff is hurting after the first of the year. My husband still has a few tricks up his sleeve."

"And you'll be feeding the whole clan on the feast of Our Lord's birth?"

"My daughters and stepdaughters will be doing most of the work. In the end I suppose I'll have to banish them all from my kitchen if I'm going to get any work done."

I sighed in loud protest. "'Tis the way of it all, isn't it? . . . No cousins invited?"

"We don't have any cousins. . . . Oh, you mean my brothers' kids. . . . They've all been raised to hate us. Won't speak to any of us. They're afraid of us too. . . . The sons are thugs like their fathers, except the one that's studying science at CalTech. The family doesn't like him either. Why waste your time with that stuff when you should be home helping us in all our small-time deals and crimes? . . . People tell me that they think now that they have the local franchise on the Sopranos."

"They kill someone every week?"

"They're too dumb to be able to do that. It would be nice if they went to Vegas or somewhere like that and leave this town alone."

"Isn't one of the daughters a nurse over at the hospital?"

"Camilla . . . or Cammy as they call her,

sister to Tammy who works at our local supermarket. Steals from the store all the time. My kids tell me that Camilla is not all bad. Wanted to be friends with them when they were teens, but too shy to try it. Shy is not fashionable in that branch of the clan."

"Cammy and Tammy, sound like a sweet pair," I said.

"I wouldn't mind having them over for Christmas dinner, but Tammy would steal the silverware."

When we were finished with our gossip, I called Mr. Casey again on his mobile. He wasn't there, so I left my message about Cammy and Tammy.

Then me poor dear Dermot Michael called me.

"Nuala Anne."

"Me first wife, is it?"

"First and best!"

"'Tis true."

"Did you get your friggin' contract?"

"Woman, I did."

"And?"

"Well, they actually want three books instead of one, though they all have to be about this ditsy woman."

"The one that's fey?"

"I wouldn't go that far. She thinks she is one of the dark ones."

"A lot you know about the dark ones . . ."

"They're petty good stretched out naked in bed, I'm told!"

"Give over, Dermot Michael Coyne! You have a dirty mind altogether!"

"I'm just saying what I hear."

"And?"

"And they have gorgeous tits."

"You know what I'm asking!"

"You mean the money?"

"I do!"

"You never tell me what Kosmic Entertainment is paying you."

"'Tis a different matter altogether! You're not the family treasurer."

"I don't remember when we elected you. . . ."

"How much are they paying?"

When me dear sweet Dermot is teasing me and also trying to stir me up from a distance, he can be a desperate man!

"Well, since you put it that way, a lot more than you told me I should ask for. You can retire now, Nuala, and we can spend the rest of our lives making love all day on a beach in the Cayman Islands."

"You're round the bend altogether. . . . But congratulations anyway! You can show me the check when you come home!"

I told him about the developments on the Donlan case that morning.

"It looks like we'll be able to fly to Ireland after all," he said. "I'll be looking forward to my annual Irish cold."

"Well, I'll keep the bed warm for you won't I and make the soup!"

When the man is teasing me, he can be a real amadon.

Stretched out naked on a bed! Well, he will be waiting a long time for that to happen, won't he now!

Till tonight anyway.

Please God, don't let him get sick this time.

— Maria Angelica —

ON THE Wednesday afternoon before Christmas, the day before Christmas Eve, I returned to Oakdale to prepare the Christmas festival. At Jackie's insistence I went home in a Reliable limo. I made him promise he'd do the same. The bad guys were still around somewhere. I didn't think they'd take time off for the holidays. I stopped at the office where my son Pete was holding down the fort while reading the Barchester saga.

"Nothing happening," he said, barely looking up from the book.

"Go home to your family, Pete," I suggested. "I have some phone calls to make."

ANDREW M. GREELEY

"Okay, but then I won't be able to finish this book today."

"Your daughter is more important."

His eyes twinkled mischievously.

"I guess so . . . How's Jackie?"

"Dutiful and obedient. He'll be out tomorrow."

"Maybe you shouldn't stay home alone tonight."

"No one would try to harm me here in Oakdale."

"If you change your mind, give us a ring. We'd be glad to have you share supper with your granddaughter who might even throw something at you if she's in a playful mood."

I almost said yes. I should have said yes, but then I wouldn't have met my late-night visitor.

There was a big stack of Christmas cards waiting for me. I opened them carefully and set aside those to whom I had not sent a card or those who merited a special note of sympathy or congratulations. There was one, astonishingly enough from Sterling Silver Stafford in which he congratulated me on my marriage and wished me many years of happiness. He added that he and his wife were going to settle down in Oakdale after the first of the year and suggested we all have dinner sometime later. It was a peace offering. I would reply that my husband and I would welcome a dinner invitation—a return offering of peace. I gathered up the cards and the other mail and asked the Reliable man to drive me home. Then I suggested that he could drive back to Chicago and collect my husband who had better feel as lonesome as I was. Well, I didn't say the last clause, but I thought it.

So when I entered our house two blocks behind the office and turned on the lights, it looked very empty and very old. Well, it should have looked that way. It was empty and old. And I was lonely. In all the years since Peter's death I had never felt lonely here. And it wasn't Peter's absence that made me feel lonely. I hoped that he wouldn't mind my bringing another man into his home and into his bedroom. The blessed in heaven are not jealous are they? I love him, Peter, I said. That doesn't mean I will ever stop loving you. But this is different.

I had yet to make love to Jack in our bedroom. I would certainly do it at Christmas, no matter how many people were in the house or in the charming motel down the street. We all had to move beyond such a critical symbol. It would be hard on Jack's daughters. Their love for me was genuine enough in the sense that they wanted to love me and had begun to love me, but still had some doubts. For that I couldn't blame them. Everyone would be on their good behavior, too good perhaps to relax. By next Christmas we would have bonded sufficiently to be able to argue and fight.

Enough philosophy. I was lonely and I wanted to tell my man that I was lonely.

"Jack Donlan."

"I think I may divorce you and yourself leaving me all alone out here."

"You're beginning to sound like that lovely Irish witch."

"I want you, Jackie, and I want you here."

"It was your idea that—"

"I know it was my idea, but you shouldn't have agreed with me. You know how besotted I have become with you."

"We'll make up for it tomorrow."

"I'll hold you to that promise. . . . I hope you have a difficult and lonely night."

"I'll try my best. I hope you have a good, quiet night with peaceful dreams about our first Christmas together."

"You too," I replied. "I didn't mean what I said. I love you."

"And I love you, Maria Angelica."

We both wept, more from love than loneliness and said good night. I made him promise to call me before he went to sleep.

I walked around the house, getting a feel for what it was like now that I had a new husband. The house was not interested in my changed state in life. It still tolerated me as did the ghosts of those who had lived in it for more than a century. I knew that their spirits checked in periodically to make sure I was being good to the house and departed approvingly. They did not live there anymore, but lived elsewhere. They were happy spirits.

Was this all my superstitious Italian soul, or my serene Catholic faith? I figured that the two were not all that far apart.

The phone rang and I jumped, startled out of my mix of nostalgic reverie and physical loneliness. It was the sheriff.

"Hi, Maria, good to have you home for Christmas. It wouldn't be Christmas here in Oakdale if you weren't with us."

The sheriff, Jake Danzig, was an elderly man, of my father-in-law's generation, but sharp and competent. Also a loyal Democrat.

"Thanks for the welcome, Jake. It is good to be back."

"We're looking forward to seeing your handsome husband."

"So am I! He won't be here till tomorrow morning. I miss him already. . . ."

"I'd say that's a pretty good sign. . . . I know that you're not the nervous Nellie type, but I thought I'd mention that the Oakdale chief of police and I have arranged to have cars cruise by your house alternately all night long. Just a precaution."

"Thanks for the reassurance, Jake. It is just a little scary being here alone on the darkest day of the year. I'll sleep more peacefully knowing that the cruisers are out there."

And thanks to Mike Casey for alerting you.

His call and his flat Midwestern voice brought everything back to normal. It was my house and my town and my county and I was perfectly safe. I took off my clothes and put on a nightgown, part of my quickly assembled trousseau, and made myself a salad and a cup of warm herbal tea and settled in to finish the mail.

The phone rang again. My husband going

to bed and calling me to tell me he was lonely too.

A woman's voice on the other end of the line trying to find words.

"Uhm . . . I . . . Aunt Maria?"

"I think so . . ." I made a quick leap. . . . "Camilla?"

A rush of relief in the voice.

"Yes! Aunt Maria! How did you know it was me?"

"A pretty voice suggested a pretty young woman."

"Thank you . . . I have to talk to you, Aunt Maria. . . . Tonight . . . I'm sorry to bother you. . . ."

"No problem . . . Can you come over here?"

"I think I'd better . . . I'm out at the hospital. . . . I'll park behind your house in the alley and knock on your back door. . . . I hope you understand. . . ."

"Of course, hon. I'll be in the kitchen getting ready for Christmas, so I'll see the lights of your car."

"Thank you, Aunt Maria, it will be nice to talk to you."

I spent the quarter hour profitably preparing cranberry sauce. Almost to the minute a tiny car turned into our alley and stopped behind the garage. The lights went out and a slender figure emerged from the car. She was wearing a dark coat and huddling against the wind. I opened the back door as she approached it.

"Camilla," I said, opening my arms.

"Aunt Maria," she said, collapsing into them.

Inside the kitchen we both sobbed.

"Thank you for visiting me."

"Thank you for letting me into your house."

"Come into the parlor and sit down. May I get you something to drink? A glass of wine maybe?"

She hesitated.

"Just one glass. I have to drive back to the hospital. I live there now."

I took her coat and hung it in the closet, opened one of my bottles of Barolo, filled two glasses, and brought them back into the parlor. I turned on the gas fire in the fire-place, and offered a toast.

"Welcome, Camilla! You will always be welcome in this house."

She was wearing a nurse's uniform into which her young body fit neatly. She looked so much like a younger Maria Angelica.

"You are more beautiful than ever, Aunt Maria," she said. "You must be happy in your new marriage."

"Thanks, Camilla. I am very happy, happier than I ever thought would be possible for me."

"I am in love with a young psychiatrist on the staff, an Irish Catholic boy who is so good. He's in love with me too, I think. We are both very careful. I couldn't ask anyone to marry into my family. My father and uncle are both psychopaths. They have terrorized and brutalized my mom and my aunt. . . . My uncle has tried to assault me several times. I will not live in that house ever again."

"How awful, Camilla!"

"They are plotting with a terrible man from your husband's office to murder you and all your family here in your house on Christmas Day. I had to tell you."

"Joseph McMahon."

"Yes, that's his name. Like my father and my uncle he is on fire with hate."

"He has been behind several attempts to hurt us, hasn't he?"

"He is such an evil man. He and my uncles delight in the thought of torturing you. They were very angry when your friends thwarted their plot to kidnap you."

I shivered.

"We will thwart them again, Camilla, and we will protect you."

"I don't think I'm a psychopath. Yet I was caught up in their plan. I have to escape from the family."

"We'll protect you, Camilla, that I promise you."

"They want me to steal some poison from the hospital. I am to bring it on Christmas Eve and they will give it to cousin Tammy who will put it in the turkey dressing she will deliver here later in the day. You know what she's like. She has no conscience at all. Everything, no matter how cruel is a big joke. I'll take something harmless. If they find out, if they test the chemicals, they will rape me and kill me."

"They will do no such thing. You are under my protection from now on. . . . You have a cell phone of course?"

She gave me the number.

"You bring the poison to the house, early in the morning. Tell them you have to return to the hospital. And you come here instead. Will Mr. McMahon be in your house all day?"

"Yes, he wants to make sure nothing goes wrong this time."

"It will be the last time. . . . Do your mother and your aunt try to resist them?"

"Not anymore. They were peasants brought over from Italy. They have been beaten into submission. They hate their husbands and their sons, except for my cousin Nino who is at CalTech, but are afraid to try to break free."

"Terrible," I murmured. So much evil at this holy time . . .

"I must go back to the hospital, Aunt Maria. . . . This is very good wine."

"I promise I will take care of you, no matter what happens."

We hugged again and she slipped out the back door. I should call someone.

My husband? No, I wanted to tell him personally tomorrow and calm him down. Mr. Casey? I was afraid to call him. Who then?

The answer was obvious. Our good angel.

I punched in her number.

"Nuala Anne."

"Maria . . . I hope I'm not interrupting anything."

"In a half hour or so, you would be, but not yet."

— Nuala Anne —

I DIDN'T tell Maria Angelica the whole truth. She was interrupting us, just before what might be called the point of no return. It didn't matter because we knew how to slip back into the proper mood again.

I grabbed the pen and pad that Dermot keeps at bedside for any stray images that he might have in the course of the night. I scribbled down her report as me husband peered over me shoulder.

"Well done, Maria Angelica," I said when she finished. "We will stop them of course and get them with the evidence. Stay in

496 ANDREW M. GREELEY

close contact with that wonderful niece of yours. . . . She sounds like a junior Maria Angelica. Tell her that Nuala Anne and Dermot guarantee her safety. I suspect Mike Casey will want her to bring some deadly stuff so they will be able to make a good case against them. It will be the endgame for them all. Yes, we'll see that the women are protected.

"I was right, Dermot Michael, I was right. They were going to poison everyone at Christmastime and the rodent was part of the plot."

"You were right indeed, magical spouse. I never doubted you for a minute. I gave that up long ago. You'd better wake up Mike Casey. He will have to work this out with the Chicago cops and the local ones out there. Then we have some matters that you and I must finish."

"Well if you think I'd be letting you escape from your solemn duties, you're wrong altogether!"

So I called that nice Mr. Casey and spilled out the whole story.

"It's ball game, Nuala. We've got them all. I'll have to do some negotiating with the locals and the CPD. And we'll protect that brave young woman, never fear. I should tell you that we began listening in to your good friend the rodent yesterday and we already have enough to put him in jail for the rest of his life or perhaps the loony bin of our choice. I'll talk to you in the morning."

"Well, Dermot Michael, we'll go to Ireland on Boxing Day after all."

"I didn't know there was any doubt."

"Your health is the only doubt. I'll not force you to come home with me if your friggin' cold comes back."

"Nuala Anne McGrail, you and the kids are going home for Christmas regardless. . . . Now let's get on with our little pas de deux."

So we did and it was a grand dance altogether—even better because we finally had good news.

— Dermot —

THE NEXT day my good wife went off on patrol down Clybourn Avenue, the new shopping center for yuppies and other denizens of the North Side who needed to shop for a bunch of kids at the last moment. She wore her black boots, jeans, sweater, leather jacket, and ski cap, enough to strike terror in the heart of someone who would dare seize a present on which she had designs.

Since school was out, this was the assigned day for the kids to pack for the Irish venture. I was deputed to supervise this agony of choice with a strict set of guidelines that herself had provided. The harshest was that each child was permitted only one toy—Nelliecoyne's camera and the Mick's sketchpad did not count as toys. Socra Marie stubbornly refused to leave any of her dollies at home. They would cry themselves to sleep every night if they were rejected. Patjo claimed that he would bring all his toys.

I enforced the rules with the indisputable rubric of "Ma said." In Ma's name I triumphed in the end despite the tears. Moreover the young 'uns were mandated to bring only two changes of clothes—sweaters and jeans which are never dysfunctional in that wet and chilly island, especially in late December when the sun, having departed for the far horizon, tentatively explores the possibility of coming back and extends daylight by tiny increments, on those rare days when the weather permits daylight. The Irish compensate with warm peat fires, even in those places which have more advanced sources of warmth, which would include our three bedrooms in the new hotel in Clifden . . . as far west in Connemara as you can go without stepping on the sands of Long Island. Carraroe, as picturesque as it is, seems to be on a direct line for the winds and the storms which blow in off the Gulf Stream. In the hotel, one could have warm showers every day without paying more, wasn't the hotel designed for Yanks? In the homes of Connemara, that was often thought to be a needless expense, especially since it would involve removing one's long underwear.

I could feel my cold coming on.

The kids responded to their shrinking lifestyle by demanding to know why we had to go to Ireland for the week after Christmas when some of the other kids on the block or in the school were headed for warmer climes, like Florida or Puerto Rico or Arizona or Mexico. My response was that Ma had the right to be with her family at Christmas and to celebrate Mother's Christmas with her own ma. There were no assaults on the propriety of such a choice.

Mother's Christmas, aka Little Christmas, Twelfth Night, and the Feast of the Epiphany, which in the present state of the confused Catholic liturgy happens around or about January 6, usually earlier. However, the kids must be back in school on January 3, so in Connemara we reschedule Ma's Christmas to happen on December 31. It is called Mother's Christmas because it is supposed to reverse the protocol of Christmas Day on which mothers do all the work. On Mother's Christmas, the ma is not supposed to do any work at all, at all. Only one who knows nothing of the compulsions of Irish and Irish-American women will accept the possibility of such a phenomenon.

Anyway, while I was pondering these mysteries of our annual pilgrimage to the West of Ireland and wondering whether my sinuses were more clogged than normal, Mike Casey called me.

"Well, I've lined it all up," he said. "The arrest of the suspected perpetrators is in the jurisdiction of Kishwaukee County and its sheriff with help from the town police of Oakdale and back up from the Illinois State Police. However, since Chicago has a claim on some of the perps and almost a monopoly on the evidence, we will offer part of Tactical One— thirty sharpshooters who will be authorized to take out any perps who emerge from the house with human shields. The local cops will arrest all of the surviving perps, with the understanding that Joseph McMahon will be delivered to the sheriff of Cook County within the week."

"And the innocent women and children?"

"Everyone understands Camilla Sabattini is working with the police of her own volition and will be treated with gratitude and respect by arresting officers. We assume that she will be with Maria Connors Donlan. Reliable will have a cordon of armed cops at her home, just in case. The other women who may be in the Sabattini house will be taken into protective custody and perhaps brought to the local hospital for such treatment as is necessary."

"The local sheriff is in command?"

"Legally there can be no question about that. Your friend Terry Glen doesn't like that, but he knows he has to live with it. He also believes that there is enough evidence from the tapes of phone messages to obtain convictions in the courts of Cook County for all previous attacks. Finally, I am convinced that the sheriff is rock solid."

"Who authorizes the thirty snipers to shoot?"

"There will be only three, two primary, one secondary. The authority has been given to a consultant who has something of a reputation for coolness under fire."

"Michael Patrick Vincent Casey."

"And you're not even psychic!"

"What do we tell the heroic Camilla?"

"We tell her to deliver the harmless material she has obtained, no one wants to take chances with any foul-ups. We also tell her to leave her house and return to the hospital or to Ms. Connors's house. Under no circumstances is she to return to her family home until I personally tell Maria Angelica that it is secure. Moreover, under no circumstance is Maria to leave her own home and the protection of the Reliables assigned there until she is authorized to do so by me personally. I will relay all these instructions to her, but you or your good wife should pass them on to her today. I will keep her informed on her mobile phone minute by minute."

"You're not going to activate Godzilla?"

"I wanted to, but the locals didn't like the idea. It's their turf."

"What time will this all go down?"

"Precisely at one P.M. and don't you dare show up. You've taken too many risks in this mess."

"Do the locals know that if this plan fails, our friends out on the West Side will handle it themselves?"

"I doubt it. No point in complicating their lives."

I wasn't a cop, never had been. Much less was my Irish Tiger. No way that Mike the cop would dictate to her where she should be and when.

— **John Patrick** —

I TRIED to persuade myself as we drove out to Oakdale that I would not climb all over my wife immediately upon arrival at her house. A proper and gentle lover should know when restraint is appropriate. However, my head throbbed as I walked up to the door of the house and my desire exploded as she opened the door and smiled at me. She was unbearably, intolerably attractive and I was wildly hungry for her. I crushed her in my arms, kissed her passionately, bore her to the floor, peeled off her red and green Christmas robe, and devoured her. We both laughed insanely as our game continued.

"Best yet," she sighed compliantly when I was finished. "Let's go to my bedroom and act like civilized people."

"I haven't had enough of you," I protested.

"I didn't think you had. But I have some news to report."

She told me that Joe McMahon, my trusted aide, was the architect of our problems and now with the eager and clumsy cooperation of her own brothers. I was dumbfounded.

"He thought the scandals would force you to sell the firm and that he could buy it for much less than it was worth. He was envious of your success and resentful of his, as he saw it, subordinate position. He became more and more obsessed with his anger as we fended off his attacks."

"He is good at what he does, I'll admit that. He saw in your firm a real bargain without reckoning that you would be part of the bargain. But he is incapable of making a decision. I often asked him bluntly whether I should buy or sell stocks which were on the edge. He saw both sides of the decision but couldn't move beyond that. That was my responsibility and, among other things, he probably resented the fact that I found it so easy. He did not want to make mistakes. I realized that making mistakes was part of the game."

"You liked him," she said.

"I did. I'll miss him. I took him for granted, but I paid him well, not well enough I guess."

"From what I'm told it was not the substance of the payment but the fact that you made it. . . . What are you doing to me, husband?"

"Amusing myself . . . What will happen to him?"

"He'll be tried and go to jail. Nuala apparently suggested to the cops that they check the number of calls from his phone in your office to my brothers' plant out here. Then they obtained permission for a phone tap. They're planning to poison the lot of us at dinner on Christmas Day. . . . I didn't say you should stop playing with me. . . . It was a long, lonely night without you."

Then she told me about the visit from her niece Camilla and her promise to, in effect, adopt Camilla as one of her own.

"I knew, Maria Angelica, when I married you that you were beautiful, brilliant, witty, and a good bedmate. I didn't know then that you were a great woman. I now know you are. You've absorbed my three daughters into your clan without blinking an eye and now you take under your wing a frightened young woman who was raised to hate you. You are, as the young people would say, like totally awesome. The longer I know you, the more I see in you all that is love."

"Just so you don't leave me in a lonely bed too often. . . . Now let's finish what you started out in the parlor before the crowds assemble."

We did finish it, but I wanted more. Perhaps I would always want more.

"I suppose young 'just marrieds' act like we do," I gasped.

"I don't remember, but they don't have the experience with the opposite gender that we do and they don't know how important it is."

"Also," I added, "just how limited time can be."

"Speaking of time, the throngs will arrive soon. I'd better be up at work when they come, instead of lolling around like a libertine. Make yourself at home. This is our bedroom. Unpack your clothes and things and put them anywhere you can find room. If you disrupt any of my stuff I may take you into court."

Naturally there was an empty closet and several empty drawers which had been assigned to me along with a place in the marital bed. I showered and dressed in corduroy clothes that said *rural gentry.* I ensconced myself in a rocking chair in an enclosed front porch where a rural magnate might belong and opened the *Times* and the *Journal* and a book about the Enron scandal. However, I could not dismiss Joe McMahon from my mind. My dad had trusted him completely. I inherited that trust. I had never seen any evidence of resentment or disloyalty. Yet his anger must have festered through the long years. And he must have resented Maria immediately. I was responsible in some way for him. The least I could do was see that he got a good lawyer. No, that wouldn't do. Conflict of interest. Would they plead him on insanity? Who was there to stand by him?

While I was pondering these painful problems, a young woman, clearly Italianate, clearly with Sabattini genes appeared at the door and pushed the bell.

I opened the door, smiled my best country gentry smile and said, "Yes?"

"I'm Tamrya. This is Mrs. Connors's usual Christmas order of turkey dressing."

I accepted the package.

"Thank you, Tamrya. I'll give it to Ms. Connors."

"Bye."

She disappeared immediately, as if she had never been there.

Young woman, you have just become an accessory before the fact to the crime of attempted murder.

I wandered around the house, which obviously had been built in many stages, in search of the kitchen which had been hidden in a new alcove. It was the kind of modern, hyperconvenient "elegant" kitchen that Maria Elegante would have built. She was in the kitchen, huddled over a huge table with several lists and two daughters, a daughter-in-law, and a granddaughter. The latter beamed and gurgled with pleasure, perhaps because her grandmother would occasionally pick her up and swing her into the air.

"A young woman named Tamrya delivered this turkey dressing by hand for Mrs. Connors."

"I thought we were making our own dressing?" one of the daughters said.

"We are. . . . Jackie, would you be a dear

and take this package out to the man in the black car in the alley."

"Certainly! Good morning, ladies!"

"Good morning, Jackie!"

Knowing where I did not belong I made a quick retreat.

"I think, Sergeant, that Mr. Casey was expecting this evidence."

"Yes sir, he was. Turkey dressing. I'll see that he gets it."

I passed the kitchen, which was beginning to smell of many good things.

"Jackie, would you answer the phone for the next half hour please?"

"Happy to do something useful."

I did finish the *Times* and the *Journal* before the phone rang.

"Jack Donlan," I said, aware that this was not really my house, though as the spouse of the owner I had some minimal rights.

"Dermot . . . Nuala is on the other phone. We're calling to make sure you're there and all right."

"Never been better."

On reflection, I hoped that comment had not seemed too suggestive.

"We want to make sure you know all the details of what's going down tomorrow."

"I think so. The allegedly tainted but really not dressing has arrived. At herself's instructions I gave it to a Reliable who is standing guard in a limo out in the alley."

"And the arrest will be . . . ?"

"Christmas at one P.M., not an ideal time for an arrest."

"Nor for a murder," Dermot said. "These are bad people, Jack."

"I know that."

"Me point, John Patrick Donlan"—Nuala's voice sounding like that of a worried member of the seraphim—"is that under no circumstance are you to be anywhere near the arrest when it goes down, do you understand?"

"I don't get to ask why?"

"Absolutely not . . . You don't argue with one of the dark ones when it's a matter of life and death, do you understand?"

"Yes ma'am. To tell the truth I have no desire to be there."

"'Tis a fine instinct altogether. Maria Angelica doesn't deserve to be a widow again quite so soon."

That was ominous. However, I had no

desire to be present at the end of the chase and even less desire to disobey a witch, even if in this case it was the good witch of the West of Ireland.

I read the first two pages of the Enron book before the phone rang again.

"Jack Donlan."

"Uncle Jack, uh, this is Camilla. I'm a niece of Aunt Maria."

"I've heard of you, Camilla. It's a pleasure to hear you. I endorse my wife's promise to take care of you and protect you. . . ."

"Thanks, Uncle Jack . . . Could I talk to her for a sec? . . . I'm on duty at the hospital."

"She's meeting with the other magnates and potentates of this festival time in the kitchen and I'm the temporary switchboard."

"Well, she invited me to come to midnight Mass and stay over tomorrow. I want her permission to bring a guest. He won't need a room because he has to be back at the hospital by morning both days, so we won't need an extra room. . . ."

"I'll tell my good wife and I'm sure she'll call you back. But I don't think there'll be a problem. . . . Might I tell her the name of this fast-moving guest?"

"Uh, he's Johnny Burns, M.D. Senior psychiatric resident. He's really cool."

"I'll tell the good Ms. Donlan and I'm sure she'll be back to you immediately."

"Thank you, Uncle Jack. Thanks a lot."

I risked my life by venturing back to the kitchen.

"There was a call for the woman of the house from a sweet young woman named Camilla. She begs leave to bring a guest to the midnight Mass and to the dinner, but not an overnight guest because he has to get back to the hospital both days. His name is John Burns, M.D."

"Thanks, Jack. I'll call her back right away."

"Camilla!" exclaimed the three young women.

"Why not!" their mother said. "What difference does one daughter more or less make, when we already have a horde of them."

As the sun set on the very short Christmas Eve day, the participants in the festivity began to pour in, including my daughters who swarmed around my rocking chair.

"What a gorgeous old house!"

"Did Maria redo it? . . . It's so *her*!"

"And the town is *her* today, picturesque but not quaint! No way!"

By repeating such assertions frequently enough, they would persuade themselves that they had been wrong about my new wife from the beginning. Evie went to her assigned room to put the baby down and unpack her and her husband's clothes. He would arrive later in time for the collation at seven thirty—hot dogs, hamburgers, pasta, wine, ice cream, an indoor picnic.

I suggested to Mary Fran that we take a walk before twilight turned into dusk.

"I'm abandoning my guard post at the door," I informed my wife and her helpers in the kitchen, "and going for a walk in the twilight."

"I'll have one of the cars follow you."

As Mary Fran and I walked down the steps from the porch and turned toward the church, a black car started up the street and followed us at a distance.

"Car following us, Dad."

"Security."

"Will that always be necessary?"

"Only a little while longer. The danger is almost over. We're going to have another

M.D. here tonight, a shrink at that. . . . One John J. Burns, a senior resident at Kishwaukee Community Hospital."

"Johnny Jim, they call him. Brilliant practitioner and so gentle. Don't tell him I want to be a shrink. I'd be embarrassed. . . . Is he part of the family *too*?"

"Too early to tell."

I told her about the call from Camilla, leaving out the plot which was to be put down tomorrow.

"Maria is such a wonderful earth mother. . . . And funny too . . . I can tell you are still happy . . . even dizzy in love."

"Dizzier every day . . . How goes the stepmother crusade?"

"We're making progress. . . . Maria is so wonderful it was always hard not to like her. It's still a struggle for poor Evie. She is determined not to be wrong again. . . . Yet there are always little things that catch her up. . . . You'll be sleeping in Maria's room tonight?"

"If she'll have me."

"Oh, she'll have you. . . . But that's a little hard, for Evie, especially."

"Don't tell her, but I was in there this morning too!"

Mary Fran laughed.

"Of course you were, Daddy. Both of you are irresistible."

We had arrived at the church. Inside people were singing "Silent Night" and the stained glass windows were glowing. We turned to walk back to Maria's house. Our house now, I guess. Two family Christmas parties, I thought, one of them about murder, the other threatened by murder.

They were singing inside powered by a determined tenor voice, one that made most of the notes. Loud applause and then "O Holy Night!"

Inside the "collation" was being distributed and the guests were gathering around tables and TV tables.

"Mom said this was for you, Dad," Irene said as she pushed a platter of pasta Bolognese and a glass of wine. "It's Barolo."

I welcomed the red-haired Irishman who was obviously the tenor and the slender young woman who was leaning on his arm, Maria Angelica Sabattini of thirty years ago.

"Camilla," I said, "you look like my wife must have thirty years ago. God bless and protect you."

"I'll do my best to be as kind and good as she is and leave the looks to God."

"Johnny Burns, sir . . . And genes can be very powerful predictors, can they not?"

"Environment is equally important, sometimes more so," Nurse Camilla insisted. "That's why I'm so happy to be part of your family."

"I don't have much to say about it, but my wife says you'll be a great asset."

"And she's absolutely right." Johnny Burns consumed her with an adoring smile. "I've just met your daughter, though I've known her work for at least a year. Her paper on grace and therapy is brilliant beyond her years. We'd love to have her do her residency up here, but she is set on Loyola or Illinois at Chicago."

"I'm afraid that she's at the state now, Johnny Burns, where she analyzes everyone she meets."

"I did that till about eighteen months ago."

"More like six," Camilla murmured.

"You don't get respect anymore."

Then my wife appeared, freshly showered, sweetly smelling, and beaming in a long loosely flowing and yet closely fitting Christmas dress, dark green and trimmed in red. There were some gasps from the crowd at how beautiful she was. She took my arm in hers and waited till all the guests were quiet.

"I welcome everyone to our annual Christmas Eve collation and Christmas party tomorrow. As you know we have a ban on liquor from this minute until we return from midnight Mass. It is a bigger party this year and we fondly hope that it gets even bigger in the years to come. I welcome all of you, especially this gentleman here who captured me body and soul a few weeks ago. Pray for us as we all pray for you and welcome new family and old."

She kissed my cheek. Everyone applauded.

Yet more physical love for me tonight before the dawn of "Our Lord and Savior's Holy Birth" as Nuala Anne called it? Where was that Irish Tiger? I didn't feel secure unless she were around.

Evie took the floor.

"I'm the oldest of the new family and this babe inside of me is, as far as we know, the youngest for the moment anyway. I want to thank you, Mom, for making my father blush with happiness and protecting us as the Bible says under the shadow of your wings. You can count on us."

Applause, hugs, and kisses.

"That is a very seductive dress you're wearing woman," I said to my wife.

"I thought you wouldn't notice."

She hugged me again, very suggestively I thought. My somewhat austere upbringing had not prepared me for such openly seductive behavior. Either no one else noticed or they expected it.

We all trooped down to the church and crowded into it when the doors opened at eleven o'clock. There were trumpets and cellos and cymbals to stir up our emotion of joy and sadness and triumph as we sang the traditional carols. Father Matt preached a beautiful and blessedly brief homily. We were home for wine and fruitcake by one fifteen. Joy and love were back in the world and as the night wore on in our bedroom.

God, you have revealed your beauty and love in the glories of my wife's body. Protect us from the terrors of the morrow.

— Dermot —

WE ARRIVED at the Sabattini plant at five minutes to one. It was at the far edge of Oakdale from the old Connors house. It consisted of two ugly modern homes (right out of *The Sopranos*) in front of a large storeroom and garage covering twice the distance of the combined length of the houses. While they had lost control of their casino to a Las Vegas company, they still received a large annual payment from the new operators and had messed around in various local projects, both straight and crooked, and made little money from either kind. The cops arrayed around the "plant" seemed disorganized, confused, and dangerously close to the house.

"A frigging mess," I murmured to Mike the cop.

"I told you two not to come, with these trigger-happy goofs, it could be dangerous."

Two characters were standing next to Mike, a study in contrasts in rural cop stereotypes, Sheriff Jake Danzig and Oakdale Chief of Police Covington Bell. The sheriff was a wizened little man in civilian clothes with a fedora that went out of style a half century ago. The chief ballooned in riding breeches and an Ike jacket with Sam Brown belt and a gun holster. He clutched a high-powered rifle with grim passion. He had come to shoot.

"Jimmie, Paulie Sabattini, Joey McMahon, we have you surrounded. We are holding warrants for your arrest on charges of conspiracy to murder. You are innocent until proven guilty. If you surrender peacefully now, you will have the right to consult your lawyers immediately. We beg you to avail yourself of this right. Please come out of the house with your hands in the air."

"Amateur night," Mike muttered. "Someone is going to get hurt."

"The men inside are frightened, terrified,"

Nuala said, her hands clasped in something like prayer. "They can't think straight, they're so afraid. Poor scared little forest creatures."

"These cops are clueless," Mike said. "You guys don't belong here."

"They're not cool," Nuala said, caressing her weapon of choice, her camogie stick. "The people inside. They are about to do something wild. Be careful . . . Mike, they are terribly scared and terribly dangerous. Warn them that there have been no killings. There are no murder charges yet. Tell them not to take any chances."

Mike reached for the PA microphone. The sheriff, confused and befuddled by it all willingly gave it up.

"This is Superintendent Michael Casey. I am talking to James Sabattini, Paul Sabattini, and Joseph McMahon. The warrants we are holding for you are for attempted murder. That is not a capital crime. Your plot has been frustrated. No one has died. No one needs to die. Please come out with your hands up. No one needs to die today."

"These locals will start shooting as soon as they come out the door," Mike whispered. "They're trigger happy, worse even than the Bureau."

The door of the house on the left swung open. Two men pushed out with two women in front of them, shields against the police bullets. Two cops, sheriff's deputies by the look of their uniforms, who had been standing casually at the door, pulled forty-fives from their holsters. Pistol fire crackled. Both cops reeled and fell to the ground. A fusillade rang out from all around the police circle.

"Damn it to hell," the sheriff screamed on his PA. "Cease fire. I told you no one shoots unless I give an order. The next one who fires a gun will be instantly dismissed from the force.

"I'm sorry, Mike," he said to Superintendent Casey. "I thought I could keep them under control."

The Oakdale chief standing next to the sheriff lowered his rifle reluctantly.

"Watch that man, Mike," Nuala warned. "He wants to kill someone!"

"I see that," Mike whispered.

"You fuckers move back and let us through to our cars or we'll waste these cunts. Anybody shoot again and they die."

The city chief raised his gun.

"I'll take those fuckers out."

Mike shoved the rifle out of his hands.

"Asshole! You are not authorized to shoot! Do that again and you'll never be a cop anywhere in the world."

"Cov, I'm in charge. You obey the rules or I'll destroy you."

He turned on his PA again.

"Jimmie, Paulie, don't do anything stupid. No one is dead. You haven't killed anyone yet. The charge isn't murder."

"Liar! They're all dead by now, that cunt Maria and all her friends! We have no choice! We gotta get out of here! We'll kill these cunts if anyone moves on us. They're fucking useless anyway."

"Hold your fire. I repeat, everyone hold your fire. . . . Jimmie, Paulie, we intercepted your poison."

"Go fuck yourself, liar!"

"I beg you," the sheriff pleaded, "give yourselves a chance."

"Just to show you I mean business, I'm going to kill this cunt. Then you get out of the way."

"Poor, crazy, stupid man." Nuala fell to the ground to pray.

"Jake?" Mike said.

The sheriff nodded his head.

"Do it, Mike!"

Mike nodded ever so slightly to three Chicago Tac men in grey who stood to one side by a tree. They raised their weapons, aimed carefully, and fired. Both Sabattinis folded up and collapsed on the ground with holes in the center of their foreheads. The two women were still standing, freed from certain death. Police began to pull weapons from their holsters and aim their rifles. Trigger-happy goons.

"Everyone hold their fire," the sheriff bellowed. "Put your guns back in your holsters, break open your rifles, and shotguns. That is an order. Both men are dead. No more shooting. Anyone who shoots I will have up on charges today. I repeat, they're dead. No more shooting. They're dead."

The cops reluctantly sheathed their weapons as the two women began to wail like banshees. That the dead men were about to kill them did not matter. We had killed their husbands. A younger woman, Tammy most likely, joined her mother wailing on the body of one of the dead.

"Get some ambulances up here so we can evacuate these survivors," the sheriff ordered. "Get them here right away."

The cops didn't seem to understand that the fight was over, they were milling around, looking for someone to shoot. Then I saw Joe McMahon shoot out of the back door running toward the woods. These stupid rural cops would let him get away. I took off after him. As I almost caught up with him I felt the whiz of a bullet as it rushed over my head.

— Nuala Anne —

"MIKE," I shouted, "this focking asshole is trying to kill my husband."

He raised his rifle to shoot again. I hit his right arm with my camogie stick with all my strength.

"Cunt!" he screamed as he fumbled for his pistol.

I smashed his hand and he dropped the gun. He bellowed curses.

"Cease fire," the sheriff begged, "no more shooting!"

The chief of policed lunged toward me. I hit him in his balls and he fell to the ground and groaned.

I glanced at where Dermot had been. He was standing up, holding the rodent. A line of grey Tac forces were deploying around him with their M-16s at the ready.

"That's enough, young woman!" the sheriff barked.

"It will only be enough when I beat his brains out and yours too. He was taking a second shot at my husband and you were letting him do it. You are as much guilty of attempted murder as he is."

"Casey here." Mike had taken the megaphone. "We have seized the principal coconspirator whom you were permitting to escape. I am a deputized officer in the Illinois State Police. I'm arresting the trigger-happy perpetrator that fired at one of my consultants as he captured the escaping Joseph McMahon. If there are any more random shots at any of my people I will authorize my men to shoot back."

My Dermot stood next to me.

"Is that the guy that shot at me?"

He pointed at the chief of police, still twisting in pain.

"Yes."

"I wanted to slug him. I see you beat me to it."

"You could always hit this asshole of a sheriff who let him do it."

My poor Dermot clutched his fist and then saw that the sheriff was sobbing.

"I'm sorry, Mike," he groaned. "I ordered them to cease fire and they kept on shooting."

"In my report on this I will say that you lost control of your men, that in fact you never seemed to have control of them and that you thereby endangered not only the success of the mission but the lives of my personnel. . . . Nuala and Dermot, get out of here. Report to Maria and her family what has happened. . . . Sergeant Reed, will you escort this couple to the red Lincoln?"

"Yes sir . . . Miss, could I carry your hockey stick for you?"

"Certainly, Sergeant! Only it's a camogie stick. My husband usually carries my weapons, but he has been rattled by the recent events. . . . And, Superintendent Casey, tell them back at the CPD that they should have sent that cute little Godzilla creature."

My spear-carrier took my arm.

"I'm glad you're on my side."

"Those poor men weren't meant to die, Dermot. They shouldn't have died. They were so frightened."

"And so stupid."

— Maria Angelica —

AS THE hands on our old grandfather clock moved from one o'clock to two o'clock, I became more uneasy. I knew that the war in heaven between good and evil—the historic conflict in my family of origin—was going on across town. I was afraid we'd lose. Yet we must begin to eat at two o'clock regardless, because some people had to leave. I moved back and forth from the parlor where our guests were sipping Cokes and coffee lest they ruin the meal that they would be expected to demolish. I was also exhausted from the trysts with my ferocious new husband. I knew what would happen when he came into the house, his eyes alight with hunger. I had brought it all on myself and loved every second of it. But I was tired.

At five to two I entered the kitchen.

"Are you ready, young people?"

"Yes, Mom!"

"Then let's eat!"

"Dinner is served!" I announced and the meal was carried out and presented on the table amid much deserved applause. The guests and young people swarmed to their places.

"Man of the house, will you ask God's blessings?"

I had warned him that I would assign the task to him.

"This is St. Brigid's grace which our friend and protector Nuala Anne taught me.

> Bless the poor
> Bless the sick
> Bless the whole human race
> Bless our food
> Bless our drink
> And all our families please embrace.
> Amen."

More applause and then our happy young people began to devour the food.

Later, as my assistants began to remove the food plates and prepare for dessert, Mary Fran whispered in my ear, "Nuala and Dermot are in the study. They want to talk to you and Dad and Johnny Burns in the sewing room."

This was a room off the kitchen where a mother could retreat momentarily to sew or read or in this era watch TV. I caught Camilla's eye and nodded toward the sewing room. She inclined her head toward Johnny Burns. I nodded. We would surely need a psychiatrist.

I took my husband's hand and said to the assemblage, "We must see to some matters before dessert." His hand was as cold as mine. Nuala was pale and somber, her lovely face frozen in sadness. Dermot looked grim and determined. Granne O'Malley's crowd coming ashore from Galway Bay.

"The battle is over," she began as mechanically as a police spokeswoman on TV. "The area is now secure. James and Paul Sabattini are dead. They hid behind their wives as they tried to fight their way out of the police cordon. They shot and wounded two Oakdale police officers who were not prepared for the onslaught. Each held the other's wife in a firm grip and held a pistol at their throat. They said they would kill the women if the police did not back off. Both wives were screaming hysterically. There was no doubt that they meant what they said. They were both terribly frightened, indeed men with fright which had deprived them of all ability to consider what they were doing. There was no choice but for two officers with telescopic rifles to kill them both. The two men fell immediately to the ground. The women were not injured. They threw themselves on the bodies of their husbands wailing and sobbing their loss. Tamrya emerged from the house and similarly mourned her father. Mr. Joseph McMahon who had been hiding somewhere in the house emerged from the rear door and ran toward the woods behind the plant. He was apprehended by one of the officers, arrested, cuffed, and warned of his rights. He laughed hysterically adding some counterpoint to the noise. Ambulances were removing the dead and the survivors as we left to come here. . . . My husband and I want to express our sorrow to everyone. . . . I want to point out that everyone at this house was a target of a mass murder plot and yet you are all still alive for which we must thank God."

The room was silent. No one knew what to say.

"Are they at the hospital?" I said hoarsely. "We must go to them and console them."

"Yes," Camilla agreed. "They need us now."

"You must do what you have to do," Nuala said softly, in the tones of a gentle mother superior. "I would suggest that you give them time, lots of time before you attempt reconciliation. They have lost their husbands who, however cruel and brutish and however they would certainly have killed them, were still their husbands. They must grieve, perhaps for a long time. Perhaps they will return to Tuscany as rich women and begin to understand. Save your consolations until they are ready to hear them."

Johnny Burns broke the ensuing silence.

"I have to say that Ms. McGrail is correct. They must be given time to hate you and to move beyond it. I can't predict how long that will take. I will monitor their short-term recovery at the hospital and keep you posted. Camilla, may I suggest that you take a brief leave so that you will not be in the ward while your mother and your aunt and your cousin are there?"

"As you know, Doctor Burns, I am reluctant to admit that you might be right on anything. This time I'm sure you are." She began to sob. He put his arm around her and she leaned against him.

"And, Johnny Jim, isn't Ms. McGrail me ma and isn't she over beyond in Ireland? I'm Nuala Anne."

We all laughed and the tension eased.

She was crying, poor child, playing the role of the wise old great grandma. Dermot put his arm around her.

I was crying too. Where was my husband's arm?

There it was around me already.

We pressed them to stay for a bite but they had to pick up their kids back beyond in River Forest.

Camilla and I dried our tears and supported by our two men returned to the festive dinner as though nothing had happened. Life is stronger than death, that's what Christmas is all about.

— Epilogue —

THE TRIP to Galway was the disaster I predicted it would be.

It began with a teary walk down the street with the hounds to the Murphy house where the dogs were greeted with glee by Katiesue and Johnnypete. Our crowd, mother included and Patjo excluded, bid them mournful farewells. I tried to explain that dogs tend to be promiscuous with human friends. So long as there are friendly humans around, they don't much care who the humans are. However, the crowd did not accept this rationalization. The dogs would miss us every minute of every day.

Despite all our frantic efforts we boarded the plane just before the doors were closed, having suffered a long delay at the security barrier because our normally well-behaved children took umbrage at the representatives of Homeland Security. The latter I suspect had a purgatorial time during the holidays and were not sympathetic to pushy kids.

The plane sat on the runway at O'Hare for two hours because of wind problems. The kids demanded to know whether we could get off and go home. The first hour of the flight was bumpy and poor Socra Marie succumbed to motion sickness. With the same bravery that had kept her alive for several months in the hospital, she did not complain. Finally when we managed to rise above the worst of the winds, she collapsed in her mother's arms and slept the rest of the trip. Patjo and I were the only ones among the rest of the crowd who were unaffected by the milkshake ride. The good Nuala Anne and the equally good Nelliecoyne prayed rosaries with great fervor for our safe transit.

"You'd think we are on one of them coffin ships," I said.

"How do you know we're not?"

Then somewhere south of Greenland I began to sneeze.

"You're not getting your cold again!" Nuala protested as if that were an optional matter with my organism.

"Certainly not!" I lied.

Our van and driver were not waiting for us at Shannon because the plane was late. I argued with the attendant at the rental car counter that the driver should have noted that the plane was posted late. She responded with I thought a deliberately unintelligible brogue. My wife spit out a steady stream of Irish words. It worked. The van with a different driver would be back at eight o'clock sharp in the morning. They had reserved three "quality" rooms for us at the airport hotel and would notify the hotel up above in Clifden that we would be a day late.

The rooms were nice, if you ignored the jets screaming overhead, the kids piled into their beds, and Nuala and I staggered into our room, large, comfortable and stocked with notes from the management and complimentary fruit and drink.

She called her mother "up above" in Carraroe and explained in mournful Irish what had happened—while discarding her clothes and donning a warm winter nightshirt.

"Och," she concluded in English, "aren't they all great travelers and themselves in fine form!"

Even by the elastic standards of Irish truth, that statement was flat out false.

"Weren't you right all along, Dermot Michael Coyne?"

"Woman, I was . . . But about what?"

"That this trip is a daft idea, that we should have planned on sleeping here before we drove up to Galway and now yourself with your cold and you'll be sick for the whole week!"

"I shouldn't sleep in the same bed with you. I don't want to give you my cold and ruin your trip."

"You know I never catch your colds," she said, turning over and wrapping herself in the blanket.

It was a claim, I thought, to a certain moral superiority. I took my temperature—ninety-nine point eight, typical of my colds. Then I fortified myself with the cold medications that I had brought along and collapsed into feverish sleep.

The next day was bright and clear. The ride

through Clare and Galway was spectacularly beautiful. It was a countryside easy to love, so long as you didn't plan to earn a living off its fields. My fellow travelers had recovered their élan and they marveled at the splendors of the West of Ireland and listened with rapt attention to the stories their mother told, in Irish now. Poor dear da, sitting dazed in the rear seat of the van, was an object of occasional sympathetic concern.

I wondered if I should carry a bell, like a leper.

Carraroe glowed in the rare winter sunlight and Galway Bay took on its Mediterranean persona. We were welcomed enthusiastically at the new bungalow which had replaced the old stone house with a thatched roof, though the latter remained in the backyard because of the Irish conviction that it is bad luck to destroy a home. "You can never tell when you might need it again."

Nuala's ma had "just the thing" for a cold. I knew from experience from my own "ma" (grandmother actually) that it would be a concoction of whiskey (Irish), hot water, and lemon juice, with some other mysterious things added. I agreed to drink it, every last drop. It would not help my cold at all, at all, but it would kill the pain. The days in bed would pass seamlessly without a care or worry. Chicago? Where was that? Joey McMahon? Who he? The hounds? Cinda-sue and her crowd could keep them. My novel? The check with the advance? It had been duly put in the bank. Me wife and gos-sons and colleens? There was enough in my accounts so the kids could attend college. So why not go back to sleep?

My family had a great time without me, all of them babbling in the Irish language, even my poor little second son. The trip was, I was assured, "great craic." My wife was attentive and caring, as though she were ministering to someone in his final agony.

The last day or two I pulled out of the worst of the cold and some of the self-pity and insisted on hosting a dinner in a Norman restaurant on the very edge of the bay, a few miles west of Galway Town, called that by the locals, though it was now the fastest growing city in Europe.

We had dinner at the house in Carraroe the night before our departure. There was much singing and dancing and storytelling and lullabying from me wife and no wasting of a single drop of the creature. Nuala had but one splasheen of the drink, because she had to drive us home in the dark.

The next day our departure from Connemara and Shannon and our flight home was uneventful, if it seemed to me interminable. The hounds did not seem nearly as happy as they should have been on our return. Why should they be? The Murphy clan had indulged them shamelessly.

The Chicago scene had not changed much. Joey McMahon was in the psychiatric unit at Cook County Hospital, set aside for patients from county jail. It was not certain that he would stand trial. The brothers Sabattini were buried from the parish church and in the little parish cemetery behind the church. Father Matt had preached powerfully about God's mercy and love. The widows had refused to recognize Maria and her sister Gina at the wake or the funeral. However, they permitted Camilla to stand in the mourners' line, but did not speak to her. Young Dr. Burns attended her with respectful attention.

The two wounded cops were recovering from their wounds. Chief Bell had retired. The capture and charging of Joseph McMahon had been reported in both the Chicago and Rockford media, but with few details.

A week after the funeral the two widows and Tamrya had departed on Alitalia for Italy, leaving no indication that they would ever return. There was apparently lots of money in the family construction business which they had promptly sold.

The now more relaxed merger of the Connors and Donlan families were proceeding and Camilla Sabattini had been included in it. John Patrick Donlan had added two employees to his team, both graduates of the University of Chicago Business School. He and his new wife had finished a belated honeymoon in the Caymans and continued to be radiant in their common life. I had left my cold behind in Ireland, where it belonged and began my new novel. Mike the cop and his wife Annie Reilly celebrated Twelfth Night with a party in honor of me wife and meself in which a number of our cop friends were among the guests—John Culhane, Nikos Mashek, and Terry Glen included. Nuala had changed back into her Irish Tiger life. She sang of course, a whole new line of songs she called "police songs."

I worried about her. She had thrown herself back into her pre-Christmas lifestyle, without ever taking the vacation she needed.

I debated within myself how to bring up the subject.

She saved me the trouble.

One night in mid January with a new blizzard assaulting our old house while we were lying in bed almost asleep, she said, "Dermot love, the small 'uns are all worried 'bout you. They think you've worn yourself out. Doesn't Da need a vacation? I say he does, but he'll never take one. They say I should make him. So I've reserved a suite in the Caymans, the same one that Maria and Jack stayed in, for two weeks. Your parents will move into our house. . . . You know how much they love being with the kids and the mutts. I'm sure you won't catch cold down below. I'm going, Dermot Michael Coyne, even if you don't come. . . ."

More Irish fibbing.

What would, in the circumstances, be a wise reply?

"Well, I've been feeling tired a lot lately. I guess I need a vacation. . . ."

Never argue with an Irish Tiger!

— Note —

The North Central section of Illinois in this story is mostly fictional. I think I have crossed the Fox River no more than half a dozen times in my life. Oakdale is entirely fictional. The Kishwaukee County and River, Rockford, DeKalb, and Northern Illinois University actually exist but my rendering is fictional. Do not search for Oakdale because, alas, you will find it only in my imagination. The tactics of the Chicago police presented in this story are also completely fictional as well as various police officers. Neither the Reliables nor Godzilla actually exist. Indeed everyone in this book is fictional. It does not follow, how-

ever, that they do not exist vividly in my imagination and haunt my dreams
   God is not fictional.

Tucson
Vernal Equinox,
St. Patrick's Week
2007

1,000 YEARS, 1,000 PEOPLE

Ranking the Men and Women Who Shaped the Millennium

AGNES HOOPER GOTTLIEB

HENRY GOTTLIEB

BARBARA BOWERS

BRENT BOWERS

KODANSHA INTERNATIONAL

New York • Tokyo • London

To our children:

Jennie, Annie, Daniel, Matthew, and Thomas

Kodansha America, Inc.
114 Fifth Avenue, New York, New York 10011, U.S.A.

Kodansha International Ltd.
17-14 Otowa 1-chome, Bunkyo-ku, Tokyo 112-8652, Japan

Published in 1998 by Kodansha America, Inc.

Library of Congress Cataloging-in-Publication Data

1,000 years, 1,000 people : ranking the men and women who shaped
    the millennium / Agnes Hooper Gottlieb . . . [et al.].
        p.   cm.
    Includes bibliographical references and index.
    ISBN 1-56836-273-0
    1. Biography—Dictionaries.   I. Gottlieb, Agnes Hooper.
CT103.A16   1998
920.02—dc21
    [B]   98-40381
                                                                  CIP

Manufactured in the United States of America on acid-free paper

99 00 01 02   10 9 8 7 6 5 4 3 2

Contents

Acknowledgments

Our search for one thousand names and their proper rankings went beyond our own collective wisdom and the expertise of historians whose works we consulted. We sought advice from friends, professional colleagues, and scholars. Their willingness to help, and their enthusiasm —which often matched our own—has made this a better book. They gave us names that had not occurred to us, helped us understand the ebb and flow of trends in fields as various as abstract art and zoology, and even acted as arbitrators when we disagreed among ourselves.

We thank our friends and professional colleagues Deirdre Yates, Dan Yates, Tom Rondinella, John Sowa, Laura Schoppmann, Angela Weisl, Liz Milliken, Suzanne Samuels, Mary Balkun, Maxine Lurie, Don McKenna, Ken Hoffman, Maribel Holsworth, Chris Sharrett, Maurine H. Beasley, Tim J. O'Brien, Lisa Brennan, Pamela Brownstein, Barry Adler, Dana Canedy, Thomas Canedy, Ellen Musikant, Peter Messeri, Kitta MacPherson, Walter Lucas, Zsuzsa Wierda, Andy Wierda, Maureen Garde, Chris Hann, Judson Haverkamp, Ann Haverkamp, Floyd Norris, Timothy O'Brien, Rebecca O'Brien, Larry Young, Sally Young, John Lettis, Judith C. Stark, and Anthony E. Lee.

Acknowledgment is also due to family members Bruce Bowers, Robert Bowers, Jason Bowers, Allison Bowers, Jay Fuhrman, Fern Denny, Gertrude and Ralph Sussman, Bernadette Hooper, Darcy and Sidney Gottlieb, Maryrose and Gene Mangan, Terry and Don Thompson, Patrick Thompson, Tom and Darla Hooper, John and Karen Hooper, Peg and Bob Huryk, Martin and Peg Hooper, Bernadette and John McVey, Jim and Marilyn Hooper, and Elizabeth and Edward Stevens.

The staffs of the West Orange, Maplewood, and Somerset County, New Jersey, public libraries and Seton Hall University Library offered valuable guidance to the resources in their collections.

We'd also like to thank our agent, Michael Cohn, and our editor, Nancy Cooperman Su. Their guidance and suggestions made this project possible.

Introduction

In the year 1001 doomsayers had to look for another line of work. God had spared the world fire and ice at the end of the first millennium. And so the curtain went up on act two of that great tragicomedy, human history, with hopes that it would play for at least another thousand years.

It did—and what a performance!

From the opening moments—a Scandinavian adventurer's tentative step on a new continent, a Japanese writer's creation of the first novel, a German priest's experiments with guns, and an Arab thinker's reveries about the mysteries of multiplication—the second millennium was a headlong rush to the edges of man's creative, and destructive, genius.

Before it was over, a man had walked on the moon, the power of the atom had been unleashed, a scientist had cloned a sheep named Dolly, Michelangelo had worked his magic on the Sistine Chapel, Shakespeare had plumbed the depths of the human soul, and Martin Luther King, Jr., had dreamed a dream. Before it was over, Hitler's war had killed 55 million people, and Stalin and Mao had turned half the world into a hell of murder and deceit.

Which brings us to what this book is about: the one thousand men and women who, over the course of the past one thousand years, did the most to shape the world, for better or for worse.

To make our exercise provocative, we ranked those people in order of importance, from number 1—Johannes Gutenberg, whose printing press made possible the Renaissance, the Reformation, and the scientific revolution—to number 1,000, Andy Warhol, who knew a zeitgeist when he saw one and declared that everyone would be famous for fifteen minutes.

Yes, this is a book about people, though we disagree with the contention of nineteenth-century historian Thomas Carlyle that history is nothing but the story of great men (and, by extension, great women). Ideology counts, and so do economics and class struggles and sexual urges and the territorial imperative and spiritual longings. But without people there would be no events, creations, isms, or cultural trends. Where would Waterloo be without Napoleon? Communism without Marx? Religion without Francis of Assisi?

Choosing the top people was easy. Columbus, Luther, Galileo, Thomas Aquinas, and a couple hundred other names leaped to our minds. To round out the list, though, we consulted encyclopedias, haunted the biography sections of libraries, and read specialized histories of eras and locales. We boned up on subjects ranging from absolutism to Egyptian popular music.

Just as important, we asked dozens of friends

and colleagues to propose names. And they did; boy, did they! Thanks to their responses, we have included relative unknowns, at least in the United States, like Bill W., Marion Donovan, and Umm Kulthum (no peeking allowed). We rejected more suggestions than we accepted, from the ridiculous Bart Simpson (only real people, please!) to the sublime Jesus Christ (sorry, wrong millennium). And we'll never forget the Thanksgiving dinner that was dominated by our debate with two art history teachers, who said we were fools for putting Da Vinci before Michelangelo. Maybe so, but we did it for a reason.

We based our ranking on a set of criteria of our own devising, the five-point BioGraph System. Using this system, we gave the greatest weight to the subject's lasting influence. But that is far from the whole picture. We also measured people by how much wisdom and beauty they added to or subtracted from the world, by their impact on their contemporaries, by the singularity of their genius or infamy, and finally by their level of fame or charisma. (You'll find a more detailed explanation of the BioGraph System on page ix.)

For our subjects, getting on the list was quite a demographic feat. While the World Population Council tells us that no feasible estimates exist for the number of people who have lived in the past millennium, we're going to go out on a limb and guess that it is around half of the 100 billion or so that the experts say have fretted their hour upon the stage ever since Homo sapiens broke away from the lower primates. After all, 5.8 billion humans walk the earth at the end of the millennium. If our calculation is correct, the chances of making the top thousand were one in fifty million.

One of the thousand who beat the odds, Oscar Wilde, said, "The only duty we owe history is to rewrite it." We hope we weren't too brutal in the process.

Nobody will say we made every call right; some historians will chide us even for trying. Yet we are confident that the book will be a catalyst for thought about the relative value of the millennium's inventions, ideas, and events, and the people behind them. We hope it finds favor among all those who love history, love arguing about history, or just love arguing.

So here it is: *1,000 Years, 1,000 People*.

A Guide to the BioGraph System

The BioGraph System is a unique method of defining that nebulous concept "importance," for the various historical figures being judged. The system is easy to apply if you know about their lives, times, and influence. Each BioGraph point is awarded on the basis of answers to five questions. In order of their significance, they are:

1. *Lasting influence.* What was the person's impact on the millennium? To what extent was the history of the world, or a region, or perhaps even a profession, changed by this person? Maximum points: 10,000.

2. *Effect on the sum total of wisdom and beauty in the world.* How much of what makes life worth living—a work of music, painting, or literature, a well-turned philosophical argument, or a scientific concept—did the person contribute to mankind, or take away? Maximum points: 5,000.

3. *Influence on contemporaries.* How much did the person affect the world of his times? Maximum points: 4,000.

4. *Singularity of contribution.* To what extent was the person's achievement a product of her own genius, and to what extent did she depend on the work of others? Maximum points: 3,000.

5. *Charisma.* Simply put, how famous was the person? To what extent was he or she a household name to contemporaries and posterity? Maximum points: 2,000.

The highest score possible is 24,000; even Gutenberg, our number 1, fell far short, with 21,768 points. Why? After all, he earned 9,982 points for lasting influence, the most of any

figure in our book (though 18 shy of perfection, because nobody's perfect). We also awarded him 4,944 points out of a possible 5,000 for his contribution to wisdom and beauty; 3,761 out of 4,000 for his influence on contemporaries; and 2,871 out of 3,000 for his singularity of contribution.

Alas, we had to give poor Gutenberg an F for personal magnetism. Far from commanding the adulation of his contemporaries, he was in some ways a pathetic character. For example, after defaulting on a loan, he had to give up the very printing press that won him fame to a creditor. Thus, for charisma, he scores a paltry 210 out of 2,000.

Had he gotten a middling 1,000, he would have towered over every other man and woman of the millennium. As it was, he barely edged out four other movers and shakers.

Had we rated our subjects according to lasting influence alone, Gutenberg would still have taken the grand prize and Columbus would still be breathing down his neck. But Newton, now ranked sixth, would have displaced Luther for the third spot, and Shakespeare would have bumped Galileo into the low triple digits.

Again, this raises the importance of the charisma wild card. Oscar Wilde, the British playwright, got heaps of points in this category for his wit and flamboyance; Hitler (may he roast in hell) got the most—1,991—for the evil spell he cast over a nation. If only Shakespeare had exhibited a bit more, he would have elbowed Gutenberg aside for top honors.

Since we mention Hitler, perhaps we should explain why he made number 20 on our list. His charisma helped, of course, but he rated high in all other categories, too, for the mayhem he sowed. Few would question the high score he got for lasting influence; after all, he changed the course of history. But some might wonder why he got rated so high in a category like "contribution" to wisdom and beauty. The answer is that the contribution was purely negative; his slaughter robbed posterity of untold geniuses and thus impoverished both the arts and the sciences.

Yes, we have included lots of villains, from Stalin to Blackbeard, history's baddest pirate. But mostly we have leaned to the good guys, because they are the ones who make us glad to be alive and part of the human race. Just about everybody you think is important is probably mentioned in this book, and lots of people you've never heard of are too, like John Gorrie, or "Mr. Cool," as we have nicknamed him, the inventor of modern refrigeration.

As we moved down the list of the millen-nium's most illustrious lights, it became some-what more difficult for us to allocate numbers. Was there anything foreordained about ranking Savonarola, fifteenth-century Florence's hector-ing ayatollah, at number 303, just one notch behind the great French humanist François Rabelais and exactly one point ahead of Helen Keller? Not at all; frankly, if we had dined on fish and chips instead of hot dogs and sauerkraut the day we considered them, the results might have been much different. It may seem that we've assigned points to historical figures for their achievements in roughly the same way that a diners' guide grades restaurants for their cuisine, decor, ambience, and price.

What you may have deduced by now is that, in making a total of five thousand calculations—five for each person—we often more or less winged it. Oh, we approached our task seriously. We closed our eyes and reflected. We paced. We perused one another's numbers. We compared the relative merits of people within the same pro-fession or trade, peeking at what we had allotted to Rembrandt, for example, before compiling the net historical worth of Rubens.

If such an exercise were a science, it would be an inexact science. If it were an art, it would be a primitive art. In fact, it is neither; it is a useful gimmick.

So take the BioGraph numbers with a grain of salt. The meat is in the reading.

The List

1–100

1. Johannes Gutenberg
2. Christopher Columbus
3. Martin Luther
4. Galileo Galilei
5. William Shakespeare
6. Isaac Newton
7. Charles Darwin
8. Thomas Aquinas
9. Leonardo da Vinci
10. Ludwig van Beethoven
11. John Locke
12. Mohandas K. Gandhi
13. Michelangelo Buonarroti
14. Karl Marx
15. Sigmund Freud
16. Napoleon I
17. Albert Einstein
18. Nicholas Copernicus
19. Jean-Jacques Rousseau
20. Adolf Hitler
21. Adam Smith
22. George Washington
23. Wilbur Wright
24. Orville Wright
25. René Descartes
26. Louis Pasteur
27. Peter the Great
28. Thomas Alva Edison
29. William I of England
30. Dante Alighieri
31. Elizabeth I of England
32. Abraham Lincoln
33. Johannes Kepler
34. Leo Tolstoy
35. Johann Sebastian Bach
36. Voltaire
37. Franklin Delano Roosevelt
38. Winston Churchill
39. Francis of Assisi
40. Niccolò Machiavelli
41. Vladimir Ilyich Lenin
42. Ferdinand Magellan
43. Genghis Khan
44. Miguel de Cervantes Saavedra
45. Mary Wollstonecraft
46. Rembrandt Harmenszoon van Rijn
47. William Harvey
48. Simón Bolívar
49. Immanuel Kant
50. Mao Ze-dong
51. Henry Ford
52. Wolfgang Amadeus Mozart
53. John Milton
54. Benjamin Franklin
55. Alexander Fleming
56. Martin Luther King, Jr.
57. Toyotomi Hideyoshi
58. Frederick the Great
59. Georg Wilhelm Friedrich Hegel
60. Chu Yüan-chang
61. Emperor Charles V
62. Geoffrey Chaucer
63. Louis XIV of France
64. Thomas Jefferson
65. Pope Urban II
66. Marco Polo
67. Antoine-Laurent Lavoisier
68. Maximilien Robespierre
69. John Calvin
70. Charles Dickens
71. Suleiman the Magnificent
72. Paul Cézanne
73. Murasaki Shikibu
74. Alexander Graham Bell
75. Marie Curie

76. John Eckert
77. Fyodor Dostoyevsky
78. Pope Innocent III
79. Frederick Douglass
80. J. Robert Oppenheimer
81. John Stuart Mill
82. Joseph Stalin
83. Joan of Arc
84. Francis Bacon
85. Filippo Brunelleschi
86. Elizabeth Cady Stanton
87. Vladimir K. Zworykin
88. Gottfried Wilhelm Leibniz
89. William Le Baron Jenney
90. Edward Jenner
91. Queen Victoria
92. Babur
93. Chu Hsi
94. Phineas T. Barnum
95. Guglielmo Marconi
96. Marsilius of Padua
97. Desiderius Erasmus
98. Alexander von Humboldt
99. Margaret Sanger
100. Henry VIII of England

101–200

101. Petrus Peregrinus
102. Otto Lilienthal
103. Father Berthold Schwartz
104. Gregor Mendel
105. Nikolaus Otto
106. Charles-Louis Montesquieu
107. Anton van Leeuwenhoek
108. Paracelsus
109. Carl Gauss
110. James Watt
111. William Thomson

112. Petrarch
113. William Tecumseh Sherman
114. Carl von Clausewitz
115. Ignatius of Loyola
116. Okubo Toshimichi
117. Isabella I of Spain
118. Otto von Bismarck
119. Michael Faraday
120. Florence Nightingale
121. B. F. Skinner
122. Joseph Lister
123. James D. Watson
124. Thomas Hunt Morgan
125. Vasco da Gama
126. Saladin (Salah ad-Din Yusuf)
127. David Ricardo
128. Ernest Rutherford
129. Raphael Sanzio
130. Auguste Comte
131. Johann Wolfgang von Goethe
132. Maimonides
133. Andrea Palladio
134. Lech Walesa
135. Eli Whitney
136. Max Planck
137. Joseph Priestley
138. Catherine the Great
139. Susan B. Anthony
140. Carl Benz
141. Anna Eleanor Roosevelt
142. Robert Boyle
143. George Stephenson
144. Blaise Pascal
145. David Wark Griffith
146. Carl Jung
147. George Boole
148. Akbar
149. Pablo Picasso
150. Hernán Cortés
151. Thomas Hobbes
152. Fakr ad-Din ar-Razi

153. Henry the Navigator
154. Sarah Bernhardt
155. Le Corbusier
156. Louis-Jacques-Mandé Daguerre
157. Gavrilo Princip
158. Vincent Van Gogh
159. Masaccio
160. Frank Lloyd Wright
161. Ibn Sīnā
162. Oliver Cromwell
163. Victor Hugo
164. Averroës (Ibn Rushd)
165. Richard Wagner
166. Hugo Grotius
167. Henrik Ibsen
168. Jane Austen
169. Allen Du Mont
170. Gamal Abdel Nasser
171. James Joyce
172. Peter Abelard
173. Mehmed II the Conqueror
174. Joseph-Marie Jacquard
175. Jean-Baptiste Poquelin Molière
176. Caravaggio
177. Emperor Henry IV
178. Robert Goddard
179. Prince Metternich
180. Edmund Burke
181. Kemal Atatürk
182. Samuel Johnson
183. Igor Stravinsky
184. George Eliot
185. David Hume
186. Albrecht Dürer
187. Ramanuja
188. Mark Twain
189. K'ang-hsi
190. Alexander Hamilton
191. Elizabeth of Hungary
192. Anton Chekhov
193. Yoshida Shoin

194. James Cook
195. Benito Juárez
196. Claude Monet
197. Daniel Defoe
198. Dominic
199. Hieronymus Bosch
200. Nicolas Appert

201–300

201. John Maynard Keynes
202. Tycho Brahe
203. Pope Leo IX
204. W.E.B. DuBois
205. James Clerk Maxwell
206. Emmeline Pankhurst
207. Marcel Proust
208. Niels Bohr
209. Jane Addams
210. Aldus Manutius
211. Robert Koch
212. Theodor Herzl
213. Thomas Starzl
214. John Adams
215. Friedrich Nietzsche
216. Jomo Kenyatta
217. Alfred Nobel
218. Matsuo Basho
219. Giotto
220. Emil von Behring
221. Henry IV of France
222. Jawaharlal Nehru
223. Balthasar de Beaujoyeulx
224. Wilhelm II of Germany
225. Bartolomeo Cristofori
226. Francis Xavier
227. Elizabeth Blackwell
228. Lorenzo "the Magnificent" de'Medici
229. Ivan the Great
230. Carl Linnaeus
231. Claudio Monteverdi
232. Oliver Evans
233. Franz Kafka

234. Andreas Vesalius
235. John McAdam
236. Vilhelm Bjerknes
237. Mikhail Gorbachev
238. Gianlorenzo Bernini
239. Bartholomé de Las Casas
240. Lucretia Mott
241. John III Sobieski of Poland
242. Ito Hirobumi
243. Ivan the Terrible
244. Ivan Pavlov
245. Anna Pavlova
246. Robert Fulton
247. Georges Danton
248. John Dalton
249. Gratian
250. Paul Ehrlich
251. Baruch Spinoza
252. Charlotte Perkins Gilman
253. Dmitry Mendeleyev
254. Honoré de Balzac
255. Bernard of Clairvaux
256. Pieter Bruegel the Elder
257. Francis Drake
258. Donato Bramante
259. Christopher Wren
260. Auguste Rodin
261. Daniel Fahrenheit
262. Mayer Amschel Rothschild
263. Samuel Adams
264. Leonardo of Pisa
265. Anders Celsius
266. Francis Joseph of Austria-Hungary
267. Antoinette Louisa Brown Blackwell
268. James Madison
269. Henri Matisse
270. Denis Diderot
271. Mitsui Takatoshi
272. Jacob Grimm

273. Wilhelm Grimm
274. Claude Debussy
275. Gottlieb Daimler
276. John of Austria
277. Wilhelm Conrad Röntgen
278. Duke of Wellington
279. Edgar Allan Poe
280. John Donne
281. Peter Paul Rubens
282. Edward Coke
283. El Greco
284. Leo Hendrik Baekeland
285. Norman Borlaug
286. Ignaz Phillipp Semmelweis
287. John Marshall
288. Leopold von Ranke
289. Clara Barton
290. Sun Yat-sen
291. Johannes Fibiger
292. William Blackstone
293. James Naismith
294. Jean-Baptiste Colbert
295. Mi Fei
296. Franz Joseph Haydn
297. John Keats
298. John II of Portugal
299. Giambattista Vico
300. Franz Liszt

301–400

301. Édouard Manet
302. François Rabelais
303. Girolamo Savonarola
304. Helen Keller
305. Ida B. Wells-Barnett
306. Thomas Malthus
307. Pierre Beauchamp
308. Elisha Otis
309. Ferdinand Ritter von Mannlicher
310. Ram Singh
311. Thomas Paine

312. David Ben-Gurion
313. Ibn Taymiyah
     (Taqi ad-Din)
314. Jonas Salk
315. William Blake
316. Barthélemy Thimonnier
317. Horace Mann
318. Walt Whitman
319. Donatello
320. John Hawkins
321. Giovanni Boccaccio
322. Louis Armstrong
323. Margaret Fuller
324. Hung Hsiu-ch'üan
325. Domingo Faustino
     Sarmiento
326. Henry Bessemer
327. Paul McCartney
328. John Lennon
329. Samuel Morse
330. Aleksandr Pushkin
331. Sandro Botticelli
332. Kublai Khan
333. Christiaan Huygens
334. Andrés Bello
335. Jan van Eyck
336. Lise Meitner
337. John Wycliffe
338. Johannes Eckehart
339. Jan Pieterszoon Coen
340. Francisco José
     de Goya
341. George Berkeley
342. Franz Schubert
343. John XXIII
344. George Marshall
345. Thomas More
346. Auguste Escoffier
347. Gerardus Mercator
348. Thurgood Marshall
349. Cardinal Richelieu
350. Ibn al-'Arabi
351. Charles Babbage
352. Elvis Presley

353. Johannes Brahms
354. Nelson Mandela
355. Maria Theresa
356. Firdawsi
357. Walter Scott
358. Betty Friedan
359. Henry II of England
360. Babe Ruth
361. Yamagata Aritomo
362. Pierre de Fermat
363. Constantin Brancusi
364. Ludwig Mies
     van der Rohe
365. Søren Kierkegaard
366. John Dryden
367. Ezra Pound
368. Giuseppe Garibaldi
369. Jean Piaget
370. Tokugawa Ieyasu
371. Ulysses S. Grant
372. Louisa May Alcott
373. Clarence Birdseye
374. Dwight D. Eisenhower
375. Henry David Thoreau
376. George P. Marsh
377. Rachel Carson
378. Pope Gregory VII
379. Margaret Mead
380. Menelik II of Ethiopia
381. Bill W.
382. Agatha Christie
383. Jeremy Bentham
384. Pierre-Auguste Renoir
385. Lord Byron
386. James Starley
387. Jan Hus
388. Ernest Hemingway
389. Jean-Baptiste Racine
390. Bernadette of Lourdes
391. John Bunyan
392. Richard Francis Burton
393. Aphra Behn
394. Samuel Taylor
     Coleridge

395. Enrico Fermi
396. Yo Fei
397. James Boswell
398. Gustave Flaubert
399. Jean-Paul Marat
400. Tomás de Torquemada

401–500
401. Mikhail Bakunin
402. Bartolomeu Dias
403. Giovanni Bellini
404. Nichiren
405. Vaslav Nijinsky
406. John Harington
407. Osman I
408. Guido of Arezzo
409. André-Marie Ampère
410. George Washington
     Carver
411. Leif Eriksson
412. Roger Bacon
413. Wallace Hume
     Carothers
414. Frederick Winslow
     Taylor
415. Friedrich Engels
416. John I of England
417. Ferdinand Foch
418. Aristide Boucicaut
419. Charles-Maurice
     Talleyrand
420. Eleanor of Aquitaine
421. Ferdinand de Lesseps
422. Yung-lo
423. Gustavus Adolphus
     of Sweden
424. Frédéric Chopin
425. Alessandro Volta
426. Eugene O'Neill
427. Philip II of Spain
428. Mathew Brady
429. Leon Trotsky
430. John Harvey Kellogg
431. Konrad Adenauer

432. Michel de Montaigne
433. Jean Monnet
434. Jean-François Borel
435. John Pierpont Morgan
436. Henry Maudslay
437. Woodrow Wilson
438. Li Hung-chang
439. John III of Portugal
440. Joseph Monier
441. Virginia Woolf
442. Jackie Robinson
443. James Buchanan Duke
444. John Roebling
445. Alan Turing
446. Louis Lumière
447. Vincent of Beauvais
448. Henry Cavendish
449. Gabriele Falloppio
450. John Gorrie
451. Wassily Kandinsky
452. George III of England
453. Heinrich Hertz
454. Gertrude Elion
455. Chiang Kai-shek
456. Ibn al-Haytham
457. Harriet Beecher Stowe
458. Booker T. Washington
459. Charles de Gaulle
460. Benito Mussolini
461. Ch'ien-lung
462. Frederick Grant Banting
463. Albert Kahn
464. Pope Clement VII
465. Konstantin Stanislavsky
466. Fidel Castro
467. Philip of Hesse
468. Eugène Delacroix
469. Irving Berlin
470. Frederick Law Olmsted
471. Thomas Cranmer
472. Walter Raleigh
473. John Montagu
474. Cesare Beccaria

475. Pope Gregory IX
476. Giuseppe Verdi
477. Hiroshige
478. Shah Jahan
479. Emily Dickinson
480. Emperor Frederick II
481. Anne Frank
482. Edgar Degas
483. Jorge Luis Borges
484. Bernardo O'Higgins
485. Harry S Truman
486. John D. Rockefeller
487. George Eastman
488. 'Abd al-'Aziz ibn Sa'ud
489. William the Silent
490. Wilhelm Wundt
491. Maria Agnesi
492. Jonathan Swift
493. Jakob Fugger
494. Walt Disney
495. Edmund Kean
496. Ambroise Paré
497. Baybars I
498. Yasir Arafat
499. Yury Gagarin
500. Amelia Jenks Bloomer

501–600

501. Aaron Montgomery Ward
502. Karen Horney
503. Luigi Galvani
504. Ralph Waldo Emerson
505. Meriwether Lewis
506. Iwasaki Yataro
507. Alfred Krupp
508. Jean de La Fontaine
509. Percy Bysshe Shelley
510. Nettie Maria Stevens
511. Tamerlane
512. Charles Lyell
513. Jan Vermeer
514. Hokusai
515. Robert E. Lee

516. Charles Lindbergh
517. Alp Arslan
518. Winslow Homer
519. Jules Verne
520. Giovanni Giacomo Casanova de Seingalt
521. William Butler Yeats
522. Emily Brontë
523. Dag Hammarskjöld
524. Johnny Torrio
525. William Faulkner
526. Duke Ellington
527. Philip II of France
528. Giovanni Pierluigi da Palestrina
529. John Jacob Astor
530. Francesco Borromini
531. Christopher Latham Sholes
532. Thomas Chippendale
533. François Villon
534. Harriet Tubman
535. Frederick Hopkins
536. Albert Luthuli
537. José Martí
538. Enrico Caruso
539. Godfrey Newbold Hounsfield
540. Levi Strauss
541. Benvenuto Cellini
542. Francisco de Orellana
543. William James
544. Washington Irving
545. Paul Gauguin
546. Tecumseh
547. John Knox
548. Margaret Bourke-White
549. Ibn Khaldun
550. Hans Christian Andersen
551. Félix Lope de Vega
552. Shaka
553. Joseph Conrad

554. Isadora Duncan
555. Fannie Farmer
556. Martin Behaim
557. Henry James
558. Jean-Baptiste Say
559. Marie LaChapelle
560. Gustave Courbet
561. Pierre Corneille
562. Benjamin Spock
563. Abigail Adams
564. Rubén Darío
565. George Frederic Handel
566. Cornelius Vanderbilt
567. Jalal ad-Din ar-Rumi
568. Jean-Baptiste-Camille Corot
569. Duncan Phyfe
570. Bartholomaeus Anglicus
571. Omar Khayyám
572. Edwin Hubble
573. Simone de Beauvoir
574. Oscar Wilde
575. George Wythe
576. Zhou Enlai
577. William Wordsworth
578. Gustav Mahler
579. Anna Comnena
580. Angela Merici
581. Mildred "Babe" Didrikson Zaharias
582. Eamon De Valera
583. Mahmud of Ghazna
584. Thomas Mann
585. Mohammed Ali Jinnah
586. Mary Mallon
587. Honoré Daumier
588. Francisco de Miranda
589. Robert Owen
590. Rashi
591. Lu Hsün
592. Henri Cartier-Bresson
593. Bertrand Russell
594. William of Sens
595. Anthony of Padua

596. Eisai
597. Ramakrishna
598. Minamoto no Yoritomo
599. Nicolás de Ovando
600. Douglas MacArthur

601–700

601. William of Ockham
602. King Gillette
603. Rowland Hill
604. John R. Pierce
605. Joseph Henry
606. Georgia O'Keeffe
607. Émile Zola
608. Robert Browning
609. Charles Goodyear
610. Mary Stuart
611. Alexis de Tocqueville
612. Robert Swanson
613. Louis IX of France
614. Helena Rubinstein
615. Sergey Prokofiev
616. Ian Wilmut
617. Niccolò Paganini
618. Christina Rossetti
619. Nikita Khrushchev
620. Regiomontanus
621. Andreas Marggraf
622. Charles Michel de L'Epee
623. Deng Xiaoping
624. Horatio Nelson
625. Berthe Morisot
626. Paul Julius Reuter
627. Pope John Paul II
628. Stephen Langton
629. Anna Freud
630. José de San Martín
631. Ernest Mach
632. Catherine de Médicis
633. Charles-Pierre Baudelaire
634. Ludwig Wittgenstein
635. John Duns Scotus

636. Dietrich Bonhoeffer
637. Konstantin E. Tsiolkovsky
638. William Gladstone
639. Benjamin Disraeli
640. Philippe Pinel
641. James Gordon Bennett
642. Inigo Jones
643. Pierre-Marie-Alexis Millardet
644. William Morris
645. Peter Goldmark
646. Robert A. Watson-Watt
647. Aleksandr Solzhenitsyn
648. Pierre-Joseph Proudhon
649. William Randolph Hearst
650. Maria Montessori
651. Ts'ao Chan
652. Nicolas Leblanc
653. Dorothy Day
654. Edward Gibbon
655. James Wolfe
656. Elizabeth Seton
657. Pierre Bonnard
658. Stephen I of Hungary
659. Henry VII of England
660. John Gregg
661. Samuel Gompers
662. Crazy Horse
663. Gotthold Lessing
664. Grandma Moses
665. Luther Burbank
666. Francisco Franco
667. Dom Pedro II of Brazil
668. Charles Atlas
669. Haile Selassie
670. Albert Schweitzer
671. Hector Berlioz
672. John James Audubon
673. al-Mahdi
674. George Gamow
675. Nathaniel Hawthorne
676. Antonín Dvořák

677. Frances Willard
678. Jim Thorpe
679. Sato Eisaku
680. Joseph Glidden
681. Muhammad Ali
682. Dorothy Crowfoot Hodgkin
683. Blackbeard
684. Alexander Parkes
685. Jacques Cousteau
686. Henry Fielding
687. Gerhard Groote
688. Chester Carlson
689. Elizabeth Kenny
690. Kwame Nkrumah
691. Thomas Carlyle
692. John L. Sullivan
693. Hannah Glasse
694. Blanche of Castile
695. Zwangendaba
696. Neil Armstrong
697. Bayezid
698. Thomas Hopkins Gallaudet
699. Unkei
700. Theodore Roosevelt

701–800

701. William Morton
702. Emperor Joseph II
703. Peter Drucker
704. Amelia Earhart
705. René Favaloro
706. Abbas I of Persia
707. Matthew Perry
708. James Monroe
709. Sophie Germain
710. John Bardeen
711. Georges Clemenceau
712. John Ford
713. Stephen Wozniak
714. Leo Szilard
715. Seymour Cray
716. Herman Melville

717. Katharine Dexter McCormick
718. Giuseppe Fiorelli
719. Margaret Thatcher
720. T. S. Eliot
721. Colette
722. Alfonso X of Spain
723. Martin Buber
724. David Livingstone
725. Gertrude Stein
726. Albertus Magnus
727. David Packard
728. Julia Margaret Cameron
729. Edward Robinson Squibb
730. Robert Noyce
731. Milton Friedman
732. Antonio Vivaldi
733. Theodor Schwann
734. Mobutu Seso Seke
735. Salvador Dali
736. Queen Margaret of Denmark
737. Alexander Nevsky
738. Friedrich Von Hayek
739. Matteo Ricci
740. Ray Kroc
741. Franz Boas
742. Helmut Kohl
743. Pierre de Coubertin
744. Ralph Nader
745. Eduard Bernstein
746. Alfred Hitchcock
747. Edward Bernays
748. Sébastien Le Prestre de Vauban
749. Charles Proteus Steinmetz
750. Friedrich Wilhelm Bessel
751. Jean Nidetch
752. Albert Camus
753. Juan Perón
754. Stephen Crane

755. Mary Cassatt
756. Robert Louis Stevenson
757. Tulsidas
758. Samuel Pepys
759. Elizabeth Barrett Browning
760. George Orwell
761. Jean-Bernard-Léon Foucault
762. James McNeill Whistler
763. John Harvard
764. William S. Gilbert
765. Herbert of Cherbury
766. Muddy Waters
767. Izaak Walton
768. Daniel Edgar Sickles
769. Buckminster Fuller
770. Charles Frederick Worth
771. Ou-yang Hsiu
772. Mother Teresa
773. Mordecai Anielewicz
774. Toni Morrison
775. Andrei Sakharov
776. Heinrich Schliemann
777. Barthold Georg Niebuhr
778. Euclides da Cunha
779. Emily Post
780. Fernão Lopes
781. Marie-Antoinette
782. Toussaint-L'Ouverture
783. Alexander Calder
784. Louise Brown
785. Jackson Pollock
786. George Fox
787. Jonathan Edwards
788. Werner Forssmann
789. Robert Baden-Powell
790. Robert the Bruce
791. Indira Gandhi
792. Peter Carl Fabergé
793. Cyrus McCormick
794. Pope Julius II
795. Charlie Chaplin

796. Thomas Babington
Macauley
797. Piet Mondrian
798. David Bushnell
799. Thomas Huxley
800. John Chapman

801–900

801. El Cid
802. Pope Gregory XIII
803. Johann Strauss
804. William Pitt the Elder
805. Henry de Bracton
806. Max Weber
807. Miguel Hidalgo
y Costilla
808. Herbert Spencer
809. Pierre Teilhard
de Chardin
810. William Wilberforce
811. Ben Jonson
812. Brigham Young
813. Leon Battista Alberti
814. Alexander Cartwright
815. Hans-Joachim Pabst
von Ohain
816. Jerzy Neyman
817. Henri Toulouse-Lautrec
818. Martha Graham
819. Charles H. Townes
820. Laurence Olivier
821. Malcolm X
822. Igor Sikorsky
823. John Pym
824. John Graunt
825. J. Willard Gibbs
826. Felix Hoffmann
827. Sarah Josepha Hale
828. Robert Frost
829. Francis Fry
830. David Sarnoff
831. Dom Pérignon
832. Friedrich Serturner
833. Stephen Foster

834. Federico Fellini
835. Edwin Drake
836. Simon Stevin
837. Pope Boniface VIII
838. Sergey Diaghilev
839. Paul Klee
840. Pele
841. Richard Rodgers
842. Louis Wirth
843. Jayavarman VII
of Indochina
844. Langston Hughes
845. Lewis Carroll
846. Algernon Charles
Swinburne
847. Umm Kulthum
848. Lord Palmerston
849. Alfred Kinsey
850. The Marquis
de Lafayette
851. Cosimo de'Medici
852. Catherine of Aragon
853. Miyan Tansen
854. Bronislaw Malinowski
855. Maurice Ravel
856. Bernardino Ramazzini
857. George Gershwin
858. Francisco Pizarro
859. George Gallup
860. Bonaventure
861. Florence Kelley
862. Anwar el-Sadat
863. John Napier
864. Karl Landsteiner
865. Johann Pestalozzi
866. Christine de Pisan
867. Harvey Wiley
868. Kurosawa Akira
869. Robert Clive
870. Anthony Van Dyck
871. Luigi Pirandello
872. John Dewey
873. Dorothea Dix
874. Alexandre Dumas

875. François-André Philidor
876. Willard Libby
877. Alexander MacKenzie
878. Isaac Bashevis Singer
879. James I of England
880. Judah ha-Levi
881. Paul Kruger
882. Thomas Nast
883. Afonso de Albuquerque
884. Marcello Malpighi
885. John Macdonald
886. Emma Goldman
887. Arthur Rimbaud
888. Bob Dylan
889. Warren Buffett
890. Henri Bergson
891. John H. Hammond, Jr.
892. Giuseppe Mazzini
893. Samuel Hahnemann
894. Golda Meir
895. Henry Moore
896. John Henry Newman
897. Rabindranath Tagore
898. Mikhail Kutuzov
899. Jack London
900. Cole Porter

901–1,000

901. John Steinbeck
902. Frances Perkins
903. Michael Jordan
904. Richard M. Nixon
905. Reinhold Niebuhr
906. Friedrich Froebel
907. César Ritz
908. Erich Maria Remarque
909. Gregory Martin
910. Karl Barth
911. William Jennings
Bryan
912. Noam Chomsky
913. Hannah Arendt
914. Martin Heidegger
915. Franklin Kameny

916. Frank Gilbreth
917. Walter Hunt
918. Joseph Goebbels
919. William Cobbett
920. Girolamo Fracastoro
921. Sri Ramana Maharishi
922. Paul Robeson
923. Grote Reber
924. John Philip Sousa
925. Antonio de Mendoza
926. Jean-Auguste-Dominique Ingres
927. Samuel Beckett
928. Peter Behrens
929. Federico García Lorca
930. Jane Cunningham Croly
931. François Truffaut
932. Robert Peel
933. Stephen Biko
934. Marcel Marceau
935. George Mallory
936. Henry Clay
937. Hugh Hefner
938. Pancho Villa
939. Ibn Battutah
940. Mata Hari
941. Che Guevara
942. Andre Malraux
943. Emperor Maximilian I

944. Rosa Parks
945. Simon Wiesenthal
946. Benjamin Lee Guinness
947. Josef Pilsudski
948. Matthew Arnold
949. Teresa of Ávila
950. Kahlil Gibran
951. Katharine Hepburn
952. Cary Grant
953. Julius Nyerere
954. Dwight L. Moody
955. Amina
956. Louis Braille
957. Edward Lear
958. Ingmar Bergman
959. John von Neumann
960. Ada Byron Lovelace
961. Andrew Carnegie
962. Mary Pickford
963. Roger Bannister
964. John L. Lewis
965. Aaron Copland
966. Srinivasa Ramanujan
967. Charles Drew
968. Captain Kidd
969. Scipione Riva-Rocci
970. Harry Houdini
971. Virginia Apgar
972. Coco Chanel

973. Francis Baring
974. René-Théophile-Hyacinthe Laënnec
975. Jethro Tull
976. Sergey Korolyov
977. Henry Shrapnel
978. Alfred Sloan, Jr.
979. Albert Lasker
980. Daniel Hale Williams
981. A.P. Giannini
982. John Pemberton
983. Marion Donovan
984. Mahalia Jackson
985. Henry Rous
986. Henry Robert
987. Al Neuharth
988. Walter C. Wingfield
989. Fela
990. Joseph Bramah
991. Hubert Booth
992. Edmond Hoyle
993. Ella Fitzgerald
994. William Levitt
995. Elijah McCoy
996. Bernard Cornfeld
997. Marilyn Monroe
998. Theodore Seuss Geisel
999. George Santayana
1,000. Andy Warhol

Ten Who Almost Made It
Lady Godiva
Amerigo Vespucci
Pocahontas
Pyotr Ilich Tchaikovsky
Ronald Reagan
John F. Kennedy
Oprah Winfrey
William Gates
Cal Ripken, Jr.
Diana, Princess of Wales

If you are looking for the unsung and the underappreciated, skip the first chapter.

From number 1, Johannes Gutenberg, to number 100, Henry VIII of England, the names of the top people of the millennium will be familiar to most readers, or should be. Of course, that won't stop the quibbling.

Was Galileo the greatest scientist, George Washington the most important American, Elizabeth I of England the foremost woman? Is Beethoven—a mere scribbler of melodies, many will argue—worthy of inclusion in the top 10? We say yes to those questions.

We also say that it is too soon to define the lasting influence of people who are alive now. So none of them is in the top 100 and neither are many of our *near* contemporaries.

Einstein, Churchill, Mao, Fleming, Stalin, King, Oppenheimer, Zworykin, Sanger, and Eckert are the only members of the top 100 to live in the second half of the twentieth century, and only computer pioneer Eckert, who died in 1995, came close to reaching the next millennium.

Our first living legend: DNA detective James Watson, who is in the second group of 100.

But we're getting ahead of ourselves . . .

1 JOHANNES GUTENBERG (1394?–1468)
our man of the millennium

If not for Gutenberg, Columbus (2) might never have set sail, Shakespeare's (5) genius could have died with him, and Martin Luther's (3) Ninety-five Theses would have hung on that door unheeded. In fact, without mass quantities of books to burn, the Inquisition could have fallen flat on its face. The printing press, developed by goldsmith Gutenberg in the 1430s, helped spread truth, beauty, and yes, heresy throughout the world. We know the Chinese had movable type for centuries before Gutenberg, but they used it for silk printing, not books. Gutenberg, however, always had publishing in mind. Copies of his first major project, the Bible, survive today. He worked for years to perfect his system of movable type and a press that could mass-produce books, leaflets, and propaganda. What little is known about Gutenberg comes from the many lawsuits filed against him for the rights to the invention. But no one successfully challenged Gutenberg's place as the Western inventor of movable type and the printing press. Because his press unharnessed the power of ideas on the world, we rank him ahead of the people whose ideas found an audience through printing. **21,768**

2 CHRISTOPHER COLUMBUS (1451–1506)
the agent of Western civilization

This Genoese weaver's son altered the fabric of civilization by convincing Spanish queen Isabella (117) to finance his plan to sail west to beat the Portuguese to the treasures of the East. Bad math helped his salesmanship; he underestimated the miles to Japan by 8,200. Lucky for him, a new world was in the way. Biographer Samuel Eliot Morison called Columbus's October 12, 1492, landing on a spit of sand on San Salvador the most important event for humanity since the birth of Christ. From prehistory, the earth had been populated by aborigines at one with nature, not above it. Columbus's arrival hastened the burial of pastoral cultures under the steamroller of Western progress. Medieval advances in seafaring made the fatal contact inevitable, but Columbus gets points for getting there first. **21,756**

3 MARTIN LUTHER (1483–1546)
the monk who divided Christendom

On October 31, 1517, Saxon monk Martin Luther tacked his Ninety-five Theses to the door of Wittenberg's castle church, and the world was never the same. His denunciation of priestly hucksters' "get-out-of-sin-free" indulgences started a revolt that ended Western Christendom's twelve hundred years of ideological unity, touched off a century and a half of religious warfare, and stimulated nationalism and capitalism. Reformer Desiderius Erasmus (97) tried to get Luther to tone down the attacks on the pope, but Luther was pigheaded. Using the new printing technology to whip up a following, Luther belittled the sacraments, argued for state power over religion, and championed heresies we now consider commonplace. Decades later Catholic emperor Charles V (61) said his worst mistake was not hanging Luther. If he had, maybe Charles would be number 3 on our list. **21,753**

4 GALILEO GALILEI (1564–1642)
founder of modern science

Copernicus (18) popularized the heretical idea that the earth was not central to the universe. For teaching how to search for what *was*, we rank Galileo highest among scientists. Galileo built the first astronomical telescope, discovered the craters of the moon, invented a better clock, and revealed the laws of bodies in motion. Better yet were his abstract contributions—yoking mathematics to physics and showing that truth comes from experiments that prove theories, not from dogma. He paid for those contributions. In 1633 the Inquisition silenced him, but not his creed. "Minds created free by God must never be enslaved," Galileo wrote in the margins of his Copernicus-championing book, *The Dialogues*. Old ideas die hard. Not until 1822 did the Catholic Church lift its ban on *The Dialogues*. In the modern world science has triumphed over superstition because of Galileo and experimenters who followed him. **21,751**

5 WILLIAM SHAKESPEARE (1564–1616)
mirror of the millennium's soul

Of all poets, said John Dryden (366), Shakespeare had the largest and most comprehensive soul. Also the largest vocabulary, employing 24,000 different words to create his works. What fools we mortals be to sing his praises in so few. But even the Bard of Avon would concede that brevity is the soul of wit. So consider this: Shakespeare gave the stage the immortal *Hamlet, Macbeth, Othello, King Lear,* and much more— but left no personal letters. Records show he was born and reared in Stratford-upon-Avon, had a solid education steeped in Latin, and, historians think, gained experience in theater before surfacing in London in 1587 as playwright, director, and actor. Shakespeare was more intent on building his family's good name and comfortable lifestyle than in preserving his works. Thankfully, seven years after his death, two associates published his plays. Poet William Wordsworth (577), a great admirer, once exclaimed in a weak moment to essayist Charles Lamb that "anyone could write like Shakespeare if he had a mind to it." To which Lamb replied: "All that's lacking is, apparently, the mind." **21,709**

6 ISAAC NEWTON (1642–1727)
the big apple of science

Yes, we judge him ahead of Copernicus (18) and Einstein (17) (and behind Galileo only because the Italian sage led the way). One would have to go back 2,400 years to meet his match (in Aristotle). Born the year Galileo (4) died, a premature baby so small his mother said he could fit into a quart mug, Newton wasn't expected to live. But live he did, and what a life! Wrote Alexander Pope: "Nature and Nature's laws lay hid in night: / God said, Let Newton be! and all was light." William Wordsworth (577) described him as "a mind forever / Voyaging through strange seas of thought, alone." He discovered the laws of gravity and motion that hold the universe together, founded the science of physical optics, and shared the invention of the calculus with Leibniz (88). Voltaire (36) spread the story, apocryphal or not, that a falling apple inspired him. Newton was hot-tempered and vindictive, but the author of *Principia Mathematica* and inaugurator of the Age of Reason can be forgiven almost any foible. **21,706**

7 CHARLES DARWIN (1809–1882)
detonator of the scientific revolution known as the theory of evolution

Just as Copernicus (18) displaced the earth from the center of the universe, so Darwin exiled man from the company of the angels, and God from the Creation story, with his doctrine of natural selection and his proposal that all living creatures evolved from a common ancestor. Ironically, the book this British naturalist took on his five-year voyage aboard the H.M.S. *Beagle* to survey South America's coasts was Milton's (53) *Paradise Lost*. We rate Darwin's *Origin of the Species,* the fruit of the *Beagle* expedition, the most influential book of the nineteenth century, surpassing even Marx's

(14) *Das Kapital.* For not only did it overthrow beliefs dating back to man's beginnings, its conclusions, unlike Marx's, endure. Despite his discovery of the struggle for survival, Darwin hated nature's "clumsy, wasteful, blundering, low and horribly cruel works." For him, the cruelest was an insect bite in an Andean village that turned him into a semi-invalid for life. Still, Nature gave him the strength afterward to marry his cousin and produce five little Darwins. **21,689**

8 THOMAS AQUINAS (1225–1274)
Christianity's voice of reason

Tommaso d'Aquino's noble Italian family was so adamant against his decision to join the Dominicans that his mother had him imprisoned in the family castle. Then, the story goes, his brothers tried to lure him from his vocation with a prostitute. It was not to be. Thomas held her off with a torch and joined the religious order. Often referred to as a "dumb ox" because he was so physically slow, Thomas's mind succeeded where his body could not. His masterpiece, *Summa Theologica,* reconciled the teachings of classical philosophers with Catholic doctrine. Since then other philosophers have merely sifted through his genius, but none has usurped his position as the church's most important philosopher. In his two-million-word tome, Thomas provided billions of Christians for eight hundred years with the proof of God's existence and answered moral questions, but he died before completing his discussion on the life of Christ. **21,685**

9 LEONARDO DA VINCI (1452–1519)
the ultimate Renaissance man

Illegitimate son of a peasant girl and a Florentine lawyer, Leonardo's amazing artistic talent surfaced when he was a mere boy. He produced few paintings—and left some unfinished—but he still created masterpieces. Best known is the celebrated *Mona Lisa,* whose eyes are said to shine with the artist's own mysterious wisdom. Da Vinci's scope was limitless; the epitome of the Renaissance man, he worked as a military architect and engineer, studied geology, botany, hydraulics, and mechanics, and did theoretical work in mathematics. Through it all he saw art as a means to intellectual growth. His mission became to observe and record—through scientific drawings and commentary—all the world's objects, including the human organism, drawn from cadavers he dissected in a hospital. Sigmund Freud (15) said, "He was like a man who wakes up too early, in pitch darkness, while everyone else is still sleeping." To contemporaries, Leonardo lived more in the future than his present; among the thousands of pages of his drawings are plans for submarines and flying machines. **21,634**

10 LUDWIG VAN BEETHOVEN (1770–1827)
music's titan

An autopsy by a doctor, aptly named Wagner, revealed that the convolutions in Beethoven's brain were extraordinarily deep and wide. Might as well dissect a sunset to explain God. Before Beethoven, the best music could transport the listener to occasional psychic realms of beauty and truth. But in Beethoven's mightiest symphonies, concertos, chamber works, and opera, *Fidelio,* the transports are infinite and unceasing. Some were written in the throes of a cruel deafness. "The thing that marks him out from all the others, is his disturbing quality, his power of unsettling us and imposing his giant moods on us," music-loving playwright George Bernard Shaw wrote. As the bridge between classicism and romanticism, Beethoven was the starting point for worship of the new, the nineteenth century's dubious contribution to art. Our favorite compositions: the magisterial Ninth Symphony, of course, and the last six string quartets. **21,631**

11 JOHN LOCKE (1632–1704)
democracy's philosopher

The asthmatic Locke found nothing more suffocating than metaphysical disputation. "Fiddling" is what he called such unproductive philosophizing. He believed in facts, facts, facts. Nothing is innate, he claimed; all knowledge is derived from experience. Such concepts had a profound influence on education and science. Even more important were his thoughts on government. He believed in checks and balances, the sanctity of property and labor, and the absurdity of hereditary rule. Looking for examples of his influence? Start with the Declaration of Independence and the U.S. Constitution. This Puritan lawyer's son was a physician and public servant whose association with fellow liberals made the uptight government of England's Charles II queasy. So Locke went to Holland, always a haven for freethinkers. No wunderkind, he didn't put his thoughts on paper until he was fifty-four, after the English Revolution of 1688 made it safe. **21,627**

12 MOHANDAS K. GANDHI (1869–1948)
the peaceful slayer of an empire

The unassertive Gandhi failed at law in India, so he took his practice to South Africa. There he found his calling: employing civil disobedience to fight injustice against minority Indians. Back home, the loincloth-clad Gandhi led a life of abstinence and prayer while he struggled to win India's independence from British rule. Indians revered him as Mahatma, "the Great Soul." The British considered him a thorn in their side. Gandhi launched widespread resistance movements in 1920–22, 1930–34, and 1940–42. In 1947 the British yielded and granted India dominion status. Even Gandhi's opponents had to admire him. While jailed in South Africa for challenging the government, he had made sandals for General Jan Smuts. The statesman returned them years later, saying, "I am not worthy to stand in the shoes of so great a man." After Gandhi, Western colonialism was doomed. On his way to evening prayers, the peace-loving Gandhi was assassinated by a Hindu fanatic. **21,614**

13 MICHELANGELO BUONARROTI (1475–1564)
first among artists

By the time Michelangelo died at age eighty-eight, Renaissance Italians believed him divine—how else could they explain his genius? Michelangelo fought the disapproval of his aristocratic father to apprentice as an artist, then studied anatomy by dissecting corpses. In 1499 he signed a contract promising to create "the most beautiful work in marble which exists today in Rome." He sculpted the *Pietà*, which still meets that description. Then his nude statue of *David*, crafted from a discarded hunk of marble, revealed his understanding of the human form. When Pope Julius II (794) conscripted him to do something with the ceiling of a small chapel at St. Peter's, Michelangelo balked. He was a sculptor, he said, not a painter. Yet this completed ceiling in the Sistine Chapel, whose creation required four years of backbreaking labor conducted seventy feet off the ground, remains the most magnificent fresco ever painted. **21,579**

14 KARL MARX (1818–1883)
founder of modern communism

Half the world was once ruled in his name; today Marxists fight for survival in university history departments. The German philosopher's central proposition was the triumph of the workers in a class struggle ordained by the iron laws of history. His writings ranged from the turgid economic analysis of *Das Kapital* ("Capitalist production begets its own negation") to the wit of the *Eighteenth Brumaire of Louis Bonaparte* with its put-down of Napoleon III (history repeats itself "the first time as tragedy, the second time as farce"). His voluminous writings formed the core of Communist ideology. In college, after a spree of carousing, he plunged so deeply into his studies that his father, a converted Jewish lawyer, rebuked him for "brooding over melancholy oil lamps." Forced to seek political refuge in London, he haunted the British Museum and wrote about Europe for Horace Greeley's *New York Tribune* while his family ate potatoes in a two-room flat. **21,566**

15 SIGMUND FREUD (1856–1939)
sage of the subconscious

As the founder of psychoanalysis, Freud altered forever our view of the human mind with his concepts of the Oedipus complex, dreams, wish fulfillment, the pleasure-unpleasure principle, transference, and the mind's division into id, ego, and superego. Reading Freud can be fun; our favorite: "Sometimes a cigar is just a cigar." Freud alienated disciples like Alfred Adler and Carl Jung (146), and lately revisionists have taken to branding him a megalomaniac and his theories unscientific drivel. But his thinking was original and profound, contributing immeasurably to our understanding of people's motives and behavior. Besides, how can you dislike a guy who wrote his betrothed nine hundred love letters? **21,550**

16 NAPOLEON I (1769–1821)
the human god of war

Napoleon Bonaparte's genius on the battlefield outweighs his shortcomings. Suffering from a classic Napoleonic complex, the five-foot-two native of Corsica fought in the French Revolution and became a general by age twenty-five, later to become France's dictator. Napoleon's civil code, which is still the law in much of Europe, reorganized the courts and guaranteed citizens the freedoms promised by the Revolution. Then Napoleon got carried away by his own success. He proclaimed himself emperor of France in 1804 and swept across Europe with his army, creating the largest European empire since the Romans. In every conquered territory he abolished feudalism and established a parliament—but make no mistake, he was still a dictator. His undoing came when he tried to conquer Russia. Europe united against him, and he met his Waterloo on a battlefield in Belgium in June 1815. He escaped to St. Helena in the Atlantic Ocean, where he lived in exile and died six years later of stomach cancer. **21,545**

17 ALBERT EINSTEIN (1879–1955)
the brain behind the revolution in physics

His general theory of relativity supplanted Newton's (6) mechanistic vision of the universe by viewing gravity as a curvature through space-time. In many ways his life was a tragedy. A pacifist, he propelled the world into the atomic age. The foremost scientific genius of the twentieth century, he rejected tenets of quantum theory with all its incertitude (because "God is not malicious") and spent his final years in futile pursuit of a unified field theory of the universe. A father figure to the world (he once asked why "nobody understands me and everybody likes me"), he let down his own children, giving up a daughter for adoption and alienating his younger son by his aloofness. Despairing over humanity's inhumanity, this German Jew who fled the Nazis to America once said, "Politics are for the moment. An equation is for eternity." His, establishing the equivalence of mass and energy, was $E = mc^2$. **21,544**

18 NICHOLAS COPERNICUS (1473–1543)
astronomer who dethroned man from the center of the cosmos

We know now that the earth revolves around the sun. But half a millennium ago the idea was incomprehensible: "No one in his senses will ever think the earth, heavy and unwieldy from its own weight and mass, staggers up and down around its own center and that of the sun," declared Jean Bodin, a sixteenth-century religious liberal. The Polish Copernicus initially challenged that orthodoxy reluctantly, but his studies of the sky and ancient texts forced him finally to reject it. His theory overthrew the fifteen-hundred-year-old Ptolemaic system and laid the foundation for modern astronomy and Newtonian physics. Historian Arthur Koestler called Copernicus a "conservative cleric, who started the revolution against his will." Indeed, he procrastinated so long in publishing his findings that the manuscript reached him only on his deathbed—by which time, wrote his friend Bishop Giese, "he had lost his memory." **21,425**

19 JEAN-JACQUES ROUSSEAU (1712–1778)
spiritual father of just about everything

Revolution, romanticism, individualism, communism, fascism, psychoanalysis, sexism—you name it, you can find its origins in the writings of Rousseau. He was a contradiction-filled Swiss-born philosopher who abandoned his offspring but then wrote *Émile,* a child-rearing guide that influenced generations of educators. He believed that humans were inherently good, and he

championed civil rights in such masterpieces as *The Social Contract,* but he argued that women belonged in the kitchen. "Man is born free, but everywhere he is in chains," Rousseau wrote, but he also called for the subjugation of the individual to the will of the state. That sounds like fascism to us. Psychohistorians say Rousseau's obsession with his deformed penis—he wrote about it without giving graphic details—made him neurotic. Hard to prove, but such revelations in his *Confessions* showed Rousseau-ridden romantics how to elevate delightful excesses of public introspection into art. **21,414**

20 ADOLF HITLER (1889–1945)
the millennium's most evil man

It is relatively easy to explain the rise of a dictator who preached national pride to a country that had been humiliated in World War I, but no words explain Hitler. Despots of centuries past were barbarians ignorant of civilized behavior. That doesn't diminish their culpability, but it underscores Hitler's. He was supposed to be a civilized man of a civilized time. Yet the extermination of Jews in death camps was his "final solution of the Jewish question." A high-school dropout who was gassed in World War I as a soldier, Hitler seized control of Germany as head of the Nazi Party in 1933. His invasion of Poland triggered World War II. By the time he committed suicide in defeat, he had killed six million Jews in the Holocaust and his country was wrenched in half—a schism that lasted more than forty years. **21,410**

21 ADAM SMITH (1723–1790)
high priest of capitalism

As Marx's theories fade into irrelevance, this Scottish scholar's star continues to rise. His

Wealth of Nations, published in 1776, is the bible of the classical school of economics, with its attacks on mercantilism and government intrusion in the marketplace, its defense of free trade, and its exaltation of private property and individual self-interest (guided always by the "invisible hand" of society's well-being). In the 1960s such principles came under relentless attack; at the dawn of the new millennium, they underpin the global economy. Smith also got in some delicious digs at bureaucrats, like: "The whole, or almost the whole, public revenue, is in most countries, employed in maintaining unproductive hands." His book's wonderful "Index of Subjects" is worth reading on its own merits. Samples: "Beggar, alone depends on benevolence, 14; once synonymous with scholar, 132," and "Cockfighting has ruined many, 859."   **21,375**

22 GEORGE WASHINGTON (1732–1799)
"Father of Our Country"

He could have been King George I. But while some architects of the Constitution favored a monarchy, Washington had a democratic vision. He refused a crown but was elected president unanimously at the Constitutional Convention in 1789. In office Washington set precedents for the workings of the executive branch. Thanks to his quiet stalwart leadership, this new government system was given a chance to flourish. Before Washington became president, he was already a legend. The apocryphal story of chopping down his father's cherry tree and then confessing because, he said, "I cannot tell a lie," illustrates the esteem Washington had earned among his countrymen. As commander of the Continental Army during the revolution, Washington showed battlefield brilliance. Again, his successes are steeped in legend—regrouping his forces in the bitter winter at Valley Forge, crossing the Delaware River, and sleeping at countless bed and breakfasts along the way.   **21,370**

23&24 WILBUR (1867–1912) and ORVILLE (1871–1948) WRIGHT
the original "Wright Stuff"

No one person invented the airplane. Like many great innovations—the automobile, the television, and the computer, for example—the airplane resulted from the work of many. But Wilbur and Orville score big points for being the first to fly a powered, manned airplane. Try as we have to pen separate entries for Wilbur and Orville, their stories are inextricably entwined—they were always a team. First they edited a newspaper in their hometown of Dayton, Ohio. Then they designed and manufactured bicycles there. Together they explored the mysteries of flight. Using the foundational research of German Otto Lilienthal (102), the Wright brothers constructed a flying machine with a twelve-horsepower engine, a sleek propeller, and a movable rudder for controlling direction. Weighing in at 750 pounds, including the pilot, the plane flew into history on December 17, 1903, when it took off from a field near Kitty Hawk, North Carolina, and stayed aloft for fifty-nine seconds. Travel was never again the same. After that first flight the Wright brothers improved their "aeroplane" and promoted it. Wilbur died of typhoid fever thirty-six years before his younger brother. Orville, however, reaped the financial benefits of their achievement. He lived to see his invention reduce around-the-world travel to hours, change the course of warfare, and transform twentieth-century life.   FOR EACH: **21,362**

25 RENÉ DESCARTES (1596–1650)
progenitor of modern philosophy and inventor of analytic geometry

The boy Descartes asked "Why?" so often, his

father dubbed him his "little philosopher." Taught by demanding Jesuits, he nevertheless found his education lacking. He was plagued by uncertainties and had "the extreme desire to distinguish truth from falsity." So, cushioned by an inheritance and his patrons' largesse, Descartes devoted 1628–49 to quiet study in the Netherlands and produced his major philosophical works, notably the *Meditations*. In it he discarded scholasticism, which arrived at "truths" based on the views of authorities, and instead applied the rational inductive methods of science and mathematics to philosophy. Vowing to consider nothing true until he could find grounds for believing it so, he established one firm fact: "I think, therefore I am." Descartes also developed the Cartesian coordinate system for graphing equations and geometric shapes, which guides mapmakers even today.   **21,348**

26 LOUIS PASTEUR (1822–1895)
human scourge of microorganisms

Pasteur's theory that disease occurs when germs attack the body from the outside triumphed over the long-held view that germs were spontaneously produced in substances themselves. Today the French researcher's name graces milk cartons for his "pasteurization" process, which safeguards beverages and foods by zapping harmful germs with heat. Countless human and animal lives have been saved with vaccines he developed against rabies and anthrax. Contemporaries hailed him as a hero for using science to master nature and aid mankind. Pasteur had almost superhuman powers of observation and was obsessed with germs both in and outside the lab. Friends said Pasteur avoided shaking hands for fear of infection, wiped his plate and glass with his napkin to remove contaminating dirt before dining, and painstakingly dissected his bread, finding tiny bits of foreign

matter, including roaches, where nobody else could see them.   **21,332**

27 PETER THE GREAT (1672–1725)
czar who built Russia into a great power by Westernizing it

Posing as "Sergeant Mikhaylov" on a trip through Holland, England, and Austria in 1697–98, Peter seized upon the technological innovations of those countries wherever he saw them. Back home, he launched a feverish program to create Russia's first navy and modernize its military, designing some of the guns himself. He banned beards—too "Asian"—and sheared recalcitrant aristocrats himself. He would sometimes smack his ministers with his walking stick, especially if he were hung over from one of his massive drinking bouts. He was ruthless in amassing power, yet once, awestruck at a conspirator's ability to withstand torture, Peter walked up to him, kissed him, and forgave him. He died from a fever after diving from his yacht into icy waters to save a boatload of drowning soldiers.   **21,317**

28 THOMAS ALVA EDISON (1847–1931)
the man who lit the world

The electric light bulb, phonograph, and movie projector were among Edison's 1,093 patented inventions, many of which revolutionized modern life. The phonograph, for one, allowed sound for the first time to be recorded mechanically. Equally worthy was his Menlo Park, New Jersey, lab, with its white-coated assistants conducting experiments in assembly-line style, a forerunner of the industrial research laboratory. The nation hailed his achievements, but making money, not headlines, had always been Edison's prime motivation. By forty he was a millionaire, yet he couldn't manage his wealth and was chronically in debt. A genius at technology, he was socially inept. He was fired from job after job for recklessness. Once he wired a washbasin and gleefully watched the near-electrocution of coworkers. The years finally sobered Edison, although they couldn't curb his zest for discovery. At age eighty-two he said: "I am long on ideas but short of time. I only expect to live to be about one hundred." One thing Edison couldn't invent was more time. He died at eighty-four. **21,310**

29 WILLIAM I (c.1028–1087)
"the Conqueror" of England

Without this French feudal lord's arrival on the scene, England could have stayed a backwater for centuries. First known as "William the Bastard," he survived childhood as the target of murderous relatives. It honed him into one of the greatest soldiers and rulers of the Middle Ages. In October 1066 William led a force of six thousand men from northern France, across the English Channel, and to landfall near Hastings, where they defeated and killed King Harold of England. William's firm hand brought unity and a centralized government to the Anglo-Saxon land, strengthened the justice system through use of juries, and linked England economically with France and Mediterranean states. Greedy and pitiless, William wanted to squeeze more taxes from his subjects when he commissioned the Domesday Book. But this massive survey of English land—village by village—is now prized as a historical gem. **21,295**

30 DANTE ALIGHIERI (1265–1321)
divine poet of vernacular verse

Modern literature owes Dante big-time. Because this philosopher-poet chose to write in his native Italian rather than clerical Latin, he paved the way for Europe's emerging lay culture. He's best known for his epic poem, *The Divine Comedy*, a challenging read for the best of us. It's his vision of Hell, Purgatory, and Paradise. Magnificent

verse on its own, the poem is rich with theology, allegory, symbol, and commentary on contemporary life. It also mirrors Dante's own life story and spiritual development. When he wrote it, the dour Dante was a lost soul exiled from his native city of Florence after political enemies condemned him to death. His writings drew inspiration from his love for the beautiful Beatrice Portinari, a Florentine aristocrat he hardly knew, who died young. In *The Divine Comedy* Dante gives her immortality as Beatrice, his fictional guide through Paradise. **21,280**

31 ELIZABETH I (1533–1603)
molder of the modern British state

In forty-five anxious years of rule, she put England in the Protestant camp, unleashed the sea dogs who started the British Empire, and best of all, put trust in that cockpit of popular sovereignty, the House of Commons. Elizabeth surrounded herself with brilliant advisers like William Cecil, Walter Raleigh (472), and Francis Walsingham, and she listened to them. Up to a point. Independence was her prized possession, and she kept it by coy avoidance of marriage-minded princes and courtiers. Elizabeth's bravest act: ordering off the wigged head of her Catholic rival to the throne, Mary Queen of Scots (610), who would have ruined England with her beautiful wickedness. The defeat of the Spanish Armada in 1588 was Elizabeth's finest hour. Winston Churchill (38), an expert in such matters, wrote, "She had a capacity for inspiring devotion that is perhaps unparalleled among British sovereigns." **21,271**

32 ABRAHAM LINCOLN (1809–1865)
savior of the American union

Born in poverty in a log cabin in Kentucky, Abraham Lincoln grew (and grew—he was the tallest president, at six foot four) to become America's second-greatest leader. Lincoln, nicknamed "Old Abe" at age thirty-eight, won the presidency in 1860. When southern states rebelled, he led the North through the Civil War. His Emancipation Proclamation freed slaves in rebel states. "If my name ever goes into history, it will be for this act," he said. A fine orator, Lincoln's brief speech at the consecration of a cemetery on the site of the decisive battle of Gettysburg has become legendary American rhetoric. His assassination during a performance of *Our American Cousin* in Ford's Theater in Washington, D.C., elevated him to folk-hero status. While his February 12 birthday no longer earns his own national holiday, Lincoln's distinct profile, bony frame, and craggy face are etched in the annals of American history. **21,255**

33 JOHANNES KEPLER (1571–1630)
discoverer of the paths of the planets

Much of Kepler's work was astrological claptrap. He cast horoscopes for German nobles, but hey, everybody's got to make a living. His best achievement was discovering the proof that Copernicus (18) was right and that the earth and other planets *do* revolve around the sun. Kepler was an assistant to Tycho Brahe (202), a Dane who gathered volumes of data on the movements of the planets, especially Mars. Kepler studied the tables until he had his brainstorm that the orbits were elliptical. Eureka! Everything fit. Kepler's work also paved the way for calculus, and his ideas about planetary attraction provided the foundation for Isaac Newton's (6) principles. Nonscientific events, like the Thirty Years War, could be a distraction; it's hard to concentrate when you are evacuating a town. **21,249**

34 LEO TOLSTOY (1828–1910)
superman of letters

For *War and Peace* alone, he earns humankind's eternal gratitude. This tale of Russia caught up in Napoleon's (16) invasion is the greatest novel, a window both on Russia and the human soul. French historian Henri Troyat called it a "hymn to man and nature whose like has not been seen in the literature of the world." Tolstoy's energy was boundless; his son Ilya recalled how he took up Greek in his fifties and within six weeks was translating Herodotus. A man of contradictions—soldier turned pacifist, philanderer turned puritanical Christian, aristocrat turned peasants' champion—he also had a spiritual pride that bordered on messianism. To British writer Paul Johnson, Tolstoy thought of himself as "God's elder brother." But his advice to fellow writer Ivan Bunin was down to earth: "There is no happiness in life, only occasional flares of it. You must learn to live on them." **21,239**

35 JOHANN SEBASTIAN BACH (1685–1750)
inspiration for three centuries of musicians

It amazes us how a man who fathered twenty children found the energy to produce so much profound music. For churches and courts in music-mad Germany, Bach wrote hundreds of works for organ, instrumental ensembles, and chorus, many dashed off like a pastor's sermon in time for Sunday service. No master was better at weaving seemingly unconnected notes into a complex but coherent whole capped by a climax, and every scribbler of music from Mozart (52) to the moderns has been his awestruck debtor. If his appeal to later generations of casual listeners were greater, we would have ranked Bach before Beethoven (10). Even before he died, Bach's baroque style made him a musical fuddy-duddy to audiences keen for the breezier homophonic styles of newcomers, including four Bach sons. Our favorite Bach: the *St. Matthew Passion* and any fugue that's handy. **21,233**

36 VOLTAIRE (1694–1778)
apostle of enlightenment

He was a lifelong hypochondriac, but the autocratic religious and civic institutions of eighteenth-century France made him truly sick. Voltaire was the most popular Continental writer of his age, and even the establishment was riveted when he argued that God was neither just nor evil. Man, employing reason, was the only force for good on earth, he wrote in works that formed the intellectual underpinnings of the revolution that burst in France a decade after his death. "There will be an explosion at the first opportunity, and there will be quite a rumpus," he predicted. *Candide,* one of the ten most influential books of the millennium, taught that laughter and resignation are mankind's hope in a world beset by horror. Unlike most writers, Voltaire was a wise investor. His estate was worth $50 million in today's money.   **21,231**

37 FRANKLIN DELANO ROOSEVELT (1882–1945)
protector of the American way of life

Most Americans think of FDR, the thirty-second president of the United States, as the creator of social welfare; we prefer to think of him as the president who preserved capitalism, restored faith in government, and saved the world from Hitler (20). When FDR became president in 1933, America wallowed in the Great Depression. His building and road projects put desperate people back to work until factories geared up to arm the Allies. Without FDR's vision, capitalism could have been destroyed and America could have fallen prey to the evils that lurked across the oceans—fascism, Nazism, and Communism. While his New Deal revived the American economy, his "fireside chats" reassured a frightened people they had "nothing to fear but fear itself." The most popular president since George Washington (22),

his election to unprecedented third and fourth terms provided the Allied leadership needed to ensure victory during World War II.   **21,215**

38 WINSTON CHURCHILL (1874–1965)
hero of England's finest hour

To pay homage to Churchill, we paraphrase the words of the twentieth century's greatest orator himself. After all, never in the field of human conflict was so much owed by so many to one man. Early in World War II, when the British fought by themselves but not for themselves, Prime Minister Churchill offered countrymen his blood, toil, tears, and sweat. In his gravelly voice and with his signature cigar, Churchill prodded the conscience of democracy to resist Adolf Hitler (20) and his monstrous tyranny, the foulest and most soul-destroying tyranny. He crafted alliances with both President Roosevelt and Joseph Stalin (82), first to give Churchill the tools of war and ultimately to finish the job. How he led his people through their finest hour, even while Britain faded as a great world power, is *not* a riddle wrapped in a mystery inside an enigma.   **21,206**

39 FRANCIS OF ASSISI (1181/82–1226)
instrument of peace

Saint Francis was a ladies' man and Italian soldier until he had a vision of Christ and gave himself over to the poor, begging with them and mingling with lepers. He revered nature as the handiwork of God, calling animals his brothers and sisters. But he was no medieval ecologist; his purpose was to walk in Christ's footsteps. Traveling with the Crusaders in Egypt, he once tried to convert a town's Muslim defenders. Another time he preached naked from an Assisi pulpit. (You can look it up.) He was the first known Christian to find himself marked with the stigmata of the crucified Christ. The Franciscan order that he founded has made immense contributions to Western scholarship, but its main influence has been spiritual. "I have done what I had to do," Francis said toward the end of his life; "may Christ teach you what is your part." **21,182**

40 NICCOLÒ MACHIAVELLI (1469–1527)
first modern political scientist

If Machiavelli had been more Machiavellian, he would have cozied up to Giovanni de' Medici. When the Medicis took over Florence in 1512, they kicked Machiavelli out of his job as a diplomat. What do ex-officials do? They write books. Machiavelli's was *The Prince,* a Hints-from-Heloise book for despots on how to get power and keep it and one of the most influential political books of all time. It pooh-poohs rectitude as a tool for governance and rates Renaissance thug Cesare Borgia the ideal ruler. "Machiavellian" has come to describe those who use unscrupulous means to achieve power. That's terribly unfair. Machiavelli was merely a creature of his times, and a thoughtful philosopher, too. He helped develop secular history and political science by championing the notion that good government is government that works and needs no moral and religious underpinnings. **21,176**

41 VLADIMIR ILYICH LENIN (1870–1924)
primal revolutionary

He founded the Russian Communist Party, formulated Marxism-Leninism (you really must read all fifty-five volumes), led the Bolshevik Revolution, created the Soviet police state, quashed the counterrevolution, centralized the economy, and preached revolution abroad, all with a fanatical will. What drove him? Fury at the czar for hanging his beloved older brother? Revenge against his childhood playmates for calling their fat friend "little barrel"? No matter;

Lenin created the nightmare of twentieth-century totalitarianism that engulfed half the globe. "Hang—hang without fail, so the people will see," he ordered police in suppressing a peasants' revolt. Toward the end of his life, he apologized: "I am, it seems, strongly guilty before the workers of Russia." And in his secret testament he deplored the accumulation of power by his "coarse" lieutenant, Stalin (82). By then, it was too late. Stalin—who some believed poisoned him—was present at Lenin's autopsy. **21,162**

42 FERDINAND MAGELLAN (c.1480–1521)
leader of the first trip around the world

When sixteenth-century Europeans realized America was not the Spice Islands, they wondered if there was a way to sail around the new continent. Magellan said yes and proved it on history's most courageous voyage. Leading 237 men in five worm-worn ships, this Portuguese traitor in Spain's service started west in 1519 on the first circumnavigation of the globe. He found the southern passage that bears his name and was the first European to cross the Pacific. One ship with a mere eighteen survivors completed the voyage home. Storms, disease, starvation, aborigines, and Portuguese captors claimed the rest, including Magellan himself; Filipinos shot him full of arrows during a skirmish. The sponsors, happy to have Spain in the spice trade, shrugged off the terrible toll. The surviving ship, *Victoria,* held twenty-six tons of cloves, cinnamon, mace, and nutmeg worth 7.8 million *maravedis,* double the cost of the five original vessels. **21,154**

43 GENGHIS KHAN (1167?–1227)
destroyer of Asia

We blame the Mongol clan Tayichi'uts for Genghis Khan. Legend says they captured the nine-year-old princeling but neglected to kill him.

Genghis Khan never made such mistakes. His armies swept out of the northern steppes, crushing cities and cultures, and slaughtering more millions than history can count. Why did he do it? Some say for loot, and some say he was merely protecting his flanks from the Chinese, whom his followers ruled for 108 years. The Mongol empire in what is now China, Russia, and the Islamic world was the largest land mass ever consolidated under one clan. Genghis Khan was barbaric on an epic scale; Arab historians go so far as to blame the present aridity of the Middle East on his destruction of irrigation systems. Nearing death, Genghis Khan sought a potion to make him immortal. Thank God that exceeded his reach. **21,143**

44 MIGUEL DE CERVANTES SAAVEDRA
(1547–1616) *creator of the most beloved fool in literature*

The peripatetic Cervantes tried soldiering—before his capture and five-year enslavement by Barbary pirates—then civil service, even tax collecting. Except for his bravery in battle, he failed at everything except writing. Even there he didn't make his mark until age fifty-seven and the publication of *Don Quixote,* a worldwide sensation. This parody of then-popular chivalric romances features the delusional Don Quixote, a country gentleman who believes he's a knight. With his earthy squire, Sancho Panza, Don Quixote sets off to pursue a noble but impossible quest. Through many generations—and translations into more than sixty languages and publication in seven hundred editions—this tale has captured the popular imagination and influenced musicians, poets, and artists, notably Picasso (149). Its impact on the development of prose fiction, and the evolution of the European novel, is immeasurable. This outcome would have floored Cervantes if he had known. The Spanish novelist, dramatist, and poet thought his crowning achievement was *The Trials of Persiles and Sigismunda.* Huh? **21,130**

45 MARY WOLLSTONECRAFT (1759–1797)
beacon for women's rights

Like a character from one of her romantic novels, Wollstonecraft developed a radical concept of womanhood after she suffered the indignity of an abusive father who squandered her inheritance and favored his firstborn son. Her *Vindication of the Rights of Woman,* published in 1792, challenged women to resist male domination. Written more than half a century before the emergence of the first women's rights movement, her book provided the philosophical underpinnings for suffragists and later equal rights advocates to use to construct their arguments of equality. While her writings caused a furor, her personal life was no less scandalous. She bore a daughter out of wedlock and then, when she discovered herself pregnant by another man a few years later, married William Godwin. She died giving birth to daughter Mary, a future writer and wife of poet Percy Shelley (509). **21,114**

46 REMBRANDT HARMENSZOON VAN RIJN
(1606–1669) *master of the Dutch masters*

In 1947 Rembrandt's famous group portrait, *The Nightwatch,* underwent a cleaning. As centuries of grit were lifted, curators discovered it was actually a daytime scene. Like his masterpiece, Rembrandt's once-sullied reputation has been rehabilitated. Well into the eighteenth century critics called him a vulgar painter, ruled by greed and vanity. We know differently now. Rembrandt reached his creative and productive heights after age fifty-five. In all he produced six hundred paintings, including numerous self-portraits, three hundred etchings, and nearly two thousand drawings. His intuitive understanding of human nature coupled with his brilliant technique has had enormous influence on artists through the centuries. Art experts now agree: no other painter has ever achieved Rembrandt's mastery of chiaroscuro effects, the play of light and dark in a scene. Our enduring favorites: *Aristotle Contemplating the Bust of Homer* and *A Girl at the Window.*   **21,096**

47 WILLIAM HARVEY (1578–1657)
the physician who unlocked the secrets of blood circulation

It's so simple, we teach it in second-grade science: the heart is a pump that circulates the blood. For centuries, however, the human body was a mystery. Aristotle suggested that blood originated in the liver; ancient physicians theorized that arteries carried special spirits. Some doctors believed blood moved in spurts through the body, but they had no idea how. Then along came Harvey, the British physician who paved the way for modern physiology with his dissections of pigs, dogs, and other small animals. He discovered it was the heart, not the liver, that pumped blood. He described the blood's path. On the subject of reproduction, Harvey again disputed Aristotle, who had hypothesized that woman's role was merely as a vessel for man's seed. Harvey, who attended to kings, suggested (accurately, it was proved some 150 years later) that mammals are produced from eggs.   **21,081**

48 SIMÓN BOLÍVAR (1783–1830)
liberator of South America

History has been kind to Bolívar. He was, in some ways, the George Washington (22) of South America. He wrestled control of his continent away from the strangling tentacles of Spain; he abhorred servitude and believed in freedom for freedom's sake; he envisioned a united South America; and he served as first president of Venezuela and Peru. One region he liberated in southern Peru was

named Bolivia in his honor. That's where the similarities to our man George end. A powerful orator and writer, Bolívar inspired and led the rebellion. Yet at his death he was feared and reviled as a dictator by the very people he had liberated. But as Bolívar himself once observed, "To judge revolutions and their leaders, we must watch them at close range and judge them at a great distance." Distance rehabilitated Bolívar. Today he is revered as "the Great Liberator."   **21,072**

49 IMMANUEL KANT (1724–1804)
metaphysician of the modern world

German existentialist Karl Jaspers once declared it was not enough to say Kant was the culmination of the Enlightenment; rather, "Kant surpassed the Enlightenment." Kant held that certain realities —"things in themselves"—lie outside reason, which can know only objects of experience. Thus, you know you stubbed your toe, but you can't be sure God exists. However, Kant's famous categorical imperative—"act as though the maxim from which you act were to become through your will a universal law"—requires you to believe in God anyway in order to live a just life. Kant's thinking underpinned subsequent Western innovations in philosophy, theology, history, psychiatry, and the physical sciences. For all the sweep of his scholarship, however, the five-foot-tall Prussian with a shrunken chest never ventured more than sixty miles from his hometown and rarely broke a daily routine that began with a five A.M. breakfast of weak tea and a pipe of tobacco.   **21,069**

50 MAO ZE-DONG (1893–1976)
China's unifier—but at horrendous cost

Mao transformed China from a backward nation into a world power with nuclear weapons. But of all the twentieth century's tyrants, his actions killed the most people. He fought a guerrilla war against the Japanese in the 1930s, civil war against Chiang Kai-shek (455) that led to the 1949 Communist takeover, and a proxy war with the United States over Korea. During his thirty-seven-year rule, he proclaimed freedom of expression ("Let a hundred flowers bloom"), then stomped on those who spoke their minds; launched the "Great Leap Forward" collectivization of agriculture that left thirty million dead; and proclaimed the Cultural Revolution that killed millions more. As a child, he impulsively gave his coat to a starving boy. As an old man, he infected hundreds of peasant girls with a venereal disease that was harmless to him. **21,054**

51 HENRY FORD (1863–1947)
mover of mass production

While many nineteenth-century inventor types claimed to be the genius behind the automobile, Ford makes our list not for being the first but for being the most innovative in putting cars together. A high-school dropout at age sixteen, Ford's knack for tinkering began with his childhood hobby repairing watches. He designed his first car in 1896, then opened his own company in an investor's garage. Next, he analyzed how cars were constructed. After seven years of study, Ford perfected an assembly line made up of forty-five different steps that produced an automobile in ninety-three minutes. Using this technique, Ford produced fifteen million of his popular Model T's over a twenty-year period, ultimately lowering the cost of an automobile so that it was within the reach of the common man, and creating a repetitive, monotonous and boring occupation—work on the assembly line. **21,041**

52 WOLFGANG AMADEUS MOZART (1756–1791)
musical mingler of art and entertainment

When Mozart was twelve, he wrote his first opera, but by then he was already a veteran; at six

he won plaudits as a keyboard artist, and at eight he wrote a symphony—not a memorable one but a symphony nonetheless. In those days Mozart was a curiosity schlepped around Europe's drawing rooms by his father Leopold. It was a life that should have burned him out at twentysomething. Not Mozart. He lasted to age thirty-four and in the ten years before his death created dozens of concertos, operas, symphonies, and chamber works that have been performance mainstays for two centuries. No one ever wrote music so joyously entertaining and profoundly artistic at the same moment—music that appeals equally to the heart and the head. Our Mozart greatest hits: *Don Giovanni,* the later piano concertos, and all the string quintets. **21,026**

53 JOHN MILTON (1608–1674)
poet of Paradise

Valued as the greatest English poet after Shakespeare (5), Milton wrote rich, dense verse that inspired writers for centuries. One of them, Alfred Lord Tennyson, called Milton "the God-gifted organ-voice of England." As a youth, Milton had longed to write a great heroic poem about England, but he got sidetracked by growing political unrest and wound up penning revolutionary pamphlets and treatises championing religious and civil liberties. He lost his eyesight while toiling as a secretary in Oliver Cromwell's (162) council. This blindness brought one blessing: it probably spared him from execution for treason when the royalists regained power. Milton later said, "The light is not so much lost as turned inwards, for the sharpening of my mind's edge." That hard-won clarity helped shape *Paradise Lost,* Milton's epic poem—ten years in the making—on man's fall from God's grace. He composed this poem, section by section, in his head, then dictated it to family members. **21,022**

54 BENJAMIN FRANKLIN (1706–1790)
America's Renaissance man

He achieved fame as writer and printer of *Poor Richard's Almanack,* laced with maxims such as "A penny saved is a penny earned." He invented bifocals, the lightning rod, and the fuel-efficient Franklin stove. In Philadelphia he founded the University of Pennsylvania, the nation's first university, and the first public library. By 1757 Franklin was wealthy enough to retire and enter public service. He told his mother he had other goals than getting rich: "I would rather have it said 'he lived usefully' than 'he died rich.'" Franklin more than achieved that aim. He fine-tuned Thomas Jefferson's (64) draft of the Declaration of Independence. Once the American Revolution was over, he negotiated peace with England and helped frame the Constitution, the fundamental law of the United States. But his greatest contribution was convincing the French, through sheer charm, to provide financial and military aid to the rebel colonies. That marked the turning point of the Revolution. **20,988**

55 ALEXANDER FLEMING (1881–1955)
discoverer of antibiotics

He is an inspiration to those of us who find mysterious fuzzy growths lurking in our refrigerators. If the British scientist Fleming had been a neatness freak, the penicillium fungus growing on his petri dish would never have flourished. But Fleming routinely let dirty petri dishes accumulate. When he finally got around to cleaning up, he'd scrutinize each dish to see if anything interesting had happened. Once, he set a dish aside for several weeks. When he came back, he discovered, to his chagrin, that mold had spoiled the specimen. But wait! He realized that the mold had actually dissolved the bacteria. Thus Fleming discovered penicillin, a drug that has saved countless lives. He shared a Nobel Prize in medicine with Harold Florey and Ernst Chain, who developed penicillin for mass production in the early 1940s. Their work created the most important series of drugs ever—antibiotics. **20,973**

56 MARTIN LUTHER KING, JR. (1929–1968)
minister to a divided nation

His doctrine of nonviolent protest stirred the compassion of millions and set the course of the U.S. civil rights movement. At age twenty-six King masterminded the bus boycott in Montgomery, Alabama. For 382 days blacks refused to ride buses until the Supreme Court shattered the "separate but equal" principle upon which segregation was based. King was jailed, threatened, and hated, but never disheartened. At the 1963 March on Washington, in a speech destined for history books and forensics competitions, King described his dream of equality to some two hundred thousand protestors. On April 3, 1968, four years after passage of a federal civil rights law that prohibited segregation, King ominously warned that trying times lay ahead: "I've been to the mountaintop . . . And I've looked over and I've seen the Promised Land. I may not get there with you." The next day King was dead from an assassin's bullet. **20,964**

57 TOYOTOMI HIDEYOSHI (1537–1598)
unifier of Japan

Contemporaries called him one of the ugliest men alive—but not to his face. Hideyoshi, born to a peasant, was a strong-willed general and nononsense ruler who unified Japan by conquest after centuries of tribalism. For these accomplishments he is often compared to Abraham Lincoln (32). He established the institutional framework for the government, economy, and society for Japan's next 250 years. Toyotomi conquered his enemies the old-fashioned way: He killed them in battle, though to those who survived he demonstrated a magnanimity rare for the era. Finally in power at age fifty, he used the census to keep tabs on his subjects, who were organized into feudal classes and castes from which they could not wander without permission. As much as power, he loved art and ostentation. Gold adorned everything from his chopsticks and bowls to the bathroom walls and roof of his Kyoto castle. Late in his reign getting close to him was dangerous. When he sired a son five years before his death, Hideyoshi ordered the previous heir, his nephew, to commit suicide. **20,963**

58 FREDERICK THE GREAT (1712–1786)
the sword of German militarism

Did King Frederick II of Prussia make Bismarck (118) and Hitler (20) possible? We say yes, so Frederick scores high for lasting influence. Other autocrats used armies to push their neighbors around; Frederick was better at it. He conquered Silesia in his first months in power and spent the next forty-six years creating the efficient army that turned his backwater kingdom into a land-grabbing European power. It took the worst wars in history to wipe this arrogant acquisitiveness from Germany's repertoire. Writer Johann Goethe (131) called the flute-playing, French-speaking, Bach-befriending Frederick the model benevolent despot. Not bad, having Goethe for a reference. But the same Frederick ordered the arrest of Voltaire (36) just for leaving town. Frederick could be kind, the Victorian historian Thomas Macauley (796) wrote. "But under this fair exterior he was a tyrant, suspicious, disdainful and malevolent." Macauley got it right. **20,959**

59 GEORG WILHELM FRIEDRICH HEGEL
(1770–1831) *philosopher for a dislocated age*

His all-embracing system posited a God-like world-spirit acting through history and guiding human reason. Eggheads like Bergson (890), Dewey (872), Feuerbach, Heidegger (914), Jaspers, Marx (14), Sartre, Strauss, Toynbee, Veblen, Weber (806), Whitehead, and Whitman (318) all came under his spell. His concepts pulsate through communism, fascism, pragmatism, existentialism, cultural anthropology, and social psychology. Reducing his philosophy to the well-known thesis-antithesis-synthesis formula of the dialectical process is a gross but convenient oversimplication. Historian Carl J. Friedrich commented that the more you read Hegel, the clearer he becomes—"clearer, but not clear." It is heartening to note that upon falling in love with his future bride, Hegel dropped his erudition and wrote love poetry. Of the New World he said: "America is the land of the future in which in times to come world history shall reveal itself." **20,921**

60 CHU YÜAN-CHANG (1328–1398)
the first Ming

Chu Yüan-chang was a starving beggar when a fortune-teller told him to join the fight against China's Mongol rulers. Good advice. Sixteen years later, as head of the rebel army, he defeated the Mongols and became the first emperor of the Ming dynasty, which governed China from 1368 to 1644. Ming craftsmen gave the world exceptional art, but Chu was a cruel paranoid who brooked no limitations on his power. Mentioning the emperor's humble origins was a hanging offense. Bungling bureaucrats were flogged on their bare buttocks with bamboo rods. Harvard historian John Fairbank wrote that Chu concentrated so much power in his hands, nothing could get done. The centralized despotism of Chu and his Ming minions helped China miss the boat of modern development. **20,909**

61 CHARLES V (1500–1558)
the emperor who gave it all away

As Holy Roman emperor, Charles's control in Europe extended from Spain and the Netherlands to Austria and the Kingdom of Naples. But the architect of the largest-ever German empire was also its destroyer. His reign was marked by conflicts with French king Francis I over control of Italy, battles against the encroaching Turks, and the start of the Protestant Reformation. By 1552 the empire was crumbling, and Charles, suffering from gout, was in failing health. He abdicated in 1556 and retired to a monastery in Spain. Some might say he dropped out. But casting off the ever-increasing burdens of leadership was an option he'd been contemplating since 1532, when an adviser told him that a ruler who couldn't preserve the peace—or was even an obstacle to it—was obligated to retire. **20,892**

62 GEOFFREY CHAUCER (1342–1400)
humanity's poet laureate

Chaucer's works, with their innovative vocabulary and meter, had a monumental impact on the development of English literature and influenced centuries of writers, including Shakespeare (5). Chaucer was a veteran civil servant, diplomat, and courtier whose career ebbed and flowed with political tides. Privately he was a prolific writer, a learned man with a heightened sense of humor and irony and tolerance for human foibles. His masterpiece is the unfinished *Canterbury Tales.* The plot features a storytelling contest by twenty-four pilgrims journeying to a shrine in Canterbury. Through them we see, as Chaucer always did, the humor and tragedy of the human condition. Our favorite narrator: the lusty Wife of Bath, who cries in Olde English, "Allas! allas! that evere love was synne." To writer C. S. Lewis, "the great mass of Chaucer's work is simply a background to the *Canterbury Tales,* and the whole output of the fourteenth century is simply a background to Chaucer." **20,861**

63 LOUIS XIV (1638–1715)
absolute monarchy in its purest form

King Louis seized personal control of France in 1661. Years of civil strife had left destruction everywhere, and the treasury was empty. But he envisioned a nation of power and grandeur. Within a decade he steered France to industrial revolution, importing thousands of craftsmen to create manufacturing centers. Good thing, too, because Louis decided to build the dream home of all time, the monumentally expensive Versailles palace. Known as the "Sun King" for the brilliance of his court and his support of the arts, Louis considered himself God's representative on earth. But his velvet-slippered feet were made of clay. His greed for land prompted neighbors to forge coalitions that checked his ambitions in two wars. Upon hearing that his fifty thousand troops had been defeated at Blenheim in 1704, Louis wailed, "How could God do this to me after all I have done for him?" **20,850**

64 THOMAS JEFFERSON (1743–1826)
author of the Declaration of Independence

When President Kennedy told a group of Nobel laureates they were the "most extraordinary collection" of minds to grace the White House with the "possible exception of when Thomas Jefferson dined alone," he was going for a laugh. But he wasn't far off the mark. Jefferson provided a liberal vision for the new republic that contrasted starkly with those who sought to create an aristocracy. His was the voice of the people. He championed the "little guy" (read: the colonial yeoman farmer), supported a free press, defended freedom of religion, and sent Lewis (505) and Clark off on their excellent adventure to explore the West. The Founding Fathers' jack-of-all-trades, Jefferson was an accomplished writer, scientist, architect, surveyor, lawyer, and farmer. Besides, anyone who can turn a phrase like "life, liberty and the pursuit of happiness" gets big points in our book. **20,837**

65 POPE URBAN II (c.1042–1099)
preacher of the Crusades

On November 27, 1095, the bearded, handsome Pope Urban II stood on a platform in a field outside the east gate of Clermont, France, and exhorted Christian soldiers to take back the Holy Land from Muslims who were mistreating pilgrims. Plus, he added delicately, it would rid Europe of pugnacious knights with nothing to do but hack up their neighbors in silly wars. Let them kill infidels for a change. It was the most effective speech of the millennium; it launched the Crusades, which spanned four centuries and stimulated the cultural intercourse that sped the westward transmission of the Muslims' superior learning. Too bad it also unleashed bestial orgies of butchery and rape on anyone in the Crusaders' paths, including a lot of Christians. Italian merchants made fortunes supplying ships and food to the warriors. And Urban died before news of Jerusalem's capture got back to Rome. **20,822**

66 MARCO POLO (1254–1324)
world's most influential traveler

Plenty of European adventurers and traders went to Asia in the early centuries of the millennium, but Polo had a publicist. The story of the Venetian's twenty-three-year trip east and his service in the stately court of Kublai Khan (332) was a Renaissance best-seller that stirred Europeans' longing to know about the Orient and its treasures. They read, they dreamed, and some acted on their dreams, most notably Christopher Columbus (2). We know Columbus read the *Travels* because he wrote in the margins of his copy. Polo's ghostwriter was a Pisan named Rustichello who debriefed the traveler while they were fellow prisoners of the Genoese in the 1290s.

Rustichello's embellishments probably insured the book's success, but it was Polo who made the trip that incited his readers' wanderlust. **20,796**

67 ANTOINE-LAURENT LAVOISIER (1743–1794)
creator of modern chemistry

Lavoisier formulated a theory of combustion, demonstrated the role of oxygen and the principle of conservation of matter in chemical reactions, and established the distinction between elements and compounds. Some say his work in human respiration made him the founder of physiology and biochemistry. His success in increasing crop yields on his farm made him a precursor of the Green Revolution. Somewhere along the line he married a thirteen-year-old girl. Lavoisier was also a public servant whose accomplishments included doubling France's gunpowder production. With powder to spare to ship to the American colonialists, France insured the success of the American Revolution. For all his contributions, Lavoisier was attacked by radicals in the French Revolution and guillotined. "It required only a moment to sever that head," commented mathematician Joseph Louis Lagrant, "and perhaps another century will not be sufficient to produce another like it." **20,768**

68 MAXIMILIEN ROBESPIERRE (1758–1794)
the terror of Europe's Old Regime

Known as the Incorruptible for his idealism, Robespierre was also a master of intrigue and the fiercest current in the political maelstrom that reshaped the Western world, the French Revolution. A champion of the poor, he declared, "We are the lower class, the scum." Moralistic, he established a "Republic of Virtue." But he smelled conspiracy everywhere and presided over the Terror that lopped off so many French heads with Dr. Guillotin's new instrument. "Without terror, virtue is impotent," he said. In the end, his enemies, fearful of being "shortened by the national razor," shortened Robespierre. Shot through the jaw in a melee shortly before his execution, the demagogue could utter no speech as the blade fell, only an animal cry that British historian Thomas Carlyle (691) described as "hideous to hear." This lover of philosopher Jean-Jacques Rousseau (19) left behind a harsh legacy: Destroy the past for a glorious future, and you will also, in all likelihood, destroy yourself. **20,719**

69 JOHN CALVIN (1509–1564)
Protestant Reformation leader

Born Jean Cauvin in France, Calvin couldn't resist tinkering with his name, much less organized religion. Abandoning Roman Catholicism, he published the most influential treatise of the Reformation, *The Institutes of the Christian Religion,* at age twenty-six. Emphasizing the Bible as sole source of God's law, the *Institutes* became the cornerstone of the Protestant movement. As ruler of Geneva, Calvin instituted an asceticism that inspired the English Puritans and American Pilgrims. He condemned "all injurious persons, adulterers, rakes, thieves, ravishers, the covetous, the drunken and the gluttonous." Calvinism spread across Europe, rivaling Lutheranism. Max Weber (806) attributed capitalism's rise to the new faith's work ethic. For all Calvin's dogmatism, his emphasis on personal responsibility and freedom and his opposition to "unjust" authority contributed to the West's secularization. Calvin, though tormented by ulcerous hemorrhoids and the "wild beast" of his temper, also had a soft side, feeding the poor and remarking, "We are not forbidden to drink wine." **20,711**

70 CHARLES DICKENS (1812–1870)
novelist of the emerging industrial age

Dickens's work is marked by rich portrayals of Victorian society, sharply etched characters—

A Christmas Carol's Ebenezer Scrooge, for one—and a crusading spirit for social reform. He was traumatized when his parents forced him to work in a shoe-polish factory. Then his middle-class father was thrown into debtors' prison. Little wonder Dickens frequently put an oppressed child at the center of his novels, including *Oliver Twist, Great Expectations, Bleak House,* and *David Copperfield,* which are widely read today. Dickens liked to describe himself as "the Inimitable"—a fitting name for someone continually churning out novels, editing magazines, and acting in plays. Ever the entertainer, Dickens craved an audience's adulation. At age forty-six he launched tours through Britain and the United States, reading from his works and acting all the parts. Friend Thomas Carlyle (691) caught his performance in 1863 and told him wonderingly, "Charley, you carry a whole company of actors under your own hat." **20,666**

71 SULEIMAN THE MAGNIFICENT (1494–1566)
paramount ruler of the seven-hundred-year Ottoman Empire

To the west, Suleiman conquered Belgrade, expelled the Christian Knights of St. John from Rhodes, annexed Hungary, and built his navy into a Mediterranean power; to the east, he launched campaigns against Persia and conquered Iraq. All this bloodshed! Not to worry; Suleiman was also a patron of the arts and a reformer, known as the Lawgiver for his commitment to justice. No wonder he was called Sultan of the Ottomans, Allah's Deputy on Earth, Lord of the Lords of this World, Possessor of Men's Necks, King of Believers and Unbelievers, King of Kings, Emperor of the East and West, Prince and Lord of the Most Happy Constellation and—last but not least—the Shadow of the Almighty Dispensing Quiet in the Earth. To be sure, he executed two of his sons for conspiracy, but then, a dad has to show tough love.   **20,637**

72 PAUL CÉZANNE (1839–1906)
founder of modern art

"He was the father of us all," a group of famous twentieth-century painters of various schools said of Cézanne in a manifesto a half-century after his death. In a thousand paintings and drawings, this self-absorbed Frenchman proclaimed the importance of capturing nature as it really was, and he did so by fusing the formalism of classicists and the color sense of the romantics in an incomparable style. His chief contribution: the notion, implicit in his teachings and his work, that visual artists should be bound only by the limits of their imagination, not by the reality of the objects they depict. The best legacies of Cézanne's genius are his sixty paintings of *Mont Sainte-Victoire* near his home in Aix-en-Provence and his paintings of figures in landscapes, like *The Great Bathers,* which he worked on from 1892 to 1905.   **20,632**

73 MURASAKI SHIKIBU (978?–1031?)
creator of the novel

Murasaki's *The Tale of the Genji* was the world's first novel and is still considered the greatest work of Japanese literature. Educated beyond feminine pastimes of calligraphy, embroidery, and painting, Murasaki studied literature and the Chinese language. Following the birth of her daughter and the death of her husband, she went to the royal court and began her great work, based loosely on her observations there. At the time Japanese men looked down upon literature written in Japanese, preferring to use Chinese characters. Women, however, were free to write in Japanese. Thus Murasaki wrote her novel, a combination dime-store romance and sweeping family saga of Genji, the charming son of the emperor. Begun in 1002

and finished about 1005, the book was written in fifty-four chapters. Some believe the last chapters were written by someone else, but hey, they said that about Shakespeare (5), too.   **20,583**

74 ALEXANDER GRAHAM BELL (1847–1922)
inventor of the telephone, which revolutionized personal communication

Prior to Bell's invention, messengers delivered notes from business to business; women spent afternoons visiting and paying social debts; and teenagers were seen, not heard. Enter Bell, from a family of vocal technicians. Bell, who emigrated from Scotland to Canada and then became an American citizen in 1882, taught speech before he began tinkering with sound. Bell hired mechanic Thomas Watson to help translate his scientific knowledge into the mechanics of a telephone. Then, on March 10, 1876, Bell brought his assistant running with his first transmission: "Mr. Watson, come here; I want to see you." Improvements followed rapidly, and Bell Telephone Company was formed in 1877. On the day of his funeral, telephones in North America were stilled for one minute to pay tribute to his genius. Now an average 1.6 billion calls are made in the United States alone every day.   **20,581**

75 MARIE CURIE (1867–1934)
pioneer of nuclear physics

Curie's dedication to science was so absolute that before her marriage, she asked a friend to find her a wedding dress that was "practical and dark so that I can put it on afterwards to go to the laboratory." Born Maria Sklodowska in Warsaw, she met Pierre Curie when she was studying in Paris. Pierre joined Marie's research project, and they sifted through a ton of soil to isolate a thimbleful of radium. They shared a Nobel Prize in physics in 1903. Marie took a back seat to her husband in the male bastion of the academy. In the laboratory, however, she reigned. She discovered polonium—named for her native country—and coined the word *radioactive.* The first woman to win a Nobel Prize, Curie won again—in chemistry—in 1913. Ultimately her passion for science was her undoing—she died from anemia caused by overexposure to radiation. **20,572**

76 JOHN ECKERT (1919–1995)
inventor of the first modern computer

John Mauchly conceived the Electrical Numerical Integrator and Computer (ENIAC) to calculate artillery trajectories for the U.S. Army, but Eckert built it. Weighing thirty tons and containing eighteen thousand vacuum tubes and seventy thousand resisters, ENIAC, which could duplicate twenty hours of human figuring in thirty seconds, used so much power that neighborhood lights dimmed. It also had four thousand red neon tubes. "Every science-fiction machine since has had flashing lights all over it," Eckert marveled. The American duo's hold on the computer crown is not final; some say British mathematician Alan Turing (445) should share it for a machine he developed in 1943. But Eckert dismissed the claims of another pretender, American John V. Atanasoff, for a vacuum tube he built in the 1930s, saying, "He never really got anything to work." ENIAC worked, and the computerization of the world followed. **20,561**

77 FYODOR DOSTOYEVSKY (1821–1881)
the maker of modern literature's antihero

Salvation through suffering was the credo of Russian Dostoyevsky's tragic life and dark novels. He is considered one of the greatest novelists in history. In 1849 the young writer was arrested with other socialists and charged with treason. He was about to be shot when his sentence was commuted—the czar's twisted intent from the start. The episode scarred Dostoyevsky for life, and he developed epilepsy. Exiled for four years

to a Siberian work camp, his only book was the Bible and his only company, fellow inmates he called "the soul of Russia." They inspired his later novels, *Crime and Punishment, The Possessed,* and his masterpiece, *The Brothers Karamazov.* Dostoyevsky's flawed heroes are consumed by a tragic sense of life and search endlessly for truth and self-fulfillment. Through these works he paved the way for the twentieth century's existential and surrealist literary movements. **20,421**

78 POPE INNOCENT III (1160–1216)
champion of papal power

The deeply religious Italian nobleman Lotario di Segni had a lofty vision of pope as Vicar of Christ, "set midway between God and man, below God but above man." A master politician, he intervened in turf battles in Germany, England, and France, arguing that only he could determine the best leader to defend church interests. By 1215, through his brilliant statesmanship, Christendom extended from Greenland to Syria. That same year he convened the reform-minded fourth Lateran Council—the climax of the medieval papacy. His reign also had darker sides: the first repressions of heretics and the Fourth Crusade, which conquered Constantinople in 1204. But peace was more his style. He died on a peace mission to the Italian town of Perugia. While his body lay in state, thieves stripped it of vestments. At burial Innocent's corpse wore only the simple garments of the poor. **20,418**

79 FREDERICK DOUGLASS (1817–1895)
abolitionist leader

A fugitive slave in the North, Douglass galvanized audiences with stories of his youth in bondage and his antislavery message. But he omitted key details—including his real name, Frederick Augustus Washington Bailey—for fear his master would track him down. Self-educated and brilliant, Douglass was so eloquent that people began doubting he had been a slave. He felt compelled to write his autobiography, *Narrative of the Life of Frederick Douglass,* and reveal the facts. When the book appeared in 1845, Douglass left for Europe on a two-year speaking tour. He returned with enough money to buy his freedom and launch his own newspaper to press for abolition through political action. During the Civil War Douglass persuaded a reluctant President Lincoln (32) to declare all slaves free and conscript them to fight for the Union. But Douglass was deeply disappointed with Reconstruction's failure to bring political and social equality to blacks. **20,401**

80 J. ROBERT OPPENHEIMER (1904–1967)
director of the first atomic bomb project

His genius at getting other geniuses to work together made possible the awful weapons that finished World War II with climactic bangs and made the world forever unsafe. Oppenheimer was a polymathic physics professor whose best theoretical work was behind him when the U.S. Army picked him to lead the construction of the atomic bomb. In three years he completed the Manhattan Project by making the right decisions and by coddling, cajoling, and cheerleading his battalion of former and future Nobel laureates. Edward Teller, who later built the first H-bomb, called Oppenheimer the best lab director he ever knew. Oppenheimer was an unlucky gambler, though. In a ghoulish lottery, he bet ten dollars that the test blast on July 16, 1945, would equal 300 tons of TNT; it was 18,000. He had uncorked an evil genie. If mankind lets it loose again, good-bye next millennium. **20,397**

81 JOHN STUART MILL (1806–1873)
promoter of individual rights

Mill's writings on philosophy, economics, political science, logic, and ethics deeply impressed contemporary thinkers. His essay "On Liberty" is the finest argument for the rights of the individual versus the state. Mill was influenced by the theory of utilitarianism formulated by his father, James Mill, and family friend, Jeremy Bentham (383). They believed that the morality of an action derives from its positive or negative outcome and that all legislation should achieve "the greatest good for the greatest number." But Mill also believed that minorities must never be subjugated to the whims of the majority. He advocated unionism, proportional representation, and women's rights. Prodded by his authoritarian father, Mill was reading Greek at age three, Latin at eight, and writing a history of Roman government at age eleven. He later observed: "I never was a boy, never played at cricket; it is better to let Nature have her own way." **20,375**

82 JOSEPH STALIN (1879–1953)
monster

If ever there was a case against child abuse, Stalin, beaten as a boy by his drunken father, is it. Killing was his sport. Only Hitler (20) ever got the better of him, and only because, as one pundit remarked, Hitler double-crossed him before he could double-cross Hitler. The impact of this evil genius on history was stupendous: He collectivized Soviet agriculture (twenty million dead of starvation); helped defeat Nazi Germany; seized half of Europe; sent millions to their deaths in slave camps; industrialized the Soviet Union; and made it a nuclear power that fought a forty-five-year cold war with the West. What good can be said of this Georgian peasant who refused to attend the funeral of his mother, a God-fearing washerwoman, and rejected a German offer to return his son from a prisoner-of-war camp? This, at least: He destroyed Communism's promise and sealed its demise. **20,361**

83 JOAN OF ARC (1411?–1431)
heroic patron saint of France

French peasant Jeanne d'Arc never learned to read or write, but she was overcome by the "voices" of saints, who told her to free France from English rule. Perhaps the original "aggressive female," Joan dressed as a man and convinced the dauphin to commission her an army of about four thousand men. By sheer persistence, some may say bullheadedness, she wore down the English at Orleans and triumphantly stood by the side of Charles VII at his coronation. It was all downhill from there. She was captured, sold to the English, and burned at the stake at the age of twenty. The national hero of France, however, has been immortalized in story, history, and art. She was canonized a Catholic saint in 1909. **20,298**

84 FRANCIS BACON (1561–1626)
formulator of the scientific method

The learned Bacon rose to attorney general, then lord chancellor under James I (879). All the while he continued writing, publishing his masterful *Essays* in 1597. His brilliant political career ended in disgrace in 1621 for bribe taking. Bacon devoted the next five years to his beloved philosophy; he planned a major work but completed only two parts, *The Advancement of Learning* and *Novum Organum.* His major contribution: proposing that inductive logic—the process of reasoning from the specific to the general—be used for scientific discovery, an approach embraced by modern science. Bacon's enthusiasm for his scientific method was his undoing. One wintry day he stopped his coach outside London, inspired by the snow-covered fields to think snow might preserve food. At a farmhouse he bought a chicken, had it slaughtered, then stood outside to pack it with snow. His resulting chill led to fatal pneumonia. **20,273**

85 FILIPPO BRUNELLESCHI (1377–1446)
inventor of linear perspective

People who erroneously credit the invention of perspective to fourteenth-century artist Giotto (219) are merely fooled by his perfect eye. Giotto did indeed pay attention to space and form, but it came to him naturally. The Italian architect Brunelleschi, however, put it down on paper. Brunelleschi worked as a goldsmith in Florence but turned to architecture when he lost a competition to create a set of golden church doors. He experimented to create depth on a flat surface, articulating what the eye already knew: that parallel lines seem to converge at some "vanishing point" on a canvas and that the closer you are to an object, the larger it appears. Brunelleschi spelled out the rules to create a three-dimensional flat surface, and his ideas were embraced by the art world. Now his concept of points and lines forms the foundation of art lessons even on an elementary level. **20,263**

86 ELIZABETH CADY STANTON (1815–1902)
founder of the American women's rights movement

If Cady Stanton hadn't been so eccentric, cantankerous, and aggressive, she probably would have ended up with her picture on the dollar coin and with all the credit for starting the women's rights movement. As it was, she organized the first women's rights conference in her hometown of Seneca Falls, New York, in 1848. Then she spent the rest of her life passionately arguing for woman suffrage and equal legal and work rights. She raised the ire of almost everyone when she rewrote the Bible from a woman's perspective. She made many enemies with her single-minded approach, which is probably why the more congenial Susan B. Anthony (139) is generally but wrongly credited as the sole force behind the movement. Cady Stanton died eighteen years before women won the vote and decades before they reached the full legal equality she championed. **20,196**

87 VLADIMIR K. ZWORYKIN (1889–1982)
television pioneer

Working for Westinghouse Electric Corporation, the Russian-born engineer invented the first electronic television system with his iconoscope camera tube and kinescope picture tube, patented in 1923 and 1924. Despite later refinements, the modern TV picture tube remains essentially his kinescope. But in the 1920s Zworykin's inventions left Westinghouse bigwigs unimpressed. Their loss was RCA's gain. RCA hired Zworykin in 1929, named him director of electronic research, and used his system to develop their own—investing $50 million "before we ever got a penny back," grumbled RCA legend David Sarnoff (830). Fifty years later Zworykin told interviewers he never expected TV to have such global impact. But the man who was the father of television technology disowned his electronic offspring. He'd envisioned television for education, not mindless entertainment. "I would never let my children come close to this thing," he said. "It's awful." **20,163**

88 GOTTFRIED WILHELM LEIBNIZ (1646–1716)
inventor of calculus and symbolic logic

The brilliant German entered the University of Leipzig at age fifteen and graduated from law school at twenty. His fellow philosophers drew from independent incomes, but Leibniz had to earn his own way. He was at various times historian, diplomat, engineer, scientist, and inventor—whatever role his royal benefactors required. As philosopher, Leibniz criticized the theories of Descartes (25) for damaging faith in God. Leibniz held that the basic components of the universe are metaphysical points he called "monads"—isolated and of infinite number but together forming an

ordered plan. He argued this harmony showed God had created "the best of all possible worlds"—a notion Voltaire (36) satirized in *Candide*. As mathematician, Leibniz discovered calculus and published his results three years before Isaac Newton (6), who maintained he had thought of it first. Naturally, the two never hit it off. **20,132**

89 WILLIAM LE BARON JENNEY (1832–1907)
architect of the skyscraper

Next time you're waiting for an elevator to the thirtieth floor or dodging neck-craning tourists on the street, remember Jenney, the American civil engineer and architect who designed the Home Insurance Company Building in Chicago, built in 1885. Some quibble that the skyscraper's forerunner came fourteen years earlier, with the Equitable Life Insurance Building in New York. Hogwash. Jenney's our man. His building was only ten stories high but was the first to have its weight supported by an iron and steel framework—not the usual load-bearing walls. Ever since, carving space from the sky has soared in crowded cities, and the skyscraper has become a symbol of the twentieth century. The current tallest: the 1,535-foot-high Oriental Pearl Television Tower in Shanghai. **20,101**

90 EDWARD JENNER (1749–1823)
inoculator of nations

If Jenner were a researcher today, he would be a pariah. After all, his guinea pig was an eight-year-old boy, who was injected first with an untested vaccine, then with smallpox. The experiment ended happily enough—Jimmy Phipps never got smallpox, and Jenner discovered a way to inoculate people against the world's most dreaded disease. Up until Jenner's discovery in 1796, not only did smallpox kill thousands, but its survivors were marked for life with disfiguring scars.

Jenner had observed a relationship between a mild disease that plagued milkmaids—the cowpox—and the deadly smallpox. Noting that milkmaids rarely came down with smallpox, Jenner developed a serum using cowpox sores, despite criticism and roadblocks from the medical establishment. He named his process *vaccination* from the Latin word for cow, *vaca,* in tribute to the source of his discovery. **20,093**

91 QUEEN VICTORIA (1819–1901)
the mother of all monarchs

Victoria of England was so dominant a personality for two-thirds of a century that her name came to represent the era when Britain had an empire and society adhered to an almost fanatical priggishness. Victoria's advice to her daughter about the duties of the marriage bed reflected the sexual repression of the time. "Lie still, and think of the empire," she said. Indeed, the empire was vast—spanning the globe at a time when England was unchallenged as a world leader. Britain's power eventually faded like the stiff chintz curtains from a Victorian parlor, but not until after her sixty-three-year reign was over. Victoria fell madly in love and married her cousin Albert and, despite her apparent distaste for marital obligations, gave birth to nine children. Their marriages to royalty throughout Europe ensured that, at least for another generation, the sun didn't set on the British Empire. **20,028**

92 BABUR (1483–1530)
the Muslim conqueror of India

His name means "lion" in Turkish, and this direct descendant of the Mongol warriors Genghis Khan (43) and Tamerlane (511) had their fighting spirit in his genes. At the age of eleven he inherited an Afghan principality, but it was too small for his ambitions, and for the next three decades his Muslim armies raided southward into India in search of gold and land. At the climactic battle of Panipat in 1525, the Hindu enemy, even with its 100,000 men and 100 elephants, was no match for Babur's 12,000 veterans. At his death all of northern India was under his power. The Mughal empire he created—and that his grandson Akbar (148) expanded—held sway in India until the British swept it aside in 1857. Besides war, Babur loved beautiful gardens, art, and music. He also indulged in alcohol, a habit that overcame his resolution to live like a good abstemious Muslim. **19,967**

93 CHU HSI (1130–1200)
most influential Chinese philosopher of the millennium

Chu Hsi essentially reinvented Confucianism to his liking, in some cases using texts that were not written by Confucius or members of his school. By virtue of the clarity of his ideas and his high moral purpose, his brand of Confucianism dominated Chinese intellectual life for centuries. He rejected the Buddhist doctrine that the world is an illusion, saying the physical universe is upheld by the same moral law that controls human affairs. "Heaven is law," he wrote. He believed man's nature was forged in Heaven and is thus incorruptible, though it can be clouded like a pearl in a bowl of dirty water. A high official in the Sung dynasty, Chu Hsi preached benevolence as the loftiest virtue, denounced corruption, and was active in famine relief. Late in life, though, enemies accused him of joining in a "rebel clique of spurious learning." **19,944**

94 PHINEAS T. BARNUM (1810–1891)
patron saint of sales and advertising

If people bought only what they needed, global trade would collapse. From Podunk to Pakistan, the world's billions are gobbling up merchandise of dubious value—rap CDs and radar detectors, Pepsi and popcorn, Milky Ways and miracle bras—thanks to demand created by advertisers and salesmen using techniques perfected by Barnum. He made his fortune in 1835, charging customers to meet George Washington's (22) 161-year-old ex-nurse. Who believed it? Nobody. Who bought the tickets? Everybody. His museums, circuses, sideshows, and presentations of stars like "Swedish Nightingale" Jenny Lind made him the model for modern marketing. "There's a sucker born every minute," he supposedly said, and without the suckers created by the Barnums in three-piece suits in modern corporate boardrooms, the world economy would be very different today. **19,921**

95 GUGLIELMO MARCONI (1874–1937)
radio man

In the 1890s, a Bolognese estate rang with Papa Marconi's pleas: Guglielmo! Stop fiddling with those electric gizmos and do your homework! In the attic, on the lawn, teenage Marconi was trying to build machines to exchange wireless telegraph signals using the electromagnetic waves that Heinrich Hertz (453) had discovered a decade earlier. Marconi got his breakthrough when he was twenty-three. The radio company he established in his mother's native Britain was a success, he won the Nobel Physics Prize at age thirty-five, and he might have invented microwave ovens and radar, too, if he had lived longer. Broadcasting became an entertainment and advertising medium in the 1920s, and radio continues to shrink the global village. In 1995 the British Broadcasting Corporation's forty-one-language world service had 160 million regular listeners in a hundred countries, including the United States, where there are now 1.2 radios for every man, woman, and child. **19,918**

96 MARSILIUS OF PADUA (c.1270–c.1342)
sower of the seeds of modern politics

We traced the development of secularism, nationalism, and popular sovereignty, and all are rooted in Marsilius of Padua. Sixteenth-century reformers read his tract, *Defensor Pacis,* which called for a church of poverty-stricken priests subservient to kings, who in turn would be subject to popular will, maybe even elected. This was radical stuff for the fourteenth century, and Holy Roman emperor Louis of Bavaria treated Marsilius like a heretic—at first. Then Louis realized that the book justified his side in a struggle with Pope John XXII; the grateful sovereign rewarded Marsilius by making him archbishop of Milan. John Wycliffe (337), Martin Luther (3), and Henry VIII of England (100) studied *Defensor Pacis,* but it's a tough read today. We take English philosopher Bertrand Russell's (593) word for its importance. **19,842**

97 DESIDERIUS ERASMUS (1466?–1536)
literary light of the Renaissance

Erasmus's literary accomplishments range from the great *Adagia,* a collection of proverbs from classical times, to his satirical masterpiece, *The Praise of Folly.* His lasting importance, though, lies in his Latin translation of the New Testament from the original Greek. Some consider him the first New Testament scholar. Though critics discerned impiety in this Catholic priest's disdain for religious dogmatism, he remained faithful to Rome, earning Martin Luther's (3) wrath for his admonitions to return to the fold. Europe's crowned heads vied to attract him to their courts, but he loved England most. In *The Praise of Folly,* written as a distraction, Folly complains of men's ingratitude: though all cherish her, "not a one has emerged in all the ages to celebrate the praises of Folly in a grateful oration." Erasmus strove to spread the Gospel among common folk, declaring, "Would that the farmer might sing snatches of Scripture at his plow." **19,810**

98 ALEXANDER VON HUMBOLDT (1769–1859)
universal scientist

His six-thousand-mile expedition through the forests of Latin America—where he marveled at "the stupendous display of wild and gigantic nature"—laid the groundwork for physical geography and biogeography. Along the way Humboldt dissected a twelve-foot crocodile and ate wild cacao beans to survive. Botanist, geographer, geologist, anthropologist, and astronomer, Humboldt even invented a system for delivering mail along wires slung from one church steeple to the next. In his lifetime he collected sixty thousand botanical specimens and identified 3,500 species. He spent his old age publishing his findings and was working on the final volume of his encyclopedic *Cosmos* when he died at age ninety. American philosopher Ralph Waldo Emerson (504) called him "one of the wonders of the world, like Aristotle, like Julius Caesar, who appear from time to time, as if to show the possibilities of the human mind." **19,777**

99 MARGARET SANGER (1879–1966)
birth control's evangelist

In the early nineteenth century women had an average of 7.04 children. Mothers often died in childbirth or languished afterward in depression. Sanger, the sixth of eleven children, was radicalized by her mother's early death, her own difficulty in delivering her three children, and her work as a New York tenement nurse. When a doctor told one impoverished woman that the only way to avoid another pregnancy was to make her husband sleep on the roof, Sanger rebelled. She wrote extensively about "birth control," a term she coined, and was jailed in 1916 after she opened America's first birth control clinic. She persisted, organizing many procontraception groups, including Planned Parenthood in 1942. In time Sanger's message became accepted wisdom, and birth rates plummeted to about 2.2 children per woman. Sanger's critics today note that she supported forced sterilization of institutionalized adults. But like her or not, she makes our list for giving modern women the knowledge and tools to control the size of their families. **19,769**

100 HENRY VIII (1491–1547)
England's first Protestant king

"How ridiculous, that the headdress of a pope governs the fly of a prince." So said eighteenth-century philosopher Voltaire (36), and Henry thought so, too. When the pope wouldn't let Henry divorce Queen Catherine (852), the king abolished Catholicism in England. That makes him a central figure in the history of England and the Protestant Reformation; we would rank him even higher had he been motivated by ideology, not lust and longing for a male heir. He was an effective ruler in the sixteenth-century mode—literate, energetic, and a practitioner of decapitation as a way of giving unwanted courtiers the pink slip, as humanist chancellor Thomas More (345) discovered when he supported the pope. Two of Henry's six wives and More's replacement, Thomas Cromwell, fared no better. Cromwell was axed for arranging Henry's marriage with Henry's terminally dowdy wife number four, Anne of Cleves. Lucky for Anne, Henry merely divorced her. **19,751**

Scan the next hundred entries, and you'll see that inventors and scientists steal the show. Look closely, and you may detect a pattern: Early breakthroughs were but the building blocks for future explorations. This led us to a quandary: Do we give more credit to the brain behind the idea or to the genius who applied it? In the end, we decided to rank doers over dreamers.

Take the automobile. Frenchman Alphonse Beau de Rochas envisioned a more efficient gas-fueled internal combustion engine with a four-stroke system. He thought about it and wrote about it, but he never built it. That task fell to Nikolaus Otto, inventor of the famous Otto Silent engine. Tailgating him is his fellow German Carl Benz, the entrepreneur who put the parts together—the engine under the hood, the chassis mounted on four wheels—and sold the first cars to a clamoring public.

The evolution of air travel is another case. In less than a hundred years, we've graduated from the Wright brothers' primitive biplane kites to supersonic airliners that can whisk passengers between New York and Paris in the time it takes to eat a five-course meal. German engineer Otto Lilienthal gets a high rating in our book because his fundamental research into gliders made flight possible. But the Wright brothers soar even higher because they made the pioneering flight.

While the Wrights took to the skies and Otto and Benz took to the road, American geneticist James Watson traveled another, interior route. Drawing on nearly a century of studies into the riddle of life, Watson discovered that the very structure of the molecule of heredity, DNA, forms a double helix. Yet his achievement, great as it was, was but one step on a path started by Moravian monk Gregor Mendel, who cultivated peas to unearth the keys to heredity, and continued by Thomas Hunt Morgan, who bred fruit flies to describe the link between genes and chromosomes.

It's fitting then that so many of these explorers land near the top of our roster. After all, their theories, experiments, and inventions have revolutionized our lives.

101 PETRUS PEREGRINUS (fl.1200s)
chronicler of the compass

With its wobbly needle suspended in water, distinguishing north from south and east from west, the magnetic compass served as primitive radar. It gave sailors the nerve to venture into uncharted seas when shorelines or stars couldn't guide them. Columbus (2) used it to sail to the New World; Da Gama (125) used it to navigate to India. We're not sure who invented it. Some say Hannibal in 203 B.C., others say the Chinese in the 1100s. With no particular point man in sight, we'll choose French Crusader Petrus Peregrinus. During the siege of Lucera, Italy, in 1269, he wrote the first detailed description of the compass in his remarkable *Epistola de Magnete*. Maybe he didn't create it, but he was the first to explain its use. Peregrinus's writings were beacons in medieval experimental research and steered the way to modern scientific methodology. **19,736**

102 OTTO LILIENTHAL (1848–1896)
pioneer of flight

Yes, Wilbur and Orville (23 and 24) were first to get off the ground in a powered plane, but Lilienthal gave his life for flight seven years earlier. As his gravestone memorializes: "Sacrifices have to be made." Before his death in a glider accident, the German engineer led the race to soar with the birds. The Wright brothers relied heavily on his research. He spent years observing birds in flight, studying their thrust and the airflow around them. He applied that information to his flying contraptions. His glider, with a body harness for the pilot, was reminiscent of a five-hundred-year-old Da Vinci sketch. Lilienthal survived one crash because he equipped his glider with a shock absorber. His detailed description of the crash helped future researchers, including the Wrights, prevent the tendency of a glider or a plane to nosedive. Lilienthal wasn't so lucky the second time he went down. **19,731**

103 FATHER BERTHOLD SCHWARTZ (fl.1300)
legendary inventor of the gun

How legendary? One historian declares that proving who invented the first cannon is impossible. Yet we'll go with scholars who target early fourteenth-century monk Berthold Schwartz, the only candidate with a name. Explosive powder was invented by the Chinese in the tenth century and was used to fire arrows by the Arabs in the thirteenth. But guns—metal pumping metal—debuted in Europe. Whereas cannons didn't exist in 1300, they thundered in the siege of Metz by 1324 and were blowing up people throughout the civilized world by 1350. So a dubious thank you, Father Schwartz, for the greatest leap in the technology of mass slaughter since the spear. **19,700**

104 GREGOR MENDEL (1822–1884)
dominant force in genetics

A Moravian monk, Mendel tended a garden in the monastery grounds and experimented with plants, primarily the pea. Over seven years he crossbred thirty thousand plants, noting patterns in coloring, seeds, and stem lengths. Based on this data, he theorized that while we inherit an equal number of characteristics from our parents, some characteristics are dominant and others are recessive. Mendel showed how his theories of inheritance work through simple mathematical laws. He told his local scientific society, but hardly anyone else, about his findings. Modest Mendel wrote only two papers, dismissing his studies as an isolated experiment. Thirty-four years later three European botanists with a similar thesis were chastened to learn that Mendel had had it first. His discovery fueled the development of genetics after 1900. Today students around the world recreate his experiments in science classes to understand the basics of heredity. **19,689**

105 NIKOLAUS OTTO (1832–1891)
engineer with drive

There are thinkers, and there are doers. Otto was the latter, a German engineer who took Frenchman Alphonse Beau de Rochas's groundbreaking theory on the ideal gas-fueled internal combustion engine and, fourteen years later, in 1861, made it real. This first practical alternative to the steam engine was the most significant invention in the history of the automobile. Before then, gas engines had relied on a less-than-efficient two-stroke cycle that basically drew in gas, ignited it, and discharged exhaust. Very slooooow going. Beau de Rochas envisioned a four-stroke system with pistons pumping four times—fast—to compress the fuel-air mixture before ignition. He patented the plan but never built the contraption. Otto did and met success. His firm, Otto and Langen, produced and sold nearly fifty thousand Otto Silent engines in seventeen years, then began to manufacture in the United States in 1878. These engines were forerunners of the gasoline-fueled internal combustion engines used today in most cars and airplanes. **19,654**

106 CHARLES-LOUIS MONTESQUIEU
(1689–1755) *democracy's tutor*

If you read nothing else in *Spirit of the Laws,* his gift to human liberty, read chapter 6 of book XI, which begins: "In every government, there are three sorts of power. . . ." This theory of the separation of power into executive, legislative, and judicial branches inspired the Constitution of the United States and the Declaration of the Rights of Man in France. Montesquieu based his doctrine on his observations of British politics, which he traced to ancient Germany. Thus, "This beautiful

system was invented in the woods," he said. *Spirit of the Laws,* a probing treatise on politics that rivals the work of Aristotle, also discusses the impact of climate on culture. As Yankees, we applaud his perceptiveness: "If we travel North, we meet with people who have few vices and a great share of frankness. If we draw near the South, we fancy ourselves entirely removed from the verge of morality." **19,651**

107 ANTON VAN LEEUWENHOEK (1632–1723)
macro figure in microbiology

Microscopes were around before Leeuwenhoek, but he perfected the art of lens-making and showed the world how these instruments could be used for scientific research. He focused his 300-power microscopes on blood, sweat, tears, spit, spices, semen, vinegar, tooth tartar, bees' eyes, flea heads, feathers, hair, and anything else he could slice thin. Then he reported his observations to the Royal Society in London so others could expand his work. Anyone who has endured an acquaintance's bad breath will appreciate what Leeuwenhoek reported first: "There are more animals living in the scum of the teeth than there are men in a whole kingdom." He identified thousands of one-celled animal species lurking in dots of marsh water and described how they were influenced by other "animacules" that we now call bacteria. **19,643**

108 PARACELSUS (1493–1541)
medicine man

Philippus Aureolus Theophrastus Bombast von Hohenheim—the full name of this Swiss Renaissance physician—cast off the accumulated superstitions of the ages and established the role of chemistry in medicine. At the age of fourteen he set off across Europe seeking wisdom, and within five years he had studied at the universities of Basel, Tübingen, Vienna, Wittenberg, Leipzig,

Heidelberg, and Cologne. But the medical scholarship he found there was based more on ancient texts than on scientific observation, and he concluded that higher education was dominated by "higher asses." Instead, he sought folk remedies for disease and as a result developed numerous drugs for previously hopeless conditions, including a mercury treatment for syphilis remarkably similar to the cure discovered four centuries later. Likewise, Paracelsus concluded that a miners' disease of his era resulted from inhaling noxious fumes, not from the anger of "mountain spirits." **19,627**

109 CARL GAUSS (1777–1855)
princely mathematician

Gauss's copious contributions to the science of numbers, from the discovery of space's curvature and the description of the bell curve to the invention of the heliotrope and his insights into algebraic equations, earned him the nickname of "prince of mathematicians" and a place close to Newton (6) and Leibniz (88) in the millennium's pantheon of mathematical geniuses. A child prodigy, he figured out at seven the formula for calculating the sum of any series of numbers, and he wrote the seminal *Disquisitiones Arithmeticae* at twenty-four. We confess our fondness for this German bricklayer's son, not for his precocity but for his serenity in letting others take credit for his discoveries if he was dissatisfied with his own proofs. Though he called mathematics "the divine science," his interests ranged widely, and he once proposed a scheme to plant geometric swaths of forest in Siberia to alert extraterrestrials to earthly intelligence. **19,626**

110 JAMES WATT (1736–1819)
inventor of a commercially viable steam engine

A quick quiz: Watt scientific genius triggered the Industrial Revolution? That's right—James Watt, who as a child liked nothing better than tinkering at his own forge in a corner of his father's workshop. Yes, there were other steam engines—Thomas Newcomen, for example, built one in 1711, and Thomas Savery had patented one in 1698. But remember, if theirs had been so great, then we'd be buying light bulbs with 100 Newcomens or Saverys. Watt, whose name today represents the fundamental unit of electrical power, worked in a lab making scientific instruments. He built a steam engine, patented in 1769, that could be applied to specific tasks. His helped drain a mine and then transformed the cotton and woolen mills. The secret to his engine was his "condenser," a gadget still in use. He also coined the term "horsepower" to describe the capabilities of his engines. **19,607**

111 WILLIAM THOMSON (1824–1907)
physics phenomenon

To be sure, Lord Kelvin—his aristocratic title—doesn't leap off the lips the way Newton's (6) and Einstein's (17) names do. Yet he was one of the sharpest scientific minds of his century. A pioneer of physics specializing in thermodynamics, he helped establish the law of the conservation of energy, advanced understanding of electricity and hydrodynamics, and was an authority on underseas telegraphy. He also inspired the Kelvin thermometer for temperature readings. Like most overachievers, he started young, enrolling in college at ten and publishing his first treatise at sixteen. Like many geniuses, he had a towering ego. C. P. Snow, the author, remarked wryly, "Lord Kelvin announced around 1904 that physics had now come to an end—presumably, with himself." Armchair intellectuals mock his miscalls: "heavier-than-air flying machines are impossible"; "radio has no future"; "X-rays are a hoax." **19,598**

112 PETRARCH (1303–1374)
first Renaissance scholar

Petrarch revived the great texts of ancient classical culture, which he regarded as history's premonition of Christianity. The innovativeness and vernacular power of this Italian's lyric poetry and the perfection of his sonnets have earned him the sobriquet of first modern poet. Petrarch is famed for his chaste love of the mysterious Laura, apparently a local housewife named Laura de Noves. Smitten with longing for her from the time he first saw her in an Avignon church on April 6, 1327, until she succumbed to the Black Death exactly twenty-one years later, Petrarch ultimately concluded that he must abandon his obsession with Laura and give himself over to God. Yet his passion for her haunts us still:

> *a heavenly spirit, a living sun,*
> *was what I saw; now, if it is not so,*
> *the wound's not healed because the bow grows slack.*

19,542

113 WILLIAM TECUMSEH SHERMAN
(1820–1891) *total warrior*

Tecumseh was Sherman's birth name, but his adoptive father tagged him William, a name befitting a Christian. Some Christian. Sherman ordered America's Union armies marching through the South to destroy crops, shell civilians, and burn Atlanta. That helped the North win the American Civil War, but it made Sherman's name synonymous with cruelty in the South. He claimed he hated war. "It is all hell," he said. American military doctrine has embraced his credo: Live in peace, but if a bully picks a fight, pound him into the ground. On Christmas Eve 1864, contemplating his attack on South Carolina, he wrote: "I almost tremble at her fate but feel that she deserves all that seems in store for her." We rank him high for innovat-

ing lightning thrusts by mobile armies living off the land. The same strategy, with modern weapons, has a name: blitzkrieg. **19,541**

114 CARL VON CLAUSEWITZ (1780–1831)
soldier who wrote the book on war

Clausewitz was a long-dead nobody until the 1880s, when someone asked Prussia's brainiest general, Helmuth von Moltke, to list the books that most influenced him. Moltke's answer: Homer, the Bible, and Clausewitz's obscure, posthumously published *On War*. In this tome Clausewitz distilled thirty-nine years of military experience and came to the conclusion that even peacetime nations should organize massive well-trained armies of regiments ready for use as instruments of policy. That's exactly what Moltke and his ilk did in the decades before World War I, making Clausewitz the ideological father of that conflict. In his thirties Clausewitz fought alongside Cossacks, whom he reviled as cowards. He died in Europe's last great cholera epidemic, having survived the Napoleonic battles of Jena, Borodino, and Waterloo, where men died like scythe-cut wheat. **19,538**

115 IGNATIUS OF LOYOLA (1491–1556)
founder of the Jesuits

How apt that the metaphor of Catholics as "soldiers of Christ" was coined by a soldier of Spain. Born Don Iñigo Lopez de Recalde in the Basque region, Ignatius pursued a military career until he was wounded by a cannonball during the war with France. During his lengthy convalescence he found God while reading a book about the lives of the saints. Poorly educated, he went to school with little children to prepare himself for study at university. Still, he envisioned a religious order that was modeled after an army and dedicated to living as teachers in imitation of the life of Christ. Ignatius created his military-style

Society of Jesus and ruled the order as its general. Although Ignatius started his Jesuits with just six followers, today it is the largest single Catholic religious order, made up of teachers, missionaries, scientists, and scholars. **19,485**

116 OKUBO TOSHIMICHI (1831–1878)
savvy and courageous bureaucrat who helped create modern Japan

"Courageous bureaucrat" sounds like an oxymoron, but not at the birth of the new Japan. Okubo needed the bulldoggedness of a Churchill (38), the iron will of a Bismarck (118), and the patience of a Mandela (354) to lead the local and imperial officials in wrenching control of Japan from feudal lords. The son of a minor warrior, Okubo was an aide to the ruler of the province of Satsuma when he realized Japan would be forced to kowtow to established nations unless the government were organized along Western lines. He and his henchmen rallied around the youthful Meiji emperor in 1868, suppressed the feudal lords, and forged a national economy and army. With dizzying speed Japan was transformed from a backwater to an industrial world player. It was the kind of group effort Japan is famous for, but Okubo stood out, which cost him his life. He was murdered by a Samurai swordsman who opposed the nationalist movement. **19,412**

117 ISABELLA I (1451–1504)
New World visionary

Christopher Columbus (2) made the great voyage, but Queen Isabella paid for his ticket. She was the only Spanish royal to believe in Columbus's plan to sail west through the "Atlantic abyss" to reach the treasure-laden East. Okay, so she strung him along for six years until court experts came around to her way of thinking. But Isabella gave Columbus the opportunity of the millen-nium. The explorer won the staunchly Catholic monarch over by promising to corral passels of heathens ripe for conversion. Ultimately, though, the queen of Castile proved to have more scruples than her protégé: she ordered the release of the natives Columbus had enslaved. After Isabella died, Italian humanist Pietro Martie mourned, "The world has lost its noblest ornament . . . she was the mirror of every virtue, the shield of the innocent, and an avenging sword to the wicked." Ornament or not, Isabella was also responsible for making the Inquisition more deadly by expelling the Jews from Spain, one of the darkest hours in that religion's history. **19,407**

118 OTTO VON BISMARCK (1815–1898)
unifier of Germany, master of Realpolitik, forerunner of Hitler

Known as the Iron Chancellor for his vow to achieve his aims through "blood and iron," Bismarck dominated Europe in the second half of the nineteenth century after winning wars he provoked with Denmark, Austria, and France, then pursuing secret alliances that many blame for World War I. He scorned moralistic namby-pambies, comparing a diplomat with principles to "a man who attempts to walk through a dense forest with a long pole clamped horizontally between his teeth." At home he flouted German laws, militarized society, jailed opponents, censored newspapers, and fought the Catholic Church. King William I couldn't control him. For all his arrogance, Bismarck industrialized Germany and, attempting to trump the socialists, introduced the world's most advanced social welfare system. **19,397**

119 MICHAEL FARADAY (1791–1867)
sparkplug of electrical theory

Like an undefeated *Jeopardy!* champion, Faraday absorbed trivia while he apprenticed as a bookbinder in London. In 1812 he attended a scientific lecture series, took copious notes, bound them (his training came in handy here), and studied. He secured a job in a laboratory and began his own work in 1825. Faraday explained the concept of force, discovered electromagnetic rotation and induction, described the "Faraday effect," formulated Faraday's law, and laid the foundation for field theory. His discovery of electromagnetic induction had practical applications in industry. When Faraday's work culminated in a radical theory of electricity in 1838, no one paid attention—his ideas were so contrary to prevailing beliefs, they were ignored. Although he turned out to be right, at the time even Faraday seemed unwilling to promote his theory. A year later he suffered a nervous breakdown and never recovered his genius. **19,388**

120 FLORENCE NIGHTINGALE (1820–1910)
modern nursing's
"lady with the lamp"

In 1851, when Nightingale defied her family and began nursing, it was a job for fallen women. Nurses were, after all, expected to accommodate doctors' sexual needs. Certainly no lady should witness a hospital's immodest sights. But Nightingale, who feared that the inactivity imposed on women of her class was pulling her toward insanity, believed God called her to nursing. After minimal training she opened a clinic in 1853. When Nightingale's "Angels" nursed the wounded in the Crimean War, mortality rates plummeted. A legend when she returned home to Britain, Nightingale took to her bed with a heart ailment and nervous afflictions. Still, she continued to direct medical reform and ensured that nurses were properly trained. Eventually senility and nerves tempered her brusque personality. When she was awarded

the Royal Order of Merit in her bed in 1907, she murmured, "Too kind, too kind." **19,340**

121 B. F. SKINNER (1904–1990)
stimulating psychologist

Skinner founded behaviorism, the theory that humans react primarily to external stimuli, not to ideas or subconscious longings. You aren't a pervert who lusts after Mom (or Dad), the Harvard professor assured us, repudiating Freud; you're a laboratory rat. But that's good, because we can build a better world through the "positive reinforcement" of desirable behavior. Skinner liked to tinker with machines that applied his principles, from his famous climate-controlled "mechanical baby tender" to a guided missile steered by pigeons. He also taught pigeons to play table tennis. Skinner had enormous influence on American psychologists in the 1950s and 1960s. Yet his writings are riddled with banalities, from his pronouncement that "better contraceptives will control populations only if people will use them" to his admonition to old people to eat well. Skinner abandoned his youthful dream of writing novels because "I had nothing to say." On coming to terms with our ultimate fate, he observed. "It is probably better not to think about death." **19,339**

122 JOSEPH LISTER (1827–1912)
surgeon who introduced
antiseptics in medicine

He didn't save the world from halitosis, but he discovered that antiseptics kill germs. Lister, a British surgeon, despaired at the forty-percent mortality rate for amputations and the almost-certain death of patients after abdominal surgery. He discovered how to kill off germs without destroying the surrounding tissue. His patients had always fared better because he was a stickler for cleanliness.

When he heard that carbolic acid aided sewage treatment, he fiddled with salves until he obtained near-miraculous results in curing and preventing infections. Because his methods gave a chance to cases once deemed hopeless, Lister was universally revered in his lifetime. It was only natural, when a pharmacist concocted a liquid antiseptic in 1879 for use during and after surgery, that the golden burning germ-killer be named Listerine. Its use for bad breath was still decades away. **19,321**

123 JAMES D. WATSON (b. 1928)
DNA detective

Watson, the American geneticist and biophysicist, had some help identifying the molecular structure of deoxyribonucleic acid, or DNA, the molecule of heredity. This two-meter-long microscopic strand in each cell determines who we are. The 1953 discovery was one of the most significant since Mendel (104) founded the science of genetics a century earlier. It earned Watson the Nobel Prize in 1962, with Britain's Francis Crick and Maurice Wilkins. We put Watson a gene above his fellow researchers at Cambridge because it was his theory that DNA's essential components, four organic bases, had to be linked in pairs. Working together, Watson and Crick relied on Wilkins's X-ray defraction studies of DNA to produce their thesis that DNA is shaped like a double helix. Their painstaking research had breakthroughs and frustrations. "Science seldom proceeds in the straightforward logical manner imagined by outsiders," Watson later wrote. "Instead, its steps forward (and sometimes backward) are often very human events." **19,311**

124 THOMAS HUNT MORGAN (1866–1945)
fruitful geneticist

Before you toss out that overripe cantaloupe, pause to acknowledge Morgan's genius. Those annoying fruit flies swarming the melon helped Morgan describe how chromosomes contribute to heredity. Picking up where Mendel left off, Morgan began in 1907 to unravel how you inherited your grandmother's red hair. From his Columbia University "fly room," Morgan described the link between genes and chromosomes. Breeding experiments had always been hampered because of an animal's gestation period, but fruit flies solved that problem because they reproduced in twelve days. An added bonus was that thousands could be housed in one milk bottle. Morgan's experiments explained the mysteries of heredity, thus shifting the focus of biochemistry, giving new understanding to inherited disease, and putting genetics on its modern course. When his first child was born in 1906, Morgan said his son inherited his mother's character. "Apparently it dominates in the first hybrid," he observed. **19,299**

125 VASCO DA GAMA (c.1460–1524)
discoverer of the sea route from Europe to India

The Portuguese were smart. While the delusional Columbus (2) was still insisting that America was some woodsy offshore island of Japan, da Gama was proving that the way to reach Asia was, yes, to go East, young man, but first go South. Da Gama's four-ship fleet rounded Africa's Cape of Good Hope and on May 20, 1498, landed in Calicut, India. It was the first all-sea trip from Western Europe to India, and it launched Portugal's 450-year empire in East Africa and Asia. Not until the Suez Canal was dug in 1869 was there a quicker all-sea route from Europe's Atlantic coast to Asia. Calicut welcomed da Gama, but jealous Arabian traders incited the local population, and he had to fight his way out. He returned in 1503, subdued the city, and skewered many of its citizens. **19,292**

126 SALADIN (SALAH AD-DIN YUSUF)
(1138–1193) *Islamic liberator of Jerusalem*

The Crusaders didn't deserve an enemy as honorable as Saladin. The Christians waded in blood when they conquered Jerusalem in 1099. When Saladin recaptured the city eighty-eight years later, he spared his enemies and opened holy sites to pilgrims of all faiths, even Christians. For money, of course. Saladin started soldiering at fourteen and fought his way to the leadership of Syria and Egypt by defeating other Islamic factions. Then he turned on the Christians. He became the hero of 1,001 breathless romances, including some that stretched the truth to pair him with the love-starved queen of France, Eleanor of Aquitaine (420). Saladin was good, but not that good; he was ten years old when Eleanor visited Palestine. However, Saladin did know Eleanor's crusading son, Richard the Lion-Hearted: they made peace in 1192. **19,258**

127 DAVID RICARDO (1772–1823)
the reason they call economics the "dismal science"

The son of a Dutch immigrant, Ricardo made a fortune on the London stock market before formulating some of the nineteenth century's most important contributions to economic thinking. Whether or not the pessimism of his friend Thomas Malthus (306), the population doomsayer, infected his thinking, Ricardo is best known for his notion that wages stabilize at subsistence levels. Thus, he reasoned, the only way for government to keep poverty in check is to limit the number of poor people—among other methods, by discouraging "early and improvident marriages." His thesis that the value of a product depends on the labor that goes into it influenced Marx (14). His theory of comparative advantage, which states that free trade is the most efficient way of allocating global resources, was instrumental in breaking down trade barriers in Europe. And his theory of rent played a part in land-reform movements in both Europe and the United States. **19,252**

128 ERNEST RUTHERFORD (1871–1937)
atom smasher

His is the stuff of science fiction. Rutherford discovered gamma rays and described alpha and beta particles and thorium X. He smashed an atom, demonstrated that it consisted of a central nucleus surrounded by electrons, and accomplished the first artificial transformation by changing one element into another. His research provided the cornerstone for the subsequent generation of physicists who put nuclear technology into warfare. A New Zealander who emigrated to England, Rutherford balked at geographic boundaries within science. At the dawn of the nuclear age, he envisioned governments pooling resources and working together. He corresponded with colleagues around the world and mentored fledgling scientists. When Jewish scientists fled Nazi Germany, he helped them find refuge. Yet another Nobel Prize winner, Lord Rutherford earned the ultimate honor in death—he was buried in Westminster Abbey. **19,228**

129 RAPHAEL SANZIO (1483–1520)
Renaissance wonder

Just about every fourteen-year-old knows that Raphael was one of the four greatest Renaissance painters. And while we can attribute Raphael's latest renaissance to four pizza-eating Teenage Mutant Ninja Turtles, it underscores, rather than diminishes, the importance of his work. Trained by his artist father, Raphael was also influenced by Leonardo (9) and Michelangelo (13); if the

Renaissance had sponsored art contests, he would have finished third behind them. Like other Renaissance artists, he studied anatomy and perspective. Concentrating especially on portraiture, Raphael was obsessed with the Madonna. He painted her in dozens of ways—with fish, rose, veil, curtain, book, carnation, child; with angels and saints, including John the Baptist, Francis, Jerome, Elizabeth, and Catherine. With the popes as his patrons, it's not surprising that his best works have religious themes. Our favorite by far—the action-packed *St. George and the Dragon.*   **19,189**

130 AUGUSTE COMTE (1798–1857)
world's first sociologist

In fact, he coined the term. The French cogitator also concocted positivism, which stipulated three stages of human understanding of the world: the theological, or superstitious; the metaphysical, or abstract; and the positive, or objective and rational. He believed we should renounce the first two and pursue the third. While many of the ideas he expressed in his main work, *The Course of Positive Philosophy,* seem ludicrous today, they represent the first great effort to redefine the good society in the industrial age. Given to grand gestures, from abandoning his parents' Catholicism to marrying a prostitute, Comte considered himself a reformer more than a thinker. An idealist, he lectured workers free of charge and went to jail rather than join the National Guard. Which is not to say he succumbed to false modesty. Otherwise he could never have written of his science of sciences, or "religion of humanity," as he also called his philosophy: "It is time to complete the vast intellectual operation begun by Bacon, Descartes, and Galileo, by constructing the system of general ideas which must henceforth prevail among the human race."   **19,175**

131 JOHANN WOLFGANG VON GOETHE
(1749–1832) *Olympian of letters*

"I am like a snake," Goethe said. "I slough my skin and start afresh." A lifetime of metamorphoses took this colossus of German literature from the turbulence of early romanticism to the serenity of classicism. He wrote brilliantly of politics, science, philosophy, history, and art. But his fame rests largely on the poetic drama *Faust,* the product of sixty years of meditation and personal regeneration. It inspired novelist Thomas Mann (584) and composers Richard Wagner (165), Hector Berlioz (671) and Charles Gounod. A towering intellect, Goethe also surged with passion. He was forever in love, casting each object of his affection as his poetic muse. That pattern persisted to age eighty-two, when he dallied with a teenager. In his weakened state he contracted fatal pneumonia. Death, Goethe's final metamorphosis, overtook him as he sat in his armchair, murmuring of his love for a dark-haired girl.   **19,162**

132 MAIMONIDES (1135–1204)
rabbi of reason

From Moses to Einstein (17), Jews have survived by staying one step ahead of tyrants. In 1148, when the new Islamic ruler of Córdoba offered Jews the depressingly familiar "convert or die" option, Maimonides took the road to Morocco and Egypt where he found safety in the court of a tolerant sultan, Saladin (126). Maimonides's family was in the jewelry business. But when his brother David was lost at sea with a stock of gems, Maimonides devoted himself full time to his other trades: philosopher, rabbi, and physician. His commentaries on Jewish law set the agenda for future rabbis and his writings on Aristotelean reason influenced Thomas Aquinas's (8) scholasticism. Maimonides's wisdom still grips us. The worst form of charity is money given grudgingly

40

with strings attached, he wrote; "The highest step and the summit of charity's golden ladder" is to teach the poor a trade. **19,131**

133 ANDREA PALLADIO (1508–1580)
divine builder

Ever wonder why the White House has columned porticoes or how those handsome curved windows gracing new homes got their name? The answer: the legacy of Palladio, the Venetian architect who drew inspiration from the Romans and whose buildings reflect his supremely rational and orderly approach to design. This Renaissance giant's influence has spanned four centuries and spread throughout Europe into the New World. With that portfolio, you'd think he was a worldly scholar. Not so. Palladio was only a bright bricklayer when a rich Venetian discovered him and tutored him in humanism. The rest is architectural history. Palladio won commission after commission, specializing in villas for the nouveaux riches and palaces for the firmly entrenched wellheeled. His treatise, *The Four Books of Architecture,* popularized classical decorative details and, some say, was the most influential architectural pattern book ever printed. **19,111**

134 LECH WALESA (b. 1943)
death knell for Communism

The most influential political leader at the end of the twentieth century aspired only to the simple life of an electrician. Yet we traced the epicenter of the earthquake that crushed Communism back to his shipyard in Gdansk, Poland. There Walesa and members of Solidarity, the trade union, staged courageous strikes and peaceful opposition to the government's raising of meat prices. Walesa and other union rabble-rousers were jailed, but the government could not turn back the tide of change. One by one Eastern European nations followed Poland's lead and turned away from stifling, restrictive governments. The Berlin Wall fell. Even the paterfamilias of Communism, the Soviet Union, abandoned it. But Solidarity was first. Walesa won the Nobel Peace Prize in 1983, and in 1990 he was chosen president of Poland in free elections. **19,102**

135 ELI WHITNEY (1765–1825)
inventor of interchangeable parts

No, Whitney didn't make our list for his 1793 invention of the cotton gin (which is, by the way, short for "engine"). Whitney, a Massachusetts native who was trained as a lawyer, lost so much money in a prolonged fight for the patent rights to his mechanized cotton-picking machine that he eventually gave up and started making weapons. Here's where Whitney's lasting influence comes in. He standardized the manufacture of parts at his rifle factory and started the country on the road to industrialization. He established a rudimentary assembly line in which workers fit the same standard part into a partially constructed musket over and over again. He had the right idea, but he was ahead of his time. It took him eight years to finish a two-year government contract for ten thousand guns. **19,077**

136 MAX PLANCK (1858–1947)
originator of the quantum theory, "the greatest mystery we've got," in the words of physicist John Archibald Wheeler

Though less acclaimed than Einstein (17), Planck sits at the right hand of the master. Their speculations form the basis of modern physics. "Planck's constant," putting a finite value on the dimensions of the subatomic world, means time and space have units that can't be made smaller. Thank heavens; otherwise, we wouldn't be able to move. Like most of the millennium's great thinkers, Planck was a religious man, and he must have called often upon his faith. Both his daughters died in childbirth, his first son was killed in World War I, and his second son was tortured to death by the Nazis. By historical coincidence, the quantum theory, which gave birth to the uncertainty principle that places a limit on the accuracy of the scientific method, was formulated in 1900—the dawn of the century of live-and-let-live moral relativism. **19,063**

137 JOSEPH PRIESTLEY (1733–1804)
experimental chemist

Priestley achieved fame and infamy for his pioneering efforts in education and his support of religious and civil liberties. But this Protestant preacher contributed to the launching of modern chemistry by discovering ten new "airs," or gases. His biggest breakthrough: observing that red mercuric oxide, when heated, gave off a colorless gas he called "dephlogisticated air." Lavoisier (67) repeated Priestley's experiment and christened the gas "oxygen." Priestley earned worldwide prestige as a scholar, but his ardent support of French revolutionaries made him hated in his native England. After French king Louis XVI was executed, mobs destroyed Priestley's Birmingham home and laboratory. He fled to the safety of the United States and there communed with American thinkers, including Jefferson (64) and John Adams (214). Priestley's intellect was so impressive—and the void he left behind so great even years after his death—that Adams once exclaimed to Jefferson, "Oh, that Priestley could live again!" **19,038**

138 CATHERINE THE GREAT (1729–1796)
empress of Russia

Her importance lies in her expansion of the Russian empire, but she is interesting for her contradictory personality. As a young bride immersed in the Enlightenment, the future despot despised despotism. A romantic, she ordered her dissipated husband's assassination. Capable of cruelty, she risked smallpox inoculation to set an example for her subjects. Vain, she shunned high-heeled shoes because they hurt her feet. Contemptuous of others' weaknesses, she was addicted to coffee and snuff. Fancying herself a thinker, she hoped Montesquieu (106), "now in heaven," would forgive her plagiarism. The story about the horse is untrue, though she was sexually active, starting with the Adonis-like Stanislaus Poniatowsky ("Stany" to her highness), who slipped into her boudoir disguised as a footman and was made king of Poland for his attentions, and ending with boy-toys in her dotage. So what? She was great, as only Peter the Great (27) had been great before her in Russian history, and Lenin (41) after. **19,011**

139 SUSAN B. ANTHONY (1820–1906)
suffrage leader and cofounder of the U.S. women's rights movement

Ironic, isn't it, that when they finally decided to put a famous woman's image on a piece of American money, they designed a coin no one wanted to use. Just before Anthony died at age eighty-six, she reminded suffragists, "Failure is impossible." Sad commentary that the vote was still fourteen years away and true equal rights elude women still. Anthony was vilified in her lifetime because her philosophy of equality, which she preached publicly and vociferously, was deemed unwomanly. Mocked for her failure to marry, described in print as "personally repulsive," and arrested for attempting to vote, Anthony argued for the vote and women's equality to three generations of American women. Like the embarrassing aunt who becomes "eccentric" and interesting with age, Anthony stayed around long enough to witness her own rehabilitation. **19,001**

140 CARL BENZ (1844–1929)
manufacturer of the first salable car

His name symbolizes the ultimate driving luxury, but when Benz successfully took to the manure-laden streets of Munich in June 1886, his automobile was a no-frills, glorified tricycle. Indeed, it would be an overstatement to assert that Benz "invented" the automobile. He was one of dozens of inventor/tinkerer-types around the globe who were racing to build a horseless carriage. Yet he managed to develop his version well enough to sell the first one in 1887. Two years later fifty workers were employed at the Benz factory. By 1890 he was turning out four-wheeled vehicles. Benz also invented electric ignition and water cooling in his cars. True luxury cars with big price tags didn't come until after the Benz company merged with Gottlieb Daimler's (275) Mercedes in 1926. **18,967**

141 ANNA ELEANOR ROOSEVELT (1884–1962)
first among first ladies

If there hadn't been an Eleanor, there wouldn't have been a Franklin (37). She refused to let her polio-stricken husband sink into self-pity, and her indefatigable campaigning in his bid for New York's governorship helped propel him into the White House in 1933. Through it all she was her wheeler-dealer husband's social conscience, championing the causes of women and the poor in her daily newspaper column. She was a voice of civil rights in an era before civil rights. Though theirs was a marriage of convenience by then, she helped mold FDR's New Deal and chewed his ear on her pet issues. When women were barred from presidential news conferences, Roosevelt held her own press meetings and allowed only women

reporters to cover them. An indefatigable worker, she said she believed, "It is not fair to ask of others what you are not willing to do yourself." Despite criticism that her activism went beyond the proper role for women, Roosevelt set the standard by which all subsequent first ladies have been measured. **18,933**

142 ROBERT BOYLE (1627–1691)
catalyst of the chemical revolution

Boyle ranks below Bacon (84), Galileo (4), and Newton (6) in the pantheon of modern science, but he was also a philosopher, linguist, and author of sermons "for proving the Christian Religion against notorious Infidels." He viewed the universe as a giant clock started by God and run on His immutable laws. The fourteenth son of the earl of Cork, Boyle replaced the Aristotelian notion of four basic elements of earth, air, fire, and water with a concept of primary particles interacting to form "corpuscles"— a precursor of modern chemical theory. He also conducted pioneering laboratory experiments, formulated Boyle's Law on the relationship between gas volume and pressure, created a system of chemical classification, and perfected the air pump. Discovering so much, he lamented how little he knew in his *Essay of Men's Great Ignorance of the Uses of Natural Things.* **18,886**

143 GEORGE STEPHENSON (1781–1848)
the engineer who could

Stephenson was a semiliterate coalyard maintenance man with a North England accent thicker than a vein of anthracite. His eloquence was in his hands. He was a whiz at improving and designing the steam-driven machines coming into vogue in the early nineteenth century, and in 1825 he built the twenty-five-mile Stockton and Burlington Railway for a mine owner who needed to transport coal to port. Copying existing tramroads, Stephenson set the iron rails 56.5 inches apart, and that's still the standard railroad gauge in Britain and the United States. Some engineers designed engines; others built the tracks. Stephenson did both and made the whole power-packed package an industrial success, forever changing the way we travel. Even his genes were mighty. In 1830 his son Robert built "The Rocket," the best engine yet, giving the golden age of rail another burst of steam. **18,853**

144 BLAISE PASCAL (1623–1662)
French scientist and born-again Christian

A mathematical prodigy whose sister said he figured out Euclid's proofs at twelve using a lump of coal on his playroom floor, Pascal founded the modern theory of probability and made important discoveries in calculus. In physics he formulated "Pascal's principle" governing hydraulics. He built the first calculating machine and helped set up the world's first regular city transport system in Paris. He was also the first writer of modern French prose. In 1654 he had a profound religious experience—his "night of fire"—and thereafter devoted his life to God. His *Pensées* posit faith as the key to understanding the universe and urge readers to "wager" God exists. His sayings rank as some of history's most memorable, including: "If Cleopatra's nose had been shorter, the face of the real world would have been changed," and "The heart has its reasons which reason does not understand." **18,821**

145 DAVID WARK GRIFFITH (1875–1948)
the first major film director

D. W. Griffith transformed movies into art. When his silent film *The Birth of a Nation* premiered in 1915, *The New York Times* noted that the "melodramatic and inflammatory" film marked the "advent of the two dollar movie." It was melodramatic because of its sympathetic treatment of two families—one from the North and one from the South—and inflammatory because of its unsympathetic, cruel portrayal of blacks. Content aside, Griffith's uncanny cinematic insight, camera techniques, film editing, and authentic sets defined the standard for future Hollywood filmmaking. Griffith's colossal epic gave the illusion of reality on battlefields and on night rides of the Ku Klux Klan. Its then unheard-of length—two and a quarter hours—coupled with a huge cast, sweeping camera work, and politically charged subject matter left audiences breathless. An advocate of using film to teach difficult concepts, Griffith called it "history by lightning!" **18,803**

146 CARL JUNG (1875–1961)
Freud's star pupil

—until he took a closer look at psychoanalysis and decided id didn't work for him. When Freud (15) urged him to hold fast to sexual theory, Jung said, the master spoke like a father saying, "Promise me, son, you will go to church every Sunday." In a classic Oedipal rebellion, the pipe-smoking Swiss sage founded his own therapeutic school, analytic psychology, based on the mystical notion that primeval archetypes lurk in the human mind as a "collective unconscious" that drives our behavior. As he put it: "Individual consciousness is only the flower and the fruit of a season, sprung from the perennial rhizome beneath the earth." Rivaling Freud's interpretation of human personality, Jung's philosophy found some surprising expressions, from his construction of a strange but beautiful house as a representation "of my innermost thoughts" to his fascination with UFO sightings as twentieth-century projections of ancient myth. **18,769**

147 GEORGE BOOLE (1815–1864)
mathematician whose logic lurks behind computer technology

Anyone who has searched a computer database is versed in Boolean logic. Use *and* to link two terms, and you narrow the search; use *or* to link the same terms, and you broaden the search. Boole created a binary system of symbolic logic based on two numbers—0 and 1—that today we call Boolean algebra. Not only do we trace the binary system used in computer technology to Boole, but we credit him with the technology used in telephone switching. Yet another scientist who rose above humble beginnings, Boole taught himself Latin, French, Greek, German, and Italian. He worked his way up to become a mathematics professor at Queen's College in Cork. Then, in his 1854 masterpiece, *An Investigation of the Laws of Thought,* he logically laid out his system in black and white (or is it, black or white?). **18,765**

148 AKBAR (1542–1605)
greatest of India's Mughal emperors

Akbar expanded his dominion throughout the subcontinent, adding Afghanistan, Baluchistan, and northern India to create the most powerful empire of his day. A Muslim, he took Hindu wives and made common cause with Hindu princes (though he also lopped off the head of a Hindu prisoner at age fourteen to prove his manhood), and he invited Christian missionaries to his realm. An enlightened ruler, he launched a renaissance of Indian painting, promoting a school of realism marked by bold colors and Western perspective. Akbar had other passions, too. Though illiterate, he was so captivated by philosophical discourse that he had to "forcibly restrain myself from listening to it." His craving for mango fruit was so potent, he planted an orchard of a hundred thousand mango trees, and

his love of polo so great, he had polo balls painted with phosphorus so he could play at night. **18,710**

149 PABLO PICASSO (1881–1973)
modern art's colossus

During Picasso's ninety-two years on Earth, this incredibly versatile artist of almost mythical energy produced more than twenty thousand works, including paintings, sculptures, drawings, illustrations, and even pottery. He influenced the cubist movement and abstraction and introduced collage. He also consumed five mistresses and two wives; his art reflected the joy of each new union and the bitterness of each breakup. He had his Blue Period and his Rose Period, but his most famous painting is largely black and white. *Guernica,* an eleven-by-twenty-five-foot canvas that interprets the German bombing of the Basque town of Guernica during the Spanish Civil War, explodes with terror and destruction. "One does not paint in order to decorate apartments," Picasso said. "Painting is an instrument of offensive and defensive war against the enemy." **18,666**

150 HERNÁN CORTÉS (1485–1547)
New World warrior

Cortés's conquest of Mexico in 1521 ranks among the most pivotal military feats ever; his forces laid siege to the Aztec capital, crippling Montezuma's mighty empire. Cortés's military campaign was bolstered by a turncoat native princess who became his interpreter/mistress and by 200,000 Indians who wanted their Aztec tormentors crushed. The victory ushered in three centuries of Spanish domination in South America. It turned out that Cortés had less to fear from Aztec spears than from infighting. Diego Vasquez, Spanish governor of Cuba, was jealous of Cortés's success and undermined his prestige in Spain. Cortés returned home in 1540 to find he meant nothing to Charles V (61) and his court. One account has it the king was entering his coach when he spotted a familiar figure in the crowd. Charles asked who the fellow was, only to have Cortés bellow back, "It's the one who gave you more kingdoms than you used to have towns." **18,619**

151 THOMAS HOBBES (1588–1679)
British philosopher and early advocate of testosterone control

Hobbes's bleak materialism was attacked in his day and ours, but his theory of a social contract between rulers and subjects had an enormous influence on the West's political evolution. Men, Hobbes maintained, are driven by a "restless desire of power" and tend to go around killing one another. Thus, he famously declared, in their natural state they live lives that are "nasty, brutish, and short." In civilized societies, however, they surrender their rights to a sovereign in return for his protection. Forget Hobbes's royalism; his assumption that the state derives its legitimacy from the people, not God, was a breakthrough in political thinking, leading eventually to democracy. Hobbes couldn't have been more unlike his imaginary ignoble savage. He tutored noblemen's sons, lived high off the hog, translated Homer in his eighties, and took what he called his "great leap in the dark"—death—at ninety-one. **18,543**

152 FAKR AD-DIN AR-RAZI (1149–1209)
Muslim theologian

Ar-Razi loved disputation above all else (even food, he said) and traveled about the medieval lands of modern-day Iran, Turkistan, and Afghanistan debating local scholars. He also expounded—too lovingly, some religious leaders griped—on heretical doctrines before skewering them with his ripostes. Merciless toward enemies and rivals, he orchestrated his brother's death in a shah's dungeon. Enemies sometimes struck back, like the fanatic who opposed rational analysis of Islam. "Here is my proof," he declared, brandishing a knife at Ar-Razi. But Ar-Razi always maintained he was doing it for the good of the faith, and in fact by forcing the sects of his troubled age to reexamine their creeds, he helped unify Islam. He wrote more than a hundred books, and his commentaries on the Koran, Islam's holy text, are regarded as masterpieces. **18,512**

153 HENRY THE NAVIGATOR (1394–1460)
founder of the Age of Exploration

He seldom left home and died thirty-two years before Columbus (2) set sail, but Portugal's Prince Henry launched the age of exploration by ordering seamen south to Africa and nearby islands. Today it seems like a jaunt, but at the time the Henry-inspired expedition that rounded the Guinea coast was a giant leap. Contemporaries called Henry's pastime a waste of money. Nobody complained, though, when his voyagers brought home slaves and gold from Africa. In 1498, after predecessors had inched their way south, Portuguese navigator Vasco da Gama (125) found a new route to India around Africa's Cape of Good Hope. That put Portugal first in the race to the wealth of the East and control of the Spice Islands. Henry's hobby had paid off. **18,492**

154 SARAH BERNHARDT (1844–1923)
the millennium's greatest performer

Known as "the Divine Sarah," this French thespian was a legend in her lifetime, thrilling audiences in Europe, the United States, Australia, South America and Canada in roles created by Victor Hugo (163), Alexandre Dumas (874), and Jean Racine (389). Hugo lauded her "golden voice." But offstage Bernhardt was temperamental and arrogant. She once said, "To be worthy of the name, an actor must be capable of a continuous dissection of his personality." Hers was fundamentally flaky; some say Bernhardt slept in a coffin. For sheer color, we rate her over rival Eleanora Duse, the Italian actress of quiet strength and subtlety. Bernhardt's name is synonymous with melodrama, on and off the stage. She also scores for her gutsy final curtain. Her right leg had to be amputated following an injury, but Bernhardt insisted on visiting troops during World War I. So she clambered onto a litter chair and was carried to the front.   **18,398**

155 LE CORBUSIER (1887–1965)
sculptor of buildings

Le Corbusier was the pseudonym of Charles-Édouard Jeanneret, a Swiss painter, writer, architect, and city planner. Largely self-taught, he was the first architect to champion the use of reinforced concrete, which he molded like plastic to give his buildings form. The man who once proclaimed, "A house is a machine for living in," created functional structures spiked with bold expression. His quintessential design: a box with strips of horizontal windows, open living spaces, and roof gardens. The United Nations Secretariat building in New York is mostly his plan. He loved to shock, which cost him points in conservative quarters. That's why his innovative design for the League of Nations building in Geneva—with its wall of heating and insulating glass—lost the 1927 competition when judges disqualified it on a technicality. While the setback embittered Le Corbusier, his entry only won him greater renown among young architects.   **18,387**

156 LOUIS-JACQUES-MANDÉ DAGUERRE
(1789–1851) *inventor of practical photography*

When Daguerre's pictures were unveiled at a lecture in 1839, Parisians combed opticians' shops and pharmacies for the equipment to duplicate his process. The "daguerreotype" was so coveted that, in a grand philanthropic gesture, the French government purchased the rights and gave the invention to the world—free of charge. The technique was not without problems: the camera was unwieldy and required subjects to sit perfectly still with their heads in clamps for thirty minutes to fix the image; the process yielded only one "positive" plate; and pictures had to be made outdoors on sunny days. Its aficionados were undeterred. By 1850 there were ten thousand daguerreotypists in the United States alone. This process remained in vogue for about twenty-five years until the development of a quicker one using negatives that could be copied onto paper. But for his vision, we dub Daguerre the "father of photography."   **18,345**

157 GAVRILO PRINCIP (1895–1918)
assassin who ignited World War I

On June 28, 1914, Princip and six other Serbian-trained Bosnian liberationists slipped into Sarajevo to kill the heir to the Austrian throne, Archduke Francis Ferdinand. One of Princip's bomb-throwing pals missed Francis, but when the archduke and his wife Sophie drove to the hospital to visit injured aides, the chauffeur took the wrong street. Purely by coincidence, Princip was walking by; he fired into the car and killed the royal couple. Austria's wishy-washy Emperor Francis Joseph (266) almost let the incident pass. But Europe was a powder keg, and Princip had supplied the spark. German warmongers goaded Austria into retaliating against Serbia, and all the nations chose sides. Before World War I ended, ten million soldiers were dead. Princip, too. The law forbade execution of teenagers, but tuberculosis claimed him in 1918.   **18,314**

158 VINCENT VAN GOGH (1853–1890)
tormented artist of haunting expressionistic paintings

In his lifetime Van Gogh sold only one painting, but in 1990 the $82.5 million paid for his portrait of his physician set a record for the world's most expensive painting. Van Gogh's torment began at birth—he was named after a dead brother and spent his life wondering if he was a substitute for the dead baby. After work as an art dealer and a minister, Van Gogh began painting. Through hundreds of letters written to his brother Theo, we see Van Gogh drift into madness. In a psychotic frenzy he cut off part of his ear and sent it to a prostitute. During his year in a mental institution in southern France, he produced some of his most memorable paintings. Unable to still the madness, he shot himself and died in his brother's arms. Our favorite Van Goghs: *Starry Night,* of course, and *The Potato Eaters.* **18,313**

159 MASACCIO (1401–1428)
humanist master

Masaccio's life was just a brushstroke on eternity's canvas, yet he changed painting forever. He established a first in painting: the use of light coming from a single source to emphasize natural form. He was born Tommaso di Giovanni di Simone Guidi. Good-hearted but absentminded and sloppy in dress, he was nicknamed Masaccio, "Big Clumsy Thomas." Like contemporaries Brunelleschi (85) and Donatello (319), Masaccio brought humanism into his art, dispensing with medievalism's God-centered view to focus on man and the world. His figures were warm and solid. He mastered the technique of perspective in *The Trinity,* but his legacy is greater: the celebrated *Life of Saint Peter*—awesome frescoes in the Brancacci Chapel in Florence. His new style of realism made him a founder of modern painting and a temple at which Da Vinci (9), Michelangelo (13), Raphael (129), and countless others worshiped. **18,278**

160 FRANK LLOYD WRIGHT (1867–1959)
innovative architect

Junior architect Wright got the residential projects while senior colleagues snagged commercial plans. Never mind. Wright's prairie houses soon formed the basis of twentieth-century residential design. Influenced by the Mayans, Native Americans, and European cubists, Wright's houses of stone, brick, and copper seemed to grow out of their grassy hills or rocky slopes. Architect Eero Saarinen described Wright's work as "all one organism, all one thing." Wright first won international recognition, then connected with Americans. His most famous work: the Solomon R. Guggenheim Museum in New York, a six-story helix that opened in 1959. Wright's wit, like the corners of some of his buildings, had sharp edges. Novelist Rex Stout once invited him to the fourteen-room house Stout had built on a Connecticut hillside. Wright took a long look, then proclaimed it "an excellent spot. Someone should build a house here." **18,198**

161 IBN SĪNĀ (980–1037)
all-purpose medieval genius

Ibn Sīnā, or Avicenna as he was called in the Christian world, mastered the Koran, Greek philosophy, and the arts of legal disputation and medicine when he was a mere teenager. Then he started writing. One of his achievements was the five-volume *Canon of Medicine.* Though most of it is now considered quackery, it was the leading authority on symptoms, herbs, drugs, and crude surgery until the seventeenth century. His many works synthesizing divine revelation and Greek logic and metaphysics were the true beginning of medieval philosophy and had an impact on the thinking of Thomas Aquinas (8), Albertus Magnus (726), and Roger Bacon (412). Ibn Sīnā was born in what is now Afghanistan, and he served various rulers in Persia. But his true service was to civilization as a thinker who helped drag the world out of the intellectual Dark Ages. **18,193**

162 OLIVER CROMWELL (1599–1658)
leader of the English Parliament's revolt

Cromwell hated absolutist rulers and bishops, and he rid England of both. He was a radical Puritan member of the House of Commons whose knack for soldiering propelled him from battalion commander to victorious leader in the civil war against the autocratic, crypto-Catholic king Charles I. "I tell you we will cut off his head with the crown on it," Cromwell replied roughly when a royalist questioned Parliament's right to try the king for treason. Charles was beheaded in 1649, and Cromwell ruled as England's dictator for the next nine years. After Cromwell's death, an England weary of gloomy Puritanism invited Charles's son to rule, and Charles II got grisly revenge. Cromwell's disinterred head was put on a pole atop Westminster Hall. But it was too late to stop what Cromwell had wrought. After him, no English king dared to claim absolute power. **18,182**

163 VICTOR HUGO (1802–1885)
the great romantic

Hugo's overwhelming personality, with its infinite contradictions, rivaled his monumental talent. Attentive husband, doting father, and lusty suitor, he kept wife, mistress, and countless conquests on the side. As a young poet, he curried favor from the monarchy, then evolved into an impassioned republican. To author Jean Cocteau, "Victor Hugo was a madman who believed himself to be

Victor Hugo." Whatever his true persona, Hugo the writer sent classicism reeling in 1830. He demolished literary conventions by introducing a new sound and beat of verses in his romantic drama, *Hernani.* But it is the sweep and drama of Hugo's poetry, *The Contemplations* and *The Leaves of Autumn,* and his novels, *The Hunchback of Notre Dame* and *Les Misérables,* that place him at the forefront of French literature. Writer Jules Renard observed: "Only Victor Hugo has spoken; other men merely stammer." Even the act of dying couldn't diminish Hugo's poetic powers. "Here is the battleground of day and night," he whispered, before darkness enveloped him. **18,105**

164 AVERROËS (IBN RUSHD) (1126–1198)
Christianity's favorite Muslim

In the late Middle Ages Averroës, as the Latins called Ibn Rushd, had a huge following in the Christian West. His analysis of the relationship between reason and faith in his commentaries on Aristotle had a profound effect on European theologians. The commentaries were helpful to Thomas Aquinas (8), though Aquinas denounced Averroës's Christian followers for being too strong on reason, too weak on faith. Some of Ibn Rushd's own Islamic contemporaries beat Aquinas to the Averroës-bashing game. In 1195 he was accused of spreading falsities, particularly ideas that subverted the notion that God created the world. His books were burned, and he was banished briefly from his home in Córdoba. Ibn Rushd was also a judge, diplomat, scientist, and author of a medical encyclopedia, which makes him a real renaissance man two hundred years before the Renaissance. **18,101**

165 RICHARD WAGNER (1813–1883)
the man who made the fat lady sing

Wagner stretches the limits of our ability to love the art of artists we hate. He was an egomaniac who stole his friend's wife, fought with former admirers like Nietzsche (215), and made anti-Semitism his ideological leitmotif. Impressionist master Pierre-Auguste Renoir (384) came to sketch Wagner's head and in return heard a tirade against German Jews. But oh, those heavenly notes. Wagner rescued the music of opera from frivolous French and Italian melody-makers and fused it with drama, motion, and spectacle. Above all, as musicologist Donald Grout wrote, Wagner's music carried its audiences to a state of mystical and sensuous ecstasy, the goal of all romantic art. Conductor Bruno Walter—a Jew, by the way—wrote that on first hearing *Tristan and Isolde,* "never had my heart been consumed by such yearning and sublime bliss." Our favorite Wagner: *Die Walküre,* all four and a half hours. **18,059**

166 HUGO GROTIUS (1583–1645)
originator of international law

He wrote Latin verse at age nine, finished law school at fifteen, was Holland's official historian at twenty, and was sentenced to life imprisonment at thirty-six, for preaching toleration in a Calvinist country. Not to worry. Grotius's wife fooled his Keystone Cop guards into carrying him to freedom in a sealed box they thought was full of weighty books. Grotius fled to France, where Louis XIII offered him a hefty pension and the freedom to write *On the Law of War and Peace,* the millennium's most important treatise on international relations. In it Grotius wrote that wars for defense and recovery of property were legitimate, but that fighting should be prevented by negotiations and battles should be fought according to rules he laid out, such as no killing of civilians. Civilized countries pay lip service to his laws today. By the way, big-hearted Louis was all talk. He never paid the pension. **18,038**

167 HENRIK IBSEN (1828–1906)
creator of the modern theater

Ibsen was to the stage what Darwin (7) was to biology and Freud (15) to sex. "Everything that isn't a copy of him is a reaction to him," said scholar Eric Bentley. Subsequent giants acknowledged their debt; George Bernard Shaw wrote an ode to him; playwright Eugene O'Neill (426) called him "my inspiration"; filmmaker Ingmar Bergman (958) said, "He has followed me all my life." Scholars divide this Scandinavian dramatist's works into three phases—poetic drama, social realism, and symbolism—but no matter; never before had any playwright probed so deeply into the human psyche. His exposure of human foibles, in *A Doll's House,* for example, offended many. One critic denounced his play *Ghosts* about syphilis as "a loathsome sore." True, his rival August Strindberg dismissed him as a "Norwegian bluestocking," but Ibsen retorted by placing a picture of Strindberg in his study and declaring, "He shall hang there and watch as I write." **17,923**

168 JANE AUSTEN (1775–1817)
homespun trend-setter of English literature

Austen was the first to weave a story from domestic circumstances, and no author has ever surpassed her uncanny mastery of the format. Unlike great classics that are praised but never read, her small stack of novels is notably readable. Indeed, Austen's stock has increased as each generation of readers comes to fancy her simple domestic plots. Her anonymously published novels, including *Sense and Sensibility, Emma,* and *Pride and Prejudice,* sold well during her lifetime although she initially had trouble finding a publisher. Austen poked fun at the fickleness of inheritance rights, scrutinized the British class system, and criticized the idleness of women.

Her critics snidely suggest that she wrote and rewrote one book—the story of an impoverished, gentrified family's attempt to find suitable husbands for their daughters. Austen herself never married, and she lived in obscurity with her sisters until her death at age forty-two. **17,921**

169 ALLEN DU MONT (1901–1965)
inventor of the cathode-ray tube, a fancy name for your video screen

Allen who? Considering that his invention anchors so many modern conveniences, it's a wonder his name fails to convey the wizardry of a Whitney or a Westinghouse. Revered and honored by television technicians during his lifetime, Du Mont is virtually unknown today. Yet he made the first commercially viable CRT, a technology that unleashed the possibilities in dozens of other areas. He used the patents of researcher Charles Jenkins to produce the first picture / sound broadcast in 1931. Within six years he was manufacturing commercial television receivers based on the thirty patents he held. The cathode-ray tube dictated the design of personal computers, word processors, oscilloscopes, automatic teller machines, and radar tracking screens. Be it Milton Berle, a Boeing 747 on takeoff, or your thirty-five-dollar bank balance, cathode-ray tubes produce the images. **17,867**

170 GAMAL ABDEL NASSER (1918–1970)
Egyptian leader and pan-Arab idol

As a child, he shouted, "God Almighty, may a calamity overtake the English," every time he saw a plane fly overhead. Yet on the night he deposed King Farouk in 1952, he spoke English to coconspirators because "Arabic is hardly a suitable language in which to express the need for calm." In power until his death, Nasser nationalized the Suez Canal, briefly united Egypt with Syria, oversaw the construction of the Aswan Dam, introduced economic and social reforms, created a police state, fought two losing wars with Israel, and joined with Nehru (222) of India and Tito of Yugoslavia to preach nonalignment with the superpowers. While he never realized his pipe dream of ruling over the world's 420 million Muslims, Nasser inspired hysterical adulation at home. Little wonder: He was the first home-grown ruler of an independent Egypt since the last pharaoh fell. **17,855**

171 JAMES JOYCE (1882–1941)
the Ulysses of modern literature

His *Ulysses,* an account, modeled on Homer's epic, of one day in the lives of a Dublin salesman, his wife, and a teacher, is the most influential novel of the twentieth century. In it the Irish writer displays amazing wordplay, powerful imagery, and thematic force, and develops his innovative stream-of-consciousness "interior monologue." Flip through *Ulysses* and read gems like: "He kissed the plump mellow yellow smellow melons of her rump, on each plump melonous hemisphere, in the mellow yellow furrow, with obscure prolonged provocative melon-smellious osculation." Sounds sorta pornographic to us, but an American judge lifted a ban on it in 1933, saying "the words criticized as dirty are old Saxon words, known to almost all men." Joyce warmed up to his style in *Portrait of the Artist as a Young Man* and took it to its impenetrable extreme in *Finnegans Wake.* George Bernard Shaw praised *Ulysses* but declined a request to purchase it, saying, "If you imagine any Irishman would pay 150 francs for a book, you know little my countrymen." **17,809**

172 PETER ABELARD (1079–1142)
brilliant bad boy of medieval philosophers

Abelard brought logic and skepticism to the forefront of scholasticism, the philosophy developed by medieval thinkers relying on Aristotle's teachings, early Christian writings, and church dogma. Abelard was a celebrated philosophy teacher in Paris and founder of that city's university when he seduced a young student, Héloise. The couple secretly married but her uncle had Abelard castrated by thugs. In shame, he joined the priesthood and pressured Héloise to become a nun. (Their love story has inspired poets ever since.) As a French Benedictine, the ever-critical Abelard argued that "the master-key to knowledge is to keep asking questions," and he applied it to matters of faith. Church leaders twice condemned him as a heretic, yet no matter whom he angered—and the monks in one abbey tried to kill him—his greatest punishment was house arrest. **17,803**

173 MEHMED II THE CONQUEROR
(1432–1481) *founder of the Ottoman Empire*

With his capture of Constantinople in 1453, the mythical turning point between the medieval and modern ages, Mehmed II destroyed the last remnants of the Roman Empire and broke Christianity's tenuous hold on southeastern Europe. The son of Sultan Murad II and a Christian slave girl, Mehmed could be cold-blooded— he ordered a high-ranking official and his two teenage sons decapitated and the heads delivered to his banquet table after the minister refused to deliver one of the boys to him for sexual pleasure—but those were cruel times. He began his reign by talking peace, but as historian Edward Gibbon (654) said, "war was in his heart." After he conquered Constantinople (and turned the great church of Hagia Sophia into a mosque), Christendom quailed in fear of a Muslim onslaught. It never came; his subsequent military campaigns were mostly failures. **17,764**

174 JOSEPH-MARIE JACQUARD (1752–1834)
machinist who loomed large in the Industrial Revolution

Four thousand years after the loom was invented in Egypt, weaving cloth in patterns was still a job for busy hands. Lots of them. Inventors tried to make a machine to do the job faster, and in 1728 Jacques Vaucanson built a mechanical loom. Unfortunately it was an unwieldy monstrosity. Then came Jacquard, a weaver-turned-tinker. In 1804 he found Vaucanson's loom in a museum and added a system of movable perforated cards to regulate the cloth patterns. Voilà! Jacquard's solo-operator looms in factories replaced hundreds of home-based weavers, making it an engine for the social changes accompanying the Industrial Revolution. Displaced Lyonnais silk workers threw Jacquard's machines into the Rhône River, but not fast enough. By 1812 there were eleven thousand of the looms in France alone, and Jacquard was rich. **17,745**

175 JEAN-BAPTISTE POQUELIN MOLIÈRE
(1622–1673) *comic genius*

Poquelin was supposed to become an upholsterer like his father. Or a lawyer, as his uncle wished. Instead he chose the scandalous life of the stage, took the name Molière, and wrote, produced, and acted in scores of his own farces and comedies that eventually earned him acclaim as the greatest of all French playwrights. He created a style of comedy that juxtaposed the normal against the abnormal. A master of style and language, his shtick was quirky human nature. In *Tartuffe* Molière ridicules the religious hypocrite; in *The Imaginary Invalid,* a hypochondriac who fears death and doctors; and in his greatest comedy, *The Misanthrope,* the antisocial man. A critic once accused Molière of borrowing plots and incidents from ancient and modern plays. "I claim my property wherever I happen to find it," Molière shot back. Ah, but whatever flowed from his pen became entirely his. **17,688**

176 CARAVAGGIO (1573–1610)
painter who followed no school but his heart

Classical and religious themes. Dark backgrounds. Illumination directly on subjects. Skin so lifelike, a seventeenth-century critic mused that the color must have been made from ground flesh. These are elements of the paintings of Michelangelo Merisi da Caravaggio, a naturalist so unbound to his predecessors, he makes us think of the canvases Édouard Manet (301) painted 250 years later. Rembrandt (46) borrowed his techniques. Caravaggio did not emulate the saints he depicted. He scandalized Rome by using a drowned prostitute fished from the Tiber as the model for *Death of the Virgin*. He fled from the city for killing a man over a tennis wager, found favor in Malta, but had to run again when a vengeful enemy hired thugs to settle a score with the painter. They finally caught Caravaggio in Naples and disfigured his face with knives. **17,675**

177 HENRY IV (1050–1106)
loser

Henry was the Holy Roman emperor whose effort to gain ascendancy over his traditional coequal in church affairs ended in spectacular failure. The idea of church–government separation didn't exist in the Middle Ages. Popes controlled territory in Italy, and sovereigns of the Holy Roman Empire —much of what is now Germany and Italy— shared religious power. When Henry asserted his rights in Italy, Pope Gregory VII (378) fought back, and Henry was forced to humble himself before the pope in the snow in the Italian town of Canossa in 1077. Henry's kowtowing didn't last

long; soon the pope and emperor warred again, until Henry was deposed by his own son. Henry's defeat provided the impetus for the papacy's control over the Catholic Church's destiny. **17,673**

178 ROBERT GODDARD (1882–1945)
the original rocket scientist

On October 19, 1899, Goddard climbed into a cherry tree and, influenced by the science fiction novels he voraciously consumed, dreamed about building a device that could travel to Mars. He dubbed the date his "anniversary" and fondly visited the tree whenever he was back home in Worcester, Massachusetts. Although he had previously struggled in math and science, his new-found inspiration propelled him to success. He began experimenting with rocketry during graduate school and, by 1914, developed a rocket fueled by solids. When World War I intervened, Goddard worked on weaponry for the U.S. Army. Although the war ended before his bazookalike weapon was put to use, it saw action during World War II. While his liquid-fuel rocket reached a height of only nine thousand feet, Goddard's work was the launching pad for future space exploration. **17,665**

179 PRINCE METTERNICH (1773–1859)
the balance-of-power dude

As Austria's foreign minister and the paramount force at the Congress of Vienna in 1814–15, he was the architect of the post-Napoleonic order in Europe that strove to prevent the dominance of any single nation. Metternich scorned democracy as a "decomposing principle" and warned a visiting Harvard professor that America "cannot end in a quiet, ripe old age." Love or hate his reactionary heart, you have to give Metternich credit for bringing stability to a war-ravaged continent. The nineteenth century was the pinnacle of

European civilization, and one-third of it—1815 to 1848—is known as the Age of Metternich. So famed for intrigue was this disciple of Machiavelli (40) that when he died, a diplomat asked, "I wonder what he meant by that." Henry Kissinger, who received a collection of Metternich's writings as a gift from French politician Valéry Giscard d'Estaing, was a pale imitation of the master, a Metternich *manqué.* **17,654**

180 EDMUND BURKE (1729–1797)
inspiration to political conservatives the world over

His *Reflections on the French Revolution* is to Barry Goldwater's *Conscience of a Conservative* what a Tolstoy (34) novel is to an Archie comic book. Burke argued that political virtue derives from tradition and moral authority, and he opposed democracy as mob rule. Perhaps surprisingly, he sympathized with the American Revolution as justified by British intransigence (though he lamented America's "savage men"). Burke also fought to ease British rule in Ireland and India. He denounced the French Revolution for its murderousness, and his loathing of all utopian contrivances looks smart today, anticipating the social-engineering horrors of fascism and Communism. "The only thing necessary for the triumph of evil is for good men to do nothing," he said. Burke dabbled in aesthetics, writing a tome in which he commented on everything from cloudy skies to the symptoms of love, including "breath drawn slowly, with now and then a low sigh." **17,528**

181 KEMAL ATATÜRK (1881–1938)
toppler of the tottering Ottoman Empire

Young Mustafa Pasa took the Arabic name Kemal, meaning "perfection," for excellent work in math. Military and political prowess were his real strengths, however. Like other young officers, he wanted Turkey freed from the Ottoman yoke. So Kemal resigned from the service, built civilian and military support, and in 1923 founded the nation and was named its first president. These developments prompted the last Ottoman sultan to flee the country. Kemal led the new republic with an iron hand, thrusting the nation once known as "the sick man of Europe" into modern times. He closed Islamic religious institutions, threw out the Arabic alphabet in favor of the Latin one, modernized legal and educational systems, and encouraged Western dress. He also pushed adoption of surnames. Of course, the one he reserved for himself was Atatürk, meaning, "father of the Turks." **17,514**

182 SAMUEL JOHNSON (1709–1784)
English man of letters

His conversation, immortalized in Boswell's biography, prompted the actor David Garrick to comment: "He shakes laughter out of you." His aphorisms ("Second marriages are the triumph of hope over experience") and putdowns ("Nobody ever wished it longer," he said of Milton's (53) *Paradise Lost*) are legendary. His works include his landmark *Dictionary of the English Language* and the ten-volume *Lives of the Poets.* Though he was a Tory royalist and was hanged in effigy by the American revolutionaries, his rise from bookseller's son to literary lion fits the American ideal of the self-made man. And his political stands resonate today, including his denunciations of capital punishment and Europe's rapine of native populations. "How is it," he asked, rebuking the colonists, "that we hear the loudest yelps for liberty among the drivers of Negroes?" **17,480**

183 IGOR STRAVINSKY (1882–1971)
the Picasso of classical music

Granted, Debussy (274) rejected music's rules of harmony, but Stravinsky rejected all the rules.

Gone were pretty melodies and conventional orchestrations; Stravinsky favored harsh, unruly, clashing noises. The son of a Russian opera singer but hardly a prodigy himself, Stravinsky abandoned law studies after endearing himself to composer Nikolay Rimsky-Korsakov. Stravinsky ranks as the most important classical composer of the twentieth century for his sounds that were "fierce, like a toothache," interspersed with "agreeable harmony, like cocaine." About his discordant *Le Sacre du Printemps (The Rite of Spring),* one horrified critic asserted the ballet was better called the "Massacre" of spring. When it premiered in Paris in 1913, the dancers couldn't hear the music over the audience's boos and catcalls. Hard on the ear yet haunting in its own way, *The Rite of Spring* abandoned musical conformity and became the standard by which modern classical music is measured.   **17,472**

184 GEORGE ELIOT (1819–1880)
probing novelist

Eliot was the pen name of Marian Evans, a plain provincial woman who evolved from Evangelical Christian to free-thinking essayist. Evans surprised friends by taking up with married journalist George Henry Lewes. Fulfilled in her personal life, she blossomed as a novelist, becoming a major literary voice in the nineteenth century. She wrote the acclaimed *Adam Bede,* the autobiographical *The Mill on the Floss,* and her masterpiece, *Middlemarch.* While her contemporaries were writing romantic tales, Eliot's probing analysis of her characters' psychology presaged twentieth-century fiction. Evans used a pseudonym for fear that critics would pan her books if they knew her living arrangements. That changed when a crackpot clergyman claimed he was really George Eliot. Evans's pride couldn't bear it, and she finally owned up. Though her

literary career flourished, Victorian society shunned her. She lived with Lewes for twenty-four years until his death in 1878.   **17,403**

185 DAVID HUME (1711–1776)
radical skeptic

When Samuel Johnson (182) was told that the dour Scottish philosopher Hume had denied the existence of God, Johnson exploded, "He lies, sir." Hume held that truth is unattainable; the mind is but a collection of sensations, and there is no such thing as cause, only the mental impression of a conjunction of events. If he were alive today, Hume would declare the mind to be a sophisticated computer. Many believe he was the most brilliant philosopher to write in English. His extreme skepticism reinvigorated scientific inquiry, even calling into question Newtonian physics, and his thought was a major influence on such figures as Immanuel Kant (49) and Auguste Comte (130). Passion was not unknown to him: He fell in love with a French countess and feuded with Jean-Jacques Rousseau (19). His fondness for food prompted a contemporary wit to write: "David Hume ate a swinging great dinner / And grew every day fatter and fatter; / And yet the huge bulk of a sinner / Said there was neither spirit or matter."   **17,401**

186 ALBRECHT DÜRER (1471–1528)
foremost German Renaissance artist

Dürer basked in the glow of Renaissance masters in Italy, then brought this influence home to Northern Europe. By 1515, his astonishing technique and inventiveness—he combined rational use of perspective and proportion with highly realistic detail—earned him international fame. Dürer created masterful altarpieces and religious works, superb nature studies, portraits, self-portraits, and copper engravings. Critics hail his prints, especially the woodcut *Four Horsemen of the Apocalypse,* depicting Pestilence, War, Famine, and Death. His graphics influenced Van Dyck (870), Rubens (281), Rembrandt (46), and El Greco (283). Dürer adored Italy and its artists. In 1506 he wrote from Venice: "Oh how cold I will be away from the sun; here I am a gentleman and at home a parasite." Always pious, Dürer met Martin Luther (3) in 1517 and became a devoted follower. Nonetheless, Catholic leaders so esteemed the work he'd done for their churches that prelates joined Protestants in mourning his death. **17,334**

187 RAMANUJA (1017–1137)
Hindu theologian

After he had a vision of the god Vishnu, he worshiped the deity daily and preached the doctrine of love for God until his death at age 120. Ramanuja thus transformed one of the world's great religions from a set of rituals aimed at liberating practitioners from the cycle of death and rebirth into a devotional faith. By holding out the promise of salvation through God's grace, he reinvigorated Hinduism. Today, four thousand years after its beginnings in the Aryan tribes that would one day conquer India, it flourishes. **17,295**

188 MARK TWAIN (1835–1910)
turning point in American fiction

We applaud Twain's body of work, from *The Adventures of Tom Sawyer* to *A Connecticut Yankee in King Arthur's Court.* But we second Ernest Hemingway (388), who said all modern American literature comes from one book. He meant *The Adventures of Huckleberry Finn,* the story of a teenager fleeing his abusive father by rafting down the Mississippi River with a runaway slave. Beyond its hijinks and humor, the 1884 novel plumbs the American psyche and its frenetic drive for new frontiers after "civilizing" old ones. Too bad some modern readers interpret it as racist. In his fiction Twain used American themes, settings, and southern vernacular to help create an authentically American literature divorced from British and European culture. "Mark twain!" the cry of Mississippi boatmen sounding shallow water, was the pseudonym of steamboat-pilot-turned-writer Samuel Langhorne Clemens. **17,292**

189 K'ANG-HSI (1654–1722)
magnanimous Chinese emperor

He was as important to China as his contemporaries who molded their European nations into dominating powers: Louis XIV of France (63), Peter the Great of Russia (27), and William III of England. K'ang-hsi established the territorial contours of modern China by conquering Taiwan and Mongolia, making Tibet a vassal state, and neutralizing Russian power on his borders. He was a conscientious monarch who cut taxes, built public works, and patronized the greatest of Chinese artists. Every child, including K'ang-hsi's own twenty-eight, learned thrift, humility, and lawfulness from his Sixteen Sacred Injunctions, a distillation of Confucian wisdom that guided daily conduct. They ranged from the spiritual injunction number three—"observe filial piety and brotherly love"—to the simple and practical number fourteen: "pay your taxes to ward off being dunned." **17,242**

190 ALEXANDER HAMILTON (1755–1804)
American statesman and monetary mandarin

Okay, Hamilton was an opportunist with monarchist leanings who quarreled with everybody—Washington (22), Jefferson (64), John Adams (214), James Madison (268), Aaron Burr—and wrote a friend that "the whole world is a mass of fools and knaves." Even so, we rate him coequal to Jefferson in his influence on the early Republic. America's first and greatest treasury secretary, he secured the nation's financial credibility by insisting the Revolutionary War debt be paid off, and he championed a strong central government that endures today. What a waste that at seven A.M. on July 11, 1804, a bullet fired in a duel by the traitorous Aaron Burr tore into Hamilton's abdomen at six hundred miles an hour, splintered his spine, and extinguished the life of this West Indies–born Anglophile bastard son of a French Huguenot tart and her Scottish lover, this pamphleteer with a weakness for pseudonyms like Pacificus, this adulterer forced to confess his "indelicate amour" for a blackmailer's wife, this brilliant Founding Father. **17,120**

191 ELIZABETH OF HUNGARY (1207–1231)
model of Christian charity

Absolute evil has more lasting influence than absolute good, and that's why despots like Hitler (20) and Genghis Khan (43) outrank Elizabeth on our list. Yet Saint Elizabeth's role of do-gooder, coupled with her position as queen of Hungary, made her a saintly model for generations. Married at age thirteen to Louis of Thuringia, Elizabeth endured the constant criticism of a mother-in-law who mocked her charitable nature. While pompous popes, corrupt confessors, and impious priests were giving Catholicism a bad name, Elizabeth demonstrated Christian charity. She established the world's first orphanage and built a hospital for lepers. She visited the sick and fed the poor. Then, under the influence of a mystic Franciscan who served as her confessor, she endured brutal beatings for piety's sake and spent the last of her twenty-four years deep in prayer and ministering to the poor. **17,106**

192 ANTON CHEKHOV (1860–1904)
literary luminary

A medical student in Moscow, Chekhov was also family breadwinner, making money by churning out short comic sketches for magazines. "Don't envy me," he wrote his brother Alexander. "Writing brings me nothing but twitches." But writing short stories and plays soon became his life's work. Chekhov always put plot second to mood and characterization. His serious autobiographical story, "The Steppe," was hailed as a masterpiece. His most acclaimed plays—*Uncle Vanya, The Three Sisters,* and the perennially performed *The Cherry Orchard*—use ordinary dialogue to probe the human heart. A kind, unpretentious man, Chekhov inspired "a desire to be simpler, more truthful, more oneself," said writer-friend Maxim Gorky. But some countrymen felt Chekhov's works fell short because he delivered no strong political or social message. Even the great Tolstoy (34) sometimes missed the point. "Where do your characters take you?" he once asked Chekhov. "From the sofa to the junk room and back!" **16,976**

193 YOSHIDA SHOIN (1830–1859)
guru of revolutionary Japan

He was obsessed with the notion that Japan would be subjugated by the West unless it overthrew traditions. When American admiral Matthew Perry steamed into Tokyo Bay and frightened Japan out of its isolation, Shoin stowed away in order to record the secrets of the West. He was caught before the ship sailed. Then he opened a school that taught young nationalists the need for a modern army, industry, central government, and an aggressive foreign policy. They absorbed his zeal and later dominated the governments that put Japan on a modern course. He was executed for plotting to kill a leader of the old regime. Novelist and Asia hand Robert Louis Stevenson (756) wrote of Shoin in 1880: "He failed in each particular enterprise that he attempted; and yet we have only to look at his country to see how complete has been his general success." **16,937**

194 JAMES COOK (1728–1779)
explorer who made the South Pacific British

Captain Cook's secret weapon was sauerkraut. Rich in vitamin C, it kept his crews healthy while other captains wondered why scurvy was killing their men. Cook needed able men. On three of the longest exploratory cruises in history, he charted the South Pacific, claimed Australia and New Zealand for Britain, brought back exotic flora, and ended speculation that there were habitable continents south of Africa. Cook, an eighteen-year-old farmer with no connections when he went to sea, advanced on merit. He could be stern, but his men admired him, never more than when he let them make love, not war, among the women of Tahiti. Not all the natives were friendly. A mob of Hawaiians stabbed Cook to death when he tried to arrest their king for being lenient with natives who stole a boat. **16,912**

195 BENITO JUÁREZ (1806–1872)
Mexican liberator

Juárez barely cleared five feet and had the dark strong features of his Zapotec Indian heritage. He battled prejudice from fellow Mexicans, who dubbed him "the little Indian." But Juárez was fortified with an iron will that helped him rise from poverty and illiteracy to become a law school graduate. He was a born executive who won national prestige as governor of his home state of Oaxaca, then justice minister, and finally president of Mexico. He helped overthrow the dictator, General Santa Anna, championed a democratic federal republic, and resisted Napoleon III's military drive to establish a Mexican empire. Santa Anna never could figure Juárez out. The two met in 1829 when Juárez was a barefoot peasant waiting on the general's table. "It is amazing that an Indian of such low degree should have become the figure in Mexico that we all know," Santa Anna mused. **16,872**

196 CLAUDE MONET (1840–1926)
leader of the impressionist school

Monet's finest achievement: his huge painted panels of lilies floating in his water garden at Giverny, France. One set hangs in the Museum of Modern Art in New York City, another in Paris. We second the dealer overwhelmed by these works, who found the water and sky had "neither beginning nor end. It is mysterious, poetic, delightfully unreal." The panels were typical of Monet, who made a habit of painting numerous studies of the same motif, be it haystacks or Rouen Cathedral, to capture changes in light and atmosphere as time passed. The very name *impressionism* comes from a critic's denigration of his *Impression: Sunrise, 1872.* Monet produced about three thousand works, mostly seascapes, landscapes, and river scenes. Artist Eugène Boudin introduced the eighteen-year-old Monet to the then-uncommon approach of painting outdoors; it changed Monet's life. "Suddenly," he said, "a veil was torn away. I had understood—I had realized what painting could be." **16,861**

197 DANIEL DEFOE (1660–1731)
cornerstone of the English novel

Defoe's two splendid novels, *Robinson Crusoe* and *Moll Flanders,* broke new ground by exploring human nature in matter-of-fact, vividly detailed narratives. But these books came late in his life. He'd given up as a tradesman after risky moves mired him in debt. A Protestant Dissenter, Defoe had written persuasive political pamphlets and even fought on the losing side against Catholic king James II. After he was pilloried by the Tories on charges of treason—for writing an ironic political pamphlet—Defoe switched to survival mode. Didn't matter which party was in power, Tory or Whig, he was their man as pamphleteer and intelligence agent. Biographers say he died while hiding from creditors hounding him for a twenty-five-year-old debt. **16,849**

198 DOMINIC (1170–1221)
the Catholic Church's teacher

Before Saint Dominic, the only good heretic was a dead one. Dominic didn't end that belief (after all, the Inquisition was just getting off the ground), but he created an approach that differed radically from the blood-and-guts way of doing business. Dominic, the first of the Catholic Church's great preachers, believed in his power to convert heretics back to orthodoxy—without drawing blood. His Order of Preachers prepared friars who traveled about Europe converting unbelievers. He established chapters near universities, and soon his order was linked to learning. In a radical departure from the monastic tradition of small autonomous monasteries, he established himself as head of his order throughout Europe. Today the Dominicans are one of only four large international orders of monks, and they continue the tradition of education and preaching. **16,842**

199 HIERONYMUS BOSCH (1450–1516)
far-out painter

Almost nothing is known of him except his forty surviving artworks, but what a tale they tell.

Think of him as a Dutch Franz Kafka (233) with a paintbrush. His imagination runs riot, concocting freak animal-human-tree hybrids and demons with rats' faces and birds' claws, snatching at fallen souls. His visions are no dilettante's panorama of the absurd, however, but a mystic's revelation of sin's perils. His depictions of man's ensnarement in evil are glued together by symbolism—an owl for heresy, bagpipes for lust, a wizard for Satan's deception. It was perhaps inevitable that twentieth-century pundits would declare his dreamlike landscapes the harbinger of surrealism, with its Freudian twists and Salvador Dali (735) turns. But other modern critics reckon him too weird to make that claim. Though he influenced others, notably Bruegel the Elder (256), says art historian Horace Shipp, "In truth he stands alone, outside all schools." **16,821**

200 NICOLAS APPERT (c.1750–1841)
inventor of canned food

Before Appert, the French army was underfed. Meat and vegetables spoiled before Napoleon's (16) soldiers could eat them. The French government offered a prize for a practical way to preserve provisions. Thus began this former candy-maker's fourteen-year flirtation with preservation. He won the 12,000-franc prize in 1810 with his method of preserving food in glass bottles that had been sealed and heated in boiling water. Eventually Appert changed his containers to steel cylinders plated with tin. Just why do we rank Appert and his "canning" invention so high? Well, his methods triggered a nineteenth-century revolution in the kitchen that eased women's burdens and changed the eating habits of people around the world. Of course, gourmets among us would argue that canned peas are inedible, but armies have marched and triumphed on them. **16,809**

The next group includes our highest ranking sports figure: a man who won no championships, broke no records, and never signed a sneaker contract.

Eat your hearts out Babe, Jackie, Michael, and Muhammad Ali. Number 293, James Naismith, beats you all because he knew how to exercise his brain. In 1891, at a YMCA in Springfield, Massachusetts, he invented basketball, the only sport that is both new and universal.

Two Neanderthals competing to skewer a speedy roebuck for dinner invented track and field. The ancients played primitive forms of polo, golf, tennis, football, and soccer. Baseball is relatively new, but it has star status only in Japan and the Americas, and its appeal has slipped among modern fans, who crave continuous action. Fast-paced basketball is popular from Brooklyn to Beverly Hills, from Tblisi to Timbuktu.

In our rating system, mere athletes were unable to match Naismith's point totals for singularity and lasting influence. What is singular about Bret Favre, whose success depends on two thousand pounds of lineman? Athleticism has no lasting influence. A race won, a home run, even a knockout punch, exists for only a moment.

To make the top one thousand, a sports figure had to be more than a player. Muhammad Ali and Jackie Robinson championed social change. Babe Didrickson Zaharias inspired women. Henry Wingfield, Henry Rous, Pierre Coubertin, and Alexander Cartwright wrote rules and organized events. John Sullivan, Babe Ruth, Jim Thorpe, Pele, and Michael Jordan helped create the global mass sports culture that emerged in the twentieth century.

The only athlete we included solely for his physical prowess was Roger Bannister, who in 1954 ran the first sub-four-minute mile.

201 JOHN MAYNARD KEYNES (1883–1946)
key economist of the twentieth century

The British scholar's seminal work, *The General Theory of Employment, Interest and Money*, overturned the prevailing laissez-faire view and argued that governments should increase spending in recessions to mitigate the dislocations of the business cycle. In a surprisingly short time his ideas triumphed in both academia and the policy-making councils of the West. A devoted capitalist—some say he saved capitalism—Keynes dismissed Marxism as "dreary, out-of-date controversializing." The Cambridge don also had an obsession with people's hands and became so entranced with President Franklin D. Roosevelt's (37) "shortish round nails" in a 1934 meeting with him that he lost his train of thought. A homosexual, Keynes nonetheless married the ballerina Lydia Lopokova, to the disapproval of his Bloomsbury literary-circle friends like Lytton Strachey, who called her a "half-witted canary." **16,789**

202 TYCHO BRAHE (1546–1601)
stargazer extraordinaire

Brahe's great gift to astronomy was his highly accurate data based on naked-eye observations. It gave his student, Johannes Kepler (33), a firm foundation for his theories on how planets revolve around the sun. When Brahe was thirteen, he witnessed a total eclipse of the sun, and it opened his eyes to astronomy. The young Dane learned to estimate distances between stars using compasses and cross-staffs. In 1563 he observed Jupiter and Saturn overlap. Copernicus (18) had predicted it would happen but got the date wrong. Brahe decided to dedicate his life to the accurate recording of heavenly sightings. His reputation blossomed in 1572 with the discovery of a supernova in the constellation Cassiopeia. The news helped shatter Renaissance security in a fixed and certain universe. **16,751**

203 LEO IX (1002–1054)
the rulemaker for priests

The Alsatian priest Bruno became Pope Leo IX because he had pull. His cousin Henry III was ruler of the Holy Roman Empire, and when emperors spoke, electors listened. It was a corrupt start to a saintly papacy. Leo dedicated his reign to rooting out deviltry in the church, and in 1049 he codified rules for priestly behavior. Churchmen could no longer marry, buy their holy offices, charge their flocks for sacraments, or go to war. Simply put, holy people were required to act—well, holy. After Leo the rules were often ignored, but they remained as beacons whenever the church chose the road to reform. Leo shouldn't have broken his own rule against fighting. In 1053 he tried to stop Normans from ravaging southern Italy, but his army was mauled at the battle of Civitate, and Leo remained a captive most of his remaining days. **16,702**

204 W.E.B. DU BOIS (1868–1963)
mover and shaker

A Harvard-educated sociologist, Du Bois became convinced that protest was the only way black Americans could change a racist system. In writings, speeches, and his newspaper, *The Crisis*, he clashed with conservative Booker T. Washington (458), who preached the status quo while urging black people to seek economic gains. Du Bois founded the Niagara Movement in 1905, a precursor to the National Association for the Advancement of Colored People in 1909. Though he embraced Marxism and frequently visited the Soviet Union, he ranks toward the top of the confrontational strain of black protest of racial injustice in America. In 1951 Du Bois was indicted as an unregistered agent for a foreign power. He joined the Communist Party in 1961, moved to Ghana, and renounced his U.S. citizenship. His autobiography, penned in Ghana, declares: "I do not apologize for living long. High on the ramparts of this blistering hell of life, as it must appear to most men, I sit and see the Truth." **16,681**

205 JAMES CLERK MAXWELL (1831–1879)
physicist with an electrifying message

In our age of corporate downsizing, we find it comforting to note that this Scottish genius who originated the theory of electromagnetic radiation, developed the field equations that set the stage for Einstein's (17) special theory of relativity, and nourished ideas that blossomed into quantum physics got laid off early in his teaching career. He got the ax in a merger of two colleges and had to hustle to find a job. "Before Maxwell, physical reality was thought of as consisting in material particles," Einstein wrote. "Since Maxwell, it has been thought of as represented by continuous fields. This change in the conception of reality is the most profound and the most fruitful that physics has experienced since the time of Newton." Maxwell died at age forty-eight of abdominal cancer, the disease that claimed his mother at the same age. He was buried without fanfare in a village churchyard. **16,671**

206 EMMELINE PANKHURST (1858–1928)
British radical suffragette

While the word *suffragette* was a snide pejorative in America, it was a badge of honor that British activists like Pankhurst wore proudly. And theirs was not a battle for the weak of heart. When Parliament failed to respond to polite entreaties for suffrage, Pankhurst got nasty. She had met with a quick and early success in 1894, when British women secured the vote in local elections. But when it came to voting on the big boys in Parliament, the legislators would not budge. Pankhurst and her comrades heckled public speakers; their suffrage meetings triggered rioting. They clashed repeatedly with the bobbies and were jailed. In prison their publicized hunger strikes created a public relations nightmare for the government. Aided by her daughters, Pankhurst lobbied strenuously for only about a decade until World War I began, whereupon she devoted her energy to the British effort. She died just a few weeks after British women won full voting rights in 1928. **16,532**

207 MARCEL PROUST (1871–1922)
literature's time traveler

Proust's literary triumph, *Remembrance of Things Past,* is one of the greatest achievements in world literature. Funny, since it was triggered by a snack. The French author dipped a cake into his tea, and the taste of it transported him to childhood teas at Aunt Leonie's and blissful family walks on sunny paths in his native Normandy. Proust's work is an archaeological dig in one man's mind to uncover meaning in his life. He employs what psychologists call mnemonic combination: the association of colors, music, and names with scenes and sensations of the past. The astounding seven-volume novel— presented entirely as an interior monologue—is the longest ever written. Proust never finished revising the last few volumes before he died. It takes perseverance to stay with the long and convoluted sentences. Ezra Pound (367) thought criticism of Proust's writings deserved to be written in one paragraph, seven pages long, and punctuated only by semicolons. **16,521**

208 NIELS BOHR (1885–1962)
giant of the subatomic world

He applied quantum theory to atomic structure, postulating that the atom could emit radiation only in "quantum jumps." Confused? Well, Bohr said anybody who didn't think quantum theory was crazy hadn't been listening. Einstein (17) called his work "the highest form of musicality in the sphere of thought." His research into atomic spectra and X-rays is an invaluable contribution to science. In essence, he discovered that electrons move around the nucleus, and he described how atoms emit and absorb energy. Asked what direction physics would take, Bohr quoted Goethe's (131) *Faust:* "What is the path? There is no path. On, into the unknown." Born of a Jewish mother, Bohr fled Denmark on a fishing boat to escape the Nazis, and he later joined the project to build the atomic bomb.   **16,507**

209 JANE ADDAMS (1860–1935)
builder of the settlement house movement in America

At the height of her popularity in 1910, reformer Addams was called "the only saint America has produced." The Mother Teresa (772) of her generation, Addams finished second behind Thomas Edison (28) in a newspaper reader survey to name the most useful Americans. Addams rebelled against the idleness imposed on middle-class women. While others shrugged off this ennui with a sip of sherry and another stitch on their petit point samplers, Addams believed it morally wrong to do nothing when so many people needed so much. She created a settlement house of women like herself who gave assistance to immigrant Chicago. Hull House was the original community house, providing shelter, education, activities, and a sense of belonging to impoverished women and children. Addams's pacifism during

World War I tarnished her reputation among contemporaries, but she was vindicated with the award of the Nobel Peace Prize in 1931.   **16,502**

210 ALDUS MANUTIUS (c.1450–1515)
publisher to the Renaissance

𝕭ut for 𝕴talian humanist 𝕬ldus 𝕸anutius, this whole book might look like this sentence.
A missionary for the wondrous learning of the ancients and a crafty businessman, Aldus made classical texts shorter than before by using Roman letters that were slimmer than Gutenberg's Gothic letters. *The most compact form was italic, a slanted typeface invented by Aldus's craftsmen in 1501.* After Aldus, most books were no longer printed imitations of manuscripts. His books were also cheaper because he printed them in editions of a thousand—five times as many as other publishers. The result was a wide dissemination of classical learning to an increasingly literate Europe. We marvel at the list of writers whose works Aldus was the first to publish in book form. Among the Greeks alone were Sophocles, Herodotus, Xenophon, Plato, and Demosthenes.   **16,482**

211 ROBERT KOCH (1843–1910)
pioneering bacteriologist

Before Koch, doctors couldn't even begin to cure certain diseases because no one knew what the germs looked like. Koch identified the bacteria that cause anthrax, tuberculosis, and cholera and started science on the road to keeping those diseases in check. We salute his accidental discovery of a way to obtain pure specimens of the deadly bugs. In the liquid gelatin cultures used up to Koch's time, bacteria would jumble together like marbles in a sock. When a discarded potato slice that was laden with germs blossomed into multicolored bacteria, Koch realized that solids were better than liquids. From then on, cultures were grown on hardened gelatin. Koch became so famous, his 1890 report on a test for tuberculosis was misconstrued as the announcement of a cure. The world was disappointed, but it was a step toward the eventual defeat of the disease.   **16,473**

212 THEODOR HERZL (1860–1904)
propagandist for a Jewish state

Herzl gave meaning and hope to the Passover incantation "Next year in Jerusalem." He grew up surrounded by rampant anti-Semitism in Austria and, when he moved to Paris to escape it, was horrified to discover the same climate of hate. Although he had advocated assimilation, journalist Herzl became convinced—after reporting on the persecution of French Jewish soldier Alfred Dreyfus—that the Jews needed their own state. Herzl ignored friends who thought him crazy and published his pamphlet *The Jewish State* in 1896. As he explained, "We want to lay the foundation stone for the house which will become the refuge of the Jewish nation." His campaign to recreate the Jewish homeland of Israel in Palestine was called Zionism. Although he died of a heart ailment more than forty years before the State of Israel became reality, Herzl's remains were moved there in 1949 to a hill overlooking the town of Mount Herzl.   **16,465**

213 THOMAS STARZL (b. 1926)
transplant pioneer

As a medical instructor at Northwestern University, Starzl decided to buck conventional medicine and devote his life's work to transplanting organs. In 1963 he performed the first liver transplant on a three-year-old boy who bled to death on the operating table. After other tragic failures and widespread criticism, Starzl immersed himself in research and spent twenty years perfecting

surgical techniques. That, together with the wonder drug cyclosporine, which suppresses the body's urge to reject foreign organs, made transplants routine. Even heart transplants, pioneered in 1967 by South African surgeon Christiaan Barnard, are performed successfully today. Recently Starzl has championed the use of the antirejection drug FK-506 as more effective than cyclosporine. Described as "volatile" by coworkers, Starzl nevertheless won admiration for his devotion to transplant patients and their cause. His interest reaches into history. "How much more complete the world might have been," he mused, "if Mozart had been treated with renal transplantation instead of dying at the age of thirty-five."   **16,442**

214 JOHN ADAMS (1735–1826)
American revolutionary

Adams was the supernova of America's most illustrious family, whose other lights included son John Quincy, the sixth president; second cousin Samuel (263), revolutionary firebrand; and grandsons Charles Francis, Brooks, and Henry, scholars. Jefferson (64) wrote the Declaration of Independence, but Adams was its fiercest proponent in the Continental Congress. As America's second president, he considered his resistance to the clamor for war with France—a decision that saved countless lives and perhaps the Union itself—"the most splendid diamond in my crown." In the national consciousness Adams has gained nowhere near the stature of Founding Fathers Washington (22), the national deity; Jefferson, the national genius; or Franklin (54), the national Renaissance man. Perhaps this is because he was, in fact, short, as well as pudgy (his enemies dubbed him "His Rotundity"), dour, and a little fussy. Yet of the four, Adams alone refused to own slaves.   **16,376**

215 FRIEDRICH NIETZSCHE (1844–1900)
mad poet of modernism

One of the most influential philosophers of all time, venerated by practically every intellectual giant of the twentieth century, Nietzsche pushed the Enlightenment to its ultimate secular conclusion. "God is dead," he said, and humans must seek meaning in religion's ashes. His ideal was the passionately creative man, or "superman." His thinking, notably his doctrines of perspectivism (the relativity of all knowledge) and man's will to power, set the stage for the modernist culture of deconstructionism, nihilism, and alienation. Poor Nietzsche! Raised with his budding-Nazi sister by a domineering mother and two maiden aunts, he was plagued by eye and stomach ailments before descending into syphilis-induced insanity. Hitler (20) adored him, but he was no anti-Semite. Historian Edward O'Brien said Nietzsche longed for the Christian and pagan godheads of Christ, Apollo, Lucifer, and Dionysus to be united in one breast—his own.   **16,359**

216 JOMO KENYATTA (1896?–1978)
African nationalist

When Henry the Navigator (153) proposed in 1434 that Portugal explore unknown worlds, the first boats sailed for the unknown continent to the south. From then on, European imperialists plundered the Dark Continent for gold, ivory, jewels, and ultimately, its people. While the slave trade had been abolished by the time Kenyatta, a member of the Kikuyu tribe, was born, he railed against white-only land laws and British colonization. Hailed as a natural leader, Kenyatta preserved rich African traditions while promoting modernization. His movement climaxed with his imprisonment for seven years during the Mau Mau rebellion against Great Britain. While in prison he was elected president of the rebel government. British colonial rule ended officially in 1964, when he was elected president of Kenya, a position he held until his death.   **16,279**

217 ALFRED NOBEL (1833–1896)
dynamite philanthropist

Nobel's story is *It's a Wonderful Life* with Swedish subtitles. When his brother Ludwig died in 1888, some foreign newspapers erred and reported it as Alfred's demise. They painted him as the inventor of dynamite who had amassed monumental wealth by becoming a merchant of death. Actually, Nobel's vision in developing the explosive, dynamite, from highly volatile nitroglycerin, was to use it for nonmilitary purposes. The rare opportunity to read his own obituary and see how some evaluated his life shattered Nobel. He decided to dedicate a large portion of his fortune to the cause of peace. Thus, according to his will, $8 million in seed money went to launch the Nobel Foundation in Sweden in 1900. Ever since, the foremost scientists, authors, and peacemakers have received the world's most coveted prize.   **16,250**

218 MATSUO BASHO (1644–1694)
high priest of haiku

Japan's most revered poet was a farmer's son who quit a job in a waterworks to devote his life to verse. He transformed the three-line, seventeen-syllable haiku, Japan's most popular poetry form, from the courtly style of his predecessors into a form with no subject-matter boundaries. "The old verse can be about willows," he said. "Haiku requires crows picking snails in a rice paddy." Basho popularized the notion that haiku could be about anything from simple domestic images ("Wrapping the rice cakes, with one hand she fingers back her hair.") to contemplation of death ("Sick on a journey, my dreams wander the withered fields.") Millions of ordinary people around the world who write haiku to express their deepest thoughts owe Basho a huge debt. Paraphrasing one of his famous verses, we say:

On haiku's high bough,
Basho alone is perching
This millennium

16,217

219 GIOTTO (c.1267–1337)
the grandfather of Italian art

Although a contemporary said Giotto was as ugly as an Italian man could be, he possessed an unnerving ability to create beauty. Before his frescoes fueled the Golden Age of Florence, painting had been fading as a flat, lifeless art form. Giotto's ability to create depth was so uncanny that some people believe he invented perspective. Not so. Giotto paid attention to color, form, and the arrangement of his subjects. He placed people in the foreground of his frescoes so that viewers could see them at eye level. He played with light to give the illusion of depth. To top it off, he always told a story. He never had the polish of Michelangelo (13) or Leonardo (9), but he generated such enthusiasm for painting in Florence that his innovations whetted the appetite of Italy for the Renaissance masters who followed. **16,203**

220 EMIL VON BEHRING (1854–1917)
pioneer of serum therapy

Behring worked in a Berlin laboratory in 1890, injecting rabbits with tiny amounts of tetanus toxin produced in bacterial cultures. Weeks later, the German doctor drew serum from the rabbits and injected it into mice that had just received deadly doses of tetanus toxin. The rodents scampered away, healthy as ever. After announcing that breakthrough, Behring published another paper describing the same successful experiment

with diphtheria toxin. He dubbed the toxin-neutralizing agent "antitoxin." But it had yet to prove effective with humans. The crucial test came on Christmas Eve 1891 when a Berlin doctor injected the antitoxin into a child dying of diphtheria. Within hours her fever broke. Thousands more would be saved the same way. For that, Behring and his Japanese colleague, Shibasaburo Kitasato, received the first Nobel Prize for physiology or medicine in 1901. **16,163**

221 HENRY IV (1553–1610)
peacemaker of France's religious wars

Let's hear it for kings like Henry of Navarre, who lack convictions. He led the Protestant army that conquered France and then cast away his faith, like an old cloak, to make himself palatable to the Catholic majority. "Paris is well worth a mass," he supposedly declared. The dynasty that Henry started lasted two hundred years, and he was a hero to later Frenchmen because he was one of them: tolerant, learned, fun-loving, amorous. He raised his legitimate children and bastards as one big happy family; his favorite among his sixty mistresses was Henriette d'Entragues. Henry loved her even when she became a gluttonous fleshy nag like his wife, Marie de Médicis. Henry craved the hunt and fine dining and was suffering from gout when he was stabbed to death in his coach by François Ravaillac, a Catholic fanatic. **16,159**

222 JAWAHARLAL NEHRU (1889–1964)
political heir of Mahatma Gandhi
and first prime minister of India

Educated at Harrow and Cambridge, cradles of British elitism, Nehru helped negotiate India's independence from Britain in 1947 and led the new nation until his death. While he paid lip service to Gandhi's (12) doctrine of nonviolence, he battled Pakistan in Kashmir, seized Goa from Portugal, and fought border skirmishes with the Chinese. And while he preached neutralism in foreign affairs, he was the only nonaligned leader to support the Soviet Union's invasion of Hungary. History will forgive him. Nehru's influence was so enormous that Adlai Stevenson said he "wore a halo." Luckily, the halo didn't enable him to foretell events. His only child, the future Prime Minister Indira Gandhi (791), was assassinated in 1984; her son Sanjay died in a plane crash; and Sanjay's brother Rajiv, the third prime minister of the dynasty, was killed by a bomber in 1991. **16,113**

223 BALTHASAR DE BEAUJOYEULX
(d. c.1587) *creator of the original ballet*

Beaujoyeulx was an Italian violinist who doubled as a servant to French queen Catherine de Médicis (632). He was so good at organizing parties for the royal court that he was placed in charge of the celebration to commemorate the marriage of the duke of Joyeuse and Marguerite of Lorraine in 1581 at the Hôtel de Bourbon in the Louvre. So he put on a show. The result, his *Ballet Comique de la Reine,* is generally regarded as the world's first ballet. It was a five-and-a-half-hour extravaganza of scenes from the legends of the mythological enchantress Circe. The dance, which cost more than 3.5 million francs, featured Roman gods spinning in circles and other dazzling geometric patterns. But because it was the first ballet as we know it, we tip our tutu to this Beautiful/Joyful kind of guy. **16,111**

224 WILHELM II (1859–1941)
militarist German kaiser blamed for World War I

If only he had listened to his mother. She was an English princess who thought Germans were uncul-

tured boors, and she tried to make Wilhelm a liberal Anglophile. But he was a pumped-up Prussian from the tip of his hobnailed boots to the top of his spiked helmet. If Grandma Victoria's (91) England could have colonies and a big navy and boss other countries around, he reasoned, Germany could, too. As kaiser, he dismissed the wily Bismarck, appointed pliant ministers, heated up the arms race, and became the aggressor in World War I. Four years and ten million deaths later, he abdicated. After the war Wilhelm lived in a safe haven provided by the Dutch government; he remained an unrepentant fool to his final days. When Hitler (20) conquered Paris in 1940, the old kaiser sent the new Führer a congratulatory note. **16,106**

225 BARTOLOMEO CRISTOFORI (1665–1731)
grand piano maker

Talk about an idea whose time hadn't come! Travel back to Florence around 1700. See how Italian harpsichord maker Cristofori tinkers with an invention we now call the piano. It's similar to the harpsichord, but instead of plucking strings, it produces loud and soft tones by using leather-covered hammers. The secret ingredient is escapement, a nifty mechanism that controls how the hammers strike strings and then rebound. But the world isn't ready for it. People swear by their harpsichords and clavichords. Even Voltaire (36), comparing the popular harpsichord to the piano in 1774, calls the latter "a boiler-maker's instrument." Years after Cristofori's death, however, something clicks and composers begin writing music for the piano. It really takes off after a pint-sized genius by the name of Mozart (52) finds its tones to his liking. **16,003**

226 FRANCIS XAVIER (1506–1552)
evangelist to the Indies

Xavier was one of seven original members of the

Jesuits, recruited by Ignatius Loyola (115) to lead lives of poverty and celibacy in imitation of Christ, and to spread the gospel. Known as the "Apostle to the Indies," Xavier found converts among the fisherfolk of India, the headhunters of the Spice Islands, and the cultural elite of Imperial Japan (whose hard-to-learn language he declared to be "the work of the devil"). His biggest contribution to the evangelical cause was his adaptation of the Christian message to local customs and his recruitment of local priests. He knew he would never again see his beloved Jesuit brothers, thousands of miles away, so he cut their signatures from the letters they sent and pinned them in his habit next to his heart. Xavier died of fever as he was attempting to storm the heathen gates of China. **15,974**

227 ELIZABETH BLACKWELL (1821–1910)
first American woman doctor

What a bunch of overachievers! Blackwell and her sister Emily became doctors; another sister was a newspaper correspondent, another a writer; one sister-in-law, Antoinette Blackwell (267), was America's first woman minister, and another was famed suffragist Lucy Stone. Elizabeth was enraged when a friend died from a simple gynecological disorder. So she worked with doctors in the Carolinas, but was rejected as an applicant by most medical schools. She gained entry to Geneva Medical College in New York only after students voted to let her attend. Once there, however, students speculated that she was insane. One professor tried to bar her from the lecture on reproduction. As a doctor, she faced prejudice from other physicians, hospital staffs, and patients. Ultimately, with the backing of reformers like Horace Greeley and Henry Ward Beecher, she opened her own hospital for women and children in New York. **15,919**

228 LORENZO "THE MAGNIFICENT" DE' MEDICI (1449–1492)
Florentine strongman with a weak spot for great art

His title was simply "first citizen," but he ruled Florence like a mafia godfather with a lawn full of statues. He stimulated the production of beautiful art simply by buying so much of it: stunning buildings, sculptures, and paintings by Michelangelo (13), Botticelli (331), Filippino Lippi, and Pico della Mirandola. Lorenzo dabbled in architectural design and wrote almost-not-too-bad verse about snoring shepherds, swooping hawks, and little bleating lambs. "If Florence was to have a tyrant she could never have found a better or more delightful one," said a contemporary with democratic leanings, Francesco Guicciardini. Lorenzo's love of art and wisdom was hyped. One hagiographer wrote that Lorenzo lamented on his deathbed that he had had no time to finish a great library he had planned. If you believe that, we've got a Ponte Vecchio to sell you. **15,906**

229 IVAN THE GREAT (1440–1505)
creator of the modern Russian state

Through conquest, diplomacy, and his renunciation of Moscow's two-hundred-year allegiance to the Mongols, Ivan made Russia a European power to be reckoned with and created a sense of Russian destiny. When he assumed the throne, his realm consisted of just fifteen thousand square miles, less than half the size of present-day Indiana. With his son Vasily, he nearly tripled Russian territory, a start toward expansion that made Russia the world's largest nation. Ivan, the grand duke of Moscow, dreamed of making Russia the Third Rome, cherishing a monk's prophecy that while "the two Romes have fallen, the third does endure. Your Christian Empire shall last forever." To fulfill his vision, he claimed to be a direct descendant of the Roman emperor Caesar Augustus, and he married the niece of the last emperor of Byzantium (the second Rome), a woman described by an Italian observer as a "mountain of fat." **15,873**

230 CARL LINNAEUS (1707–1778)
eighteenth-century Adam

Kingdom: Animalia; Phylum: Chordata; Class: Mammalia; Order: Primates; Family: Hominidal; Genus: Homo; Species: Homosapien. That about sums him up. Linnaeus's 1735 treatise *Systema Naturae* laid down a simple method of classifying plants by the way their flowers were formed. Then he turned his attention to the animal kingdom. His work was embraced by the scientific community because of the rapid discoveries of more and seemingly endless forms of life. Linnaeus's method, often sketched out like a massive family tree, is simply a filing system that allows researchers to sort out all life-forms. The genius of his system is that everything, from the minuscule amoeba to the elegant Easter lily to the massive elephant to as-yet undiscovered life-forms, has its niche. **15,866**

231 CLAUDIO MONTEVERDI (1567–1643)
first composer of music drama as we know it

Monteverdi's first published works appeared when he was fifteen, and he spent much of his career directing music at Venice's magnificent St. Mark's Church. Before he wrote the opera *Orfeo* in 1607, musical plays were just that: plays with music. Monteverdi intertwined the words and notes and added arias rich in new harmonies. That makes *Orfeo* the granddaddy of every opera and musical comedy, from those composed by seventeenth-century Frenchman François Lully to twentieth-century Englishman Andrew Lloyd Webber. Monteverdi was both a learned innovator and a sycophant in search of patrons. "There is nothing in me that does not spring from your infinite goodness," he gushed to Cardinal Ferdinand Gonzaga in 1611. His apple polishing worked. The duke of Mantua paid most musicians with bread, veal, fish, candles, and salt; Monteverdi got gold. **15,854**

232 OLIVER EVANS (1755–1819)
industrial troubleshooter

Evans pioneered the development of high-pressure steam engines and created the automatic production line. This man never met a production snafu he couldn't unravel. What a pity the public didn't appreciate his vision. Consider the production line he created in the 1790s that used power from waterwheels and employed only machines to pummel grain into flour. One incredulous miller exclaimed, "It will not do! It cannot do! It is impossible it should do!" But it worked. Then there was his steam engine, which he adapted to process cotton, tobacco, and paper and, most importantly, to power steamboats. Evans predicted that the steamboat, together with the railroad, would help people travel "as fast as birds fly." Of course he didn't envision the airplane, but given a few more years, he would have. **15,762**

233 FRANZ KAFKA (1883–1924)
apostle of alienation

In the twentieth century perhaps only Proust (207) and Joyce (171) rival his impact on literature. The opening of *The Metamorphosis* captures modern man's neurotic self-absorption: "As Gregor Samsa awoke one morning from uneasy dreams, he found himself transformed in his bed into a giant insect." So powerful a hold does Kafka's surrealist imagery have on us that *Kafkaesque* has entered the popular vocabulary to describe everything from the Nazi Holocaust that consumed his three sisters to the incongruities of our daily lives. Kafka's own torments read like a checklist of twentieth-century anxieties: the Oedipal revolt; the dead-end job; the troubled relationship with the opposite sex (he was horrified by the "hellish luster" of his fiancée's gold teeth). Fame eluded Kafka, and he died at age forty of tuberculosis. A friend disobeyed his instructions to destroy his manuscripts, giving the world the fruits of what Kafka called "a form of prayer." **15,755**

234 ANDREAS VESALIUS (1514–1564)
the body's tour guide

For more than a millennium, the medical world followed the anatomical theories of the ancient physician Galen, who had dissected pigs, goats, and monkeys to formulate his ideas about the structure of the human body. Then Vesalius published his tome, *De Humani Corporis Fabrica,* proving that Galen's description of "animal" structure actually was strikingly different from "human" anatomy. By methodically dissecting cadavers, Vesalius showed the skeletal and muscular makeup of humans, creating the modern science of anatomy. A steady supply of corpses was provided by a criminal court judge who was interested in Vesalius's theories. The judge even delayed executions to fit Vesalius's dissection schedule. The Flemish Vesalius commissioned a series of anatomical drawings to illustrate his book, which provided a scientific description of the human body's skeleton, muscles, and nervous, reproductive, and digestive systems. **15,742**

235 JOHN MCADAM (1756–1836)
guru of gravel

The next time you head down the lonesome highway, think of John McAdam, the Scottish businessman-engineer. He taught road building so well, the word *macadam* is still a synonym for street pavement. He earned a fortune as a banker in British-occupied New York during the American Revolution, giving him the leisure to go home and live his youthful dream of improving Britain's abominable dirt highways. In 1823 Parliament adopted his plan. The solution was a veneer of stone that could bond with the dirt below. The type of stone didn't matter, as long as the pitch of the road permitted the water to drain away and keep the underlying dirt from turning mushy. Tar, asphalt, and cement came later, but McAdam's principles paved the way. **15,666**

236 VILHELM BJERKNES (1862–1951)
weather wizard

The son of a Norwegian scientist, Vilhelm mastered the academic specialties of mechanics and mathematical physics. After years of studying hydrodynamics and thermodynamics, he devised a theory of air masses that is central to modern weather forecasting. He even crafted plans for predicting what the heavens held in store, based on conditions in the atmosphere and oceans. Pretty darn good for the early 1900s, when people trusted their lumbago to presage rain or looked to woolly caterpillars to warn of brutal winters. Now the heirs of Bjerknes use satellites, balloons, and radar to warn humanity of approaching storms. **15,651**

237 MIKHAIL GORBACHEV (b. 1931)
catalyst of Communism's collapse

Gorbachev, last ruler of the Soviet Union, first sought to fix an evil system with sops he called *glasnost* and *perestroika.* But recognizing that his politically bankrupt and economically moribund empire had lost the cold war, he negotiated its surrender. "If you can't beat them, join them," his press spokesman Gennadi I. Gerasimov said. We debated whether to rate this baptized grandson of a devout Russian Orthodox woman higher. After all, he helped avert nuclear war. But if he hadn't put Communism on the trash heap of history, somebody else would have. A turning point in his waltz with the West was his 1984 trip to London, where he wowed Prime Minister Margaret Thatcher (719) while his wife snapped up a $1,780 pair of earrings in Harrod's with her American Express credit card. After ceding power, Gorbachev toured America in *Forbes* magazine's corporate jetliner, *Capitalist Tool*. **15,589**

238 GIANLORENZO BERNINI (1598–1680)
Rome's decorator

While many of us must be content to lie peacefully beneath a two-by-four-foot gravestone, all of Rome is a monument to Bernini. A full three centuries after his death, his genius lives on in fountains, churches, statues, altars, piazzas, and other people's tombs. Although the quick-tempered Bernini was born in Naples, he lived, worked, and thrived in Rome. Pope Paul V, seeing the child Bernini's copies of the great sculptures of antiquity, declared he was destined to be "the Michelangelo of his age." And like that great master before him, Bernini spent his career doing the artistic and architectural bidding of cardinals and popes. He was so busy that he was forced to hire just about all the stone carvers in and around Rome to complete his commissions. When in Rome, do as the Romans do: sit in a café at the Piazza Navona and admire Bernini's fountains. **15,581**

239 BARTHOLOMÉ DE LAS CASAS
(1474–1566) *conscience of a new continent*

The conquerors of the West Indies killed the conquered without scruple. The natives weren't considered human until Pope Paul III decreed it thirty-nine years after Columbus's discovery. Las Casas was a planter-turned-priest who witnessed massacres in Cuba and Hispaniola and cried out in anguish untypical of his times. When humanist Juan Ginés de Sepúlveda declared it was no crime to kill heathens, Las Cases replied, "All the peoples of the world are men, and the definition of men, collectively and severally, is one: that they are rational beings." His lobbying led to a law abolishing Indian slavery, though when he tried to enforce it as bishop of Chiapas in Guatemala, Las Casas was forced to return to Spain. Eventually the law prevailed, and Las Casas is remembered as an early champion of social justice. **15,524**

240 LUCRETIA MOTT (1793–1880)
first voice of American women

Mott was the first woman to speak up for women's right to speak out. This was ignited after abolitionists refused to let her participate at an international conference. Her militancy began years earlier after she discovered male colleagues at her school were earning double her salary. In 1848 she teamed with Elizabeth Cady Stanton (86) to launch the organized women's rights movement in the United States. Mott and her husband James shared a rare marriage of equals. Both Quakers, they were staunch abolitionists who hid escaped slaves in their home. Mott always had the angels on her side. At one antislavery meeting thugs were attacking speakers outside. Mott told her male escort to assist other ladies who were alone and fearful. Then she turned to a mean-looking hoodlum, placed her hand on his arm, and said, "He will see me safely through." Thunderstruck, the heavy did as Mott instructed. **15,473**

241 John III Sobieski (1629–1696)
Polish king and legendary savior of Christian Europe

In one of the decisive battles of European history, Sobieski broke the Turkish siege of Vienna in 1683, turning back the Turkish "menace." Earlier he had displayed his military genius by defeating the Tatars four times in eleven days in a raid on Ukraine. To be sure, the Polish warrior had warts. A French artist sketched him being heaved by his men up the battlements of a conquered city because he was too fat to climb them. And before he became king, he switched sides twice in a war between Poland and Sweden. Why he wasn't executed for treason, we'll never know. Moreover, it seems, the terror of the Turks was also a henpecked husband, "the obsequious slave" of his beautiful French wife. His greatest failure was posthumous; within years of his death, independent Poland ceased to exist.   **15,468**

242 Ito Hirobumi (1841–1909)
modernizer of Japan

Educated in a pro-Imperialist school and made samurai by age twenty-two, Ito was sent on a mission to Europe. In England, when he saw the technology of the Industrial Revolution, he shed his anti-West prejudices and became an advocate of opening Japan to foreign influences. After putting down rebellions by samurai and divisions within the government, Ito drafted a constitution that insured the continuity of the imperial line. As prime minister from 1889 to 1901, he presided over Japan's industrialization. Then he served as resident general of Korea, an unwilling Japanese protectorate. A man of unusual sensitivities for a politician—he wrote Chinese poetry under the pen name Spring Field—Ito was assassinated by a Korean nationalist.   **15,421**

243 Ivan the Terrible (1530–1584)
first Russian czar

He expanded the empire started by his grandfather, Ivan the Great, made Moscow the capital, and created the basis of Russian absolutism that endured into the late twentieth century. But he is most remembered for his reign of terror against the Russian nobility. Even as a boy, he savored brutality; a favorite game was tossing dogs from the Kremlin's two-hundred-foot walls. As ruler, he was prone to bizarre political moves, like his creation of an autocratic state-within-the-state, and his false abdication. "The czar's nocturnal birdsong / was the screams of folk in towers and in dungeons," Russian poet Yevgeny Yevtushenko later wrote. Ivan once kissed a foe's infant child, then slit its throat. He killed his son Ivan during a quarrel, striking him in the temple with the iron-pointed staff he carried everywhere. Years later, as Ivan lay dying, he beseeched God's forgiveness. Tolstoy (34) imagined him confessing: "I allowed the devil to rule my deathless soul."   **15,410**

244 Ivan Pavlov (1849–1936)
dogged researcher

Next to the legend of Galileo (4) dropping balls from the leaning tower of Pisa to learn about gravity, our favorite research story is about Pavlov's dogs. Pavlov proved that pooches who are repeatedly given meat after a bell rings will eventually start salivating when the bell sounds, even if no meat is in sight. These experiments on what Pavlov called "conditioned responses" spread the idea that social behavior can be altered by scientific controls. Behaviorist B. F. Skinner (121) lapped up the theory. Given the Soviet government's mechanistic views, no wonder the Kremlin watchdogs never muzzled Pavlov's research. His father was a country priest; Pavlov was trained in a seminary, but he was drawn to physiological studies from an early age. He was in his fifties when he embarked on his dog experiments, and he won the Nobel Prize for medicine and physiology in 1904.   **15,399**

245 ANNA PAVLOVA (1881–1931)
prima ballerina

The inspiration for ballet-master Michel Fokine's 1905 *The Dying Swan* came from the flowing style of unorthodox dancer Isadora Duncan (554). But Fokine had Pavlova in mind when he choreographed it. Her perfect execution of classical ballet techniques to evoke emotion in an audience made her the greatest ballerina of her time, maybe all time. Her interpretation of the swan's feeble last attempts at life, for example, is ballet history's most famous solo performance by a woman. The St. Petersburg–born dancer learned her craft at Russia's Imperial Ballet Academy. She began appearing abroad in 1907, and in twenty-three years of almost nonstop touring, she was the number-one missionary for the art of classical dance, prompting a famous successor, Allegra Kent, to call her a balletic combination of Ferdinand Magellan (42) and the missionary Junípero Serra. Her grace and intensity are evident even today; the miracle of film captured Pavlova dancing at the height of her career.   **15,361**

246 ROBERT FULTON (1765–1815)
launcher of the first viable steamboat

Others produced prototype steamboats, but Fulton made the dream work. He tested his first steamboat in the Seine, then offered the ship to the French. But Napoleon (16), who had rejected Fulton's newfangled submarine as dishonorable warfare, said *non* again. "A charming man and brilliant conversationalist," said French minister Talleyrand (419) about Fulton, "but I'm afraid the poor fellow's cracked." When the British turned him down, too, a frustrated Fulton returned to America. With partner Robert Livingston, he launched a steamboat run on the Hudson River between New York and Albany in 1807. The 150-foot steamship, with huge paddlewheels on each side, was named the *Clermont*, but the jeering public called it "Fulton's Folly." Nobody laughed long; the boat cut the trip from four days to thirty-two hours. Fulton's commercial success knocked tows, barges, and horse ferries right out of the water. Another giant step in the evolution of transportation.   **15,360**

247 GEORGES DANTON (1759–1794)
the Great Compromiser of the French Revolution

Instrumental in ridding France of the monarchy and creating and defending the French Republic, Danton moderated Robespierre's (68) excesses before falling victim to the Terror. A ditty in the 1792 legislative election urged: "Only vote for such men / As Danton and then / We'll be happy forever, / Forever, Amen." But happiness eluded France as the bourgeois revolt against king and clergy degenerated into a bloodbath. Danton's efforts to forge compromises among political factions and save the innocent from the gallows proved futile. At the foot of the scaffold, he cried out: "O my wife, my well beloved, I shall never see thee more!" Then he rebuked himself: "Danton! No weakness!" Finally he asked the executioner to show his decapitated head to the people. "So passes," wrote Thomas Carlyle (691), the nineteenth-century British historian, "like a gigantic mass, of valour, ostentation, fury, affection and wild revolutionary force and manhood, this Danton."   **15,343**

248 JOHN DALTON (1766–1844)
physicist who laid the foundation for atomic theory

Dalton's Quaker clothing sometimes drew attention, but behind his facade lurked a keen scientific mind. The son of a weaver, Dalton showed such academic ability that by age twelve he was running the school he had attended in an English village. Barred from Oxford and Cambridge because he was a Quaker, Dalton was largely self-taught. He formulated the theories that matter is made of atoms, that different elements have different atoms, and that a reaction is a readjustment of atoms. He didn't get everything right—for example, his formula for water was one hydrogen atom too short—but he put scientific thinking on the right track. He spent a lifetime making observations, and by the time he died, he had accumulated more than 200,000 entries in his diary.   **15,341**

249 GRATIAN (fl. 1140)
author of the millennium's first great law book

He was a twelfth-century writer, probably Italian, and probably a monk. That is all any honest medievalist can claim to know about the life of Gratian. Whoever he was, Gratian had a profound influence on the law and on scholarship by writing *The Concord of Discordant Canons,* better known as the *Decretum.* Catholic Church laws handed down by tradition often disagreed with each other; the *Decretum* tried to reconcile the contradictions, making it the prototype of legal opinions and treatises that settle disputes over the meaning of laws and precedents. Like a lot of scholars of the law, Gratian was neither objective nor riveting. His chapter on sex, for example, was so boring, it gave us a headache, which Gratian may have intended, given his view that coition was sinful, even in marriage. **15,269**

250 PAUL EHRLICH (1854–1915)
father of chemotherapy

Where Emil von Behring (220) and Shibasaburo

Kitasato left off with their antitoxin work, Ehrlich began. As a student in Berlin, Ehrlich shone in subjects he loved and faltered in those he disdained. Fortunately for us, this cigar-puffing, moody genius adored science. He invented a new staining technique on slides for the tuberculosis bacterium—a development of major importance for diagnosing TB and one that is still used. Behring came to use Ehrlich's pathfinding research in standardizing diphtheria serum. But the two clashed when Ehrlich decided serum therapy couldn't conquer the many infectious diseases not triggered by bacteria. Ehrlich's experiments with drugs to kill or stem the growth of these diseases marked the start of chemotherapy. When his arsenic compound proved effective against the organism that causes syphilis, nations took notice. At his death, the London *Times* praised Ehrlich's many achievements, saying, "The whole world is in his debt." **15,244**

251 BARUCH SPINOZA (1632–1677)
religious rationalist

One critic said his philosophy "devoured thought." It is hard to get emotional about his observation that "emotion towards a thing contingent, which we know not to exist in the present, is fainter than an emotion towards a thing past." But his influence on the modern world view is overwhelming; thinkers from Kant (49) through Freud (15) adopted his habit of picking everything apart. This secularist son of refugees went about Amsterdam trying to persuade his fellow Jews that the Talmud was not binding on them. The shocked Jewish leaders excommunicated him. His religious rationalism was his revenge. Einstein (17) called his ideas "heroic illusions." And the playwright Dimitri Frenkel Frank imagined a conversation in which the artist Rembrandt (46) confides he has gone bankrupt. "Is that all?" Spinoza asks disparagingly. "It's better to think." Rembrandt replies: "It's better to feel." **15,236**

252 CHARLOTTE PERKINS GILMAN (1860–1935) *women's economic equalizer*

Gilman did not suffer foolish women gladly. She dubbed the twentieth century the "woman's century" and lamented that "the world waits while she powders her nose." Gilman described the mental breakdown she suffered after her child's birth in the now-celebrated short story "The Yellow Wallpaper." In that piece a new mother is driven mad by inactivity and the limitations placed on middle-class women. Gilman herself had been overwhelmed by a paralyzing postpartum depression that lifted only when she fled her husband and began writing. During a prolific career she published books, essays, short stories, poems, articles, and even her own magazine. In 1898 her *Women and Economics* asserted that until women became self-reliant and prepared themselves for careers, they would be economically disadvantaged. Society, she argued, would improve only when the lot of women was ameliorated. **15,204**

253 DMITRY MENDELEYEV (1834–1907) *classifying chemist*

The ghost of Mendeleyev hovers behind the huge periodic tables of the elements on the walls of chemistry classrooms. The Russian succeeded where other brains had failed, developing the first known relationship of the elements by classifying them according to atomic weight. His work, with later additions by German Julius Meyer, is known as the Periodic Law, a basic principle in chemistry. Savvy Dmitry even left space for elements he suspected were out there— somewhere. He was right; three more were dis-

covered within twenty years with the properties he predicted, and there were more to come. Chemistry was Mendeleyev's forte. Politics was another story. In 1890 the progressive Professor Mendeleyev sent the government a letter from students protesting unjust conditions at the university in St. Petersburg, where he was teaching. Not only did the oppressive czarist regime take great offense, but it put Mendeleyev in a new category: retired. **15,191**

254 HONORÉ DE BALZAC (1799–1850) *chronicler of the human comedy*

The French Realist writer helped mold the modern novel through use of sequenced events, realistic characters, and forceful language. He wrote to pay never-ending bills. For twenty years, Balzac clocked twelve- to eighteen-hour workdays writing ninety-five novels, numerous short stories, plays, and essays. He decided to compile the novels and stories into one massive work called *The Human Comedy,* which includes the novels *Le Pere Goriot, Eugenie Grandet,* and *La Cousine Bette.* Author W. Somerset Maugham said Balzac's "greatness lies not in a single work, but in the formidable mass of his production." Balzac's workaholism matched an extravagant lifestyle of gambling, gluttony, and materialism. A memorable character himself, he created two-thousand others ranging from innkeepers, clerics, and journalists to bureaucrats, merchants, and prostitutes. They were so lifelike even Balzac believed in them. While dying, he called for his medical character: "Send for Biachon," he implored. "Biachon will save me." **15,167**

255 BERNARD OF CLAIRVAUX (1090–1153) *spiritual peacemaker*

Burgundian nobleman Bernard de Fontaines sought a life of meditation and established a

Cistercian monastery at Clairvaux. Existence was austere, and Bernard soon developed anemia, migraines, gastritis, and hypertension. But his sufferings only strengthened his spirituality. Word soon spread of this mystic, ascetic, and saint, and the world summoned him from solitude. He mediated civil and church disputes, was confessor to five popes, and countered heretical teachings. God's grace that "had possession of this frail man burst into flame in the hearts of all who heard him speak," wrote Thomas Merton. Bernard's one mistake: championing the Second Crusade without envisioning its bloody outcome. Church fathers call him the "Mellifluous Doctor," for his teachings as sweet as honey. "The reason for loving God, is God," Bernard said. "The measure of this love is to love without measure." Bernard was canonized in 1174. **15,150**

256 PIETER BRUEGEL THE ELDER
(c.1528–1569) *patriarch of Flemish painters*

Like father, like sons. Pieter the Younger and his brother Jan never quite equaled the eminence of their father. As a triumvirate, however, they gave the Flemish school of painting its luster. While other artists were immortalizing the Madonna, saints, and other heavenly bodies, Bruegel the Elder hobnobbed with peasants. In fact, his paintings could only have been painted in the Low Countries. Even today the gray skies there and the broad simple Flemish faces make Brussels look like an ad for a Bruegel exhibit. Bruegel deliberately rejected the Renaissance preoccupation with the ethereal and mystical in favor of earthy peasant life and realistic settings. One of our favorites, *The Census at Bethlehem*, portrays Joseph and a very pregnant Mary in a sixteenth-century Flemish winter scene. Bruegel also liked to arouse emotion: in his *Wedding*

Dance just about all the men are cavorting in various states of arousal. **15,147**

257 FRANCIS DRAKE (c.1540–1596)
Mr. Mission Impossible for Queen Elizabeth I

Good morning, Mr. Drake. Your mission, if you choose to accept it, is to keep England independent by singeing the beards of Spaniards and taking their treasure. If you or any member of your force is caught or killed, the queen will disavow any knowledge of your actions. Drake was the best seafaring warrior in outgunned England's war against Spain. And though Queen Elizabeth (31) pretended he was an unauthorized brigand, she was able to repay her entire foreign debt with the wealth he captured from the Spanish during his three-year trip around the world in the *Golden Hind*. The booty was worth $30 million in today's money. This red-haired fanatical Protestant and music lover—he brought an orchestra on his trips—died of fever on an expedition. When the Spanish heard, they danced in the streets. This entry will self-destruct in ten seconds. **15,145**

258 DONATO BRAMANTE (1444–1514)
beauteous builder

How would you like to have St. Peter's Basilica in your portfolio? Bramante did, and a host of smaller but equally distinguished edifices. Pope Julius II (794) tapped him for chief architect of St. Peter's—quite an honor for this peasant's son. Bramante began his career by painting architectural fantasies—fake archways and columns—on murals. He graduated to building the structures themselves. In 1499 he went to Rome expecting to retire and study ancient buildings. Enter Julius and his commission to construct the world's largest church, where his own tomb would be enshrined. Work was still under way when Bramante died at age seventy. He was buried in St. Peter's, one year after Julius. Bramante's body was borne there, said artist Giorgio Vasari, "by the papal court and by all the sculptors, architects and painters." **15,103**

259 CHRISTOPHER WREN (1632–1723)
awesome architect of London

He never went to Italy to marvel at the craftsmen who preceded him, and he had no formal architectural training. Yet Wren became the most important architect in England, someone who envisioned London's churches and palaces that we ogle today. Educated in mathematics, Wren was consulted for his expertise in that area to help solve a building problem. Traveling to Paris, he watched with curiosity the construction of the Louvre. Back in England, his opportunity for great architectural accomplishments came about after the Great Fire ravaged London in 1666. Nearly all the city—including some eighty churches and the cathedral—was destroyed. Wren rebuilt London. Lacking the financial backing of the Catholic Church or benevolent royalty, his visions of architectural splendor were always toned down to accommodate financial realities—even St. Paul's Cathedral, the ultimate monument to his genius. **15,089**

260 AUGUSTE RODIN (1840–1917)
the thinking man's sculptor

He was a perfectly fine sculptor who became one of the greatest by breaking from realism and turning to the romanticism that marks his best works. As the model for the breakthrough, *The Age of Bronze,* Rodin picked one of nine musclebound soldiers sent by an acquaintance in the Belgian army. His most famous works are *The Burghers of Calais, The Kiss, Balzac,* and of course, *The Thinker*—so familiar, it is a cliché. "Life flows like a river from his fingers," an admirer said, and

Rodin loved putting those fingers on beautiful models. "Your skin has the whiteness of a turbot that one sees lying on the marble slabs of your wonderful fishmongers," the Frenchman told English subject Mary Hunter. Dancer Isadora Duncan (554) lamented late in life that she kept her virginity at age twenty-two when sixty-year-old Rodin offered to take it. **15,031**

261 DANIEL FAHRENHEIT (1686–1736)
originator of the first widely used thermometer

Of thirty-five temperature scales circulating in the early eighteenth century, Fahrenheit's mercury thermometer became the best known, and its proliferation helped scientists the world over compare temperatures in experiments. Fahrenheit put water's freezing point at 32 degrees and its boiling point at 212. He arrived at ideal human body temperature by sticking gauges in a healthy man's mouth or under his armpit. Fahrenheit thought he was patterning his scale after Dutch physicist Ole Romer's prototype. He got it wrong, but Fahrenheit's scale turned out to be more logical and practical. So much so that the United States has been loath to change to the more recently adopted Celsius scale. Until that happens, just figure F = (9/5 x C) + 32. **15,004**

262 MAYER AMSCHEL ROTHSCHILD
(1744–1812) *founder of the world's greatest banking dynasty*

From selling old coins in Frankfurt's Jewish ghetto, Rothschild graduated to money changing before becoming Prince William of Hesse-Hanau's financier. Setting up his five sons in the financial centers of Frankfurt, Paris, London, Vienna, and Naples, Rothschild hooked Europe's princes on low-cost credit discreetly advanced. In the Napoleonic Wars, he financed the duke of

Wellington's (278) military campaigns under the French dictator's nose. The Rothschilds cherished secrecy, from the false bottom of the family coach to the artificial language they invented. After the patriarch's death the sons spurred Europe's economy by investing in the Industrial Revolution. In 1849 their aging mother reassured a visitor, "There will be no war. My sons won't finance it." That power eluded them, but their empire still flourishes.   **14,943**

263 SAMUEL ADAMS (1722–1803)
propagandist of the American Revolution

We tell our journalism history students that Adams is the real father of public relations. More than a hundred years before P. T. Barnum (94) or Edward Bernays (747), Adams whipped up public sympathy for revolution. He wanted the American colonists to hate the British so much that they'd pick up their bayonets and fight. Adams and his "Sons of Liberty" buddies wrote scores of articles that set out logical arguments against British domination. The articles were penned in simple terms so that even the barely literate—the men who would be footsoldiers—could understand. Adams hung out in the offices of the *Boston Gazette* and used the newspaper to rally "patriots" against the British redcoats. When the British fired on a crowd in Boston, Adams dubbed it the "Boston Massacre." Rumor has it he was one of the Indians who invited the British to a tea party.   **14,937**

264 LEONARDO OF PISA (c.1170–c.1240)
the Western world's math teacher

Which problem is easier to solve? (a) XVI + CCCXII + IX = ? or (b) 16 + 312 + 9 = ? If you said (b) you are adept in the new math. New, that is, in 1202 when Leonardo, also known as Fibonacci, published the *Liber Abaci* or *The Book of Calcula-*

tion. It was a compilation of wisdom he had picked up as a merchant in Islamic territory, and though it was old stuff to the Arabs and Hindus, it was new to the West. Leonardo's widely circulated book put Roman numerals on the road to being useless, except to count world wars and Super Bowls. Leonardo taught how to add, subtract, multiply, and divide the Arabic numbers and in later works wrote about esoteric equations and trigonometry. For the record, the answer to the first problem is CCCXXXVII. Thanks to Leonardo, you can do the other one yourself.   **14,898**

265 ANDERS CELSIUS (1701–1744)
developer of the centigrade temperature scale

Astronomer Celsius spent years observing the aurora borealis, determining the size of stars, and confirming Newton's (6) theory that the earth pancakes at the poles. Only late in life did he dabble in temperature scales, but there he made his mark. In 1742 Celsius invented a centigrade scale, which was the first to allow for atmospheric pressure in its measurements. His "constant degrees," or fixed points, were zero, for where the mercury stood when the thermometer was plunged into boiling water at a particular barometric reading, and one hundred, when it was placed in melting snow. The scale was reversed by Sweden's Uppsala observatory in 1747 and became known as the Swedish thermometer. It wasn't until the 1800s that folks started tacking Celsius's name to it. Use of the centigrade thermometer has now spread throughout most of the world.   **14,876**

266 FRANCIS JOSEPH OF AUSTRIA-HUNGARY (1830–1916)
last of the emperors

He was a big old lumbering guy in mutton chops, presiding over the decline of a big old slumbering state of multinational chaps. Francis Joseph issued the ultimatum to Serbia that led to World War I and the resultant horrors of fascism and Communism. Many of his family came to a sad end. His brother Maximilian, the would-be emperor of Mexico, was shot to death. His son, Crown Prince Rudolf, blew his mistress's and his own brains out. His wife Elizabeth was hacked to death by an anarchist. And it was the assassination of his great-nephew Francis Ferdinand that provoked Francis Joseph's ultimatum. Then the Habsburg dynasty that he had headed for sixty-eight years came crashing down. As historian A.J.P. Taylor wrote, "the crimes and errors of centuries were exacting their penalty." The emperor told Teddy Roosevelt (700) that he was "the last monarch of the old school." With his death it was time for history to say adieu to empires. **14,870**

267 ANTOINETTE LOUISA BROWN BLACKWELL (1825–1921)
first ordained woman minister in the United States

No matter that, about a century earlier, the old blowhard Samuel Johnson (182) said, "Sir, a woman preaching is like a dog's walking on his hind legs. It is not done well; but you are surprised to find it done at all." Blackwell, despite such Neanderthal attitudes, became an ordained Congregational minister in 1853. After a year at her parish in South Butler, New York, her liberal religious beliefs clashed with those in the traditional parish. Then she switched to the Unitarian Church. She married into the prominent reform family, the Blackwells, and gave birth to seven children. She helped establish a parish in Elizabeth, New Jersey, and occasionally preached at other free-thinking churches. Blackwell vocally supported suffrage and education for women.

She dabbled in poetry and also wrote books on religion and women's rights. Take that, Mr. Johnson! **14,861**

268 JAMES MADISON (1751–1836)
father of the U.S. Constitution

He called it "a system which we wish to last for ages," and it has. The Ten Commandments aside, there is no better set of written rules. Its provisions flowed in large part from Madison's erudition and ability to form compromises among the delegates to the 1787 Constitutional Convention in Philadelphia. Madison prepared for the drafting by studying a hundred books on government sent from France by ambassador Thomas Jefferson (64). (In return, Jefferson asked Madison to send him fruit trees and a possum.) Madison successfully preached ratification of the Constitution as coauthor of a persuasive series of newspaper articles that are known collectively as the *Federalist Papers.* Elected to the nation's highest office in 1808, the sixty-inch Madison was America's shortest president. But "Jemmy" and his ice-cream-making wife Dolley stood tall against the British in the War of 1812—except when redcoat raiders temporarily burned them out of the White House. **14,837**

269 HENRI MATISSE (1869–1954)
French painter of bestial force

Matisse said he became an artist because his mother gave him a set of paints while he was recuperating from appendicitis at age twenty. He led a group of pals who were influenced by the Tahitian paintings of Paul Gauguin (545), and when they exhibited their works at a Paris show in 1905, a critic dubbed them, the "wild beasts"—*fauves,* in French—for their bold colors and broad brushstrokes. His most famous painting is *The Dance.* Even before he became a trendsetter,

Matisse had graduated from outrageousness to marketability. His popularity was boosted when celebrity Gertrude Stein (725) and her brothers collected his works. Matisse and Pablo Picasso (149) had a famous friendship, but Picasso's hangers-on decided that Matisse was old hat, and they loved to throw lit cigarettes at his 1906 *Portrait of Marguerite,* hanging in Picasso's studio.   **14,821**

270 DENIS DIDEROT (1713–1784)
encyclopedia editor

One of the most original thinkers of his time, French philosopher Diderot's essays presaged Darwin's (7) ideas on natural selection and Braille's (956) reading system for the blind. But Diderot is best known as editor of the *Encyclopédie,* twenty-eight volumes of erudition printed in forty-three editions during a quarter-century. Though often flawed and biased, the *Encyclopédie* became the most important publication of the century, with contributions from Voltaire (36), Rousseau (19), Diderot, and other distinguished authors, mathematicians, and scientists. It had a profound influence on thought during Europe's Age of Enlightenment, preaching reason over religion and knowledge over dogma. Fueling Diderot's brilliance was his insatiable appetite for ideas. "I let my mind rove wantonly, give it free rein to follow any idea, wise or mad, that may come uppermost," he wrote. "I chase it as do young libertines on the track of a courtesan. My ideas are my trollops."   **14,816**

271 MITSUI TAKATOSHI (1622–1694)
Japanese business visionary

Starting off as a rice merchant and money changer, Mitsui branched out into dry-goods stores and expanded rapidly by applying two principles: Keep your prices low and your workers happy. Sounds obvious? Even in the twentieth century a lot of companies have forgotten those rules. In the seventeenth century they were revolutionary ideas. Mitsui kept his prices low by maintaining razor-thin profit margins. And he kept his workers happy by giving them bonuses (an early form of "worker empowerment"). Scan any directory of corporate Japan today to see Mitsui's legacy, a conglomerate that spans every conceivable industry: Mitsui & Co., Mitsui Bank Ltd., Mitsui Construction Co., Mitsui Engineering and Shipbuilding Co., Mitsui Mining & Smelting Co., Mitsui Mining Co., Mitsui OSK Lines Ltd., Mitsui Petrochemical Industries Ltd., Mitsui Real Estate Development Co., Mitsui Sugar Co., Mitsui Toatsu Chemicals Co., Mitsui Trust & Banking Co., and Mitsui Warehouse Co.   **14,804**

272 & 273 JACOB (1785–1863) and WILHELM (1786–1859) GRIMM
publishers of children's fairy tales

Once upon a time there were two brothers who were inseparable. They went to school together, and when their father died and the family lost all its money, they found a way, through the kindness of others, to attend graduate school. Together they studied ancient German literature and folklore. When Wilhelm married the daughter of a druggist, the three of them lived as a family, and she dutifully cared for the domestic needs of the two brothers. They wrote down the tales of storytellers throughout the region and published 156 stories in two volumes. The stories reinforced nineteenth-century morality and upheld the Protestant ethic. Goodness always prevailed. Even today, despite criticism from feminists and parents who think the tales are a little too grim, children are enthralled by the plight of Little Red Riding

Hood, Cinderella, Rapunzel, Snow White, and dozens of other fairy princesses and damsels in distress. One day a wicked king took over their part of Germany, and the brothers Grimm were ordered to sign an oath of allegiance to him. When they refused, the penniless Grimms were cast out of their jobs. Then the kind king of Prussia invited the brothers to Berlin, gave them jobs at the university there, and they lived happily ever after. The End. **FOR EACH: 14,801**

274 CLAUDE DEBUSSY (1862–1918)
liberator of music from harmony

We date the beginning of modern music to December 22, 1894, when a Paris audience heard a flutist play the opening passage at the premiere of Debussy's *Prelude to the Afternoon of a Faun*. In an instant music was freed from the conventional harmonic rules that had reigned for almost three centuries, and out rushed the color and improvisatory feeling associated with modern music. "I want to sing my interior landscape with the simple artlessness of a child," Debussy wrote. He was shy like a child, but he loved whiskey and food, could roll a perfect cigarette without licking the paper, and was an uncompromising craftsman; he delayed publication of one piece for months while he fiddled with four measures. He loved France and hated most things Germanic, including the music of Mozart (52) and Wagner (165). "They had spoiled a lot of paper," he said. **14,741**

275 GOTTLIEB DAIMLER (1834–1900)
inventor of the gas guzzler

The development of the automobile was stalled because the existing steam engine was slow and so heavy that it weighed down the horseless carriage. But Daimler, who worked initially in engineer Nikolaus Otto's (105) factory, literally fueled the budding automobile industry with his inven-

tion—a high-speed, gasoline-powered, internal combustion engine. Just one cog in the big wheel that was to become the automobile industry, Daimler's invention solved the biggest problem in developing a practical car. The Daimler engine later powered boats and airplanes, but its first success was in November 1885 on a motorcycle—the world's first—that Daimler drove in his garden. By the turn of the century, the German Daimler was marketing a "Mercedes" automobile to French buyers who sought the latest expensive toy. It took Henry Ford (51) and his innovative ideas to finally mass-produce these novelties. **14,738**

276 JOHN OF AUSTRIA (1545–1578)
defender of Christendom

John won the naval battle of Lepanto over the Turks in 1571, ending the Ottoman threat to Christian Europe in the Mediterranean. He had other adventures, attacking pirates off North Africa and scheming to invade England and wed the imprisoned Scottish queen, Mary Stuart (610). But it was his annihilation of the Turkish fleet that turned the tide of history and inspired paintings by Titian, Tintoretto, and Paolo Veronese. On one of the Holy League's two hundred ships, legend has it, a wooden statue of Christ twisted to one side to avoid a Turkish cannonball; the statue survives in a Barcelona cathedral. On another, the left arm of the future Spanish novelist Cervantes (44) was wounded, though his right emerged unscathed to pen *Don Quixote* years later. The Turkish sultan shrugged off the debacle; having just conquered Cyprus, he declared, "They have cut off my beard; I have cut off their arm." **14,731**

277 WILHELM CONRAD RÖNTGEN
(1845–1923) *the X-man*

In November 1895 the German physicist was experimenting in his office with cathode rays when he witnessed an eerie fluorescence. He abandoned his line of research and became absorbed in examining this phenomenon. After discovering the rays' ability to penetrate matter, he brought his wife to the laboratory and photographed her hand using them. The result was an image of her bones. When his research was made public in January 1896, illustrated with a similar X-ray of a human skeleton hand, the excitement in the scientific community and the public at large was huge. Röntgen presented his findings to the kaiser himself. The rays' diagnostic qualities were put to use almost immediately. While in Germany they're called *Röntgenstrahlen* after the inventor, the rest of us use the term the discoverer himself coined, "X-rays." **14,708**

278 DUKE OF WELLINGTON (1769–1852)
Waterloo wunderkind

Without this blue-eyed British dandy's military genius, the world might be ruled today by Napoleon VII. But on a field near Brussels in 1815, the Iron Duke shattered Napoleon I's (16) last-ditch bid for power. His soldiers called him "Old Nosey"; one private told him, "God bless your crooked nose; I would rather see it than ten thousand men." Wellington (born Arthur Wellesley) later became a political reactionary and father figure to Queen Victoria (91), but Waterloo—a synonym for utter defeat—remains his legacy. Alas, the prayer said in British churches after he crushed the French dictator went unfulfilled: "Grant that the result of this mighty battle may put an end to the miseries of Europe." Wellington was as successful in love as in war. Retorting to Lady Shelley's boast that she had resisted his advances, he wrote his niece: "In my own justification, I was never aware of this resistance." **14,695**

279 EDGAR ALLAN POE (1809–1849)
master of the macabre

A giant of American literature, Poe wrote short-story masterpieces of supernatural horror like "The Fall of the House of Usher," and produced haunting poetry, most famously "The Raven," with its half-mad student's cries for consolation and the ill-omened raven's repeated reply of "Nevermore." Poe invented the detective story and was an important literary critic. His influence on future American and European writers, and on modern literary theory, is huge. But his life was as tortured as his fiction. A gambler, boozer, and opium user, Poe got kicked out of West Point, legend has it, for showing up naked for a parade. He married his thirteen-year-old cousin and, after her death at twenty-four, went downhill fast. "I became insane, with moments of horrible sanity," he wrote his mother-in-law. He was found dead on a Baltimore street. His funeral drew four mourners. **14,685**

280 JOHN DONNE (1572–1631)
God's poet

Born Catholic, Donne converted to Anglicanism, took his orders, and rose to dean of St. Paul's Cathedral. Years before, he had written love poems marked by cynicism, sensuality, and realism. His later religious poetry dealt with death and the soul's union with God, earning him the reputation as the greatest metaphysical poet. Donne was nearly undone by his secret marriage to Anne More. When her wealthy father heard about it, he had Donne imprisoned and stripped of his job. Eventually the marriage was ruled valid. Donne remained devoted to Anne and was grief-stricken when she died in 1617 after their twelfth child was stillborn. Her death only intensified his religious convictions. Donne, the preacher, could rivet his congregation. Consider this, from which more than one writer has borrowed: "No man is an island, entire of himself . . . any man's death diminishes me, because I am involved in mankind; and therefore never send to know for whom the bell tolls; it tolls for thee." **14,680**

281 PETER PAUL RUBENS (1577–1640)
the Rubens in Rubenesque

He should be every woman's hero. In an age of anorexia, waifs, and diet pills, we are comforted by Rubens's taste in women. He celebrated cellulite, fantasized about fat, and paid homage to heavy hips. If Rubens were the arbiter of today's popular culture, most women would be goddesses. We would have ranked Rubens higher for the sheer beauty of his work, except it's hard to know which canvases are real Rubenses and which are from his "paint factory." He had so much influence in the art world that he had dozens of students and professionals working for him to fulfill all his commissions. He drummed up projects for himself when he served as a part-time Netherlands diplomat in Spain and England. He also was the Calvin Klein of the baroque world, affixing his name to tapestry designs, book title pages, engravings, and all sorts of decorative pieces. **14,671**

282 EDWARD COKE (1552–1634)
uncommon common lawyer

In his decisions and commentaries, Justice Coke taught jurisprudence to generations of Englishmen, and he was an early leader of the fight to make common law superior to kings' power. These were lofty achievements for a moneygrubbing know-it-all who was jealous of other office seekers, notably philosopher-lawyer Francis Bacon (84). The humbly born Coke made his fortune by marrying an heiress worth thirty thousand pounds sterling and got to be attorney general in 1594 by fawning on Lord Burghley, Queen Elizabeth's (31) chief counselor. A. L. Rowse, the chronicler of Elizabethan history, wrote of Coke: "It was through this unpleasant man, selfish, and opinionated, greedy of power and money, rasping and grasping, pedantic and shrewish, for all his good looks crabbed and inasthetic (he loathed poets), that English liberties were upheld and defended." **14,644**

283 EL GRECO (1541–1614)
painter of religious ecstasy

Born Doménikos Theotokópoulos on Crete, he soaked up Titian's teachings in Venice, where they called him El Greco, "the Greek." When King Philip II (427) needed artists to create altarpieces for a major new monastery, El Greco packed his bags, moved to Spain, and never left. Some place his portraits on a pedestal with Rembrandt's (46). Consider the triumphant majesty of his masterpiece, *The Burial of the Conte de Orgaz.* Among his great works: *Baptism, Crucifixion,* and *Resurrection.* He painted figures stretched to superhuman lengths, with bold colors and emotional intensity. El Greco never lacked for confidence. He once dismissed Michelangelo (13) as "a good man but he couldn't paint." A prolific artist, El Greco was equally creative in launching lawsuits to collect his fees. Artists for ages can thank him for championing their rights against the finicky demands of philistine patrons. **14,632**

284 LEO HENDRIK BAEKELAND
(1863–1944) *plastic man*

Love him or hate him, he's the guy who gave the world the most durable, ubiquitous, useful, and maddening material since clay. Maybe it was because he grew up in perpetually overcast Belgium and craved a better raincoat, but after he emigrated to the United States in 1889 and sold his Velox photographic-paper invention to George Eastman for $1 million, Baekeland set out to find a synthetic substitute for shellac. In 1909 he combined phenol with formaldehyde to produce Bakelite, the first totally synthetic plastic and the first that didn't soften in heat. Today plastic is used in everything from life-saving medical devices to the shopping bags that waft across our parks. The man in the movie *The Graduate* was alluding to career options when he uttered one of cinema's most memorable one-word lines to Dustin Hoffman, but he might have been predicting the fate of the human race: "Plastics!" Thanks, Leo.   **14,587**

285 NORMAN BORLAUG (b. 1914)
savior of one billion lives

Borlaug sparked the Green Revolution, which tripled world grain output in the second half of the twentieth century, feeding a booming population and saving vast tracts of pristine forest from slash-and-burn farmers. It all started with the high-yield dwarf wheat he developed in Mexico and took to Pakistan and India in the mid-1960s to avert famine there. In 1984 former President Jimmy Carter and Japanese industrialist Ryoichi Sasakawa talked Borlaug out of retirement to help them take the Green Revolution to Africa. "I'm seventy-one; I'm too old to start again," the Iowa-born agronomist said. Retorted Sasakawa: "I'm fifteen years older, so I guess we should have started yesterday." Borlaug went to Africa, saw the poverty and hunger, and said, "Let's just start growing." He continued working on projects there well into his eighties.   **14,582**

286 IGNAZ PHILLIPP SEMMELWEIS
(1818–1865) *medicine's Mr. Clean*

Before Lister (122), before Pasteur (26), there was Semmelweis. He unraveled the mystery of why women died from childbed fever. The disease, with the medical name "puerperal fever," had plagued maternity wards. Mortality rates were astronomically higher among women who had been attended by physicians rather than midwives. Semmelweis deduced that the only difference between the groups was that midwives were barred from performing autopsies of dead women. Horrors! Doctors went from the morgue to the delivery room without cleaning up! Simple solution: *Wash your hands!* Semmelweis required doctors to use a strong lime solution on their hands before delivering babies. The result was near miraculous—mortality rates dropped from 18 percent to 1.27 percent. Nonetheless, Semmelweis's ideas were never accepted until Lister reinforced them, a sorry fate for Semmelweis, who died of a raging infection after cutting his hand during an autopsy.   **14,571**

287 JOHN MARSHALL (1755–1835)
most important American jurist

When death stilled Marshall's brilliant legal mind, the Liberty Bell tolled in mourning. It cracked. Coincidence, maybe; eerily apropos, absolutely. As chief justice, Marshall raised the Supreme Court to an equal third branch of government. When Marshall was appointed by President John Adams (214), the high court's responsibilities were murky. In the landmark *Marbury v. Madison* decision of 1803, the Supreme Court overturned an act of Congress because it was unconstitutional, thus establishing the right of courts to review laws. Marshall, born in a log cabin in Virginia, the eldest of fifteen children, had turned down President Washington's (22) request that he serve as first attorney general. A loyal Federalist, Marshall clashed with presidents during his thirty-four years as chief justice. Most memorably, he incurred Jefferson's (64) wrath when he presided at the treason trial of Jefferson archrival Aaron Burr. Burr was found innocent. **14,562**

288 LEOPOLD VON RANKE (1795–1886)
founder of modern historical method

"My object is simply to find out how things actually occurred," he wrote, a novel goal at a time when antiquarians glossed over truths that clashed with their philosophies. All good historians since then have followed his precept. He used his friendship with Austria's powerful Prince Metternich (179) to gain access to official archives throughout Europe and wrote sixty books packed with what he had learned. Early twentieth-century critics suggested, unfairly, that Ranke was a boring historiographical version of Sergeant Joe Friday, the TV detective who wanted "the facts, ma'am, just the facts." Yet in classics such as *History of the Popes* and *German History in the Time of the Reformation,* Ranke touched on broad themes, not just dates and events. Call it optimism or chutzpah, he started his *Universal History* when he was eighty-six years old and had covered events through the fifteenth century when he died. **14,543**

289 CLARA BARTON (1821–1912)
whirlwind disaster-relief organizer

Barton was called the "Angel of the Battlefield" for her courage and compassion in helping victims of the Civil War, the Franco-Prussian War, and the Spanish-American War. She was the driving force who brought the United States into the International Red Cross in 1881. More important, Barton convinced the International Red Cross to provide relief not just during war but after natural disasters. Privately, this schoolteacher-turned-rescue worker was one of the walking wounded. Emotionally crippled in childhood, Barton waged a lifelong battle against depression. She couldn't stomach criticism and was an imperious boss. All her life she was a formidable presence. In old age she once heard noises in her house at night. She crept downstairs in her nightgown and nightcap, armed with a toy pistol. She discovered a burglar, threw him out, and then returned to bed, tucking the toy pistol under her pillow. **14,519**

290 SUN YAT-SEN (1866–1925)
leader of the Chinese nationalist revolution that overthrew the 250-year Manchu dynasty

A poor farmer's son, Sun was influenced by Western ideas and baptized by an American missionary at age nineteen. He abandoned a medical career to embroil himself in Chinese politics. He wasn't very good at it, failing in all ten attempts at fomenting revolt. But his cause prevailed, aided by financial support he drummed up in Europe, Japan, and the United States, and he became the first leader of the Chinese Republic, proclaimed in 1911. Still, he didn't let affairs of state overwhelm him. In his late forties, married and the father of three, he took a second wife, the daughter of a Bible salesman. After he died, everybody from the Kuomintang he once ran to the Chinese Communist Party, and even the Japanese occupiers of World War II, claimed his mantle. **14,493**

291 JOHANNES FIBIGER (1867–1928)
pioneer cancer researcher

If you asked Fibiger, he would have said his work to eradicate diphtheria earned him a place in our book. Wrong! It was good stuff, but Fibiger makes the grade as the man who made cancer a scientific research priority. Before him, cancer was such an unknown that the medical world was afraid to fiddle with it. This Danish physician who had developed a serum against diphtheria pursued an educated hunch that chemicals and environmental factors could trigger cancer. He trapped more than a thousand wild rats and used a toxin to induce tumors in their stomachs. Today we know that his research lacked scientific controls and that he jumped to unproven conclusions. But that's immaterial. Fibiger's research and Nobel Prize in 1926 signaled to researchers that cancer was an important unexplored field. We've begun to tame cancer today because he dared to study it at all. **14,477**

292 WILLIAM BLACKSTONE (1723–1780)
teacher of the law

In 1768, when he fought to keep a troublemaker named John Wilkes from taking a seat in the House of Commons, Blackstone the politician was trumped by Blackstone the scholar. Wilkes's claim was supported by Blackstone's own four-volume *Commentaries on the Laws of England,* and that settled the argument for the parliamentarians. The commentaries were history's most influential one-man synthesis of the inchoate corpus of common law. One of his admiring students at Oxford was young John Adams (214), the U.S. president-to-be. Abraham Lincoln (32) wrote of his first encounter with Blackstone's books at age twenty-six, "Never in my whole life was my mind so thoroughly absorbed." The bad side of Blackstone was his knee-jerk traditionalism; to liberal philosopher Jeremy Bentham (383), Blackstone was a reactionary boob who failed to understand that the law evolves. His poetry was bad, too. A sample couplet: "There in a winding, close retreat / Is Justice doom'd to fix her seat." **14,444**

293 JAMES NAISMITH (1861–1939)
inventor of basketball

What has ten legs, rises nearly thirty-five feet, and clears big bucks in product endorsements? Your average pro basketball team. Naismith developed the game these swift giants play, but he couldn't have dreamed it would reach such heights. In 1891 Naismith was a gym teacher in Springfield, Massachusetts, under orders from the department head to create a fun yet safe game for students to play indoors during snowy winters. He rose to the challenge, mixing elements of soccer, football, field hockey, and other outdoor sports. The result: basketball, pretty much as we know it today—only then, you had to dunk a soccer ball in a peach basket. **14,419**

294 JEAN-BAPTISTE COLBERT (1619–1683)
architect of French economic grandeur

Finance minister and navy chief under Louis XIV (63), Colbert pushed France into the industrial age and made it Europe's dominant power. A ferocious worker, he instituted administrative and tax reforms, subsidized domestic industry, and built roads and canals. So bent was he on the nation's economic revival that he complained that too many promising young men were taking holy orders instead of going into business. Colbert started the company St. Gobain—still going strong—to produce mirrors so his compatriots wouldn't waste their money on Italian imports. In 1670 he ordered the planting of acorns in central France to provide timber for the navy for the next two hundred years. Three centuries later the hundred-foot-tall oaks of the forest of Troncais stand as a tribute to his farsightedness. **14,412**

295 MI FEI (1051–1107)
premier Chinese artist

Chinese artists ignored perspective, preferred watercolors to oil paints, never learned to draw the human body, and relied heavily on cultural symbolism, which is lost to the untrained eye. Mi Fei was no exception. He was a Chinese bureaucrat whose big mouth annoyed his bosses so much that he was bounced from department to department. For relaxation he painted sparse landscapes—a few mountains in the background, some pine trees in the foreground, and a simple hut at eye level—in a century when Chinese artists crammed as much as they could into pictures. Although he fell into disfavor with the ruling emperor, centuries of artists vindicated him by copying his style, the highest compliment the Chinese bestow on an old master. **14,397**

296 Franz Joseph Haydn (1732–1809)
symphony stylist

Austria, 1809: Napoleon's (16) advancing armies occupied Vienna, home to famed composer Haydn. Even the emperor was awed by the musical genius who had composed 104 symphonies, establishing the symphony's basic form. "Papa Haydn" also crafted choral works, including *The Creation,* and more than eighty string quartets and fifty sonatas. As the great man lay dying, Napoleon ordered an honor guard stationed outside. Seventy years earlier, Haydn had arrived in the city as a peasant boy to sing in the choir. He'd gotten excellent musical training—until his voice changed. Eventually he became music director for Prince Esterházy and spent twenty-five years in his employ. Haydn adored Vienna but welcomed the writing respite of summers in the countryside with the prince's entourage. "There was no one to confuse and torment me," he explained, "and so I was obliged to become original." **14,358**

297 John Keats (1795–1821)
British romantic poet

From his blazing but too brief life, Keats bequeathed us a wealth of poems rich in imagery, melody and exquisite language. A sample, from his long poem *Endymion:*

A thing of beauty is a joy for ever:
Its loveliness increases; it will never
Pass into nothingness; but still will keep
A bower quiet for us, and a sleep
Full of sweet dreams, and health, and quiet breathing.

Tuberculosis killed Keats's mother and younger brother and claimed Keats, too. He died in agony in Rome, where he had gone to seek a cure. Thanks to Lord Byron (385), the belief arose that Keats's death was hastened by scathing reviews of *Endymion.* Not really. Keats had weathered the lashings of sniveling critics with calm resolve. He once wrote, "I think I shall be among the English Poets after my death." He was right. **14,353**

298 John II of Portugal (1455–1495)
early imperialist

King John is probably best remembered as the man who turned Columbus (2) down eight years before the navigator's 1492 voyage. He made up for that lapse, however, by sending expeditions down the coast of Western Africa to build forts and trade in gold, slaves, spices, and ivory. Obsessed with the European quest for Prester John, a mythical Christian potentate who reigned somewhere in "the Indies," he also sent exploratory voyages eastward. Prester John, who supposedly held banquets for thirty thousand knights at an enormous table made of emeralds, was viewed as Europe's natural ally against Islam. King John never found Prester John, but he did reach an agreement with Spain in 1494 to divide up the New World. At home he was known as the "Perfect Prince" for beheading a couple of dukes to reassert royal power *à la* Machiavelli. **14,350**

299 Giambattista Vico (1668–1744)
first modern historian

Vico wrote and rewrote his ideas and then published them in a tome with a rambling twenty-four-word title. We dug up a few clichés to express his ideas more succinctly: what goes around, comes around; history repeats itself; or as Yogi Berra put it so elegantly, it's déjà vu all over again. Vico fell off a ladder at age seven and injured his head so severely that doctors predicted he would die or be an idiot. Not so. After his recovery, he studied law. Vico's masterpiece (the short title is *The New Science*) described how man rises from bestial behavior, only to lapse again. His cyclical stages of history were the ages of gods, heroes, and finally men. Vico warned that despite the cycles of history, the changing nature of man prevents any kind of accurate prophecies. Oh well, *veni, vidi, vico.*   **14,345**

300 Franz Liszt (1811–1886)
musical Don Juan

He was a pale, sad-eyed, long-haired Hungarian-born French pianist whose dazzling public performances of works like his own *Liebestraum* helped make serious music an art form for mass consumption. And he invented the musical groupie. "It was impossible to count the ravishing celestial women who came to fall trembling, like poor little larks, at the feet of the terrible enchanter," a contemporary wrote. A teenage Russian lover spurned by the sixty-year-old Liszt was so distraught, she threatened to shoot him. Normally, though, he had long-term relationships like the ten-year affair with novelist Marie d'Agoult, who bore him three children. Their daughter, Cosima, married Richard Wagner (165), who was influenced by Liszt's orchestral styles in such pieces as *Les Preludes.* Today modern piano students learn techniques handed down by the pupils who flocked to the aging Liszt's studio.   **14,308**

As we stacked up the movers and shakers of the millennium against one another, we could almost hear apoplectic readers rising in protest and screaming: "You're nuts!"

Take the next batch. How on earth, Elvis fans will moan, could we have rated those Liverpool mopheads ahead of the King? In truth, it was a close call. The first vote was 2–2, but then a Presley supporter weakened and the lone holdout conceded defeat. Our collective conclusion: Both the British crooners and the American hip-swiveler exerted enormous influence on popular music and popular culture, but the Beatles wrote most of their own music and sold more records.

Even so, one of us still believes that decision is all wet. And all of us bridle at some of the choices forced upon us by the other three. So we can imagine how much grumbling our rankings will provoke in readers. Scan the next thirty-odd pages, and you'll no doubt make your own list of dopey verdicts. Here is a sampling of seeming incongruities, and our reasons for them.

• What?!? Barthélemy Thimonnier, inventor of the sewing machine, gets more points than Samuel Morse, father of the telegraph? Yes, because Morse was but one of many minds who contributed to the evolution of the telegraph— he hit upon the idea while listening to an account of another scientist's experiments—whereas Thimonnier, a simple Parisian tailor, made his breakthrough pretty much on his own.

• What?!? Horace Mann—what did he do again?—trounces Babe Ruth, the greatest athlete in the history of the universe? Is that possible? Yes, because while Ruth scores high on charisma, Mann's championing of public schools makes his influence on American society incalculable.

• What?!? Two more popes? Do we really need all these popes? Yes. John XXIII turned the Catholic world on its head with his modernization program, while Gregory VII was a beacon of reform in the medieval church.

We can reason all we want; nobody is going to agree with us 100 percent of the time. And so we make this bold and unequivocal declaration: We stand by every one of our choices, except the really dumb ones. And you know which ones those are.

301 ÉDOUARD MANET (1832–1883)
rebel with a palette

Frenchman Manet painted light-filled gardens, sunny seascapes, and alluring women. His groundbreaking style, using contemporary subjects and working in broad flat splashes of color, encouraged the Impressionists to break conventions, too. But it was his daring nudes that electrified the public and generated widespread scorn. Consider the large canvas, *Luncheon on the Grass,* and its naked female models picnicking in the woods with two clothed male artists. Or *Olympia,* the cream-skinned whore lounging on a divan, her eyes coolly appraising. *Olympia* so inflamed people in 1865 that it had to be hung high to avoid umbrella attacks. "Insults rain down on me like hailstones," Manet moaned to poet-friend Baudelaire (633). Only after his death, in a memorial exhibition in Paris, did sentiments soften. In 1907 then–Prime Minister Clemenceau (711) had *Olympia* brought down from her perch and transferred to the Louvre. **14,300**

302 FRANÇOIS RABELAIS (1483–1553)
French humanist and comic genius

The defrocked monk jested that he wrote *Gargantua and Pantagruel,* his masterpiece about a giant and his son, "whilst I was eating and drinking." His opening line was, "Most noble and illustrious drinkers, and you thrice precious pockified blades." After denouncing the "sneaking jobbernol" who condemned Homer for spilling wine on his verses, Rabelais added, "A certain addle-headed coxcomb saith the same of my books, but a turd for him." Does that give you a flavor of his humor? Yet, saith French writer Anatole France, his real thirst was not for wine but to "drink knowledge; drink truth; drink love." The human comedy fascinated him. He poked fun at the pedagogic and parodied the

powerful. Czech writer Milan Kundera said that through Rabelais, "the art of the novel came into the world as the echo of God's laughter." The laughter echoes through Voltaire (36), Honoré de Balzac (254), Jonathan Swift (492), and Anthony Trollope. **14,281**

303 GIROLAMO SAVONAROLA (1452–1498)
fanatical reformer

Some historians say the Dominican friar who was dictator of Florence for four years was a throwback to the Dark Ages. We agree with others who say Savonarola was the prototypical modern politician who is swept to power on a wave of popular support and then becomes a power-mad dictator. Like some hectoring ayatollah, Savonarola preached so eloquently against the licentiousness of Florence's oligarchy that ruler Piero de' Medici was forced to flee and Savonarola took over. At first the people adored their priestly autocrat. When Savonarola built a pyre of decadent art, Sandro Botticelli (331) gladly contributed his own sensuous paintings to the flames. But the Florentines grew tired of Savonarola's bombast. So did Pope Alexander VI, a fun-loving man with six sons. When Savonarola warned the pontiff to prepare for a trip to hell, Alexander had his Florentine allies torture and burn Savonarola and throw his ashes in the Arno River. **14,271**

304 HELEN KELLER (1880–1968)
human miracle

Blind, deaf, and mute, Keller likened her early childhood to "a phantom living in a no-world." Then when she was six, Anne Sullivan, the woman she would call Teacher, arrived. The two battled for weeks, but persistent Sullivan won. The breakthrough came as water splashed Keller, and Sullivan spelled the word *water* in Keller's hand in sign language. Knowledge lit

Keller's face, and she spelled the word back. It opened the floodgates to Keller's brilliant mind. With Sullivan tirelessly spelling out lectures in Keller's hand, she was able to attend Radcliffe College and graduate cum laude. This remarkable woman devoted her life to aiding the deaf and blind, traveling the world to raise money for the cause, and impressing all she met. On her seventy-fifth birthday she said, "My birthday can never mean as much to me as the arrival of Anne Sullivan. . . . That was my soul's birthday." **14,270**

305 IDA B. WELLS-BARNETT (1862–1931)
crusader for justice

Wells-Barnett could have remained an obscure schoolteacher stomaching injustices against blacks in the South. But not Ida Bell. Ousted from a whites-only train car in 1895, she sued the railroad, winning in circuit court but losing in Tennessee's Supreme Court. When she decried inadequate schooling for black children, she was sacked from her teaching job. And when three friends were hanged by a white mob in 1892, she launched a national crusade against lynching through her writings in the newspaper *Memphis Free Speech,* of which she was half-owner. "I felt that one had better die fighting against injustice than to die like a dog or a rat in a trap," she later wrote. She helped found the National Association of Colored Women and the National Association for the Advancement of Colored People. **14,212**

306 THOMAS MALTHUS (1766–1834)
population doomsayer

Malthus, an English economist who wore his hair in ringlets and powdered them pink, worried that the poor were having too many babies. Sound familiar? "A half-starved Highland woman frequently bears more than 20 children, while a pampered fine lady is often incapable of bearing

any," he fretted. He urged people to marry late and employ the "vice" of contraception. Though his methodology was questionable (he used American data supplied by Benjamin Franklin (54) but forgot to ask if they included immigrants), Malthus talked Prime Minister Pitt into dropping his support for poor relief. To his credit, he deflated the faith in human progress of utopian thinkers like his father's friend, Jean-Jacques Rousseau (19). Malthus also influenced Darwin's (7) thinking and helped instigate the population control movement. He had three children, 0.9 above the zero-population-growth replacement level. **14,202**

307 PIERRE BEAUCHAMP (1636–1705)
choreographer of ballet's basics

Ballet students know the five fundamental positions that dictate most classical ballet movements. These range from the first, in which the feet, pointing out, form a straight line, to the fifth, in which the feet are parallel and facing opposite directions. It's the fifth that does most of us dancer-wannabes in. Some historians credit the creation of these positions to Beauchamp, but others say he was merely the first one to write them all down. No matter. His work promoted ballet as a discipline that could be studied and learned. Born in Versailles, France, Beauchamp was from a family of troupers. He served as the superintendent of ballets of the king and had an impressive career as a dancer himself. He makes our book not for his performance but for codifying the art of ballet. **14,176**

308 ELISHA OTIS (1811–1861)
uplifting inventor

A prehistoric human trying to hoist something up a tree invented the elevator by throwing a rope over a limb. Otis invented a way to avoid disaster if the rope broke. He built the first elevator with an automatic safety brake—a steel spring meshing with a ratchet—and unveiled it at the 1854 Crystal Palace Exposition in New York. Otis, standing on the platform halfway up a shaft, had an assistant cut the hoisting cable, and the brake held. After that, buildings could be as tall as architects could design them, which makes Otis a towering figure in the history of skyscrapers. He was a Vermont farm boy turned mechanic who perfected his elevators in the service of a Yonkers, New York, bedstead company that needed to lift heavy machinery to the upper floors of a factory. In 1857 he constructed a passenger lift, and the name Otis has been associated with elevators ever since. **14,151**

309 FERDINAND RITTER VON MANNLICHER (1848–1904)
inventor of the cartridge clip

Only a blip in the million-year history of warfare technology, Mannlicher nevertheless played a key role in creating the repeating rifle and thus holds indirect responsibility for millions of battlefield deaths. For us, he symbolizes man's ageless impulse to improve upon the means of mass slaughter, from the prehistoric putterer who tipped his stone spear with bronze to the makers of the nuclear bomb. Mannlicher epitomizes the nerdy side of warcraft, the tinkerer entranced with technological advance, as opposed to the general who commands or the soldier who fights. We could have chosen any number of Industrial Revolution innovators for this spot, like William Armstrong, the British solicitor who designed the modern rifle with its "fine spiral grooves" (as one enthusiast called them) to assure a spinning projectile. But Mannlicher, an Austrian railroad engineer who created 150 types of repeating guns and automatic rifles, will do. **14,142**

310 RAM SINGH (1816–1885)
Sikh advocate of ousting the British from India

Many Americans learn about British rule in India by watching Cary Grant (952) in the film *Gunga Din* or Shirley Temple's *The Little Colonel.* The truth of Britain's domination of India was much harsher than anything Hollywood dished up. Singh was moved to action. He served in the Sikh army, then organized a group called the Kukas. They wore white robes and turbans, chanted prayers in a special way, and followed secret rituals. Because these men were poor and from low castes, they had unquestionably accepted British domination until Singh came along. When an all-out revolt appeared inevitable, the British tied Kukas to cannons and blew them to pieces. Singh advocated civil disobedience and boycott of British goods. The British threw Singh in prison and then exiled him until his death. **14,138**

311 THOMAS PAINE (1737–1809)
writer with a Common Sense message

Englishman Paine's life changed upon meeting fellow lover of liberty, Benjamin Franklin (54), in London in 1774. Franklin gave Paine a letter of introduction for the colonies. There the political philosopher wrote his famous fifty-page pamphlet *Common Sense,* which galvanized public opinion in favor of independence. The pamphlet sold a half million copies in three months and paved the way for the Declaration of Independence. During the ensuing war Paine reminded the suffering, half-starved troops of their higher mission in *The American Crisis.* "These are the times that try men's souls," he wrote. "Tyranny, like hell, is not easily conquered; yet we have this consolation with us, that the harder the conflict, the more glorious the triumph." Paine's other immortal work was *The*

Rights of Man, written in 1791. In it he defended the French Revolution and condemned monarchies. It inflamed British leaders, who had Paine charged with treason and tried in absentia. **14,101**

312 DAVID BEN-GURION (1886–1973)
founder of Israel

When Ben-Gurion was growing up in Poland, Jews were so passive that whenever a pogrom destroyed their villages and killed their families, they did not resist. Ben-Gurion, who grew up among Zionists, urged comrades to fight in self-defense, but always he dreamed of a Jewish state. Born David Gruen, he changed his name to honor an ancient Jewish hero who defended Jerusalem from the Romans. After relocating to Jerusalem in 1910, Ben-Gurion lobbied for a Jewish state. Decades of struggle and negotiation followed, culminating in Ben-Gurion's announcement of Israel's formation in a radio address on May 14, 1948, the day the British pulled out of the region. The next day, five Arab countries attacked the infant nation. With Ben-Gurion as prime minister, Israel weathered the hostilities. Jews affirmed they were no longer passive victims, and the Israeli army became known as one of the best, and most dreaded, in the world. **14,087**

313 IBN TAYMIYAH (TAQI AD-DIN)
(1263–1328) *Islam's keeper of the fundamentalist flame*

Ibn Taymiyah's philosophy can be summed up in the title of his essay, *The Steps Leading to the Knowledge That the Messenger of God Has Already Made a Clear Exposition of the Roots and Branches of Religion.* Medieval Islam was buffeted by revolutionary tendencies, and a sense of permissiveness about doctrine began to take root. Ibn Taymiyah espoused a philosophy that put on the brakes and called for strict adherence to the literal word of the Koran and a commitment to community institutions, particularly the state. Every future Islamic thinker who rejected over-intellectualism—and there have been many, down to Iran's Ayatollah Khomeini—is a philosophical descendant of Ibn Taymiyah, though he was never a fanatic. He spent time in jail for his beliefs, but to Ibn Taymiyah, "only someone who has shut out God from his heart is a prisoner." **14,083**

314 JONAS SALK (1914–1995)
physician who crippled polio

When Dr. Salk injected dead poliomyelitis virus into monkeys and caused antibodies to form, the scourge of this paralyzing disease was about to be over. Epidemics in the United States had afflicted 27,000 people in 1916, 25,000 in 1946, 58,000 in 1952, and 35,000 in 1953. By 1957, with Salk's vaccine in use, cases dropped to 5,000. Salk developed the vaccine at the University of Pittsburgh School of Medicine. His breakthrough: creating a tissue culture lab that produced quantities of vaccine like never before. Almost two million children were guinea pigs in the largest field trial ever. Rival Albert Sabin, who later produced his own live virus vaccine (the one that is now in wide use), criticized the process as rushed and questioned the Salk vaccine's safety. But it was proven effective and released in 1955, making Salk an international hero. Asked who owned the patent on the vaccine, Salk replied, "There is no patent. Could you patent the sun?" **14,044**

315 WILLIAM BLAKE (1757–1827)
mystic poet

It is for the lyrical magic of his verse (illustrated by his own engravings) and for his influence on English romanticism that we rate Blake so high. Think of his powerful imagery: "Tyger! Tyger! burning bright / in the forests of the night." A. E.

Housman pronounced him "more poetical than Shakespeare." We are almost as entranced by his otherworldly visions as by his verbal inventiveness. He saw God's head in a window at the age of four. The biblical Lot sat for a portrait in his studio. Just before he died, a witness reported, "he burst out singing of the things he saw in Heaven." Was he mad? Endowed with "eidetic vision," the ability to project mental images into the physical world? Enraptured of the Holy Spirit? It doesn't matter; Blake was filled with such a furious and joyful imagination, you just gotta love him!   **14,039**

316 BARTHÉLEMY THIMONNIER (1793–1859)
inventor of the sewing machine

In the American schoolchild's litany of great inventors, Elias Howe has this category sewn up, but that is just another example of American cultural imperialism. Thimonnier, a Parisian tailor, constructed the first crude mechanical sewing machine and secured patents in 1830, sixteen years before Howe. His wooden device required skilled operators to feed fabric manually to make even stitches. Sadly for Thimonnier, he never publicized how crucial seamstresses would be to the operation. After he constructed eighty machines to fill a contract for army uniforms, a gang of seamstresses and tailors, fearful that they would be displaced by new technology, broke into the workshop. They pummeled Thimonnier and destroyed his machines. While Thimonnier continued to improve his designs in France, Howe and Isaac Singer took their patent battle to court. Howe won the money, but Singer's name has been associated with sewing machines ever since.   **14,022**

317 HORACE MANN (1796–1859)
public education's champion

Public schools, or common schools back then, failed Mann miserably. A poor boy in Franklin, Massachusetts, he went to common school but left because the teachers were inept. He educated himself at the local library, attended Brown University, and graduated valedictorian. With a law degree he entered politics, later heading the Massachusetts Board of Education. Public schools then were offering the bare minimum, and people didn't expect more. Mann changed their thinking by railing against unqualified teachers, shoddy management, and short school terms. He believed a republic's survival depended on informed citizens and that this necessitated free universal education. Deeply religious, Mann nevertheless insisted that religion be purged from state-supported schools. Weeks before his death, he advised Antioch College graduates to "be ashamed to die until you have won some victory for humanity." His victory: starting the movement that produced the most extensive public school system in history.   **13,994**

318 WALT WHITMAN (1819–1892)
America's poet

Nineteenth-century America was a place where poets glorified daffodils or turned to England for romanticized iambic guidance—that is, until our man Walt arrived on the scene. Whitman was an unknown and a bit of a ne'er-do-well journalist when he sent his *Leaves of Grass* to Transcendentalist high priest Ralph Waldo Emerson (504). Emerson loved it: "I find it the most extraordinary piece of wit and wisdom that America has yet contributed." Whitman dipped into his own pockets to publish it, then spent his life rewriting and promoting it. He even wrote a favorable review—anonymously, of course. It's a shame so many Americans remember Whitman for his schmaltzy eulogy to the fallen Abraham Lincoln (32), "O Captain! My Captain!" That's Whitman at his rhyming best, but it's his audacious use of free verse and celebration of common people in a democracy that earns Whitman a place in our hearts (and our book!). **13,976**

319 DONATELLO (c.1386–1466)
innovative Renaissance sculptor

Born Donato di Niccolo de Betto di Bardi in Florence, Donatello came of age in the art world by helping create bronze doors on the city baptistery. He switched to marble and wood to create his most memorable sculptures. Generally considered one of the four greatest artists of the Italian Renaissance—along with Michelangelo (13), Leonardo (9), and Raphael (129)—Donatello worked closely with the architect Brunelleschi (85). When Donatello sculpted a slumped, weakened Christ on the crucifix, Brunelleschi criticized its realism. Legend holds that Donatello had such a hair-trigger temper that he once hurled a bronze head out a window when a client protested that he was being overcharged. Genius, however, has its privileges. Donatello, who developed techniques to enhance depth in sculpting, is also hailed today as one of the greatest artists who ever lived and a developer of perspective in sculpture. **13,954**

320 JOHN HAWKINS (1532–1595)
sea dog of the slave trade

A picture of a chained African adorned Hawkins's coat of arms in recognition of his daring early voyages. The English raider swooped down on Portuguese slavers, who had started the evil trade, stole their cargo, and sold the slaves in the Spanish West Indies. Those who refused to buy risked having their villages sacked by Hawkins's crews. So began the English slave trade that flourished for more than two centuries. In the 1580s Hawkins was treasurer of the navy, and though suspected of graft, he outfitted

the fleet so well, it defeated the Spanish Armada in 1588. That gives Hawkins a niche in some histories as founder of the modern British navy. He blamed God for his failure to capture the Spanish treasure fleet in 1590, prompting a disappointed Queen Elizabeth (31) to swear, "This fool went out a soldier, and has come home a divine." **13,953**

321 GIOVANNI BOCCACCIO (1313–1375)
curtain raiser on the Renaissance

The *Decameron,* completed by the Italian in 1353, was the first great comedic book of the millennium, though its backdrop is far from funny. In Florence ten people who are in quarantine together during a plague each tell ten stories about love, sex, religion, and politics—stories full of mistaken identities, ribaldry, and satire that skewers just about everything and everybody. In one story a pious Jew refuses to convert to Christianity until he visits Rome and is dazzled by lustful, slothful, and gluttonous priests. Biographer Thomas Bergrin called Boccaccio's masterpiece "skeptical, affable, and all but dangerously open-minded," qualities that demonstrated the new spirit of irreverence that was soon to flower in the Renaissance. Boccaccio would not be politically correct today. He was fat, and one of his other books was a venomously misogynist tome, *The Corbaccio.* **13,922**

322 LOUIS ARMSTRONG (1900–1971)
Mr. Jazz

Known as Satchmo, short for "Satchel Mouth," Armstrong grew up in New Orleans, where jazz was born. He played cornet in marching bands and on Mississippi riverboats until his career took off in 1922, with a stint with King Oliver's band in Chicago. Armstrong's wild and dramatic trumpet-playing set jazz on fire. He launched the instrumental solo in jazz performances and later, with ensemble recordings, established himself as a jazz virtuoso. He's also credited with creating "scat," the stringing together of meaningless syllables using the voice like an instrument. People kept asking him when he was going to quit, Armstrong said at age sixty-one. "I tell them, musicians don't quit; they just stop when there ain't no more gigs." His gigs ended a decade later—but not his influence. "Without him," said trumpeter Clark Terry, "we wouldn't have had anything to follow." **13,901**

323 MARGARET FULLER (1810–1850)
rebel against women's dismal status

Mary Wollstonecraft (45) had been dead nearly fifty years and no one was talking about suffrage or equality when Fuller's *Woman in the Nineteenth Century* revived interest in women's rights. Published in 1845, the book boldly decried women's lowly economic, social, and political status. A protégée of Ralph Waldo Emerson (504), Fuller was among the early female newspaper writers. Horace Greeley hired her as New York's first literary critic. So biting was her commentary that competitor Edgar Allan Poe (279) lamented the world had three types of people: "Men, women, and Margaret Fuller." Hers is a tragic story. On a fateful European trip, she met up with an Italian revolutionary and gave birth to an illegitimate son. The priggish Greeley fired her. Fuller was forced to return to America with her lover, child, and a book-length manuscript, but the boat sank in a storm off Fire Island, New York. Everyone perished. **13,877**

324 HUNG HSIU-CH'ÜAN (1814–1864)
delusional destroyer

This self-proclaimed younger brother of Christ parlayed his messianic complex into a religious movement that almost toppled the Manchu dynasty and culminated in the deaths of twenty million people. It was one of the oddest and saddest episodes in history. Hung had a nervous breakdown at twenty-three after failing a civil service exam for the third time, then fell into a delirium in which two men urged him to purge the world of devils. Years later, skimming through a Christian tract, he concluded that the figures were God and Christ—and he was God's second son. In America today the guy would be ranting on a street corner. But in China in 1850 he found a receptive audience in the impoverished masses, raised an army, captured Nanking, declared a Heavenly Kingdom, ordered his top generals assassinated, locked himself in his palace with eighty-eight concubines, and committed suicide as government troops moved in. **13,844**

325 DOMINGO FAUSTINO SARMIENTO
(1811–1888) *beacon of freedom to Latin America*

Sarmiento's 1845 essay, "Culture and Barbarism," should be required reading. It is a beautifully written plea to Latin Americans to shed the thuggishness and strongman politics spawned by the culture of the plains-riding gauchos and to adopt European manners and the gung-ho spirit of the United States. After traveling widely in North America, Sarmiento returned home and led efforts to bring modern education to his country. Turning to politics, he helped lead the forces that in 1852 overthrew Argentina's prototypical dictator, Juan Manuel de Rosas. Sarmiento had a chance to put his teachings into practice; he was president of Argentina from 1868 to 1874. Democracy has been short lived in many South American countries, but Sarmiento's life and work are an inspiration to all people who love freedom and reason. **13,842**

326 HENRY BESSEMER (1813–1898)
metallurgy master

Briton Bessemer helped usher in the Age of Steel by inventing a converter that produced steel at lower costs. American William Kelly first realized malleable iron could be produced by blasting pig iron with oxygen. Bessemer stumbled upon the same chemical change eight years later. "All this was a revelation to me," he said, "as I had in no way anticipated such violent results." But Bessemer gets kudos for designing machinery to mass-produce steel: a brick-lined cylinder that stayed upright during the heating process, then was tipped on its side to load hot pig iron or pour molten steel. The Bessemer converter produced twenty tons of steel in twenty minutes. Soon the new railway industry was replacing wrought-iron rails with cheaper and sturdier steel rails. To honor Bessemer's contribution, at least six steelmaking towns and counties in America were named after him.   **13,819**

327 PAUL MCCARTNEY (b. 1942)
singer/songwriter and bassist for the Beatles

Imagine our dilemma if Beethoven (10) had been born in 1942. Sure he's important, but how can we gauge lasting influence? With his fellow Englishman John Lennon (328), McCartney wrote and performed for the most influential band in the twentieth century, but rock 'n' roll is a mere blip on the timeline of the last thousand years. Will citizens of the world in the year 2100 sing a tune like "Yesterday" the way we hum Beethoven's Fifth? We're betting they will. McCartney's first instrument was a trumpet, but he traded it in because he couldn't sing and play at the same time. Then he restrung his guitar to play left-handed. The mop-topped "Fab Four" revived rock 'n' roll, pioneered music videos, and starred in full-length movies. By the time the

Beatles split up in 1970, their records had outsold every other performer in history. When they write the book for the third millennium, the Beatles might just roll over Beethoven.   **13,808**

328 JOHN LENNON (1940–1980)
founder and songwriter for the Beatles

Beatlemania ruled. Girls fainted in hysteria. Crowds surged. The Beatles filled football stadiums. The year was 1966, and Lennon, the first Beatle, observed that his group was now "more popular than Jesus." Always the heretic and most political member of the Beatles, Lennon generated storms of criticism from religious zealots, the political right, and parents who didn't want their children influenced by these demons. Time has quelled the maelstrom. Today the Beatles have multigenerational appeal. Lennon was still in high school in Liverpool, England, when he organized The Quarry Men in 1957. Lennon, Paul McCartney (327), George Harrison, and Ringo Starr topped the record charts with such early songs as "Love Me Do," "She Loves You," and "I Wanna Hold Your Hand." After the Beatles' breakup in 1970, Lennon recorded with his poet wife, Yoko Ono, but was silenced too soon by a gunman in New York.   **13,796**

329 SAMUEL MORSE (1791–1872)
inventor of the first practical telegraph

Sailing home to America from Europe in 1832, Morse overheard an amateur scientist's remark that the flow of electricity is unhindered by the length of the wire. "If this be so," he recalled responding, "I see no reason why intelligence might not be instantaneously transmitted by electricity to any distance." So he set out to make a telegraph. When he demonstrated a primitive model in his

Manhattan apartment in 1835, a friend derided it as a "mantel ornament." Morse persisted and in 1844 built the first American telegraph line, from Baltimore to Washington. Using his Morse code of dots and dashes, he sent his famous message: "What hath God wrought?" By century's end telegraph wires crisscrossed the globe. It was the biggest advance in the speed of communications since the horse. Morse was also an accomplished painter, whose *Gallery of the Louvre* fetched $3.2 million in 1982, the most ever paid for an American work of art at the time.   **13,788**

330 ALEKSANDR PUSHKIN (1799–1837)
Russia's national poet

The French-loving Russians believed that their language was too barbaric for literature. Pushkin proved them wrong with romantic poems, short stories, essays, and a novel, *Eugene Onegin,* his chef d'oeuvre, or should we say шедéвр. This verse tale of love and redemption proved that Russian writers could create beauty without using another country's voice. English scholar A.D.P. Briggs wrote, "Anyone who takes the trouble to learn Russian in order to read Pushkin will never regret it." Pushkin's paternal great-grandfather was a black African who was ennobled after serving Peter the Great (27), and like other spirited Russian blades, young Pushkin was a gambler, girl-chaser, and sometime soldier. He also had liberal leanings, which disturbed czarist censors from time to time. But he died like an aristocrat, shot in a duel with a French diplomat he had accused of seducing Mrs. Pushkin.   **13,754**

331 SANDRO BOTTICELLI (1445–1510)
Florentine Renaissance master of color and rhythmic line

Sandro inherited the name Botticelli from older brother Giovanni, whose nickname was "little barrel." After an apprenticeship with Filippo Lippi, he became the favored painter of the all-powerful Medici family. Botticelli's masterpieces, *The Birth of Venus* and *Primavera,* show his love of classical myth and idealistic portrayals of beauty and grace. At the height of his career, Dominican priest Savonarola (303) came to town, preaching a more puritanical religion. Botticelli listened, and his paintings changed. In *The Calumny of Apelles,* his lines became sharper, his themes more tortured. He withdrew from the artistic community and plunged into his long-held mission of illustrating Dante's (30) *Divine Comedy.* The world soon forgot him and warmed to Leonardo (9), Raphael (129), and Michelangelo (13). It took over three centuries before Botticelli's genius was rediscovered by some English intellectuals. Did fate decree that one of them would be *Dante* Gabriel Rossetti?   **13,751**

332 KUBLAI KHAN (1215–1294)
Mongol ruler of the empire's apex

The only reason history has recorded so much about the Great Khan is that he provided safe passage to China for two Venetian merchants and one of their sons, the famed Marco Polo (66). Young Marco's diary of his adventure illuminates life in the Mongol empire. So appealing was Kublai's story that writer Samuel Taylor Coleridge (394) immortalized the ruler's palatial summer home in every schoolchild's nightmare poem, "Kubla Khan." Kublai, grandson of notorious bad boy Genghis Khan (43), built one of the biggest empires in history, encompassing eighty percent of Eurasia and unifying China under one ruler. Before amassing his territories, however, Kublai fought a civil war against his younger brother for the title of Great Khan. Then he led his armies through China and proclaimed himself heir to that country's Dragon Throne. His troops conquered Burma and Indochina, but typhoons thwarted attacks on Japan. **13,708**

333 CHRISTIAAN HUYGENS (1629–1695)
scientific light

The Dutch Huygens is best known for his wave theory of how light travels. We don't wish to get too Freudian, but . . . he also discovered the pendulum, with its *steady, rhythmic motion;* was the first to propose that Earth is an *oblate spheroid;* did pioneering work on *rotating bodies* and mathematical *curves;* developed a new method of *grinding* lenses for telescopes; and discovered the rings that *caress* Saturn. The guy was obsessed! Huygens was also a contender with Pascal for the title of father of probability theory, and he came up with early calculations for winning or losing at games of chance, like his third proposition: "To have p chances to win a and q chances to win b, the chances being equivalent, is worth $(pa + qb)/(p + q)$ to me." **13,701**

334 ANDRÉS BELLO (1781–1865)
South American statesman and intellectual

The Venezuelan-born Bello roamed Europe with his pupil, Simón Bolívar (48), the future liberator of much of South America, to rally support for his continent's independence. Even revolutionaries must eat, so Bello took a job sorting files for the liberal English philosopher Jeremy Bentham (383). Bello read what he sorted. In 1829 he went to Chile and helped its revolutionary government write a constitution based on Bentham's liberal principles. Bello authored a civil code that other countries copied and that is still in effect throughout much of South America. He founded the University of Santiago. As a literary figure, Bello was anything but revolutionary, a

rare classical poet among Byron-bedazzled romantics. After three hundred years of evil colonialism, many writers of Spanish-speaking America were prepared to denounce everything that had emanated from the former mother country. But Bello taught South Americans to love what was good in Spain's culture. **13,699**

335 JAN VAN EYCK (1390–1441)
maestro of oil painting

Van Eyck, the founder of the Flemish school of painting, was first to master the new technique of oil painting. His works glow from within, the pleasing products of countless coatings. Using an oak panel, he'd first spread thin layers of chalk and animal glue to smooth out the wooden surface and reflect light. Painstakingly he'd add colors diluted with turpentine. So precise was he—and so attuned to the smallest detail—that we can see silvery hairs on his figures' legs, the result of Van Eyck's scraping the surface with a pointed tool to expose the white layers below. His greatest work, *Adoration of the Sacred Lamb,* was so esteemed, it figured in the Treaty of Versailles. A clause required the Germans to return the masterpiece to Belgium before peace officially could be declared after World War I. **13,654**

336 LISE MEITNER (1878–1968)
mother of nuclear fission

Meitner's description of the splitting of a uranium atom put her on the cutting edge of nuclear physics, but she refused to help build the nuclear bomb. In her heart she hoped that that kind of destruction would not be achievable. As a woman in a man's world, Meitner faced the predictable uphill battle: her parents insisted she take a teacher's exam so she could support herself; her first lecture in 1922 on cosmic physics was reported in a newspaper as "cosmetic physics." She worked with such scientific luminaries as Max Planck (136) and Otto Hahn. When a supervisor barred her from Hahn's Berlin laboratory, they set up shop in a tiny workroom. Meitner, who was Jewish, was forced to flee Berlin in 1938 for Sweden. There she worked with her nephew to describe fission, which provided the key that unlocked the Pandora's box of nuclear war.   **13,650**

337 JOHN WYCLIFFE (1330–1384)
the Reformation's herald

"It is hard to say whether Luther and Wycliffe would have differed if they met," mused British scholar George Macaulay Trevelyan. Wycliffe's writings started Christendom questioning church authority, and the Reformation exploded across Europe in the sixteenth century. Wycliffe, who is credited with the first translation of the Bible into English, was violent in his attacks on Rome. He implored the "Church of wicked Spirits" to renounce its worldly possessions, assailed the doctrine of the transubstantiation of the bread and wine of the Eucharist into the body and blood of Christ as idolatry, and denounced the pope as a spiritual despot, asking, "Lord, where is freedom in Christ, when men are casten in such bondage?" Pope Gregory XI compared his heresies to "the perverse opinions and unlearned learning of Marsiglio of Padua (96) of damned memory." Perverse or not, Wycliffe coined the phrase "government of the people, by the people, and for the people."   **13,645**

338 JOHANNES ECKEHART (c.1260–c.1328)
the meister of mysticism

Eckehart preached that the godhead was an empty nothingness. If men renounced all sense of self and created their own nothingness, there would be a spark—a *Seelenfunklein*—and a miraculous union between man and god would be forged. If you think this sounds like heavy-duty mysticism, go to the head of the *schola*. Meister Eckehart was the most influential Christian mystic of the Middle Ages, more like an Eastern philosopher than a scholar of Western Catholicism. His sermons were written in German—rare for speculative works until that other troublesome priest, Martin Luther (3), came along two centuries later. Pope John XXII condemned many of Eckehart's propositions as heretical, but Eckehart died before he could be punished. His philosophy is imbued with the mystical strain of Christianity that, even today, is one of its most powerful attractions. Among his famous sayings: "As man cannot live without God, so God cannot live without man."   **13,609**

339 JAN PIETERSZOON COEN (1587–1629)
empire builder

Pepper, nutmeg, cloves: no cooks worth their salt would be without them. Trade in these commodities was so lucrative in Coen's day that the Dutch carved out a Southeast Asia empire, known as Indonesia, to safeguard their commercial interests. They kept control of these spice-producing lands—Sumatra, Borneo, Java, Celebes, the Moluccas, and some of the Lesser Sunda Islands—until 1949. Coen was instrumental in grabbing these territories. As director general of the trading group the Dutch East India Company, he fortified outposts on the archipelago, pushed out the Portuguese, and quashed English initiatives. He also was a merciless defender of Dutch (really, his own) interests. In his role as governor general, he dispatched a fleet to conquer the Banda Islands in 1621. The few natives who survived the bloody massacre were bound into slavery.   **13,599**

340 FRANCISCO JOSÉ DE GOYA (1746–1828)
an artist at war with tradition

Like Beethoven (10), he was deaf (Goya's deafness may have been caused by lead poisoning), and like Beethoven, he was disturbed by the excesses of Napoleonic violence. Both men created revolutionary works of art that inspired the romantics and realists who followed. Goya was a social-climbing Spaniard who churned out paintings of kings, queens, and courtiers. Then the Napoleonic war ravaged Spain, and in 1814 he produced his masterpiece, *The Third of May 1808,* a painting of faceless French soldiers shooting civilians. That and his collection of etchings depicting the horrors of the conflict are among the greatest war art of the millennium, though it's not clear whether they were expressions of Goya's true outrage or Spanish propaganda. Even critics who dislike Goya's work credit him with starting something new. "With Goya the modern anarchy begins," art historian Bernard Berenson lamented.   **13,553**

341 GEORGE BERKELEY (1685–1753)
perceptive philosopher

Poor Berkeley; his insights into the nature of perception and his theory that the physical world exists only in our senses are a monumental contribution to Western thought, in some ways presaging quantum theory. Yet how the world has mocked him for his ideas! "Whether the external world exists or not, the wine at Bologna is extremely good," an Oxford don quipped. Even poet William Butler Yeats (521) belittled "God-appointed Berkeley, that proved all things a dream." Berkeley, an Anglican bishop, had his own dream—a college in Bermuda to spread the gospel among the New World Indians. So he sailed to America in 1728 and lived for three years in Newport, Rhode Island, waiting in vain for a grant promised by London. After returning home, he wrote a brilliant treatise on mathematics, a discourse on economics, and a tome that combined philosophical ruminations with a discussion of the medical benefits of tar water.   **13,551**

342 FRANZ SCHUBERT (1797–1828)
prolific composer at the gateway to romanticism

At least Mozart (52) was famous before he died. Though other composers knew of Schubert's brilliance, all but a tiny fraction of his towering compositions—symphonies, sonatas, chamber works, and songs—went unpublished until after his death at age thirty-one. Schubert's music straddled two eras: the classical of Haydn (296), Mozart (52), and Beethoven (10), and the romantic of Mendelssohn and Schumann, who created audiences for Schubert's work. Pop music–besotted moderns take note: Schubert's musical settings of Goethe (131), Friedrich Schiller, and Heinrich Heine poems have transported audiences for almost two hundred years, which is why we rate him over Irving Berlin (469) and Stephen Foster (833). And instrumental works, such as the piano impromptus and the "Trout Quintet," have not gone out of date either. There is a romantic myth that Schubert died from a fever he caught in the rain at Beethoven's funeral, but the truth is he died of syphilis.   **13,544**

343 JOHN XXIII (1881–1963)
the pope for a new age

English-speaking Catholic children guffawed at this chestnut: What's the pope's telephone number? *Eccum spiritu tuo.* You can still coax a nostalgic smile with that joke from anyone who remembers the phrase's incantation in the Latin mass, but John XXIII sent the Catholic world to its knees with his modernization program. No one expected any departure from tradition when

Angelo Giuseppe Roncalli was elected pontiff at age seventy-seven in 1958. He surprised the complacent by convening the Second Vatican Council. The visible ramifications of "Vatican Two": Catholics talk less about sin and more about love; the mass has been translated into local languages; bongo drums, guitars, and folk songs make ceremonies appealing to youth; altars have been turned around to bring priests before the people; nuns have shed their habits; and Catholics have given up heavy-duty fasting in Lent and eat meat on Fridays.   **13,512**

344 GEORGE MARSHALL (1880–1959)
Axis axer

Winston Churchill (38) called the U.S. Army chief of staff in World War II "the organizer of victory," and we rate Marshall the greatest American general who never commanded troops in war. He was General John Pershing's chief planning officer in World War I and rose to army chief in 1939. When the war came, he directed the mobilization and strategy and picked the field generals, notably the commander in Europe, Dwight Eisenhower (374). Marshall had qualities that democracies require of military leaders: disdain for personal glory, respect for political authority, and intolerance for underperformers. After the war President Harry Truman (485) appointed him secretary of state and called America's generous European Recovery Program the Marshall Plan, in hopes that the former general's popularity would rub off on what was then a controversial idea. It did.   **13,506**

345 THOMAS MORE (1478–1535)
a man for all seasons

. . . is what Desiderius Erasmus (97) called his friend More because the author of the Renaissance classic *Utopia* never changed his cloak of rectitude with the political weather. When England's Henry VIII (100) demanded allegiance to royal religious supremacy, his witty and learned friend and former supporter refused and was beheaded. He was canonized for his martyrdom in 1935. Young More wanted to take holy orders and he wore a hair shirt most of his life, but he liked women and preferred being a good husband to being a bad priest. Biographer Richard Marius called More a man torn between the necessities of making his way in the secular world and preparing his soul for the eternal world to come. More taught the world how to be a hero by choosing the latter.   **13,477**

346 AUGUSTE ESCOFFIER (1846–1935)
a man for all seasonings

Kaiser Wilhelm II (224) lauded his French culinary maestro Escoffier by observing, "I am the emperor of Germany, but you are the emperor of chefs." Escoffier's brilliant culinary career led him to the posh Savoy Hotel in London in 1890. There he created the now-famous peach Melba— poached peaches on vanilla ice cream, topped with raspberry puree—named for singer Nellie Melba. He moved on to the prestigious Carlton Hotel, also in London, where his reputation soared. In his cookbooks, which set the standard for haute cuisine, Escoffier never minced words. "Stock is everything in cooking, at least in French cooking," he said. "Without it, nothing can be done." Grudgingly he included recipes on appetizers and snacks but sniffed, "They have no raison d'être on a good menu." Despite the hefty cholesterol count in his dishes, Escoffier lived to the ripe old age of eighty-nine. Pass the butter, please.   **13,456**

347 GERARDUS MERCATOR (1512–1594)
worldly cartographer

Mercator came as close as anybody to achieving the impossible—drawing an accurate world map by taking this sphere we call Earth and flattening it on paper. Okay, his famous Mercator projection in 1569 had inevitable distortions, but navigators still loved it. Its oh-so-precise and parallel lines of longitude and latitude allowed mariners to draw a straight line between two points and plot a course without resorting to frequent adjustments of compass readings. However, the Flemish mathematician and engraver wasn't the first to bind maps in book form; that distinction went to his rival, Ortelius, in 1570. But fifteen years later Mercator did launch his ambitious project to publish a collection of maps. He called it the *Atlas,* after the Greek demigod who cradles the world on his shoulders. In Mercator's lifetime the Low Countries became the world center of cartography. You might say he put them on the map. **13,444**

348 THURGOOD MARSHALL (1908–1993)
legendary civil rights attorney and first black U.S. Supreme Court justice

Don't get mad, get even. Before Marshall made history as the champion of civil rights, he zapped the University of Maryland Law School, which had refused to admit him, with a lawsuit. The great-grandson of a slave crafted a civil rights legal strategy before the movement spilled over to lunch counters and the backs of buses. He persuaded the National Association for the Advancement of Colored People to attack the policy of "separate but equal" public schools. In his arguments in *Brown v. Board of Education* in 1954, he convinced the Supreme Court that segregated schools were a form of discrimination. Integration followed slowly. As a Supreme Court justice for twenty-four years, the liberal Marshall often penned dissenting opinions. A jokester who nurtured his reputation as a curmudgeon, Marshall quipped that he often voted with the majority on only one issue—when to have lunch. **13,441**

349 CARDINAL RICHELIEU (1585–1642)
creator of the modern French state

He accomplished his two goals: to undermine the Spanish-Habsburg domination of Europe, and to establish royal absolutism in France. The portrait of Richelieu by Philippe de Champagne in the Louvre depicts a face, foxlike and sinister, that one would hesitate to cross even 350 years after his death. Alive, Richelieu was pitiless toward plotters against his beloved Louis XIII. (It took two jailbirds thirty-six swings of their dull-bladed axes to chop off the groaning head of the marquis of Chalais.) After all, the cardinal declared, "kings are the true images of God," and thus "subjects must blindly obey the prince." Richelieu could also be pragmatic, siding with Protestants to foil the Catholic Habsburgs' designs. After Richelieu's death Louis XIII sank into decline, but the stage was set for the glorious reign of his son, the future Sun King (63). **13,408**

350 IBN AL-'ARABI (1165–1240)
master of Sufism, Islam's mystical creed

Young Ibn al-'Arabi frequented cemeteries because he liked to talk to dead people. He roamed North Africa and his native Spain in search of wisdom wherever he could find it. One of his masters was a ninety-five-year-old woman. In 1198, a vision told him to go east, so he settled in Mecca and wrote—actually, it was dictated by another vision, he said—the 560-chapter *Meccan Revelation.* Another of his books, *Bezels of Wisdom,* was dictated by Muhammad himself, Ibn al-'Arabi said. His works, still read today by his Sufi followers, teach that God can be discovered by those with the fortitude to make a spiritual journey aided by silence, isolation, fasting, and sleep deprivation. That path has been tried by millions of ascetics, be they lovers of Ibn al-'Arabi's brand of Sufism or members of other religions. **13,400**

351 CHARLES BABBAGE (1792–1871)
inventor of the first computer

Think of it: Here's a Brit who was born when George Washington (22) was president, and he built a Calculating Engine in 1822 capable of computing mathematical tables and printing the results. Then he designed his Analytical Engine, the forerunner of the modern digital computer. Unfortunately, Babbage struggled for funding to complete the project, despite his mother's urgings to continue "even if it should oblige you to live on bread and cheese," and his dream was forgotten until his unpublished notebooks were discovered in 1937. We would have ranked him higher, but his machine was so primitive and its applications so limited that its importance is mainly symbolic. In 1995 a section of his earlier engine was auctioned off to an Australian science museum for $282,000. Babbage, who gave parties with performing dolls, wrote to Tennyson that the poet's line "Every moment dies a man, / Every moment one is born" should read "Every moment dies a man, / Every moment one and one-sixteenth is born." **13,391**

352 ELVIS PRESLEY (1935–1977)
the king of rock 'n' roll

Presley's contribution was artistic and economic. More than any American singer, he produced enjoyable music in every popular genre: ballads, blues, jazz, gospel, rock, country, western, folk, even Christmas carols. Most important, he borrowed the sounds of black rhythm and blues, which had had a limited audience, and converted them into something new and acceptable to a mass international public. Adults were amused or shocked at the sneering kid with the swiveling hips, but no one did more than Presley to legit-imize the sound and the culture that made rock music the art form and multibillion-dollar industry that it became. Biographer Albert Goldman wrote that on the day Presley's fading career ended with his drugged-up death, a Hollywood cynic quipped, "Good career move." The cynic was right. Cultural historians are beginning to find similarities in the mystical aura that surrounds the Presley legend and the way early Christians felt about Jesus. **13,347**

353 JOHANNES BRAHMS (1833–1897)
classical music's great romantic

Johannes's piano teacher saw his prodigy as a concert pianist. But the nine-year-old preferred writing scores based on musical works. "It is a pity," teacher Otto Cossel said. "He might be such a good pianist, but he won't leave this everlasting composition alone." Thank goodness, for Brahms gave us his choral work *A German Requiem,* four symphonies including number 4 in E minor with its emotional finale, concertos, chamber music, his famous lullabies, and more than two hundred songs. Composer Robert Schumann heard twenty-year-old Brahms play his sonatas, and it was a revelation. "He began to open up regions of wonder," Schumann wrote. "We were drawn more and more into charmed circles." Germans took their musical disputation very seriously. From the moment of Schumann's endorsement of the young genius, Brahms was in his conservative camp, opposite the "enemies," the school led by Liszt (300) and Wagner (165). The division persisted past their lifetimes. **13,319**

354 NELSON MANDELA (b. 1918)
nemesis of apartheid

For 342 years, the minority whites ruled South Africa and enforced a policy of racial segregation called apartheid, a regional term for "apartness." Mandela, born to be chief of the Thembu tribe, joined the guerrillas seeking to overthrow the government. Rising to the top ranks of the rebel army, he was captured in 1962 and jailed for twenty-seven years. During his incarceration, Mandela became an international legend, a symbol of resistance to the last openly racist regime on earth. When he was freed in 1990, he led negotiations with then-President F. W. de Klerk to transfer power to the black majority. A graying distinguished elder statesman when he finally ascended to the presidency in 1994, Mandela summed up his personal philosophy in his autobiography: "People must learn to hate, and if they can learn to hate, they can be taught to love." **13,318**

355 MARIA THERESA (1717–1780)
archduchess of Austria

At twenty-three she inherited much of the Netherlands, Bohemia, Austria, and Hungary, along with toothless rheumy advisers with no diplomatic or political skills. It was a scary start for Maria Theresa, but she found able ministers and generals and kept the Austrian empire from succumbing to the power of her neighbors, particularly Frederick the Great of Prussia (58). Without Maria Theresa's leadership, the Austrian empire would have been gobbled up long before its demise after World War I, and the map of Europe would have looked different for 150 years. She was an implacable defender of Catholicism, conservativism, and old-fashioned morality, but like her daughter Marie-Antoinette (781), she loved entertainment. Her Viennese court became the music capital of Europe. There an eight-year-old Mozart leaped into Maria Theresa's plump arms and kissed her. **13,317**

356 FIRDAWSI (c.940–1020)
the Homer of Persia

His sixty-thousand-verse *Shah-nameh* is the national epic of Persia, and no Islamic poem matches the beauty of its language. Sultan Mahmud of Ghazna (583) decided he wanted a work that glorified his country, and he picked Firdawsi to write it after a competition among a dozen of the best court poets. The pay was to be one gold coin per verse. It took Firdawsi thirty-five years to finish, and when the sultan sent silver instead of gold in payment, poet and potentate had a falling-out. Firdawsi complained, Mahmud threatened to have him trampled by elephants, Firdawsi retaliated by writing a satire about Mahmud's slavish origins and had to flee for his life from the angry ruler. Years later, legends say, the sultan realized how great Firdawsi's poem was and sent the gold, but it arrived on the day of Firdawsi's funeral. **13,288**

357 WALTER SCOTT (1771–1832)
inventor of the historical novel

Scott's tales, from *Rob Roy* to *The Heart of Midlothian,* make history come alive. Most enduring is *Ivanhoe,* a romantic adventure tied to Richard the Lion-Hearted's return from the Crusades. Scott was crippled by polio as a boy, suffered a debilitating illness in midlife, and faced financial disaster in his fifties. He met each setback with stoicism and nobility—much like his characters. Scott grew wealthy but was disastrously free-spending, purchasing an estate in Scotland and investing heavily in his publishing house. The financial crash of 1826 ruined him. When Scott finally acknowledged authorship of the popular *Waverley* novels, published anonymously, he joked he had ceased to be the "Great Unknown" and become the "small known." Still, as he later wrote in his journal: "I had the crown." **13,276**

358 BETTY FRIEDAN (b. 1921)
the center of feminism's second wave

Friedan struck a national nerve when she described "the problem that has no name" in her landmark *The Feminine Mystique* in 1963. A journalist, she decried the fact that although women were being educated for careers, they were forced to retire when marriage and motherhood intervened. Then their biggest challenges were "ring around the collar" and the "heartbreak of psoriasis." Her ideas—published forty-three years after the feminist movement stalled when American women won the right to vote—opened act two of feminism. In 1966 Friedan founded the National Organization for Women and was one of the most vocal supporters of women's equality in the home, the workplace, and the political arena. Although the proposed Equal Rights Amendment to the U.S. Constitution failed, the vocal and visible international women's rights movement that Friedan triggered did much to improve the lives of women around the world.   **13,270**

359 HENRY II OF ENGLAND (1133–1189)
judicious nation builder

English justice in the Middle Ages was meted out by self-serving barons until Henry shifted power to royal judges. They roamed the country in the king's name, an important start toward the national justice systems so crucial to democracy in the English-speaking world. Henry's desire to run a good kingdom was matched by his vigor in battle, but like a lot of workaholics, he should have spent more time with his family. Egged on by Henry's wife, Eleanor of Aquitaine (420), his four sons rebelled from time to time, and when Henry died in bed, he was mourned by few of his countrymen. Not so his martyred friend Thomas Becket, whose appointment as archbishop of Canterbury Henry had fostered. When the two men struggled over administration of the church, Henry's henchmen murdered the archbishop on his own altar.   **13,214**

360 BABE RUTH (1895–1948)
the Sultan of Swat

During World War II Japanese soldiers storming Marine lines on the Pacific island of New Britain cried, "To hell with Babe Ruth!" Such was George Herman Ruth's status as an American icon. Ruth revitalized baseball, the Great American Pastime, by making it a game of power as well as finesse. The left-handed "Babe" was among the American League's best pitchers when his Red Sox manager switched him to the outfield, and his overwhelming hitting power surfaced. During his glory days with the New York Yankees, Ruth led the American League in home runs for twelve years. Successors have broken a string of his records, but no one has come close to replacing him as the millennium's most famous hitter. A big man at six foot two and 215 pounds, Ruth was a warm-hearted womanizer and boozer whom fans always forgave. Indeed he was, as sportswriter Paul Gallico said, a "swashbuckler built on gigantic and heroic lines."   **13,197**

361 YAMAGATA ARITOMO (1838–1922)
statesman who built Japan into a military force

We don't like to point fingers, but if you're looking for a fall guy for the Japanese attack on Pearl Harbor in 1941, the yen stops here. Yamagata planted the idea of war with the United States in 1904. The Plan of National Defense of the Empire was a strategic blueprint that guided the Japanese war plan three decades later. Born to a family of low samurai rank, Yamagata advocated a modern military after he was wounded in a skirmish with a Western army. He traveled to the West to observe armies and returned in 1870 to Japan, where he patterned the Japanese force after the successful Prussian army. Yamagata instituted conscription to build his forces and ultimately commanded the modernized Imperial Guard. A soldier at heart, he served as prime minister in the 1890s and later was the head of the military dictatorship. **13,164**

362 PIERRE DE FERMAT (1601–1665)
author of history's most famous mathematical puzzle

Forget that Fermat discovered or codiscovered the modern theory of numbers, the fundamental principle of analytic geometry, differential calculus, and the theory of probability, all in his spare time. (He was a French judge who once condemned a priest to be burned at the stake.) Fermat's celebrity rests on a tantalizing note he jotted in a textbook on his "last theorem," that "$x^n + y^n = z^n$" has no whole-number solution when n is greater than 2. "I have discovered a truly marvelous proof, which, however, this margin is too narrow to contain," he wrote. But what proof? For 350 years the enigma defeated all comers. *Scientific American* even printed postcards declining readers' requests to evaluate their solutions. Then in 1993 Princeton University mathematician Andrew Wiles solved the theorem after eight years of toil. Did Fermat have a simpler demonstration? We know the answer, but the margin of this book is too narrow to contain it. **13,157**

363 CONSTANTIN BRANCUSI (1876–1957)
molder of abstract forms

Brancusi turned a Paris atelier into a rustic Romanian hut to recreate his peasant origins. His sculpture was just as simple, with pure lines and smooth textures. "Don't look for obscure formulas or mysteries," he said. "I am giving you pure joy." His artistic vision deeply influenced the way modern sculptors, painters, and industrial designers view the concept of form. Brancusi liked to carve in wood, then recreate the piece in bronze or marble. Two of his favorite organic shapes: the egg and the elongated cylinder. Another was the flying bird. But his very abstract *Bird in Space* was grounded by U.S. customs officials, who thought he was sneaking an industrial part into the country. Brancusi sued. In 1928 the Supreme Court ruled in his favor, declaring the object a "new direction" in art. It's now perched in New York's Museum of Modern Art. **13,155**

364 LUDWIG MIES VAN DER ROHE (1886–1969) *the man who made glass houses*

You might want to throw stones at him, but Mies makes our list because he's behind the glass and steel that shapes city skylines. Born in the ornate Victorian Age, Mies decreed "less is more" and launched minimalistic modernism in architecture. A German by birth, Mies moved to the United States after the Gestapo closed his Bauhaus School of Design in 1933. Mies believed design needs to represent "the very innermost structure of the civilization from which it springs." And so for him, buildings needed to reflect the technological society of the twentieth century—"an architecture that anyone can do." Nearly every city boasts a Mies original. It's hard to pick a favorite when you're talking glass monoliths, but there's a warm place in our hearts for Newark's Colonnade Apartments, which we've been driving by rather regularly since it went up in 1958. **13,119**

365 SØREN KIERKEGAARD (1813–1855) *progenitor of existentialism*

The Danish philosopher's influence on modern thinkers, from Freud (15) to Sartre, was enormous. He held that existence means making moral choices and acting on them, with the most important being a "leap of faith" to overcome despair. The reward is great: "God sees that which is hidden and knows the torment; He counts the tears and forgets nothing." As a child, Kierkegaard was shaken by "the great earthquake"—his pious father's revelation that he had once climbed a hill and cursed God. A handsome, sad-eyed hunchback gripped by a lifelong melancholy he called "my castle," Kierkegaard broke an engagement to his beloved Regine Olsen to pursue God. He attacked the church in Denmark as a static "Christianity of nincompoops" that "perishes in the palaver" of its pastors. But he had bigger game in mind, the Hegelianism then sweeping Europe, arguing that its attempt to systematize reality was futile. **13,088**

366 JOHN DRYDEN (1631–1700)
literary leopard who changed his spots

Making enemies was a habit for him. First he praised dictator Oliver Cromwell (162). Then he welcomed King Charles II from exile and was rewarded with the post of poet laureate. Then he was declared poet *non grata* for converting to Catholicism. Dryden suspected, but couldn't prove, that the assailants who almost beat him to death in a London alley in 1679 were hired by an aristocrat who believed Dryden had mocked him in an anonymous verse. Through all these crises his plays packed in audiences and made him the most famous writer in England for four decades. English professors are his plays' only big fans now, but his literary criticism still sings, particularly essays that helped make Shakespeare (5) a god. And his poetry endures. "None but the brave, deserve the fair," he wrote in "Alexander's Feast," one of our favorites. **13,084**

367 EZRA POUND (1885–1972)
mad gadfly of American letters

Few writers in history have so dominated the literary scene: as an American in Europe,

Pound promoted T. S. Eliot (720), James Joyce (171), D. H. Lawrence, Robert Frost (828), and Marianne Moore and profoundly influenced William Butler Yeats (521) and Ernest Hemingway (388). Eliot dedicated "The Wasteland" "To Ezra Pound, il miglior fabbro" ("the better smith"), and indeed, Pound's wordsmithery was masterful. As a boy, he resolved to "know more about poetry than any man living," and he succeeded. Listen to the sea in the *Cantos,* his masterpiece: "And the blue water dusky beneath them, / pouring there into the cataract, / With noise of sea over shingle." Alas, the great mind misfired. Pound made Jew-baiting, pro-Fascist broadcasts from Italy in World War II and, indicted in the United States for treason, spent twelve years in a mental hospital. Maybe novelist Ford Madox Ford wasn't joking when he called him "the kindest-hearted man who ever cut a throat." **13,037**

368 GIUSEPPE GARIBALDI (1807–1882)
unifier of Italy

What a life! Banished as a rebel to Latin America, Garibaldi fought as a pirate in a Brazilian civil war. During the conflict he spied a beautiful girl on a hillside through his ship's telescope and sailed away with her forty-eight hours later. Back in Italy he fought with such ferocity against the Austrians and French to free his homeland that he became known as "the hero of two worlds." In his great campaign of 1860 against Sicily and Naples, he triumphed against impossible odds with his mythical "thousand men," and the following year the Kingdom of Italy was born. Abraham Lincoln (32) tried without success to recruit Garibaldi as a major general in the American Civil War. The most charismatic of the triumvirate of Italian liberators, Garibaldi has been claimed by every conceivable political movement of the twentieth century. During the cold war he was the only historical figure to appear on both American and Soviet postage stamps. **13,019**

369 JEAN PIAGET (1896–1980)
reader of the juvenile mind

We know that the Swiss psychologist Piaget is pivotal to understanding early childhood development, but he's so hard to comprehend—even in English—that scholars have built their careers on trying to simplify his ideas for educators and parents. We'll do our best: Thinking comes before language; and knowledge is learned, not inherited, by children through their environments. The bottom line to Piaget's revolutionary theories: Adults need to foster children's development from the earliest stages. Although Piaget first studied zoology and wrote a dissertation about mollusks, he was moved to analyze infant behavior. He observed his own children and others before concluding that normal children pass through four stages of development—from the reflex stage of crying and sucking, to rudimentary thought processes, to an understanding of abstract concepts, and finally to analytical thinking. A child prodigy himself, he published his first scientific article at age eleven. **13,003**

370 TOKUGAWA IEYASU (1543–1616)
founder of a 254-year Japanese dynasty

Feudalism in every country is like a Mafia organization, and so it was in Japan. The warlords lived by a treacherous code based on family connections, violence, and honor—except that they didn't have to worry about the police. They were the police. From the age of four to six Ieyasu was a hostage to his samurai father's enemies. By twelve he was an experienced fighter, and at seventeen he was the head of his family.

Almost forty battles later he had conquered Japan, establishing the Tokugawa line of shoguns that ruled until 1867. Although he approved of trading with the West early in his reign, he realized that the openness that accompanied commerce would undermine feudal rule, and he instituted restrictions that led to more than two centuries of Japanese isolation. **13,000**

371 ULYSSES S. GRANT (1822–1885)
Civil War victor

Grant said he attended West Point for an education, not a military career. He distinguished himself in the Mexican War and other campaigns, however, making captain before leaving the army in 1854. A failure at farming and real estate, he was saved by the Civil War. The career of this plain, quiet, but determined man proved meteoric. Because of his astute leadership, he shot from regiment colonel to brigadier general, then general of all United States armies in three years. But adversary Robert E. Lee (515) had only disdain for Grant. "His talent and strategy consists in accumulating overwhelming numbers," Lee wrote. Exactly—that's why Grant beat Lee and won the conflict. He taught generals of all nations how to win wars of attrition. Grant forced Lee's surrender in April 1865 and, three years later, was elected president. His career was far from illustrious; his second term was marred by political scandals. But he deserves credit for supporting amnesty for Confederate leaders and protection of blacks' civil rights. **12,956**

372 LOUISA MAY ALCOTT (1832–1888)
enduring American author

If you want to know about Alcott, read *Little Women* with attention to the assertive Jo March. Alcott's classic about four impoverished but gentrified sisters was autobiographical fiction that she said "simmered" for years in her mind. Her first story, which she called "great rubbish," was written when she was sixteen. For ten years she supported her family on macabre, risqué "blood and thunder" stories with plots about opium parties and murder. It wasn't great literature, but as Alcott observed, it "paid the butcher's bill." In four months in 1868 she dashed off *Little Women,* a favorite among preteen girls that has remained in print ever since. It was so successful that Alcott continued the saga through *Little Men* and *Jo's Boys.* Her novel *A Long Fatal Love Chase* was rejected because the tale of adultery and bigamy was too sensational, but it enjoyed great success when it was finally published in 1995.   **12,954**

373 CLARENCE BIRDSEYE (1886–1956)
Frosty the chow man

Those fishsticks in your freezer stay fresh because of this Yankee entrepreneur, who described himself as "just a guy with a very large bump of curiosity." At age ten he hawked muskrats he captured in a park for one dollar each. In college he sold rare black rats he spotted behind a butcher shop to Columbia University for breeding experiments. But it was in Labrador in 1916, where he had taken his new bride to trap foxes in a region two hundred miles by dogsled from the nearest town, that he hit upon his brainstorm for fast-freezing food. He noticed that fish he brought up through ice holes froze almost instantly and, thawed weeks later, tasted fresh. He later applied the same principle to vegetables and mass-marketed his products in small packages. The frozen-food industry was born. **12,926**

374 DWIGHT D. EISENHOWER (1890–1969)
war hero with a winning grin

The unemotional Eisenhower wrote in his diary on June 11, 1942, "The C/S says I'm the guy."

U.S. Army chief of staff George Marshall (344) had chosen him to command the forces that would attack Nazi Germany in Western Europe. Until then Eisenhower was unknown outside the army, but in its chummy upper ranks he was appreciated for his planning skills. While other Allied generals led the troops that did the killing, Eisenhower kept the egomaniacal generals like American George Patton and British Bernard Montgomery from killing each other. He directed the D-Day invasion of Normandy and the conquest of Germany and rode his fame to the White House in 1953. Eisenhower presided over America during the feel-good 1950s, but he lacked distinction as a president—except for his unflinching enforcement of desegregation rulings that he disagreed with. We're not complaining. Better than his successors who made big mistakes with their activism—John F. Kennedy, Lyndon Johnson, and Richard Nixon (904)—we like Ike.   **12,908**

375 HENRY DAVID THOREAU (1817–1862)
America's down-to-earth philosopher

Most deep thinkers are a day late and a dollar short when it comes to implementing ideas. We like Thoreau because he didn't just talk about man's return to nature, he lived it. Thoreau and pal Ralph Waldo Emerson (504) laid down the tenets of Transcendentalism, which paid homage to nature and the individual. Emerson was cozy in his Concord, Massachusetts, home when Thoreau chopped down some trees, built a cabin on Walden Pond, and wrote about his two-year experiment. He parlayed an overnight jail visit for failing to pay his poll tax into *Civil Disobedience,* which made him the patron saint of the 1960s antiwar movement. At the time no one paid much attention: one night in prison—commuted when an unknown benefactor paid the tax— hardly seemed fodder for lofty ideals of resistance to an unjust civil authority. Decades later, however, even India's Mohandas Gandhi (12) and civil rights leader Martin Luther King, Jr. (56), found inspiration in Thoreau's disobedience. **12,877**

376 George P. Marsh (1801–1882)
conservation crusader

Marsh's lifetime of observations produced the landmark *Man and Nature* in 1864, which advanced world knowledge of resources management. Marsh was an American diplomat with more than protocol on his mind. A congressman tapped for international posts, he used his travels to observe the human impact on the natural world. In Turkey he saw how development affected the landscape around the Mediterranean. In Italy he chronicled how deforestation of alpine regions led to erosion, then landslides and floods. His mastery of languages—he spoke twenty—steered him through foreign environmental studies that bolstered his views. In his book he argued that human abuse of forests, lands, and waterways had more long-term, destructive consequences than did natural disasters. And although it's gospel today, Marsh was among the first to recognize the importance of food chains—and the ensuing harm if one link is broken. **12,871**

377 Rachel Carson (1907–1964)
our environmental conscience

Imagine a world where spring does not come—a world with no birds, or crops, or children at play. "No witchcraft, no enemy action had silenced the rebirth of new life in this stricken world. The people had done it themselves," Carson wrote. Years before Earth Day became an annual April event, Carson's 1962 best-seller, *Silent Spring*, warned that man-made pesticides were destroying life. So potent was her message that she was condemned by the chemical industry and the crop growers' champion, the U.S. Department of Agriculture. Yet a special committee appointed by President Kennedy supported her ominous predictions. Carson spent her early career as a writer for the U.S. Bureau of Fisheries. She once wrote an introduction to a bureau booklet that was so eloquently passionate that it was published instead in *The Atlantic Monthly*. When we traced the modern environmental movement to its roots, we found Carson lobbying on behalf of springtime. **12,844**

378 Gregory VII (1020–1085)
reform pope

An early advocate of the separation of religion and government, Gregory also insisted on the separation of priests from their concubines. (Back then, men of the cloth took wives and even shacked up with their girlfriends.) Gregory reasserted the authority of the Holy See, starting with his attack on "lay investiture," the installation of bishops and abbots by secular rulers. This led to his clash with Holy Roman emperor Henry IV (177) and the latter's famous capitulation. After crossing the Alps in the winter of 1077, Henry stood, barefoot and in sackcloth, for three nights outside the castle where Gregory was staying in Canossa, before finally gaining absolution. The standoff ignited the great struggle between church and state in medieval Europe. Gregory also attacked the sale of church offices, or simony; laid the groundwork for the doctrine of papal infallibility; and founded the College of Cardinals. Oh, yes—he also decreed clerical celibacy. **12,819**

379 Margaret Mead (1901–1978)
anthropologist with a popular touch

As a twenty-five-year-old graduate student, Mead studied Samoan child-rearing and sex practices, spurning one villager's offer of a personal demonstration. In *Coming of Age in Samoa* and other writings, she taught that the ills of civilized society are cultural, not biological, and can be eliminated if people emulate primitive people. She found, for example, that the generation gap was unknown in Samoa. Mead spread wisdom on these subjects for half a century as an ethnologist at New York's Museum of Natural History and as a globe-trotting lecturer. When she turned preachy about family life, though, some critics noted she had been divorced three times; detractors said she fabricated some of her Samoan findings. And her mentors Franz Boas (741), Ruth Benedict, and France's Claude Lévi-Strauss are considered greater theoreticians. But no one surpassed Mead in efforts to help the general public apply the lessons of anthropology to modern-day living. **12,804**

380 MENELIK II (1844–1913)
Ethiopian emperor

Menelik's grandfather prophesied the child would restore Ethiopia to greatness—a reasonable expectation for the namesake of the son of King Solomon of ancient Israel and Sheba, queen of south Arabia. Menelik united Ethiopia after centuries of dynastic struggles, restored religious liberty, and ushered his country into modern times. He also beat back Italy's attempt to envelop Ethiopia as part of its colonial empire. The canny Menelik marshaled a hundred thousand barefoot but well-armed warriors to crush advancing Italian forces in 1896 at Aduwa. It was the bloodiest defeat ever for a colonial power on that continent. Through it Menelik, the "King of Kings" and the "Lion of Judah," ensured that his country would not suffer the fate of the rest of Africa during the great wave of colonization. As he told Europe's leaders, "I have no intention of being an indifferent looker-on if the distant Powers have the idea of dividing up Africa." **12,797**

381 BILL W. (1895–1971)
founder of Alcoholics Anonymous

His name was Bill Wilson, and he was an alcoholic. After recovering from his own drunken odyssey with the support of other alcoholics, Bill W. articulated a twelve-step recovery program that gave drunks, as he called them, the courage to stand up in a crowded smoke-filled room and admit they had a problem. Founded in 1935 by Bill W. with the help of an Ohio physician, Dr. Bob, AA grew into a worldwide organization. Members join on a first-name-only basis that cuts across sex, class, race, and religion. AA has no dues, bylaws, or officers. Bill W. realized that giving up alcohol forever seemed impossible, but most drunks could stop drinking for just a day. The "one day at a time" approach was so successful in helping alcoholics that its group support philosophy has been applied to gambling, drug addiction, and overeating. **12,782**

382 AGATHA CHRISTIE (1890–1976)
the Dame whodunit

The works of grandmotherly, tweedy Dame Agatha are the world's most read after the Bible and Shakespeare (5). Her novels, including *Murder on the Orient Express* and *Death on the Nile,* have sold more than 400 million copies. This prolific writer from an upper-class British family created two recurring characters: eccentric Belgian detective Hercule Poirot and elderly sleuth Miss Jane Marple. Ever the lady, Christie bristled when an American publisher put a nude woman on her book jacket. "There's nothing immoral in my books," she said, "only murder." Christie created ingenious fictional puzzles, and her narrative skill made every story a page-turner. One mystery, though, she declined to unravel: her much-publicized disappearance in 1936. People thought it was a stunt, but Christie apparently suffered a breakdown when her husband left her. She was found in a country hotel, registered under the name of her husband's mistress. **12,781**

383 JEREMY BENTHAM (1748–1832)
philosophy's Dr. Feelgood

He was the prime expounder of utilitarianism, which he described as "the greatest happiness of the greatest number." This formula underpinned his life's campaign for social reform. Early in his career, he said, he was disillusioned to discover that "people in power were against reform," following their "sinister interest" rather than the general good. In studying the obstructionism of the powerful, this Ben Franklin lookalike categorized their four basic tactics for quashing reforms: the "fallacies" of invoking higher authority, warning of the risks of change, delaying debate, and if all else failed, sowing confusion. Bentham's plan for a model prison, the "Panopticon," was never implemented in Britain, though penitentiaries in the United States copied it. And he loved fancy language. The writer Lucie Duff recalled how as a child she was escorted by the elderly Bentham around his garden in an activity he called "ante-prandial circumgyration." **12,777**

384 PIERRE-AUGUSTE RENOIR (1841–1919)
dishmaking's loss,
the art world's gain

While fellow impressionists preferred landscapes, Renoir became a master of figure painting. His trademark: voluptuous female nudes cavorting in streams, their skin pink and radiant. Renoir was happy painting dishes for six francs a day, but his workshop was driven out of business by mass production. So he went to art school and met Claude Monet (196), Alfred Sisley, and Camille Pissarro and for the next dozen years went hungry producing paintings that defied conventions and lacked buyers. For dumbest landlord of the millennium, we nominate the one who discarded twenty canvases that Renoir presented in lieu of rent. Finally Renoir found an audience at the most famous art exhibit in history, the April 15, 1874, show by thirty rebel painters spurned by the stuffy jurors of the Paris art establishment. Renoir got two good reviews and sold a painting, *La Loge,* for a respectable 425 francs. He lived long enough to become a celebrated master and see his paintings in the Louvre. **12,776**

385 LORD BYRON (1788–1824)
the romantic body beautiful

George Gordon Noel Byron was the male sex symbol of the millennium—dark, handsome, and tremendously appealing to women, whom he treated with contempt. Lamed by a clubfoot, he nevertheless exuded courage. Guilt-ridden, emotional, and defiant, he was the mold for the Byronic heroes of his writings. Byron gained fame in 1812 with publication of *Childe Harold's Pilgrimage.* But of all his works, his masterpiece was the mock epic *Don Juan,* a poetic satire of English society. A sample:

> *In her first passion woman loves her lover,*
> *In all the others all she loves is love.*

A daring adventurer who captivated Europe with his exploits, Byron died of exposure while fighting in the Greek war of independence. His legendary amours included liaisons with his half-sister, poet Shelley's (509) sister-in-law, and novelist Lady Caroline Lamb. After the affair with Lamb,

Byron warned, "Keep clear of her." She labeled him, "Mad, bad, and dangerous to know." **12,773**

386 JAMES STARLEY (1830–1881)
big wheel in bicycle history

We faced the same problem with the bicycle that we did with the automobile, television, gun, and airplane: Sure it's important, but who the heck invented it? We could have selected Jean Theson, who invented a self-propelling machine in 1645, but his version had four wheels and in no way resembled the sporting vehicle we know today. We considered giving the nod to Baron Karl de Drais de Sauerbrun, whose contraption required riders to power it by moving their feet along the ground; or to Kirkpatrick Macmillan, whose 1839 model featured cranks, rods, and levers. Then there was Pierre Michaux, whose "velocipede" also relied on cranks. Eureka! We settled upon Starley, affectionately considered the "father" of the bicycle in England. His 1870 "penny-farthing" model had a massive front wheel but was basically similar to what we know today as the bike. **12,770**

387 JAN HUS (1372/73–1415)
the playboy who became a prophet

As a youth, Hus was something of a gadabout, with a weakness for stylish clothing, chess, and feasts. "But when the Lord gave me knowledge of the Scriptures, I discarded from my foolish mind that kind of stupid fun-making," he said. Hus and John Wycliffe (337) were the two great medieval precursors of the Protestant Reformation. As usual, Britain proved more hospitable to dissent than the continent; Wycliffe died of a stroke while scribbling in his rectory, while the Czech Hus was burned at the stake three decades later. The irony was that while Hus approved of Wycliffe's campaign to purify the church, he

rejected most of his doctrinal challenges. "Seek the truth," he wrote in a famous prayer, and:

> Listen to the truth
> Teach the truth
> Love the truth
> Abide by the truth
> And defend the truth
> Unto death.

12,687

388 ERNEST HEMINGWAY (1899–1961)
imitated but rarely surpassed literary stylist

Then you were young and you read *A Farewell to Arms* and *For Whom the Bell Tolls* because Hemingway wrote them and Hemingway was good. You tried to write like Hemingway but you were not Hemingway. You were a Hemingway wannabe.

"Hemingway's style taught writers the beauty of prose that is spare, simple, clean," a critic said.

"Yes," you said. "He was splendid."

Your wife did not understand. "I spit on Hemingway the obscenity. I do not care about the old man. I do not care about the sea. Hemingway was a bully and impotent," she said.

"*Tu sais rien.* You do not understand. You are a woman," you said.

Then there was Paris, and bullfights, and the Spanish Civil War, and Havana and Key West and his Nobel Prize. He posed beside fish and lions that were big and dead. In the summer he shot himself in the head. **12,653**

389 JEAN-BAPTISTE RACINE (1639–1699)
magnificent obsessive

Racine's grandmother took the penniless orphan with her when she joined a convent at Port-Royal, and it changed his life. Port-Royal was the hotbed of Jansenism, a somber cult that leaned toward predestination—in violation of the Catholic Church's teachings. Outstanding scholars of the day also espoused Jansenism, so Racine had first-rate teachers. At nineteen he left for Paris to study law but instead prowled the royal court, theaters, and boudoirs. His decision to become a playwright scandalized the folks back home. Racine's eleven tragedies exploring the destructiveness of obsession have remained popular in French theaters and classrooms. His lofty dramas melded the formal beauties of neoclassical structure and verse with Greek mythology. His finest works: *Phaedra* and *Iphigenia*. Racine was at the pinnacle of his career when he abruptly stopped writing plays. His biographer-son ascribed this to a religious conversion. It seems that Racine reverted to the cult of his youth, costing him the king's favor. **12,617**

390 BERNADETTE OF LOURDES (1844–1879)
last hope of the sick and lame

Saint Bernadette was puny, sickly, and illiterate, yet she convinced the Catholic world that she had seen the Virgin Mary near her sleepy French town at the foot of the Pyrenees. At first, *paysans* said Marie-Bernarde Soubirous was a fool when she lapsed into ecstatic trances. At the direction of a "lady in white," the fourteen-year-old girl dug a hole and, when water sprang up, washed herself. Then a miner, blinded in an accident, washed his injured eye and regained his sight. Today millions of pilgrims trek to drink the grotto water. The streets of Lourdes are as crowded as a suburban mall the day after Thanksgiving, while local shops hawk religious souvenirs. Lourdes provided handicap access decades before government mandates. Railroad cars and ramps are designed to accommodate people on stretchers and in wheelchairs who come to Lourdes in a last-ditch, and usually fruitless, effort to find a cure. **12,604**

391 JOHN BUNYAN (1628–1688)
author of Pilgrim's Progress, *one of the millennium's most influential books*

An allegory of the Christian journey of faith, *Pilgrim's Progress* was the most widely read religious tome in the Anglo-Saxon world after the Bible for more than two hundred years. In it the hero, Christian, sets off from the City of Destruction with a huge burden on his back to seek the Celestial City. On the way he encounters endless snares and enemies, from serpents to a horrible giant, prompting one twentieth-century book reviewer to call him the Indiana Jones of Protestant Christianity. But the nineteenth-century British scholar Benjamin Jowett placed *Pilgrim's Progress,* alongside *Arabian Nights, Plutarch's Lives,* and *Robinson Crusoe,* as one of four books all boys should read. Bunyan, the son of a poor English tinker, said he led a sinful life before turning to religion, "with few equals for lying and blaspheming the Holy name of God." **12,603**

392 RICHARD FRANCIS BURTON (1821–1890)
roamer of the last frontiers

On a passage to India in 1853, an English civil servant spotted a fierce mustachioed man exercising on deck and exclaimed, "That Arab has an intelligent look." That Arab was the sun-blackened Burton, still in disguise from the first known trip by a non-Muslim to Mecca and Medina, the holy cities barred to infidels. Risking his life to see things no Western eyes had encountered makes this glory-seeking sometime spy, diplomat, scholar, soldier, and naturalist one of the greatest explorers of the millennium. He plunged into Amazon jungles, remote India, Afghanistan, Arabia—even Utah—and his crowning achievement was exploration of the source of the Nile River. Packing courage, cunning, and knowledge of twenty-nine languages, Burton survived a Somali warrior's spear in the face and lived among cannibals in Gabon. In his spare time, he wrote best-selling translations of the *Kama Sutra* and the *Arabian Nights*. **12,599**

393 APHRA BEHN (1640–1689)
first Englishwoman to earn her living as a writer

Contemporaries, scandalized that she presumed to take up the manly art of writing, and perhaps threatened by her talent, accused Behn falsely of plagiarism. One critic called her authorship "a reproach to her womanhood and a disgrace even to the licentious age in which she lived." Even today intrigue surrounds her. She served as a spy during the Anglo-Dutch War, but her warning that the Dutch planned to attack by sailing down the River Thames went unheeded. Later she was shipwrecked in the English Channel but survived, only to be incarcerated briefly in debtor's prison. She turned to writing to earn her keep and, by 1671, had two plays performed at England's Duke's Theatre. In all she wrote more than twenty plays, five novels, and numerous poems. She was buried in Westminster Abbey, proof positive that, despite her gender, she was numbered among the literary elite. **12,577**

394 SAMUEL TAYLOR COLERIDGE
(1772–1834) poet, philosopher, and opium eater

We include Coleridge not because he was a junkie, of course. We include him for the power and wildness of his poetry, including his most famous work, *The Rime of the Ancient Mariner*, which makes him one of the greatest of the English romantics. Yet Coleridge's addiction tarnished his poetry, eroded his imaginative powers, damaged his marriage, soured his friendships, and has even been blamed

for his other great failing, his plagiarism. "I was seduced into the ACCURSED Habit ignorantly," he complained. It became "a slavery more dreadful than any man who has not felt its iron fetters eating into his very soul, can possible imagine." In "The Pains of Sleep," he describes the agony of withdrawal: "Fantastic passions! maddening brawl! / And shame and terror over all!" **12,509**

395 ENRICO FERMI (1901–1954)
elemental physicist

Old dictionaries defined uranium as a rare but worthless metal. Fermi helped prove how worthless those dictionaries were. Building on work by Frédéric and Irène Joliot-Curie, Fermi bombarded elements with neutrons in experiments that led to the discovery that atoms of uranium could be split. For this work he won the Nobel Prize for physics in 1938. On December 2, 1942, he led a group of U.S. government researchers who started the first nuclear chain reaction in a lab under Stagg Field in Chicago. Afterward they drank Chianti from paper cups in a joyless celebration befitting the nightmarish next step: bottling the reaction in bombs that destroyed Hiroshima and Nagasaki to end World War II. Physicist Emilio Segrè, who worked on the bomb project, too, called Fermi "the last individual of our times to reach the highest summits in both theory and experiment and to dominate all of physics." **12,502**

396 YO FEI (1103–1141)
Chinese military hero

The peasant Yo Fei was a muscled wonder at age eleven. He mastered wrestling and archery but also taught himself to read and write. When Mongolian invaders threatened, Yo Fei's mother urged the twenty-year-old to lead the battle and burned "Do your best for your country" with a hot knife into his back. Fellow officers were suspicious of this literate giant who shunned silks and robes to dress like his men. He abandoned predictable military stratagems to embrace guerrilla tactics and trained his troops as crack archers. "It is easier to pull down a mountain than defeat Yo Fei's army" went the saying among enemy soldiers. Yo Fei was made general and became a national hero, only to be done in by evil Prime Minister Ch'in Kuei. To this day, Chinese revere Yo Fei and revile Ch'in Kuei. They eat fried cakes dubbed "Yu Cha Kuei," for "Kuei has been fried in oil." **12,478**

397 JAMES BOSWELL (1740–1795)
author of the world's greatest biography, The Life of Samuel Johnson

If there is a link between genius and lust, Boswell is exhibit A: This son of a dour Scottish Presbyterian blazed a trail of fornication across Europe, frequenting whores and seducing actresses, house servants, his friends' wives and daughters and even the mistress of his hero, the French philosopher Rousseau (19), saying she became "agitated, like a bad rider galloping downhill" in their lovemaking. An egotist, a celebrity hound, and a drunk, Boswell was nevertheless a charmer. Samuel Johnson (182), England's towering intellect of his age, said Boswell was "never in anyone's company who did not wish to see him again." Boswell has his detractors; Edmund Wilson called him "a vain and pushing diarist," and others have complained that he painted a crude portrait of his brilliant subject. But most critics say his eye for detail and his accounts of the intellectual give-and-take in London society are unparalleled. Historian Thomas Carlyle (691) said his prose "woundrously brought back to us" a lost era. **12,444**

398 GUSTAVE FLAUBERT (1821–1880)
ultimate realist

When the novel *Madame Bovary* appeared in 1856, the Parisian authorities tried Flaubert on a charge of outraging public morals, but art won. He was acquitted, and the critics cheered. This still-popular story of a woman crushed by the tyranny of provincial society showed future novelists that pure realism could convey truth and beauty. A fanatical perfectionist in all his novels, Flaubert ripped up eight pages of every ten he wrote. He also had a weird habit of screaming himself hoarse while he scribbled, to release the demons that blocked creativity. He suffered from syphilis, violent epileptic seizures, and disgust at novelists he found to be lacking in talent. One was Harriet Beecher Stowe (457), whose *Uncle Tom's Cabin* he considered too preachy. Flaubert's credo guides all great writers: "The author in his work must be like God in the universe, present everywhere and visible nowhere." **12,431**

399 JEAN-PAUL MARAT (1743–1793)
the guillotine's best friend

Second only to Robespierre (68) in France's Reign of Terror, Marat once demanded that 270,000 enemies be beheaded. His end was as grisly as the fate he decreed for others. The scene: He is soaking himself in a bathtub to assuage a skin disorder that is driving him insane with itching and is scribbling an editorial for his newspaper. He hears a woman pleading with the guard he has posted at his door to be allowed entry so she can reveal a conspiracy against him. "Let her in," he commands. Hmm. Lovely, he thinks, giving her the once-over. But she is agitated; here is a list, she declares, of your enemies, plotting against you! "They shall be guillotined," he roars, intending to impress her. At which point she draws a knife from the fold of her dress and plants it into his chest. End of itching problem. **12,430**

400

Tomás de Torquemada (1420–1498)
evil grand inquisitor

In an age when most Spanish churchmen loved splendor, Torquemada's asceticism appealed to the humorless Queen Isabella (117). She gave her Dominican confessor freedom to eradicate heresy, and Torquemada and his assistants tortured thousands of suspected nonbelievers. Men who implicated others were treated with relative leniency: Their hands were *not* cut off before they were castrated, hanged, drawn and quartered, and burned.

When Torquemada recommended the expulsion of Spanish Jewry in 1492, Isabella and King Ferdinand suggested a fat ransom instead, but Torquemada got his way. "Judas sold Christ for thirty pence; and your highnesses wish to sell Him again for 300,000 ducats," he complained. Now the good news. He died from gout after months of excruciating pain. By then, though, the culture of conformity that Torquemada had done so much to foster helped Spain achieve the domestic unity required of a great world power.   **12,414**

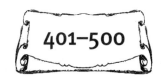

The business of America is business. So said "Silent Cal" Coolidge, the thirtieth president of the United States, in a rare burst of loquaciousness. He was right, and in this section, we pay homage to some of the great pioneers of capitalism.

What a cast of characters they are. Frederick Winslow Taylor, the world's first great efficiency expert, thrilled to productivity gains the way some men take to liquor. Management guru Peter Drucker ranked him up there with Marx, Darwin, and Freud in his influence on posterity.

Then there is John Harvey Kellogg, the doctor who hooked the world on corn flakes; J. P. Morgan, the bulbous-nosed financier who created the first billion-dollar corporation; James Buchanan Duke, the master marketer who convinced consumers that smoking was good for them; Albert Kahn, designer of the modern factory; John D. Rockefeller, oil monopolist and philanthropist; George Eastman, who framed the human race with his hand-held camera (just think: people snapped seventy *billion* photos in 1996 alone); and Walt Disney, cartoon king.

To be sure, our next group of one hundred luminaries is loaded down with the usual weight of national leaders, military men, scientists, inventors, artists, writers, musicians, and religious figures. (Yes, two popes pop up, but trust us: in the great unfolding drama of history, popes are big.) Nevertheless this is the first section to contain such a concentration of business folk, and—with a few exceptions, like Aristide Boucicaut, a Frenchman who had a lot in store for shoppers, and Jakob Fugger, a Renaissance-era moneybags—they are an American crowd.

Most of them were born in the nineteenth century and died in the twentieth. We salute them because so much of what they accomplished lives on so visibly all around us. We'd say more, but as soon as we finish our Kellogg's Raisin Bran, we're going to watch Disney's *Beauty and the Beast* for the fortieth time.

401 MIKHAIL BAKUNIN (1814–1876)
arch anarchist

"The passion for destruction is creative," the Russian Bakunin declared. While Marx (14) sat in libraries, Bakunin mounted the ramparts—in Paris, Prague, and Dresden—before being seized and turned over to Czar Nicholas I. In prison, wracked by scurvy, he subsisted on sour cabbage until his teeth fell out. He escaped and fled to the United States. His famous quarrel with Marx divided Europe's revolutionary movement for years. The fussbudget Marx triumphed, but the swashbuckling Bakunin was his contemporaries' darling. "Everything about him is colossal," remarked the composer Richard Wagner (165). And poisonous. A century later American black revolutionary Eldridge Cleaver said he "fell in love" with this antibourgeois, antiliberal, anti-German, anti-Communist, anti-intellectual, anti-Christian anti-Semite. And the murderous Shining Path guerrillas of Peru and the Khmer Rouge of Cambodia owe an intellectual debt to the man who craved "the annihilation of everything." **12,411**

402 BARTOLOMEU DIAS (c.1450–1500)
first European to round Africa's southern cape

Dias is a mystery man because of Renaissance Portugal's fanatical secrecy about its explorations. We know enough to laud Dias for one of the millennium's influential voyages. A three-ship fleet under his command, with Christopher Columbus's (2) younger brother Bartelomeo among the pilots, sailed from Portugal in August 1487 and headed south. The African coast was to the east. Before Christmas they were three hundred miles farther south than any previous expedition, and on February 3, 1488, after wandering in a tempest, they sighted land. This time, though, the land was to the north, not the east.

They had rounded the Cape of Storms—later renamed by Portugal a more upbeat Cape of Good Hope—and the route to the Indies and its riches lay open for Vasco da Gama's (125) voyage of 1497. Dias was lost at sea in 1500 after exploring the coast of Brazil. **12,409**

403 GIOVANNI BELLINI (c.1430–1516)
atmospheric artist

While other artists may have known the difference between day and night, Bellini was among the first to paint it. He paid strict attention to the time of day and weather conditions and figured out how to use paint to emphasize daylight and atmosphere. His skill at creating a moment on canvas makes him one of the leading, although oft overlooked, artists of the Renaissance. His achievements are impossible to ignore in Venice itself, where tourists are left breathless by his magnificent altarpieces. Son of an artist and brother of the lesser known but accomplished Gentile Bellini, Giovanni extended his artistic influence by training the next generation of painters. He counted both Titian and Giorgione among his students. Our favorite: *Saint Francis in Ecstasy* at the Frick Collection in New York City. **12,356**

404 NICHIREN (1222–1282)
Japanese seer without peer

Unlike fellow Japanese Buddhists who tolerated other beliefs, Nichiren called those who disagreed with him liars, demons, and hypocrites. This "robust, intransigent sincerity," as scholar Martin Collcutt called it, made Nichiren an influential figure in the creation of Japanese-style Buddhism; almost twenty million people today belong to sects influenced by his teachings. More important, followers through the ages have championed his belief in Japan's preeminence in the world as well as his teachings that the way to salvation was repeated recitation of "homage to the Lotus Sutra," *nam-myoho-renge-kyo*. He had an uncanny knack for foretelling disasters—earthquakes and plagues followed his predictions—but exile was his reward for being such a crank. He claimed in his memoirs that he escaped execution when a divine light blinded the swordsman, though in truth he was reprieved.   **12,333**

405 VASLAV NIJINSKY (1890–1950)
ballet's soaring superstar

By sixteen, Nijinsky's extraordinary talent in ballet earned him the title "eighth wonder of the world." The Russian youth joined Sergey Diaghilev's (581) Ballets Russes and fell under the master's artistic and sexual sway. Innovative Nijinsky dazzled world audiences with solos in *Le Spectre de la Rose* and *Petrushka*. Filmmaker Charlie Chaplin (795) called Nijinsky's dancing "hypnotic, godlike, his somberness suggesting moods of other worlds." Known for spectacular leaps, Nijinsky said staying aloft wasn't difficult: "You have to just go up and then pause a little up there." As choreographer, Nijinsky's avant-garde approach to *L'Après-midi d'un Faune*, and *Le Sacre du Printemps* created an audience for modern dance. In 1913 he shocked associates by marrying a Hungarian aristocrat. The spurned Diaghilev fired him. Within six years—at age twenty-nine—Nijinsky's genius was eclipsed by madness, and he was diagnosed a schizophrenic. He never rebounded.   **12,321**

406 JOHN HARINGTON (c.1560–1612)
the bard of the bowl

Indoor plumbing ranks high among the millennium's achievements, and we give Elizabethan wit John Harington credit for popularizing the need for the toilet, maybe even inventing it. Medieval and Renaissance homes, rich and poor, stank with human waste. Harington's remedy—cistern, stop

tank, lavatory-pan and seat, sluice, and sewage tank—looks like a modern toilet. More jokester than inventor, Harington put the plans in his ribald pamphlet, *The Metamorphosis of Ajax*, making the melancholy Homeric character, later shortened to "Jakes," a synonym for privy. So is John, in Harington's memory. In a sonnet advertising his invention, Harington wrote, "Sith here you see, feel, smell that his conveyance / Hath freed this noisome place of all annoyance." Some rich people installed the devices, though municipal water systems took more than two hundred years to catch up and make toilets feasible. **12,311**

407 OSMAN I (1258–1326)
founder of the Ottoman Turks

The son of a tribal chieftain, Osman and his fellow Turkmen warriors fought skirmishes with Byzantine troops along the fringes of the vast Byzantine empire. Then he dreamed of a tree that grew from his loins, its branches casting a shadow over the world, and its leaves turned into sword blades pointing toward Constantinople, the Byzantine capital. Osman subsequently conquered several thousand square miles of Byzantine territory. Though a minor power at his death, his realm grew into one of history's greatest empires, stretching at its zenith in the sixteenth century from the gates of Vienna, through the Balkans and the Middle East and all across North Africa. While Osman could be cruel—he slew his elderly uncle with a crossbow for questioning policy—he was considered benevolent for his age, and the prayer for his successors was "May he be as good as Osman."   **12,301**

408 GUIDO OF AREZZO (c.990–c.1050)
noteworthy musical theorist

We sing Guido of Arezzo's praises for developing the prototype of musical notation so familiar today: dots representing specific pitches marching up and down the lines and spaces of a staff. Guido called his pitches *ut, re, mi, fa, sol.* Later, *la* and *ti* came and *ut* was replaced by *do.* Thank goodness. If that famous Rodgers (841) and Hammerstein song had started with the words "*Ut* a deer, a female deer," *The Sound of Music* could have flopped. Guido's textbook, the *Micrologus*, was the top music theory book for four hundred years. Its short dedication is the source for what little we know about Guido's life: he was a monk who wrote and taught music. Few musicians today remember the *Micrologus*, but if you hum a few bars, they can play along. **12,254**

409 ANDRÉ-MARIE AMPÈRE (1775–1836)
magnetic researcher

This guy was so advanced that before he was old enough to know numbers, he figured out math problems using stones and cookie crumbs. He said that by the time he was eighteen, he had learned all the math he would ever know. After a Danish scientist noticed that a compass needle jumped when it was brought in contact with electrical current, Ampère explained why. He outlined the theoretical "swimmer's rule," which described what would happen when a compass, a swimmer, and an electrical wire came together. Of course, Ampère didn't mention that a swimmer would die if placed in contact with an electrical wire. Oh well, that's a different lesson. In his most famous experiment, now replicated ad nauseam at elementary school science fairs, Ampère showed how electrical wires can behave like magnets, attracting and repelling at the poles. **12,209**

410 GEORGE WASHINGTON CARVER
(1860–1943) *the nutty professor*

Carver, the botanist who revolutionized Southern agriculture, is best known for his research on peanut derivatives. From childhood he loved plants and flowers. Barred by many schools because he was black, Carver was middle-aged before he graduated from college. Educator Booker T. Washington (458) lured Carver to the all-black Tuskegee Institute by offering him "the task of bringing a people from degradation, poverty and waste to full manhood." Carver's association with Tuskegee lasted nearly fifty years. But he felt his movable school was his finest achievement. Driving a wagon and mule, he took seeds, tools, and plants across Alabama, teaching sharecroppers about cross-fertilization and coaxing them to replace the nutrient-depleting King Cotton with sweet potatoes and tomatoes. On campus Carver was a familiar figure in his old wool suit, the trousers baggy at the knees from the kneeling he did to collect plant samples. But he never neglected one sartorial touch: his lapel always held a fresh flower. **12,197**

411 LEIF ERIKSSON (fl.1001)
first European to set foot in the New World

Another Icelander, Bjarni Herjulfsson, sailed there first, in 986, after being blown off course on his way to Greenland, but he turned around without disembarking because the land looked "pretty useless" to him. Leif, son of Erik the Red, the Norwegian outlaw who colonized Greenland, followed Bjarni's directions and went ashore on "Vinland" in 1001. The site was probably on the northern tip of Newfoundland, where the ruins of a Norse village have been found in L'Anse aux Meadows. In any case a German crew member named Tyrk wandered off and got drunk on fermented berries—thus, perhaps, the "Vin" in Vinland—and Leif boasted back home that Vinland's rivers overflowed with salmon. In 1009 an expedition of 250 Icelanders established another settlement, and other Vikings apparently made their way as far south as Rhode Island and Cape Cod, but the Native Americans expelled or killed them. **12,196**

412 ROGER BACON (c.1213–c.1292)
early experimentalist

The English Franciscan friar would be in the top hundred if we had proof that he actually made, or even possessed, the gadgets ascribed to him: telescopes, eyeglasses, and gunpowder. We don't know much about what Bacon did, only that he said experimentation—not just revelation or the classical wisdom touted by Thomas Aquinas (8)—is a path to the truth. Bacon's fellow friars were skeptical about his experiments with chemicals and lenses, but Pope Clement IV was intrigued and gave Bacon permission to write an encyclopedia. Bacon threw in the view that science should reign supreme in education, and that or some other "suspected novelty," as they called heretical thinking then, put Bacon in prison for most of his last fourteen years. **12,188**

413 WALLACE HUME CAROTHERS
(1896–1937) *inventor of nylon*

Those polyester leisure suits of the 1970s would never have been possible without Carothers. While he had absolutely nothing to do with curing John Travolta of his *Saturday Night Fever*, Carothers invented the first artificial, man-made fiber. Although rayon was developed first, it was made with natural products, not chemicals, and was a poor substitute for silk. Meanwhile the silk supply from Japan dwindled as the United States' relationship with that country deteriorated. Working as a chemist for Du Pont, Carothers produced strong elastic nylon threads in 1935. By 1938 nylon stockings were marketed, and Du Pont began developing industrial applica-

tions. When World War II intervened, women had to sacrifice their nylons so the fibers could be devoted to war uses, especially fabric for parachutes. Carothers never enjoyed the spoils of his invention. He lapsed into a deep depression and committed suicide just two years after he developed nylon. **12,174**

414 FREDERICK WINSLOW TAYLOR
(1856–1915) *industrial control freak*

Taylor, the son of a wealthy lawyer, developed a theory for improving factory efficiency that essentially involved reorganizing workers' routines—down to the way they bent over—to eliminate wasted effort. "He couldn't see an idle lathe or an idle man," John Dos Passos wrote of Taylor in *U.S.A.*, his trilogy about America. "Production went to his head and thrilled his sleepless nerves like liquor or women on a Saturday night." Taylor called his system scientific management, and its influence on modern mass-production and management techniques is incalculable. He knew his innovations would infuriate workers, but he also figured the increased productivity would lead to higher wages. And he was right. Taylor's other passion was sports; at age twenty-five he won a national tennis championship, and in later years he invented a Y-shaped putter, but it didn't meet the standards of the U.S. Golf Association. **12,129**

415 FRIEDRICH ENGELS (1820–1895)
Karl Marx's sidekick and paymaster

Okay, so Marx (14) was the intellectual giant of this duo. But without Engels's wealth—squeezed from the proletariat slaving away in his English textile mills—Marx might have been forced to seek gainful employment instead of railing against the capitalist system that was lining his pockets. For a while Engels sent him the occasional five-pound note, a princely sum then, but when he sold out his share of the family textile business, Engels guaranteed his collaborator an annual stipend of 350 British pounds. Though preaching the coming of a communist utopia was his main shtick, Engels had time for other pursuits. He sang in a choral society, loved to go fox hunting, spoke twenty-four languages, and shacked up with an uneducated Irish working girl named Mary Burns. After she died, he shacked up with her sister Lizzy. **12,111**

416 JOHN I (1167–1216)
monarch who signed the Magna Carta

Cited as the forerunner of the Declaration of Independence, the Magna Carta was less prized by contemporaries than by later generations. Over centuries it has become a symbol of resistance to oppression. When his barons forced John to sign the document at Runnymede in 1215, it was considered a policy statement asserting the rights of king and people and a way to redress wrongs. Its text had the first expression of due process and a stipulation that the governed be consulted before taxes are levied. John, youngest son of Henry II (359) and Eleanor of Aquitaine (420), was his father's favorite. However much Henry loved him, England did not. John was a tyrant who swept aside established rule of law, brought in foreign mercenaries, and heavily taxed and fined his subjects. Little wonder people said John "trusted no man, and no man trusted him." **12,098**

417 FERDINAND FOCH (1851–1929)
French leader of the Allied victory in World War I

Without Foch, Europe might be united today— under the jackboot of the kaiser. Foch's mother was a friend of Saint Bernadette (390), the woman who had a vision at Lourdes; his brother was a Jesuit; he himself attended mass daily. But a greater passion than religion drove him: his dream of recapturing the province of Alsace-Lorraine from the Germans, who had seized it in 1870. At France's War College, Foch taught that "the will to conquer sweeps all before it." After war broke out, he issued his famous report at the second battle of the Marne: "My center is giving way; my right retreats; situation excellent. I am attacking." In March 1918, with the Germans near victory, the Allies finally united their forces under a single commander—Foch. Within two weeks he reported, "The [German] wave is dying on the beach." In November the Germans capitulated. Alsace-Lorraine was won. **12,076**

418 ARISTIDE BOUCICAUT (1810–1877)
inventor of the department store

Archaic French law had once prohibited shops from selling more than one type of merchandise or establishing set prices. So tradition was certainly against him when Boucicaut scandalized polite French society with his selling method. He opened Bon Marché as a small dry-goods store in 1838, and by midcentury it was a vast enterprise featuring many different departments and goods. Boucicaut, the son of a banker, established Bon Marché (the name means cheap) in a poor neighborhood of Paris and lured customers to his store by giving away needles and thread. He was among the first retailers to encourage browsing, established fixed prices that eliminated bartering, and slowly built a clientèle by allowing customers to return merchandise. So successful was Boucicaut at his enterprise that American merchants like Macy and Woolworth toured the Paris original to glean ideas for their own ventures. **12,065**

419 CHARLES-MAURICE TALLEYRAND
(1754–1838) *revolving-door duke*

The great French statesman preserved the territorial integrity of France and helped negotiate a post-Napoleonic balance of power in Europe that lasted a century. In his first vocation as a womanizing priest, the clubfooted aristocrat defended church privileges until the French Revolution loomed, then denounced them. In his later career as a bribe-taking diplomat, he abandoned French heads of state at the first whiff of danger, thereby managing to serve as foreign minister under the revolutionary regime, Napoleon (16), and the restored monarch Louis XVIII. He justified his opportunism by declaring that "after shipwrecks, there must be pilots to save the victims." When Napoleon uncovered a plot by him, the emperor shook his fist in his underling's face and vilified him as "shit in a silk stocking." Talleyrand took the abuse without flinching but afterward commented to a companion, "What a pity that such a great man should be so ill-bred." **12,019**

420 ELEANOR OF AQUITAINE (c.1122–1204)
queen of two kingdoms

In England and France the last half of the twelfth century could be called the Age of Eleanor because she used brains, beauty, and an inheritance to manipulate the government of three kings who ruled from 1137 to 1199. The first was Louis VII, whom she married, bringing her inheritance, the huge region of Aquitaine, under France's control. Then she took it back. Their marriage was annulled, and she married Henry II of England (359) and made the Aquitaine their wedding gift. They had four sons, and the romance faded. He locked her in a castle for years for meddling in affairs of state. But Henry's death put her back in business as First Mom in the kingdom of her son Richard the Lion-Hearted. It

was Eleanor—not the apocryphal Robin Hood and his Merry Men—who kept the conniving Prince John (416) from stealing Richard's realm while he was off crusading. **12,009**

421 FERDINAND DE LESSEPS (1805–1894)
ditchdigger—but what a ditch!

Lesseps was the mastermind of the Suez Canal. At age forty-four his career fizzled. A distinguished diplomat, he had resigned in disgust from French public service after the government blamed him for a zealous general's takeover of Rome. Idleness allowed de Lesseps to pursue a dream he had shaped years before as consul in Cairo: construction of a canal across the hundred-mile Isthmus of Suez, connecting the Mediterranean and Red seas to open the shortest sea route between Europe and the Indian and western Pacific oceans. It took ten long years of battling engineering problems and shoring up shaky international support, but de Lesseps's charm and chicanery finally triumphed. When the canal opened in 1869 amid fanfare and fireworks, the first flotilla sailed past. One observer said: "There was something solemn and imposing about this group of vessels, surrounded by desert, anchored on an artificial lake created by the genius of one man." **12,008**

422 YUNG-LO (1363–1424)
the Ming dynasty's brilliant ruler

The word *ming* means "brilliant," but before Yung-lo could show his brilliance, he had to establish his authority. He was born Chu Ti, the lowly fourth son of the first Ming ruler, Chu Yüan-chang. Called the Prince of Yen, Yung-lo was popular in North China, where his troops guarded the borders. His nephew succeeded Chu Yüan-chang as emperor, but Yung-lo justified insurrection by arguing that the youth had been led astray by corrupt advisers. The three-year civil war ended when the nephew died in a fire and Yung-lo became emperor by default. He moved the capital from Nanking to Beijing in 1407 and reconstructed the Grand Canal so ships could navigate inland. He extended Chinese borders beyond the Great Wall into the Gobi Desert and, nearly a century before Europe's great explorations, sent his loyal eunuch, Cheng Ho, on sea expeditions throughout the east, as far south as Africa. **12,001**

423 GUSTAVUS ADOLPHUS OF SWEDEN
(1594–1632) *father of the modern professional army*

Gustav inherited three wars and concluded them by making peace with Denmark, beating back Russia from the Baltic (and thus delaying its emergence as a European power for a century), and fighting Poland to a draw. More important, the Swedish monarch entered the Thirty Years' War on the side of the Protestant princes of Germany and their allies against the forces of the Counter-Reformation, delivering Europe from Catholic domination. Gustavus instituted a highly disciplined, professional army organized into squadrons and brigades, and he actually paid his soldiers on time. These and other innovations enabled him to sweep victorious through Germany, gaining the title of "Lion of the North." But on November 6, 1632, leading a cavalry charge on a mist-shrouded battlefield, Gustavus was separated from his men, knocked from his horse into the mud, and shot through the head with a pistol. Adieu, Adolphus. **11,987**

424 FRÉDÉRIC CHOPIN (1810–1849)
the prince of the piano

Rarely has the millennium seen a greater flowering of art in one place and time than Paris in the 1830s. Hugo (163), Balzac (254), Musset,

Delacroix (486), Ingres (926), Mendelssohn, Heine, Liszt (300), and Berlioz (671) worked and played together, and they welcomed Chopin, newly arrived from Poland in 1831. Chopin was smart. He shrugged off an offer of lessons from the great Frederick Kalkbrenner (the great who?) and cozied up to Baron Rothschild, whose rich friends left coins discreetly on mantelpieces after Chopin taught their children. "A really perfect virtuoso," the sweet Felix Mendelssohn wrote of Chopin the performer. We revere Chopin the composer of short piano pieces—the waltzes, ballads, études, and mazurkas. So often heard, they are as familiar as the whistling of the wind. He died of tuberculosis, spurned at the end by his former lover, the intriguing woman with a man's pen name, novelist George Sand. **11,944**

425 ALESSANDRO VOLTA (1745–1827)
inventor of the battery

Try this. With a silver spoon connect the back of your tongue to a bit of tin on the tip of your tongue. The sour taste you get is from the electricity sparking between the two metals. You have turned your tongue into a primitive battery. Luigi Galvani (503) tried a similar experiment with the nerve and muscle of a frog's leg and thought the electricity he generated was caused by the frog. Volta proved it was the wires. He experimented with different metals, wires, and buffers and built what came to be known as the voltaic pile, the first battery. That jump-started the electrical revolution of the nineteenth century. The volt, the measure of electromagnetic force, was named for him in 1881. **11,911**

426 EUGENE O'NEILL (1888–1953)
America's greatest playwright

O'Neill, a taciturn man whose youth was spent backstage wherever his actor-father performed, bounced around the world, lost himself to alcohol, abandoned a wife and child, and even attempted suicide. Then he studied playwriting. His troubled childhood provided fodder to create bleak characters like the drunken riffraff in *The Iceman Cometh*. His realistic, disturbing plays established American theater as art, beyond vaudeville and melodrama. He won four Pulitzer Prizes and was the only American playwright to win the Nobel Prize for literature. O'Neill wrote his masterpiece, the autobiographical *Long Day's Journey into Night*, in 1940 but had it locked in a vault until after his death. In the foreword, O'Neill called it "this play of old sorrow, written in tears and blood." Near the end of his life, suffering from Parkinson's disease and unable to write, he became reclusive, a mirror of the tragic characters he had created in his dramas.   **11,910**

427 PHILIP II OF SPAIN (1527–1598)
mightiest monarch of his age

Philip ruled Spain at the height of its power, yet sowed the seeds of its decline. He is best known for championing the Counter-Reformation and sending his "Invincible Armada" to destruction against England. Philip executed thousands of Protestant rebels in the Netherlands and even sent soldiers to Florida to clean out the "nest of heretics" there. But more than his religious fanaticism, his bureaucratic procrastination undermined his reign. The foot-dragging reached comic proportions when he placed his empty suit of armor outside the palace to review the troops while he fussed inside over his wordy replies to urgent dispatches. Historian Barbara Tuchman called him "the surpassing woodenhead of all sovereigns." Yet under him Spain's literary Golden Age began. And his passel of wives included a Portuguese princess, Bloody Mary of England, and the daughters of a French king and an Austrian emperor.   **11,893**

428 MATHEW BRADY (1823–1896)
photography's first witness to war

Brady and his staff captured the Civil War on film, marking the first time a major conflict was so fully documented by camera. It all started when Brady learned how to make daguerreotypes and opened a Broadway studio in 1844. He envisioned himself as the "instrument chosen to express the American spirit," said biographer Philip Kunhardt, Jr. Presidents posed willingly, putting up with long periods of remaining still, a metal brace immobilizing their necks and heads, because they knew the publicity value of a Brady photo. When civil war broke out, Brady turned delivery wagons into darkrooms, and he and employees shadowed Union troops, capturing the quiet of camp life and the gruesome corpse-strewn battlefields. Brady invested $100,000 in the project and was ruined when the government failed to buy his photos afterward. Deeply in debt and hounded by creditors, he died an alcoholic in a charity ward. The collection is now housed in the Library of Congress.   **11,844**

429 LEON TROTSKY (1879–1940)
fiery Russian revolutionary

On an October morning in 1902, Trotsky rapped three times on the door of a London flat. "The Pen has arrived," Vladimir Lenin's (41) wife announced. So met the two most influential Russian revolutionaries of modern times, Lenin, the exiled grand strategist, and Trotsky, the Jewish-born wordsmith and rabble-rouser who had escaped from a Siberian penal colony. In 1917, after years of planning and conniving—sometimes in different factions—they established the Soviet state. It was Trotsky who performed the hardest task: leading the armies that defeated the czarist generals. At his hour of triumph he told a liberal opponent: "You are miserable bankrupts, your role is played out; go where

you ought to be: into the dustbin of history."
Today Marxism is played out. Trotsky, stripped of
power by Stalin in 1926, was murdered in Mexico
by an assassin with an ice pick.   **11,793**

430 JOHN HARVEY KELLOGG (1852–1943)
champion of breakfast

How do you spell breakfast? For millions of Americans who grew up on television, it's "K-E-double
L-O-double good, Kellogg's best to you." Dr. Kellogg's vegetarian regimen at his health sanitarium
in Battle Creek, Michigan, couldn't accommodate
eggs over easy, bacon, and sausage. He started
serving little flakes of corn for breakfast. They
were an instant success, even though his flaked
wheat—Granose—didn't make it as the breakfast
of champions. Will Keith (W. K.) Kellogg toiled
under his brother's thumb at the clinic for years,
then formed his own company in 1906 to market
John Harvey's cornflakes. Back at the sanitarium,
patient C. W. Post was so taken with the breakfasts that he formed a competing cereal company.
But it was John Harvey's healthier idea that put
the snap, crackle, and pop into breakfast.   **11,719**

431 KONRAD ADENAUER (1876–1967)
*the man who made Germany
respectable again*

As mayor of Cologne when the Nazis came to
power, Adenauer refused to greet Hitler (20) and
was dismissed and subsequently imprisoned three
times during World War II. As chancellor from
1949 to 1963, he presided over West Germany's
economic rebirth and its integration into Western
Europe. A Roman Catholic from the Rhineland,
he distrusted the Protestant Prussians and their
militaristic mentality, muttering as he headed east
across the River Elbe on trips to Berlin, "Now we
enter Asia." Adenauer supported the Atlantic
alliance and fought attempts to neutralize Ger-

many. His realism bordered at times on unscrupulousness, prompting one rival to quip that the aging
chancellor had read a version of Machiavelli (40)
edited by Ignatius Loyola (115). Franz-Josef Strauss,
a powerful German politician, once exploded,
"Herr Chancellor, we have not come here to say
'Yes' and 'Amen' to all that you say." Adenauer
retorted, "'Yes' will be quite sufficient."   **11,718**

432 MICHEL DE MONTAIGNE (1533–1592)
permissive essayist

The essay form that Montaigne perfected has been
useful for thinkers as diverse as the bearded sage
Martin Buber (723) and the bemusing comic Dave
Barry. Montaigne also contributed a compelling
message: There is no absolute morality, only the
morality in the eye of the beholder, which makes a
cannibal as worthy as a curly-wigged duke. "The
world is but a perennial movement," Montaigne
wrote. He received the best education his French
aristocrat father could afford and became a lawyer
and government official. But he spent most of his
time in his study writing things that were pithy,
witty, and wise. When he was elected mayor of Bordeaux in 1581, Montaigne said, "We offer our blood
and sweat." Winston Churchill (38), who added
"toil and tears" to his speech accepting British
leadership in World War II, was just one of many
writers who stole lines from Montaigne.   **11,676**

433 JEAN MONNET (1888–1979)
*uncommon visionary of
the Common Market*

For two millennia tyrants failed to do it with
guns, swords, and elephants; Monnet used coal,
steel, butter, and wine to bring nations of Europe
together peacefully. A Frenchman from Cognac,
Monnet advocated Allied economic cooperation
during World War I, then served in the ill-fated
League of Nations. His vision of a united Euro-

pean Coal and Steel Community stemmed from a desperate need to pool dwindling resources after World War II. From there came the Brussels-based Common Market, now the fifteen-nation European Union, which has its own passport and a planned single currency for the new millennium. Monnet, a talented negotiator one-on-one with adversaries, was so secretive that his office had two doors—one to show people in and another to usher them out. A witness to the near-destruction of Europe in two wars, Monnet believed "the greatest risk of all would be to do nothing and change nothing." **11,671**

434 JEAN-FRANÇOIS BOREL (b. 1934)
wonder drug maker

Borel, an immunologist at the Swiss company Sandoz Pharmaceuticals, made a life-saving discovery in 1970. Soil from Norway yielded a previously unknown fungus, *Tolypocladium inflatum*. Sandoz technicians cultured it in hopes of producing a medicine to fight fungus infections. Borel noticed this new substance, called cyclosporine, could kill lymphocytes—the cells our bodies summon to attack foreign cells—on a selective basis without destroying surrounding tissue. It was a miracle breakthrough for the fledgling arena of organ transplants, where a patient's immune system could prove fatal to a donated liver, heart, lung, or kidney. But this wonder drug also threatened cancer and kidney damage. Eventually that risk was lowered when doctors mixed cyclosporine in a "cocktail" with other drugs. Cyclosporine won federal approval in 1983, and since then one-year survival rates for transplant patients have soared from 50 to 90 percent. **11,669**

435 JOHN PIERPONT MORGAN (1837–1913)
the wizard of Wall Street

J. P. Morgan financed the industrialization of the United States after the Civil War, hobnobbing with presidents and kings along the way. First speculating in gold and arms, he later dominated the railroads and created industrial trusts. In 1901 he put together United States Steel, the world's first billion-dollar corporation. John Gates, owner of a steel company Morgan coveted, commented on losing a huge poker pot, "I'll put it on Old Livernose's bill," a reference to Morgan's bulbous schnozzle. So vast was Morgan's wealth that he singlehandedly saved the U.S. Treasury from collapse in 1895 and halted a Wall Street panic in 1907. A legendary womanizer, Morgan also made wrong calls, once rejecting an offer to buy General Motors for $500,000. **11,653**

436 HENRY MAUDSLAY (1771–1831)
the lord of the lathe

The only thing more important to the Industrial Revolution than machines were the machines that made machines, and Maudslay built both. The best of his inventions was a metal lathe that cut screws quicker and more precisely than the screws made by hand. That makes Maudslay the father of the nuts and bolts industry. The shop he built in 1798 to make pulley blocks for the royal dockyards—some of the blocks were still in use in World War II—was one of the world's first automated factories. Ten laborers replaced a hundred skilled craftsmen. From his first job in a bullet factory at age twelve to the day he died and was buried in a cast-iron coffin, Maudslay was a happy man when he was in his shop tinkering. **11,644**

437 WOODROW WILSON (1856–1924)
president with a pointed plan for ending war

Wilson, president of Princeton University turned New Jersey governor, won the 1912 Democratic nomination for president on the forty-sixth ballot. Then he was elected to his first term without a majority in a three-way race. Many of his social welfare programs and financial reforms, like the Federal Reserve System, provided the roots for the New Deal of Franklin Roosevelt. Wilson ran for his second term on a "read my lips" campaign doozy: "He kept us out of war." Not for long. Wilson led America's better-late-than-never effort in World War I, negotiated the Treaty of Versailles, then suffered a tremendous blow when Congress rejected his fledgling League of Nations peace plan. The idea was resurrected, and Wilson's fourteen-point plan vindicated, when the United Nations rose out of World War II's ruins. But in 1919 Wilson couldn't have predicted that, and the stress of the presidency cost him his health. Wilson suffered a stroke so debilitating that his doctors and his second wife, Edith, secretly acted as president for three months until he recovered sufficiently to finish his term. **11,601**

438 Li Hung-chang (1823–1901)
leading Chinese statesman of the nineteenth century

As head of China's central province, Li began to modernize his nation militarily to guard against Western and Japanese encroachments. He built three Western-style arsenals and established a railroad, telegraph line, and modern naval bases, the first steps on the road to Chinese modernization. As China's chief negotiator with outside powers, his abiding philosophy was "Let us use the foreigner, but do not let him use us." Westerners soon found he had not one but ten faces. "He united the traits of cordial philanthropy and heartless cruelty, of truthfulness and mendacity," said American John Foster, Li's assistant at peace talks with the Japanese in 1895. To his credit, Li was a staunch patriot. He took the bullet of a Japanese fanatic during those negotiations. That

loss of face for the Japanese forced them to soften their humiliating peace terms. **11,579**

439 John III of Portugal (1502–1557)
imperialist and persecutor

Amazingly for a nation the size of present-day Maine, Portugal under John III projected its sea power to the far reaches of the globe. In a single decade beginning in 1529, it gained control of the Spice Islands in Indonesia, settled Brazil, conquered the city of Diu in India, and established a colony in Macao, China. At home most of the king's energies were directed at persecuting the hapless third or so of the population suspected of being tainted with Jewish blood. Though early in his reign John hired a disciple of the Dutch humanist Erasmus as his court chronicler, he turned increasingly orthodox in religion as the hated Lutheranism spread. In 1536 he instituted the Inquisition in Portugal, primarily to destroy any vestiges of the Jewish faith among the descendants of forced converts to Christianity. **11,574**

440 Joseph Monier (1823–1906)
gardener with a concrete idea

The Frenchman made concrete planters for orange trees and had the bright idea of making the concrete stronger by forming it around iron rods. Voilà—reinforced concrete, now one of the most popular materials for buildings, bridges, and roads. Concrete had always been a bulwark against compressive forces; Monier's rods prevented crumbling and added the tensile strength needed for large structures that swayed. He patented his idea in 1867 and built a fifty-foot-diameter reservoir with his new product. Within twenty years the formula was known throughout Europe by its German name, *Das System Monier*. It revolutionized architecture. Some of the most stunning buildings in the world, such as the TWA terminal at Kennedy Airport, are made of reinforced concrete, and some of the ugliest are, too, like the grim housing developments of Eastern Europe. **11,540**

441 VIRGINIA WOOLF (1882–1941)
modern literature's lighthouse

Woolf shed the trappings of the traditional novel to recapture, she said, the "essence" of life. She used stream of consciousness and interior monologues to put readers in her characters' minds. Her impressionist style and her struggle to describe the relationship between feminism and writing make her work beacons to readers of twentieth-century literature, particularly women. Her finest works: *To the Lighthouse, The Waves,* and *Mrs. Dalloway.* Woolf's quick intelligence made her the center of the famed Bloomsbury group, intellectuals who included John Maynard Keynes (201), T. S. Eliot (720), and Lytton Strachey. Her niece, painter Angelica Garnett, described Woolf's personality as "a diamond stream of water, hard and scintillating, transparent, bubbling, austere and life-giving." Woolf, who battled insanity throughout her life, drowned herself in fear that another breakdown was near. We now understand her illness: contrary to popular images of her "idyllic" Victorian childhood, Woolf was sexually abused for years by her stepbrothers. **11,529**

442 JACKIE ROBINSON (1919–1972)
athlete who changed the color of sports

When Brooklyn Dodger president Branch Rickey decided to integrate baseball after World War II, he knew he needed a black superman with unbelievable athletic credentials who had "guts enough not to fight back" against verbal abuse and worse. He picked Robinson, a formidable four-sport college athlete, veteran of World War II, and star of the Negro League's Kansas City Monarchs. Despite jeers, threats, and segregation from teammates on the road, Robinson began a ten-year career with the Dodgers in 1947. The pressure was tremendous for this one-man traveling civil rights movement. When Boston fans taunted shortstop Pee Wee Reese for playing with Robinson, Reese sauntered over to second base, put his hand on Robinson's shoulder, and chatted quietly with him to show solidarity. The fans shut up. After Brooklyn won the National League pennant that first season, Robinson was named Rookie of the Year, and American sports, indeed America, was never the same. **11,522**

443 JAMES BUCHANAN DUKE (1856–1925)
cancer-stick king

The world's addiction to tobacco goes back to Columbus's (2) encounter with the peace pipe, but it was "Buck" Duke, the southern farm boy, who mass-marketed cigarettes. At age nine he wandered the North Carolina countryside with his father and two blind mules, peddling homemade chewing tobacco. Two decades later their business was using the latest technology to churn out 120,000 prerolled cigarettes a day. By slashing prices from a dime to a nickel for a pack of ten, inventing snappy brand names, designing colorful packages, and using promotional gimmicks—from coupons redeemable for picture cards of "sporting girls" to massive billboard and newspaper advertising—Buck turned his American Tobacco Company into a colossus that sucked up competitors and controlled half the national market by 1889. The company was broken up in 1911 on antitrust grounds. But by then America was hooked. **11,511**

444 JOHN ROEBLING (1806–1869)
suspension bridge builder

The philosopher G.W.F. Hegel (59) was one of his teachers at Berlin's Royal Polytechnic School, but Roebling cared less for cyclical theories of history than cylindrical strands of steel. He invented a process to bind wire rope into thick cables for the suspension bridges he built across the mighty rivers of his adopted America. Roebling bridges spanned the Ohio, the Monongahela, and the Niagara before he designed his masterpiece, the Brooklyn Bridge. In its time it was America's greatest construction feat, a symbol of the nation's preeminence in engineering. The four cables holding up the bridge have a combined strength of 180 million pounds, and every builder of suspension bridges from Australia to Zaire has studied Roebling's work as intensely as military cadets study the campaigns of Napoleon (16). Roebling's foot was crushed in an accident during construction of the bridge, and he died of tetanus before it was finished in 1883 under the direction of his son. **11,508**

445 ALAN TURING (1912–1954)
code-cracking computer theorist

"On Computable Numbers," a paper written when Turing was just twenty-five, ushered in the age of digital computers by figuring out how to make machines "think." Turing also masterminded the British Intelligence team in World War II that cracked the German "Enigma" codes, which provided Allies with knowledge of Germany's land and sea movements and helped secure victory. It was a nice piece of work: Germany's encoding machine provided 403,291,461,126,605,635,584,000,000 alphabet combinations. One of the first messages decoded with the British "Bombe" came from the German U-Boat admiral to his captains and ended with the ominous command: "Defeat England." Afterward, Turing applied himself to automated computers and described "artificial intelligence." He suggested that machines could think like people if they were equipped with a random factor similar to a roulette wheel. When Turing's homosexuality was discovered, he was forced to undergo a "cure" or face prison. Instead he committed suicide by snacking on a cyanide-coated apple. **11,489**

446 LOUIS LUMIÈRE (1864–1948)
innovator in motion

Brothers Louis and Auguste Lumière presented the world's first projected motion picture on December 28, 1895. At one franc per head, Parisians filled a hundred chairs in a basement below the Grand Café, Hotel Scribe, and watched the twenty-minute "Workers Leaving the Lumière Factory." *Fantastique.* The images on the screen were generated by a hand-cranked apparatus moving at sixteen frames per second. The Lumières' Cinématographe was both projector and camera, and light enough to carry. This device set the standard for movie-making for years. Louis deserves top billing because he alone created a new brand of photographic plate that enriched the family business, making it financially feasible for the Lumières to experiment with film. Also, Louis dispatched sales reps not just to sell Lumière cameras and movies but to film new scenes that would add to the brothers' inventory. **11,466**

447 VINCENT OF BEAUVAIS (1190–1264)
chronicler of knowledge

Vincent, a French Dominican priest, synthesized ancient and medieval knowledge in eighty books, the *Speculum Majus* or *Great Mirror*. Widely considered the greatest encyclopedia until the eighteenth century, *Speculum Majus* covered the history of the world from the biblical creation to Vincent's own time, helping to set the stage for the explosion of learning known as the Renaissance. Among future authors who drew on it were Geoffrey Chaucer (62) in the late 1300s and Sir Walter Raleigh (472) in his *History of the World*, published in 1614. **11,465**

448 HENRY CAVENDISH (1731–1810)
scientist whose genius spoke for itself

Legend says that the neurotically shy Cavendish spoke fewer words in his lifetime than any other man who lived eighty years. He left his London home and laboratory only to attend the Royal Society Club, but when he was approached there once by a noted physician eager to meet the famous scientist, Cavendish fled in terror. He communicated to his servants with notes. Cavendish's work, including the discovery that water is a compound of oxygen and the mysterious gas we now call hydrogen, helped early nineteenth-century scientists discover the chemical and physical properties of matter. He was the first scientist to measure gravitational forces between small bodies, which led to extrapolations of the weight of the planets. Some of his scientific methods were crude: to study electric currents, he shocked himself. **11,438**

449 GABRIELE FALLOPPIO (1523–1562)
tube tracker

Falloppio described the tube in the ear. Just kidding—we wanted to see if you were paying attention. Actually, Falloppio's pal, Bartolommeo Eustachio, takes credit for the ear. Falloppio, a pioneer in the systematic study of the human body, analyzed blood vessels, kidneys, and—okay, okay—female anatomy. He described female reproductive organs, including the trumpet-shaped fallopian tubes that bear his name. He created the term

vagina and explained how the thin membrane called a hymen covers the vagina of a virgin. Falloppio turned to anatomy because he was such a failure as a surgeon that he had trouble keeping patients alive. He studied the writings of Vesalius (234), then dissected dead lions at the Medici zoo in Florence. He began describing human anatomy based on dissections of the corpses of men, women, fetuses, newborns, and young children. Although he was falsely accused of working on living creatures, he became a university lecturer of great stature and taught other luminaries who further unraveled the mysteries of human anatomy. **11,422**

450 JOHN GORRIE (1803–1855)
Mr. Cool

Yes, some historians will note that other nineteenth-century tinkerers helped develop modern refrigeration, but to them we say: Chill out! Gorrie got there first. As a physician in Apalachicola, Florida, he invented an air-conditioner for fever patients and by 1844 was cooling two hospital rooms and his own home with it. The apparatus, which employed the basic cooling principle still used in most refrigerators, also made ice. For all his technical wizardry, Gorrie was unable to raise money for a factory to build his invention. So hostile were religious folk in those days to artificial refrigeration that he wrote on the subject under a pseudonym, plaintively declaring that it could "become accessory to the extension of commerce." *The New York Globe* was unimpressed. "There is a crank down in Florida," the newspaper snorted, "that thinks he can make ice by his machine as good as God Almighty." **11,407**

451 WASSILY KANDINSKY (1866–1944)
the Jerry Seinfeld of art

Like the television comedian's sitcom, Kandinsky's art was about nothing. Picasso (149) was preoccupied with abstracting inanimate objects and the human form when Kandinsky took painting to new levels with *Composition I*, considered to be the first completely abstract painting. Finished in 1910, it was inspired by music and depicted no recognizable objects. The Russian Kandinsky moved to Munich, mingled with German expressionists, and helped form the Blue Rider group. He exerted influence on contemporary art as a teacher and theorist at the famed Bauhaus school from 1922 to 1933. "The observer must learn to look at the picture as a graphic representation of a *mood* and not as a representation of objects," Kandinsky wrote. He hawked his paintings with an audacious lack of subject matter to well-to-do trendy Americans. When one American commissioned four Kandinskys for his apartment, another noted it required "a good deal of courage" to hang such modern paintings "in a place where everybody must see them." **11,399**

452 GEORGE III (1738–1820)
the king who lost America and helped Britain find itself

Master propagandists that they were, the rebel leaders of America demonized the English king George. They said in the Declaration of Independence, "A Prince, whose character is thus marked by every act which may define a Tyrant, is unfit to be the ruler of a free people." Tyrant? Not really. George makes our list because he lacked the vision to realize that conciliation might have kept America in the empire. "The idea that he was a dunce dies harder than the old notion that he wished to be a despot," biographer Stanley Ayling wrote in praise of George's love of learning. Yes, he lost the colonies, and yes, dementia caused by a metabolic imbalance called porphyria made him insane for long periods. But for most of his sixty-year reign, George helped provide the stability

that allowed pastoral England to move peacefully into the industrial age. **11,349**

453 HEINRICH HERTZ (1857–1894)
the wave of the future

The Scot James Clerk Maxwell (205) theorized that radio waves existed, and Hertz, a German, proved him right in experiments in the late 1880s. Without Hertz's work, Guglielmo Marconi (95) could not have built the transmitters and receivers that made radio possible. Hertz was an all-around genius, tops in his high-school class in Greek, a student of Arabic, and a skillful draftsman and mathematician. In his honor radio frequencies are measured in hertz; that's what those numbers on the radio dial signify. He died of a blood disease at age thirty-six. **11,348**

454 GERTRUDE ELION (b. 1918)
pathfinder in drug research

A star in biochemistry without the requisite doctorate, American Trudy Elion revolutionized the way drugs are developed. And during her long years of research, she never forgot that her mission was curing people. With collaborator George Hitchings at the drug firm Burroughs Wellcome, Elion studied normal and abnormal cells, then created drugs to interrupt the reproductive process in maverick cells while leaving healthy ones alone. In 1950 she synthesized 6-MP, a compound that, combined with other drugs, has boosted survival rates for leukemia to eighty percent. She also developed acyclovir, the first antivirus drug, which fights herpes viruses. Though she had retired by the time her team created the successful AIDS drug AZT, her colleagues used all her painstaking experimental techniques. In 1988 she received the Nobel Prize. "It's very nice," she said upon hearing the news, "but that's not what it's all about." **11,344**

455 CHIANG KAI-SHEK (1887–1975)
America's bad bet in China

Heir to the revolutionary leader Sun Yat-sen (290), Chiang headed the Nationalist government of China from 1928 until he lost the civil war to Mao's (50) Communists and was driven to exile on Taiwan in 1949. From then on he was a thorn in Beijing's side, threatening to retake the mainland and building up an economy that was the envy of the developing world. The political right in the United States never forgave Harry Truman (485) for abandoning Chiang in 1949, but the American president claimed that the ineptness and corruption of Chiang's regime gave him no choice. "I bet on a bad horse," he said. The United States, however, supported Taiwan with economic aid and a defense treaty, until Nixon's (904) rapprochement with China led to a break in diplomatic relations in 1979.   **11,340**

456 IBN AL-HAYTHAM (965–1039)
a lens on Arab learning

Many people know that the Crusades stimulated European contacts with the works of brilliant Muslims who had preserved and expanded classical learning. But few have any idea who those Muslims were. Here's one: Ibn al-Haytham, known in Western Europe as Alhazen. His book *Treasury of Optics*, available in Latin translations after the thirteenth century, provided a theoretical foundation for European lens crafters. He taught that light emanates in a straight line from every point on a luminous parabola, and he stimulated inquiry by challenging scientists to discover the law governing the refraction of light. The question, known in the West as "Alhazen's problem," was finally solved by Dutchman Willebrord Snell in 1621. Being a copycat was another of Ibn al-Haytham's contributions: he copied works by Euclid, Apollonius, and Ptolemy, and those manuscripts found their way west.   **11,333**

457 HARRIET BEECHER STOWE (1811–1896)
source of the abolitionist outcry heard 'round the world

When Abraham Lincoln (32) met Stowe a decade after *Uncle Tom's Cabin* was published, he asked, "Is this the little woman who made this great war?" Stowe's novel, which described in great detail the harshness of slavery, spurred international outrage when it was published in 1852 and acted as a catalyst for antislavery activities. Although she had never traveled farther south than Cincinnati, Stowe said she wrote what she saw, explaining that the story came to her in visions. Condemned by Southerners but an instant best-seller, *Uncle Tom's Cabin* sold more than 300,000 copies its first year. Stowe, a member of the prominent New England Beecher family of ministers and authors, was a prolific writer whose works fill sixteen volumes. But she makes our list solely on the weight of her first novel, which forced America to confront its shameful conduct.   **11,331**

458 BOOKER T. WASHINGTON (1856–1915)
no Uncle Tom

Washington, son of former slaves, was determined to get an education. He worked his way through agricultural school and studied at a seminary before being tapped to head a new college for black students at Tuskegee. In thirty-four years Washington built Tuskegee Institute from two small buildings into a sprawling campus with nearly two thousand students. Tuskegee's endowment rose to $2 million, thanks to Washington's cordial arm-twisting of white philanthropists. He believed that vocational skills and good work habits were the keys to economic prosperity for his people, maintaining that "no race can accomplish anything till its mind is awakened." His pacifism and emphasis on vocational education over academic skills drew criticism from black contemporaries such as W.E.B. Du Bois (204). Publicly, Washington never rocked the white world's boat. Privately, he helped fund lawsuits battling segregation and championing the right of blacks to vote. **11,327**

459 CHARLES DE GAULLE (1890–1970)
embodiment of France

François Mauriac said of the obscure official who fled the collaborationist Vichy regime in 1940 and appealed to his compatriots from London to resist their Nazi overlords, "A madman imagined he was France, and the world believed him because it was true." De Gaulle actually declared, "I am France." Churchill (38) couldn't stand him, saying, "Of all the crosses I have to bear, the cross of Lorraine is the heaviest." Roosevelt (37) dismissed him as "a nut." Big mistake! From his triumphal march down the Champs-Élysees after the liberation of Paris, to his election as president in 1958 and his creation of the Fifth Republic, to his extrication of France from Algeria (including his plea during a 1961 crisis, "Frenchmen! Frenchwomen! Help me!"), to his independent foreign policy that included withdrawal from the Atlantic alliance, the six-foot-five general obsessively pursued his only ambition: to restore the grandeur of France. **11,326**

460 BENITO MUSSOLINI (1883–1945)
the first fascist

Mussolini, the supreme opportunist, abandoned his youthful socialism and, in 1919, created the Fascist Party, named after the ancient Roman symbol for authority, with the slogan "Believe! Obey! Fight!" In 1922 he seized power by threatening a march on Rome by his Black Shirt followers.

"Il Duce," a former editor, then abolished freedom of the press but made the trains run on time, winning accolades abroad from the likes of Winston Churchill (38) and numerous American congressmen. "Statesmen of his ability only occur once in a century," an American biographer gushed at the time. Mussolini wasn't racist or anti-Semitic, but he earned history's damnation for allying himself with the archdemon Hitler (20) and leading his nation to defeat in World War II. Shortly before Italian partisans shot him and his mistress and hanged their bodies upside down at a gasoline station, Mussolini pondered whether he and Hitler "might not both be slightly mad." **11,311**

461 CH'IEN-LUNG (1711–1799)
emperor who lived too long for his country's good

He is the millennium's best argument for term limits. Imperial China reached its apex in the first forty years of Ch'ien-lung's sixty-three year reign, the longest in China's recorded history. Agriculture and the arts flourished, taxes were low, the peasants were happy, and warlike tribes on the borders were subdued. Then Ch'ien-lung turned into a tax-levying, war-mongering, grumpy old tyrant. Books that offended him were burned—13,862 titles, by his advisers' count. He let the underpaid civil service slide into corruption led by his foppish imperial counselor, Ho-shen. Ch'ien-lung's successor ordered Ho-shen to kill himself and tried to reform the government, but it was too late. British imperialists were waiting in the wings and turned China's emperors into powerless puppets. **11,304**

462 FREDERICK GRANT BANTING
(1891–1941) *tamer of diabetes*

Banting gets kudos for turning a killer disease into a chronic one. For years doctors diagnosed diabetes by tasting a patient's urine for the telltale sweetness of sugar. But doctors didn't know how to treat it. Enter Banting, a Canadian, and his junior colleague Charles H. Best. Eight months after he began research in May 1921, Banting isolated insulin, the hormone that was causing all the trouble in the pancreas. He injected his serum into a fourteen-year-old boy who had failed to respond to other treatments. The insulin worked. By October 1922 insulin was marketed. When the Nobel Prize was awarded jointly to Banting and the now obscure professor who supervised the laboratory, Banting quelled controversy by splitting his prize money with Best. Today the side effects of diabetes can still kill, but Banting took the starch out of the disease that affects twelve million Americans. **11,300**

463 ALBERT KAHN (1869–1942)
creator of modern factory design

In an era when designing a factory was considered more an engineering than an architectural challenge, Kahn stepped forward to change all that. Kahn, a Detroit industrial architect and planner, answered the summons of automaker Henry Ford (51) who considered multistory factories inefficient. Kahn developed huge single-level, steel-framed structures with walls of glass that housed all assembly processes on one floor, a factory scheme that became the norm. Leading architect for most of America's car manufacturers for three decades, Kahn designed more than a thousand projects for Ford, including the 1917 River Rouge auto plant near Detroit, one of the largest in the world. As Kahn saw it, the "avoidance of unnecessary ornamentation, simplicity, and proper respect for cost of maintenance" make for a kind of structure that, while "strictly utilitarian and functional, has distinct architectural merit." **11,206**

464 CLEMENT VII (1478–1534)
pontifex minimus

If ever an institution needed a dynamic leader and didn't get one, it was the Catholic Church under Pope Clement VII. The world might be more Catholic today if in 1523 the cardinals had picked someone better than this ineffectual illegitimate son of a Medici banker. When he should have been healing Europe's spiritual wounds, he played politics—and did it so badly that in 1527 an army of mercenaries under a French count sacked Rome. They locked Clement in his castle, murdered a quarter of the eternal city's people, and demanded a 400,000-ducat payoff. Clement raised part of it by selling eight cardinal's seats to clergymen as unworthy as himself. Meanwhile, Protestantism was taking root in Scandinavia, Poland, England, and parts of France. England turned Protestant because the officious Clement wouldn't annul Henry VIII's (100) marriage. Surprising scruples for a pope who cooed over the bastard son he sired with a serving maid. **11,199**

465 KONSTANTIN STANISLAVSKY
(1863–1938) *the plumber of actors' souls*

There's madness to his method. Stanislavsky taught actors that by casting aside inhibitions, they could reach new depths of reality and emotion in their roles. Before he articulated "method acting," he spent years in Russia theorizing about his own work. Cynical critics say he developed his acting theories to compensate for his unfortunate dearth of ability. Whatever the motivation, Stanislavsky founded the Moscow Art Theater in 1898 to teach his system, which he likened to unearthing the actor's "superconscious intuition." On a world tour Stanislavsky spread his ideas about "the Method." As he explained it, "Technique is all right so far as it goes, but . . . before it come talent, inspiration, superconsciousness, and the living over of a part." In *On the Waterfront*, America's greatest method man, Marlon Brando, muttered, "I coudda bin a contender." Thanks to Stanislavsky, he was. **11,146**

466 FIDEL CASTRO (b. 1926)
the Communist who couldn't

Castro, lawyer turned guerrilla leader, assembled a revolutionary force that fought its way to victory in Cuba in 1959. His stated intent: to free the island nation from military dictatorship. Let's revisit Cuba now. Cubans supposedly have more educational opportunities, free health care, and guaranteed employment. But the same Marxist-Leninist government won't tolerate dissent, stifles intellectuals, and through overcentralization hobbles the economy. Mismanagement is rife, production is shoddy, and shortages are common. Judging from this, Castro's main place in history will be as accessory to a tension-filled weekend in October 1962 when Soviet premier Khrushchev (619) and American president Kennedy faced off over Soviet placement of missiles on Cuban soil. Khrushchev finally blinked, and the missiles were removed. If Castro hadn't appealed for Soviet military protection amid fears of an American invasion, there wouldn't have been a crisis. It's the closest the world has come to nuclear war. **11,144**

467 PHILIP OF HESSE (1504–1567)
patron of the Protestants

Without support from this German ruler, Protestant upstarts Martin Luther (3) and Huldrych Zwingli would have been crushed like acorns under the heel of Catholic emperor Charles V's (61) boot. Philip's defeat of imperial armies in 1534 was said to have done more for the Protestant cause than a thousand Lutheran books, and at Marburg he founded the first

Protestant university. He was a moral man, and that led to his downfall. Unwilling to commit adultery with his beloved, he married her in 1540 without divorcing wife number one. Luther was willing to bend the rules for a powerful patron and declared that bigamy wasn't a sin. But Philip's scandalized allies deserted him. In 1547 he was taken prisoner by Charles, and leadership of the Protestant cause that he had nurtured so well passed to other rulers. **11,132**

468 EUGÈNE DELACROIX (1798–1863)
storm-struck painter

No placid pastoral scenes for Delacroix. As he explained, "The wickedness of my expression almost frightens me." The dapper Delacroix relished his reputation as a mysterious figure among French *artistes* and dipped into mythology and history to paint gory, massive, imaginative canvases. He even turned to literature to depict Shakespearean scenes from *Macbeth, Romeo and Juliet, Hamlet,* and others. Delacroix distanced himself from his subject matter because, as he wrote in his journal, "Feeling must not be expressed to the point of nausea." In addition to sweeping epics such as *Death of Sardanapalus* and *Murder of the Bishop of Liège*, Delacroix illustrated the works of writer friends Victor Hugo (163) and Alexandre Dumas (874). We've included Delacroix on our list because he represents the best of romanticism. And his novel use of color foreshadowed and influenced the impressionists of the next generation. **11,125**

469 IRVING BERLIN (1888–1989)
composer of America's old favorites

Forget Barry Manilow; Irving Berlin wrote the songs that made the whole world sing. Ironic but true: A Russian Jewish immigrant, born Israel Baline, immortalized Christmas, Easter, and just about every American holiday in music. An early Berlin tune, "Smile and Show Your Dimple" flopped in 1917, but he resuscitated it sixteen years later with new lyrics that left everyone humming "Easter Parade." When it came time to compose a Christmas melody for the Bing Crosby and Fred Astaire movie *Holiday Inn*, Berlin dashed off "White Christmas," the nostalgic ditty that charmed homesick GIs in World War II. Berlin refused to let dance bands perform "God Bless America," an honor he reserved for the Republican Party and soprano Kate Smith, who made it her signature song. As composer Jerome Kern put it, "Irving Berlin has no place in American music. He *is* American music." **11,122**

470 FREDERICK LAW OLMSTED
(1822–1903) *breath of fresh air for American cities*

Olmsted and British partner Calvert Vaux designed some of the greatest public oases in urban America, including Central Park in New York City and Prospect Park in Brooklyn. Solo, Olmsted did even more, creating Boston's park system and the grounds of the U.S. Capitol and the Washington Monument. "As artist, he paints with lakes and wooded slopes, with lawns and banks and forest-covered hills," said Chicago architect Daniel Burnham. Olmsted's career as landscape architect took root after stints as a topographic engineer, seaman, scientific farmer, and journalist. En route he labored successfully for the preservation of Yosemite and Niagara Falls, which led him to a role in founding the National Park Service. High-minded Olmsted saw his parks as a proving ground for democracy, mingling everyone from tenement dwellers to Fifth Avenue swells. That still holds today, only add skateboarders, bikers, and joggers to the mix. **11,121**

471 THOMAS CRANMER (1489–1556)
Protestant flame over England

Cranmer, the first Protestant archbishop of Canterbury, stumbled into the role of Henry VIII's (100) ecclesiastical consultant in the murderous monarch's divorce from Catherine of Aragon (852). On voiding the marriage, he warned Henry against further cohabitation with Catherine, prompting a churchman to ask, "How did you manage not to laugh at yourself while with such judicial severity you made these threats to the king?" Instrumental in the Church of England's break with Rome, Cranmer disseminated the English Bible in churches and reformed the liturgy. Mary I, hating him for his part in her mother's divorce, had him condemned as a heretic and burned at the stake. In one of the most riveting spectacles in Protestant history, Cranmer held his hand in the flames so it would be consumed first, because it "had offended" God by signing a false recantation of his beliefs. **11,107**

472 WALTER RALEIGH (c.1554–1618)
the courtier who turned a queen's head and lost his own

Raleigh showed that it is possible to live a life more dramatic and full of diverse accomplishments than any fiction writer could imagine. A war veteran and law student in his teens, he went to Queen Elizabeth's (31) court in 1581, charmed his way into her favor, became captain of her guard, fought the Spanish at sea, and organized the first, ill-fated, English colony in Virginia. He wrote blissful verse, like these lines to his incandescent wife Bess Throckmorton:

Serena be not coy
Since we freely may enjoy
Sweet embraces, such delights
As will shorten tedious nights.

Elizabeth's appeasement-minded successor, James I (879), beheaded Raleigh for fighting with the Spanish during an exploration of the Orinoco River of South America. James also hated Raleigh for popularizing tobacco. How awful, the king wrote, "that the sweetness of man's breath, being a gift from God, should be wilfully corrupted by this stinking smoke." **11,070**

473 **JOHN MONTAGU** (1718–1792)
*fast-food innovator,
but did he hold the mayo?*

We could be munching peanut butter and jelly montagus, but lucky for us his title was Fourth Earl of Sandwich. The story is so good, it can't be true, can it? All sources, however, point to Montagu as the earl who gave his title to fast food in 1762, about two centuries before the Big Mac and the Whopper. Montagu was so absorbed at the gaming table that he ordered up sliced meat and bread. He stuffed meat between the bread slices and—voilà!—food history! Of lesser importance but still noteworthy, Captain Cook (194) named the islands now called Hawaii after the earl because he was popular in England for supporting exploration. Since we've shared with you our favorite symphonies, oil paintings, and buildings, we may as well tell you that we have an affinity for pastrami and turkey on rye with coleslaw and Russian dressing. **11,064**

474 **CESARE BECCARIA** (1738–1794)
criminal justice reformer

Beccaria's slim volume, *An Essay on Crimes and Punishments*, attacked the criminal and penal systems and galvanized Europeans to press for reforms. The young Italian lawyer was sickened by the state of contemporary prisons. Accused were housed with hardened criminals. Men and women, young and old, were thrown into the same filthy compounds with no bedding or sanitation. Torture was commonplace. Defendants were rarely permitted legal counsel. Punishments were cruel; even petty theft could lead to the gallows. Beccaria, who was strongly influenced by the Enlightenment and liberal philosophers such as Montaigne (432), recoiled at these conditions. He argued that the seriousness of a crime should determine the degree of punishment, and that the effectiveness of the justice system lay in the certainty of punishment, not its severity. Beccaria's call for the end of capital punishment launched abolition movements that continue today. **11,034**

475 **GREGORY IX** (1147?–1241)
instigator of the papal Inquisition

Gregory, about age eighty when elected pope in 1227, was an enlightened figure for his era, a friend of Saints Dominic (198) and Francis of Assisi (39). Kindly toward women, he approved the Order of Saint Mary Magdalene as a refuge for rehabilitated prostitutes. In 1234 he promulgated a code of canon law that twentieth-century management guru Peter Drucker (703) called the world's first "management text." Gregory expended an immense amount of time quarreling with Emperor Frederick II (480). In 1232 he appointed an inquisitor to hound heretics in Germany, and a year later he commissioned the sadistic Dominican Robert le Bougre to harass religious renegades in France. The papal Inquisition proved to be Gregory's most fateful accomplishment. Yet it was never as nasty as the Spanish Inquisition, set up by the Spanish monarchy in 1478 to root out unreconstructed Jews and Moors. **11,008**

476 **GIUSEPPE VERDI** (1813–1901)
opera boffo

Verdi's reputation among the masses has suffered from what historian Lawrence Levine calls the "sacralization" of culture: the transformation of popular entertainment, like Verdi's music, into highbrow art that is good for you but not fun. Yet Verdi's operas are as tasty as Tuscany's finest wines: Try them—you'll like them. The snooty Milan Conservatory rejected eighteen-year-old Verdi, but he took private lessons and spent the rest of his life composing melodramatic shows with hummable tunes like the "Anvil Chorus" from *Il Trovatore* and grisly moments like the jester's-murdered-daughter-in-a-sack scene that the censors were talked out of cutting from *Rigoletto*. Verdi's rival, Richard Wagner (165), wrote that *Aïda* was, "in the crucial moments, bad all the time," but paying customers have disagreed for 130 years. Verdi was so loved that when he was on his deathbed, the police detoured traffic away from his house so he could die in peace. **11,001**

477 HIROSHIGE (1797–1858)
on-the-road Japanese print artist

Hiroshige was just another struggling woodblock artist until he found inspiration on a trip from his native Edo (Tokyo) to Kyoto. He joined a group bearing an annual gift of horses from the shogun to the emperor. His landscape drawings from that journey, published in 1834 as *Fifty-Three Stations of the Tokaido Road*, brought him phenomenal and instant success. Unlike traditional landscape artists, Hiroshige infused his outdoor scenes with the common people he met along the way. His work bridges classical and modern painting. Some say he was a victim of his success. His later prints lacked the depth of *Tokaido Road*—perhaps because he hurried to meet the public's demand for his works. In Japan he is considered greater than Japanese artists who are better known in the West, like Hokusai (514). Hiroshige completed about 5,400 illustrations, prints, and paintings, including a thousand diff-erent views of his native Edo, and a thousand studies of birds and flowers. **10,954**

478 SHAH JAHAN (1592–1666)
builder of the Taj Mahal

The most beautiful monument of the millennium is this memorial to a love story. Shah Jahan, the biggest spender of the extravagant Mughal emperors of India, had his minions build this mausoleum in memory of his wife, who died in childbirth. The project—on the southern bank of the Yamuna River, outside Agra—took twenty-two years to complete. Its perfectly proportioned design has a double dome and four identical facades, each with an arch rising 108 feet. The building's opalescent marble surface changes shades with the light, making it stunning from every vantage point. The man who built the Taj Mahal must have had a loving heart. Not so his next of kin. When Shah Jahan fell ill, his four sons battled each other to succeed him. The winner, Aurangzeb, promptly put his father under house arrest until his death. **10,945**

479 EMILY DICKINSON (1830–1886)
virginal voice of American poetry

Dickinson lived all her life in the family home in Amherst, Massachusetts. From her youth on she attached herself to older men with whom intimacy was impossible. She fell in love with her "dearest earthly friend," the Reverend Charles Wadsworth, on hearing him preach in Philadelphia, and pined for him for decades, though seeing him only four times. Another great love/mentor, Thomas Wentworth Higginson, was blind to her genius and urged her not to publish her work. Thus only seven of her nearly eighteen hundred poems made it into print in her lifetime. In her later years she became increasingly eccentric, wearing only white and lurking on landings while her spinster sister entertained visitors. Higginson described her "soft frightened breathless childlike voice." But that voice, in poetry that explores the themes of unconsummated love, separation, nature, a half-open door, God, death, and immortality, ripples vibrantly across the ages.   **10,911**

480 FREDERICK II OF THE HOLY ROMAN EMPIRE (1194–1250)
the wonder of the world

In forty years of intermittent warfare and conniving, Frederick conquered, lost, conquered, lost, and so on, chunks of his native Italy, the German empire, and the Holy Land. The significance of those fights has faded, but they had a huge impact on his contemporaries, especially the thousands butchered in his wars. His charisma prompted admirers and foes alike to call him *stupor mundi*, wonder of the world. To medievalist Norman Cantor, this handsome brawler was "a megalomaniac who considered himself beyond the ethical standards of Latin Christianity." He read philosophy, patronized Arab scholars, and kept a harem. His books about birds were masterpieces. He was excommunicated twice: once for siding with the pope's enemies in a war for northern Italy, and once for turning back from a Crusade. When he finally went to the Holy Land in 1228, he tried diplomacy for a change and took back Jerusalem for Christianity without a fight.   **10,876**

481 ANNE FRANK (1929–1945)
the Holocaust's most famous victim

Abel Herzberg, a survivor of Hitler's death camps, observed that the Nazis did not kill six million Jews; they murdered one Jew six million times. Frank's life in hiding, immortalized in *The Diary of Anne Frank*, gave Hitler's victims a face. Frank, her family, and four other people hid in a cramped annex above an office in Amsterdam from July 1942 until an anonymous caller betrayed their secret to the police in August 1944. Their story—poignantly interspersed with the mundane and profound thoughts of a teenage girl as she comes of age—was chronicled in the diary Frank received on her thirteenth birthday. A month before the hiding place was uncovered, Frank wrote that she clung to her hopes for a good life "because in spite of everything I still believe that people are really good at heart." She died in the Bergen-Belsen concentration camp in March 1945.   **10,832**

482 EDGAR DEGAS (1834–1917)
artist who was tu tu brilliant

Other impressionists outranked him in artistry, but Degas is the guy the public loves to love. He maintained that he learned his craft by studying the techniques of the old masters. Interested in technology, he used photography to capture a subject in motion. Obsessed with both women and horses, he became noted for his scenes at the race track and the ballet. He lived a monklike existence and never married, but he played voyeur by painting women taking baths and dressing. When in advanced years he went blind, Degas used his hands to "see" what he had previously committed to the canvas and created a series of horse and ballet dancer sculptures. Our favorites: *Woman in the Bath Washing Her Leg* and *Women Ironing*.   **10,822**

483 JORGE LUIS BORGES (1899–1986)
most influential Latin American writer of the twentieth century

John Updike said the Argentine poet, essayist, and short-story writer "proposes some sort of essential revision of literature itself." Borges's short-story masterpieces brim with apparitions, prophecies, wizards, hallucinations, literary allusions, and flights into the past. But they are muscular and compelling. In "The Gospel According to Mark," a medical student stranded on a ranch with a family of primitive gauchos whiles away the evenings reading Mark to them. They hang on to his every word. The kicker: "They asked his blessing; then they mocked at him, spat on him. . . . The shed was without a roof; they had pulled down the beams to make the cross." The son of an Anglophile father and a mother who translated American novels into Spanish, Borges learned English before Spanish. He said the chief event in his life was reading in his father's library. **10,814**

484 BERNARDO O'HIGGINS (1778–1842)
Chile's founding father

The illegitimate son of an Irish-born Spanish governor of Chile, O'Higgins grew up on the periphery of the family, unrecognized by his father. He studied in London, where he took up with Venezuelan revolutionary Francisco Miranda, who was trying to work up fervor for South American independence from Spain. O'Higgins was willing to listen. He fell in with rebels in Chile, and in scenes reminiscent of a Gabriel García Márquez novel, the upstarts skirmished with the Spanish for years. Forget the lofty sentiments of freedom they had bandied about: O'Higgins was declared supreme dictator in 1817. When O'Higgins's gestures toward social reform—including tolerance of Protestantism in an overwhelmingly Catholic country—angered aristocrats and church authorities, he was deposed and lived out the rest of his days in exile in Peru. **10,788**

485 HARRY S TRUMAN (1884–1972)
cold war warrior

Vice president just eighty-two days when Franklin Roosevelt (37) died, the untested Truman inherited the job of winning World War II and rose to the challenge, authorizing the dropping of atomic bombs on Japan to prevent huge American casualties. After the war he curtailed Soviet territorial advances by developing a containment policy, thus setting the course of foreign policy for decades. His Truman Doctrine protected Greece and Turkey from Communist domination. This honest and feisty chief executive was never swayed by the public's whimsies; he fired the insubordinate General Douglas MacArthur (600) and withstood the outcry. In 1948 the Gallup poll and others predicted that the former haberdasher from Missouri would lose the presidential race. They were dead wrong. Truman, said comedian Fred Allen, was "the first president to lose in a Gallup and win in a walk." **10,761**

486 JOHN D. ROCKEFELLER (1839–1937)
ruthless industrialist

Rockefeller applied only to large companies for his first job. "I did not guess what it would be," he said of his ultimate ambition, "but I was after something big." Within fifteen years he had it; his instincts for economy and management propelled him from shipping clerk to partner in a business, then owner of an oil refinery, and finally founder of Standard Oil Company, the first major U.S. trust. The company's cutthroat competitiveness and the public's hatred for monopolies prompted Congress to pass the Sherman Antitrust Act in 1890. Rockefeller outmaneuvered it, however, by transferring the trust's properties to companies in other states. By 1913 his fortune totaled $900 million. Rockefeller hired a publicity man to rehabilitate his tarnished image. He started giving away chunks of his massive wealth. With $80 million, he founded the University of Chicago. And he created major philanthropic institutions that, by his death, had received $500 million to support the arts, education, and medical research. **10,760**

487 GEORGE EASTMAN (1854–1932)
first Kodak moment

Eastman invented film and the box camera, transforming photography from a specialty of professionals who lugged around seventy pounds of equipment to a hobby for the masses. The first hand-held Kodak, a word he concocted for its punchiness, was a phenomenon in 1888. "The craze is spreading fearfully," the *Chicago Tribune* reported. In England Rudyard Kipling exclaimed, "I am amazed at the excellence of the little Kodak's work." In Gilbert (764) and Sullivan's new opera *Utopia*, two maidens sang, "To diagnose / Our modest pose / the Kodaks do their best." Eastman, a lifelong bachelor, gave away more than half his fortune, $1 billion in today's dollars, and once paid to remove the tonsils of every child in his home town of Rochester, New York, an operation that was believed beneficial at the time. His suicide note read: "My work is done. Why wait?" **10,700**

488 'ABD AL-'AZIZ IBN SA'UD (c.1880–1953) *potentate of petroleum*

Warrior chieftain Ibn Saud swept out of the desert and captured the city of Riyadh in 1901 to begin a campaign that made him the founder and ruler of a unified Saudi Arabia thirty years later. Two American companies paid him $170,000 for oil-drilling rights and found one fourth of the world's oil reserves. Even with all that wealth under his feet, Saud was habitually short of cash because he loved to indulge his free-spending sons, forty-five of them by twenty-two wives. His successors demanded higher prices for oil, but they stuck to his foreign policies: lip service to the holy war against Israel, anti-Communism, and preference for Americans over Britons. Britain didn't help its cause when it gave Saud a right-hand-drive Rolls-Royce. When Arabs sit together, the place of honor is on the right. Ibn Sa'ud did not cede honor to any man, certainly not a chauffeur. **10,659**

489 WILLIAM THE SILENT (1533–1584)
the quiet man of Dutch independence

This story has more subplots than a Dickens novel: William was the good guy who fought intolerance and tyranny. Born to Lutheran parents, he was brought to the court of Holy Roman emperor Charles V (61) and converted to Catholicism. He clashed with the emperor's son, Philip II of Spain (427), over governance of the Netherlands. Philip hated Protestants; William didn't. William damaged his relationship with Philip irreparably when he took a runaway nun as his third wife. Although history records William as a man of few words, he made an impassioned plea in the national council of state against nobility's attempts to rule their subjects' consciences. No one listened. When William led the uprising, Philip offered a reward for his assassination. William was killed by a Catholic fanatic before independence was secured. He is generally recognized as the hero of Dutch independence. **10,654**

490 WILHELM WUNDT (1832–1920)
founder of experimental psychology

Wundt's 1874 textbook, *Principles of Physiological Psychology* was a landmark. He analyzed the immediate experiences of consciousness, including feelings and sensations. A true innovator, Wundt converted his laboratory at the University of Leipzig into the first institute for research in experimental psychology, attracting students from around the world. But feelings were frosty between the German giant in this new field and his American counterpart, William James (543). Wundt advised students not to waste time on such "a second-rate philosopher." Wundt's own writings were voluminous; it would take about three years to complete them, reading fifty pages a day. An irritated James noted that when "critics make mincemeat" of one of Wundt's views, "he is meanwhile writing a book on an entirely different subject. Cut him up like a worm, and each fragment crawls." **10,634**

491 MARIA AGNESI (1718–1799)
world's first great woman mathematician

At eleven Agnesi joined the disputations in her Milanese father's salon, conversing on topics from ontology to hydromechanics in Italian, Latin, French, Greek, German, Spanish, and Hebrew. At age twenty, dissuaded by her father from entering a convent, she devoted herself to mathematics. Her masterpiece, *Analytical Institutions for the Use of Italian Youth*, was a sweeping and groundbreaking treatment of algebra. The all-male French Academy was properly impressed, declaring in 1749, "There is no other book, in any language, which would enable a reader to penetrate as deeply into the fundamental concepts of analysis." An elderly British mathematician learned Italian just so he could translate the work into English. Yet nearly two hundred years later, Agnesi wasn't even mentioned in a four-volume, 2,500-page American survey of mathematics. After her father died in 1752, she abandoned mathematics for religion, ultimately joining the order of Blue Nuns. **10,623**

492 JONATHAN SWIFT (1667–1745)
the dean of English satirists

Swift's master work, *Gulliver's Travels*, was published anonymously in 1726 and has been a world classic ever since. Moreover, this brutal put-down of human folly has evolved into a favorite fantasy for children. Written, as Swift said, to "vex the world rather than divert it," the book's political allegory may not be clear to moderns, but we do get the biting wit, irony, and sparkling language. The hero is Lemuel Gulliver, a ship's surgeon, shipwrecked on the island of Lilliput, where natives are only six inches tall. Swift uses Gulliver's adventures to ridicule war, political parties, scientists, philosophers, and human vices and failings. Swift, an Anglo-Irishman, was an Anglican priest appointed dean of St. Patrick's Cathedral in Dublin. In 1729 he became a hero to the Irish in their bitter conflict with the British after his tongue-in-cheek suggestion in *A Modest Proposal* that Irish babies be fed to the rich as a way of reducing Ireland's poverty. **10,610**

493 JAKOB FUGGER (1459–1525)
renaissance Rockefeller

Jakob the Rich, as he was called, ran a conglomerate as powerful in its time as IBM, Wal-Mart, and Citibank combined. From their compound in Germany, Fugger and his brothers controlled mines, land, cloth factories, and wholesale establishments, and they were the richest bankers, too. Fugger was the papal collection agent for indulgences, making him a target of Martin Luther's (3) reformist anger, but Luther, always the nationalist, couldn't hide his pride that it was a German making all that money. Fugger lent Charles V (61) 500 guilders so Charles could rig his election as Holy Roman emperor over Francis I of France. Then Fugger sent the millennium's cheekiest dunning letter. He reminded Charles: Without me, you wouldn't be absolute ruler of Germany, Austria, Spain, and the Netherlands, so pay me back! Charles, not the last politician to heed a big contributor, did. **10,609**

494 WALT DISNEY (1901–1966)
animator without equal

Disney's Mickey Mouse and Donald Duck appeal to children of all ages. He mixed sound and animation to introduce the world's most famous mouse in the 1928 cartoon phenomenon *Steamboat Willie*. Next, he mastered color with his premier full-length cartoon, *Snow White and the Seven Dwarfs*. Disney immortalized on film such childhood classics as *Cinderella*, *Sleeping Beauty*, and *Winnie the Pooh*. He then turned his Midas touch to live-action films. Perhaps most spectacular was Disney's transformation of the ideal family vacation from a week at the beach into total immersion in his fantasy worlds. When Disneyland opened in California in 1955 to a never-ending stream of oh-so-happy patrons, Walt planned a bigger and better theme park in Orlando, Florida. After he died, rumors spread that he had his body frozen until medicine advanced enough to thaw him out. We still don't know if that's true, but we think that's a Goofy idea. **10,599**

495 EDMUND KEAN (1789–1833)
curtain-raiser for modern acting

Kean changed acting from formalized and mechanical to natural and romantic. The bastard son of an actress, he was adopted by his uncle's mistress, who played in London productions. At age sixteen he began acting in the provinces. Ten years later he was starring in London. Kean specialized in Shakespearean villains: Shylock, Richard III, Macbeth, and Iago. Unlike more regal rivals, he'd crawl on the stage, if necessary, for dramatic effect. "His acting is like an anarchy of the passions, in which each upstart humor, or frenzy of the moment, is struggling to get violent possession of some bit or corner of his fiery soul and pigmy body," wrote critic William Hazlitt. What Kean lacked in stature, he made up for in

monumental magnetism. He also was the first to market star quality by commanding high fees for limited engagements in England and the United States. **10,597**

496 AMBROISE PARÉ (1510–1590)
Frenchman on the cutting edge of surgery

Paré was trained as a lowly "barber-surgeon," not a physician. But as he accompanied France's armies on their campaigns, he experimented endlessly with ways to heal the wounded. He learned from an old woman the effectiveness of applying crushed onions to burns. He treated wounds with ointment instead of burning oil, adding brandy and turpentine into the mix to combat gangrene. To curb bleeding during amputations, he tied the arteries of the wounded rather than sear the vessels with a hot iron. After he saved a soldier stabbed twelve times with a sword and left for dead, the troops showered Paré with silver coins and carried him around "like a holy body." His fame spread, and he ultimately served four French kings. His book on treating gun wounds was mocked because it was written in French, not Latin, but he retorted that God "understands all languages well." **10,595**

497 BAYBARS I (1223–1277)
savior of Islam

In the thirteenth century Mongol armies led by Genghis Khan (43) and his kin swept west, killing or conquering everyone in their path. But on September 3, 1260, the advance was stopped at an oasis near Jerusalem by an Islamic army headed by a former slave, Rukn ad-Din Baybars. The decisive battle saved southwestern Asia and North Africa for Islam. A month later Baybars assassinated his sultan and began seventeen years of rule that shrank the territory of the Christian crusaders and solidified the fledgling Mamluk dynasty that ruled Egypt and Syria for the next two centuries. This founding father was a statesman of the highest caliber, "unimpeded by any scruple of honour, gratitude, and mercy," as historian Steven Runciman wrote. Baybars was a victim of his own cruelty; he died when he accidently drank poison intended for a foe. **10,590**

498 YASIR ARAFAT (b. 1929)
terrorist peacemaker

After Palestinians lost control of their homeland with the creation of Israel in 1948, Arafat smuggled arms to Arabs and trained others in terrorism. Elected head of the Palestine Liberation Organization in 1969, he wandered the globe, wreaking terror, dodging enemies, and raising money for his countryless comrades. With his trademark checkered kaffiyeh headdress and a three-day growth of facial hair, Arafat publicized the Arab agenda to Western nations sympathetic to Israel. Meanwhile, the PLO hijacked and bombed airplanes, murdered Israeli schoolchildren, and blew up buses, restaurants, and other places where innocent people gathered. Then the unthinkable happened. An aging Arafat, worn out from decades of combativeness, renounced terrorism and recognized Israel. In return the Israelis accepted Arafat and his PLO as representatives of the Palestinian people. For this Arafat shared the 1994 Nobel Peace Prize with Israeli prime minister Yitzak Rabin and defense minister Shimon Peres. **10,589**

499 YURY GAGARIN (1934–1968)
first man in space

Soviet Air Force lieutenant Gagarin made his historic 108-minute swing around planet earth on the *Vostok I* spacecraft in 1961. This feat fueled an undeclared American-Soviet race to the moon. The flight "reflected the heroic accomplishments of the Soviet people," crowed Soviet leader Nikita Khrushchev (619). President Kennedy pledged to put Americans on the moon within a decade. Only after the Soviet Union crumbled did the secret come out: Gagarin had almost been killed on reentry when his spacecraft failed to separate from its braking rocket, sending *Vostok* into convulsions. "Malfunction!" screamed notes taken by Gagarin's flight commander on earth. "Everything was spinning around," Gagarin later told debriefers. The crisis lasted ten minutes before separation was achieved and the craft descended safely. Had the world known the truth, the space race might have slowed to a crawl, with NASA first sending more chimps into the vast unknown. **10,588**

500 AMELIA JENKS BLOOMER (1818–1894)
girdle slayer

Before the Civil War an outdoor stroll was an ordeal for women, with heavy petticoats hanging beneath their skirts dragging through muck and manure in urban streets, and with girdles and corsets, according to one magazine, "trammeling their genteel thorax with springs of steel and whalebone, screwing in the waist to Death's hourglass contraction, and squeezing lungs, liver, and midriff into an unutterable cram." Bloomer ditched the whole mess for Turkish-style trousers. Though not the first to wear them, as a public figure—she edited a women's publication, *The Lily*—she popularized them as "bloomers" and became a national object of both admiration and mirth. Women in the Midwest held Bloomer balls, but an editorialist in the South thundered, "Our ladies blush that their sisters anywhere descend to such things." Bloomers never really caught on, and Bloomer herself gave up the garb in 1859. But she had made her point, and women today breathe easier. **10,561**

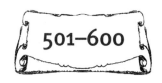

501–600

Too many writers.

That's what some of our friends said when we showed them advance copies of the book you now hold in your hands.

And it is true that we have included more literary figures—novelists, poets, playwrights, and essayists—than any other category. Wordsmiths account for nearly twelve percent of the first five hundred people on our list, far outstripping the representation of scientists, say, or inventors, or warriors, or kings—all groups that would seem to have a greater practical impact on our lives than these muses' apprentices.

Yet now, rather than making amends for this imbalance, we have abandoned all restraint. In the next chapter, fully *one-fourth* of all our subjects are writers. And what writers! Emerson, La Fontaine, Shelley, Verne, Yeats, Casanova, Brontë, Faulkner, Irving, Villon, Martí, and Andersen are all there. So are Lope de Vega, Conrad, James, Corneille, Beauvoir, Abigail Adams (for her diaries), Darío, Khayyám, Wilde, Wordsworth, Mann, and Lu Hsün.

And that litany doesn't even include an additional dozen or so people—historians, religious thinkers, psychologists, a cookbook author, an encyclopedist, a sociologist, a social activist, and a legal scholar—who made the grade by putting their thoughts on paper.

Compare this army of scribblers to the puny tally of just one inventor (of the typewriter), one economist (a truly ugly Frenchman), one sports hero (a real Babe), two architects, two explorers, two saints, four freedom fighters, and not a single pope.

What's our excuse? You get four writers together, and—we just can't help ourselves.

We'll make you a bet. Far from reproaching us for squeezing too many authors into our compendium, you'll take us to task for excluding one of your favorites. But you know what? We really wanted to put him (her) in, honest; we swear he (she) ended up as number 1,001.

501 AARON MONTGOMERY WARD
(1844–1913) *mail-order merchandiser*

Ward wooed isolated farmers by providing everything a settler needed—from bullets to corsets to pianos to tombstones. He undercut general stores by eliminating sales clerks and offering a money-back guarantee. His first catalog, in 1871, was a one-page sheet that he and his wife personally addressed to thousands of members of the farmers' collective, the National Grange. Customers were skeptical, and orders trickled in. The Great Chicago Fire wiped out Ward's inventory, and the panic of '73 nearly destroyed him. He persevered. In 1875 his thirty-two-page catalog ranked among the best-read books of the day. By 1893 his "wishbook" weighed two pounds, numbered 544 pages, and was used in rural schools to supplement reading primers and in outhouses to—well, you know. In the 1940s the Montgomery Ward catalog, which had promoted ready-to-wear and created the national consumer, was named one of the most influential books in America.   **10,520**

502 KAREN HORNEY (1885–1952)
Freudian who shrank
Freud's influence

For most of his career, Sigmund Freud (15) taught that female hysteria was caused by penis envy, but in 1922 Horney offered a different explanation that was so good, even Freud adopted it. She said many women suffered from feelings of being *geschlagen,* struck down, by their fathers, a kind of psychic castration. Horney emigrated from Berlin to New York in 1932 and as dean of the American Institute of Psychoanalysis, continued to voice anti-Freudian ideas, such as the notion that mental health is affected as much by environment and culture as by sex. Her teaching gave psychoanalysis a perspective that had eluded the German

and Austrian men who dominated the field in its early years. Not that Horney disliked men. She cheated on her husband Oskar regularly for most of their seventeen-year marriage, and one of her lovers had been her patient. Our analysis of that: naughty, naughty.   **10,508**

503 LUIGI GALVANI (1737–1798)
electricity galvanizer

Galvani was teaching anatomy at Bologna when he began studying the effects of electricity on frogs. By chance, he noticed that frogs' legs being dried on brass hooks would twitch when the hooks were hung on an iron railing. He concluded that animal tissue contained a force he called "animal electricity." Galvani thought this "electric fluid" flowed from the brain, with nerves acting as conductors to the muscles. Electrician Alessandro Volta (425) found Galvani's theory "one of the most beautiful and surprising discoveries." But Volta's own experiments showed that the electrical current originated in the metals, not the frogs. Galvani got it wrong, but we honor him for sparking the scientific inquiry into electricity. His name is in *galvanizing,* the process of protecting iron or steel with zinc coating, and *galvanometer,* a device for detecting electric current. We also owe him for inspiring Volta to invent the first battery, another "beautiful" discovery that led to the age of electric power.   **10,492**

504 RALPH WALDO EMERSON (1803–1882)
transcendent poet

His most famous line describes the outbreak of the American Revolution: "Here once the embattled farmers stood / And fired the shot heard round the world." But Emerson was more interested in proclaiming America's literary independence than its political separation from England. He yearned for the appearance of a poetical genius equal to the young nation's grandeur—and found him in Walt Whitman (318). Meanwhile, the ex-Unitarian minister joined Henry David Thoreau (375) in preaching Transcendentalism, a kind of mystical union with nature. In his books and lectures Emerson railed against the sterile scholarship and religious orthodoxy that he believed hindered man's discovery of the divine spark within himself. For all his intellectual daring, however, he adhered to his era's delicacy in expressing sexual longing, declaring to his future wife Lydia Jackson, "I do sympathize with the homeliest pleasures and attractions by which our good foster mother Nature draws her children together." **10,482**

505 MERIWETHER LEWIS (1774–1809)
the Lewis in Lewis and Clark

In 1803 President Thomas Jefferson (64) feared that the English would occupy the unmapped land west of the new Louisiana Territory. So he commissioned his Virginia neighbor and secretary, Lewis, to trek across the continent first and report on the animals, plants, mountains, deserts, rivers, and Indians in that forbidding wilderness. It was the most celebrated journey in American history, and the land Lewis claimed became Washington, Oregon, and Idaho. The explorers proved that there was no all-water route across the continent. In 1805 Lewis and his lieutenant, William Clark, reached the Pacific Ocean. Romantic legends say the Shoshone woman Sacajawea showed them the way, but it was Lewis's skill as a backwoodsman and leader that kept the expedition together for its three and a half years and six thousand miles. **10,460**

506 IWASAKI YATARO (1835–1885)
Japanese industrialist who founded Mitsubishi

There's a lot more to Mitsubishi than cars. In fact, when Iwasaki got started, the automobile was just a gleam in the eye of some distant mechanical geniuses. Ships were the thing—magnificent steamships that chugged around Asia. Iwasaki acquired the remnants of a feudal shipping industry, renamed it Mitsubishi, and built it into the second largest *zaibatsu* (family-owned industry), just behind Mitsui. Government officials wanted to end Japanese dependence on foreign shipping, and Iwasaki accommodated them by taking over the state shipyards in 1884. The rest is industrial history—Iwasaki's empire expanded into banks, copper, coal, gas and electric utilities, warehouses, machinery, chemicals, oil, paper, textiles, and yes, cars. Mitsubishi survived the Japanese defeat in World War II, but its two-hundred-plus companies were split during Allied occupation. **10,435**

507 ALFRED KRUPP (1812–1887)
entrepreneur gone ballistic

Minus the driven Alfred, there would have been no Krupp dynasty to arm Germany in three major wars. The Krupp family business was making pots and pans. Then Alfred's father founded a steel-making firm in Essen in 1811. He died a failure, leaving his fourteen-year-old son in charge. Alfred struggled for years. Through sheer determination, he turned the business around. To demonstrate the strength of his steel, Alfred began manufacturing munitions, earning the nickname "the Cannon King." Krupp guns soon thundered in the Franco-Prussian War of 1870. After Krupp died, his 42-centimeter howitzers pummeled Allied forces in World War I. The Krupp family's secret buildup of German military might and support of Hitler (20) paved the way for World War II. Alfred's great-grandson was tried as a war criminal at Nuremberg. From pots to Panzers. Some legacy. **10,411**

508 JEAN DE LA FONTAINE (1621–1695)
fabled French poet

In mocking human foibles, La Fontaine has few equals. One of our favorite characters is the frog who, beholding the mighty ox, tries to puff herself up to his size until "the stupid midget blew herself in two." Adds the author: "The world is full of people not one whit more sage." His morality tales are familiar the world over. One of the more famous ones, about a grasshopper and an ant, preaches the virtue of industriousness. "Locust, having sung her song / All summer long, / Saw her larder running low / As the wind began to blow." So she begs for food from the ant. The ant refuses with this withering response: "Sang songs, eh? I am so glad. Now's your time to dance." La Fontaine could be selfish (he married a fourteen-year-old girl, then abandoned her) and sycophantic to the rich. But he showed the world how to laugh at itself; what greater achievement could any author want?   **10,389**

509 PERCY BYSSHE SHELLEY (1792–1822)
master of sweeping sentiment

Oh, for the time when the languid recitation of Shelley's "To a Skylark" and "Ode to the West Wind" was the preferred foreplay of the English-speaking young. Alas, Shelley's writings have less mass appeal today than his wife Mary's novel *Frankenstein*, but for almost two centuries Percy's poems made the world tingle. Shelley was expelled from Oxford for writing an atheistic tract, eloped with a sixteen year-old beauty, dumped her for the more intellectual Mary, and traveled through Europe with other poetic supernovas, Leigh Hunt, John Keats (297), and Lord Byron (385). Contemporary critics appreciated him little. When his body washed up on an Italian beach after a sailing accident, the *London Courier* reported, "Shelley, the writer of infidel poetry, has been drowned; now he knows whether there is a god or no."   **10,379**

510 NETTIE MARIA STEVENS (1861–1912)
geneticist with a fertile mind

Henry VIII (100) discarded his first wife Catherine of Aragon (852) because she failed to give him a male heir. Thanks to Stevens, we know Henry had only himself to blame. Stevens demonstrated that, contrary to the folk wisdom of the ages, the man, not the woman, determines the sex of an offspring. Working with beetles, Stevens described two different kinds of sperm, one with an X chromosome and the other with a Y chromosome. She observed that only eggs possess two X chromosomes and concluded that eggs fertilized with X sperm produce females, while eggs with Y sperm produce males. Stevens, who started her career as a librarian, then earned a doctorate in biology, was centuries too late to change the fate of Henry VIII's wives. But she erased one of genetics' big question marks.   **10,358**

511 TAMERLANE (c.1336–1405)
definitely not Mr. Nice Guy

His Persian enemies contemptuously called him "Timur the Lame," but it didn't do them any good. This cutthroat Mongol gobbled up principalities like porridge. His mounted archers spilled blood from Mongolia to the Mediterranean. Whole villages and cities were destroyed. Damascus was occupied and its treasured artisans shipped off to beautify Samarkand, Tamerlane's home city. In 1401 twenty thousand residents of Baghdad were massacred and the city's monuments destroyed. Those who dared revolt against his iron rule rarely lived to regret it; Tamerlane's forces bludgeoned rebels in Persian territories and built towers out of their skulls. Tamerlane, the last of Central Asia's conquerors, then set out to subdue China but died en route. His body was entombed in a mausoleum in Samarkand. In 1941 Soviet archaeologists opened it and found the skeleton of a tall, powerfully built man, lame in his right leg and arm.   **10,342**

512 Charles Lyell (1797–1875)
old-world geologist

The Scottish scientist forged the modern view of the earth's structure and encouraged a young naturalist named Charles Darwin (7) in his scientific inquiries. As an infant, Lyell was called "the most indefatigable squaller of all the brats of Angus." That energy went to good purpose in later years. In his endless field trips—to the Scottish lakes, the riverbeds of central France, Italy's Mount Etna, the Pyrenees, Niagara Falls—Lyell collected data on rock formations that persuaded him that the earth's surface had evolved through incremental physical and chemical processes over vast stretches of time, not through periodic cataclysms like the biblical Flood. Though an amateur, he disseminated his theory in his acclaimed *Principles of Geology*, which he revised and updated eleven times over forty years. Lyell was first a mentor to, then a disciple of Darwin, who said the older man's work "altered the whole tone of one's mind."   **10,333**

513 Jan Vermeer (1632–1675)
Dutch master of realism

This son of a Delft art dealer was the deft early painter of ordinary people doing ordinary things. He did it with photographic precision by using a camera obscura—a primitive projector—to display the images of his models on a flat surface to get the perspective right. Vermeer's works were unappreciated in his lifetime. A court-appointed receiver, Anton van Leeuwenhoek (107), later to become a famous microbiologist, forced Vermeer's wife to sell twenty-five of his paintings for a pittance to pay a grocery bill. Two centuries after his death Vermeer emerged from obscurity when connoisseur Etienne Thoré-Burgër wrote pamphlets trumpeting the painter's genius. After that, owning a Vermeer was as good as finding gold in the attic, and forging Vermeers became a cottage industry. A guard at the war crimes trial after World War II said Hilter's (20) henchman Hermann Goering showed more emotion when his prized Vermeer was exposed as a fake than when he was sentenced to death.   **10,327**

514 Hokusai (1760–1849)
the Japanese artist most renowned in the West

We toyed with saying Hokusai was the Toulouse-Lautrec (817) of Japan, but in truth Lautrec was the Hokusai of France. Western artists, especially impressionists like poster prince Lautrec, Edgar Degas (482), and Claude Monet (196), collected Hokusai's prints and studied them. He is the most famous woodblock print artist of the *ukiyo-e*, which means "pictures of the floating world" but which actually depicted everyday life. Toward the end of his career he signed prints "the old man, mad on drawing." Indeed he was. Estimates number his output at about thirty thousand illustrations, woodblocks, silk screens, drawings, and paintings. We like *Beneath the Wave off Kanagawa* from his most famous print collection, *Thirty-six Views of Mount Fuji*. When he was well into his seventies, Hokusai traveled around Japan, creating prints. He returned home to Edo to find residents dying from famine. He fed himself by trading prints for rice.   **10,321**

515 Robert E. Lee (1807–1870)
hero of a civilization gone with the wind

Aristocratic Lee was an unlikely hero to rally the rebel South during the Civil War. He denounced slavery as evil, likened secession to revolution, and detested war. Dedicated to the union, he was offered command of the Federal army. But after weeks of agonizing over service to his country or duty to his state, he chose his cherished Virginia and was made Confederate commander. "Duty," he told his son, "is the sublimest word in our language." The Union's greater numbers and resources doomed the Confederacy. But West Point–trained Lee, the finest military tactician this country has ever produced, outmaneuvered Union forces at nearly every turn, prolonging the conflict into an anguished four-year struggle. After surrendering to Grant (371) at Appomattox, Lee was asked to write his memoirs. He declined, saying he would be "trading on the blood of my men." **10,301**

516 CHARLES LINDBERGH (1902–1974)
aviation demigod

Lindbergh's epochal flight from New York to Paris on May 21–22, 1927, in *The Spirit of St. Louis*, the first nonstop solo crossing of the Atlantic, triggered a worldwide outpouring of adulation. Perhaps he was the last true hero; perhaps he was just an irresistible love object for the masses, an all-American boy, brave and incorruptible. At Le Bourget Airport in Paris, a crowd of several hundred thousand mobbed his plane. *The New York Times* proclaimed: LINDBERGH DOES IT! TO PARIS IN 33½ HOURS; FLIES 1,000 MILES THROUGH SNOW AND SLEET; CHEERING FRENCH CARRY HIM OFF FIELD. The aviator's welcome home was even more tumultuous. In time Lindbergh would be pitied for his two-year-old son's kidnap-murder and maligned for opposing America's entry in World War II. But posterity will honor him for that magical moment when he conquered the heavens—and humanity's heart. **10,287**

517 ALP ARSLAN (c.1030–1072)
conquering sultan

His name means "valiant lion," and legend says his moustaches were so long, he tied them behind his head before a battle lest they foul up his longbow. This Persian conquered much of the Middle East for the emerging Seljuk dynasty, and his victory at the Battle of Manzikert in 1071 was a turning point in history. His cavalry defeated a hundred thousand soldiers of Christian Byzantium, secured eastern Turkey for Islam, and started the Byzantine Empire on the road to extinction. Reports of Alp Arslan's cruelty and arrogance—he used the captured emperor Romanus Diogenes for a footstool—whipped up anti-Islamic fervor that led to the Crusades. One afternoon a condemned prisoner with nothing to lose rushed at Alp Arslan with a knife. The haughty sultan put an arrow in his bow and moved toward the assailant, but he stumbled—on his feet, not his moustache—and was stabbed to death. **10,263**

518 WINSLOW HOMER (1836–1910)
the artist of the elements

Quiet and reclusive, Homer warmed to the outdoors. After stints in a lithographer's shop and as artist-correspondent at the Union front during the Civil War, Homer turned to oil painting. He developed a unique style that was realistic and bold, painting nature as he saw it: forests and lakes of the Adirondacks, palm trees and glistening waters of Florida and the Caribbean. Homer's watercolors and oils exert a strange pull; we feel the grim determination of rescuers in *The Wreck* and the lone fisherman's fear in *Fog Warning*, as gray mists rise on the horizon. In 1883 the crusty Homer retreated to a desolate fishing village in Maine to paint increasingly abstract seascapes. "The life that I have chosen gives me my full hours of enjoyment for the balance of my life," Homer wrote. "The Sun will not rise, or set, without my notice, and thanks."   **10,237**

519 JULES VERNE (1828–1905)
sci-fi guy

Earlier science-fiction novels exist, like Mary Shelley's *Frankenstein*, but Verne's were the first to spin futuristic fantasies on painstakingly scientific foundations. The wonders he depicted in *A Journey to the Center of the Earth, Twenty Thousand Leagues Under the Sea*, and other tales have stirred readers' imaginations ever since. Verne foresaw airplanes, submarines, gas-powered cars, computers, and hundreds of other twentieth-century contraptions. The space pioneers in *From the Earth to the Moon* were launched from the same spot, Florida, in a capsule built of the same material, aluminum, at almost the same escape velocity, and splashed down in the same ocean, the Pacific, as America's *Apollo 8* astronauts. Writers H. G. Wells, Ray Bradbury, and Arthur C. Clarke (author of *2001*) all acknowledged their debt to the Frenchman. "Who can say," asked astronaut Frank Borman, "how many of the world's space scientists were inspired by their boyhood reading of Jules Verne?"   **10,201**

520 GIOVANNI GIACOMO CASANOVA DE SEINGALT (1725–1798)
the original Casanova

"When the lamp is taken away, all women are alike, but without love this great business is a vile thing," Casanova wrote, showing his seedy and sentimental sides in *The History of My Life*. It's the millennium's prototypical dirty book, though it's more charming than pornographic. The Venetian-born diarist was expelled from a seminary for cuddling with another boy, and he became a Europe-trotting diplomat, journalist,

spy, gambler, con man, and sometime jailbird. At every stop Casanova seduced women, including three sisters he met on a trip in 1744. (The sister posing as a castrated man was a challenge.) A bowdlerized version of his memoirs, published in 1821, made the word *Casanova* a synonym for womanizer. The world had to wait until 1960 for the unexpurgated edition based on the mildewing original manuscript, which survived World War II in a Leipzig bank vault.   **10,165**

521 WILLIAM BUTLER YEATS (1865–1939)
the Irish bard

In his poetic eulogy to Yeats, W. H. Auden wrote, "mad Ireland hurt you into poetry," and it's true that Yeats had an ambivalent relationship with his homeland. He hated the conservativism and violence, yet loved the land, the simple folk, the legends, and the rhythm of the English language. It all seeped into Yeats's poetry and plays.

I find under the boughs of love and hate,
In all poor foolish things that live a day,
Eternal beauty wandering on her way.

That's what he wrote in *To the Rose Upon the Rood of Time*. Yeats loved many women, especially the fierce nationalist Maud Gonne. His wife Georgie—he was age fifty-two, she was twenty-five when they wed—tolerated his flings and shared with him a love of the occult. Anthologist M. L. Rosenthal called him "the most widely admired, by common reader and sophisticate alike, of all modern poets who have written in English."   **10,158**

522 EMILY BRONTË (1818–1848)
writer of demonic love

Not even her tight-knit family realized that shy homebody Emily Brontë harbored the passion and intensity to write *Wuthering Heights*, now a classic in English literature. "It is a fiend of a book," wrote author Christina Rossetti (618) in 1854. "The action is laid in Hell—only it seems places and people have English names there." It's the turbulent tale of ill-fated lovers Catherine Earnshaw and the brooding orphan Heathcliff, who seeks revenge on those who have stood in their paths. The backdrop is the desolate Yorkshire moors, Emily's treasured turf since childhood. Unlike her sister Charlotte, who won praise for *Jane Eyre*, Emily's book irritated critics, who termed it "disagreeable" and "gloomy." Today her contribution is considered the greater of the two. A year after publication of *Wuthering Heights*, Emily died of the family scourge, tuberculosis. She never lived to see her poetic genius inspire others, including the equally enigmatic writer, D. H. Lawrence. **10,147**

523 DAG HAMMARSKJÖLD (1905–1961)
Mr. United Nations

From 1953 until his death in a plane crash on a peace mission to Africa, Hammarskjöld built the United Nations into a formidable force in international politics and fought off efforts by the superpowers to make it a pawn in the cold war. Hammarskjöld also initiated the organization's peacekeeping role, notably in settling the Suez crisis of 1956 and containing the fighting in the Congo in the early 1960s. Best described as asexual, the Swedish statesman once dragged a woman out of his bed who had sneaked there hoping to trade her favors for a secretarial job, slapped her, and called the police. Deeply religious, he befriended Martin Buber (723) and undertook to translate the Jewish philosopher's *I and Thou* into Swedish. Twelve pages of the manuscript were found in the wreckage of the crash that killed him. "The road to holiness," Hammarskjold once wrote, "passes through the world of action." **10,101**

524 JOHNNY TORRIO (1882–1957)
organized crime's organizer

Torrio rubbed out his own uncle, but argued crime would pay even more if gangsters worked together. His 1934 crooks' summit drew together Lucky Luciano, Bugsy Siegel, and Meyer Lansky. They carved the country into bootlegging territories, then wreaked murder and mayhem to give the organization muscle. Torrio had been a two-bit cutup in New York when he was summoned to Chicago by Uncle Jim Colosimo, who ran a chain of brothels but lacked ambition to expand into other lucrative areas. When Torrio wanted Big Jim bumped off, he called in a young punk who was trying to evade a murder charge in New York—Al Capone. Torrio lost his taste for day-to-day delinquence after he was wounded by a gunman from another crime family and went to prison for brewing beer. He retired, handed Capone the daily crime operation, and built his national syndicate. **10,071**

525 WILLIAM FAULKNER (1897–1962)
southern stylist

Nobel laureate Faulkner wrote brooding tales of America's post–Civil War South and its decaying values. Many Faulkner novels unfold in Yoknapatawpha County, a fictionalized version of his northern Mississippi haunts. He specialized in dysfunctional families with foul secrets. His best novels: *The Sound and the Fury* and *As I Lay Dying*. Meat-and-potato readers don't warm to Faulkner's run-on sentences, frequent flashbacks, and stream of consciousness. Sure he's difficult— but mighty rewarding. To make a steady living while he wrote novels, Faulkner worked odd jobs, including a stint as scriptwriter in Hollywood— one project was the script for Hemingway's (388) *To Have and Have Not*. But one day he went AWOL from a set. His angry agent tracked him down to Mississippi and demanded what the hell was going on. "Ah asked my producer if ah could work at home," Faulkner related by phone, "and he said fine, so heah ah am."   **10,065**

526 DUKE ELLINGTON (1899–1974)
royal riffer

Ellington was an instrumental figure in American jazz and a founder of big band music and swing. Picture a jazz fest in the White House in 1969. President Richard Nixon (904) toasts "the greatest Duke of them all." The prez plays the piano. Then Clark Terry blasts the trumpet, Gerry Mulligan plays sax, and Joe Williams sings. Even Marine band members join in. They rock until the wee hours in honor of Ellington's seventieth birthday. Only fitting for the man born Edward Kennedy Ellington, composer, bandleader, and pianist famous for "Sophisticated Lady" and "Satin Doll." As a boy, Duke sensed his would be a unique contribution to the world. Some mornings he would descend the staircase in his middle-class Washington, D.C., home and tell his mother and aunt, "Now listen, this is the great, the grand, the magnificent Duke Ellington." Then he'd bow and command, "Applaud, applaud!"   **10,048**

527 PHILIP II OF FRANCE (1165–1223)
precursor of French power

The most important king of the 350-year Capetian dynasty, Philip tripled the royal domains. Before his birth his father Louis VII had a dream in which his future son drank human blood from a chalice. Certainly rivers of blood spilled during Philip's reign, as he reconquered French territories held by English kings. To consolidate royal power, he was "hard on the evil barons and wishful to sow discord among them," a contemporary chronicler reported. In 1190 he went on the Third Crusade

with Richard the Lion-Hearted of England but was stricken with malaria that "wrought havoc with his bones so that his fingernails and his hair fell out," according to his court chaplain, and he returned home. One critic, Gille de Paris, lamented that France was "torn apart by the extortioners of her prince," but conceded that other European monarchs were worse.   **10,032**

528 GIOVANNI PIERLUIGI DA PALESTRINA (c.1525–1594)
musical master of the Mass

The Italian composer of 105 masses whose works fill thirty-three volumes, Palestrina has been called the "savior of church music." He learned about church music as a choirboy; later he played the organ at the church in his native Palestrina. He sang with the pontifical choir for a time but got tossed out because of a rule prohibiting participation by married men. Palestrina refused several prestigious positions, including a request to direct music for the court of Austria's emperor Maximilian II, because the salaries were miserable. Eventually he became the Vatican's master of music. When his wife died, Palestrina delighted the pope by announcing he would enter the priesthood. Palestrina was so admired by the church hierarchy that he was allowed to keep his church position even after he was wooed from his studies and married a wealthy widow. **10,018**

529 JOHN JACOB ASTOR (1763–1848)
first American monopolist

Before Rockefeller (486) and oil, Ford (51) and cars, Gates and software, there were Astor and furs. He came from Germany to America to sell musical instruments but there was more money in pelts than flutes, and by the 1820s his American Fur Company had just about monopolized the market. He did it by bribing officials to give him exclusive rights to set up trading posts in various wilderness territories. Michigan governor Lewis Cass, for example, got $35,000 from Astor in 1817. Such payoffs were a bargain. Astor spent a mere two dollars in trade goods for every package of furs that fetched $140 in London markets. Astor invested his earnings in New York real estate. His wealth at his death in 1848 was the foundation for the fortune that the Astors who followed him lavished on society parties, Newport mansions, and charities like New York's public libraries.   **9,998**

530 FRANCESCO BORROMINI (1599–1667)
go-for-baroque architect

Borromini's fame spread throughout Europe for his crowning achievement: the daring creation of the small church and monastery, S. Carlo alle Quattro Fontane in Rome. While contemporary architects based their designs on the proportions of the human body, Borromini modeled his on geometric forms. And he treated space and light as architectural components. Inside, S. Carlo is diamond-shaped with a curving outline alternately convex and concave. Borromini's use of lighting makes the dome almost seem to float above worshippers. Borromini and the great Bernini (238) collaborated on projects such as the famous baldachin in St. Peter's, with its four undulating columns crowned by S-shaped volutes. Borromini could be withdrawn and subject to rages that alienated patrons. In the throes of one fit of fury, after having suffered from depression for months, he seized a sword and killed himself.   **9,985**

531 CHRISTOPHER LATHAM SHOLES
(1819–1890) the #@!* father of the asdfjkl;

How many billions of fingers have flown over the infamous *qwerty* keyboard, named for the letter sequence on the second row, since the Wisconsin journalist designed it in the 1860s? Sholes, whom we consider the inventor of the typewriter, separated the most-used letters to prevent the typebars from jamming under the assault of speed freaks. He also put all the letters of *typewriter* on the same row to make it easier for salesmen to peck out the new name. The typewriter revolutionized business. The Remington Arms Company promoted it with the slogan, "The typewriter is to the pen what the sewing machine is to the needle." After Mark Twain (188) submitted the first typewritten manuscript to a publisher, few wordsmiths were able to avoid the machine, though English poet Robert Graves declared grumpily, "I have never used one and have warned my daughters not to." Today the typewriter can rest in peace, but *qwerty* lives on—on computer keyboards.   **9,978**

532 THOMAS CHIPPENDALE (1718–1779)
wondrous woodworker

Chippendale targeted the emerging middle class of mid-eighteenth-century England as his market. Knowing that their finances were slimmer than the mansion crowd's, he built his London business by simplifying fashionable furniture styles, notably rococo, and keeping embellishments to a minimum. His mahogany cabinets were masterful, his chairs elegant and comfortable. Chippendale won greatest fame, however, for *The Gentleman and Cabinet Maker's Director*, the most important collection of furniture design published to that date. In his book Chippendale dissected his designs, showing cross-sections of moldings and exact dimensions. The catalog appeared in 1754 and had run to three editions by 1760. Furniture makers in the American colonies bought it and made Chippendale knockoffs. Because the book became a bible for borrowers, it's difficult even for experts to tell if antiques are real Chippendales or masterful copies.   **9,962**

533 FRANÇOIS VILLON (b. 1431)
brawling poetic chronicler of the late Middle Ages

If not for French police records, we would know nothing of Villon's life, nothing of his riotous student days at the University of Paris, nothing of the men he killed (he stabbed a priest in the groin, but it was a fair fight) or of his close call with the gallows. Parliament pardoned Villon just before he was to be hanged in 1463, and then he vanished from history. He left behind poems that show that his times were like our own. English writer Wyndham Lewis called Villon "a companion of thieves and whores and vagabonds, producing from the dregs of his life an exquisite flower of pure poetry; a temper as flecked with dark and light as an April day." His most famous lyric is the "Ballad of the Ladies of Bygone Times," with its finale, "*Mais où sont les neiges d'antan?*" "But where are the snows of yesteryear?"   **9,958**

534 HARRIET TUBMAN (c.1820–1913)
the Moses of her people

Tubman, a slave on a Maryland plantation, couldn't bear her cruel treatment. "There was one of two things I had a right to, liberty or death," Tubman said. "If I could not have one, I would have the other, for no man should take me alive." She escaped to Pennsylvania, aided by the Underground Railroad, a series of secret safe houses for runaway slaves heading north. Tubman soon became the preeminent guide on the Railroad, making nineteen trips south and back and leading more than three hundred slaves—including her parents—to freedom. With a $40,000 bounty on her head, Tubman

still spoke out against slavery and, when civil war erupted, turned spy for the Union. Despite her contribution, Tubman had to lobby more than thirty years to gain a government pension. **9,942**

535 FREDERICK HOPKINS (1861–1947)
the one-a-day man

The British biochemist received the 1929 Nobel Prize for medicine for his discovery of "essential nutrient factors"—today known as vitamins—in animal diet. Hopkins might shudder at the pill-popping mania he touched off in people eager to prolong their lives or just fight off the flu. Linus Pauling, another Nobel laureate, famously ingested enormous quantities of vitamin C to ward off colds and cancer. Many vitamins have indeed been shown to forestall or reverse diseases and disorders like cancer, heart disease, rickets, calcium deficiency, impotence, and even carpal tunnel syndrome. But many specialists say a healthy diet is the best source of these nutrients, and they disparage many of the claims made by the vitamin-pill industry. Dr. Victor Herbert, an American crusader against nutrition quackery, said a one-a-day vitamin dose "just gives you expensive urine."   **9,921**

536 ALBERT LUTHULI (c.1898–1967)
African freedom fighter

As president of the African National Congress in the 1950s, Luthuli organized his "Defiance Campaign" against apartheid. South African authorities tried to silence him. They exiled him, arrested him, and tried him for treason. They banned his writings and outlawed his speeches. Nothing worked. The steamroller that was Luthuli thundered on, providing the initial oomph in what was to be a decades-long battle. Under Luthuli's direction, blacks organized resistance to curfew and segregation laws. At one rally police fired at unarmed blacks, killing 70 and injuring 250. The son of a washerwoman, Luthuli also served as the Zulu chief. He won the 1960 Nobel Peace Prize for leading the ANC's passive resistance at a time when, a continent away, American blacks were also boycotting segregated public buses and lunch counters. Luthuli was crossing a railroad bridge near his farm, when he was hit by a train and died.　**9,899**

537 JOSÉ MARTÍ (1853–1895)
Cuban revolutionary with a pen

As a teenager, Martí was known briefly as 113, his number in the Cuban prison where he was sent for anti-Spanish agitation. Then he was an exile in Paris, Mexico City, and New York, using his pen to rally support for Cuban independence. From his anguish came haunting poetry, some political, some as apolitical as the writing of other symbolist geniuses. A sample: "And on the backs / Of giant birds / Endless kisses / Awaken." He wrote: "Without profound pain, man never produced truly beautiful works." He could write fast, too. To help a friend with writer's block fulfill a contract, Martí ghostwrote the classic novel *Lucia Jerez* in seven days. His martyrdom in a guerrilla skirmish rallied Cubans to the revolution that made the country independent four years later.　**9,873**

538 ENRICO CARUSO (1873–1921)
the golden voice

Caruso was a poor factory worker in Naples earning extra *lire* by serenading the lady loves of Neapolitan swains, then a fill-in tenor for operas in Naples, Rome, and Milan. His big break came in 1898 with his creation of the role of Loris in *Fedora*. Acclaim spread worldwide. In 1903 Caruso performed at the opening night of the Metropolitan Opera in New York in *Rigoletto* and opened each season there for the next seventeen years. He also left another legacy: He was the first opera star to record his voice on gramo-phone records. Composer Giacomo Puccini recognized Caruso's enormous talent. It was 1897, and Puccini was sitting at the piano, playing from his *Bohème* while the then-unknown Caruso was singing. Suddenly Puccini whirled around on the piano stool to face Caruso. "Who sent you to me?" he asked. "God?"　**9,851**

539 GODFREY NEWBOLD HOUNSFIELD (b. 1919) *CAT scanner*

Hounsfield, an English engineer, helped design the first all-transistor computer in Britain in 1959. But his company refused him money for a project to make images of human organs because nobody could figure out what he was talking about. So Hounsfield wangled a government grant and, as one technology specialist described it, "borrowed spare parts from a half-dozen different devices and added to that a technology of his own creation that no physicist, physician, or radiologist had ever imagined before." What he was talking about turned out to be computerized axial tomography, an X-ray technique for obtaining clear cross-sectional images of internal organs. The development of the CAT scan in the early 1970s revolutionized diagnostic medicine and won Hounsfield and Allan MacLeod Cormack, an American who did his own research into CAT technology, the Nobel Prize in 1979.　**9,828**

540 LEVI STRAUSS (1829–1902)
blue jeans genie

San Francisco merchant Strauss wanted to ensure that the grizzled, cantankerous misfits who bought his trousers to mine the California gold rush were satisfied. He double-stitched seams and used tentcloth. He hired a tailor who had come up with the novel idea of using copper rivets to reinforce pockets, which had to hold tools and rocks. Then he imported an even sturdier fabric, denim, to make the pants. So confident was he that his "Levi's" would stand up to even the harshest abuse that his label featured two horses in an unsuccessful tug-of-war with a pair of jeans. What started as work clothes became America's uniform in the 1950s, when some fashion arbiter teamed a pair of jeans with saddle shoes. Since then jeans have been rolled up, frayed, bleached, torn, patched, embroidered, beaded, and dyed; they're still the single most popular clothing item in the world.   **9,795**

541 BENVENUTO CELLINI (1500–1571)
artist, rogue, and writer

Cellini the artist made bronze figures and gold medallions with exquisite grace and detail. Victorian admirer W. M. Rossetti said Cellini's statue, *Perseus Holding the Head of Medusa,* is "full of the fire of genius and the grandeur of a terrible beauty." Cellini the rogue claimed to have fired the shot that killed the constable of Bourbon, leader of the French attack on Rome in 1527. He killed commoners, too, but always there was a patron to bail him out. When Cellini murdered a man in a dispute over a horse, an art-loving cardinal arranged his safe passage to France. But it is Cellini the writer whom we celebrate most. *The Autobiography of Benvenuto Cellini,* his account of his art and adventures, the best memoir ever written by an artist, conveys the rowdy spirit of the Renaissance. It makes riveting reading, even today.   **9,778**

542 FRANCISCO DE ORELLANA
(c.1490–1546) *first explorer of the Amazon*

Orellana's voyage down the world's mightiest river was for survival not adventure. He was a lieutenant in a Spanish land force searching for cinnamon and gold east of Quito. Instead his party met starvation. When Orellana and fifty

men sailed downriver to find food, they were eating hides, straps, and the soles of their shoes. The explorers found nourishment but realized the impossibility of returning upstream. So they drifted, hoping to reach the sea. We now know the Amazon has eleven hundred tributaries, with twenty percent of the world's river water. Orellana's voyage took sixteen harrowing months. Back in Spain he told of treasures and female tribes, after whom he named the river "Amazon." But his return to the region ended with losses of ships and men, and the river claimed Orellana, who drowned near its mouth.   **9,759**

543 WILLIAM JAMES (1842–1910)
philosopher of the American way

Americans consider themselves a practical people; James came up with a creed to match. James, brother of the novelist Henry James (557), was among the first to treat psychology as a science subject to laboratory testing. But what really shook up the academic establishments of Europe and America was his philosophy of pragmatism, which said any doctrine was true only insofar as it was useful—a notion that anticipated the relativism of the twentieth century. "It is absolutely the only philosophy with no humbug in it," James boasted. Friends loved his ebullience more than his ideas. One student described him as an "irresistible gust of life coming down the street." James thought religion was useful. Did he think it was true? He told his dying father his deepest hope was "that on the other side, dear, dear old Mother is waiting for you." But maybe he was just being pragmatic.   **9,748**

544 WASHINGTON IRVING (1783–1859)
America's first fiction writer

So legendary is Irving's association with Tarrytown, a New York village nestled in the Hudson

River valley, that residents recently renamed their shopping district after the writer's most famous fictitious setting, Sleepy Hollow. Tarrytown and its Dutch influences inspired much of Irving's quirky fiction, which helped him earn international fame in developing the short story as a respected literary form. Irving fostered an intriguing reputation as a man-about-town lawyer-turned-diplomat-turned-writer. His fiction's popularity was due in no small part to his uncanny knack for characterizing eccentrics and oddballs, like the pontificating, satirical Diedrich Knickerbocker, the pompous, gangly schoolteacher Ichabod Crane, and the ne'er-do-well somnambulant husband Rip Van Winkle. Named for the Revolutionary War hero George Washington (22), Irving enjoyed his first dubious success at writing when he traded English compositions to school chums for completed arithmetic homework.   **9,733**

545 Paul Gauguin (1848–1903)
artist gone native

Gauguin the stockbroker left his wife and five children to be a vagabond painter. It's one of art history's most-told stories. Less known is how this insecure but megalomaniacal imitator pandered to anyone who could help him get an audience: impressionists Edgar Degas (482), Pierre-Auguste Renoir (384), and Camille Pissarro; Vincent Van Gogh's (158) art dealer brother Theo; hack journalists, and finally poet Stéphane Mallarmé, the leader of the symbolists. Mallarmé helped Gauguin obtain a government grant to go to Tahiti, and there he stopped imitating other painters and unleashed his genius. The eroticism and extravagant colors and shapes of his South Sea paintings—some depicting his Melanesian teenage wives—inspired the best of the twentieth-century artists who followed. "Everything I learned from

other people merely stood in my way," he wrote to a friend a month before he died of syphilis.   **9,718**

546 Tecumseh (1768–1813)
chief chief

The Shawnee Indian leader organized a confederation of Great Lakes tribes to stem the flow of white settlers into Indian territory north and west of the Ohio River after 1800. (As a boy, he had played with white boys, including Daniel Boone, captured by his adoptive father.) Though the English supported his campaign, his grand alliance collapsed with his death in battle in 1813. It was probably doomed anyway; there were too many whites, and they were too well armed. Yet he pursued his hopeless cause with valor, believing he must resist a merciless foe. "Brothers," he told one gathering of Indian warriors, "the white people are like poisonous serpents. When chilled, they are feeble and harmless, but invigorate them with warmth, and they sting their benefactors to death."   **9,701**

547 John Knox (1514?–1572)
founder of Presbyterianism

The turning point in Knox's life was a fiery anti-Catholic sermon he preached to rebellious followers of a martyred Lutheran evangelist in 1547. "Others lopped the branches of the Papistry; he strikes at the root," one witness exclaimed. Thereafter Knox, a converted Catholic priest in Scotland, considered himself a prophet. Arrested, he spent nineteen months as a slave on a French galley. The ordeal broke his health but not his spirit; when a statue of the Virgin Mary was thrust into his face, he wrote, he "grabbed the idol, cast it into the river and said, 'Let her learn to swim.'" Knox went on to preach in England, befriend Calvin (69), and espouse radical ideas, from his denunciation of women rulers in *The First Blast of the Trumpet against the Monstrous Regiment of*

Women to his call for God-fearing men to take up the sword against godless rulers. **9,684**

548 MARGARET BOURKE-WHITE
(1904–1971) *photographer of life and times*

As a glamorous celebrity, Bourke-White helped change the image of the sleazy photographer, fueled in the 1920s by the first tabloid newspapers, into that of adventurer and artist. Although her shots of the human drama at German concentration camps in World War II are her most poignant, Bourke-White found the most satisfaction photographing industry. When publisher Henry Luce saw her pictures of steel factories, he invited her to join his fledgling magazine world, which eventually would include *Time*, *Life*, and *Fortune*. The military recruited her as a photographer in World War II, but her pictures also appeared in *Life*. When she asked permission to photograph the African invasion, the Pentagon wouldn't let her fly there because it was too dangerous. So she went by ship, and it was torpedoed. When she climbed into the life raft, she took a tiny camera and film instead of supplies. **9,649**

549 IBN KHALDUN (1332–1406)
medieval historian with modern ideas

In his book *The Universal History*, the Berber courtier and historian analyzed society, politics, and economics in scientific terms shockingly similar to the ideas, centuries later, of pioneering sociologist Auguste Comte (130), groundbreaking political scientist Charles-Louis Montesquieu (106), and revolutionary economist Karl Marx (14). Unfortunately, no great Western thinkers read Ibn Khaldun's book until the nineteenth century, when it was found in musty libraries. Still, the work shows how advanced Islamic civilization was at a time when Europe remained in the grip of hidebound ideas. When he wasn't in a monastery thinking, Ibn Khaldun was a judge and adviser for rulers from Spain to Egypt. The sultan sent him on a diplomatic mission to Damascus in 1400, just as Mongol scourge Tamerlane (511) was arriving at the gates with his bloodthirsty minions. Ibn Khaldun, being both brilliant and prudent, paid homage to the conqueror and left on the next available camel. **9,620**

550 HANS CHRISTIAN ANDERSEN
(1805–1875) *the ugly duckling of children's literature*

Andersen wrote novels, plays, and travel books, but his exquisite fairy tales are what he's known for today, from "The Ugly Duckling" and "The Emperor's New Clothes" to "The Nightingale," "The Little Mermaid," and "Thumbelina." All were autobiographical. "Children," he said, "understood only the trappings." Andersen's insecure childhood scarred him. His grandfather and father went mad; his aunt ran a brothel. Despite later success Andersen always feared his disreputable background would be discovered. As a teenager, he left his Danish hometown to seek fame as a playwright. The effort failed, but a patron secured Andersen a grant to pay for his education. At age twenty-three Andersen resumed writing plays and won acclaim. His friends valued his wit and humor and tolerated his emotionalism—he overreacted to criticism by bursting into tears. "Bear with me," he wrote one close friend, "you know I have a screw loose." **9,612**

551 FÉLIX LOPE DE VEGA (1562–1635)
golden boy of the Spanish Golden Age

Lope's prodigious output—he claimed he wrote fifteen hundred plays; 470 survive—earned him the title "Monster of Nature." His love life was like a monstrous French farce. He seduced wives, widows, actresses, and even the sixteen-year-old sister of the king's earl marshal. He renounced debauchery and entered the priesthood in 1614—but soon abandoned Sunday masses for Saturday night lasses. In his plays Lope abandoned convention for naturalness of structure and dialogue. We like the scene in *Peribáñez* where a bull, chasing a peasant, "kept him hopping like an Italian tightrope walker." And Lope's sixteenth-century description of sexual harassment in *Fuenteovejuna* is as powerful as any we've read:

> *The knight's shadow falls where the maiden cowers,*
> *She cannot avoid the searching eyes.*
> *Why do you hide from me, sweet girl?*
> *For my desires, lynx-eyed, can see through walls.*

9,598

552 SHAKA (c.1787–1828)
founder of the Zulu empire

South Africa today numbers 8.5 million Zulu-speaking people—by far the largest ethnic group in a country of 36 million—mostly concentrated in a ten-thousand-square-mile tract along the Indian Ocean. Shaka built up the Zulu tribe after he inherited a tiny group with a ragtag army of about fifteen hundred men in 1816. He replaced soldiers' spears with knives for hand-to-hand combat; then he wreaked havoc. During the 1820s displaced clans who feared the Zulus clashed with each other in battles for land in southern Africa. By the time Zulu supremacy was established, two million people were dead. Shaka, insane with grief when his mother died, ordered the slaying of pregnant women, and cows so their calves could feel maternal loss. He banned milk, a staple of the Zulu diet, and forbade planting crops. His psychotic frenzy ended only when he was murdered by his half brothers. **9,561**

553 JOSEPH CONRAD (1857–1924)
novelist at the heart of darkness

He wrote of ships and seamen, but calling Conrad a spinner of sea stories is like saying Michelangelo (13) was an interior decorator. Conrad's adventure tales are about the big themes: love, death, redemption, and the meeting of East and West. A Pole born Józef Teodor Konrad Walecz Korzeniowski, he served in the English merchant marine for twenty years and learned English so well, he became a master stylist. He did not adopt English, he said. "It was I who was adopted by the genius of the language." His best book, *Lord Jim*, about a seaman who makes a life-haunting mistake, was a critical success, but it took four years to sell two thousand copies, some readers finding it difficult. Many still do. On first reading Conrad's dense prose, some high school students wail, as Mister Kurtz did in *Heart of Darkness*, "the horror, the horror." **9,545**

554 ISADORA DUNCAN (1878–1927)
ballet's liberator

The genius of Duncan's career has often been overshadowed by the legendary oddity of her death. She was strangled when her trademark flowing scarf tangled in the wheel of a sports car as she was riding along the Côte d'Azur in France. During her lifetime Duncan rattled the classical world of dance by challenging its rituals. She urged dancers to liberate themselves through free and sweeping movements unseen in classical ballet. She rejected tights, toe shoes, and tutus and danced barefoot in scarves and loose shifts. She took a few ballet classes but hated them. Her debut in Chicago in 1899 was a resounding flop, but her tour of Europe gained her many fans and followers. Duncan influenced traditional choreographers to loosen the movement in their dances, and she opened schools in Berlin, Paris, London, and Moscow, to pass on her techniques to the next generation of dancers. **9,519**

555 FANNIE FARMER (1857–1915)
precision cook

Whenever Farmer tasted an interesting dish, she'd wrap a sample in her lace handkerchief so she could take it home to figure out its ingredients. Farmer standardized measurements in recipes for her first cookbook, *The Boston Cooking School Cookbook*, published in 1896. As the school's director for eleven years, she taught cooks to measure ingredients accurately rather than haphazardly throw in a dash or a pinch. Her interest in ethnic cooking and regional specialties was reflected in her recipes. She was a primary force in the creation of an "American" cuisine. In simple language that any novice could understand, Farmer explained how to choose a melon, boil an egg, or cook a roast. After her death the cookbook was renamed for her. Still the bible in many kitchens, it has sold more than four million copies. **9,480**

556 MARTIN BEHAIM (c.1459–c.1506)
globe-trotting globe-maker

Behaim was an erudite German merchant and mathematician who emigrated to Lisbon and claimed later to have taken part in Portuguese expeditions down the coast of Africa. When Behaim visited his hometown of Nuremberg in 1490, the town fathers were so impressed by his stories, they asked him to build a globe depicting the new discoveries. Still on display in Nuremberg, the *Erdapfel*, or earth apple, as they called it, proves that the flat earth theory was dying before Columbus's (2) voyage. Columbus didn't see the globe, but Magellan (42) had a copy when he set out to circumnavigate the world. A Behaim fan, German astronomer Hieronymous Muntzer, wrote to King John II of Portugal (298) in 1493 suggesting that Behaim be hired to lead an expedition West to find Asia. Nice idea, but too late. Columbus had already tried it. **9,477**

557 HENRY JAMES (1843–1916)
novelist of the mind

A master craftsman and innovative stylist, James helped launch the twentieth-century stream-of-consciousness movement and influenced authors from James Joyce (171) and Graham Greene to Joseph Conrad (553) and Virginia Woolf (441). Probing every nuance of his characters' psyches ran in the family; Henry's older brother was American psychologist William James (543). The theme of many Jamesian novels, including *Daisy Miller, The Portrait of a Lady*, and *The Ambassadors,* was the conflicting values between innocent America and sophisticated Europe. James became a transatlantic cultural figure after moving from the United States to England. His life was devoted to writing, and he never married. Gregarious at social gatherings, he could be aloof in private. Some critics found him too refined and passionless in his writing. "He is never in deep gloom or in violent sunshine," conceded Conrad. "But he feels deeply and vividly every delicate shade. We cannot ask for more." **9,469**

558 JEAN-BAPTISTE SAY (1767–1832)
incredibly ugly French economist

We regret having to get personal, but everybody knows economics is the dismal science, and we feared losing your attention. Anyway, Say postulated—what else?—Say's law, which states that supply creates its own demand. Thus economic recession or depression has nothing to do with demand and everything to do with temporary disequilibriums in production. Say's law held sway until John Maynard Keynes (201) repealed it following the Great Depression of the 1930s. But it popped up again in the 1980s, reincarnated as President Reagan's supply-side economics. Maybe if Say had spent more time working on his theory, he would have perfected it, but he seemed to have trouble sticking to any single career, earning his keep variously as an insurance adjustor, journalist, bureaucrat, cotton-mill entrepreneur, and think-tank guru before settling down as an economics professor. (And, yes, he really was ugly.) **9,455**

559 MARIE LaCHAPELLE (1769–1821)
mother of modern obstetrics

Male physicians started poking their noses into the process of childbirth in the sixteenth century. Then in 1721 a male midwife in London invented forceps. Used incorrectly, the instrument could be deadly to both mother and child. Enter LaChapelle, who persuasively argued that doctors and midwives should return to the ways of "natural childbirth." She believed professionals should intervene only when a serious problem occurred. As head of obstetrics at the Hôtel Dieu in Paris, LaChapelle argued against the use of forceps to shorten labor. The daughter of a midwife, LaChapelle trained midwives throughout Europe. Her three-volume *Pratique des accouchements*, the standard text for many years, chronicled some forty thousand cases, and promoted her laissez-faire treatment of childbirth but described intervention techniques for difficult cases. LaChapelle was the first obstetrician to immediately stitch up new mothers to repair the damage that nature caused. **9,437**

560 GUSTAVE COURBET (1819–1877)
art's radical

The gentility reviled Courbet's paintings and his politics. The paintings were influential milestones in the history of realism—hunters killing stags,

portraits that showed warts and fat folds of flesh, pictures of the poor. When the prudish Paris salon of 1864 rejected Courbet's *The Awakening*, a picture of nude lesbians, his friend Jean Millet complained that the really indecent paintings in the show were the ones that appealed to stockbrokers and bankers. Courbet's politics were a mixture of aggressive anarchism, communism, and socialism. "What fabulous intercourse between a slug and a peacock, what genetic antitheses, what bristly slime, could have spawned the thing called M. Gustave Courbet?" novelist Alexander Dumas, Jr., wrote after Courbet was arrested for blowing up an imperial war monument during the aborted Paris revolution of 1870–71. Courbet's fame saved him from a firing squad. Free on parole, he went on painting. **9,431**

561 PIERRE CORNEILLE (1606–1684)
dutiful French dramatist

Playwright Corneille was the father of French classical tragedy, a genre admired throughout Europe during the seventeenth and eighteenth centuries. He dropped Greek tragedy's conventions, with its heroes merely puppets of the gods. In his master work, *Le Cid*, as well as in *Horace*, *Cinna*, and *Polyeucte*, Corneille's characters confront impossible moral and emotional dilemmas but manage to prevail through judgment and will. With Corneille, love always runs a distant second to duty. "You must never allow love to reach the stage when you cannot help loving," Corneille wrote in the dedication to his first play. That was a prevailing theme in his thirty-two other eloquent plays, some of which are performed to this day. Corneille's career had astounding highs and lows. For two decades he was France's premier playwright. After 1659, however, the public tired of his heroic plots, and he was upstaged by younger rival Jean Racine (389). **9,408**

562 BENJAMIN SPOCK (1903–1998)
the parents' pediatrician

Before Spock, experts preached rigidity. Behaviorist John Watson admonished parents to "never hug or kiss" their kids. Aw, go ahead, hug 'em, Spock advised. "Trust yourself. You know more than you think you do," he wrote in *Dr. Spock's Baby and Child Care*, published in 1946. The Connecticut-born pediatrician said parents should smile at, talk to, play with, and fondle their babies. His bible of parenting has sold fifty million copies worldwide, making it the second best-seller of all time after the real Bible. Not bad for a how-to tome that originated with an editor's remark, "It doesn't have to be very good, we're only going to charge a quarter." During the Vietnam War Spock became a peace activist, and critics accused him of spawning the youthful rebellion and drug culture of the 1960s with his "permissiveness." Nonsense, Spock retorted; he merely wished to treat parents like "sensible people."　　**9,395**

563 ABIGAIL ADAMS (1744–1818)
first lady of letter writing

What we know about the real people behind the American Revolution comes in part from Adams's letters. She was the *People* magazine of colonial America. Her lifetime of letter writing began with love notes to beau John Adams (214) then continued through his presidency. Although Adams hoped her letters would be tossed away as "trash," the more than two thousand that survive describe colonial politics and social life. "Remember the ladies," Adams, an early feminist, chided her husband at the Continental Congress. "Do not put such unlimited power into the hands of the Husbands. Remember all men would be tyrants if they could." The United States could have avoided more than a century of discontent if the Founding Fathers had heeded Adams's warning.

Numbered among the most influential first ladies, Adams was criticized for meddling. John Adams's secretary of state charged that the second president was "under the sovereignty of his wife." She died seven years before her son, John Quincy, was elected president.　　**9,371**

564 RUBÉN DARÍO (1867–1916)
savior of Spanish poetry

To break up a teenage romance, Darío's parents sent him from his native Nicaragua to El Salvador, and there he succumbed to his lifelong mistresses: poetry, and the alcohol addiction that eventually killed him. A friend gave him works by French symbolists Stéphane Mallarmé and Paul Verlaine, and Darío adopted their style, rescuing Spanish poetry from a stuffy romantic tradition. "I seek a form that my style cannot discover, a bud of thought that wants to be a rose," he wrote in his 1896 book, *Profane Hymns*. We laud him for the beauty of his work and because he was among the first Latin American writers to portray the United States as a mechanistic bully, an enduring depiction. In a poem entitled "Roosevelt," he wrote, "And though you have everything, you are lacking one thing: God!"　　**9,348**

565 GEORGE FREDERIC HANDEL
(1685–1759) *the hallelujah man*

Handel's superb oratorio, *The Messiah*, with its famous "Hallelujah" chorus, took twenty-three days to write. Some speculated he had divine guidance. "I did think I did see all Heaven before me," Handel conceded, "and the great God himself." Thirty years before, the brilliant German-born composer had won over England with his opera *Rinaldo*. He remained in London, composing forty operas and his celebrated *Water Music*, for George I. English disenchantment with operas in "unintelligible" foreign languages prompted

Handel to compose oratorios—large musical compositions for solo voices, chorus, and orchestra. Soon he made this the most popular musical form in England. Though *The Messiah* was not the last composition for this master of the baroque, it was his swan song. In failing health and nearly blind, Handel fainted in the orchestra pit during a performance of his master work on April 6, 1759. He died eight days later. **9,339**

566 CORNELIUS VANDERBILT (1794–1877)
money-making machine

While Marx (14) brooded over the evils of capitalism, the wily Yankee Vanderbilt was turning a hundred-dollar investment in a leaky boat into a shipping and railroad empire worth $100 million—serious money then. His trick was to cut prices and improve service, though his two first rules for business success were "1. Buy the railroad. 2. Stop the stealing that went on under the other man." Frugality helped, too; Vanderbilt scribbled money orders on scraps of paper rather than buy preprinted checks. Though he was famous for saying "The public be damned," he once helped prevent a financial panic by committing money to stave off speculators' attempts to corner the gold market. At his fiftieth wedding anniversary, his son-in-law sang a ditty he had composed to honor the aging tycoon:

In Wall Street he is a tornado;
He blows stock about as the dust;
When speculators have made their pie, Sir,
The Commodore breaks in the crust.

9,303

567 JALAL AD-DIN AR-RUMI (c.1207–1273)
mystic founder of the whirling dervishes

Rumi's sons were so disturbed by their father's devotion to a charismatic dervish (holy man) that they had the dervish murdered. Rumi, a native of the region that is now Afghanistan, turned to poetry to explore his sorrow. Writing in Persian, he produced about thirty thousand mystical verses, which he often performed with a whirling dance. When Rumi found new love and devotion with an uneducated shopkeeper in the Konya bazaar, his free-form poetry again flowed—this time his *Mathnavi* was numbered among the Persian classics. In fact, the *Mathnavi* is still so popular that it is often sung. His ideas often contradicted one another, but Rumi wanted to explore the depths of clashing human emotions. He inspired many disciples who organized after his death into the Mawlawiyah order of whirling dervishes. His mausoleum in Turkey remains the destination of pilgrims. **9,280**

568 JEAN-BAPTISTE-CAMILLE COROT
(1796–1875) *"a rare genius and the father of modern landscape painting"*

So said Eugène Delacroix (468), who took tips from Corot on how to paint trees. Obscure until his sixties, Corot lamented that his success came after his father's death. "He resented my paintings and could never find anything good in it because it didn't sell," Corot said. Finally, after Napoleon III paid a hefty 18,000 francs for Corot's *Solitude* in 1865, Corot's landscapes became so popular that he was the most-forged painter of his time. If the forgery was good enough, Corot would sometimes lend his signature. He sought veracity with a dash of drama. "While aiming at truth and accuracy, let us never forget to clothe it with the appearance of what has touched us," he wrote in 1856. He was humble and charitable. When artist Honoré Daumier (587) couldn't pay his rent, Corot bought him a house. **9,275**

569 DUNCAN PHYFE (1768–1854)
crafter of a furniture phyfedom

Before Phyfe, elegant furniture was imported from Europe. The Scottish-born cabinetmaker, who started life as "Fife," then changed the spelling perhaps to lure business from established French furniture firms in New York, opened a workshop there. Business boomed after the Embargo Act of 1807 prohibited European furniture trade. While other craftsmen imitated ornate French furniture, Phyfe developed a simple, graceful style. He disliked cabinets of ostentatious size, dubbing them "butcher furniture," and used rich mahogany imported from the West Indies. His furniture was expensive for the day—$122 for a sofa, $22 for a chair, and $80 for a dining set. The distinctive Phyfe style, especially his lyre design in chairs and tables, is often imitated, but you have to visit a museum to see the originals. **9,261**

570 BARTHOLOMAEUS ANGLICUS
(fl.1220–1240) chronicler of knowledge, part two

Bartholomaeus, an English-born Franciscan friar, was a disseminator of knowledge, hastening medieval Christendom's intellectual awakening. His great *De Proprietatibus Rerum (On the Nature of Things)*, begun in Oxford, polished in Paris, and completed in Germany, was meant as a tool for biblical study. Though generally ranked a shade behind the work of his contemporary Vincent of Beauvais (447), it marshaled in a single nineteen-volume set the opinions of the greatest Christian, Jewish, and Arab scholars of his time, as well as ancient Greek wisdom. Books one and two deal with God and the angels; books three through seven cover man, both body and soul; books eight through

eighteen examine the "corporeal substances"; and book nineteen treats the "accidents" of color, odor, taste, and liquidness. The encyclopedia was enormously popular, finding its way into libraries throughout Europe for centuries and getting translated into several vernacular languages from the original Latin. **9,248**

571 OMAR KHAYYÁM (1048–1131)
the tentmaker's poetic son

Omar billed himself as an astronomer. The modern world, however, knows him as the poet who said, "A jug of wine, a loaf of bread—and thou." Unfortunately, he probably didn't write it. Omar's poetry stock soared centuries after his death when his "quatrains"—poems consisting of four rhymed lines—were translated and embellished upon by Edward FitzGerald in *The Rubaiyat of Omar Khayyam*, published in 1859. Scholars differ on where Omar ends and FitzGerald begins, but they agree that at least 50 of the 250 verses can be attributed directly to the Persian. FitzGerald himself said that the "drink and be merry" theme that runs throughout his *Rubaiyat* showed that "the old Tentmaker, who, after vainly endeavoring to unshackle his Steps from Destiny, and to catch some glimpse of Tomorrow, fell back upon To-day." **9,233**

572 EDWIN HUBBLE (1889–1953)
astronomical heir to Galileo (4)

In the 1920s, the Missouri-born stargazer discovered the existence of galaxies beyond our own Milky Way and, even more astonishing to scientists, detected evidence for the universe's expansion that physicist George Gamow (674) would later use to formulate his Big Bang theory of creation. The Hubble space telescope is named after him, as is the Hubble constant that measures the velocities at which heavenly bodies are flying apart. Who cares that Hubble was a vainglorious self-promoter who lied about boxing French champion Georges Carpentier to a draw, faked two dueling scars on his face, and affected an English accent? To his credit, Hubble loved wild animals, was kind to underlings, and had the wisdom to renounce an early career as a lawyer. Besides, vanity is fleeting; Hubble's constant is, well, constant. **9,208**

573 SIMONE DE BEAUVOIR (1908–1986)
thinker for the second wave

Hailed for feminist writings, Beauvoir considered them only one facet of her work: "I am a writer. I have written novels, philosophy, social criticism, a play—and yet all people know about me is *The Second Sex.*" That classic treatise examined the second-class status of women and provided a theoretical framework for the international women's movement. To write it, Beauvoir plumbed her masterful knowledge of philosophy, economics, biology, literature, and sociology. Actually, she'd been preparing for years. Child of a proud bourgeois family, she had an embossed calling card by age three. Her autocratic father praised her for having "the mind of a man." Her parents' unhappy marriage made her compulsive about establishing order in chaos. One example: During her lengthy liaison with philosopher Jean-Paul Sartre, she was the one to introduce him to students he later seduced. Supporters dubbed them "the kingly couple"; critics called her "the most public sinner in all of France." **9,191**

574 OSCAR WILDE (1854–1900)
the wit that launched a thousand quips

Wilde's greatest literary accomplishment was his play *The Importance of Being Earnest*, a farce brimming with epigrams that exposed the hypocrisy of Victorian society. A fop who dressed in a velvet jacket, black silk stockings, and lavender gloves, the Irish dramatist had plenty of enemies, including American writer Ambrose Bierce, who called him the "sovereign of insufferables," and American painter James McNeill Whistler (762), who said he had "the courage of the opinions—of others." His two-year imprisonment for sodomizing an English lord won him a dubious place of honor in pederasty's pantheon. But he is most remembered for the quips that peppered his prose and public utterances. Samples: "I can resist anything except temptation;" "Nothing succeeds like excess"; and on his deathbed, the apocryphal "Either that wallpaper goes, or I do." **9,189**

575 GEORGE WYTHE (1726–1806)
America's first law professor

As chair of law at the College of William and Mary from 1779 to 1790, this signer of the Declaration of Independence oversaw the evolution of American jurisprudence and articulated a court's right to overturn an unconstitutional law. We've argued that U.S. Chief Justice John Marshall (287) carved a powerful role for the Supreme Court on this basis, but guess who taught Marshall? Wythe also suggested that the federal government's power should be subservient to that of individual states. Sounds like Thomas Jefferson (64)? Guess who taught Jefferson? Wythe eventually left William and Mary and started his own school, where he mentored Henry Clay (936). After Wythe chose his nephew as heir, the nephew sprinkled arsenic into Wythe's coffee. The brilliant lawyer died, but not before he disinherited his scheming nephew. The only witness was a black cook whose testimony was discounted. The nephew went free. **9,167**

576 ZHOU ENLAI (1898–1976)
consummate diplomat

A staunch Chinese Communist from his youth, he emerged unscathed from party purges and forced exiles. Zhou even managed to die before the infamous Gang of Four could discredit him. Charming, urbane, and astute, he was prime minister of the world's most populous country for twenty-five years. Among his achievements: arranging the historic meeting between Mao Ze-dong (50) and President Nixon (904) in 1972. But lest the West forget, this reasonable negotiator at the Geneva Conference in 1954 was the same man who approved the slaughter of millions of landowners at the start of the Communist revolution. To political writer Theodore White, this paradoxical man "could act with an absolute daring, with the delicacy of a cat pouncing on a mouse. Yet he was capable of warm kindness, irrepressible humanity, and silken courtesy." **9,151**

577 WILLIAM WORDSWORTH (1770–1850)
wordsmith

One of the great British romantics, Wordsworth is the poet of the dreamer, the wanderer, the oddball, the nature lover. And since we are all, sometimes, all of those things, we love him. His famous definition of poetry as the "spontaneous overflow of powerful feelings" found expression in lines like these:

I wandered lonely as a cloud
That floats on high o'er vales and hills,
When all at once I saw a crowd,
A host of golden daffodils.

Yet writing was such an ordeal, it gave him chest pains. Wordsworth, admirer of revolutionary France in his youth, Tory churchgoer in his old age, was a complicated creature. But his poetry was simple; he described ordinary events and people at a time when poetry was cerebral and stale. Dismissed at first as a producer of "dawdling, impotent drivel," he lived to become an icon to the world. **9,129**

578 GUSTAV MAHLER (1860–1911)
symphonic master

Mahler told his analyst—Sigmund Freud (15) no less—that his musical mood swings were caused by a boyhood episode. Panicked by a nasty argument between his parents, he ran into the street and heard a hurdy-gurdy man playing the amusing "O Du Lieber Augustine." Let's hear it for transfiguring experiences. Mahler's nine and a half lush, long, and mercurial symphonies kept the classical tradition alive in central Europe and rival those of Johannes Brahms (353) as the darlings of today's symphony concert programmers. We like best the eighty-one-minute roller-coaster ride that is the Sixth Symphony. A riveting conductor, too, Mahler ran the New York Philharmonic until bossy benefactresses and mediocre players drove him home to Austria. There he met a new muse, his wife Alma, who had a talent for marrying artistic geniuses. After Mahler, she wedded architect Walter Gropius and writer Franz Werfel. She revealed years later that Mahler was as flat in the bedroom as he was sharp on the podium. **9,121**

579 ANNA COMNENA (1083–c.1150)
witness to the Crusades

The Alexiad, Anna's chronicle of the reign of her father, Byzantine emperor Alexius I, is a major source of modern knowledge about the First Crusade and its effect on Byzantium. It's also how we know that the Crusaders were free-booting louts, always vicious, and sometimes cowardly. Anna told how Bohemond of Normandy, to escape from a besieged town, had his death proclaimed, hid in a sealed coffin with a stinking, decomposing chicken, and was carried through enemy lines. At her father's funeral in 1111, Anna organized a coup to put her soldier husband Bryennius on the throne instead of her brother John. The rebellion fizzled, and Anna was sent to a convent where she took a pen and etched her name into the history of the Middle Ages. **9,085**

580 ANGELA MERICI (1474–1540)
the teaching nun

We've tracked the roots of Catholic parochial education to Merici, founder of the Ursuline sisters. Orphaned at age ten, Angela studied as a Franciscan tertiary, the noncloistered religious who tended to worldly concerns. She had visions throughout her life; one showed singing women moving up and down a ladder while a voice said they were members of a religious order she would create. As the years passed, Angela devoted herself to educating Italy's poor children until she found a way to fulfill her dream. She trained women in Brescia, supervised orphanages, and established schools for former prostitutes. They were Catholic nuns' first formal classrooms. So if you had your knuckles rapped in third grade, or wake up in a sweat from a recurring nightmare that you forgot to give Sister Agnes Marie your term paper, thank Saint Angela. She was canonized in 1807. **9,066**

581 MILDRED "BABE" DIDRIKSON ZAHARIAS (1911–1956)
the greatest woman athlete

On July 16, 1932, Babe singlehandedly won the national women's amateur *team* track championship as the only member of the Dallas Golden Cyclones, scoring thirty points to twenty-two for the second-place Illinois Women's Athletic Club, with twenty members. Another time she won six gold medals and broke four world records in one

afternoon, "the most amazing feat by any individual, male or female, in track and field history," according to one account. In the 1932 Los Angeles Olympics, the nineteen-year-old Didriksen won gold medals in the hurdles and the javelin. Turning to golf in 1933, she practiced until her hands bled, a display of tenacity that ultimately made her the world's greatest woman golfer, with seventeen straight golf championships in 1946 and 1947. Nicknamed for her idol Babe Ruth, she married a three-hundred-pound professional wrestler in 1938, scotching rumors she was a man. **9,061**

582 EAMON DE VALERA (1882–1975)
first prime minister of an independent Ireland

A strange last name for an Irish hero, but then De Valera was not your typical Irishman. Born in the United States to an Irish mother and a Spanish father, De Valera was baptized Edward and adopted Eamon when he began public life. He was sent to live with relatives in Ireland after his father's death. De Valera fought in the 1916 Easter Rebellion against British rule and escaped a death sentence only because of his American citizenship. De Valera was elected to parliament as the candidate for Sinn Fein, the nationalist party. When he was sent again to prison, he escaped to America, where he sought financial support from Irish immigrants. A revolutionary parliament, the Dail Eirann, elected him president in absentia, and De Valera became the official head of government who ensured his country's independence after his party won a majority in the Dail in 1932. **9,024**

583 MAHMUD OF GHAZNA (971?–1030)
India's Islamic invader

We last encountered Mahmud in entry number 356 as he was refusing to pay the gold he owed to the poet Firdawsi for writing Islam's greatest epic, the *Shah-nameh*. Mahmud's cruelty to Islamic poets paled next to his cruelty to Hindu everybodies. His armies swept into India sixteen times, sacking, raping, killing, and looting. In 1018, in a fever of Islamic zeal, he ordered the destruction of the Hindu temple of Mathura, a gold-and-gem-encrusted shrine that had taken two hundred years to build. Indian historians consider Mahmud a bandit, albeit a bandit with a big appetite. His effect, though, was to spread Islam deep into the Asian subcontinent, an accomplishment that led to the unceasing Hindu-Islamic rancor in that region since. **9,001**

584 THOMAS MANN (1875–1955)
a magical mountain of talent

The writings of the German Nobel prizewinner constitute an imaginative analysis of European culture. He established his literary reputation with *Buddenbrooks* in 1901, then followed with *Tonio Kröger* and *Death in Venice*. But his triumph is *The Magic Mountain*, a novel ranked with the finest works of art of the twentieth century. Protagonist Hans Castorp is a simple young German visiting his cousin at a mountain-top sanitarium when he, too, falls ill with tuberculosis. Castorp's visit stretches to seven years. As he interacts with other patients, Castorp grows spiritually, mentally, and emotionally. We soon recognize, however, that each of these patients represents a philosophy of Western culture. Mann touches on a host of issues: psychoanalysis and spiritualism; the links connecting art, disease, and death; the relative nature of time; the relations between artist and society. A gigantic tour de force. "Only the exhaustive is truly interesting," Mann said. Many readers agree. **8,998**

585 MOHAMMED ALI JINNAH (1876–1948)
founder of Pakistan

The name Gandhi (12) is known the world over, but even some educated Westerners draw a blank at the name of the man who created Asia's seventh-biggest country. In part, that is because most histories of the Indian independence movement have been penned by British and Indian scholars, who have played down Jinnah's role or portrayed him as a fanatic bent on carving out a separate Muslim state, whatever the cost in blood. And flow the blood did in the Hindu-Muslim massacres that accompanied the partition of British India. Ironically, Jinnah began his political career as an apostle of Hindu-Muslim unity but changed course in the 1930s. Lord Mountbatten, the last British viceroy, spent three hours alone with him in April 1947 in a desperate effort to preserve Indian unity, but concluded that "Mr. Jinnah was a psychopathic case." Four months later Pakistan was born. **8,972**

586 MARY MALLON (1869–1938)
Typhoid Mary

Everyone loved Mallon's cooking. Only trouble was, sickness followed her. From 1900 to 1907 the Irish immigrant cooked in six New York homes and one hospital. Forty-seven people fell ill, and three died from typhoid fever. Doctors hypothesized typhoid was spread by microscopic bacteria; then health investigators tracked the outbreak to Mallon. They isolated her on Quarantine Island in New York's East River. Newspapers dubbed her "Typhoid Mary." Two years later officials released her after securing her promise never to cook again. She lied. She was arrested after two more people died. Mallon, a healthy carrier of typhoid, lived another twenty-three years in isolation. She makes our list because, aside from being a colorful legend, she illustrates the unresolved conflict between society's right to health and individual freedom. **8,951**

587 HONORÉ DAUMIER (1808–1879)
skewer of the rich, the reactionary, and the ridiculously bourgeois

As he grew old, Daumier pined to be recognized as a fine artist, not as a caricaturist and draftsman. Sorry. Though the literary lion Honoré de Balzac (254) wrote of twenty-three-year-old Daumier, "there is something of Michelangelo in this youth," what makes this messenger-boy-turned-artist important are his sculptures and lithographs—four thousand of them. Collectively, they expressed his belief in democracy and equality and his hatred of France's rulers and ruling class. In 1832 he was sentenced to six months in jail for depicting King Louis Philippe as Gargantua feeding on office-seekers' gold. Characters invented by Daumier to personify stock manipulators, usurers, corrupt journalists, and exploiters of workers became fictional celebrities. Blindness ended his career, and he died poor. **8,937**

588 FRANCISCO DE MIRANDA (1750–1816)
torchbearer of Latin American liberty

The dashing Venezuelan was an early inspiration to Simón Bolívar (48), liberator of South America. Miranda dreamed of freeing Latin America from Spanish domination. To Yale president Ezra Stiles, Miranda was "a learned man and a flaming son of liberty." After two decades of appeals to world leaders, this charismatic and eloquent dandy won British support. He sailed a ragtag crew to Venezuela in 1806, but peasants refused to rally round and Miranda retreated. A second break came in 1811, when revolutionary leaders summoned him to Venezuela to lead their forces. With independence secured, Miranda assumed

dictatorial powers. But the Spanish counterattacked, Miranda declared himself "struck to the heart" when Bolívar's negligence lost a key fort to the enemy, and Miranda surrendered. He tried to flee but was captured and nearly killed by a seething Bolívar, his former general. **8,928**

589 ROBERT OWEN (1771–1858)
Utopia's draftsman

After improving the workers' lot at his cotton mills with such innovations as free medical care, Owen launched his most famous experiment, a cooperative village in New Harmony, Indiana, in 1825. Populated by intellectuals, reformers, and crackpots who, one historian said, were more inclined to furrow their brows than the fields, the community collapsed three years later. Undeterred, Owen returned to Britain and got involved in the workers' movement, eventually heading a national trade-union federation before it, too, fell apart. Owen preached an atheistic social doctrine with an oddly religious edge, frequently announcing the arrival of a new millennium of peace and brotherhood. In his later years he took up spiritualism, claiming he had spoken with the ghosts of Thomas Jefferson (64) and the Duke of Kent. Whatever his failings, his campaign to ameliorate factory conditions early in the Industrial Revolution had an enduring impact on governments' social policies. **8,918**

590 RASHI (1040–1105)
interpreter of the Bible and the Talmud

The stories about Rashi probably aren't true, but they make good legend. For example, Rashi's mother was pregnant when she was crushed against a wall by two carts. The wall miraculously formed a protective niche around her belly. Another story says Rashi nursed a sick monk who later became a Catholic bishop and protected Jews from annihilation to return the favor. What we do know about Rashi is that he was born Solomon ben Isaac and trained as a rabbi. Lacking family riches, he worked in French Champagne vineyards. He wasn't an eminent thinker like Maimonides (132), but his commentaries are important even today because he simplified complex Talmudic thoughts and explained confusing Bible passages. He was smart enough to know when he was out of his league. "I do not know what it is," he wrote on more than one occasion. **8,884**

591 Lu Hsün (1881–1936)
greatest modern Chinese writer

A medical student in Japan during the Russo-Japanese war, Lu Hsün saw a newsreel of the execution of a Chinese spy and was appalled that the Chinese spectators depicted in the film showed no anger or shame. At that moment Lu Hsün decided that waking up his countrymen's souls was more important than healing their bodies. His writing received little attention until 1918 when his short story, "Diary of a Madman," caused a sensation by attacking Chinese cruelty, hypocrisy, and commitment to outworn traditions. The madman reads a history book that extols Chinese benevolence, but hidden in every line are the words "eat men." Later, in "The True Story of Ah Q," Lu Hsün mocked peasant revolutionaries, but in 1929 he joined the Communist Party. No wonder the Chinese now consider him their most important modern writer, though even anti-Communists agree that Lu Hsün's deification is warranted. **8,867**

592 Henri Cartier-Bresson (b. 1908)
photography's decisive moment

Frenchman Cartier-Bresson raised photojournalism to an art form. He intended to be a painter until he acquired a 35-millimeter Leica. It soon became, he said, "the extension of my eye." For forty years, as he traveled throughout the world, that eye captured poignant scenes of humanity: a Gestapo informer heckled by jeering French; the saucy gazes of two Mexican prostitutes; a working-class family picnicking by the Marne. "He sees through the lens as a sniper sees through the telescopic sight on his rifle," said historian Peter Pollack. And like a hunter, he preferred camouflage, applying black tape to shiny parts of his camera to make it less noticeable. Cartier-Bresson believed in the "decisive moment" in picture taking. "Photography," he said, "is the simultaneous recognition in a fraction of a second of the significance of an event." **8,859**

593 Bertrand Russell (1872–1970)
British jack-of-all-intellectual-trades

His influence lay in his ability to force his unorthodox views into the social mainstream. A brilliant mathematician, Russell, an atheist, found comfort in that discipline's "cold and austere beauty." He churned out scores of books, from *The ABC of Atoms* to *Marriage and Morals*. Married four times, he "pursued anything in skirts," according to his friend Sidney Hook. His greatest fame came from his social activism. Imprisoned for pacifist activities in World War I, he switched ground to urge a preventive war against the Soviet Union in the late 1940s, only to turn into a nuclear-disarmament advocate with an anti-Western bent. Russell declared that British and American leaders "Macmillan and Kennedy are fifty times as wicked as Hitler." And in the late 1960s he and other leftist grandstanders convened the International War Crimes Tribunal to denounce American intervention in Vietnam. **8,851**

594 WILLIAM OF SENS (d.1180)
cathedral builder

History has recorded little about the master builders who designed the world's great cathedrals at Chartres, Paris, Mont-St.-Michel, and elsewhere. We are in a position to pay homage here to William of Sens because his rebuilding of England's Canterbury Cathedral after a fire in 1174 was documented by a scribbling monk. Gervase, who witnessed the blaze, described in his diary how William came from France to rebuild the choir and expand the church. William's innovations, especially his use of contrasting stone in the interior, coupled with some interesting flying buttresses that owe their design to Paris's Notre Dame, can still be seen at Canterbury. In 1178 William barely survived a fifty-foot fall from scaffolding, but for a time he directed the construction from his bed. Then the project was passed on to yet another William—known to history simply as "the Englishman."   **8,832**

595 ANTHONY OF PADUA (1195–1231)
most-prayed-to saint

Since the seventeenth century countless Catholics have appealed to Saint Anthony to help locate lost objects. Many swear he's come through. Some say this started after a novice borrowed Anthony's psalter without permission, then saw a fearful apparition. During his lifetime, however, Anthony's mission was finding lost souls. This priest from a noble Portuguese family dreamed of martyrdom at the hands of Saracens in Morocco, but poor health prevented him from traveling that far. He became a Franciscan and preached the word closer to home, in France and Italy. With his fine voice and charisma, he drew overflow crowds that could be accommodated only in marketplaces. Anthony died at thirty-six, exhausted by his heavy workload. He was canonized in 1232. His devotion to the poor inspired the nineteenth-century institution, St. Anthony Bread, a fund for the needy that continues today, especially in developing countries.   **8,821**

596 EISAI (1141–1215)
tea-totaling monk who brought Zen Buddhism to Japan

Our idea of a great ritual is an annual martini on New Year's Eve. Still, we want to toast the man who authored *The Essentials of Tea Drinking*, in which he described for the shogun the use of tea to maintain health and ensure longevity. Today, remnants of his methods can be found in the formal Japanese ceremony, which was perfected in the sixteenth century by Sen No Rikyu. The ritual *Chanoyu*, which literally means tea's hot water, uses tea to promote harmony, peace, and one perfect moment. Eisai spent four years studying at the Song monasteries in China and then returned to Japan and founded the Rinzai Sect of Zen Buddhism in his native land. He also brought home tea seeds that are believed to be at the root of much of Japan's tea crop. Variations of Eisai's tea method became so popular that the fourteenth century Buddhist monk Ikkyu observed one could find enlightenment more quickly in a tea ceremony than from hours of meditation.   **8,802**

597 RAMAKRISHNA (1836–1886)
Hinduism's charismatic leader

The Hindu holy man Gadadhar Chatterji was born into a poor Brahman family. He suffered epileptic seizures, standing stock-still for long periods, and in adulthood he sank into trances anytime. His immersion in Islam produced a vision of Muhammad; his study of Christianity made him "see" Jesus Christ. He concluded that all religions are essentially the same and valid. This revered wise man could also be most human. Calcutta elite were shocked when Ramakrishna burst into childlike laughter and dance, and spoke the coarse dialect-spiked obscenities natural to his village. He had no patience with rituals of the faithful in which they twisted their bodies like pretzels to gain mystical insights. "Shun them like filthy excrement," he said of yoga exercises. His follower, Vivekananda, helped spread the master's teachings through the Ramakrishna Mission, a religious society that today continues its educational and philanthropic work throughout the world.   **8,796**

598 MINAMOTO NO YORITOMO
(1147–1199) Japan's first shogun

Yoritomo established a system of rule by feudal lords that lasted seven hundred years. His story starts with the rivalry between the Minamoto and Taira clans. Their clashes were particularly grisly. One example: Minamoto legions raided a palace, setting it afire. Nobles, courtiers, and ladies-in-waiting fled. "When they rushed out, so as not to be burned by the fire, they met with arrows," one account said. "When they turned back, they were consumed by the flames." The Taira eventually won that round. But in the Gempei War, Minamoto no Yoritomo led his faction to victory in 1185, crushing the Taira in a sea battle. He then established constables and district stewards in the provinces, thus undermining the central government's local control, and took the title of shogun, or supreme commander.   **8,768**

599 NICOLÁS DE OVANDO *(1451–1511)*
West Indies tyrant

Ovando established the cruel system of exploitation of natives in the Americas that was copied throughout Spanish America. The callous Spanish nobleman arrived in Santo Domingo in 1502 to govern the Spanish colonies in the West Indies; he brought with him more than two thousand settlers and the largest fleet the New World had ever seen. The natives, however, refused to work for the occupying force, and colonists soon dubbed them "dirty dogs." Ovando's soldiers tracked down and killed Indians who sought to escape, including their princess, Anacaona. Under the *encomienda* system, the defeated natives were forced to work the settlers' estates in exchange for food and security. When word reached Spain of Ovando's brand of brutality, he was recalled. Even in those days, though, he got a book deal out of it.   **8,737**

600 DOUGLAS MacARTHUR *(1880–1964)*
the general who had a great fall

World War I hero, victorious World War II general, benevolent despot of occupied Japan, scourge of Asian Communism, nationalist idol, MacArthur veered dangerously close to Bonapartism in old age but, being an American, became a businessman instead. It was MacArthur who uttered the defiant vow, after being driven out of the Philippines by the Japanese, "I shall return!" And it was MacArthur who, fired by President Truman (485) for insubordination in the Korean War, nearly triggered revolution in the streets with his farewell speech to Congress that quoted an old barracks ballad: "Old soldiers never die, they just fade away." Popular adulation waned, however, after the septuagenarian general faded into a lucrative job as head of the Remington Rand Corporation. MacArthur wanted to drop fifty atomic bombs on China. Truman scorned him as "Mr. Prima Donna, Brass Hat, Five Star MacArthur." In that battle of titans, happily, Truman prevailed.   **8,711**

Call them, if you will, the fomenters of quiet revolutions; These statesmen, writers, teachers, environmentalists, and humanitarians discovered their noble callings— or had their causes thrust upon them—and remained true to their messages no matter what the fallout.

On the following pages you'll meet a few of the millennium's great moral voices. One is Russian writer Aleksandr Solzhenitsyn, who endured eight hellish years as a political prisoner in the Soviet gulag and lived to write his vengeance. Another, fiery French novelist Émile Zola, swayed his countrymen with a dramatic open letter pleading for justice for the unjustly accused Alfred Dreyfus.

German doctor Albert Schweitzer inspired the world with his selfless devotion to the sick and lame of Africa, and with his philosophy of reverence for all living things. Undersea explorer Jacques Cousteau had the same deep respect for nature. In films of his many underwater explorations, Cousteau kept hammering away at the verdict few wanted to accept: The industrial world was endangering the earth's oceans with its wastes.

Some of the notables in the next pages bettered the lives of the disabled. Elizabeth Kenny, a pioneer in physiotherapy, created soothing massages and exercises to help the paralyzed. And the Frenchman Abbé de L'Epee wanted to extend the Christian message of salvation to deaf students but first had to learn to communicate with them. He devised a manual alphabet that enabled these children to study the same academic subjects as hearing youngsters.

Blessed, too, are the pure of heart: German Protestant theologian Dietrich Bonhoeffer opposed the Nazis during World War II and could have saved himself by remaining in America. Instead, he chose to return to his native land and stand with his compatriots. He was executed weeks before the war's end, but his ecumenical spirit lives on.

601 WILLIAM OF OCKHAM (c.1285–c.1349)
sharp-witted philosopher

The Englishman developed a fundamental principle of modern thought: Once a problem has been solved, additional solutions are unnecessary. It's called "Ockham's razor" because it shaves a lot of time-wasting work. Just as important was Ockham's view, new in its time, that objects had no universal meaning independent of their existence. The concept, called nominalism, is a philosophical seedling of the empiricism that flowered in the Renaissance. Ockham was a Franciscan monk who taught at Oxford, but in 1328 he took refuge with Holy Roman emperor Louis IV to escape punishment for teaching heresy about transubstantiation, the belief that bread and wine are transformed into the body and blood of Christ. For an explanation of Ockham's heresy, see our next book, *1,000 Years, 1,000 Religious Disputes That Are Incomprehensible Today.*   **8,692**

602 KING GILLETTE (1855–1932)
speaking of razors

For most of the millennium cutting whiskers with a straight razor was a chore and often a bloody one, except for those who could afford to hire barbers. Then came Gillette, a bottle-cap salesman from Boston with the capitalistic dream of inventing a product, any product, that customers would have to buy over and over. He claimed that he got the idea for the safety razor and disposable blade while he was shaving, and in 1904 he patented the system that changed the face of, well, faces. The Gillette Safety Razor Company blade was sharp because it was thin and flexible, and customers kept coming back because the blades were only a couple of cents each. The invention made Gillette a millionaire, but only briefly. He was shorn of his fortune by the Great Depression.   **8,662**

603 ROWLAND HILL (1795–1879)
the post's impressionist

Hill created the modern postal system. Letters used to be postmarked by hand and postage was paid by the receiver, not the sender. Hill, a teacher, envisioned a system that used a "bit of paper just large enough to bear the stamp and covered at the back with a glutinous wash"— in other words, a postage stamp. Hill's plan included a standard fee for delivering a letter—a penny—no matter what the distance throughout his native England. Britain's first stamp featured a profile of young Queen Victoria. Because it was difficult to see a cancellation on the "penny black," the ink was switched to red. Millions of the penny reds imprinted with a teenage queen circulated during Victoria's long reign. In 1842 Hill's idea caught on in the United States when a New York postmaster began selling a stamp with George Washington on its face.   **8,649**

604 JOHN R. PIERCE (b. 1910)
space-age networker

With live television coverage of a missile attack on Kuwait or police storming a rebel stronghold in Peru, the world is in our living rooms. Communications satellites whirling through space link continents like a vast electronic spider web. Pierce gets our thanks for starting the process. An engineer at Bell Labs in 1936, he improved the traveling-wave tube, the most common source of microwave power for transmitting signals from satellites. His paper envisioning unmanned communications satellites spurred the 1960 launch of the experimental balloon, *Echo I.* Two years later the first commercially funded satellite, *Telstar I,* was launched into orbit and relayed data, voice, and television transmissions. In August 1964 *Syncom 3* made history by transmitting the Olympic Games from Tokyo. To

Pierce, this was déjà vu. A lifelong writer of science fiction, he'd built plots around such space-age communications back in high school. **8,635**

605 JOSEPH HENRY (1797–1878)
the thinker who didn't tinker

If he had been interested in the practical application of his groundbreaking research, Henry might have built the first intercity telegraph, the first telephone, maybe the first commercial electric motor. Instead, as biographer Thomas Coulson wrote, "Like a child he went on asking 'Why?' without seeking a final answer." Henry's greatest discovery was self-induction, which makes possible the transmission of electrical pulses through long wires. He built the first laboratory-size electromagnetic telegraph, and when Samuel Morse (329) was having trouble making his Washington-to-Baltimore line work, Henry helped with technical advice, such as using glass to insulate the relays. Electromagnets perfected by Henry were central to Alexander Graham Bell's (74) telephone. After working at Albany Academy and Princeton University, Henry finished his career at the Smithsonian Institution. President Lincoln (32) had reviled the Smithsonian as a warehouse of useless curiosities. But after he met Henry, the president declared: "It must be a grand school if it produces such thinkers as he is." **8,591**

606 GEORGIA O'KEEFFE (1887–1986)
artist of the American Southwest

The willowy O'Keeffe once was hounded by a fellow art student who was determined that she pose for him. "It doesn't matter what you do. I'm going to be a great painter, and you will probably end up teaching painting in some girls' school," he warned. Eugene Speicher (Eugene who?) erred on both counts. Although women artists of previous generations had indeed been the captives of classrooms, O'Keeffe took a different route. She destroyed all her paintings just before her thirtieth birthday because she thought they were unoriginal. Then she found inspiration in the New Mexico desert. She painted haunting scenes of the landscapes she found there, as well as her seductively sensual, decidedly female flowers. This passion for painting, coupled with her marriage to photographer/gallery owner Alfred Stieglitz, who nursed her talent and managed her career, sealed O'Keeffe's destiny as an American original. **8,569**

607 ÉMILE ZOLA (1840–1902)
writer who told it like it was

He founded the naturalist school of fiction with his objective, almost scientific probes into the dark corners of a character's life. This led critics to label his works pornographic. His first book, *Thérèse Raquin*, spurred his publisher-bosses to order him to stop writing or quit. He quit. His twenty-novel cycle, *The Rougon-Macquart*, is one family's social history, and each novel presents a different profession, trade, or class. Of these, *Nana*, a study of prostitution, caused a scandal; and the leftist-leaning *Germinal*, an exploration of mining conditions, was a novel of class warfare. While Zola defended Manet (301) and other impressionist artists, he's best known for his open letter, "J'accuse," which helped win a new trial for Alfred Dreyfus, a Jewish army officer unjustly accused of treason in an anti-Semitic climate. "When truth is buried underground," Zola wrote, "it grows, it chokes, it gathers such an explosive force that on the day it bursts out, it blows up everything with it." **8,567**

608 ROBERT BROWNING (1812–1889)
perfecter of the dramatic monologue

A major poet of the Victorian era, Browning created psychological studies in verse that influenced the writings of poets Ezra Pound (367) and Robert Frost (828). Consider this Browning dialogue in the chilling, "My Last Duchess": The duke, peering at a portrait of his late wife, tells a visitor, "Oh Sir, she smiled, no doubt, / Whene'er I passed her; but who passed without / much the same smile? This grew; I gave commands; Then all smiles stopped together." Browning won greatest fame for *The Ring and the Book*, a chronicle of a seventeenth-century Italian murder trial. To novelist Henry James (557), Browning had two personalities: bon vivant of London society and fiercely private artist. In 1846 Browning married the poet Elizabeth Barrett (759) after a courtship kept secret from her domineering father. They moved to Italy for her health. Their happy, though complicated, union lasted sixteen years—until Elizabeth's death in Browning's arms. **8,541**

609 CHARLES GOODYEAR (1800–1860)
tire squire

Goodyear was a hapless manufacturer who was periodically jailed for debt because he put his capital into products nobody wanted, such as natural rubber mailbags that turned to mush. Then in 1839 he discovered vulcanization, a process of applying hot steam to chemically treated rubber. No longer did rubber ooze in summer, freeze in winter, and stink all year around. Vulcanization made Goodyear a big wheel in the history of industry. What would cars and bicycles ride on without rubber tires? Tinkering was in Goodyear's genes. His father invented Goodyear's Patented Spring Steel Hay and Manure Fork, a winning item in 1812. Suits over patent rights to vulcanization threatened to make Charles Goodyear's waning years depressing, but he bounced back after he hired a good lawyer, Daniel Webster. **8,519**

610 MARY STUART (1542–1587)
Queen of Scots

Was she history's tragic figure or a scheming adulterer-turned-murderer? Catholics loyal to Mary were willing to overlook rumors that she killed her husband after she took a lover. Protestants abhorred Mary for her vampish role in sixteenth-century intrigue. A great beauty, Mary was a statuesque five foot eleven with amber eyes and copper hair. Queen of Scotland since infancy, she grew up in France and married Francis II, son of King Henry II and his queen, Catherine de Médicis (632). When he died, Mary returned to Scotland a refined Frenchwoman uncomfortable with her country's earthy lifestyle. After the birth of son James (879) and her second husband's murder, Mary was imprisoned for eighteen years for her involvement in plots to overthrow her cousin, Elizabeth I (31). Elizabeth eventually ordered Scotland's femme fatale beheaded because the mere fact that Mary lived gave England's Catholics reason enough to plot treason. **8,475**

611 ALEXIS DE TOCQUEVILLE (1805–1859)
the Homer of America's odyssey

French aristocrat Tocqueville's observations on the new republic form *Democracy in America*, one of the greatest political treatises ever written. Under the guise of studying America's prison system, Tocqueville arrived in New York in May 1831 intent on learning what made this country tick. For nine months he and Gustave de Beaumont traveled by horse, steamer, and stagecoach from Boston to New Orleans, searching for the essence of democracy. Beaumont focused on race relations. Tocqueville targeted politics. His analysis was astute (even then he noted "the ablest men are rarely placed at the head of affairs"), but he sometimes stumbled. Ultimately, Tocqueville predicted, the equality of America would spread to

Europe. "To attempt to check democracy would be to resist the will of God," he wrote. **8,472**

612 ROBERT SWANSON (b. 1947)
entrepreneur who launched the biotechnology revolution

Swanson was a twenty-nine-year-old former frat rat when he cofounded Genentech in 1976 with gene-splicing pioneer Herbert Boyer. The company, conceived over beer in a San Francisco pub, spawned the biotechnology industry of genetically altered products. Genentech's products, ranging from a blood clot buster to a human growth hormone, accounted for nearly half of those on the market in the late 1990s, and scores of its scientists started their own firms. Swanson has his lighter side, manifested in antics like showing up at Genentech's Friday afternoon beer bashes in a grass skirt. When we last looked, the MIT-trained chemist headed a company that was trying to make drugs capable of switching off disease-causing genes. "It's people who make the difference," he once said, "people who have dreams of catching the big fish." **8,451**

613 LOUIS IX OF FRANCE (1214–1270)
Saint Louis the king

Louis was a monarch at twelve, and his wise mother, Blanche of Castile (694), taught him to love God and humanity, though Louis made an exception for Muslims and for French nobles who disturbed the peace. In 1250, after quelling unrest in France, Louis went on a Crusade, but the Arabs captured him and extracted a ransom equal to a year of royal income. He went again twenty years later, caught a fever, and died. Louis wore simple clothes and denied himself such pleasures as salt, and he was that rare medieval royal who liked to read books. His blend of piety, physical courage, and intellect made him a

model king to generations of admirers, though his canonization in 1297 was mostly a political act. Pope Boniface VIII (837) gave him a halo to appease a potential enemy, Louis's grandson, King Philip IV. If looking at famous skulls is your idea of fun, visit Louis's in the treasure room of Notre Dame cathedral in Paris. **8,427**

614 HELENA RUBINSTEIN (1882–1965)
empress of beauty

Cleopatra may have used eyeliner and rouge to lure Mark Antony, but by 1900 good girls no longer wore makeup. Today the cosmetics industry is worth $6 billion annually. Who changed women's minds? Rubinstein. The Polish native studied medicine but switched to cosmetics after she emigrated to Australia in 1902. There her family's face cream was a big hit—in large part because Rubinstein relied heavily on advertising. By 1915 she had salons in Paris, London, and New York. Her polished look found a ready market with modern women who were raising their hemlines, cutting waist-length tresses, shedding whalebone corsets, lobbying for suffrage, and working in factories and offices. Called the Princess after she married royalty, Rubinstein coined nicknames for her competition: Charles Revson of Revlon was "The Nail Man," while she contemptuously referred to Elizabeth Arden as "the Other One." **8,401**

615 SERGEY PROKOFIEV (1891–1953)
twentieth-century traditionalist

Prokofiev was a prolific composer, penning symphonies, concertos, operas, ballets, program pieces, and film scores. A prodigy who was writing music at age six, he left Russia in 1918 during the revolution. First stop, the United States, where his now well-known opera, *The Love for Three Oranges*, nearly bombed in the

Big Apple. Critics, Prokofiev snarled, were "a pack of dogs." Disillusioned, he moved to Western Europe, then returned to the Soviet Union of Joseph Stalin (82). While his early works had been modern and dissonant, he now shifted his style to the lean and near-classical. However, he resisted the Communist regime's pressure to compose only works of social realism. Prokofiev's output remained monumental, including the symphonic fairy tale *Peter and the Wolf* and the ballet *Romeo and Juliet*. Still, Stalinists censured him for "modernistic techniques." Eventually, the composer's workaholism weakened his health, and he died just three hours ahead of Stalin. **8,397**

616 IAN WILMUT (b. 1944)
world's first cloner

In 1997 Wilmut, a British embryologist, created a lamb named Dolly using DNA from an adult sheep. The feat stunned the scientific world—an American biology professor scrambled to revise a book that said it couldn't be done—and raised visions of carbon-copying animals capable of producing prodigious quantities of milk, wool, proteins for drugs, even organs for humans. But critics said "Bah!" to Dolly's *ba-a-a-h*. They worried somebody would try to clone people. In no time one American researcher declared his intention to do just that. "I would find that offensive," Wilmut said, as if the idea had never occurred to him. Others mulled the possibilities of duplicating Michael Jordan (903) or Mother Teresa (772). A Jesuit priest hastened to declare that a cloned human would have a soul. Wilmut, a reclusive sort with a penchant for solitary strolls in the Scottish mountains and a nobody until his deed was publicized, said all he wanted was "to understand things." Goodbye Frankenstein, hello Dolly. **8,368**

617 NICCOLÒ PAGANINI (1782–1840)
virtuoso of all virtuosi

A Viennese concert-goer insisted he spotted the devil perched on Paganini's shoulder during a recital. How else to account for the cadaverous-looking but loose-limbed Genoese violinist's supernatural skills and eye-popping performances? He played the highest notes and harmonics with clarity and moved his bow so dexterously, his Guarneri-made violin sometimes sounded like a mini-orchestra. Paganini hyped his evil image by not denying wild stories that he ravished women and performed black magic, but those tales were mostly myth. An evil man wouldn't have given 20,000 francs—a lot of money, then—to impoverished, yet-to-be-recognized Hector Berlioz (671), as Paganini did. Paganini's compositions, notably the pyrotechnical twenty-four caprices, challenged generations of stringed-instrument players to match his skills. No one succeeded, except maybe twentieth-century violinist Jascha Heifetz, but trying made them better players. **8,347**

618 CHRISTINA ROSSETTI (1830–1894)
the poet's poet of Victorian England

"I wrote such melancholy things when I was young that I am obliged to be unusually cheerful and robust in my old age," Rossetti once said. She wasn't kidding. How's this for starters?

> *He did not love me living; but once dead*
> *He pitied me; and very sweet it is*
> *To know he still is warm though I am cold.*

Filled with haunting, sensual images of love, death, illness, and loneliness, Rossetti's poetry found an enthusiastic audience in the Pre-Raphaelite Brotherhood, a band of artists who worked together to unite painting and poetry. As a woman, Rossetti never had official membership in the group; her relationship to it was through her brother, Dante Gabriel, himself a poet and painter of some note, though not of Christina's stature. We include the reclusive, introverted Christina for her position as England's greatest female poet. **8,322**

619 NIKITA KHRUSHCHEV (1894–1971)
first human Soviet leader

After Stalin's (82) horrors, Khrushchev's reign from 1953 to 1964 was almost fun. Certainly this plain-spoken miner's son, who taunted the West by declaring, "We will bury you," and pounded his shoe on a table at the United Nations, was colorful. But his great accomplishment—de-Stalinization—was deadly serious. It began in his secret speech to the Communist leadership in February 1956, denouncing Stalin's brutalities. "Peaceful coexistence, different paths to socialism, revolution without violence, and the abandonment of the doctrine of the inevitability of war: the Soviet Union formally renounced her role as the spearhead of violent revolution," said historian Edward Crankshaw. The next eight years were action-packed: The Hungarian Revolution was crushed; Sputnik was launched; Khruschev toured America; the Chinese-Soviet alliance collapsed; the Berlin Wall rose; the Cuban missile crisis erupted; the superpowers signed a nuclear test-ban treaty. An ousted Khrushchev then wrote his memoirs. **8,310**

620 REGIOMONTANUS (1436–1476)
mathematician with the right angle

His name is Latin for "from Konigsberg," or royal mountain, his hometown in Germany. Copernicus (18) and other stars of Renaissance astronomy built on work by Regiomontanus, notably his *On Triangles of Every Kind*, published fifty-seven years after his death. "Knowing these ideas will open the door to all of astronomy and to certain geometric problems," he wrote. The book was full of easy solutions to important problems, such as how to measure the right angles of triangles. He found errors in translations of Ptolemy's *Almagest*, a second-century book that placed the earth at the center of the universe. Regiomontanus's math helped later scientists prove that even the correctly translated Ptolemy was wrong. A quarrel with a fellow savant forced him to flee Rome in 1468, but he was welcomed in Austria, Hungary, and Germany, and he went back to Rome in 1472 to be science adviser to Pope Sixtus IV. **8,287**

621 ANDREAS MARGGRAF (1709–1782)
sweetie pie of the sugar industry

The U.S. Department of Agriculture estimates the average American consumes sixty-five pounds of sugar annually. That's an awful lot of bonbons. We rooted out Marggraf, a German who extracted sugar from beets in 1747—a discovery that eventually spawned the multibillion-dollar sugar industry. Marggraf learned chemistry from his father, the court apothecary in Berlin. He figured out how boiling alcohol could coax the juice right out of the beet. The crystals that formed were identical to cane sugar. His discovery was important because beets grew well in Europe (and the United States, for that matter), while cane sugar, the previous sole source of sugar, needed a balmier climate. Marggraf's success in the laboratory extended far beyond this discovery. A pioneer in analytical chemistry, he was first to use a microscope in the laboratory to analyze elements. How sweet it is! **8,261**

622 CHARLES MICHEL DE L'EPEE
(1712–1789) *hero of the deaf*

Deaf people always were able to communicate with one another using basic hand gestures. It was the hearing who felt left out. Then came Abbé de l'Epee, who taught deaf children a manual alphabet, the better to learn academic subjects. He called this "methodical signing" and his instruction became known worldwide as "the French method." Noble Epee's motive: "to reach heaven by trying at least to lead others there." He put on grand public performances, reeling off questions that deaf pupils answered in up to seven languages. In an age when deaf children were a scandal, to be hidden or abandoned, Epee demonstrated they were as intelligent as hearing youngsters. His system prevailed for nearly a century, until educators known as oralists, including Alexander Graham Bell (74), insisted the deaf needed to speak, not sign. That conflict continues to this day.   **8,255**

623 DENG XIAOPING (1904–1997)
architect of China's economic miracle

One of Mao Ze-dong's comrades in founding Communist China in 1949, Deng launched a market liberalization three decades later, saying, "It doesn't matter if a cat is black or white, as long as it catches mice." The economy took off, prompting speculation it might outstrip America's in the twenty-first century. Deng opened China to the world, even donning a cowboy hat at a Texas rodeo. But ever the tyrant, he ordered the Tiananmen Square massacre of prodemocracy demonstrators in 1989, the greatest blot on his legacy. He said he wanted to avoid the chaos that had killed millions under Mao. (The pragmatic Deng had bounced back from two Maoist purges to become China's "paramount leader" in 1978.) The four-foot-eleven chain smoker was unencumbered by human affection, declining to attend his father's funeral and earning his daughter's description as "a man of introverted character and few words."   **8,221**

624 HORATIO NELSON (1758–1805)
seagoing hero

Britannia ruled the waves for three centuries, and here's the dirty secret: The British navy's most celebrated fighting commander had no stiff upper lip. Nelson cried easily. He was a self-promoter. He abandoned his wife for a married woman, Emma Hamilton. He often forgot that his men were fighting for England's welfare, not his glory. They didn't care; he had the "Nelson touch" for victory. "Among all the warriors of his generation, Napoleon alone was a greater master of the souls of men," biographer David Hannay wrote. Nelson went to sea at twelve and won fame against the French at the battles of Copenhagen, Aboukir Bay, and Cape St. Vincent, where he lost his right arm. "England expects that every man will do his duty," he signaled before the Battle of Trafalgar. Minutes later, a French sharpshooter killed him. Nelson was so revered, Parliament ennobled his heirs and paid them £5,000 a year until 1951, when the government said, enough already.   **8,210**

625 BERTHE MORISOT (1841–1895)
impressionist master of the ordinary

Our favorite Morisot painting, *Mother and Sister of the Artist*, celebrates a simple domestic scene. A friend of Cézanne (72), Pissarro, Monet (196), and Renoir (384), Morisot exhibited in all the Parisian impressionist shows, except in 1879, when she was pregnant. Women in her day were often disqualified from intellectual endeavors by their very femaleness. As writer Virginia Woolf (441) wryly noted, historically in literature, "Anonymous" was a woman. The art world was no different, but Morisot and American impressionist Mary Cassatt changed all that. That the impressionists were themselves outcasts in France made it more logical that women flourished in this untraditional environment. Morisot fell in with the boys after she and her sister struck up a friendship with Édouard Manet (301). "It's a pity they are not men," Manet remarked about them. He mentored Berthe; she posed for him and married his younger brother. **8,177**

626 PAUL JULIUS REUTER (1816–1899)
wire service whiz

No idealistic journalist, Reuter was a canny German businessman who recognized how the telegraph could deliver news fast. Born Israel Beer Josaphat, he changed his name and converted from Judaism to Christianity. Better for business, Reuter said. He launched a prototype of the news service in Paris in 1849, using carrier pigeons to bridge gaps in the unfinished telegraph system. Two years later in London he founded the service that retains his name today. Reuters first relayed market developments via telegrams. Later it supplied newspapers with first-hand accounts of world events. Reuters's first scoop: transmission of Napoleon III's speech to French legislators as he delivered it in 1859. He alluded to impending war between France and Austria. These days the agency is refocused on financial news. "Reuters has turned itself into nothing less than the world's leading supplier of computerized information," said *Forbes* magazine in 1989. Julius would be pleased. **8,160**

627 POPE JOHN PAUL II (b. 1920)
amazing Grace

The first non-Italian pontiff since the Dutch Adrian VI died in 1523, John Paul wasted no time in flying around the globe to greet adoring throngs from his popemobile. His impact was immense; his historic visit to his native Poland in 1979, one year after his ascent to the throne of Saint Peter, inspired the creation of the Solidarity trade-union movement that became the catalyst

of Communism's collapse. He energized the Catholic Church with his youthfulness and intellect, though some liberals lambasted his doctrinal orthodoxy. He sought reconciliation with the Jews. A poet and playwright since adolescence, John Paul greeted the people of Rome after his election with the words, "Be not afraid." He met with the Turkish gunman who tried to assassinate him and called him "my brother." He railed against abortion, euthanasia, economic injustice, and capitalist decadence. Four words summarize his life: He preached the Gospel. **8,158**

628 STEPHEN LANGTON (c.1155–1228)
the cleric who stared down a king

He was the archbishop behind the Magna Carta, the document that started the West on the road to popular sovereignty. After preaching a sermon at London's St. Paul's Church on August 25, 1213, Langton told a group of rebellious barons that he had found a copy of a promise by King Henry I, 113 years earlier, to respect the rights of his vassals. It was just the legal precedent the barons needed to support their demands against Henry's great-grandson, the power-grabbing, money-grubbing King John (416). The barons used Henry's promises as a model for the Magna Carta, and Langton helped convince John to sign it in 1215. Langton was a biblical scholar at the University of Paris in 1207 when Pope Innocent III (78) picked him to be England's chief prelate, the archbishop of Canterbury. When John's successor, King Henry III, sought Langton's permission to tax the clergy, the archbishop said, yes, but don't make it a habit. **8,124**

629 ANNA FREUD (1895–1982)
the daughter who analyzed children

How Freudian! The child of the father of psycho-analysis (15) dedicated her career to analyzing kids.

First a teacher, Anna studied psychiatry under her father's tutelage. She wasn't her father's favorite, but she sure got his attention by caring for him after he became ill with cancer of the mouth. She became his voice at professional conferences, his nurse and confidante. Father and daughter fled Vienna in 1938 to escape the Nazis and settled in England. After her father's death in 1939, Anna Freud became a leading figure in child psychiatry. She developed ways for analysts to interpret the play of children, founded a British clinic for child therapy, and coined the phrase "separation anxiety" to describe the fear children feel when they are removed from their parents. **8,093**

630 JOSÉ DE SAN MARTÍN (1778–1850)
South America's liberating lion

Spanish army officer San Martín heard the call of his native Argentina and joined the revolution against Spain in South America. Under orders from the junta in Buenos Aires, he organized the crack Army of the Andes, telling conscripts, "I want only lions in my regiment." San Martín led them boldly across the mountains—a military feat ranking him with Hannibal and Napoleon (16)—to invade Chile in 1817, defeating royalists at Chacabuco. Eventually his forces crossed into Peru and occupied Lima. But after fifteen years of struggles, San Martín grew dispirited and began proposing monarchies, not republics, for the new countries. When revolutionary giant Simon Bolívar (48) arrived, San Martín retreated and allowed Bolívar to finish the fight for Peru. Before leaving for exile in Europe, San Martín told his rival: "Time alone will tell which of us has foreseen the future more clearly." Bolívar had. **8,092**

631 ERNEST MACH (1838–1916)
scientist of sound and fury

The Austrian's experiments with the speed of pro-

jectiles were so innovative, engineers now measure the velocity of sound in Mach numbers. At thirty-two degrees Fahrenheit, Mach One is 1,180 feet per second. Mach the philosopher of science had an impact as large as Mach the physicist, in a perverse way. He rejected commonsense extrapolations and taught that science should describe only those phenomena that can be observed. Albert Einstein (17), Max Planck (136), and Werner Heisenberg ultimately disagreed, but their agonizing explorations of Mach's views when they were young made them better scientists. Lenin (41) thought Mach was so wrong, he wrote a book, *Materialism and Emperio-Criticism*, sounding off against "Machism." Mach's son Heinrich committed suicide, and Mach blamed himself for failing to prepare the lad for life's difficulties. That conclusion was based on common sense, a very un-Machian concept. **8,077**

632 CATHERINE DE MÉDICIS (1519–1589)
the Mommie Dearest of the Renaissance

Behind every great man there is a woman, and behind some wishy-washy kings there was Catherine. Daughter of the Florentine Medicis, she married France's King Henry II, then mothered three French kings and two queens of Spain. When her weak son, Charles, was king, Catherine masterminded the 1572 St. Bartholomew's Day Massacre of Protestant leaders who were attending the wedding of Catherine's daughter. The slaughter spread, and seventy thousand Protestants eventually were killed. The stout Catherine's hearty interest in food fueled creation of a national cuisine. When her penchant for spinach became known, dishes were served "à la Florentine," after her city of origin. Although Catherine's husband preferred the company of his mistress, the queen had the last word. When Henry died, she confiscated the enchanting Loire Valley château, Chenonceaux, which the king had given to his lover. **8,050**

633 CHARLES-PIERRE BAUDELAIRE
(1821–1867) *rebel with a verse*

Moody and introspective, Baudelaire wrote poems of inner despair that spoke directly to twentieth-century British and American poets. His masterpiece, *Flowers of Evil*, shows brilliant phrasing and expressive lyrics, but its eroticism shocked fellow French on publication in 1857. A sample from the poem "Jewels":

> *Her long legs, her hips, shining smooth as oil,*
> *Her arms and her thighs, undulant as a swan,*
> *Lured my serene, clairvoyant gaze to travel*
> *To her belly and breasts, the grapes of my vine.*

Baudelaire was convicted of obscenity and ordered to suppress six poems. He complied, then wrote thirty-three more. "This book is almost good," he wrote his doting mother. "It will endure as testimony of my disgust and my hatred of all things." He wanted to write a vitriolic autobiography, too, but suffered a stroke that left him paralyzed. **8,048**

634 LUDWIG WITTGENSTEIN (1889–1951)
searcher for the meaning of meaning

The Austrian-born Wittgenstein studied in Cambridge under philosopher Bertrand Russell, who called him "perhaps the most perfect example I have ever known of genius." His 1921 masterpiece *Tractatus Logico-Philosophicus*, based on jottings he made while fighting in World War I, explores the relationship between language, thought, and the world. The final sentence reads: "Whereof one cannot speak thereof one must be silent." Wittgenstein, a homosexual and born-again, if idiosyncratic, Christian, was an intense man. After giving away a huge inheritance in 1919, he supported himself teaching school in rural Austria. He contemplated committing suicide,

as three of his four brothers had done. He once stormed out of a room after the German philosopher Karl Popper joked that he felt threatened by the way Wittgenstein was waving a poker around to emphasize a point. "I am a worm," he wrote, "but through God I become a man." **8,042**

635 JOHN DUNS SCOTUS (c.1277–1308)
the smartest dunce in Christendom

Contemporaries called Duns Scotus the "subtle doctor" because he ruminated on divinity, will, being, and intellect until every shade of meaning had been catalogued ad nauseam. To future generations it was gibberish. That's why the word *dunce* was derived from his name. At the risk of getting an F for flippancy, we say his contribution to mankind was this: a body of teaching that was brilliant, yes, but so convoluted that more focused successors, such as William of Ockham (601), were challenged to make sense of what Duns Scotus had written, and did. Duns Scotus entered the Franciscan order in his native Scotland at age fifteen and spent his adult life teaching in Oxford, Cologne, and Paris. King Philip IV of France understood Duns Scotus well enough to exile the scholar for siding with Pope Boniface VIII (837) in a political quarrel. **7,982**

636 DIETRICH BONHOEFFER (1906–1945)
hero in a sea of hate

A German Protestant theologian who opposed Hitler, Bonhoeffer studied in New York in the early 1930s. On an American lecture tour in 1939, he was beseeched by friends to remain in order to avert persecution at home. "He paced the room upstairs here at Union [seminary], smoking his cigarettes, fighting his conscience," a classmate recalled. Finally he decided: "I will have no right to participate in the reconstruction of Christian life in Germany after the war if I do not share the trial of this time with my people." He was arrested in 1943 for anti-Nazi activities, imprisoned, and hanged weeks before Germany's surrender. Since then his influence as a foe of injustice and champion of ecumenism has soared. Contemptuous of the "cheap grace" many seek, Bonhoeffer insisted that action speaks louder than words, saying, "Only those who can cry out for the Jews can sing Gregorian chants." **7,979**

637 KONSTANTIN E. TSIOLKOVSKY (1857–1935) *cosmic dreamer*

Before the close of the nineteenth century and the advent of the airplane, this Russian researcher's gaze saw rockets hurtling through the universe. In *Investigation of Cosmic Space by Reactive Machines*, published in 1903, he solved theoretical problems of space flight, paving the way for Soviet efforts half a century later. At ten Tsiolkovsky contracted scarlet fever and lost his hearing. Shunned by neighborhood children, he withdrew into himself to read, concentrate, and dream. "The thought of communicating with cosmic space never left me," he said. Self-taught in higher mathematics, physics, and astronomy, this high school teacher dedicated his spare time to the research of flight in his homemade wind tunnel. Underpinning his life's work: recognition that the entire universe is mankind's domain. "Earth is the cradle of the mind," Tsiolkovsky said, "but one cannot live in the cradle forever." **7,977**

638 WILLIAM GLADSTONE (1809–1898) *pillar of British politics in the British century*

Gladstone's evolution from Tory theocrat to Liberal champion of free trade and a free Ireland is one of the more compelling political conversions of history. But then, Gladstone was no ordinary man. The son of a Scottish corn merchant who got rich in the West Indies sugar-and-slave trade,

he wandered London's streets at night trying to persuade prostitutes to change their ways. He read twenty thousand books and chopped trees for exercise, prompting Lord Randolph Churchill to quip, "The forest laments in order that Mr. Gladstone may perspire." Four times prime minister, his political reforms doubled the British electorate. While he never achieved home rule for Ireland, he sought to ease that land's suffering. He was called the Grand Old Man of Victorian England, even though Queen Victoria (91), goaded by his archrival Benjamin Disraeli (640), despised him as "that half-mad firebrand." **7,962**

639 BENJAMIN DISRAELI (1804–1881) *the other pillar*

Disraeli was the quirky Conservative to the straight-arrow Liberal Gladstone (638), his archrival. Early in his career, he condemned his own party to the political wilderness by attacking the free-market policies of the Tory prime minister Robert Peel (932). After finally "climbing to the top of the greasy pole" of power, as he put it, he championed social reforms and an aggressive foreign policy as prime minister in 1868 and 1874–80. Baptised a Christian at age thirteen, Disraeli reveled in his Jewish roots. To enemies who called him a "Jewish scamp," he retorted, "Half Christendom worships a Jewess, the other half a Jew. Which should be the superior race, the worshiped or the worshipers?" Besides, the person who counted, Queen Victoria, adored him. No wonder; everyone loves flattery, he said, "and when it comes to royalty, you should lay it on with a trowel." **7,935**

640 PHILIPPE PINEL (1745–1826) *advocate of humane treatment for the insane*

He abhorred his age's cruel treatment of the dangerously mad and believed that mental illness could be cured. Pinel taught that asylums—like the one he established at Salpêtrière hospital in Paris—should be run by medical doctors like himself, not jailers. He built a halfway house so the newly cured could adjust to society. "I am convinced that the only reason these insane people are so intractable is that they are deprived of air and liberty," he wrote. Pinel's theories eventually became accepted wisdom, and they also saved his life during the French Revolution. When a mob that had sacked a church turned on Pinel for denouncing them, he was protected by a recently unchained mental patient.   **7,912**

641 JAMES GORDON BENNETT (1795–1872)
molder of the modern newspaper

As editor of the penny paper *The New York Herald*, Bennett discovered that scooping the competition would sell papers. Getting it first was more important than getting it right. Bennett commissioned a fleet of boats to meet incoming steamers so he'd be first to print news from Europe. More than any other nineteenth-century editor, Bennett defined news as we know it. In his paper stories were timely and sensational. He focused on crime and local events, and he used the telegraph to print stories from distant battlefields. Bennett closed the coffin on the era of partisan newspapers in America when he announced in his inaugural edition in May 1835 that his *Herald* would serve no party. It didn't, but it sure served Bennett. He used the columns of his newspaper to attack his enemies, poke fun at liberal causes, and promote himself as a man-about-town.   **7,901**

642 INIGO JONES (1573–1652)
architectural purist

Jones refined Renaissance architecture, giving it restraint and proportion. For two centuries his innovative image of beauty distinguished English architecture. Jones was a clothmaker's son but rose to royal service through sheer talent. He wowed the court with costume and scenery designs before joining the earl of Arundel's entourage to Rome in 1613. There he visited ancient ruins and studied the architect Palladio's (133) works. Back home he was designated Surveyor of the Works, the chief architect of the land. Among his contributions: the first major urban development in London, Covent Garden. He created a large open space bordered by arcaded houses, a garden, and a church. Today only St. Paul's Church (not to be confused with the cathedral) survives. Jones's finest achievement was the Banqueting House, the royal building in Whitehall, with its ceiling covered by Rubens (281) paintings. Ironically, this was the site Puritans chose for the execution of Jones's patron, Charles I, in 1649.   **7,884**

643 PIERRE-MARIE-ALEXIS MILLARDET
(1838–1902) *fungus fighter*

The French botanist noticed that a foul-looking mixture of copper sulfate, lime, and water that local farmers slathered on their grapevines to discourage grape-grabbing thieves also destroyed a common mildew. He took the ingredients into his laboratory, tinkered with them for several years, and emerged with an even more effective formula, creating the first scientifically engineered fungicide. Since his technological breakthrough, researchers have developed untold recipes for preserving plants against parasitic blights, helping to ensure an adequate food supply for the world's billions. Striking another blow for human happiness, Millardet saved France's vineyards from an insect pest by grafting resistant American vines onto the domestic plants. Monsieur, we who are about to dine salute you. **7,863**

644 WILLIAM MORRIS (1834–1896)
designing Victorian

It's controversial, but we rank Morris first among poet-novelist-socialist-environmentalists who were also in the chintz wallpaper business. His work in all forms conveyed his belief that industrialized England should remember the sense of community, and respect for craftsmanship, of the past; his lasting contribution to design and the environmental movement was his advocacy of a future based on an idealized conception of the past. "Forget the snorting steam and piston stroke," he wrote. "Think rather of the packhorse on the down, and dream of London, small, and white and clean." He celebrated the past in novels and fantasy epics, such as *The Earthly Paradise*, and there was a medieval feel to the furniture, wallcoverings, stained glass, and books that he produced in his workshops. He was a founder of England's Socialist League but quit when its program became as mechanistic as the society it wanted to change.   **7,841**

645 PETER GOLDMARK (1906–1977)
groovy inventor

He made the first color television and the first miniature TV, but he wins gold marks for his invention that revolutionized the music industry. Annoyed that a full symphony couldn't be recorded on a single 78 rpm record, Goldmark improved the technology. Along with a team of researchers at CBS Laboratories, he reduced record grooves from 0.01 inch to 0.003 inch. His "microgrooves" pressed into vinyl records improved the sound and allowed six times as much music to be played at a new speed of 33⅓ rpm. The first LP, short for "long playing," featured Goldmark on cello, a secretary on piano, and an engineer on violin. LP records lasted only about forty years before they, too, were made

obsolete, but not before they gave birth to a multibillion-dollar recording industry.   **7,820**

646 ROBERT A. WATSON-WATT (1892–1973) *a huge blip in the history of inventions*

Next time your plane lands safely, thank your lucky stars for amazing radar, short for "radio detection and ranging." It's the air traffic controller's bible, the pilot's electronic equivalent of a compass. Without it, air travel would be as hairy as a bumper-car ride, and we'd all be shaving wingtips with props from Cleveland and saying our prayers. Mercy! Commercial air travel wasn't uppermost in Watson-Watt's mind as he labored in Britain's National Physical Laboratory in 1935, honing a system of aircraft location. Late that year the Scottish physicist was able to pinpoint a plane's location as far as seventy miles away by beaming radio waves at it, receiving the reflections, and calculating its distance by time passed. Experimental work with radar goes back to 1904 in Germany. But Watson-Watt's achievement led to the design of the world's first practical radar system, which warned the British of incoming German air raids in 1940.   **7,803**

647 ALEKSANDR SOLZHENITSYN (b. 1918)
voice of rage against totalitarianism

In 1945 Solzhenitsyn was sent to the Stalinist labor camps for eight years on trumped-up charges. The Russian dissident got his revenge, first in his 1962 challenge to the Kremlin, *One Day in the Life of Ivan Denisovich*, the tale of one inmate's endurance of oppression in the camps, and later in his descriptions of the terrors of prison life in *The First Circle, Cancer Ward,* and *The Gulag Archipelago*. Not only did his works undermine the Soviet system, they established Solzhenitsyn as a literary genius; some consider another novel, *August 1914*, his supreme achievement. Asked the secret of his art, he replied, "When you've been pitched headfirst into hell, you just write about it." Expelled from Russia in 1974, Solzhenitsyn spent twenty years in Vermont before returning to his homeland after it abandoned Communist rule. He found it "tortured, stunned, altered beyond recognition."

7,778

648 PIERRE-JOSEPH PROUDHON
(1809–1865) *anarchist, before anarchism got a bad name*

Nineteenth-century anarchism evokes images of bushy-bearded men making bombs in basements. The French Proudhon created the philosophy of anarchism, but armed insurrection was not his bag; government would disappear peacefully when labor fell into the hands of the community of all people, he taught. Proudhon was an impoverished, gentle family man who abhorred the revolutionism of his critic, Karl Marx (14), but shared Marx's goals. "I dream of a society where I would be guillotined as a conservative," Proudhon told a friend. It was all very nebulous, but his call for workers' organizations as a prelude to anarchism stimulated the worldwide union movement. Proudhon later regretted his service as an elected deputy in the Second Republic because he believed that democrats were no better than Emperor Napoleon III, who jailed him briefly in 1851.

7,769

649 WILLIAM RANDOLPH HEARST
(1863–1951) *colorful creator of yellow journalism*

After Hearst sent artist Frederic Remington to Cuba on the eve of the Spanish-American War, Remington telegraphed that there would be no war. Hearst cabled back: "Please remain. You furnish the pictures, and I'll furnish the war." Some say the story's apocryphal, but even history books record with relish how Hearst's outrageously sensational coverage fueled previously lukewarm public sentiment for war. His *New York Journal* invented "yellow journalism" with exaggerated—and sometimes just plain false—stories of murder and mayhem under bold "screaming" headlines. Locked in a down-and-dirty circulation battle with Joseph Pulitzer's *New York World*, Hearst raided Pulitzer's staff and hired away the cartoonist who drew the popular "Yellow Kid." When both papers published versions of the kid, people started calling them "the yellows." The name today describes the seediest side of journalism.

7,741

650 MARIA MONTESSORI (1870–1952)
children's educational champion

Montessori's epiphany was a child's smile. Harassed by male classmates in medical school, she decided to quit. En route home, she spied a street urchin delightedly playing with a piece of paper. That image sent Montessori back to the books. She became Italy's first woman doctor, then tackled a greater mission: reforming the educational system, infusing it with respect for children and a belief in their creative potential. She succeeded with Rome's mentally retarded, then with children in a squalid neighborhood. Ever since, her approach linking biological and mental growth has influenced education worldwide. The free-willed Montessori rejected restrictive classrooms with regimented rows of desks and teachers drumming information into little heads. "Before such dense and willful disregard of the life which is growing within these children," she said, "we should hide our heads in shame and cover our guilty faces with our hands!"

7,740

651 TS'AO CHAN (1715–1764)
author of China's greatest novel

Dream of the Red Chamber, a tale of the tragic love between Chia Pao-yu and his cousin Lin Tai-yu, chronicles the decline of a great family whose greed symbolizes the decadence of the ruling Ching dynasty. A sample chapter title reads: "A Henpecked Young Profligate Takes a Concubine in Secret." A feast of realistic detail, *Dream of the Red Chamber* has been compared to a Henry James (557) novel for its delineation of the manners and morals of high society and to Proust's (207) *Remembrance of Things Past* for its subtlety and metaphor. Elements are autobiographical; Ts'ao's grandfather was a wealthy official who hobnobbed with the emperor, but his father fell on hard times and Ts'ao ended up in a Beijing slum, boozing and scratching away at his novel. Grief-stricken at his son's death, he fell fatally ill, leaving behind his unpublished manuscript. **7,723**

652 NICOLAS LEBLANC (1742–1806)
soda's pop

Not soda as in Coke and Pepsi, but soda as in the common name for sodium carbonate. Without it, you couldn't make thousands of everyday products as diverse as aluminum, soap, and paper. Frenchman Leblanc put the fizz in the Industrial Revolution in 1789 by discovering how to produce soda quickly, cheaply, and in huge quantities. He combined sulfuric acid, seawater salt, limestone, and charcoal, and there was no better formula until the mid-nineteenth century. Leblanc was the duke of Orleans's private physician, but he lost his job when the duke lost his head in the French Revolution. So Leblanc concentrated on sodium carbonate. His factory was nationalized in 1794, and by the time Leblanc got it back in 1800, he had too little capital to exploit his own process. Depressed and sick, he shot himself to death. **7,701**

653 DOROTHY DAY (1897–1980)
Catholicism's grassroots rebel

Day was no fly-by-night Catholic, but she routinely rattled the church's stodgy establishment when she advocated civil disobedience, ignored the tax man, and went to jail for antigovernment activities. Day abandoned a loose life in New York when she converted to Catholicism. In 1933 she and Peter Maurin founded the Catholic Worker movement based on a philosophy of anarchism, voluntary poverty, pacifism, and activism. Maurin took a back seat while Day promoted their ideas as editor of the *Catholic Worker* newspaper, which she began distributing on May Day 1933 to New York's unemployed. She paid for the printing with her already-overdue rent money, funded the second edition by selling her typewriter, and then relied on donations. "When we need money, we pray for it," she explained. People touched by her ideas gave up material wealth, joined Day at her barebones New York headquarters, and pitched in to spread her message. **7,684**

654 EDWARD GIBBON (1737–1794)
grandest historian of history's grandest civilization

Presented with the second volume of Edward Gibbon's *History of the Decline and Fall of the Roman Empire*, the duke of Gloucester exclaimed, "Another damned thick, square book! Always scribble, scribble, scribble, eh Mr. Gibbon?" Some scribbling. One of modern times' most-read history books was instantly celebrated and controversial, too, for suggesting that it was Christianity that doomed Rome. The book's popularity showed that the right blend of facts, analysis, and vivid writing could make history appealing to a mass audience. Gibbon was squat and unlovely, but the beautiful Swiss intellectual Suzanne Curchod would have married him if Gibbon's father hadn't forbidden a match with a foreigner. The spurned Suzanne married France's finance minister, Jacques Necker. For years Gibbon neglected a testicular tumor that finally grew observably huge, to the amusement of his political enemies. Soon after he had the growth punctured, he died of a fever.　**7,665**

655 JAMES WOLFE (1727–1759)
soldier who made Canada English

Imagine if France had repelled the British invasion of Quebec during the French and Indian War. Would today's Canada be dominated by French culture? Would cash-poor Napoleon (16) have sold Canada to the United States, as he did the Louisiana Territory? Wolfe made these questions moot. On September 12, 1759, after reciting Thomas Gray's "Elegy in a Country Churchyard," with its line "The paths of glory lead but to the grave," the thirty-two-year-old major general sent his disciplined redcoats up the weakly guarded cliffs next to Quebec. They routed the surprised French the next day. Wolfe and the opposing commander, the Marquis de Montcalm de Saint-Véran, were both killed. French rule in Canada was over a year later. Wolfe's sickliness and his youth made him an odd choice for so important a command, but he had distinguished himself in earlier battles. His last words were "Now God be praised, I die happy."　**7,632**

656 ELIZABETH SETON (1774–1821)
America's first native-born saint

The pious and selfless Elizabeth became "Mother Seton," founder of the first American religious society, Sisters of Charity, and the parochial school system in the United States. Long before

that Seton had her own five children to guide. In 1803 her husband died in Italy, where the family had traveled to seek a cure for William Seton's tuberculosis. But it proved too late. Grief-stricken, Elizabeth clung to a mental mantra: "My God, You are my God—how alone I am in the world except for you and my little ones; but You are my Father and doubly theirs." Help came. William's friends, the Filicchis, took the family in, and Seton, an Anglican, was impressed by their devout Catholic faith. Two years later in New York, she stunned family and friends by converting. Her adoptive faith honored her with canonization in 1975.　**7,609**

657 PIERRE BONNARD (1867–1947)
high colorist of modern art

Vibrant color was Bonnard's calling card, and he passed it out to generations of artists. Pulsating oranges. Blood-rich reds. Lemony yellows. This, from an unassuming man with a drab childhood. A dutiful student, Bonnard graduated with a law degree as his father wished. Then he chose to paint. "What attracted me then was less art itself than the artistic life," Bonnard said. "I wanted to escape from a monotonous existence." As a member of the Nabis school of painting, Bonnard recorded daily life during France's Belle Époque, from the bustle of a crowded café to a table being set in a sunlit kitchen. No heavy social messages here. Our favorite Bonnards: the mournful *Circus Horse*, and the tenderly intimate *Nude at Her Toilette*. Toulouse-Lautrec (817) saw Bonnard's 1889 lithograph poster for *France Champagne* and decided he could do that, too. The rest is art history.　**7,588**

658 STEPHEN I (977–1038)
apostle of Hungary

Stephen, who brought Hungary into Christendom, defeated a pagan insurrection, but not before the rebels stuffed an Italian missionary into a barrel lined with spikes and rolled him down a hill. On Christmas Day in the year 1000, Stephen was anointed Hungary's first king with a papal crown that to this day is revered as a sacred relic that, in some mystical way, *is* Hungary. Stephen was a monarch's monarch, who counseled his son in his famous *Admonitions* to "rule over all without anger, pride or hatred, but with love, tenderness and humanity." The son, Emeric, or Emericus in Latin, died young and became Saint Emericus, a name that was bestowed in Italianized form on the fifteenth-century Florentine Amerigo Vespucci. Thus, some argue, America gets its name from this eleventh-century Hungarian prince. **7,565**

659 HENRY VII (1457–1509)
unifier of England

The founder of Britain's Tudor dynasty won the throne by defeating his predecessor, Richard III, at the Battle of Bosworth Field in 1485. That victory ended the War of the Roses, a half century of feudal skirmishing that had made life in England as risky as the Wild West. Henry VII cemented Britain's unity by marrying his predecessor's niece, and then he put his inherent frugality to good purpose and built a bulging treasury. Compared with Henry VIII (100), his glorious son, and Elizabeth I (31), his brilliant granddaughter, Henry VII seems like a mere dark schemer. But without him his successors would have lacked a stable foundation for their splendid feats. **7,559**

660 JOHN GREGG (1867–1948)
the secretary's best friend

We'll keep this one short. Gregg was the unchallenged master of speed writing. With his system, developed in 1888, the writing hand could keep up with the spoken word. Gregg Shorthand,

which is indecipherable to the untrained eye, was so successful for office work that it spawned numerous secretarial courses and was eventually adapted for thirteen languages. Sure, the dictaphone and the personal computer ultimately transformed the secretarial job by the end of the twentieth century. But Gregg's shorthand, coupled with Sholes's (531) typewriter, first created a revolution in offices and provided women a career path that freed them from dreaded factory work. **7,533**

661 SAMUEL GOMPERS (1850–1924)
founder of the modern American labor movement

Teenaged Gompers emigrated from London to the United States and worked as a cigar maker. Under his leadership his tradesmen split from the Knights of Labor in 1886 to form the future giant American Federation of Labor. Gompers was AFL president for thirty-seven years. "He believed in his work with a deep, almost religious fervor, yet he was too practical to become a fanatic," said George Meany, a successor as union president. Staunchly conservative, Gompers strove not for revolution but for economic gains in workers' lives. In an era hostile to labor, he pressed for higher wages, a shorter work week, and binding, written trade agreements. His principles of "voluntarism" urged unions to use economic means such as strikes and boycotts to pressure management. Lenin (41) dismissed this as a "rope of sand." But to Gompers and others, democratic trade unionism proved more powerful than "chains of steel." **7,528**

662 CRAZY HORSE (1842–1877)
strategist of Custer's last stand

Ta-sunko-witko, Sioux chief of the Oglala tribe, was a bold leader in his nation's battle to stem white settlement of the northern Great Plains. His nickname, Crazy Horse, stuck after a wild horse dashed through camp at his birth. After General George Custer's troops attacked his tribe's encampment in South Dakota, Crazy Horse led Sioux warriors down a valley, across the Little Bighorn River, and in a sweeping arc to attack the Seventh Cavalry on June 25, 1876. Overwhelmed, Custer and his men fought to the death. The slaughter was the beginning of the end of the Indian wars. American troops subsequently overran the plains, and after the harsh winter of 1877, Crazy Horse and other Indian leaders surrendered. While in custody at Fort Robinson, Nebraska, Crazy Horse was bayoneted in the back. His dying words: "Tell the people it is no use to depend on me anymore now." **7,507**

663 GOTTHOLD LESSING (1729–1781)
intellectual star of the Age of Enlightenment

Lessing ushered in the indigenous German theater with his 1763 comedy-drama, *Minna von Barnhelm*, about a Prussian soldier and his Saxon fiancée. Until then, German plays had followed stuffy French conventions and portrayed French characters. Literature seduced Lessing when he was training for a career as a Lutheran minister, and in his twenties he captivated his countrymen with poems, fables, criticism, epigrams, and silly songs, like this:

> *It rains and rains and will not stop,*
> *So grieves the peasant for his crop.*
> *But what care I for wet or fine,*
> *So be it rains not in my wine.*

It's better in German. Of higher brow is Lessing's 1766 *Laokoon*, one of the first comparisons between the aesthetics of literature and visual art. That, and his deistic moral philosophy—he taught that the search for the truth is as satisfying as finding it—made Lessing one of the giants of eighteenth-century learning. **7,488**

664 GRANDMA MOSES (1860–1961)
the grand old woman of painting

Grandma Moses lived a lifetime before she started painting. She gave birth to ten children and raised five to adulthood. She was past age seventy and had worked a farm and buried her husband before finally finding time for art. In 1938 an art collector passing through Hoosick Falls, New York, saw her work displayed in the local pharmacy. He tracked Moses to her farm at nearby Eagle Bridge. With his patronage three Moses paintings were included in a New York Museum of Modern Art exhibition of "Contemporary Unknown American Painters." Cubism and abstraction were *au courant*, but Moses's primitive scenes of farm and rural life touched a nerve with people fearful that the Great Depression and, later, World War II could destroy that American way of life. Moses kept on painting. One of her last projects, finished at age one hundred, was a set of illustrations for "'Twas the Night Before Christmas." **7,461**

665 LUTHER BURBANK (1849–1926)
the green thumb

Burbank was a self-taught horticulturalist who plowed ahead without knowledge of Mendel's (104) work on heredity. As a farm boy, he pored over Darwin's (7) *Variation of Animals and Plants Under Domestication*, later pronouncing it "without question the most inspiring book I had ever read." Burbank took Darwin's theory of natural selection and applied it to producing better plants through hybridization. His big discovery: the Burbank, also known as the Idaho potato, a superb variety generated not from standard tubers but from select seeds. Selling the rights to that spud paid Burbank's way from Massachusetts to

California, where he bought a little spread and proceeded to make horticultural history. By taking native and foreign strains, then nurturing seedlings and grafting these onto growing plants, Burbank created more than eight hundred new varieties of fruits, flowers, ornamentals, vegetables, grains, grasses, and forage plants. **7,459**

666 FRANCISCO FRANCO (1892–1975)
America's totalitarian buddy

Aside from driving Spain into economic ruin with his statist policies, Franco played a pivotal role in the great struggle between Western democracy and totalitarianism. El Caudillo, as he was known, won the 1936–39 Spanish Civil War with the help of Hitler (20) and Mussolini (460) and gave his fellow Fascist potentates aid and comfort in World War II. Yet after Hitler's defeat, Franco rehabilitated his image as the anti-Communist "Sentinel of the West" allied with America. Despite his reactionary politics, he turned Spain over to technocrats in the 1960s, setting the stage for economic revival. Likewise, he bequeathed power to a liberal king who fostered democracy after the generalissimo's tediously drawn-out death. A man of courage who took a bullet in Spain's Moroccan wars, Franco was also a dour functionary with a penchant for vengefulness. He executed thousands of opponents during the civil conflict and ordered the garroting of Basque terrorists with piano wire. **7,433**

667 DOM PEDRO II OF BRAZIL (1825–1891)
the magnanimous monarch

His father, Pedro I, led Brazil's peaceful break from Portugal in 1822, but that was no feat: the country was ready for plucking like a ripe coffee bean. Pedro's six-foot-four son, Pedro II, had more influence and charisma. Brazil's boundaries were set during his fifty-nine-year reign, and he presided over the nation's modernization. He earned the nickname Pedro the Magnanimous for being kindly, learned, and as liberal as an emperor can be. He loved peace, except when he insisted on an unpopular war with Paraguay. Though he took a gradualist approach to the abolition of slavery, that scourge ended in Brazil during his reign. Pedro had a working knowledge of eighteen languages, and he traveled in the United States and Europe, where he met Victor Hugo (163), Charles Darwin (7), and Richard Wagner (165). He was so magnanimous, he let his generals overthrow him without a fight in 1889. **7,419**

668 CHARLES ATLAS (1893–1972)
the original ninety-eight-pound weakling

Angelo Siciliano began his journey to physical perfection after his scrawny self brought a girlfriend to the beach at Coney Island. As he explained it, "A big, husky lifeguard, maybe there were two of them, kicked sand in my face. I couldn't do anything and the girl felt funny. I told her that someday, if I meet this guy, I will lick him." She dumped Angelo anyway, but he created a "Dynamic Tension" isotonic program to strengthen his pecs; he changed his name to honor the Greek god of muscles, sold his "Atlas" bodybuilding techniques, and made a fortune. The Atlas method fueled today's muscle-pumping phenomenon. For generations advertisements in popular comic books convinced nerdy teenage boys that the only thing standing in the way of a date with the homecoming queen was their wimpy physique. **7,402**

669 HAILE SELASSIE (1892–1975)
last emperor of Ethiopia

Viewed early in his reign as a benevolent dictator who introduced reforms and defied an Italian invasion, Haile Selassie became a greedy oppressor in his later years. Still, he centralized authority in Ethiopia and brought it into the twentieth century. His appeal to the League of Nations in 1936 for military help against the Italians struck a chord in the West, but Ethiopians were dismayed by his flight to Britain. The emperor, who traced his ancestry to the biblical queen of Sheba, returned home in 1940 and sank slowly into decadence. By one account he fed ribs of beef to leopards in the royal zoo while his subjects starved. Twenty-three Mercedes Benzes stood ready to whisk him to and from his nine palaces. He was ousted by a Marxist junta in 1974 and "strangled in his bed most cruelly" the following year, according to a 1994 court proceeding. **7,399**

670 ALBERT SCHWEITZER (1875–1965)
medical missionary

Accomplished organist and respected theologian, thirty-year-old Schweitzer shocked friends by announcing he would "render direct service" to mankind by becoming a mission doctor. He earned his medical degree, his wife studied nursing, and the two set off in 1913 for French equatorial Africa. With locals' help they built a hospital in Lambaréné, Gabon. Natives came by canoe from two hundred miles away, suffering from malaria, leprosy, and sleeping sickness. While ministering to these patients, Schweitzer also evolved his ethical philosophy of "reverence for life" applied to all living things. He published these thoughts in *Philosophy of Civilization* in 1923. "If you study life deeply, looking perceptively into the vast and animated chaos that is creation, the profundity of it all will stun you," the German scholar once said. "You will recognize yourself in everything." His dedication to humanity earned Schweitzer the Nobel Peace Prize in 1952 and made his name a synonym for selflessness. **7,397**

671 HECTOR BERLIOZ (1803–1869)
orchestrator of the new orchestra

His 1830 *Symphonie Fantastique* liberated the symphony from conventions. It not only told a story, it came with a program that let the audience follow along. The score included instruments new to symphonies: English horns and bells, for example. This helped create the modern, anything-goes attitude toward instrumentation. Like the subjects of his work—Faust, Romeo and Juliet, Dido and Aeneas—Berlioz was a lovestruck, tragic figure. His early works were denounced by critics such as Friedrich Zelter, who called *Eight Scenes from Faust* "an excrescence, the remains of miscarriage from a hideous incest." Twice Berlioz tried to kill himself. His smothering courtship of Irish actress Harriet Smithson bordered on stalking. She finally agreed to marry him, but then died of a stroke. Their only child, Louis, died of yellow fever. Yet much of his music was rousing and joyous and has charmed generations of listeners. **7,363**

672 JOHN JAMES AUDUBON (1785–1851)
the bird artist

The cardinal focus of Audubon societies around the world is preservation of the wilderness. Audubon, however, was hardly a conservationist. He often killed his subjects, then wired them into poses. Not surprisingly, critics grouse that his birds were painted in unnatural positions and inappropriate settings. They also poke fun at the almost human expressions some of them display. Nonetheless, Audubon wins points for his masterpiece, *The Birds of America*, which included 1,065 life-size paintings and introduced North America's feathered friends to an audience of bird lovers in Europe. For the project Audubon painstakingly tracked birds throughout the continent, ultimately identifying one new genus and close to two dozen species. Before he died, Audubon squawked about the vanishing frontier, endangered bison, and the dubious hobby of collecting bird eggs. To honor his memory, the first preservation society was named after him. **7,349**

673 AL-MAHDI (1844–1885)
African nationalist idol

A religious ascetic, Muhammad Ahmad ibn as-Sayyid 'Abd Allah declared himself the Mahdi, or savior of Islam, in 1881 and set out to purge the Sudan of its Egyptian rulers. Starting with a ragtag army equipped with sticks and spears—the Fuzzie-Wuzzies, poet Rudyard Kipling called them—he quickly united the Sudan's quarreling tribes and disparate social groups, from slave traders to devout Muslims, and destroyed the forces sent against him. In 1885 he captured Khartoum, killing the city's British commander, Charles Gordon—a terrible blow to Victorian England's pride. The victory sealed al-Mahdi's creation of a vast Islamic state. Five months later the self-proclaimed heir of the prophet Muhammad died of typhus. Today anti-Western Islamic fundamentalists find fertile recruiting ground among his ten million Sudanese disciples. **7,331**

674 GEORGE GAMOW (1904–1968)
begetter of the big bang theory

Gamow (pronounced *gam-uff*), a Russian-born American nuclear scientist, held that a thermonuclear explosion billions of years ago blew the elements apart from a single point and accounted for the continuing expansion of the universe. This explanation ultimately triumphed over the so-called steady-state hypothesis of an eternal, and rather dull, cosmos advanced by British physicist Fred Hoyle. In short, we say:

In the beginning, if you please,
Was the Big Squeeze
Of all matter. Hence,
Things got quite dense.

Uncomfortably hot, too.
Well, wouldn't you,
If in some lab test,
You were thus compressed?

After this implosion,
Came a huge explosion
That, for better or for worse,
Produced the universe.

This (pardon the slang)
Was the Big Bang.
Things just went "puff."
Or so says Gamow.

7,319

675 NATHANIEL HAWTHORNE (1804–1864)
Puritan man of letters

With his psychological insight Hawthorne explored the guilt and anxiety of the human soul. His first novel, *The Scarlet Letter*, gained him immediate fame in 1850 and remains an American classic. This is the story of Puritan Hester Prynne, who must wear a scarlet letter "A" as punishment for adultery but steadfastly refuses to name her lover. Hawthorne grew up in a guilt-ridden, sin-obsessed Puritan household in Salem, Massachusetts. Except for his father's death, he had an uneventful childhood. "Few men of equal genius and of equal eminence can have led, on the whole, a simpler life," wrote author Henry James (557). Hawthorne knew this. "I have seen so little of the world that I have nothing but thin air to concoct my stories of," he said. But from that rarefied air he produced other esteemed works, including

The House of the Seven Gables and *The Marble Faun.* **7,298**

676 ANTONÍN DVOŘÁK (1841–1904)
composer for a new world

He was an innkeeper's son, but every middle-class Czech learned music in those days, and Dvořák learned better than others. His symphonies, choral music, concerti, and chamber music are among the best of the late romantic period—far better, in our opinion, than the middlebrow bombast of his Russian contemporary, Pyotr Ilich Tchaikovsky. Behind most of Dvořák's great melodies lurked folk tunes from Bohemia, and even his most famous composition, the *New World Symphony*, a supposed compilation of American themes, is really a chip off the Bohemian block. Native tunes from regions as diverse as Appalachia, the Hebrides, and Eastern Europe use similar scales and sound hauntingly alike. If he had not been a composer, Dvořák might have been a conductor. Be it a mile-long freight or a New York City elevated train, Dvořák loved railroad travel and would spend hours watching trains rumble by. **7,258**

677 FRANCES WILLARD (1839–1898)
the nineteenth-century equivalent of Mothers Against Drunk Drivers

The most prominent promoter of Prohibition was the Women's Christian Temperance Union, and Willard was the heart and soul of the organization. The WCTU, founded in 1874, blamed whiskey for most social problems. Men drank their paychecks, beat their wives, and abandoned their families when booze got the better of them. WCTU members draped in white ribbons published poetic pamphlets and proselytized as they pleaded with America to just say no. Schoolchildren sang rhymes to warn parents of whiskey's evil.

"Tremble, King Alcohol, We Shall Grow Up!" kindergartners chanted. Grow up they did. National Prohibition became a reality in 1919, and its fourteen-year failure proved emphatically that America was not a nation of teetotalers. While legendary saloon-smasher Carry Nation was indeed a member of the WCTU, the organization disavowed any knowledge of her actions, saying its methods were "not carnal but spiritual." **7,233**

678 JIM THORPE (1888–1953)
the All-American athlete

A Native American with Sac, Fox, Potawatomie, and Kickapoo blood, Thorpe's Indian name Wa-tho-huck meant "Bright Path." That's exactly what he blazed on tracks, football fields, and baseball diamonds. "He had speed as well as strength," said "Pop" Warner, Thorpe's earliest football coach. "He knew how to use his strength and speed as well as any football player or track athlete I have ever known." Thorpe earned greatest fame for winning the decathlon and pentathlon in the Stockholm Olympics in 1912. But he was stripped of his medals after officials learned he had earned twenty-five dollars a week playing semiprofessional baseball. When age forced Thorpe from the sports arena, he couldn't adjust and drank heavily. In 1950 the Associated Press named him best all-around athlete of the first half of the twentieth century, and we say he belongs at the top of the second half, too. In 1983 apologetic Olympic officials returned Thorpe's medals to his children. **7,199**

679 SATO EISAKU (1901–1975)
navigator of Japan's economic reemergence after World War II

As prime minister from 1964 to 1972, Sato presided over an export boom that created Asia's top economy. His diplomacy was marked by the time-tested Japanese genius for obfuscation; responding to President Nixon's (904) demand for export restraint, he promised, "I will do my best." Nixon thought he had a deal and was furious when the trade gap widened. Sato's political accomplishments included signing the nuclear nonproliferation treaty, renewing the U.S.–Japanese security treaty, and regaining Okinawa for Japan. Sato apparently had a weakness for handouts; he was accused of accepting bribes from Japanese shipbuilders in 1954 and, four years later, "tried to put the bite on us for financial help in fighting Communism," the American ambassador in Tokyo reported. **7,163**

680 JOSEPH GLIDDEN (1813–1906)
the barb in barbed wire

The six-shooter didn't tame the West—barbed wire did. Cattlemen ruled the plains until farmers put up fences that kept bovine herds off the cropfields. Until about 1950 most barbed-wire fences used Glidden's 1873 process of attaching steel points to plain wire. Glidden got the idea from a crude version he saw at a county fair in DeKalb County, Illinois. He tinkered until he improved the process well enough to receive three patents. In 1875 he sold his share in his factory for $60,000, plus royalties, and that made him rich. Glidden's contemporaries used barbed wire to keep animals out. Future generations used it to keep people in. Hitler (20) used it in concentration camps, and until the cold war ended, a curtain of barbed wire snaked across Europe from the Aegean to the Baltic seas, a barrier to freedom for Communism's captives. **7,182**

681 MUHAMMAD ALI (b. 1942)
the greatest!

He avoided tackle football because it was too rough; he almost missed the 1960 Olympics because he was afraid to fly; and he claimed conscientious objector status during the Vietnam War because, he said, warfare was against his religion. Yet Muhammad Ali was the greatest boxer of his time. He weaved, jabbed, danced, and shuffled his feet to a 56–5 professional record. The only three-time heavyweight champion in history, he pulled no punches outside the ring. Ali was harshly criticized by white America after he converted to the Nation of Islam, changed his name from Cassius Clay, and refused to enter the army. Around the globe Ali's message of black pride touched as many people as the civil rights movement. In addition to his mantra "I am the greatest!" Ali, debilitated in later years from taking too many punches, claimed his was the most famous face in the world. It was. **7,171**

682 DOROTHY CROWFOOT HODGKIN
(b. 1910) decipherer of organic puzzles

Soft-spoken but resolute, Hodgkin mastered X-ray crystallography to forge significant breakthroughs that led to the proliferation of wonder drugs. In crystallography X-rays are beamed through crystals, and the resulting waves strike a photographic plate, creating thousands of spots. After analyzing these photos and making untold mathematical calculations over four years, Hodgkin deciphered the structure of penicillin in 1946. Drug makers used her model to create varieties of penicillin to attack specific bacterial infections. It took another eight years for Hodgkin to identify the atomic structure of vitamin B-12, which fights pernicious anemia. This accomplishment won the British scientist the Nobel Prize in chemistry in 1964. She didn't stop there. Five years and seventy thousand X-ray spots later, she built a model of complex three-dimensional insulin. She accomplished all this despite crippling rheumatoid arthritis that left her hands like twisted stumps. **7,152**

683 BLACKBEARD (d. 1718)
history's baddest pirate

Unlike Captain Kidd (968), a lame excuse for a brigand, Blackbeard was a bloodthirsty ogre who loved debauchery and once forced a captive to eat his own ears. Author Daniel Defoe (197) said he engaged in "frolics of wickedness so extravagant as if he aimed at making his men believe he was a devil incarnate," including locking himself and three companions in a ship's hold and setting a smoldering fire to see who could withstand the fumes the longest. Born Edward Teach in England (or perhaps Jamaica), Blackbeard launched a reign of terror in the Carolinas and in the Caribbean from 1716 to 1718, seizing booty from gold coins to bales of cotton before being killed and decapitated by the British. A ballad celebrated his end:

> *When the bloody fight was over,*
> *We're informed in a letter writ,*
> *Teach's head was made a cover*
> *To the jackstaff of the ship.*

7,141

684 ALEXANDER PARKES (1813–1890)
England's Edison

Most inventors in our pantheon had a single triumph: Bell (74) hooked up the telephone, Nobel (217) exploded dynamite. Parkes is obscure because he flitted from project to project, but he patented sixty-six processes that energized the manufacturing revolution of the nineteenth century. He made breakthroughs in electroplating, even silverizing a spider's web for Prince Albert, to show the brilliance of his process. He figured out how to rubberize textiles, a discovery that was purchased by the Mackintosh Company to make waterproof raincoats. He developed an efficient method for extracting silver from lead. His greatest invention was Parkesine, the first crude plastic. He pressed acid-soaked cotton into solid cylinders, which could be made malleable with solvents, oil, and resins and molded into any shape. Parkesine was too flammable for mass application, but it was a first step toward celluloid, Baekelite, and other durable synthetics. **7,125**

685 JACQUES COUSTEAU (1910–1997)
Magellan under the oceans

You can argue all you want about whether Columbus (2) really discovered America, but the oceans belonged to Cousteau. His *Undersea World of Jacques Cousteau* made public television fans out of millions of viewers who were mesmerized, as was the oceanographer, by the vibrant, colorful world beneath the waves. Cousteau began his exploration of the depths as a French naval officer during World War II. With engineer Émile Gagnan, he invented the self-contained underwater breathing apparatus (scuba), which allowed divers to venture deeper and stay under longer. Other seaworthy inventions included diving boats and research facilities that permitted explorations for days in the depths. He founded the Cousteau Society to popularize preservation of the oceans, and his research boat, *Calypso*, achieved such stature that it was celebrated in a hit song by the late pop singer John Denver. Considered by some the greatest explorer of the twentieth century, Cousteau won two Academy Awards for his documentaries. **7,116**

686 HENRY FIELDING (1707–1754)
nurturer of the English novel

Samuel Richardson and Daniel Defoe (197) wrote earlier novels, but Fielding took the genre further. He showed the extraordinary potential of the new literary form with *Joseph Andrews* and his masterpiece, *The History of Tom Jones*. Fielding turned to fiction after stints as a playwright, newspaper editor, and magistrate. Although *Tom Jones* is built around a romance, it teems with observations on eighteenth-century life and amusing characterizations of people from all ranks of society. The book throbs with energy like its lusty hero, Tom, who sins repeatedly but always wins forgiveness. "I have endeavored to laugh mankind out of their favorite follies and vices," Fielding said. Critic Walter Bagehot pictured Fielding as "a reckless enjoyer. He saw the world—wealth and glory, the best dinner and the worst dinner, the gilded salon and the low sponging-house—and he saw that they were good." **7,089**

687 GERHARD GROOTE (1340–1384)
copycat priest

One of our favorite cartoons features the arrival of a rotund monk with the obligatory fringe of hair around a marvelously bald head, quill pen in hand, with the caption: "Your new copier is here." That's how we envision Groote, who founded a center for book copying, which grew into a religious order, the Brethren of the Common Life. He's the fourteenth-century version of a Xerox machine. He helped the impoverished intelligentsia financially by setting them to work copying books. Members of his religious community pooled their incomes earned through teaching and book copying. While they lived a monasticlike existence, Brethren members never took vows. His order, which flourished in Groote's native Netherlands and in Germany, was the first to give grades for schoolwork, provide textbooks, and create the structure for elementary and secondary schools in Europe. **7,061**

688 CHESTER CARLSON (1906–1968)
copycat inventor

At a boring job retyping plans in a patent office, Carlson fantasized about a machine that would reproduce pages instantly. So he made one. The secret was photo conductivity, the power of light to make chemical changes in substances—in this case paper. The Smithsonian Institution has Carlson's first copy, a sheet of waxed paper with the blurry words "10-22-38 Astoria," the name of his apartment building, and the date. IBM, RCA, and Remington weren't interested in his crude process, but the fledgling Haloid Company bought Carlson's ideas in 1947 and perfected his work. Haloid marketing gurus called the process xerography and changed the company's name to the Xerox Corporation. Carlson's biggest failure was an attempt to give away the entire fortune he had accumulated from royalties. He gave $150 million to charity but died before he could disperse the final $50 million. History does not record the name of the office worker who first asked, "What's wrong with the @&%$#$ copier?" **7,038**

689 ELIZABETH KENNY (1880–1952)
physiotherapy pioneer

Victims of the poliomyelitis scourge writhed in agony when their twisted arms and atrophied legs were immobilized in casts. Kenny, a nurse in the Australian bush country, figured out a better way to rehabilitate damaged limbs. The first time she saw a victim of the dreaded disease, her little patient was crying in agony. The child found no relief when Kenny straightened the legs with sandbags. In desperation Kenny wrapped the girl's legs in hot wet rags. The whimpering stopped. Kenny developed massages and exercises to revive a patient's strength. She had first witnessed exercise's power when she helped her sickly younger brother strengthen his frail body. Today she's called "sister," the British title of respect for a nurse, but doctors then called her a quack and a charlatan. Kenny was vindicated when she was invited to share her unorthodox methods at the Mayo Clinic in Rochester, Minnesota, in 1940. **7,012**

690 KWAME NKRUMAH (1909–1972)
Ghana's shining light

Nkrumah was president of Ghana, the first of the European colonies in Africa to gain independence. He wanted to enter the priesthood until he was drawn into the African nationalist movement and became a Marxist. He outlined his plan for Africa's anticolonial struggle in his 1947 book, *Towards Colonial Freedom.* As Ghana's president, Nkrumah opened more jobs to Ghanaians and built roads, schools, and hospitals. He told cheering crowds in 1957 that Ghana "would be a shining light throughout the whole continent of Africa, giving inspiration beyond its frontiers." He spoke too soon. The faltering economy—a problem to plague Ghana for decades—churned labor unrest. Nkrumah tightened control, having himself declared president for life. In 1966, however, he was ousted in an army coup. Nkrumah's lasting achievement: assembling eight African leaders in Accra in 1958, a precursor to the Organization of African States. **6,980**

691 THOMAS CARLYLE (1795–1881)
English historian and prose stylist

Historical evidence suggests that after twenty-five years of marriage, Carlyle's wife Jane was a virgin, proving that the pen is indeed mightier than the sword. Carlyle's stirring book, *The French Revolution*, is one of the millennium's best-selling histories. He had to write it twice; he lent his only manuscript to philosopher friend John Stuart Mill (81), and a servant used it for tinder. In *Past and Present* Carlyle extolled the simplicity of the Middle Ages and railed against laissez-faire capitalism's human toll. *On Heroes, Hero-Worship, and the Heroic in History* championed the idea that to understand history, all we need to do is study great men—a notion swept aside in the determinist wave of the late nineteenth century. In all his books—inaccurate, dated, and overly sentimental though they may seem today—Carlyle's romantic prose energized the study of history and elevated historical writing to the status of literature. **6,963**

692 JOHN L. SULLIVAN (1858–1918)
fist-swinging hero of the masses

When Sullivan won the heavyweight boxing championship in 1882, loser Paddy Ryan said, "I thought that a telegraph pole had been shoved against me endways." Sullivan, the "Boston Strong Boy," was champ for ten years, and when he bellowed his famous challenge, "I can lick any son-of-a-bitch alive," he spoke for the immigrants and city dwellers thirsting for power in an America that had been dominated by the rural gentility. Sullivan's prowess and strength, his gusto, his genius for self-promotion, and his earnings—$1.2 million in the pretax years from 1878 to 1915—made him the model for every celebrity athlete from Babe Ruth (360) to Michael Jordan (903). He remained popular even when he beat his wife, tore up saloons, and kicked newsboys. Sullivan's toughest opponent was booze, but he licked it in 1905 and became a well-paid temperance preacher. **6,921**

693 HANNAH GLASSE (1708–1770)
the simple chef

Mrs. Glasse couldn't cotton to the nonsense in French kitchens. Why cook like a "*French* Booby" when you can learn from "a good English cook?" she asked. *The Art of Cookery, Made Plain and Easy, which far exceeds any Thing of the kind ever yet Published . . . By a Lady* was the first commercially successful cookbook in English and the only one geared to housewives and servants. With recipes for hare, calves' feet, and other eighteenth-century staples, Glasse rejected French techniques. She scoffed at one cook who used six pounds of butter to fry a dozen eggs; only a half-pound was needed, she argued. Thirty-four editions of her cookbook circulated for a century after its 1747 publication. Today one thousand new cookbooks are published annually, but as Glasse herself pointed out, she did it first. **6,914**

694 BLANCHE OF CASTILE (1188–1252)
the power behind the throne

Blanche's grandmother, Eleanor of Aquitaine (420), journeyed to Spain to fetch the eleven-year-old for marriage to the French prince Louis. Blanche soon adopted French ways and dedicated herself to forging France's unity. You'd want this lady on your side. A woman of strength and devout faith, she twice ruled France: first when her husband, King Louis VIII, died of dysentery after fighting southern heretics; then when their son, the saintly Louis IX (613), left to fight in the Crusades despite Mama's wishes. The strain of Louis's capture by the Muslims, and Blanche's trip to Egypt to free him, weakened her frail heart. After she collapsed en route to a retreat house, aides brought the dying queen mother back to the palace of the Louvre, dressed her in a nun's habit, and laid her to rest on a bed of hay. **6,907**

695 ZWANGENDABA (c.1780–1848)
African apostle of assimilation

In 1818, when Europe was settling into a post-Napoleonic peace and the United States was enjoying the "era of good feeling" under President Monroe (708), southern Africa was being ravaged by the Mfecane, or Crushing, a social collapse engendered by Zulu expansionism and European colonialism. Whole tribes crisscrossed the region in search of food and safety from marauding bands. In the midst of this chaos, King Zwangendaba led his Jere people on a thousand-mile, twenty-five-year trek, molding his warriors into a formidable fighting force. But instead of killing off the stragglers of other mass migrations, he absorbed them

into his tribe, creating one of the most powerful kingdoms in East Africa, the Nguni nation. He ended up on the southern shores of Lake Tanganyika, where he founded the city of Mapupo. After his death the Nguni split into five divisions and continued their expansion. **6,882**

696 NEIL ARMSTRONG (b. 1930)
first moon walker

July 20, 1969, 10:56 P.M.(EDT). Spellbound, we watched on television with more than a half-billion others as spacesuit-clad Armstrong emerged from his spacecraft. Carefully the veteran combat pilot descended the ladder from the lunar module perched 240,000 miles away on the moon's Sea of Tranquillity. One short jump off the bottom rung, and he planted his boot in lunar soil and proclaimed, "That's one small step for [a] man, one giant leap for mankind." It also sealed U.S. supremacy in the eleven-year-old space race with the Soviet Union. For two hours Armstrong and fellow astronaut Buzz Aldrin hopped across the moonscape collecting rock samples. "Isn't it fun?" Armstrong asked. Reluctantly they reboarded their spacecraft, leaving behind an American flag, instruments to yield scientific data, and a plaque commemorating their landing. "I hope some wayward stranger in the third millennium may read it and say, 'This is where it all began,'" Aldrin said. **6,863**

697 BAYEZID (c.1360–1403)
founder of the first centralized Ottoman state

In three short years Bayezid steamrolled across much of the Balkans and conquered portions of Asia Minor in his drive to extend Ottoman rule. He was the first of the Osman dynasty to use the title sultan, but the many who feared him also called him "the Thunderbolt." When his forces occupied Bulgaria and put Constantinople under siege, Hungarians and Venetians led a major Crusade in protest, but Bayezid crushed them in 1396 at Nicopolis on the Danube River. Terrified, Europe braced for Bayezid's invasion. Instead he returned to unfinished business—his conquest of Anatolia, now part of Turkey. That made him Rival Number 1 to the equally brutal Tamerlane (51), the Tatar invader of India. Their armies clashed near Ankara in 1402. The mightier Tatar forces destroyed Bayezid's army, and captured Smyrna and the sultan himself. In that one decisive battle Tamerlane stole Bayezid's thunder. **6,835**

698 Thomas Hopkins Gallaudet
(1787–1851) *schoolmaster to the deaf*

Gallaudet directed the first American school for the deaf in Hartford, Connecticut, in 1817. It led in training educators of the deaf for decades. After graduation from Yale, Gallaudet had planned to become a minister, but his health failed. Recovering at home, he tutored deaf neighbor Alice Cogswell, and this service stirred his missionary zeal to educate the deaf and save their souls. With financial backing from Alice's father, Gallaudet studied in France with Abbé Sicard, successor to legendary teacher of the deaf Abbé de L'Epee (622). Gallaudet also imported Sicard's star teacher, Laurent Clerc. Unlike some profiteers, Gallaudet's motives were lofty in operating a school for the disabled. "His religious life was his whole life. His life was a living sermon," said Henry Barnard, U.S. commissioner of education. The school founder's son became president of Gallaudet University, the world's first college for the deaf, fittingly named after his father. **6,798**

699 Unkei (1148–1223)
Japanese blockbuster

Wood sculptures grew lifelike in Unkei's hands. He lived during the transition from regency to feudalism and, in contrast to the delicate prettiness of art in the early twelfth century, Unkei's new school stressed strength and realism. He was influenced by the emergence of the Zen sect in Buddhism with its emphasis on simplicity. But he also injected naturalism into sculpture through his new system of joining parts with double-pronged iron staples. No more would artists have to straddle entire tree trunks to chisel some august figure's body and head. Now they could work sensitively with each piece, even to the point of holding the head in their hands to carve fine features. Our favorite Unkei work: the standing figure of the ancient Indian teacher Mujaku, so quietly powerful and noble. Unkei carved this statue in 1208 for Kofukuji Temple. **6,771**

700 Theodore Roosevelt (1858–1919)
celebrity president

The egomaniacal, body-building, buffalo-hunting, former assistant secretary of the navy led the charge up San Juan Hill in the Spanish-American War and came home a hero. As governor of New York, he invented his motto, "Speak softly and carry a big stick," to describe how he cowed the state legislature. When the progressive-minded Roosevelt was elected vice president in 1900, conservative Republican Party chairman Mark Hanna complained, "Don't you realize that there's only one life between this madman and the White House?" An assassin ended that life—President William McKinley's—and Roosevelt was in the White House from 1901 to 1909. He built the Panama Canal, flexed America's muscle abroad, busted monopolies, and won the Nobel Peace Prize for mediating the Russo-Japanese War. After the exciting Roosevelt, presidents were no longer content to be the head of a government. For better or worse, they were now America's celebrities-in-chief. **6,759**

701–800

Previous generations went gaga over the telephone, over the automobile, over plastic, over atomic power, over television, over space travel. All were huge leaps in technology that transformed our lives. But none ushered in—dare we use the metaphor?—a new millennium.

Computers are different. They are more important than any of the above. Bigger even than the automobile. More far-reaching in their ultimate impact on civilization, perhaps, than the printing press itself. If we could declare one soul to be the creator of the computer, the Great Pilot of the Age of the Internet, we might have to bump Gutenberg from our number 1 spot to make room.

But there is no king who can lay claim to the computer crown. So we are forced to divide the prize among a passel of princelings, five of whom make our next honor roll. So pause with us to salute John Bardeen, the transistor meister; Robert Noyce, the chip champion; Stephen Wozniak, the PC pioneer; Seymour Cray, the computer superman; and David Packard, the computer supersalesman.

Every advance in computing has been engineered by groups of researchers, which made it tough for us to pick individuals responsible for, say, the transistor, the chip, or the personal computer. We're sure to be criticized for choosing Wozniak over Steven Jobs and William Gates as the progenitor of the personal computer, Noyce over Jack Kilby as the chip champ, and Bardeen over William Shockley as the transistor inventor. (In Shockley's case, we plead guilty to being negatively influenced by his well-publicized musings that blacks are genetically inferior.)

As we gaze at the other names on our next group of one hundred, we can't help but notice the presence of an unusually dense concentration of free-market economists: Friedrich von Hayek, the libertarian foe of collectivism; Peter Drucker, the management guru; and Milton Friedman, the monetarist mandarin. A coincidence? We think not. Capitalism and computers go together. One is all about the free flow of goods and services; the other is all about the free flow of information. These days, you can't have one without the other.

701 WILLIAM MORTON (1819–1868)
a knock-out in anesthesia

One thirteenth-century surgeon anesthetized his patients with a sponge cooked in opium, hemlock berries, unripened mulberry juice, spurge flax, climbing ivy, and other plants. Later, resourceful physicians intoxicated their patients first with whiskey and told them to "bite the bullet," literally. Morton, a dentist, studied the anesthetic properties of nitrous oxide (laughing gas) with Connecticut dentist Horace Wells. Wells's early work was discredited, however, when he attempted to demonstrate for colleagues at Massachusetts General Hospital the use of nitrous oxide during a tooth extraction. The patient howled in pain. Two years later, in 1846, Morton instead used ether before pulling a tooth. Then he anesthetized a printer who needed a tumor removed from his neck. Doctors around the world hailed this discovery, which helped bring about the era of modern surgical techniques. **6,733**

702 JOSEPH II (1741–1790)
priggish potentate of the people

In his vast Austrian Habsburg domains, Joseph abolished serfdom, established religious equality, founded universities and hospitals, balanced the budget, granted press freedom, and supported the arts. Adored by the common people, he complained that his overpaid ministers "often ruin everything, thinking they know everything without reading or experience." Both his wives died of smallpox, but his great love was his mother, the empress Maria Theresa (355), coruler with him from 1765 until her death in 1780, to whom he wrote, "Your glance is more to me than all the kingdoms of the world." He chastised his sister, Marie-Antoinette (781), queen of France, for her partying and gambling. "Why do you mix with this mob of libertines, prostitutes, strangers?" he asked in a letter. In a remarkable display of self-loathing, the enlightened despot ordered his epitaph to read, "Here lies Joseph, who was unsuccessful in all his undertakings." **6,719**

703 PETER DRUCKER (b. 1909)
Mr. Management

In two dozen books, from *The End of Economic Man* in 1939 to *Managing in a Time of Great Change* in 1995, Drucker espoused a practical approach to sharpening managers' skills. Some consider him the inventor of the science of modern management. Certainly he found a mass audience; his 1974 tome, *Management,* rocketed past *The Joy of Sex* on the bestseller list. Yet he was no fusty academic. He studied corporations close up and showed how success is a matter of seizing opportunities, like the fledgling IBM's realization that business, not government, would be the biggest market for computers. Many of the Austrian-born guru's admonitions are management gospel today: Never charge the maximum you can get; treat employees as a resource, not a cost. Asked what the best-managed organization is, Drucker replied, "The Girl Scouts. Tough, hard-working women can do anything." **6,711**

704 AMELIA EARHART (1897–1937)
advertisement for adventure

Decades before "Air Jordan" transformed the Chicago Bulls basketball star into the most famous name in America, Amelia Earhart signed her name to make a buck. Earhart wasn't interested in money, but endorsements and publicity stunt flights provided the capital to maintain her oh-so-expensive toy, her airplane. Public appearances were interspersed between such adventures as being the first woman pilot to solo across the Atlantic. Clothing and a full line of luggage carried her name; her endorsements ranged from cars to cameras to sunglasses. Publisher G. P. Putnam created her image, orchestrated her career, and then married her. Earhart was in the midst of an around-the-world jaunt when her plane disappeared in the South Pacific. The mystery surrounding her fate made her as huge a celebrity in death as in life. **6,682**

705 RENÉ FAVALORO (b. 1923)
coronary bypass surgeon

Television anchorman Walter Cronkite had it done; so did interviewer Larry King; tennis great Arthur Ashe did, too, and maybe former Vice President Nelson Rockefeller should have. At the heart of bypass surgery is Favaloro, an Argentine surgeon at the Cleveland Clinic. In 1967 Favaloro spurted to the forefront of open-heart surgery when he used a vein from his fifty-one-year-old patient's leg to bypass a diseased artery surrounding the heart. The man lived. When Favaloro presented his techniques at a cardiology conference, doctors jammed into the room. Physicians in the hallway literally knocked down the door to hear him. Since then, bypass techniques have been perfected. Using artificial valves, surgeons routinely perform quadruple bypass. This surgery is so commonplace, it has given new life to millions of patients. In 1996, for example, more than 309,000 bypass operations were performed in the United States alone. **6,678**

706 ABBAS I (1557–1629)
Persian powerhouse

Persia was a snakepit of unruly chieftains until Abbas the Great won control with a professional army and English advisers. Then he defeated Turkish and Uzbek invaders to create a centralized nation. His capital at Isfahan, with its walled parade ground ten times larger than Rome's St.

Peter's Square, is still one of the world's architectural triumphs. Abbas was superstitious, canny, and cruel. In 1591 an astrologer predicted the king would die, so Abbas abdicated temporarily and had his replacement killed to satisfy the prophecy. Abbas celebrated a victory over the Turks in 1603 by having twenty thousand enemy skulls heaped before him, and he kept his ambitious sons at bay by having one murdered and two blinded. Ironically, by making his temporal power so strong, Abbas created a target for advocates of priestly power, and his country—modern-day Iran—has been bedeviled by conflicts between mullahs and monarchs ever since. **6,652**

707 MATTHEW PERRY (1794–1858)
American crowbar who opened Japan to the West

All Perry's other adventures, from suppressing the African slave trade to hunting pirates in the West Indies, pale beside his expedition to pry Japan out of two centuries of isolation. In 1853 "Old Bruin" anchored four ships in lower Tokyo Bay and demanded a trade treaty. Local authorities dithered, and Japanese suits of armor quadrupled in price. Historian Samuel Eliot Morison said it would be as if Americans today discovered that "weird-looking spacecraft were on their way to earth." But Perry said his naval force merely sought to "bring a singular and isolated people into the family of civilized nations." After making a greater show of force the following year, he got his wish. Japan entered the modern era, and the world has never been the same. **6,621**

708 JAMES MONROE (1758–1831)
doctrinaire president

Monroe's message to Congress on December 2, 1823, later known as the Monroe Doctrine, was the basis of U.S. foreign policy for more than a century. It also marked the young republic's step on the road to world superpower. Monroe, the fifth president of the United States, told European powers the American continents were closed to colonization. Attempts to counter this policy, he added, would be considered threats to U.S. security. Behind the declaration were fears that a coalition of European powers would send a major force to quash rebellious Spanish-American colonies. Monroe had struck a political nerve. "The depth and permanence of American feeling on the subject has been repeatedly demonstrated," said historian John A. Garraty. One recent example was the 1962 Cuban missile crisis, when President Kennedy ordered the Russians to remove missile bases from Cuba.　**6,615**

709 SOPHIE GERMAIN (1776–1831)
proponent of good vibrations

The French Germain articulated the formula behind the physics of vibrating elastic surfaces, paving the way for the construction of massive structures like the Eiffel Tower and skyscrapers. She came to mathematics with no formal training. Her parents were so against her career choice that they kept her bedroom without light or a fire so that she would not study at night. Her ink froze in the well, and she had to wrap herself in blankets to study in near darkness, but she was not deterred. Germain surreptitiously gained the support of Europe's leading mathematicians by sharing her research with them under an assumed name. She made such an impression on Carl Friedrich Gauss (109) that he recommended her for an honorary doctorate from a German university.　**6,587**

710 JOHN BARDEEN (1908–1991)
the incredible shrinking scientist

The age of consumer electronics began on December 23, 1947, when a team at Bell Labs built the first transistor. The tiny metal gizmo replaced cumbersome tubes for amplification and switching of electric signals. A world without transistors would lack home computers, space shuttles, VCRs, microwaves, and other modern, electronics-filled products. William Shockley and Walter Brattain had been working on transistors, but the breakthrough was made possible by Bardeen, a theoretical genius who joined them in 1945. The three shared the Nobel Prize for physics in 1956, and Bardeen later became the first person to win two Nobel Prizes in one field. He shared the 1972 physics award for superconductivity theories that led to small powerful electromagnets used for such wonders as magnetic resonance imaging.　**6,578**

711 GEORGES CLEMENCEAU (1841–1929)
French tiger in World War I

Clemenceau, a dominant figure of the Third Republic, also defended the Jewish officer Dreyfus in the Dreyfus affair that tore apart France. Luckily for Dreyfus, Clemenceau urged Émile Zola (607) to change the title of his famous denunciation of corrupt officials to the majestic "J'accuse" from the bureaucratic "Open Letter to the President of the Republic." In 1917, with the Germans winning the war, France's president appointed Clemenceau premier. Winston Churchill (38), visiting the French parliament the day Clemenceau took power, said the seventy-six-year-old Frenchman "looked like a wild animal pacing to and fro behind bars. . . . France had resolved to let her tiger loose upon all foes." Queried about his policy, Clemenceau replied, "Home policy? I wage war. Foreign policy? I wage war." He won the war, but his demands for crushing reparations from his defeated foe fueled German resentments that led to World War II.　**6,555**

712 JOHN FORD (1895–1973)
director who did what a director's got to do

If you've been looking for actor John Wayne's niche in the millennium, stop here. This is the entry for Wayne—and it's all about Ford. As one of Hollywood's greatest directors, Ford not only discovered stuntman Marion Morrison, he changed his name to John Wayne and made him a star. But Wayne's got just a bit part in this big picture: Ford perfected camera work, told poignant stories, and directed some of the most important and enduring films ever. He won Academy Awards for *The Informer, The Grapes of Wrath, How Green Was My Valley,* and *The Quiet Man.* Although not honored with an Oscar, Ford's *Stagecoach* is universally considered the perfect film of the Western genre. The way he directed the camera to create panoramic, breathtaking scenes of the Wild West was such a trademark that today film buffs call the technique *Fordian.* **6,543**

713 STEPHEN WOZNIAK (b. 1950)
personal computer wizard

Maybe there was something in the water; after all, Wozniak grew up in Silicon Valley. As a kid, his teachers thought he was deaf because it was so hard to get his attention. He won first place in the junior high science fair when he built a computer. At age twenty-four he designed the first Apple computer in his bedroom. It never occurred to him that he could make millions with his design. That was the idea of his high school buddy, Stephen Jobs, who had the business acumen to make Apple one of the most important computer companies. Before Apples, only "techies" had PCs and they had to assemble the unwieldy, complicated models themselves. When the Apple II was first sold in 1977, however, it introduced such computer terms as *floppy disk, icons, mouse, point and click,* and *drag down.* Affordable, attractive, and "user friendly," it revolutionized American life. **6,528**

714 LEO SZILARD (1898–1964)
A-bomb's anguished author

On a London street in 1933, an idea flashed in the Hungarian physicist's brain as he watched a traffic light turn green. If he could find an element that could emit two neutrons after being split by another neutron, he could start a nuclear chain reaction. And it would make a big bang. That was the theoretical genesis of the atomic bomb, and Szilard had a political role, too. In 1939 he convinced Albert Einstein (17) to write the historic letter that stirred President Franklin Roosevelt (37) to construct an A-bomb before the Nazis could build one. But the day after a bomb was dropped on Japan, Szilard was so mournful about the loss of life, he suggested that his lab staff at the University of Chicago wear black armbands. "Hiroshima shows that moral inhibitions can no longer be counted on," he said. He devoted the rest of his life to nuclear disarmament. **6,501**

715 SEYMOUR CRAY (1925–1996)
creator of the supercomputer

Cray hated organizational charts and other trappings of corporate bureaucracy. Asked to draw up a five-year plan for an early company he worked for, he wrote, "Five-year goal: Build the biggest computer in the world. One-year goal: Achieve one-fifth of the above." What he loved was breakneck computing speed, and he tinkered with his machines until they became the fastest in the world. The payoff was enormous. His supercomputers, capable of simulating nuclear-bomb explosions and deciphering enemy codes, assured American military superiority in the cold war. They also helped agriculture, by predicting weather patterns, and mining and oil drilling, by analyzing geological formations. Eventually advances in computer technology reduced the demand for supercomputers, and Cray Computer Corporation went bankrupt in 1995. That didn't stop Cray, though; he was planning another supercomputer project when he was killed in a car crash at age seventy-one. **6,498**

716 HERMAN MELVILLE (1819–1891)
one whale of a writer

"Call me Ishmael," begins Melville's masterpiece, *Moby-Dick,* the leviathan of nineteenth-century American literature. It's the story of the insane whaling captain, Ahab, on a disastrous quest for Moby-Dick, the white whale that ripped off his leg. Plunging deeper, the novel is a strongly symbolic look at good and evil. Melville's magnificent prose is "like an organ with all the stops out," said critic Clifton Fadiman. The final scene, the ship sinking: "Now small fowls flew screaming over the yet yawning gulf; a sullen white surf beat against its steep sides, then all collapsed, and the great shroud of the sea rolled on as it rolled five thousand years ago." Those looking for an easy read didn't appreciate *Moby-Dick* on publication. "Though I wrote the Gospels in this century, I should die in the gutter," Melville told author Nathaniel Hawthorne (675). Almost. He worked twenty years as a customs inspector before dying in obscurity. **6,489**

717 KATHARINE DEXTER MCCORMICK
(1875–1967) pill pusher

Biologist Gregory Pincus developed it; biologist Min-Chueh Chang tested it on rabbits; obstetrician John Rock tried it on patients; but it was McCormick who planted the idea and provided cold cash—$2 million—to create "the pill." The blue-blooded McCormick, a graduate of the Massachusetts Institute of Technology, was an heiress herself before she wedded the wealth of International Harvester. Decades in a childless marriage to a man who was insane moved her to endow a foundation to study mental illness and its link to hormones. After her husband's death, McCormick and friend Margaret Sanger (99) decided to buy themselves birth control that women could take like aspirin. Pincus said it was possible to develop but costly. So McCormick wrote a check for $40,000, then kept the money flowing. When the pill was first marketed in 1960, it provided sexual freedom for women and ushered in that decade's swinging sexual revolution. **6,470**

718 GIUSEPPE FIORELLI (1823–1896)
careful intruder in the dust

Many countries have a candidate for the title, "first great modern archaeologist." France has J.-F. Champollion, who deciphered hieroglyphics; Denmark has J.J.A. Worsaee, who proved the existence of the stone, bronze, and iron ages; England has Sir Flinders Petrie, who introduced scientific methods into Egyptology. For the greatest of them all, we chose an Italian, Fiorelli, who from 1860 to 1875 directed the excavation of Pompeii, the city covered in A.D. 79 by volcanic ash from the eruption of Mount Vesuvius. Fiorelli pioneered stratigraphy—careful digging layer by layer to avoid destruction of evidence—and founded a school to teach the method. He also developed the idea of pouring plaster into the depressions left by human remains to recreate the victims' body contours. At a time when archaeology was often just the recovery of treasures from graves, Fiorelli showed the world how to recover history. **6,465**

719 MARGARET THATCHER (b. 1925)
Britain's Iron Lady

Her Conservative Party colleagues quaked in her presence, and the Labor Goliath collapsed at her feet. Prime minister from 1979 to 1990, Thatcher dismantled Britain's welfare state and replaced it with free-market capitalism. Like Ronald Reagan, whom she called "the American dream in action," she attacked government spending at every turn (earning the nickname "Maggie the milksnatcher" early in her career for cutting school-milk programs). At first reviled for her austerity moves, Thatcher rebounded in the polls after going to war with Argentina over the Falkland Islands, and her economic policies ultimately bore fruit. You either loved her or hated her. George Bush lauded her as "the greengrocer's daughter who shaped a nation to her will," while a Dutch pundit called her "the witch in the European fairy tale." But Thatcher had the last laugh; her economic model triumphed over socialism worldwide. **6,442**

720 T. S. ELIOT (1888–1965)
poetic voice in the wasteland

The erudite Eliot plumbed Donne (280), Dante (30), and nineteenth-century symbolist poets for inspiration, creating an experimental style that rejuvenated English poetry. Eliot's early poems ache with the anguish and sterility of modern life, but later ones, such as "Ash Wednesday" and "Four Quartets," radiate hope. His spare yet elegant lines create indelible images, like this from "The Love Song of J. Alfred Prufrock":

Let us go then, you and I,
When the evening is spread out against the sky
Like a patient etherised upon a table;

Or from "The Waste Land":

April is the cruelest month, breeding
Lilacs out of the dead land

Prufrock, Eliot's first important publication, was so radically different that his publisher held it for a year, unsure it was poetry. By 1948 doubts had turned to acclaim, and the American-turned-Englishman was awarded the Nobel Prize for literature. **6,439**

721 COLETTE (1873–1954)
France's literary darling

Calling Colette an author is like saying Ben Franklin (54) was a printer. It's accurate, but it leaves an awful lot out. Colette was a bona fide Renaissance woman with careers as a mime, actress, playwright, journalist, essayist, novelist, short story writer, critic, and music hall dancer. Most of all, she liked to write about herself, but she loosely cloaked her books in fiction. She was so adored in France that when she died, she received a state funeral. Thousands crowded the streets of Paris to see her coffin pass. Her mystique has grown in death. The country is so devoted to her memory that the Colette Museum opened in May 1995; streets are named after her. Outside France the world embraces Colette for her novel *Gigi,* which found great success as a 1958 musical film starring Maurice Chevalier. Ah, yes, we remember it well. **6,394**

722 ALFONSO X (1221–1284)
learned king of Castile and León

The *Alfonsine Tables* were crafted under his patronage, and we're not talking about furniture. They were charts of the movement of stars and planets. Fifty astronomers did the work, and the printed copies that first appeared in 1483 helped scholars such as Copernicus (18) and Tycho Brahe (202) make breakthroughs that ended belief in the geocentric universe. Alfonso the Wise, as he was known, also wrote legal treatises and poetry, some of it raunchy. Bookishness aside, Alfonso was a typical medieval European ruler: acquisitive, cunning, warlike; when he wasn't fighting Muslims, he was trying to put down his children's rebellions. He badgered four successive popes to make him Holy Roman emperor, until Gregory X offered a deal: The king would be granted ten percent of papal revenue in Spain if he would stop pressing his claim to the imperial throne. Being Alfonso the Wise, the king agreed. **6,388**

723 MARTIN BUBER (1878–1965)
philosopher who preached the wonder of you

His central tenet was the need for dialogue to give meaning to life—the "I–Thou" relationship that defines love between two humans and between man and God (His most famous book is titled, not surprisingly, *I and Thou*). Though a Zionist who fled Nazi Germany to Palestine, Buber strove for Jewish dialogue with Christians and Arabs and said the central dilemma of his time was that "spirit and life have fallen apart from one another." The point was to think of other beings, even plants and animals, as "thou," not as "it." Buber remembered stealing to his grandparents' stable as a boy to stroke the neck of a dapple-gray horse. "It confided itself to me, placed itself elementally in the relation of Thou and Thou with me," he wrote. "It was as though the element of vitality itself bordered on my skin." **6,367**

724 DAVID LIVINGSTONE (1813–1873)
explorer of the Dark Continent, we presume

Livingstone trained to become a medical missionary and dreamed of Christianizing Africa and finding the source of the Nile River. He accomplished neither goal. But this Scotsman's discoveries during his amazing journeys across southern Africa over thirty years fired competition among European powers for control of the continent. After reports of Livingstone's death, the *New York Herald* sent journalist Henry Morton Stanley to track the legendary adventurer. "Dr. Livingstone, I presume," was Stanley's now-famous greeting when he caught up to him in 1871. "You have brought me new life," Livingstone told him. Stanley returned to England with Livingstone's writings on the horrors of the Arabs' slave trade in East Africa. It gave abolitionists ammunition to pressure for reform. Livingstone shaped Western attitudes toward Africa, and in death as in life, he was revered by African followers. They preserved his body and carried it from the interior to the coast, an eight-month journey of fifteen hundred miles. **6,355**

725 GERTRUDE STEIN (1874–1946)
name-dropping social commentator and patron of the arts

Stein would have ranked higher if only we could forgive her that awful "Rose is a rose is a rose." What *was* she talking about? Alas, Stein played with words; the consequences be damned. Then there's her most famous book, *The Autobiography of Alice B. Toklas.* Where does she get off writing someone else's autobiography? Sure, Toklas was her other half in a union that lasted longer than most marriages, but come on. The 1933 book, with its eyebrow-raising observations of the world's beautiful people, was an instant bestseller. Stein held her *très chic* salons in Paris in the decadent decades after the Great War. She entertained and encouraged the work of Picasso (149), Matisse (269), Hemingway (388), F. Scott Fitzgerald, and others. They painted her, wrote about her, and forgave her her insults—like the time she told Hemingway that he was "ninety percent Rotarian." **6,339**

726 ALBERTUS MAGNUS (c.1200–1280)
sainted philosopher

He was short in stature but a towering figure in the history of knowledge as Western Europe's first great champion of Aristotelian learning. He copied that old Greek so much, his critics called him Albert the Ape. Albertus was a German noble who joined the Dominican order and spent his life teaching. Thomas Aquinas (8) was his prize pupil. The pious Albert, sainted in 1622, walked barefoot on inspection tours of his church domains, and he owned nothing, not even the manuscripts he wrote. He succeeded so well in making Aristotle's science, philosophy, and mathematics known that the medievalist Henry Osborn Taylor wrote, "Perhaps the world has no greater purveyor of knowledge not his own." Albert would occasionally study nature. He wrote about plants and may have been the first man to produce arsenic in free form. **6,322**

727 DAVID PACKARD (1912–1996)
archetypical American entrepreneur

With his partner William Hewlett, he launched the modern computer industry from a Palo Alto, California, garage with $538 in cash in 1938. Their company, Hewlett-Packard, developed electronic testing and measuring devices and moved into computers in the 1970s, becoming a $31 billion colossus by 1995. But Packard was known as much for his management philosophy, the so-called "HP way," as he was for his company's size and innovativeness. A plain-spoken man who worked in short-sleeve shirts, he believed that management should encourage workers to be creative problem-solvers rather than assembly-line cogs. He gave most of his money to charity, and his garage is now a California state landmark inscribed "the birthplace of Silicon Valley." **6,313**

728 JULIA MARGARET CAMERON (1815–1879) portrait artist
with a camera

Cameron received a camera as a gift in 1863. She began making portraits at her home on the Isle of Wight, revamping the family's chicken coop into her studio. She photographed her children as well as distinguished figures, including Alfred Lord Tennyson, Henry Wadsworth Longfellow, Ellen Terry, Thomas Carlyle (691), and Charles Darwin (7). She experimented with poses and lighting, creating portraits that were haunting and intense. In those early days of photography, most critics focused on her technical shortcomings, including hazy outlines and negatives marred by tears, spots, and fingerprints. But some likened her shots to paintings of the old masters. Cameron's pictures were "admirable, expressive and vigorous, but dreadfully opposed to photographic conventionalities and proprieties," said critic Thomas Sutton. "They are the more valuable for being so." Legend has it Cameron died taking a photo. Her last word: "Beautiful!" **6,294**

729 EDWARD ROBINSON SQUIBB (1819–1900) pharmaceutical
phenomenon

Squibb, an American navy doctor, dosed himself with rhubarb and bicarbonate of soda to cure a bad stomach. He got sicker. Then he discovered sand in the bicarbonate and worms in the rhubarb. He was appalled. After he recuperated and left the navy, E.R., as he was called, opened a pharmaceutical company dedicated to product purity and uniformity. He was seriously burned when a supply of ether caught fire and for the rest of his life sported a beard to hide the scars. He also had to tape his damaged eyelids shut at night. Undeterred, he rebuilt the factory and lobbied unceasingly for government regulation of the drug industry. He died six years before passage of the Pure Food and Drug

Act, but his company grew to become one of the giants in the pharmaceutical industry and merged in 1989 with Bristol-Myers. **6,268**

730 ROBERT NOYCE (1927–1990)
chip's champ

Noyce's creation of the first silicon chip in 1958 puts him in our hall of fame, by a hair. That's the thickness of a single modern processor ten thousand times more powerful than early computers that filled a room. The first chip, built just months before Noyce's by Jack Kilby of Texas Instruments, was made of germanium. Noyce's silicon version became more popular, and as a businessman he was the central figure in the rise of Silicon Valley as the cradle of electronics invention in America. Veterans of Noyce's Fairchild Semiconductors started more than fifty other companies. At his company, Intel, he instituted a collegial, anything-goes-if-you're-successful managerial style mimicked by the Apples, Microsofts, and Netscapes that emerged at the close of the millennium. As Tom Wolfe wrote of Noyce and his entrepreneurial clones, "If you created the right type of corporate community, the right type of autonomous congregation, genius would flower." **6,239**

731 MILTON FRIEDMAN (b. 1912)
inflation fighter

Friedman, whose mother was a sweatshop seamstress, is most famous for his doctrine of monetarism, which states that the money supply is the most important factor influencing economic activity and that central banks should regulate its growth to keep inflation down and the economy humming. First, Israel bought into his theory; then Ronald Reagan and his Federal Reserve chairman, Paul Volcker, did; then Margaret Thatcher (719) did; then the whole world did. And inflation went down. A libertarian disciple of

Friedrich von Hayek (738), Friedman surpassed his teacher. He was ahead of his time in opposing government subsidies and regulations and in promoting an all-volunteer army, a negative income tax for the poor, and school vouchers. One admirer called him Adam Smith's (21) "most distinguished spiritual son," while a detractor reviled him as the "bastard progeny" of John Maynard Keynes (201). What he really wanted, he said, was to "keep government in its place." **6,203**

732 ANTONIO VIVALDI (1678–1741)
concerto creator

Known as "the Red Priest" for his red hair and ecclesiastical background, Vivaldi also was one of the most influential composers of his time. He established the three-movement format for the concerto, making it the model for its genre throughout Europe. Celebrated during the late baroque period, Vivaldi's work was neglected after his death. Scholars rediscovering Bach (35) a hundred years later found his transcription of a Vivaldi concerto. That led to Vivaldi's current revival. Unlike the compositions of his student, Bach, Vivaldi music never seems dated. His quartet of concertos, *The Four Seasons,* an early example of orchestral program music, delights every time. Vivaldi composed at lightning speed. As musical director for a celebrated Venetian school, he continuously churned out new compositions. He boasted he could "compose a concerto faster than a copyist could copy it." In all, he wrote more than five hundred concertos, over seventy sonatas, and forty-five operas and religious works. **6,194**

733 THEODOR SCHWANN (1810–1882)
cell's theorist

The truth was right under their noses, but scientists peered into microscopes for almost two hundred years before anyone postulated the theory that all organisms are made of cells. We gave Leeuwenhoek (107) credit for his microscope and subsequent inspection of blood cells, sperm, and other organisms. For the next two centuries scientists discovered brave new worlds of life but formulated no accurate theories. Schwann worked as a researcher for only five years, but they were highly productive. He discovered pepsin, described yeast as a living organism, and explained cell theory. What Schwann did for animals, Matthias Schleiden, another German biologist, did for plants. Together they presented an accurate portrait of cells, including the membrane and nucleus. When other scientists attacked Schwann for his ideas, he gave it all up and became a mystic. Then he settled down in Louvain, Belgium, and taught anatomy to college students.   **6,181**

734 MOBUTU SESO SEKE (1930–1997)
African kleptocrat

Mobutu, the prototype of the Third World autocrat, single-handedly ruined Zaire (now Congo), a mineral-rich nation four times the size of France. From the day he seized power in 1965 until his inglorious flight from rebels in 1997, he looted Zaire, squirreling billions in foreign bank accounts and building a personal fleet of five hundred Mercedes-Benzes while his compatriots' average annual income fell to $125 from $225. True, Mobutu restrained communism in Africa and unified a conglomeration of 450 ethnic groups— but at what cost! "Nothing worked there," wrote author Rand Richards Cooper. "Telephones didn't work. Electricity didn't work. Roads had dissolved back into the bush. Policemen robbed people. Atop this pyramid of thieves perched Mobutu." In a comic twist to the personality cult, Zaire's evening news opened with a scene showing Mobutu descending from the heavens. On his way, some would say, to hell.   **6,150**

735 SALVADOR DALI (1904–1989)
reality bender

Madness made Van Gogh (158) lop off his ear. For Spanish painter Dali, insanity was the lifelong source of artistic inspiration. "I dream of cadaverous shapes, distended breasts, oozing flesh," the self-proclaimed genius wrote. He read Freud's (15) theory on the erotic significance of subconscious images and was inspired to paint the landscape of his dream world—an approach that made him the leader of surrealism. Consider one of the century's most famous paintings, *Persistence of Memory,* with its watches melting on a barren landscape. Or *Daddy-Longlegs of the Evening—Hope,* showing a child-angel shielding his eyes from a penis-cannon firing a decomposing horse. A breast also oozes from the cannon, and a limp woman, broken in two on a branch, plays a liquid violoncello. "The limpness, the viscousness, the gelatinousness do portray in my mind the vital feeling I long had of my body and of the life of my being," Dali said. The artist-paranoid once encountered Freud, who found Dali's tottering mental state fascinating.   **6,131**

736 QUEEN MARGARET (1353–1412)
unifier of Scandinavia

What chutzpah! After Margaret's father died, she convinced the Danish council to ignore daddy's heir and name her five-year-old son Olaf king. Margaret ruled as regent until Olaf almost ruined everything by dying suddenly at age seventeen. No woman had ever reigned as Denmark's queen, but Margaret didn't let a few laws of succession stand in the way. She adopted her six-year-old nephew and had herself named the "sovereign lady" of Denmark and Norway. When the Swedish nobles agreed a month later to accept Margaret as their "rightful master," they dubbed her "Lady King." Meanwhile, rumors abounded in Norway that Olaf wasn't really dead. Margaret managed to convince her subjects that the man who would be king was an imposter because he lacked Olaf's huge wart on his neck. Margaret remained sovereign of Norway, Sweden, and Denmark, Europe's second largest territory, until her death from the plague.   **6,122**

737 ALEXANDER NEVSKY (c.1220–1263)
Russian hero with a sycophantic streak

Grand Duke Alexander of Novgorod was the sainted dynastic forefather of the czars. Even the commissars of the Soviet Union revered him. Alexander was a young warrior prince when he saved his homeland from the Swedes on the River Neva in 1240; hence his name Nevsky. In 1242 he beat the Teutonic Knights in a battle on frozen Lake Peipus, a struggle as important to Russia's nationalistic pride as the battles of Lexington and Concord are to America's. Alexander knew how to kowtow, too. He appeased Russia's Tatar overlords to gain a measure of independence for his kingdom and helped the Tatars suppress his own brothers' rebellions. Alexander, always hostile to Roman Catholicism, was canonized by the Russian Orthodox Church during the reign of his sixteenth-century descendant, Ivan the Terrible.   **6,103**

738 FRIEDRICH VON HAYEK (1899–1992)
worst nightmare of government central planners

The Austrian-born British subject first challenged British economist Keynes's (201) tax-and-spend gospel with his get-the-government-off-our-backs libertarianism at the height of the 1930s Depression—and was laughed out of academia. Hayek kept tilting at the Keynesian windmill, getting a direct hit with his 1944 diatribe against socialist collectivism, *The Road to Serfdom*. But it wasn't until the 1980s that the windmill finally collapsed. That's when Reagan in America and Thatcher (719) in Britain took up the free-market cause that he and disciples like Milton Friedman (731) espoused. "Hayek's central insight," wrote Friedman, "was that coordination of men's activities through central direction and through voluntary cooperation are roads going in very different directions: the first to serfdom, the second to freedom."   **6,082**

739 MATTEO RICCI (1552–1610)
bridge between the cultures of East and West

Ricci, an Italian Jesuit missionary who mastered Chinese and studied the Chinese culture, was allowed entry into the traditionally closed society in 1583. Over the next twenty-seven years, he introduced Christian teaching to the Ming dynasty through his writings and often-heated debates with leading Buddhist scholars. His book *History of the Introduction of Christianity in China* was published in the West. Ricci made conversions among the Chinese, but it was slow going. "The fruit here is at the stage of sowing rather than that of harvest," he wrote. Cultural clashes were inevitable. Once Ricci shocked townspeople with the carved wooden crucifix he carried. They summoned soldiers, who threatened to beat Ricci and his entourage. He tried to explain the Christian's relationship to the crucified Christ, but they didn't understand. "It's really not good to have someone looking like that," one Chinese villager said.   **6,065**

740 RAY KROC (1902–1984)
he did it all for you

McDonald's corporate biography claims that a staggering ninety-six percent of Americans scarfed down fast food at McDonald's in the past year. Sound impossible? In 1994 the master of fast food sold its 100 billionth hamburger. The instantly recognizable golden arches began with Dick and Mac McDonald, who developed a simple menu of shakes, burgers, and fries, sans silverware. Kroc bought the name and the quick preparation method, then marketed it to the max. Since Kroc's intervention in the lone hamburger restaurant outside Pasadena, California, in 1955, the company has built its arches in eighty countries. It buys five percent of the U.S. edible potato crop for fries and sells about $26 billion worth of fast food annually, edging out Mom and apple pie as America's emblems. Kroc built his empire with good old American elbow grease. "Work is the meat in the hamburger of life," he confided. **6,033**

741 FRANZ BOAS (1858–1942)
nurturing anthropologist

People who say that race determines intelligence are now viewed as hopeless bigots. But at the turn of the twentieth century, many serious researchers, influenced by Charles Darwin (7), believed that the brains of nonwhites were biologically inferior. We salute anthropologist Franz Boas for teachings and writings—like his 1904 article "What the Negro Has Done in Africa"—that routed the determinists and taught that culture is what counts in human development. Boas left his native Germany to escape anti-Semitism and from 1899 to 1937 headed the anthropology department at Columbia University. There he taught Margaret Mead (379), Ruth Benedict, and other famous anthropologists his techniques for studying disappearing aboriginal cultures. Boas also did field work among the natives of Canada and Siberia. But his central contribution was to refute the nativists of the so-called civilized world. **6,012**

742 HELMUT KOHL (b. 1930)
unifier of Germany

In 1982 a left-wing political foe warned that a victory of the supposedly bumbling, slow-witted Kohl in upcoming elections "would be a disaster" for West Germany. Well, the six-foot-four, three-hundred-pound, sauerkraut-loving conservative not only won, he became the nation's longest-reigning German chancellor since Bismarck. And far from driving his country to ruin, he presided over its triumph: the destruction of the Berlin Wall in 1989 and the $600 billion fusion of the two Germanys into a single capitalist fatherland. His other legacy may prove just as enduring: leashing Germany to Western Europe by monetary union, thereby containing the Teutonic penchant for adventurism that has cost the world so dearly. In 1993 *Der Spiegel* prematurely proclaimed "the end of the Kohl era." Five years later, he was still riding high. **6,005**

743 PIERRE DE COUBERTIN (1863–1937)
reviver of the Olympics

Like a runner in the four-hundred-meter hurdles, French educator De Coubertin overcame all the obstacles to win world support for resumption of the Olympic games after a fifteen-hundred-year hiatus. The Greek government balked at financing the competition in Athens, so money was raised privately to reconstruct the ancient Olympic site. On April 6, 1896, a jubilant De Coubertin joined the crowd of seventy thousand to hear King George of Greece proclaim the opening of the First International Olympic Games. They featured 311 athletes from thirteen nations. De Coubertin hoped the competition, besides easing world political tensions, would inspire youths to study ancient history. "They need something more alive, more real," said De Coubertin, president of the International Olympic Committee from 1896 to 1925.

"Olympic dust is what excites their emulation best and most naturally." Thanks to De Coubertin, the world pauses every two years to watch the best athletes compete. However, his dream of world peace through athletics has been elusive. In 1936 Hitler staged the Berlin games to demonstrate Aryan superiority, but American black sprinter Jesse Owens made the "master race" eat his dust. And in 1972 black-hooded terrorists slaughtered Israeli wrestlers at the Munich competition. **6,002**

744 RALPH NADER (b. 1934)
America's Don Quixote

He never lets up. In rumpled, ill-fitting suits and army-issue shoes, Nader marches through life tilting at windmills and, unlike literature's Don Quixote, sometimes knocking them down. Nader and his dogmatic "gift of rage" have championed consumers since 1965, when his bestseller *Unsafe at Any Speed* exposed automakers' lack of interest in safety and singled out the Chevy Corvair. Four years later, when General Motors took the Corvair off the market, its sales had slumped ninety-five percent. Nader has taken on just about everybody and everything—from Congress to insurance companies to Giants Stadium (artificial turf injures players). "We have government by the Exxons, of the DuPonts, and for the General Motors," Nader charged as he accepted the Green Party's 1996 presidential nomination. He's behind the Consumer Product Safety Act and the Freedom of Information Act. He crusaded for seat belts, airbags, no-smoking sections, and a fifty-five-mile-per-hour national speed limit. Okay, so he lost the last one. You can't win 'em all. **5,988**

745 EDUARD BERNSTEIN (1850–1932)
socialist with a human face

For the first half of his life, he was an ardent Marxist, but he realized that the collapse of capitalism was not around the corner, as Marx had predicted. So he shifted gears. Bernstein's 1898 book, *Evolutionary Socialism,* made him the leader of the German socialists who rejected communism and believed that the political system as it existed could be a vehicle for bringing about safe factories, better wages and hours, and health and retirement benefits. His German Social Democratic Party, and socialist parties like it in other countries, helped make the industrialized West safer for the working class. Bernstein's biggest failure was his inability to get white-collar workers to join his party; the year after his death, the petite bourgeoisie flocked to the Nazis. **5,966**

746 ALFRED HITCHCOCK (1899–1980)
master of the macabre

Janet Leigh gets it in the shower in the nail-biter *Psycho;* Cary Grant (952) carries a luminous glass of milk up the stairs in *Suspicion;* Jimmy Stewart clings to a ledge in *Rear Window.* Hitchcock was responsible for some of movies' most memorable scenes. He didn't talk much about why he liked thrillers, except to trot out that apocryphal tale of being locked in jail as a boy for five minutes after he had done something naughty. He confessed to scaring easily and traced his fear of the dark to the time his parents left him alone at night. The most universally recognizable film director, the rotund Hitchcock showed up in cameo roles in most of his fifty-four films and hosted a weekly TV suspense program. Hitchcock lamented that he and his literary hero, Edgar Allan Poe, were captives of suspense. "If I was making 'Cinderella,' everyone would look for the corpse," he said. **5,932**

747 EDWARD BERNAYS (1891–1995)
original spin doctor

What Barnum (94) did with elephants and midgets, Bernays did even better with subtlety and psychology. Perhaps it came naturally because he was Freud's (15) nephew, but Bernays knew how to get people to do exactly what he wanted. He coined the highfalutin phrase *public relations* for a business designed to lead people where they don't know they want to go. He called his strategy "the engineering of consent." In a career that spanned most of the twentieth century, he improved the images of presidents, including the taciturn Calvin Coolidge. He revived the failing hairnet industry, convinced women it was okay to smoke in public, and got children to wash with Ivory soap. When fashionable women refused to smoke Lucky Strikes because the green package clashed with their clothing, he manipulated consumers and manufacturers with green parties and balls. Green became the color of the season, and Lucky sales soared. **5,910**

748 SÉBASTIEN LE PRESTRE DE VAUBAN
(1633–1707) *engineer whose forte was forts*

Siegecraft used to be a military science as important as nuclear bomb-building became; Vauban was the Robert Oppenheimer (80) of his age. Vauban learned engineering from a Carmelite priest, and as a rebel soldier against France's Louis XIV (63), he helped build his first fortress, Clermont. In 1655 he switched sides and led the forces that destroyed it. Over the next half century he built 160 fortresses and directed forty sieges, helping Louis dominate continental Europe. Vauban's lasting contribution was a method of trench warfare that saved attackers' lives by giving them cover from defenders' cannons. Finally Vauban became an exponent of mobile warfare when he realized that swift-moving armies, not bricks, are a country's best defense. His remains were dug up and scattered by French revolutionaries, but his heart was

recovered in 1808, and Napoleon (16) had it buried in the vault of a Paris church. **5,872**

749 CHARLES PROTEUS STEINMETZ
(1865–1923) *night light to America*

Steinmetz, a bearded hunchback with an ever-present cigar in his right hand, fled to the United States from Germany to escape a crackdown on socialists. A brilliant mathematician, he turned his genius to electrical engineering at a research company owned by a fellow German refugee. His discovery of the law of hysteresis, which describes electrical power loss resulting from alternating magnetism (got that?), helped launch the electrification of America. To snag the loyal Steinmetz, General Electric had to buy his benefactor's company. Steinmetz was also an early ecologist, railing against pollution from burning coal, and a campaigner for the rights of the disabled. He gave himself his own middle name, Proteus, after the sage of Greek mythology who could assume many shapes if caught but, if he were held fast, would always return to his original form—a deformed dwarf with love in his heart. **5,843**

750 FRIEDRICH WILHELM BESSEL
(1784–1846) *star marker*

From his Königsberg observatory, German astronomer Bessel accurately measured positions of about fifty thousand stars. This helped the scientific community determine distances between stars, understand planetary orbits, and grasp the scale of the universe. Bessel began with a painstaking eighteen-month observation of the star 61 Cygni in the constellation Cygnus. Scotsman Thomas Henderson was pondering the same problem, but Bessel published his findings first. Later Bessel also speculated that blips in Uranus's orbit were caused by an unknown planet, thus opening the way for the discovery of Neptune. When young, Bessel was apprenticed to a commercial firm in Bremen but spent his free time studying astronomy and mathematics. By age twenty he had fine-tuned two-hundred-year-old calculations on the orbit of Halley's comet and shown them to noted astronomer Heinrich Olbers. An astonished Olbers persuaded Bessel to become a professional astronomer. Olbers called this his greatest contribution to astronomy. **5,820**

751 JEAN NIDETCH (b. 1923)
weight watcher

Here's another success story: Jean Nidetch lost seventy-two pounds and kept them off. She also spawned a $30 billion-a-year industry when, as a dumpy thirty-eight-year-old housewife, she gathered six fat friends in her Queens, New York, apartment for a weekly weigh-in and moral support session. The year was 1963; iceberg lettuce and tuna fish were about the only diet products; and dieters were supposed to stop eating anything that tasted good. Nidetch used the common sense diet that was given away free by the New York Department of Health. She dubbed her group Weight Watchers and began charging two dollars a week for members. Imitators sprang up, but none were quite as successful as the original. Nidetch sold the company to Heinz in 1978. With more than one million members, Weight Watchers lends its name to a monthly magazine and dozens of diet foods that not only promote weight loss but actually taste good. **5,817**

752 ALBERT CAMUS (1913–1960)
writer for a disillusioned century

If the people of the year 3000 want to understand the state of humanity in the twentieth century, they will need but three novels, all by Camus: *The Stranger, The Plague,* and *The Fall.* The central characters in these books—a murderer, a doctor, and a self-loathing lawyer—dramatize the absurdity of life and the redemption achieved by confronting that absurdity. Camus was an editor of *Combat,* the voice of French resistance in World War II, and a leader of the postwar literati of Paris. Leftist existentialist gadfly Jean-Paul Sartre was his best pal until 1952, when Sartre denounced Camus for being an anti-Communist and worse: an optimist. But when Camus was killed in a car crash, Sartre wrote, "His stubborn humanism, strict and pure, austere and sensual, delivered uncertain combat against the massive and deformed events of the day." **5,815**

753 JUAN PERÓN (1895–1974)
Don't cry for Juan, Argentina

"If Argentina were an orange, Peron would be the juice," the saying went, and decades later many Argentines defined themselves by their attitude toward the founder of the populist *Peronista* movement. President of South America's second-most-populous country from 1946 to 1955 and again in 1973–74, Peron was actually a right-wing dictator. He set himself up as the defender of the poor workers he called the "shirtless ones," advocated state intervention in the economy, tweaked Uncle Sam's nose, and admired Mussolini (460) and Hitler (20) as strong leaders. He himself was a softie, an animal lover with "penguin arms" who had a weakness for teenage girls. He derived his political strength from the bed-hopping babe who seduced first him, then Argentina—Eva Duarte, the *Evita* of Andrew Lloyd Webber's fantasies. **5,800**

754 STEPHEN CRANE (1871–1900)
writer of uncompromising realism

Crane's early death from tuberculosis silenced a powerful literary voice whose novel, *The Red*

Badge of Courage, has become an American classic. Written when Crane was only twenty-five, it was, he said, "a psychological portrayal of fear" set against the Civil War. "This young man has the power to feel," said writer Ambrose Bierce. "He knows nothing of war, yet he is drenched in blood." Crane later witnessed the horrors of battle as a journalist reporting on the Spanish-American War in 1898. Earlier, his assignment to cover the Cuban insurrection in 1896 left him shipwrecked off Florida, adrift for thirty hours. That adventure produced "The Open Boat," a short story masterpiece. Critics couldn't pigeon-hole Crane, labeling him an impressionist, decadent, realist, naturalist, even romantic. He said he was merely a "true artist" who "leaves pictures of his own time as they appear to him." **5,799**

755 MARY CASSATT (1845–1926)
the impressionist from Pittsburgh

She's the Rodney Dangerfield of the art world—Mary Cassatt gets no respect. Perhaps this is because she was the only American in her impressionist group; perhaps because she was struggling in a man's world; perhaps because she favored maternal subjects. No matter. We include Cassatt for just those reasons, and one more: she financially backed the only art dealer willing to sell the French impressionists' work and steered rich American buyers to him. Despite her father's objection that "I would rather see you dead," Cassatt became an artist. Childless, she often chose feminine and domestic subjects in contrast to the landscape and urban scenes her colleagues favored. Cassatt drew inspiration from her platonic relationship with the confirmed misogynist Edgar Degas (482). When he saw prints Cassatt had completed for her first solo exhibition, Degas commented: "I am not willing to admit that a woman can draw that well." **5,790**

756 ROBERT LOUIS STEVENSON
(1850–1894) *writer of tales kids love*

After Scottish novelist Stevenson died in his home in Western Samoa, literary critics dismissed his books as adventure tales lacking literary merit. Maybe so, but a century later the world reads *Kidnapped, Treasure Island, The Master of Ballantrae, A Child's Garden of Verses,* and *The Strange Case of Dr. Jekyll and Mr. Hyde,* the book that made Stevenson famous in 1886. He may have been on cocaine when he wrote it. Stevenson burned the first draft because the sexual imagery was too strong for his wife Fanny, a crabby bourgeois American ten years his senior. He suffered from tuberculosis, and the adulation of the masses failed to dispel his gloom because he wanted to be considered a serious writer, like Herman Melville (716). "There must be something wrong in me or I would not be popular," he lamented to a friend. **5,777**

757 TULSIDAS (1532–1624)
messenger of universal love

His monumental *Sacred Lake of the Deeds of Rama* has had an enduring impact on Hindu culture. Mohandas Gandhi, for one, devoured its ideals. Little is known of Tulsidas's life, save that his parents abandoned him as a child because he was born under an "unlucky star," but his epic is filled with the power of religious passion. He taught a doctrine not unlike Christianity: God, or Rama, is a benevolent father, and all men and women are brothers and sisters. In one psalm to Rama, he writes: "Those who consider other men's women as mothers and others' wealth as more poisonous than poison, those who rejoice to see others flourish and are acutely pained to see them afflicted, those to whom Thou art dearer than life, in their minds is Thy blessed abode." **5,768**

758 **SAMUEL PEPYS** (1633–1703)
recorder of life's tumult and tedium

Pepys's disarmingly candid writings of public and private affairs capture life in Restoration England, making his eleven-volume diary the most famous literary journal in world history. Industrious Pepys rose from tailor's son to secretary of the admiralty. For nine years he kept a diary affording an insider's view of ordinary and extraordinary events. We are there as Pepys witnesses the Great Fire of London in 1666: "It made me weep to see it," he wrote. "The churches, houses and all on fire and flaming at once, and a horrid noise the flames made." In June 1665 Pepys watched thousands flee the plague. "By water to Whitehall, where the Court full of waggons and people ready to go out of town. The Mortality Bill is come to 267." Pepys "turns his head to us across the centuries," wrote biographer Richard Ollard, "and addresses us as though we were across the room." **5,730**

759 **ELIZABETH BARRETT BROWNING**
(1806–1861) *love poet*

How do we love her? Let us count the ways. We love her for the depth and breadth and height of her *Sonnets from the Portuguese,* the most popular collection of love poems in English. That slim volume of fourteen-liners found inspiration from her own touching love story. Elizabeth Barrett, a frail invalid, became a celebrity with publication of her first book, *Poems,* in 1838. Poet Robert Browning (608) liked it so much that he struck up a correspondence. Love blossomed. Their courtship, despite her father's objections to the poor, younger Robert, inspired Elizabeth's most compelling work. Browning called her his "little Portuguese," and *Sonnets,* published in 1850, was dedicated to him. Elizabeth, considered during their lifetimes the more talented poet of the pair, has lost stature because of her sometimes-schmaltzy sentimentality. Her vow to Robert, for example: "If God choose, I shall but love thee better after death." **5,725**

760 **GEORGE ORWELL** (1903–1950)
Big Brother's biographer

Two of Orwell's frightening but entertaining novels have taught the dangers of propaganda and other forms of dictatorial mind control. In *Animal Farm* a group of Bolshevik-style pigs captures a farm. In *1984* the state is controlled by an anonymous, all-knowing Big Brother. Orwell abandoned a career as a policeman for the iffy business of literature, and his first book, *Down and Out in Paris and London,* was rejected by one publisher on the advice of poet and critic T. S. Eliot (720). *Homage to Catalonia,* a memoir of Orwell's months as an antifascist soldier in the Spanish Civil War, is one of the best war books of the twentieth century. Orwell believed that democracy was fragile, even in England, though he said that totalitarianism could never flourish in a country devoted to cricket. **5,684**

761 **JEAN-BERNARD-LÉON FOUCAULT**
(1819–1868) *scientific swinger*

Foucault was a French inventor who proved that the earth rotates. We like him because of the utter simplicity of the pendulum he created to establish a law of physics. In 1851 he suspended a sixty-two-pound ball on a 220-foot steel wire from the dome of the Pantheon in Paris. The ball swung back and forth, the plane of its motion unchanging with reference to the stars but shifting against the rotating planet below. Apparently Foucault's pendulum, which is still swinging at the Conservatoire des Arts et Métiers in Paris, exerts a hypnotic fascination on viewers; a character in the novel *Foucault's Pendulum* by the Italian writer Umberto Eco says, "You feel a very strong sensation—the idea that everything else is in motion and up above is the only fixed point in the universe." Foucault also helped develop a technique for measuring the speed of light, but it was his pendulum that earned him his scientific stature.   **5,682**

762 JAMES MCNEILL WHISTLER (1834– 1903) *artist son of a famous mother*

Whistler, a proponent of art for art's sake, defined the role of artist in modern society by rejecting Victorian admonitions that art should convey a moral message. "Art should be independent of all clap-trap—should stand alone, and appeal to the artistic eye or ear," Whistler declared. He produced striking portraits, paintings of nighttime London, masterful pastels, brilliant etchings, and lithographs. His most famous portrait, *Arrangement in Gray and Black,* is known as *Whistler's Mother.* The artist posed his mother standing, but she flagged and flopped in a chair. American-born Whistler studied painting in Paris, then moved to London. He cultivated an eccentric image but took his work seriously. When a review of *Nocturne in Black and Gold: the Falling Rocket,* blasted Whistler for "flinging a pot of paint in the public's face," he sued and won the celebrated case. But the damages were so paltry, Whistler had to declare bankruptcy. **5,678**

763 JOHN HARVARD (1607–1638) *college benefactor*

Harvard, the son of a London butcher and member of the Massachusetts Bay Colony, was a Cambridge man with a firm commitment to education. Thus, when he died at age thirty-one, Harvard bequeathed half his estate—a whopping £780—and his library of 320 books to the fledgling college, then two years old and struggling. Harvard College, the first in the colonies but the fourth in the New World, had a rocky

start. The first headmaster was dragged into court for beating students and subordinates, and his wife confessed to serving them "ungutted mackerel" and failing to supply them with enough beer. As we enter the next millennium, Harvard is the United States' most prestigious university and counts among its graduates U.S. presidents and a host of other global movers and shakers. Today it is one of the world's best-endowed colleges, and its library collection numbers more than eight million volumes.   **5,670**

764 WILLIAM S. GILBERT (1836–1911) *Victorian satirist*

Arthur Sullivan wrote the music. But the brilliance of Gilbert and Sullivan's comic operettas is in Gilbert's satirical thrusts at stuffy conventions, his silly rhymes, and his madcap staging, starting with their first show, *Thespis,* in 1871. That show, *H.M.S. Pinafore, The Pirates of Penzance, The Mikado,* and ten other collaborations set the tone for all subsequent musical comedy. Gilbert was a master of the one-liner; he invented the joke, "Call me a cab"; "Yes sir, you're a cab." When an ample ingenue sat down during a rehearsal, Gilbert declared, "I always knew you'd make an impression on the stage." He drowned in a lake at age seventy-five while trying to aid a girl struggling in deep water. To highbrows who scoff, we say of Gilbert what he said in *Patience* about aesthetes like Oscar Wilde (574); "Though the Philistines may jostle, you will rank as an apostle."   **5,661**

765 HERBERT OF CHERBURY (1583–1648) *godfather of deism*

Never heard of him? Well, this English courtier's challenge to religious orthodoxy echoes through the centuries, even into many churches and synagogues of modern America. Unlike Calvin (69) and Luther (3), Herbert wasn't trying to reform organized Christianity in his writings; he was blasting away at its foundations. Caught up in the rationalist ferment inspired by Bacon (84) and Descartes (25), he rejected divine revelation and said reason was the only sure path to truth. He believed in God and asserted that religious impulses were implanted in man by God, but otherwise, he decided, God just sort of sat back and watched his creation unfold. Herbert's concept of God as a passive observer of human affairs spread, and several of America's founding fathers, including Benjamin Franklin (54) and Thomas Jefferson (64), essentially embraced deism.   **5,656**

766 MUDDY WATERS (1915–1983)
he had a right to sing the blues

Born McKinley Morganfield, he earned his childhood nickname because he liked to play in the Mississippi River's muck. Muddy Waters's influence in bringing the blues, once the exclusive domain of black musicians, into music's mainstream is incalculable. When his band booked gigs in noisy Chicago nightclubs, he turned up the volume by switching to an electric guitar. His mournful laments, such as "Got My Mojo Workin'" and "Hoochie Coochie Man," introduced blues to Carnegie Hall in the 1950s. A successful appearance at the Newport Folk Festival in 1960 again drew applause from white audiences. Later in his career he fretted that blacks were turning away from the blues "because the blues recalls hard times, when you was struggling to make a living." Dubbing music his "religion," Muddy Waters set the beat for generations of musicians, including legends Bob Dylan (888) and the Rolling Stones.   **5,640**

767 IZAAK WALTON (1593–1683)
nature boy

Walton's *The Compleat Angler* is more than a book about fishing. It is the most enduring how-

to book of the millennium, and it exhorts us to love things that "nature utters in her rural shrine," as William Wordsworth (577) wrote in a poem praising Walton. Walton was an ironmonger-turned-church-deacon and biographer of friends such as John Donne (280), but his true love was sitting by a stream and catching trout, perch, pike, salmon, or carp. He recommended the right frogs to use as bait (yellow ones) and commended the eating of grayling (mixed with honey, it would cure swarthiness). He warned that no dull man could be taught the art of fly-tying. Some men loved hawking, hunting, tennis, and mistresses, he conceded, "But these delights I neither wish / Nor envy, while I freely fish."   **5,620**

768 DANIEL EDGAR SICKLES (1825–1914)
first killer to win freedom through a plea of temporary insanity

In 1859 Sickles shot his wife's lover to death. In those days, murderers got the noose. What to do? "The Devil made me do it," Sickles claimed, and the jury bought the argument. Sickles led an eventful life, helping create Manhattan's Central Park, losing a leg in the Civil War, botching a job as a military governor in the Reconstruction South, and seducing the queen of Spain as ambassador to Madrid. But it was his trailblazing acquittal that earned him a place in judicial history and in the hearts of evildoers everywhere. As we write this, the lawyer for a teacher who killed and ate a student was petitioning for his client's release because "he is now able to handle stress successfully." Which just goes to show that the temporary insanity plea is, well, ins-a-a-n-e.   **5,616**

769 BUCKMINSTER FULLER (1895–1983)
dome designer

Fuller's geodesic dome, the strongest, most cost-effective structure ever invented, can be erected swiftly and airlifted to sites. It symbolizes architect and engineer Fuller's global approach to solving housing problems by doing more with less. A navy flyer during World War I, he lived with his family on base. After his daughter died from a series of illnesses, Fuller blamed the inadequate housing. That tragedy, compounded by business failure, pushed him close to suicide. Instead, he spent two years in silence, contemplating life. He emerged with his unique vision of world peace obtainable only through comprehensive housing design. If everyone could share in the earth's bounty, Fuller theorized, war would be unnecessary. He attracted a cult following, and his futuristic domes were erected on selective sites throughout the world. "I just invent," he said. "Then I wait until man comes around to needing what I've invented." Fuller gets our kudos as a forward thinker for the third millennium. **5,600**

770 CHARLES FREDERICK WORTH (1825–1895) *fashioner of haute couture*

Sure, Worth was a genius for design (after all, he invented the bustle), and he certainly had an eye for fabric, but let's give credit where credit is due. His best client, Empress Eugénie, discarded dresses after only one wearing, in keeping with the etiquette of aristocratic women in France's Second Empire. They changed clothes twice a day. Worth, an Englishman who arrived in Paris at age twenty and worked his way up to ownership of a shop on the Rue de la Paix, charged the equivalent of about $64 for his simplest dress. Eugénie helped the House of Worth's reputation by routinely passing her hours-old dresses to her attendants, who in turn sold them to Paris's elite partiers. Of course, mass circulation of trendy fashion magazines also fueled the fire for French fashion on both sides of the Atlantic. **5,585**

771 OU-YANG HSIU (1007–1072) *Confucian reformer and poet*

China's Sung period, 960–1279, was a time of intellectual and political flowering. Next to the great Chu Hsi (93), the brightest bud was a member of the ruling oligarchy, Ou-yang Hsiu. He reformed the bureaucracy, helped bring Confucianism—the religion of tradition—back to power over Buddhism, and wrote poetry that sings, even in translation. His description of a cicada: "Here was a thing that cried / Upon a treetop, sucking the shrill wind / To wail it back in a long whistling note." He was famous early in his career for railing against incompetent, nepotistic public officials and equally famous late in life for saying radical reformers had gone too far. Ou-yang Hsiu certainly was no democrat. In 1055 he recommended that books by commoners critical of the government should be burned. **5,572**

772 MOTHER TERESA (1910–1997) *Heaven-sent do-gooder*

The daughter of an Albanian grocer, Mother Teresa founded the order of the Missionaries of Charity in Calcutta in 1948 and later established a home for the dying in the city's slums. By 1997 the order was active in one hundred countries, including the United States. Mother Teresa traveled widely, opening a soup kitchen in the Bronx, bullying the pope into installing a shelter inside the Vatican, and helping evacuate mentally ill children from the fighting in Beirut in the 1980s. "We didn't expect a saint to be so efficient," exclaimed a Red Cross official. Her defense of Roman Catholic beliefs inspired loathing in some quarters. One screed asserted she was an evil old woman. Somehow, though, we find it hard to imagine the five-foot nun, dressed in her white sari and sandals and praying,

"Let us thank God for our people, the poor people," consorting with the devil. **5,509**

773 MORDECAI ANIELEWICZ (1919–1943)
hero of the condemned

Anielewicz and his forces battled to the death rather than submit to extermination in Hitler's ovens. Their courage during the Warsaw ghetto uprising of World War II marked an end to European Jewry's passivity to oppression. When the Germans occupied Warsaw, they sealed off the Jewish quarter and imprisoned 400,000 there. Mass deportations and executions over nearly four years shrank those numbers to about 60,000. In April 1943 Nazis thought they could annihilate the rest in a three-day assault. But Commander Anielewicz and the Jewish Fighting Organization battled from bunkers for over a month before they were silenced. "What has happened has exceeded our dreams," Anielewicz wrote shortly before his death. "Jewish armed resistance and the retaliation have become a reality." Dylan Thomas urged his dying father, in a poem, "Do not go gentle into that good night." Anielewicz didn't. **5,498**

774 TONI MORRISON (b. 1931)
"Beloved" African-American author

When Morrison won the Nobel Prize for literature in 1993, some critics described her as the greatest living American author. Not everyone was enthusiastic. Columnist Edwin Yoder, for example, called her "an eccentric selection." He conceded, however, that he'd never read her novels. Morrison, the first African-American to win literature's top prize, gave literary voice to the black experience. Her first novel, *The Bluest Eye,* published in 1970, blasted prejudice and stereotypes through the story of a poor black woman who wishes for white people's eyes. *The Song of Solomon,* which appeared in 1977, celebrated the tradition of story-telling in black culture. "Parents don't sit around and tell their children those classical, mythological archetypal stories that we heard years ago," she lamented. Morrison predicted wrongly that no one would read her novel about the slave experience, *Beloved.* It became her most popular book and won the Pulitzer Prize in 1988. **5,492**

775 ANDREI SAKHAROV (1921–1989)
bomb-maker turned peacenik

We could argue that the cold war ended on December 16, 1986, when Soviet president Mikhail Gorbachev (237) telephoned Sakharov to announce the release of an army of political prisoners. Centuries of Russian oppression were soon over. Protected from the gulag because he was a national hero—he had built the first Soviet H-bomb in 1953—Sakharov spent two decades pushing for peace with the West and human rights at home. The work won him the Nobel Peace Prize in 1975. Harassment by the secret police, the loss of his job as a physicist, internal exile in the city of Gorky for nine years, and forced feedings during a hunger strike did not deter him. His heroism was a rallying point for those who helped topple the Soviet Union from within. **5,491**

776 HEINRICH SCHLIEMANN (1822–1890)
excavator of Homer's Troy

A flamboyant German-born American who married a Greek schoolgirl at the age of forty-seven, Schliemann made a fortune trading indigo in Russia and gold dust in San Francisco before turning his attention full time to archaeology. As the world watched enthralled, he directed a massive dig at Hisarlik, in present-day western Turkey, that culminated in the 1873 discovery of the "Treasury of Priam," the king in the Homeric epic, and other Trojan remains. A few years later, he unearthed the "Mask of Agamemnon," the death mask of the king who led the Greeks against Troy, in the Bronze Age city of Mycenae. Despite accusations that have dogged his reputation to this day of fabricating some of his evidence, Schliemann was a giant of archaeology and the first great popularizer of his field. **5,474**

777 BARTHOLD GEORG NIEBUHR
(1776–1831) *historiography's hero*

The German historian's method of analyzing ancient texts to extract facts from the tapestry of truth, myth, and fabrication, a talent he displayed in his three-volume history of Rome, opened a new chapter in Western scholarship. Niebuhr inherited his obsession with accurate detail from his father, the explorer Carsten Niebuhr. "When we read Caesar, he would spread out D'Anville's map of ancient Gaul on the table, and I had to find every place," Barthold recalled. At age ten he wrote a history of Africa and at sixteen dazzled a local poet as a "miracle of knowledge and intellectual maturity." The German scholar Theodor Mommsen said all historians worthy of the name are Niebuhr's pupils. Niebuhr himself proclaimed, "In laying down the pen, we must be able to say in the sight of God, 'I have not knowingly nor without earnest investigation written anything which is not true.'" **5,465**

778 EUCLIDES DA CUNHA (1866–1909)
writing rebel of the backwoods

Cunha's book, *Rebellion in the Backlands,* was the first literary protest against Brazil's injustices to the rural poor. To commemorate his effort, Brazilians honor his memory with a week-long observance every August. Journalist Cunha wrote a compelling eyewitness account of the War of Canudos, which pitted federal forces against cult leader Antonio Conselheiro and his farm-worker followers in Canudos, a backwoods village they called their "empire." Beginning in 1896, wave after wave of ever-strengthening military muscle failed to suppress these monarchist rebels who refused to recognize the authority of their state government and were labeled heretics by the Catholic Church. Finally the minister of war waged a full-scale military assault with an artillery bombardment that decimated the settlement and massacred everyone. Cunha's book pleaded for a government commitment to bring people of mixed race into the cultural mainstream. **5,460**

779 EMILY POST (1872–1960)
etiquette's expert

She minded your manners. During World War II people stole Post's *Etiquette* book from libraries the way they take Bibles from hotel rooms. Sales soared after war correspondent Ernie Pyle reported that her book was, in fact, the bible of army officer training schools. *Etiquette,* which sold more than a million copies in her lifetime and remains on library shelves, doled out Post's down-to-earth advice, tempered by her wit, on everything from a presidential visit to a whirlwind wartime wedding. Post, a magazine writer, wrote the book at the behest of her editor. After publication of the first edition of *Etiquette* in 1922, Post became a syndicated columnist and radio host. She cautioned girls against frequenting cabarets, warned everyone but Fred Astaire away from dapper walking sticks, and reminded readers that the best manners "do not suggest 'manner' at all." **5,403**

780 FERNÃO LOPES (c.1380–c.1460)[1]

Lopes had an idea that was unusual for his time: He based his history books on documents and evidence instead of hearsay. He was Portugal's royal

---

1. *father of the footnote*

archivist in 1434 when King John I asked him to chronicle the previous reigns, starting in the 1380s. Lopes took his information from state papers and moldy records in monasteries. Before he wrote about wars, he walked the battlefields. When he disagreed with a previous writer's slant, he said why and quoted from long passages of primary sources to make his case. And in his writing of his *Chronicles of Pedro, Ferdinand, and John I,* the humbly born Lopes eschewed the overblown flattery of kings that make other medieval historians' objectivity suspect. We won't violate Lopes's principles and write about his early life and death; there's no information on that in any archive. **5,396**

781 MARIE-ANTOINETTE (1755–1793)
French queen who lost her head

It took the impotent Louis XVI seven years to consummate his marriage to his Austrian-born queen, Marie-Antoinette. What's a lonely wife to do? Decorate. The money for the garden at the Petit Trianon palace near Versailles could have fed a hundred thousand peasants for a year, and she also spent lavishly on parties, concerts, and dressing up. There's no evidence that she ever said "Let them eat cake" when she heard of a shortage of bread. But her spendthrift ways inflamed the masses against the very notion of royalty, and helped intensify the French Revolution. She and her husband were so accustomed to free spending, they set aside the equivalent of $2 million for an ostentatious flight from revolutionary Paris when they should have slipped to safety quietly. They were caught, and when it was her turn to face the guillotine, she did so without tears, like a true queen. **5,347**

782 TOUSSAINT-L'OUVERTURE (1743–1803)
Haiti's opening to independence

François-Dominique Toussaint, the son of an African king, led the Haitian independence movement during the French Revolution, freed the slaves, and established a black-ruled French protectorate. He took the name L'Ouverture, French for "opening," from a remark by a French official that, in attacking enemy lines during his conquest of Haiti, "this man finds an opening everywhere." Under him Haiti prospered, and the United States was sufficiently alarmed to bribe him not to invade the American South. France's Napoleon (16), calling Toussaint "that miserable Negro," ordered the recapture of the former colony in 1802. The following year Toussaint was imprisoned in the French Alps. A fighter to the end, he castigated his jailers for taking his watch and money and demanded their return "to my wife and children on the day I am executed." The year after his death Haiti became the second independent nation in the Americas, after the United States. **5,338**

783 ALEXANDER CALDER (1898–1976)
artist with the right moves

Calder launched the art movement known as kinetic sculpture by inventing the mobile, an abstract design of metal, steel rods, and wood, moved by motors, wind, or water. Son and grandson of illustrious sculptors, Calder first opted for mechanical engineering. Then he saw painter Piet Mondrian's (797) Paris studio with its colored rectangles of paper pasted on the walls and thought it might be fun to make those rectangles move. Hello, mobile. Calder's largest creation soars 140 feet at the Federal Reserve Bank in Philadelphia. His reputation soared, too, after his Museum of Modern Art exhibit in 1943. Artist Fernand Léger ranked this burly American among "those incontestable masters of an inexpressive and silent beauty." Calder's sister, Margaret Hayes, said he refused to have anything in his home—whether pots and pans or staircase steps—that wasn't well designed. That's because, Calder explained, "bad taste boomerangs." **5,304**

784 LOUISE BROWN (b. 1978)
baby in a bottle

She made a spectacular splash even before her birth. George Orwell meets Dr. Spock. Her conception in a test tube—actually, a petri dish—and her birth in Great Britain gave birth to futuristic treatments for infertility. While in vitro fertilization remains a last-ditch and costly procedure, more than 100,000 babies have been born through the technology begun by Robert Edwards and Patrick Steptoe. They were a team: Edwards, the obstetrician who wanted to help infertile couples, and Steptoe, the researcher fascinated with the mechanisms of conception. Brown was the fruit of their labor. Oh, yes, she's the biological daughter of John and Lesley Brown. But in a very special way she was fathered by Edwards and Steptoe. After Brown completed her schooling, she went to work, appropriately, we think, at a day-care center. We recognize Edwards and Steptoe for their breakthrough in the treatment of infertility, but unable to choose between them, we give the nod to the baby they (and the Browns) produced. **5,292**

785 JACKSON POLLOCK (1912–1956)
Jack the dripper

Realist painter Thomas Hart Benton said of his pupil, "Pollock was a born artist. All I ever taught him was how to drink a fifth a day." He became the general public's best-known master of abstract expressionism—the dominant painting style of the twentieth century—by making the dripping of paint on canvas a signature technique. At his first show of splatter paintings in 1948, he sold only one, for $150. He became famous a year later when *Life* magazine asked in a headline, "Is He the Greatest Living Painter in America?" Art critic Clement Greenberg suggested he was, though a museum curator spoke for many people when he said of Pollock's work: "I suspect any picture I think I could have made myself." Two years before he killed himself driving drunk, Pollock sold his painting *Blue Poles* for $6,000. It was resold for $2 million in 1973. **5,218**

786 GEORGE FOX (1624–1691)
the first Quaker

At first we thought Fox might be a stretch for our list. After all, the English sect he founded counts only 200,000 adherents worldwide. But then we reviewed the causes Quakers have championed—the abolition of slavery, women's rights, prison reform, nonviolence—and that was all the Friendly persuasion we needed. Fox preached that an inner light from Christ takes precedence over church creed. He likewise loathed official oaths and titles. His group, the Society of Friends, was nicknamed the Quakers because he once admonished a judge to "tremble at the name of the Lord." The pacifist Fox told one follower, William Penn, the son of a British admiral and the founder of Pennsylvania, "Wear thy sword as long as thou canst." Weeks later, he asked, "Where is thy sword?" Penn replied, "I wore it as long as I could." **5,197**

787 JONATHAN EDWARDS (1703–1758)
preacher of an angry god

He was the foremost theologian of Puritanism in America. In his writings Edwards tried to resurrect the zealous spirit of Puritan forefathers. In 1741 congregants in Enfield, Connecticut, shrieked for salvation as Edwards delivered his now-famous sermon "Sinners in the Hands of an Angry God." He warned, "The God that holds you over the pit of hell, much as one holds a spider, or some loathsome insect over the fire, abhors you, and is dreadfully provoked . . . and yet it is nothing but his hand that holds you from falling into the fire every moment." Edwards launched a religious revival that spread along the Connecticut River valley in 1734. And this helped spark the Great Awakening, a massive spiritual frenzy from Massachusetts to Georgia. Although his image is that of a fire-breathing evangelist, Edwards also was a respected scholar and prodigious writer. On strolls through meadows he was even known to burst into song, delighted at God's creation. **5,169**

788 WERNER FORSSMANN (1904–1979)
invader of the human heart

When the chief of surgery at a clinic near Berlin refused to let Forssmann attempt a catheterization of a patient's heart, Forssmann did the next best thing: He catheterized himself. In a daring experiment in 1929, Forssmann enlisted the help of a nurse who held a mirror for him as he inserted an oiled tube that was normally used for bladders into his arm. The nurse then helped him walk upstairs to the X-ray department, where he tracked the tube by fluoroscope. After Forssmann's paper on his experiments was published, some researchers called him a charlatan and he lost his job. Forssmann, who abandoned cardiac research and became a urologist, was vindicated in 1956 when he shared the Nobel Prize with two other surgeons who pioneered catheter technology. Today doctors use cardiac catheterization and its stepchild, angioplasty, as a routine procedure that allows them to diagnose and treat heart ailments. **5,155**

789 ROBERT BADEN-POWELL (1856–1941)
founder of scouting

He made his fame as the general who led the heroic British stand at Mafeking in the Boer War and created the Boy Scouts in 1907 to teach kids to be as brave and resourceful as the men he had commanded in battle. Boys occupied with outdoor pursuits and community service, he reasoned, would learn self-reliance and be too busy to engage in bad habits like cursing, smoking, gambling, and masturbation. He also founded the Girl Guides, the model for the Girl Scouts. Recent biographers have noted that Baden-Powell enjoyed watching naked boys bathe and developed excruciating headaches after marriage, at age fifty-six, to a woman thirty years younger. But we have no interest in outing this outdoorsman. What counts are Baden-Powell and scouting's influence in teaching millions of kids to appreciate good deeds and the glories of nature in the increasingly mechanistic and urban twentieth century. **5,104**

790 ROBERT THE BRUCE (1274–1329)
liberator of Scotland

Bruce's rebellion against the immense power of the English throne has been called one of history's greatest heroic enterprises. On the run after crowning himself Scottish king in 1306, Bruce supposedly hid in a cave and watched a spider failing time and again to secure his web but never giving up until he succeeded. Drawing inspiration from the arachnid's adamancy, Bruce went forth to engage the oppressor. When an enemy knight charged him with his lance but "myssit the nobill kyng," in the words of a contemporary, Bruce swung down his ax with such force that he split his poor adversary's head in two. He could also be kind, once halting his army to comfort a washerwoman in labor. He gained Scottish independence by demolishing Edward II's forces in the Battle of Bannockburn in 1314. To our mind, that makes him a good auld boy. **5,091**

791 INDIRA GANDHI (1917–1984)
*Indian prime minister
with mass appeal*

Gandhi, daughter of Jawaharlal Nehru (222), dominated India's political scene for two decades. Prime minister for four terms, she was a steely ruler who inspired either hate or adoration. On her watch India won its war with Pakistan in 1971, resulting in the creation of India-friendly Bangladesh. When accused of election violations, Gandhi declared a state of emergency, imprisoned opponents, and suspended democracy for nineteen months. But the crowds forgave her. India's poor and downtrodden loved her, believing she understood their plight. Domestically Gandhi continually battled threats to national unity. An army attack on the Sikhs' holiest shrine—where separatists were storing ammunition—killed 492 Sikhs in June 1984. Five months later, Gandhi was shot to death by bodyguards who were Sikh extremists. In her will she avowed: "No hate is dark enough to overshadow the extent of my love for my people and my country." **5,048**

792 PETER CARL FABERGÉ (1846–1920)
eggstraordinary jeweler

He learned the jeweler's craft in Italy, Germany, and France, and the family business he headed in St. Petersburg in 1870 created some of the most beautiful objects of the millennium. His best baubles were made for the Russian royal family every Easter from 1885 to 1917. The gem-encrusted "eggs" had surprises inside; the 1897 egg hid a miniature gold replica of the coach that Czar Nicholas II rode to his coronation. Rothschilds, Texas millionaires, and the king of Siam bought Fabergé's jewelry, silverware, stone miniatures, bejeweled clocks and picture frames, onyx and nephrite figurines, and lifelike flowers carved from colored stones. "Fabergé is the greatest genius of our time," the czar's mother wrote in 1914. World War I and the Russian Revolution destroyed Fabergé's business, but his trade name, purchased by a company known mostly for perfume, still connotes elegance. **5,033**

793 CYRUS McCORMICK (1809–1884)
the reaper's keeper

McCormick was the inventor of the mechanical reaper. His earliest reaper cut as much grain as twenty-four laborers with sickles. Inadvertently it aided the Union cause in the Civil War. With his machines harvesting wheat, thousands of men could be freed to beef up Northern forces, a factor credited with securing Union victory over the smaller Southern army. But McCormick never set out to change history. He was just an entrepreneur who knew a good invention when he saw it. Never mind that his reaper was patented six months after Obed Hussey's; McCormick had the savvy to corner the market. He also loved a good fight. In 1862 he sued the Pennsylvania Railroad when family luggage was misrouted and destroyed. He won, but the railroad appealed. The case ricocheted to the Supreme Court five times. Finally the court ordered the railroad to pay up. It did, with interest. By then McCormick was dead. **4,981**

794 JULIUS II (1443–1513)
papal patron of the arts

The Italian Giuliano della Rovere sought magnificence for the papacy and, to that end, commissioned sublime works by Bramante (258), Raphael (129), and Michelangelo (13). Raphael painted frescoes for Julius in the Vatican. Bramante was chosen to design a new basilica for St. Peter's in Rome. Michelangelo's assignment was to paint the ceiling of the Sistine Chapel, a feat he accomplished over four years with the close supervision and friendship of Julius. As the project wore on, the impatient Julius threatened Michelangelo that if he didn't finish soon, he'd have him thrown off his scaffolding. Michelangelo recognized a real warning from Julius when he heard it and worked at double speed. For all of Julius's artistic refinement, he lacked the priestly virtues. As cardinal, he fathered three illegitimate daughters. Also, he became pope by buying the office in 1503, then immediately decreed that such purchasing practices were banned. **4,974**

795 CHARLIE CHAPLIN (1889–1977)
silent star

In 1914, during a lull in filming for *Mabel's Strange Predicament,* Chaplin entertained his fellow actors by pasting on a paper moustache and doing antics with a cane and derby. "Put that in the picture," director Mack Sennett suggested. So was born the Little Tramp, the character whose popularity did much to launch movies—particularly Hollywood movies—as the transcendent form of international popular culture of the twentieth century. Chaplin, Douglas Fairbanks, and Mary Pickford (962) were the royalty of Hollywood between the world wars, but Chaplin had a flaw: a lust for teenage girls, three of whom he married, including playwright Eugene O'Neill's (426) daughter Oona. Chaplin had retained British citizenship, and in 1952 he was driven from the United States by tax trouble, publicity about his morals, and his refusal to shun Communist friends. He settled in Switzerland and in death is a star subject in the study of film as art. **4,963**

796 THOMAS BABINGTON MACAULEY
(1800–1859) *peddler of progress*

He was a reform politician and wrote colonial India's penal code, but Macauley the history maker was dwarfed by Macauley the history writer. As the first great practitioner of narrative social history, the Englishman is the author most closely associated with the idea—exposed in the twentieth century as wishful thinking—that history is the story of mankind's march from ferocity to humanity, from ignorance to light, from tyranny to democracy. In his 1828 essay "History," Macauley called for stirring factual accounts of the "noiseless revolutions" of the common people that made positive changes occur. Just such a book was his 1848 *History of England from the Accession of James II,* an account of the Glorious Revolution of the seventeenth century. The book sold three thousand copies in its first ten days of publication and was read as avidly as books by Walter Scott (357) and Charles Dickens (70). **4,962**

797 PIET MONDRIAN (1872–1944)
new Dutch master

Nobody would confuse Mondrian's paintings of straight lines and rectangles with works by anyone else, and his style influenced the movement toward minimalism in architecture and fashion in the mid-twentieth century. First he painted bad imitations—a *faux* Pierre Renoir (384) here, a mock Dante Rossetti there—but he produced his first work in his mature style in 1916 and rarely painted a curved line or a representational form after that. A solitary bachelor, he spent a lot of time sitting and thinking in rooms as spare as his paintings. The Nazis enhanced Mondrian's reputation by including two of his paintings in their 1937 exhibition of what they believed to be execrably decadent art, and when war came, he fled to New York City. At a 1943 exhibit there he said a work by then-unknown Jackson Pollock (785) was the best painting he had seen in years. **4,961**

798 DAVID BUSHNELL (1742–1824)
builder of the first fighting submarine

Bushnell constructed the *Turtle,* an egg-shaped vessel of wood reinforced with iron hoops. This one-man propeller-operated sub could plunge twenty feet and remain submerged for thirty minutes. In 1776 rebels sent the *Turtle* in an unsuccessful foray against the British fleet blockading New York Harbor. *Turtle's* pioneering work didn't save that day, but it led to years of experimentation and refinement. By World War I the Germans were using submarines, called U-boats, to torpedo Allied ships. During World War II both sides had submarines prowling the depths. Today supersubs carry atomic missiles. While use of submarines for ocean exploration is increasing, they largely remain machines of destruction. Renaissance visionary Leonardo da Vinci (9) feared as much. He wouldn't show anyone his designs for a submersible craft "on account of the evil nature of men," he said, "who would practice assassination at the bottom of the sea." **4,905**

799 THOMAS HUXLEY (1825–1895)
Darwin's bulldog

Fearing ridicule when he wrote *The Origin of Species* in 1859, Charles Darwin (7) said, "If I can convert Huxley I shall be content," and he was. "How exceedingly stupid not to have thought of that," biologist Huxley said when he read Darwin's theories, and he devoted the rest of his life to preaching evolution. Unlike the conservative Darwin, Huxley conceded the possibility of apes in mankind's family tree. Huxley was a self-educated genius born above a butcher shop. He started conducting biology experiments when he was a naval surgeon, never met a fossil he didn't like, and rose to the heights of Britain's scientific establishment. After his oldest son died of scarlet fever, Huxley, the unwavering agnostic, wrote that even if his entire family faced imminent death, he would not try to save them by praying to God. Aldous Huxley wrote *Brave New World,* but it was his grandfather Thomas who helped Darwin create it. **4,877**

800 JOHN CHAPMAN (1774–1845)
Johnny Appleseed

Chapman, a professional nurseryman, wandered forty years through Ohio, Indiana, and western Pennsylvania, clearing land and planting apple nurseries. The fruit nourished pioneers on their westward journey. He collected seeds from cider presses, then sold seedlings to frontier folks. Chapman made some money but also gave away thousands of seeds to pioneers. Settlers gave him his nickname, and the friendly, nature-loving eccentric spawned Bunyanesque legends. People believed he slept in a treetop hammock, played with a pet wolf, and cavorted with bears. "When a folktale attains the status of a myth and embodies a cherished ideal of the people," said Chapman's biographer Robert Price, "then its true worth no longer lies merely in the dead facts that may have inspired it, but in the new, living, and creating force that it has become in the present." **4,867**

We scoff at people who say history is boring. Granted, rote memorization of the causes of the War of the Roses and oh-so important dates like December 20, 1620, is sure to make you snooze. But we assert that the past is fascinating when it re-creates the personal stories of people who, little by little, changed the world. We want to tell you about the folks who invented candy bars, aspirin, champagne, the remote control zapper, and laser beams. And about the greatest singer in the Arab world. And a Japanese filmmaker whose movies are art. And an African-American who energized his rage into a philosophy of equality.

We wanted this book to be more than a litany of great dead dudes—you know, presidents, generals, and founding fathers. History books are a-changin' along with the times, as Bob Dylan might say, but it took creativity to smoke out the stories of people who subtly altered our lives. We posed quirky questions: Who invented chess? Where did painkillers come from? When did homeopathic medicine begin? And why does Santa Claus wear a red suit and smoke a pipe? You'll find the answers in this next group.

We scoured dusty reference books to come up with Friedrich Serturner, Miyan Tansen, and Francois-André Philidor. Nope, they don't show up in history survey texts, but you'll discover in this next group of one hundred just how they've changed the world.

Sure, when it comes to history, you can't get away from warriors who sacked, pillaged, and ruled the world throughout the millennia. But we also want you to know about the contributions of a sweatshop reformer, a magazine editor who popularized mass culture, an advocate for the mentally ill, and the matriarch of modern dance.

Yes, you'll find a great number of predictable names (look for Brigham Young, Robert Frost, David Sarnoff, and George Gallup, for starters), but we like to think that this group of one hundred is especially rich in little-known people who revolutionized your world a little bit at a time.

801 EL CID (c.1043–1099)
national hero of Spain

Russia has Alexander Nevsky (737), Britain has Alfred the Great, and France has Joan of Arc (83). Spain has its national hero, too: El Cid. He was a master Christian warrior who won battles against great odds and was the first general to defeat the Almoravid clan of Muslims, which controlled Spain in the eleventh and twelfth centuries. An equal-opportunity soldier, he battled Christians, too. His name comes from *sayyid*, Arabic for "lord." Two years after his death—in bed, by the way—the Almoravids recaptured Valencia, the site of El Cid's greatest victory, and held the city for 130 years. In 1929 historian Ramón Menéndez Pidal pumped up El Cid's reputation with his book *El Cid and His Spain.* Despite inaccuracies, it placed El Cid on a par with the great national heroes of Europe. **4,842**

802 GREGORY XIII (1502–1585)
calendar fixer

We wouldn't give Pope Gregory the time of day if he hadn't created the modern calendar. A millennium and a half after it was used by the Romans, the 365-day Julian calendar was moving faster than the seasons; by 1582 the calendar was out of sync with the equinox, and churchmen were concerned because the link between holidays and their traditional seasons was breaking. Gregory made a momentous decision. He decreed that the day after October 4, 1582, would be October 15. Henceforth years at the end of each century would be leap years if they were divisible by 400 (1900 no, 2000 yes). Many non-Catholic countries ignored the reform. George Washington celebrated his birthday on February 11 before 1752, when England and America switched. The calendar is now almost perfect; in 3,300 years it will only be one day ahead of the seasons again. **4,816**

803 JOHANN STRAUSS (1794–1849)
Viennese waltz king

The waltz craze of the early nineteenth century was a milestone in cultural history. It was the first dance to combine sensuous grace and peasantlike athleticism—a formula repeated in popular dance sensations ever since, from the tango to the jitterbug to the macarena. The far-from-prudish Lord Byron (385) was so scandalized by the body contact required by the waltz, he considered it a prelude to rape. A German doctor predicted that overindulgence would cause mental illness. Queen Victoria (91) certainly didn't care; composer-conductor Strauss played at her coronation eve ball, and she was swept off her feet. Johann Jr. (1825–1899) wrote "Blue Danube." But Strauss senior's 251 compositions established the model, and his touring orchestra was as popular as any rock group today. **4,793**

804 WILLIAM PITT THE ELDER (1708–1778)
freedom-loving British imperialist

That might sound contradictory today, but it made sense in the eighteenth century. Pitt presided over Britain's transformation into a great imperial power, notably by outwitting the French in the Seven Years War. "He made England the first country in the world," English historian Thomas Macauley (796) said. But Pitt also loved freedom. His nickname was the "Great Commoner" for his defense of constitutional rights. America is forever in his debt for standing up to mad King George (452) and urging an end to taxation without representation. "The Americans are the sons, not the bastards of England," he declared in Parliament. Pitt, though plagued by "gout in the head" (manic-depression), managed to educate his five children himself, often conversing with them in Latin. One of those children, William Pitt the Younger, became prime minister at age twenty-four and rivals his father in fame. **4,730**

805 HENRY DE BRACTON (d. 1268)
lawgiver

He was a royal clerk, archdeacon, and judge in the time of English king Henry III and at his death left a book, *On the Laws and Customs of England.* It was his country's first great legal treatise. Bracton explained how specific judicial decisions interpreted the statutes, notably the law that protected landholders from arbitrary eviction. Bracton's most famous line was, "the king should not be under any man, but under God and law." (That's *Rex non debet esse sub homine, sed sub Deo et lege,* for those who don't trust legal principles that aren't in Latin.) Bracton's notion that rulers are subject to the law is a pillar of democracy. Chief Justice Edward Coke (282) used Bracton's book to argue against the divine right of kings when James I (879) tried to foist that theory on the English in the seventeenth century. **4,702**

806 MAX WEBER (1864–1920)
workaholics' best excuse

Weber's great book, *The Protestant Ethic and the Spirit of Capitalism,* explored the relationship between Calvinist dogma and the beginnings of modern capitalism. It was an analytical tour de force that admirers say rivals *Das Kapital* and in some ways—its emphasis on objectivity, the exactness of its methodology—surpasses Marx's (14) great oeuvre. To oversimplify a bit, Weber noted that according to the Calvinist doctrine of predestination, God has already decided whether you will go to heaven or hell, and there's nothing you can do about it. But wait! If you lead an exemplary life—working hard but living simply—surely that is a *sign* that God loves you. So Protestants worked their tails off, triggering modern capitalism. The neurotic son of a Calvinist mother and authoritarian father, Weber wrote on topics as varied as the nature of bureaucracy, American Indians, and the "piano as the instrument of the middle classes." **4,681**

807 MIGUEL HIDALGO Y COSTILLA
(1753–1811) *el padre de Mexico*

Hidalgo was just a country priest with flair—he loved dancing the minuet, hunting, and street bowling—when he seized the moment. Facing arrest as a member of a secret society opposed to Spanish rule, he rang his church bell to summon his tiny flock of farmhands and cowboys to insurrection. Incredibly, the revolt spread, and Hidalgo led an army of sixty thousand to the gates of Mexico City. But he was defeated and captured and soon thereafter repudiated the revolution, lamenting "the multitude of souls that dwell in the abyss because they followed me." Was it a forced confession? All we know is he requested candy for his executioners. Though he failed, Hidalgo is revered as the father of his country. Not bad for a man whose name, derived from the words *hijo de algo,* means simply "son of somebody." **4,662**

808 HERBERT SPENCER (1820–1903)
evolutionary English philosopher

In 1840, for the first and last time in his solitary bachelor life, Spencer flirted with a girl; the next year he was fired from his job as a railway engineer. "Got the sack—very glad," he wrote in his diary. So Spencer had no job or loved one to distract him from starting his life's work: writing books that applied evolutionary theory to biology, psychology, and sociology. The popular appeal of his writings made Spencer a champion of evolution to a skeptical public. *Principles of Sociology* helped found the modern study of sociology, though few scholars now think, as did the determinist Spencer, that the world is moving in fits and starts toward a perfect harmony of the individual and society. Spencer occasionally clung to outdated theories. He believed that he inherited beautiful small hands because his immediate ancestors were members of the nonlaboring class. **4,659**

809 PIERRE TEILHARD DE CHARDIN (1881– 1955) *mystic for the modern age*

As science and religion spun apart in the twentieth century, Teilhard sought to fuse them back together. Both a world-famous paleontologist and a Jesuit, he developed a theory about humanity's evolution to a higher state—"the fantastic Cosmogenesis revealing itself before our eyes." Science was in his bones. When he was six, his frantic parents found him miles from his home in Auvergne, France, making a beeline toward the mountains "to see what is inside the volcanoes." But his greatest passion was his faith; the great-great-grandnephew of the atheist Voltaire (36), he said his role in discovering Peking Man's skull made him "madly in love with the Divine Influence which governs the World." His own influence was to make the secular world take another look at that good old-time religion. **4,612**

810 WILLIAM WILBERFORCE (1759–1833) *scourge of the slave trade*

Wilberforce shamed Britain, and Britain the world, into outlawing one of the most ancient human evils. In young adulthood, the amiable Wilberforce seemed destined for no higher a calling than sipping port in the gentlemen's clubs of London. But in 1785 John Newton, a former slave trader and author of the hymn "Amazing Grace," converted him to evangelical Christianity and impressed upon him the horrors of the traffic in human flesh. Two years later his Cambridge chum, William Pitt the Younger, the famous prime minister, urged him

to take up freedom's cause in Parliament. From then on Wilberforce doggedly fought to end the slave trade and was the chief force behind the Slavery Abolition Act of 1833—enacted one month after his death. It would be decades, of course, before slavery was banned in the United States and parts of Latin America. **4,598**

811 BEN JONSON (1572–1637) *Shakespeare's little brother*

Jonson was the only English Renaissance playwright and poet to give Shakespeare (5) a run for his shillings. Jonson's most famous line, "Drink to me only with thine eyes, / And I will pledge with mine," has set hearts a-pounding for four centuries. (Never mind that he had a complexion "like a rotten russet apple when 'tis bruised," according to one contemporary.) His comedies, like *Volpone* and *The Alchemist,* expose the foibles of his age with biting satire. He was a favorite of King James I (879) and a hero to a group of younger poets called the sons of Ben. Shakespeare even acted in one of his plays, and the two men engaged in "wit-combats" in taverns. For all that, as a contemporary of Shakespeare, this one-time bricklayer's apprentice and literary light will be eternally judged against the supernova of the bard from Stratford-on-Avon. **4,517**

812 BRIGHAM YOUNG (1801–1877) *Moses of the Mormons*

That's what they called Young, who had a major impact on development of the American West. The former carpenter assumed leadership of the Church of Jesus Christ of Latter-Day Saints when founder Joseph Smith was murdered in 1844. Continuing threats prompted Young to lead his flock from Illinois to Salt Lake City, Utah, where the Mormons established settlements in 1847. "This is a good place to make

Saints, and it is a good place for Saints to live," Young declared. They called the area Deseret and named Young governor. But public outcries over Mormon polygamy (Young had twenty-seven wives) and the Christian sect's power led the United States to send a military expedition to Utah in 1857. Young was forced out as governor but remained president of the church, effectively ruling Utah until his death. Today his followers number 9.5 million, constituting one of the world's fastest-growing religious groups. **4,496**

813 LEON BATTISTA ALBERTI (1404–1472)
Renaissance know-it-all

An anonymous reader wrote in the margins of an early edition of a book by the Florentine humanist, "Is there anything this man doesn't know?" He wrote perceptively about philosophy, mathematics, morality, music, architecture, painting, and optics. Plus, he was a legendary showman; he wowed audiences by throwing coins high enough to hit the ceiling of the highest cathedral. Most of his ideas were incorporated by greater practitioners. "Leonardo Da Vinci was to Alberti as the finisher to the beginner," Jakob Burckhardt wrote in 1860. A few of Alberti's edifices are still standing, but his best contributions were treatises on perspective and architecture, though some scholars praise him more for the spirit than the substance of his lessons. He was among the first to preach the Renaissance creed: Happiness and morality are achieved by action, creation, and reason. **4,461**

814 ALEXANDER CARTWRIGHT (1820–1892)
baseball's rule maker

Every fan has opinions. Ken Griffey, Jr., is better than Joe DiMaggio was. The designated hitter rule stinks. Pete Rose belongs in the Hall of Fame, and Don Drysdale doesn't. Here's a fact: Abner Doubleday didn't invent baseball. It evolved over hundreds of years. But if anyone was father of the game, it was Cartwright, a bank clerk who wrote the first rule book, played on the original organized ball club, the New York Knickerbockers, and helped arrange the first recorded contest—Hoboken, New Jersey, October 6, 1845. Cartwright established such basics as three-strikes-you're-out and nine men on a side. His finest achievement was putting the bases ninety feet apart, creating a magical balance between offense and defense. Cartwright joined the California gold rush in 1849 and later moved to Hawaii. If there is baseball in heaven, he's the commissioner. **4,438**

815 HANS-JOACHIM PABST VON OHAIN
(b. 1911) *builder of the first jet plane engine*

High on the list of the 1,000 Dumb Mistakes That Saved The World was Adolf Hitler's (20) decision to deemphasize the development of jet warplanes at the beginning of World War II. If *Der Führer* had shelved Werner von Braun's erratic rockets and built more fighters powered by Ohain's turbojet engines, the Allies might have been swept from the skies. Ohain's Heinkel HE-178 flew in August 1939, but production stalled, and by 1944 when a few German jet fighters became operational, it was too late for the Germans. Britain's Frank Whittle designed a jet in the 1930s, too, but his government was even less interested than the Germans. After the war Von Ohain joined the army of German scientists who became U.S. citizens, and he worked on military projects. The last we heard, he was living in Florida, an eight-hour jet plane ride from Berlin. **4,405**

816 JERZY NEYMAN (1894–1981)
statistical phenomenon

We blame Neyman for taking the suspense out of democracy; pollsters using Neyman's teachings announce who won elections before the voting booths close. The ones who said in 1948 that Thomas Dewey, not Harry Truman (485), would be president were not paying attention. In papers between 1928 to 1938, Neyman wrote the mathematical principles that instruct statisticians how to test hypotheses, make samples the right size, and reduce the risk of error. He built on work by his teacher Karl Pearson, who invented the term *biometrics,* but if you have to choose which is the father of the modern poll, why not the Pole? "We have all learned to speak statistics with a Polish accent," said colleague David Kendall, bowing to Neyman's vast influence. Neyman studied and taught in Warsaw, but he settled in Berkeley in 1938 and made the University of California a mecca for students of statistics. **4,390**

817 HENRI TOULOUSE-LAUTREC (1864–1901) *poster boy of the art world*

He was Vicomte de Toulouse-Lautrec, but you'd never know it from the subjects he painted. Contemporaries produced traditional portraits and academic nudes, but Lautrec captured actresses, dancers, and prostitutes in Montmartre haunts—cafés, theaters, even brothels. His honest paintings (one is the bar scene *At the Moulin Rouge*) were shunned by fellow artists and critics. He fared better with his posters, which vibrate with intense color and flowing lines. We love the series on red-headed dancer Jane Avril. Lautrec raised the poster to creative eminence, said biographer Carlton Lake, because "he achieved more with less than any other artist of the Western World." Lautrec suffered bone disease as a youth and was a misshapen dwarf. Disgusted by his deformity, he turned to heavy drinking and debauchery, dying young. Still, he left his mark on successors like Picasso (149), and helped set the course of avant-garde art. **4,387**

818 MARTHA GRAHAM (1894–1991) *dance revolutionary*

Who gets a front page, above-the-fold obituary in *The New York Times*? Statesmen, dignitaries of the highest order, the publisher's mother, and—well, Graham. How fitting that America's newspaper of record acknowledged that Graham did for dance what Stravinsky (183) did for music. Graham said she was inspired to revolutionize classical ballet movements after she saw an abstract Wassily Kandinsky (451) painting. "I will dance like that," she said. Graham established modern dance as a separate force outside ballet and then ruled for more than sixty years as its Grande Dame. She formed her own New York dance company, choreographed more than 180 dances, and often cast herself in the starring role. From her New York debut in 1926 until her retirement from the stage at age seventy-five, Graham said she eschewed realism in favor of "life through movement." **4,381**

819 CHARLES H. TOWNES (b. 1915) *laser-sharp physicist*

Townes was sitting on a bench in Franklin Square Park in Washington, D.C., admiring azalea blossoms when he was zapped by the possibility of lasers. The year was 1951, and Luke Skywalker wasn't even a gleam in Darth Vader's eye when the notion of harnessing the force came to Townes. When Townes hashed out the idea over lunch with his students at Columbia University in New York City, they invented the acronym *laser,* for Light Amplification by Stimulated Emission of Radiation, and *maser* for the microwave device that would produce the effect. The actual laser was first produced by Theodore Malman in 1960, but Townes gets credit for focusing scientific inquiry on this path. Townes never envisioned just how useful lasers could be.

He thought they would provide a method for precise measurements, but we've got to thank this guy for revolutionizing everything from surgery to supermarket checkouts. **4,341**

820 LAURENCE OLIVIER (1907–1989)
lord of the actors

Though they were separated by more than three centuries, you've got to wonder if Shakespeare (5) had his countryman Olivier in mind when he wrote his plays. After all, Olivier sets the standard by which other performances are measured: Olivier's Hamlet, Olivier's Henry V, Olivier's Richard III, et cetera. His acting career began with Shakespeare—he played Brutus at age nine in London's All Saints Choir School production of *Julius Caesar.* His brother played the title role. Not only was Olivier the twentieth century's best actor, but his screen adaptations of the bard's work revived a fading Shakespeare for new generations. A master of both stage and screen, Olivier wooed women as a romantic leading man. His portrayal of Heathcliff in Hollywood's *Wuthering Heights,* for example, reduces even the hardhearted to sniffles. Actor Charles Laughton told Olivier that he was so good in the role of Henry V because "You are England." **4,306**

821 MALCOLM X (1925–1965)
self-proclaimed
"Angriest Negro in America"

Malcolm X called civil rights leader Martin Luther King, Jr. (56), "the best weapon that the white man, who wants to brutalize Negroes, has ever gotten in this country." Born Malcolm Little, he was an angry, street-smart kid who fell into robbery, drugs, gambling, and prostitution. While imprisoned in 1946, he studied the philosophy of the Nation of Islam and replaced his surname with the letter "X." After his release in 1952, he began preaching rage.

Malcolm founded his own militant Muslim mosque and changed his name once again to el-Hajj Malik el-Shabazz. He adopted a more conciliatory tone, moving away from outright support of violence within the civil rights movement, but continuing to assert equality for blacks "by any means necessary." The question of who planned the killing of Malcolm X has generated as many conspiracy theories as the assassinations of both King and President Kennedy. Malcolm's best-selling autobiography and a 1992 Spike Lee film about his life ensured his position as hero for subsequent generations of black youths. **4,262**

822 IGOR SIKORSKY (1889–1972)
inventor of the helicopter

Contemporaries, including the Wright brothers (23, 24), were designing planes that barreled down runways to achieve liftoff. But Russian-born Sikorsky shared Leonardo da Vinci's (9) vision of a machine that could fly straight up. By 1910, though, a frustrated Sikorsky knew the time wasn't right and shelved his plans. He developed a line of successful fixed-wing planes, the S-40s, first in Russia, then in the United States, to which he had emigrated in 1919. In the late 1930s aerodynamic theories and construction techniques caught up to Sikorsky's dream, and he tried again to create an airship with a horizontal rotor. This time it worked. The first VS-300 took off with Sikorsky at the controls in September 1939. Sikorsky foresaw the helicopter performing rescue and relief missions. He probably had no clue that it also would evolve into an offensive weapon, used in Vietnam, Afghanistan, and the Persian Gulf war. **4,212**

823 JOHN PYM (c.1584–1643)
Puritan lash of kings

Pym served in Parliament from 1621 to his death and led the Commons' resistance to the absolute monarch Charles I. During the Long Parliament beginning in 1640, Pym forced Charles to agree that Parliament could not be dissolved without its consent. But Charles only gave this lip service. "To have printed liberties, and not to have liberties in truth and realities, is but to mock the kingdom," Pym declared. He orchestrated the Solemn League and Covenant, a treaty with Scotland, and in January 1644 a Scottish army invaded England to join Parliamentary forces battling the royalists. Years later when the monarchy was restored, Charles II had Pym's body removed from Westminster Abbey and buried in a churchyard. Still, the new regent vowed to honor agreements from Pym's Long Parliament, meaning that the concept of "divine right" was dead and buried, too. **4,186**

824 JOHN GRAUNT (1620–1674)
Grim Reaper's bookkeeper

His 1662 book compiling and commenting on the births and deaths in London from 1604 to 1661 was a breakthrough in statistical research. He is variously credited with launching probability theory, sampling theory, the science of demographics, and the life-insurance industry. A shopkeeper who got up early to read, Graunt estimated the population of London by extrapolating from the number of annual births, figured out that country folk outlive city dwellers and that women outlive men, and calculated average life expectancy at birth to be sixteen years, though he himself beat the odds by advancing to the ripe old age of fifty-four. Graunt was also an early proponent of workfare, suggesting that London's beggars be put to work, "each according to his condition and capacity." **4,164**

825 J. WILLARD GIBBS (1839–1903)
the quiet man of American science

While his contemporary Thomas Edison (28) grabbed headlines, Gibbs pondered great thoughts. His most influential paper, "On the Equilibrium of Heterogeneous Substances," solved many of the problems of chemical manufacture, notably the conversion of ammonia into nitroglycerin (for explosives) and nitrates (for fertilizer). Some consider Gibbs one of the greatest scientists America has produced. The Scottish physicist James Clerk Maxwell (205) recognized his genius but died before he could tell the world. German, French, and Dutch luminaries bowed before him, but America's scientific establishment, uncomprehending, yawned. And he didn't care, figuring posterity would reward him. The bearded bachelor lived with two sisters (and one brother-in-law) in their father's house in New Haven, Connecticut, where he insisted on making salads for the evening meals, on the grounds that he was best qualified to mix heterogeneous substances. **4,109**

826 FELIX HOFFMANN (fl.1893)
headache reliever

A chemist in a Bayer laboratory in Germany, Hoffmann was assigned the job of developing a safe version of salicylic acid. Pharmacists had known for years that this derivative of willow bark, the stuff of Native American medicine men, was an effective analgesic, but it had a nasty tendency to eat people's stomachs and cause them to bleed to death. Hoffmann, whose father had crippling rheumatism and begged his son for relief, transformed salicylic acid into a safer form—aspirin. Doctors prescribed it initially to reduce joint pain and lower fevers, but imagine their delight when they discovered it effectively erased headaches. Hoffmann never got rich on the discovery, but Bayer did. Aspirin was the most popular drug in the United States by 1906. Today thirty billion aspirin tablets are consumed annually in the United States—a sharp increase since doctors discovered its use in reducing the risks of heart disease.   **4,093**

827 SARAH JOSEPHA HALE (1788–1879)
trendsetting editor

How can you not honor the woman who wrote "Mary Had a Little Lamb" and convinced President Lincoln (32) to make Thanksgiving a national holiday? But forget those things. Hale scores big points as one of the original proponents of a fledgling popular culture. As editor of *Godey's Lady's Book,* the nineteenth-century popular magazine for women, Hale was among the first opinion makers to reach a national audience through mass communication. In fact, the phenomenal success of her publication helped bolster the magazine as a literary format. Hale's writings dictated acceptable behavior for women and glorified the home as woman's proper sphere. Hale and her magazine, which printed the latest fashions from Paris alongside articles by important literary figures, have been credited by historian Barbara Welter with creating the refined, domestic woman celebrated in "The Cult of True Womanhood."   **4,042**

828 ROBERT FROST (1874–1963)
poet of the road less traveled

America's favorite twentieth-century poet immortalized the climate, character, and spirit of New England with his images of woods on a snowy evening and roads that diverge in a yellow wood. Before earning his keep as a poet, Frost worked in a cotton mill, taught school, and spent time as a chicken farmer. He observed, however, that a man who knew the pleasure of molding a metaphor was unfit for other work. Enormously popular in his lifetime, Frost won the Pulitzer Prize four times and served as a goodwill ambassador for the United States. He wrote a poem to read at the 1961 inauguration of President John Kennedy, but when the glare of the sun was too bright for his failing eyes, Frost stood in front of the Capitol and recited "The Gift Outright" from memory.   **4,037**

829 FRANCIS FRY (1803–1886)
the candy man

For centuries, chocolate was an indulgence of the world's upper classes. Marie-Antoinette (781), that decadent cake-eating queen of France, so lost her head over chocolate drinks that when she traveled, she brought along her own Viennese chocolate maker. The Fry family of chocolatiers not only transformed a ritzy beverage into a solid but marketed it to the masses of sweet tooths. Francis's company in Bristol, England, was first to manufacture a tasty chocolate bar in 1849. Sales of the exotic-sounding "Chocolat Delicieux à Manger" made J.S. Fry & Sons (Francis was the son who counted) the world's biggest chocolate manufacturer. So we lick our lips and thank Fry, who did it first, but we blow dozens of kisses to Milton Hershey, who did it best. The "Henry Ford of Chocolate," Hershey began manufacturing candy in 1893. As the millennium melted, the Pennsylvania-based company was making 33 million chocolate kisses daily.   **4,028**

830 DAVID SARNOFF (1891–1971)
electronic window on the world

Sarnoff was first to envision radio and television as entertainment media. In 1915, at age twenty-four, he suggested that the Radio Corporation of America could make its product a "household utility" by using airwaves to transmit music. Fast-forward two decades: During the depths of the Depression, after Sarnoff became president of RCA, he invested $50 million to develop television. When World War II sidetracked television research, Sarnoff served as General Eisenhower's (374) adviser on communication technology. Nicknamed "the General" in deference to his rank, Sarnoff focused big guns on television after the war and crafted network broadcasting. While its subsidiary, NBC, broadcast shows like *Amos 'n Andy*, RCA sold receivers. Today there are more than 200 million televisions in the United States. Called ruthless by some and a genius by others, Sarnoff was voted "the father of television" by the broadcasters themselves. **4,011**

831 DOM PÉRIGNON (1638–1715)
monk who perfected the "devil's wine"

He discovered that the secret to sparkling wine is a subtle blend of grapes, imprisoned in a well-shaped bottle, and sealed by a good cork. Dom Pérignon didn't invent the modern glass wine bottle (that came from, of all places, England) or the cork (ancient Greeks, thank you very much), but he mastered the fermentation process at his Benedictine abbey in Champagne. His straw-colored wine with the amusing effervescence that tickled the nose was nicknamed "the bubbling wine that makes corks jump." A favorite at Louis XIV's (63) court, champagne today represents all that is luxurious and decadent. After Perignon's death, Claude Moët cornered the sparkling wine market, helped in large part by Madame de Pompadour, who ordered about two hundred bottles at a pop. In a gesture to the master, however, the *Dom Perignon* label, the cadillac of champagnes, was marketed in 1936 by Moët & Chandon. **3,989**

832 FRIEDRICH SERTURNER (1783–1841)
pain's killer

During the American Civil War, precious drops of morphine were administered to wounded soldiers to erase pain and calm nightmares.

Physicians discovered after the war that they had created America's first massive group of drug addicts who needed daily injections to feed their dependency on this purified form of opium. Morphine today is a painkiller for the terminally ill but is used sparingly elsewhere because of its addictive lure. Serturner, a pharmacist's assistant in Prussia, isolated "morphium" in 1805. He experimented on himself and nearly died of an overdose. Opium had been used as a treatment for centuries, but the beauty of morphine was that doctors could regulate the dosage. By the 1830s morphine was used regularly for pain. It could be chewed, but doctors sometimes blistered the skin and applied morphine to be absorbed. After the hypodermic needle was invented in 1853 by Charles Gabriel Pravaz, morphine injections became commonplace. **3,927**

833 STEPHEN FOSTER (1826–1864)
composer for the good old days

Last year's hits fade, but not Foster's "Oh Susannah," "My Old Kentucky Home," "The Old Folks at Home," "Camptown Races," and "Jeannie with the Light Brown Hair," a love offering to his wife Jane. German kids still sing *"Ich komm von Alabama, mid der banjoy auf dem knie."* The Pittsburgh-born Foster spurned a career as a bookkeeper and wrote more than two hundred songs, first for the blackface Christy Minstrels and then for sheet music publishers who paid Foster two cents for every score they sold. They may have cheated him; his total take for his most creative years, 1849 to 1860, was a measly $15,000. Ruined by the alcoholism that eventually killed him, Foster spent the Civil War years dashing off forgettable songs, like "My Boy Is Coming from the War," and sold them to the owners of New York Bowery honky-tonks for fifteen dollars. **3,904**

834 FEDERICO FELLINI (1920–1993)
fantasizing director

He started as a caricaturist, got into film production while dodging Mussolini's (460) draft in wartime Rome, and cowrote the screenplay for *Open City*, a 1944 masterpiece of naturalism. As a director, Fellini's depictions of Italian society were unrivaled, but his movies are really about Federico Fellini—his childhood in fascist Rimini *(Amarcord)*, his wife, actress Giulietta Masina *(Juliet of the Spirits)*, the decadence of his rich friends *(La Dolce Vita)*, and his artistic struggles *(8½)*. That 1962 movie, starring Marcello Mastroianni, was picked by international critics in 1987 as the best European film of all time. Four of his films, starting with *La Strada*, won Academy Awards for Best Foreign Film. No director of any nationality was as good at making audiences care about sexual and psychic outcasts, be they slum-dwelling prostitutes, failed social climbers, or down-and-out circus clowns. Producer Bernardino Zapponi said, "Fellini loves squalor. It never ages."   **3,882**

835 EDWIN DRAKE (1819–1880)
first oil driller

Before Drake, oil was scooped from pools or salt wells. Drake was the first person to drill for the gooey stuff. On August 27, 1859, his Rock Oil Company drillers hit black gold at sixty-nine feet below Oil Creek outside Titusville, Pennsylvania, and soon they were pumping eight to ten barrels of petroleum a day. Drake's method was to dig to bedrock to tap only the oil veins, not clay, salt, brine, and other junk. Today, from Alaska to Arabia, from Siberia to southern Indonesia, drillers building on Drake's crude technology bring up fifty million barrels of oil a day. Drake stupidly ignored friends' advice to patent his process, and stock market losses claimed the pittance he

earned from oil operations. At his death he was subsisting on a fifteen-hundred-dollar annual pension from the Pennsylvania legislature.   **3,866**

836 SIMON STEVIN (1548–1620)
decimal doer

Multiply 34/68 by 215/86, and after a lot of scribbling and common denominator stuff you get 1¼. Now multiply the same numbers expressed as decimals, 0.5 x 2.5. The second way is easier, for which we thank Stevin. His widely translated pamphlet, *The Tenth*, popularized the use of decimals in calculation, coinage, weights, and measures. Stevin taught mathematics to the Dutch ruler Maurice of Orange and was a leading hydraulics engineer—an important job in waterlogged Holland. He invented a drainage windmill that beat back the tides, wrote the best book on water pressure since Archimedes, and supported the Copernican theory that the planets revolve around the sun. Some scholars say Stevin—not Galileo (4) standing atop the leaning tower of Pisa—was the first scientist to drop balls from a high place to prove that weight does not affect the rate of acceleration.   **3,862**

837 BONIFACE VIII (1235–1303)
the pope who would be king

No pope claimed more temporal powers and no pope fell so flat trying, which made Boniface an instrumental figure in the decline of church influence. After engineering the abdication of his ineffective, ascetic predecessor, Celestine V, the nobly born Italian Boniface declared that no clergy could be taxed without his permission. Then, in his famous decree, *Unam Sanctum*, he asserted papal supremacy over all kingdoms. An incensed Philip IV of France had Boniface arrested, and the pope died a month later. Papal power never recovered from his pigheaded arrogance. Poet Dante

(30) was so angry about Boniface's meddling in Florentine politics, he put the pope in hell in the *Divine Comedy.* Predecessor Celestine's comment about Boniface was apt: "He shall come in like a fox, reign like a lion, die like a dog." **3,816**

838 SERGEY DIAGHILEV (1872–1929)
Russian ballet czar

A founder of the Ballets Russes in Paris in 1909, Diaghilev injected new life into this art form with his lavish productions. He attracted greatness: famed dancers Anna Pavlova (245), Vaslav Nijinsky (405), and Michel Fokine; artists Dali (735) and Picasso (149), who created sets; composers Debussy (274), Ravel (855), and Prokofiev (615). Diaghilev brought the world three ballet masterworks by Igor Stravinsky (183): *The Firebird, Petrushka,* and *The Rite of Spring.* Although he had a law degree, Diaghilev decided his true calling was patron of the arts. That's tough if you're strapped for cash. But Diaghilev's charm and domineering personality always saved him—except in London in 1921, with his production of Tchaikovsky's *Sleeping Beauty.* Stravinsky thought the impresario had presented "something classical and dignified" demonstrating "the greatness and freedom of his mentality." Critics and public disagreed. The ballet ran only three months—not long enough to save Sergey from bankruptcy. **3,794**

839 PAUL KLEE (1879–1940)
fountainhead for modern art

He was an abstract expressionist, but the Swiss-born Klee's linear style and theory of color also influenced surrealists and nonobjective artists. After rejecting the conformist art classes of his adoptive Germany, Klee searched for a new beginning. He found it in North Africa, where the sun-splashed terrain dazzled him. "Color possesses

me," he wrote. "Color and I are one." Klee was preoccupied with the real versus the unreal. "Art does not reproduce the visible—it makes visible," he maintained. In 1932 the Nazis attacked Klee for his "decadent art," and he left Germany for Switzerland. In deteriorating health, he became obsessed with death, "the tragic path." One of his last paintings, *Death and Fire,* foreshadows his cremation. But carved into his memorial stone is this diary entry: "I cannot be understood in this world, for I am as much at home with the dead as with those yet to be born." **3,778**

840 PELE (b. 1940)
the foot that launched a thousand goals

Edison Arantes do Nascimento, nicknamed Pele, became a Brazilian national hero for his amazing speed and uncanny ability to kick a ball at almost any angle and score a goal. "In Brazil we live, eat and drink soccer," Pele said. And of all Brazilians, he was the leading fanatic. The soccer superstar dominated the sport that dominated the world. In his twenty-two-year career, he scored 1,281 goals when 30 goals a season was considered outstanding. He led the Brazilian national team to three victories in the World Cup. Even North Americans cool to soccer knew Pele's name. He announced his retirement from World Cup competition in 1974, but the following year he accepted a three-year, $7 million contract to play for the New York Cosmos and promote soccer in the United States. It worked. The sport caught on big-time in schools across the country. **3,751**

841 RICHARD RODGERS (1902–1979)
the sound of the musical

If the musical is America's greatest contribution to world theater, then Rodgers made it so. He shunned musical comedy themes of the early

1920s to strike out in new directions. His music wasn't decoration but essential to the unfolding of the plot. Rodgers's lengthy collaboration with lyricist Oscar Hammerstein II created the unforgettable *Oklahoma!, Carousel, South Pacific, The King and I,* and *The Sound of Music.* His most moving songs include "Younger Than Springtime," "If I Loved You," and "You'll Never Walk Alone." And his thirteen-hour score for the documentary *Victory at Sea* showed he also could write in a classical vein. Rodgers was the rare, well-adjusted artist in a maelstrom of neurotics. Some songwriters plucked inspiration from the air, but Rodgers always needed a story or plot to uncork creative juices. "Songs never come to me," he said. "I have to go after them." **3,737**

842 LOUIS WIRTH (1897–1952)
sociologist of the sidewalk

Wirth's classic essay "Urbanism as a Way of Life," published in 1938, unleashed a debate still simmering today. He suggested that life in modern industrialized cities, with their greater density of population and greater anonymity, weakens families and destroys neighborhoods. Many contemporary sociologists dispute that, saying research shows that many city dwellers can maintain strong family ties and a sense of community. But his arguments still exert a powerful influence, both in academia and in the popular culture. Wirth was one of the Chicago urbanists, a group of theorists on city life who gathered at the University of Chicago. He also taught there, founded the American Council on Race Relations, and advised local and federal policy makers. Born in Germany, Wirth emigrated to the United States at age fourteen. From his youth he was committed to social reform. "He became a sociologist," said colleague Eleanor Bernert Sheldon, "because he believed that a science of human

behavior was not only possible but indispensable to social betterment." **3,729**

843 JAYAVARMAN VII OF INDOCHINA
(1181–c.1218) *the George Washington of the jungle*

In the early thirteenth century this Khmer king dominated Southeast Asia. We include him for commissioning the stone shrines of Angkor Thom, a wonder of the world hidden from the West for years in Communist Cambodia. Inscriptions on those shrines say Jayavarman liberated his country from evil invaders. Then his armies ranged from Burma to Malaya. The stones say he was compassionate and built 120 hospitals; they hinted that he had leprosy. That would make anyone compassionate. One inscription says: "His feet were a chaplet of lotus on the heads of all the kings; he overcame his enemies in battle; loaded with jewels of virtue he took the Earth to wife, and gave her his glory for a necklace." **3,683**

844 LANGSTON HUGHES (1902–1967)
the Shakespeare of Harlem

Hughes said he was elected class poet in elementary school because he was one of the few black children and "everybody knows, except us, that all Negroes have rhythm." He was so good at it that the title stuck through high school in Cleveland. In search of adventure, he hopped a freighter to Africa and impulsively tossed all his books overboard so he could see the world through his own eyes. Back in New York, Hughes became inextricably linked with the flowering of literature, music, and drama that has become known as the Harlem Renaissance of the 1920s. He was incredibly versatile. He worked as a journalist and wrote short stories, novels, librettos, plays, and most of all, poetry. "What happens to a dream deferred," he asked in a memorable poem that inspired a critically acclaimed play by Lorraine Hansberry. "Does it dry up like a raisin in the sun?" **3,649**

845 LEWIS CARROLL (1832–1898)
the author who peered through the looking glass and saw Alice

Freudians see sexual references under every giant mushroom in Carroll's classic *Alice's Adventures in Wonderland.* Carroll, the pseudonym of Englishman Charles Dodgson, spun the yarn just to entertain young Alice Liddell on a boat trip in 1886. He wrote it down, then presented the literary gift to the girl. The tale became the most widely read children's story for generations and is still popular today. It couldn't have happened to a weirder Victorian eccentric. Dodgson was a math scholar who became an ordained deacon. Painfully shy with a bad stammer, he relaxed only in the company of children, especially little girls. Some say he fell in love at age thirty-four with famed actress Ellen Terry, then but a teenager. Their bond was a solid friendship, nothing more. Terry later wrote, "He was as fond of me as he could be of anyone over the age of ten." **3,644**

846 ALGERNON CHARLES SWINBURNE
(1837–1909) the swooning poet of Victorian England

The early works of this impressionist poet were so sensual, a critic called him "Swine-born." Smarter contemporaries knew better. John Ruskin read twenty-eight-year-old Swinburne's *Atalanta in Calydon,* and declared, "his foam at the mouth is fine." Swinburne wrote about classical subjects, and there was a simplistic edge to some of his poems, such as today's most famous, "The Garden of Proserpine," with its ending, "even the weariest river winds somewhere safe to sea." His best work used words to create effects never heard before—what his friend and biogra-

pher Edmund Gosse called "the thunder of the waves, and the lisp of leaves in the wind." When he read his poems at parties, Swinburne swooned with fervor, perhaps because one glass of wine made him tipsy. For an effete aesthete, he was unusually jingoistic. He thought England's war on Boer South Africa was just swell. **3,627**

847 UMM KULTHUM (c.1900–1975)
the Great Pyramid of Arab song

That is the actor Omar Sharif's phrase, and it barely does justice to the greatest Arab musical performer of all time. A simple country girl, Umm Kulthum mesmerized first her native Egypt and then the entire Middle East with her rhythmic celebrations of love and Arab culture. She captivated both Egyptian king Farouk and the nationalist who overthrew him, Gamal Abdel Nasser (170); she was adored by rich and poor, men and women, young and old, desert dweller and urban sophisticate. At her last concert her voice faltered, tears trickled down her cheeks, and she sang no more. More than four million Egyptians poured into the streets for her funeral. Nearly a quarter century later, in recordings, her voice—so strong, she had to stand three feet from the microphone, yet so smooth it lulled babies to sleep—still ripples across the Arab world. **3,601**

848 LORD PALMERSTON (1784–1865)
supreme British nationalist

As foreign secretary for most of the 1830s and 1840s and prime minister, with one interruption, from 1855 to 1865, Henry John Temple, or Lord Palmerston, was the architect of the aggressive foreign policy that made Britain the dominant power of the nineteenth century. He supported the Continental revolutions of 1848, befriending Italian freedom and more or less creating Belgium. Palmerston believed the British form of government was the most perfect imaginable, and he declared that Britain would protect its subjects anywhere in the world, just as ancient Rome had done. To a Frenchman who declared that, were he not French, he would wish to be an Englishman, Palmerston retorted, "Were I not an Englishman, I would wish to be an Englishman." Outside of politics Palmerston indulged in the pleasures of the flesh, often scarfing down nine meat courses for dinner and bedding so many society ladies, he was known as "Lord Cupid."　**3,591**

849 Alfred Kinsey (1894–1956)
masseur of the sexual revolution

In high school Kinsey was an Eagle Scout without a girlfriend. After becoming an entomologist and studying the gall wasp for twenty-five years, he switched to humans. He alone interviewed eight thousand people on their sexual habits, asking not whether but how often they did this or that. And that was the problem: His questions were loaded, and his subjects were volunteers. Thus, critics say, his findings were skewed, exaggerating the incidence of homosexuality, for example. Still, by recording people's reported sexual behavior, his best-sellers, *Sexual Behavior in the Human Male* and *Sexual Behavior in the Human Female,* opened a new era of eroticism and candor about sex. A bisexual, Professor Kinsey seduced male students and organized group sex among his staff and their spouses, filming the goings-on in the interest, presumably, of research. "If there'd never been a Kinsey," mused writer Stanley Elkin, "I'd never have seen Jacqueline Bisset's breasts" in the movies.　**3,569**

850 The Marquis de Lafayette
(1757–1834) standard-bearer of liberty

At nineteen the French aristocrat sailed to America to fight with the Colonists against Britain. Sleeping in the frozen huts of Valley Forge and masterminding the American victory at Yorktown,

the last big battle of the war, Lafayette earned a spot second only to Washington's in the pantheon of the American Revolution's soldiers. Active also in the French Revolution, he was hailed as the "Hero of Two Worlds." Lafayette championed the rights of French Protestants, fought slavery, and advocated universal suffrage, free education, free trade, freedom of the press, and freedom for captive European nations and Latin America. Simon Bolívar called him "master." Nobody's perfect; as an old geezer, Lafayette pawed at pretty girls. But hey, he was French. The United States provided an urn of soil from Bunker Hill, mixed with the earth of France, to cover his grave.　**3,535**

851 Cosimo de' Medici (1389–1464)
patriarch of Italy's greatest family

The Medicis ruled Florence, and later Tuscany, from 1434 until 1737, married into the royal lines of Europe (Cosimo's great-great-granddaughter became queen of France and bore three future French kings), and produced four popes, including Leo X, famous for failing to notice a German monk named Martin Luther (3). Cosimo was a Machiavellian operator before Machiavelli (40) was born. To secure power, he expelled the high-born from Florence, saying he would restore the nobility by wrapping "a few lengths of expensive cloth" around the rabble. He outwitted his opponents by guile, bribery, and when necessary, violence, once ordering an infantry captain hurled out of a palace window. A patron of the arts, Cosimo used his riches to erect magnificent monuments like the Medici palace in Florence. **3,528**

852 Catherine of Aragon (1485–1536)
*charter member of
the first wives' club*

She gave Henry VIII of England (100) the best twenty-four years of her life and six children. Then he divorced her because her child-bearing time had ended without a male heir. Plus he was infatuated with Anne Boleyn, a giggly trophy wife. Henry's split with Catholic Catherine led to the Protestant Reformation of Britain, which makes her one-half of the millennium's most important divorcing couple—bigger than Di and Charles, Liz and Dick, even Sonny and Cher. Catherine failed to get her Catholic allies to save the marriage, and she died in a convent. Lacey Baldwin Smith, a perceptive biographer of Henry, says Catherine was lucky. If Henry had been a true Renaissance prince, he would have poisoned Catherine and saved himself and Christendom a lot of trouble.   **3,507**

853 MIYAN TANSEN (1508–1590)
India's music teacher

His name means "master who commands an army of notes," and he put Indian music on its modern course. He did it by studying thousands of overlapping ragas—the melody types at the heart of India's improvisational music—and honing the list to four hundred good ones. As a boy, Tansen could scare away trespassers by hiding in a bush and imitating a tiger. Legends say his singing was so beautiful, his voice could cause spontaneous combustion, make plants flower, and start thunderstorms. It was said that he sang a traditional nighttime raga at noon, and the sky blackened. Tansen, like Johann Sebastian Bach (35), had many sons who became noted musicians, but none approached his greatness. "For a thousand years there has not been a musician like Tansen," said the court historian of Tansen's patron, Akbar the Great (148).   **3,497**

854 BRONISLAW MALINOWSKI
(1884–1942) founder of social anthropology

The Polish-born Malinowski revolutionized the study of native cultures through his groundbreak-ing field studies of the Trobriand Islands off New Guinea. Previous researchers might have viewed the islands' natives with cultural arrogance, as specimens "to be measured, photographed, and interviewed," wrote American anthropologist George W. Stocking, Jr. But in 1916 Malinowski pitched his tent in the village, spoke the dialect, and recorded his subjects' behavior for two years. From it came his major work, *Coral Gardens and Their Magic.* Malinowski said his theory "insists upon the principle that in every type of civilization, every custom, material object, idea and belief fulfills some vital function." His was such a new field that Malinowski, a professor at the London School of Economics, had to campaign hard for funding. He also nurtured young aspirants "for the sake of anthropology and so that they in turn may breed new anthropologists," he said.   **3,481**

855 MAURICE RAVEL (1875–1937)
jazzy classicist

If Ravel's compositions remind you of trumpeter Wynton Marsalis, it's because Ravel was one of the first composers to integrate jazz harmonies and orchestration into classical works. His master-pieces include *Daphnis and Chloé, Le Tombeau de Couperin,* and *Sonatine.* We had to raise Ravel's point score for a dubious accomplishment: composing *Bolero,* the millennium's most annoying classic. Boil us in oil, put us in a locked room with a life-insurance salesman—anything but the ubiquitous, pulsating *Bolero.* Ravel was a five-foot-three, book-loving dandy—one of the first Frenchmen to wear pastel shirts—and was a member of an avant-garde clique of artists called the Apaches. At the age of forty-one his fierce nationalism drove him to volunteer as a medical corpsman in World War I, though he refused to sign a manifesto calling for a ban on performances of new works by German composers.   **3,476**

856 BERNARDINO RAMAZZINI (1633–1714)
the doctor who warned
that work can make you sick

Italian physician Ramazzini's *Diseases of Tradesmen*, published in 1700, presented the first systematic account of job-related diseases. It also marked the initial step toward enactment of factory safety and workers' compensation laws. Ramazzini cited the hazards in workers' environments and the physical toll of their labors. Goldsmiths and surgeons were exposed to harmful mercury, potters and painters to poisonous lead. Cobblers developed round shoulders, and tailors, debilitating neuritis. Ramazzini urged doctors to ask a patient "what trade he is of" to better diagnose his complaint. Associates lauded Ramazzini, a professor at the University of Modena, and later Padua, for his sweet personality, his candid judgment, and his upright intentions. In his preface to the English translation of Ramazzini's work in 1746, a Dr. James wrote that Ramazzini was created "honorary fellow of almost all academies and universities of Europe and courted by all his learned contemporaries." **3,472**

857 GEORGE GERSHWIN (1898–1937)
magical music man

When Gershwin's parents bought a used piano for older brother, Ira, twelve-year-old George sat down and played a tune. His parents wisely consented to lessons. Still teenagers, George and struggling dancer Fred Astaire fantasized that someday the hoofer would star in a Gershwin musical. A decade later, Gershwin's *Lady Be Good,* featuring Astaire and his sister Adele, opened on Broadway. With hindsight, we see the niche Gershwin carved for himself in music history. His compositions bridge many forms, including classical, show tunes, and jazz. Big brother Ira penned lyrics and Gershwin wrote the music for more than twenty Broadway musicals and movies. Memorable are "Swanee" (Al Jolson's signature song), "The Man I Love," and "I Got Rhythm." As a classical composer, Gershwin gave us *An American in Paris, Rhapsody in Blue,* and *Porgy and Bess.* He died at age thirty-eight following surgery for a brain tumor. **3,448**

858 FRANCISCO PIZARRO (1475–1541)
conqueror of Peru

Conquistadore Pizarro battled in local wars in Spain, then fought in Italy. In 1502 he shipped out to Hispaniola (now Haiti and the Dominican Republic), where compatriots pegged him as the strong, unmotivated type. Yet by 1524 a prosperous Pizarro accompanied Balboa as he discovered the Pacific Ocean. That same year Pizarro set off in an unsuccessful search along the west coast of South America for the fabled Incan empire. A second try led him to Incan emperor Atahualpa. Claiming peaceful intent, his party took Atahualpa prisoner, then executed him. Incan resistance dissolved, and Pizarro established Lima as Peru's capital in 1535. Meanwhile, the empire's gold was pouring into Spanish coffers. Greedy and ambitious, Pizarro also could be courageous and cunning. Historian John Hemming saw him as "a magnificent leader, infinitely tenacious and determined." **3,431**

859 GEORGE GALLUP (1901–1984)
opinion-poll pioneer

In a world where presidents carry poll results in their pockets to remind themselves what principles to profess, who can doubt his influence? Gallup first won fame by predicting Franklin Roosevelt's (37) victory in 1936, confounding experts who had used haphazard sampling methods instead of his scientific cross-section of the population. From the beginning, however, polling had its detractors. "Nothing is more dangerous than to live in the temperamental atmosphere of a Gallup poll, always taking one's temperature," Winston Churchill (38) grumped. Retorted Gallup: "If government is supposed to be based on the will of the people, somebody ought to go out and find out what that will is." Gallup called himself a statistician and liked to say, "I'll give you ten to one you die of cancer, twenty to one you die of heart disease." He died of a heart attack. **3,429**

860 BONAVENTURE (1217–1274)
God-intoxicated saint

Bonaventure believed he was saved from death as a boy by the divine intervention of Saint Francis of Assisi (39), and he devoted much of his life to defending the Franciscan order from its critics and internal divisions. His mystical theology had an enduring impact on Christian doctrine. His argument for the existence of God wasn't some elaborate proof but the observation that "every creature cries out that God is." He urged every man and woman to seek God through contemplation and the imitation of Christ. Though compassionate, the Italian could be ruthless in puncturing his contemporaries' pretensions. Writing on pride, he declared: "An example from the monkey: The higher it climbs, the more you see of its behind." Pope Leo XIII called Bonaventure the "prince who leads us by the hand to God." **3,419**

861 FLORENCE KELLEY (1859–1932)
scourge of the sweatshop

Kelley was such a rabid lobbyist for laws to protect women and children in factories that she reluctantly withdrew support for a proposed Equal Rights Amendment. She feared it would compromise her struggle to limit women's work hours and improve the sweltering, airless, haz-ardous conditions in America's factories. The suffragist Kelley had spent too many years as a labor activist to let a constitutional amendment destroy her life's work. Secretary of the National Consumer League, she fought for the eight-hour day and government enforcement of factory safety regulations. In fact, she was the first woman factory inspector in Illinois. Kelley scores big points with us as a prolific writer, a passionate speaker, and a most effective lobbyist against the squalor wrought by the Industrial Revolution. **3,413**

862 ANWAR EL-SADAT (1918–1981)
peace-loving twentieth-century pharaoh

Sadat had a flair for the grand gesture. After taking power in Egypt in 1970, he publicly burned tape recordings made by the secret police of his predecessor, Gamel Abdel Nasser (170). In the years that followed he repudiated Nasser's one-party socialist rule by liberalizing the country's economy and lifting the government's ban on political parties. His most notable undertakings were his expulsion of Soviet military advisers in 1972, freeing Egypt from Moscow's grip; his surprise attack on Israel in 1973, restoring his nation's self-respect; and the peace treaty he signed with Israel in 1979, cooling one of the hottest threats to world peace. No saint, Sadat could be dictatorial, lazy, and acquisitive. But he also had a large heart. Thinking his assassins were putting on a special salute to him at a military parade, he broke out into his famous grin and rose to greet them. **3,407**

863 JOHN NAPIER (1550–1617)
inventor of the logarithm

The logarithm is the exponent of a base number that produces a larger number; thus in $10^2 = 100$, the 2 is the logarithm of 10. Seems simple, but it is one of the most remarkable single achievements in the history of mathematics and has saved astronomers, actuaries, and others untold billions of hours of computation. "It came to the world as a bolt from the blue," said the scholar Lord Moulton in 1914. "It stands isolated, breaking upon human thought abruptly, without borrowing from the work of other intellects." Napier was also a fanatical Protestant doomsayer who calculated that the world would end between 1688 and 1700. One of his hobbies was designing instruments of war, from burning mirrors and "devises for sayling under water" to an artillery piece capable of killing "thirty thousand Turks without the hazard of one Christian." **3,400**

864 KARL LANDSTEINER (1868–1943)
scientist who wrote the ABCs of blood types

Before Landsteiner, physicians avoided surgeries that would be especially bloody; hemophiliacs always died young. After the Austrian-born Landsteiner described three major blood groups—A, B, and C—in 1901, transfusions of compatible blood from one person to another were feasible. Two colleagues later identified a fourth group—AB—and the C type was renamed O. Transfusions became widespread in 1914 after Richard Lewisohn perfected a way to preserve blood. Landsteiner's method of sorting blood types was in use throughout the twentieth century. In 1930 Landsteiner, who had become an American citizen the year before, won the Nobel Prize in medicine for his work. Then, just three years before his death, Landsteiner's collaboration with researcher A. S. Weiner led to the identification of blood's Rh factor, a crucial discovery that allowed treatment of a deadly blood disorder found in some newborns. **3,398**

865 JOHANN PESTALOZZI (1746–1827)
molder of modern elementary education

Swiss reformer Pestalozzi's progressive approach to educating the young seems like A B C now: Dispense with traditional lecturing, memorization, and strict discipline and recognize children's individual differences and stages of development. He valued drawing, writing, singing, exercise, model- and map-making, and nature walks. He was the first to introduce music into the primary school curriculum. Influenced by French philosopher Jean-Jacques Rousseau (19), Pestalozzi spent thirty years promoting his own ideas (*How Gertrude Teaches Her Children* was an influential work) before putting them into practice. His break came after the French Revolution when he was asked to open a school for orphans and peasants in Yverdon. "First form the mind and then furnish it" was his motto. He worked on reasoning and logical thinking first, then reading. His spirit lives on in every grade-school classroom. **3,374**

866 CHRISTINE DE PISAN (1365–1429?)
feminist before it was fashionable

This began as an entry about Novella D'Andrea, an Italian law professor who hid behind a screen so her students would not be distracted by her beauty. We unearthed a reference to D'Andrea in the French De Pisan's *The Book of the City of Ladies*, published in 1405. De Pisan convinced us that our fourteenth-century Marcia Clark was but a footnote in the millennium. (D'Andrea only occasionally substituted for her dad, the professor.) But hey, we liked De Pisan's flair. De Pisan, France's first woman author and about the earliest professional woman writer we could find, may have been the world's first feminist. When De Pisan debated military ethics in *The Book of Feats of Arms and Chivalry*, her editor made it appear to have been written by a man. He didn't have the same qualms when she penned the oldest surviving treatise on women's rights, her *City of Ladies.*   **3,361**

867 HARVEY WILEY (1844–1930)
leader of the healthy food fight

Wiley, a government chemist, was troubled that formaldehyde was used to preserve milk and that copper sulfate colored canned peas. Believing that additives couldn't possibly be healthy, Wiley created a poison squad to find out. He hired strapping college graduates and fed them three square meals a day. The catch was that the food from his kitchen was laced with additives and chemicals. In exchange for food they submitted to physical examinations and collected their urine and feces for analysis. The results confirmed his suspicions. A progressive scientist in a progressive era, Wiley's work received lots of publicity and the backing of America's women's clubs, although industrial lobbies tried to sidetrack him. When President Teddy Roosevelt (700), who liked his saccharin and balked when Wiley attempted to ban it, signed the Pure Food and Drug Act in 1906, Wiley was appointed to oversee its enforcement as head of the first Food and Drug Administration.   **3,359**

868 KUROSAWA AKIRA (1910–1998)
Asia's greatest filmmaker

He started working in movie studios in the 1930s and directed his first feature during World War II. U.S. Army censors banned his 1945 samurai flick, *Those Who Tread on the Tiger's Tail,* because they felt it glorified Japan's military traditions; they didn't realize it was a parody. In 1950 Kurosawa made one of the most acclaimed movies ever, *Rashomon,* four versions of a single event from the perspectives of the ghost of a murdered man, his wife, a bandit, and a witness. In the artistry of the millennium, it's hard to find a

more effective depiction of the elusiveness of truth. Among the best of his three dozen movies are so-called Eastern Westerns, including *The Seven Samurai, Yojimbo,* and *Ran,* action movies made art by riveting characterization and photography. Kurosawa decided to kill himself after a bout with depression in 1971, but he botched the job and went back to work.   **3,352**

869 ROBERT CLIVE (1725–1774)
the soldier of Britain's fortune

His victories did more than anything to make India the jewel in Britain's imperial crown. The "heaven born general," as Prime Minister William Pitt the Elder (804) called Clive, thwarted the Dutch and French in southern and western India. Then, with the loss of just eighteen soldiers, he won control of East India in 1757 at the Battle of Plassey, near Calcutta. Clive started as a clerk in the British East India Company, but fighting suited him better. His decision to become a soldier was lucrative; trading in India made him a rich man. In the House of Commons in 1773 he defended himself successfully against a charge of embezzlement, complaining he was being treated like a common "sheep stealer." A year later, depressed by the pain of constant illnesses, he cut his throat and died.   **3,343**

870 ANTHONY VAN DYCK (1599–1641)
profound portraitist

Van Dyck was one of the most brilliant colorists in art history. He idealized his subjects while conveying their individuality, an approach that enormously influenced later artists, including Sir Joshua Reynolds and Thomas Gainsborough. After he became the renowned Rubens's (281) assistant at age eighteen, Rubens reportedly steered his young charge to portraits so he couldn't overshadow the great one at religious art. A trip to Italy introduced Van Dyck to the Venetian masters, notably Titian, who also influenced his work. Van Dyck excelled in combining warmth with dignity as evidenced in his portrait *Maria Louisa de Tassis*. Proud and ambitious, he also was hard-working and the most prolific artist of his century; five hundred Van Dyck portraits survive. He loved luxury and entertained lavishly. As court artist for England's King Charles I, he treated patrons to elaborate meals and wine. Some say these indulgences prompted his early death. **3,325**

871 LUIGI PIRANDELLO (1867–1936)
playwright in search of illusion

His invention of "the theater within the theater" had a marked influence on modern drama. Like his other works, Pirandello's world-famous 1921 play, *Six Characters in Search of an Author,* is a complex fantasy exploring the nature of illusion and reality, the permanence of art versus ever-changing life. Pirandello's characters think, debate, and try to resolve emotional problems in rational ways—an intellectual dimension Pirandello considered his true achievement, said biographer Renate Matthaei. The playwright was traumatized by his early years in Sicily's repressive and violent society. His father was a raging despot; his wife went insane and had to be institutionalized. Pirandello's output also included novels, short stories, essays, and poems. "My art is full of bitter compassion for all those who deceive themselves," he said, "but this compassion cannot fail to be followed by the ferocious derision of destiny which condemns man to deception." **3,309**

872 JOHN DEWEY (1859–1952)
professional educator

He developed the chief principle of American education: Children learn best when their lessons are related to the real world. He gave rote learning and abstract theorizing an F and taught that children must learn to think critically, using analysis and logic. Even modern educators who think children need a broad foundation of facts don't argue for a return to the pre-Dewey days when the facts had no social context. Dewey was a lecturer at the University of Chicago and Columbia University and, surprisingly, less than riveting in the classroom. "The wonder was how one who so stressed the role of interest in the educative process could himself fail so abysmally to create it in his own classes," wrote biographer George Dyukhuizen. Many people think he had something to do with the Dewey Decimal System of library classification. That was Melvil Dewey, who didn't make our list because his system is only one of many used around the world. **3,298**

873 DOROTHEA DIX (1802–1887)
crusader for the mentally ill

Thanks to family and friends, the impoverished Dix gained an education and opened her own grammar school. She returned these kindnesses by dedicating her life to improving conditions for the mentally ill. In 1841 Dix taught Sunday school at the East Cambridge, Massachusetts, jail and was shocked to see the shivering mass of mental patients herded into one clammy room. Don't worry, a guard said, these people can't feel the cold. Dix toured other Massachusetts jails and recorded similar horrors. Her report to state legislators in 1843 triggered widespread reforms. Dix extended her crusade, seeing special hospitals built for mental patients in fifteen states and Canada. Except for the Civil War, when she supervised the Union's nursing staff, Dix continued her campaign until she was eighty years old. "The more I do for the mentally sick and the poor," Dix said, "the more I see to do." **3,292**

874 ALEXANDRE DUMAS (1802–1870)
master of the historical melodrama

Dumas's swaggering romantic novels, *The Three Musketeers* and *The Count of Monte Cristo,* have delighted generations and been translated into almost every language. He produced four hundred books, sometimes relying on ghostwriters to maintain his output and revenue. Even so, the flamboyant Dumas was always short of cash. Known as Dumas *père,* he sired an illegitimate son, Alexandre Dumas, whose fame rests on the play *Camille,* the story of the tragic love affair of a consumptive courtesan. It inspired Verdi's (476) opera *La Traviata.* In old age the once exuberant and triumphant Dumas *père* began doubting his worth, wondering if any of his writings would survive. The son once came upon his elderly father reading *The Three Musketeers.* Dumas *père* explained he had promised himself to read the novel when he was old to see if it was good. "And what's your opinion?" the son asked. "It's good," Dumas answered. **3,289**

875 FRANÇOIS-ANDRÉ PHILIDOR
(1726–1795) *the chess king*

The game of kings was developed in China or India before the sixth century. But it was French opera composer Philidor who conceived of the modern game with every piece on the board—even lowly pawns—having a separate value. This unleashed upon the world a game that has challenged the intellects of millions. Philidor's gamesmanship in the Café de la Regence in Paris when he was a teenager made that city the chess center of the world. He became the greatest chess master of his time, helping to promote national schools to teach the game. His instructional book, *Analysis of Chess,* was published in 1749 and remained popular for generations. He astonished London audiences with his blindfolded exhibitions, playing as many as three opponents simultaneously. When death came, however, he was alone and poverty-stricken. "On Monday last," one London newspaper intoned, "Mr. Philidor, the celebrated chess player, made his last move." **3,275**

876 WILLARD LIBBY (1908–1980)
atom time-keeper

When researchers pinpoint the ages of Renaissance paintings or investigate the validity of Christ's supposed burial cloth, they use techniques based on Nobel Prize–winner Libby's "atomic clock." Libby, a chemistry professor at the University of Chicago, found a way to measure tiny amounts of radioactive carbon-14, an element that all organic matter absorbs from the earth's atmosphere, then gradually loses after death. The older the object, Libby theorized, the less radioactivity it gives off. He found, for example, that the final phase of North America's ice age was ten thousand, not twenty-five thousand years ago. Libby's scientific career spanned fifty years and included work on the atomic bomb and leadership of the worldwide Atoms for Peace project. "If we treat the atom well and handle her wisely," Libby said, "the awful aspect of the warlike atom will be softened by the great power for good that she has brought us." **3,261**

877 ALEXANDER MACKENZIE (1764?–1820)
fur-flung traveler

He was a Scottish-born fur trader who sought a river route to the Pacific Ocean from Canada's cold heartland. That way pelts could be shipped around the world from Pacific ports. To do it, he made two of the most arduous voyages since the Odyssey. In 1789 he canoed up the river that bears his name and reached the Arctic Ocean, a frozen dead end. In 1793 he set out again, discovering the Fraser River and carving the first overland route across the Canadian Rockies to reach the Pacific coast in British Columbia. MacKenzie's deeds may have hurt England in the long run. They frightened Anglophobic president Thomas Jefferson (64) into sending Lewis (505) and Clark to secure a U.S. foothold in the Northwest. MacKenzie was the prototypical Canadian doer—self-effacing, respectful of his inferiors, and blessed with mythic stamina. He lamented that the frenzy of his explorations left him little time to study the geography, plants, and animals along the routes. **3,256**

878 ISAAC BASHEVIS SINGER (1904–1991)
literary magic-maker

The sometimes impish Singer wrote in Yiddish about the Jews of his native Poland and adopted America. His world was populated by rabbis, cobblers, housewives, lovers, and oddballs, as well as demons, witches, and ghosts. "Thousands of years of Jewish history are embedded in him," the critic Alfred Kazin said. And in the magic of Singer's storytelling, a biographer wrote, "the ice freezes harder and the sun shines hotter than in other places." When he was awarded the Nobel Prize for literature in 1978, he said, "I am sorry writers greater than I didn't get it." But told he would get $163,000, he added, "Since it came, I will take it like a man." Asked whether he really believed in imps, Singer answered yes. But then, how could someone so full of fun and mischief say no? **3,242**

879 JAMES I OF ENGLAND (1566–1625)
the wisest foole in Christendome

That appellation was meant to convey both James's erudition and his weakness of character. His reign is most famous for things that happened with scant input from him: the King James Version of the Bible; the gunpowder plot; the colonization of America; Shakespeare (5). James had the misfortune to be caught between two of the strongest-willed women in history: his mother, Mary, Queen of Scots (610); and Elizabeth I (31), who had Mary beheaded. James's absolutism set the stage for the English Civil War, which ended in the beheading of his son, Charles I. All those beheadings! Even peace-loving James couldn't resist lopping off poor Sir Walter Raleigh's (472) noggin. But he had his P.C. moments, likening tobacco fumes to "the horrible Stygian smoke of the pit that is bottomless." He sought refuge in books, dreaming of being imprisoned in a library and "chained together with these good authors." **3,239**

880 JUDAH HA-LEVI (c.1075–1141)
poet of spiritual longing

A Jewish physician in medieval Spain, Judah ha-Levi described his yearning for Jerusalem in words of haunting beauty. "When I dream of the return of thy captivity, I am a harp for thy songs," he wrote in "Ode to Zion," his most famous poem. Elsewhere, he imagined the city of David: "Beautiful height! the whole world's gladness! / O great King's city, mountain blest!" Overcome by awe of God, he proclaimed, "The endless whirl of worlds may not contain Thee." The German poet Heinrich Heine pronounced him "God-kissed." In old age Judah ha-Levi left Spain to seek the land of his ancestors but died in Egypt before he got there. Legend has it he was slain by a Muslim as he entered Jerusalem's ruins. Assessing his greatness, another medieval poet said Judah ha-Levi "broke into the treasure house of song" and, leaving, "shut the gate behind him." **3,228**

881 PAUL KRUGER (1825–1904)
Boer pit bull and architect of the Afrikaaner nation

As a boy, Kruger accompanied his family on the Great Trek of the Dutch-speaking Boers into the African interior to escape British rule. A founder of the Transvaal republic, he led the fight for independence after Britain annexed it in 1877. He became president in 1883 and governed until his flight to Europe in 1900 after the outbreak of the Boer War. An unlettered man who believed the earth was flat, Kruger exhorted his troops: "Brothers! Act with all promptness and zeal. Read Psalm thirty-three, from verse seven to the end." His sense of divine mission foreshadowed the stubbornness of the white-minority regime that ruled South Africa for most of the twentieth century. The British won the war but left in 1931. The Boers changed the course of African history, dominating southern Africa into the 1990s and still exercising immense influence.   **3,217**

882 THOMAS NAST (1840–1902)
visions of Santa Claus danced in his head

We had considered Nast as top political cartoonist, but chose instead Honoré Daumier (587). Then a friend suggested that Nast had created the modern image of Santa. We took a second look. She was right. Although Clement Moore's 1823 poem, "'Twas The Night Before Christmas," described Santa as a jolly old elf, it wasn't until Nast began drawing for *Harper's Weekly* decades later that the chubby and plump version of Santa in a red velvet suit appeared. Nast also created the myth of Santa's workshop at the North Pole. In addition to his role as Mr. Christmas, Nast drew some of America's most defining emblems: Uncle Sam, Columbia, the Tammany tiger, the Republican elephant, and the Democratic donkey. As a political force, he was respected. Ulysses S. Grant (371) said he was elected president thanks to "the sword of Sheridan and the pencil of Thomas Nast."   **3,210**

883 AFONSO DE ALBUQUERQUE
(1453–1515) *the hammer that forged Portugal's Asian empire*

On a mission for King Emmanuel in 1503, Albuquerque established the first European trading station in India and put the Arabs out of the spice business by raiding their posts. Then he added the rich cities of Calicut, Malacca, and Goa to Portugal's possessions. Albuquerque thought big when it came to destroying Muslims, whom he hated for killing his brother Martin. He mused about diverting the Nile to make Egypt a wasteland, and he killed every Muslim man, woman, and child in Goa in 1510. Yet it shows how much worse his successors were that for almost a century, Muslims and Hindus remembered Albuquerque as a man of justice and prayed at his tomb in Goa for deliverance from Portuguese cruelty. (Albuquerque, New Mexico, was named for someone else, an eighteenth-century Spanish viceroy.)   **3,203**

884 MARCELLO MALPIGHI (1628–1694)
physiologist with a microscope

As a teenage medical student in Bologna, he amused himself by looking in microscopes. His fun became the foundation of the study of the minute structures of animal and plant organs. He explored the secrets of the lungs and demonstrated the existence of blood circulation in the capillaries. He was the first man to describe the layers of the skin—one section is called the Malpighian layer in his honor—and he studied the nervous system and secretion glands. Just as important, Malpighi showed that examination of easier-to-study lower organisms such as silkworms and chick embryos provides lessons that could be applied to human physiology. He looked at entire bodies too; he was personal physician to Pope Innocent XII for three years.   **3,198**

885 JOHN MACDONALD (1815–1891)
*first prime minister
of a united Canada*

"The story of Canadian nationality seemed to write itself around him from the start," declared historian Donald Creighton. All the wily Scot's policies—western settlement, trade protectionism, transcontinental railways—were aimed at unifying his vast and underpopulated adopted country. Late in his career he fought off a movement for commercial union with the United States, saying he would oppose this "veiled treason with my utmost effort, with my latest breath." And while he was pro-British—he had even wanted to call the new confederation the Kingdom of Canada—he was determined to keep Canada out of the British imperial orbit, declaring there was no reason to send troops to the Sudan "to get Gladstone and Company out of the hole they have plunged themselves into out of their own imbecility."   **3,191**

886 EMMA GOLDMAN (1869–1940)
anarchist without a country

"Red Emma" was deported from the United States after she protested the draft during World War I. A rabble-rouser for years, Goldman had spent a year in prison for suggesting that the starving unemployed during the 1893 depression should steal bread. The official charge was inciting a riot. Goldman also was suspected but never charged in the 1901 assassination of President McKinley. She clashed with authorities over birth control and her support of anarchism in her magazine *Mother Earth,* which was banned in 1917. When the Russian-born Goldman was shipped back to the Soviet Union in 1919, she discovered it wasn't what she had expected. The United States refused to let her back, and Goldman died in exile. Now she's everybody's darling—she's a victim who put principles ahead of her own comfort, or an enduring reminder of the right-wing bumper sticker: "America: Love it or leave it."   **3,184**

887 ARTHUR RIMBAUD (1854–1891)
poet adventurer

Scratch the verse of many twentieth-century poets, and you'll uncover French genius Rimbaud. He introduced a revolutionary theory of poetry aimed not at pleasing or instructing but at changing life, said critic Martin Turnell. The most prized books of Rimbaud's poems: *Illuminations* and *A Season in Hell.* Many consider the poem "Le Bateau Ivre" (The Drunken Boat), his finest. It shows the stages of a man's development from restricted childhood, to free manhood, then disillusionment with liberty. Rimbaud's short, thirty-seven years were packed with creativity, travels, and dangerous liaisons. Older poet Paul Verlaine shot him in the wrist when Rimbaud ended their tempestuous affair. Verlaine got a jail term. After Rimbaud finished *A Season,* he renounced literature to spend his final years in Africa as an explorer and gunrunner. Letters show he knew of his growing celebrity at home but apparently didn't care. **3,179**

888 BOB DYLAN (b. 1941)
poet laureate of the counterculture

There was folk music before Dylan lent it his raspy, nasal, and off-key voice. But after Dylan it was never the same. He gave a sound to a generation in search of something to feel bad about. First came his protest songs, "Blowin' in the Wind" and "The Times They Are A-Changin'," the anthems of 1960s restlessness. But like the decade he personified, Dylan kept shocking America, abandoning his simple folk style for hard rock in 1965, switching to blues music after a near-fatal motorcycle accident in 1966, and turning to religious themes after his conversion to Christianity in

1979. Born Robert Zimmerman, the son of a Jewish hardware-store owner in Duluth, Minnesota, Dylan reputedly adopted his new name after the poet Dylan Thomas, though some say his idol was really Matt Dillon, the sheriff of *Gunsmoke*. Joan Baez, another folk star, said of him, "He is a complicated, problematic, difficult person. I see Bobby with a slightly damaged diamond in his head." But don't think twice; it's all right. **3,172**

889 WARREN BUFFETT (b. 1930)
the investment oracle from Omaha

More than anyone, Buffett embodies the universal human itch to get rich. And as hundreds of millions of people throughout the globe pump every spare penny, pfennig, or yen into stocks as their hope for financial salvation, Buffett stands tall—about $15 billion tall at last count—as the man to emulate. He amassed his fortune using a method called "value investing," which he learned from a college professor. Basically it involves buying good stocks and holding on to them. "It's just so simple," Buffett said. "It's like studying for the priesthood and finding out that the Ten Commandments were all you needed." Maybe it helps to lust after lucre from the time you're a tot, like little four-year-old Warren running around the house with a money changer. Anyway, if you had invested ten thousand in his company in 1956 . . . Naw. You don't want to know. **3,169**

890 HENRI BERGSON (1859–1941)
debunker of scientific rationalism

Bergson, an influential philosopher, acknowledged the laws of physics but denied they could reveal ultimate truth. On a walk in 1884, he had an illumination: "I saw that scientific time does not endure." Time was not a mathematical line, he concluded, but a living reality "experienced within ourselves through consciousness." In *Cre-*

ative Evolution he argued that the essential force at work in the universe was a "vital impulse." From his youth this slight, cerebral Frenchman exerted a powerful magnetism on friends. "From your whole personality emanated a singular charm," a high-school classmate told him years later in a toast. Bergson showed uncommon courage as anti-Semitism reared its head in France. A Jew drawn to Catholicism, he refused to convert because he wanted to remain with the persecuted. He died in bed before the pro-Hitler Vichy regime could get its hands on him. **3,166**

891 JOHN H. HAMMOND, JR. (1888–1965)
remote controller

The son of a famed mining engineer, Hammond found inspiration from Daddy's friends, who included Edison (28), the Wright brothers (23, 24), Bell (74), and Marconi (95). Hammond's first successful invention was a circuit breaker that he connected to the door of his boarding school bedroom so he could circumvent the eight P.M. lights-out rule. After applying himself to more noteworthy areas, Hammond pioneered radio remote control. In 1914 he launched an unmanned yacht and sailed it 120 miles from Gloucester, Massachusetts, to Boston and back by remote control. In the eighty-some years since that first experiment, remote control has been used as a cornerstone of missile technology. More important in our day-to-day existence, it has allowed us to wallow at home as couch potatoes, "zapping" our way past dozens of television stations without touching the dial. **3,159**

892 GIUSEPPE MAZZINI (1805–1872)
Italian unification's remote controller

We rank Mazzini, one of the founding fathers of a united Italy, behind the military hero Giuseppe

Garibaldi (368) but ahead of politician Camillo Bense-Cavour (who didn't make our list). Mazzini preached insurrection to rid Italy of foreign rulers. "Neither pope nor king. Only God and the people," he declared. Mazzini briefly organized a republic in Rome in 1848 and was instrumental in uniting Italy under King Victor Emmanuel II of Sardinia in 1861. For much of his career his detractors mocked him for fomenting rebellion from the safety of exile abroad. But British historian Thomas Carlyle (691) called him "a man of genius and virtue" and took him on walks in the English countryside to counter the effects of heavy smoking and coffee-drinking. An opponent of communism and an early advocate of women's rights, Mazzini saw "the finger of God in the pages of history." Sick of the poverty that forced him to frequent London pawnshops, he tried his hand at selling imported Genoa salami. The business failed. **3,152**

893 SAMUEL HAHNEMANN (1755–1843)
original homeopathic physician

The German Hahnemann was so frustrated with the purging, blistering, and bloodletting routines in medicine that he abandoned his medical practice and became a translator. Then, in the midst of translating a medical text, he found a reference to the use of Peruvian bark to treat malaria. Today we know the bark contains quinine, which does indeed ease malaria's dreaded symptoms. But for Hahnemann, the reference provided the spark he needed to explore alternative treatments. He eventually concluded that natural remedies that produced symptoms similar to a disease should be used in minuscule amounts to cure illness. He used deadly belladonna to treat scarlet fever and camphor to counter cholera. They worked. Hahnemann, who documented about one hundred untraditional remedies for

diseases, dubbed his approach "homeopathy"—*homeo* for similar and *pathos* for suffering. **3,148**

894 GOLDA MEIR (1898–1978)
Israeli prime minister who extended her hand to the enemy

When Meir died, former U.S. secretary of state Henry Kissinger said her life symbolized the "idealism that made ordinary men and women fulfill an historic vision in a barren land." Indeed, Meir had never seemed headed for greatness. Raised in Milwaukee, she emigrated to Israel in 1921, where she worked on a kibbutz and took in laundry. After a stint in local politics, Meir helped craft the Israeli state. She joked that Moses had done the Israelites dirty: "He dragged us forty years through the desert to bring us to the one place in the Middle East where there was no oil." Meir served as foreign minister, then as prime minister. But the surprise Arab attack on Israel in 1973 led to criticism of her government, and she resigned the following year. Still, she had earned her niche in history by promising that Israel would negotiate wherever the Arabs chose—a promise fulfilled months before her death when Menachem Begin and Anwar Sadat (862) shook hands. **3,126**

895 HENRY MOORE (1898–1986)
sculptor of sensuous shapes

While other artists were blowtorching steel beams to depict the sterility of modern life, Moore was carving wood and casting bronze molds of warm curvaceous forms. His vision of art is so much more appealing. Moore said the human form mesmerized him but that he turned to the shapes of rocks, bones, and tree branches for inspiration. His massive hunks of wood, stone, marble, and bronze, all looking vaguely human and interspersed with holes and nooks, cry out to be caressed. Like great artists before him, Moore turned again and again to the mother/child theme, but his abstract interpretations bear little resemblance to classic Renaissance madonnas. During World War II his drawings in London underground stations, then shelters from German bombs, inspired Londoners and made a name for Moore among his countrymen. Today his sculptures grace museums and outdoor parks around the world.   **3,121**

896 JOHN HENRY NEWMAN (1801–1890)
Catholic prize in Protestant England

Lifelong Catholics marvel at the fervor of converts—they're like reformed smokers in their zeal. Newman was no exception. The Anglican vicar at St. Mary's in Oxford, Newman organized and led the Oxford Movement to reform the Church of England. Followers soon suspected, however, that something was rotten in Oxford: The more Newman studied, the more fascinated he was by Catholicism. On September 18, 1843, he preached his last sermon in the Church of England and, two years later, converted to Catholicism. His poems, hymns, novels, and essays, coupled with his stature among British clergy, revived Catholicism in England. Cardinal Newman's most important work, *Apologia pro Vita Sua,* traces the journey to his conversion and establishes him as one of Catholicism's greatest thinkers. Considered an autobiographical masterpiece, the book responded to criticism by Anglican clergyman and author Charles Kingsley, who argued that Catholics were uninterested in truth.   **3,099**

897 RABINDRANATH TAGORE (1861–1941)
Bengal's poetic seer

He was the first Asian Nobel laureate for literature, and he won it in 1913 after publication of *Gitanjali,* a book of inspirational verses that prompted his editor, William Butler Yeats (521), to write: "We are not moved because of its strangeness, but because we have met our own image." *Gitanjali* seems dated now, but the prize and praise by the likes of Ezra Pound (367) and Albert Einstein (17) made Tagore an international celebrity. He makes the list for using his fame well. He became the leading spokesman for an independent India that would include the best of both Eastern and Western cultures. For this Tagore was reviled by the uncompromisingly nationalist Mahatma Gandhi (12), but love of Western culture didn't make Tagore a toady for the British Raj. He preached anti-imperialism everywhere, including his school near Calcutta, where many of independent India's future leaders were students, including Prime Minister Indira Gandhi (791).   **3,091**

898 MIKHAIL KUTUZOV (1745–1813)
Russian boot to Napoleon's butt

The "sly old fox of the north," as Napoleon (16) called Kutuzov, understood that keeping an army intact to threaten an invader is more important than winning battles. In 1812 Kutuzov fought Napoleon to a draw at the Battle of Borodino near Moscow and then withdrew his forces. With the Russian army in the field, Napoleon could not dictate a surrender, and his retreating army lost almost 500,000 men to the Russian winter and Kutuzov's guerrillas. The defeat set the stage for Napoleon's ultimate downfall at Waterloo in 1815. Czar Alexander hated Kutuzov's drinking and womanizing, and critics accused the general of sleeping during battles. But his wisdom about when to fight and when to run prompted military strategist Karl von Clausewitz (114) to write that of those who fought Napoleon, "the prudent and wily Kutuzov was his most dangerous adversary."   **3,084**

899 JACK LONDON (1876–1916)
macho writer and socialist

Before he was twenty-two, London was a seaman, seal hunter, pirate, hobo, jailbird, and Klondike gold prospector—experiences he mined for some of the millennium's most popular adventure stories. His best novels are *White Fang,* the autobiographical *Martin Eden,* and his masterpiece, *The Call of the Wild,* written from the perspective of a dog. In the years just before World War I, he was the highest-paid writer in the world, and his no-nonsense narratives about tough guys with poetic sensibilities influenced Ernest Hemingway (388), Eugene O'Neill (426), and Henry Miller. London's own favorite was *The People of the Abyss,* an account of slum-dwelling. The book aired the ardent socialism that made London so popular with the Soviet hierarchy. No American novelist's works, save Mark Twain's (188), have sold so many copies in Russian translation. Ill health and alcoholism finally dragged London down, and he died of a self-inflicted overdose of morphine. **3,076**

900 COLE PORTER (1892–1964)
sophisticated songwriter who got under our skin

Porter not only gave us urbane, clever lyrics, he also wrote melodies that begged to be sung, classics like "I Get a Kick Out of You," "Begin the Beguine," and "I've Got You Under My Skin." Consider the haunting "Night and Day," from his 1932 blockbuster musical *Gay Divorcee:* "Day and night, why is it so / that this longing for you follows wherever I go? / In the roaring traffic's boom / In the silence of my lonely room / I think of you night and day." Of the many shows he wrote, Porter's crowning achievement was *Kiss Me Kate,* a musical within a musical based on Shakespeare's (5) *Taming of the Shrew.* The public never knew Porter was plagued by physical problems. A horse riding accident in 1937 led to thirty-seven operations and eventual amputation of his leg. Professionally, however, he never lost his sangfroid. Composer Richard Adler called Porter "an aristocrat in everything he did and wrote. Everything had class—even a little pop song like 'Don't Fence Me In.'" **3,065**

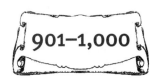

901–1,000

Welcome to the land of the almost-didn't-make-its. We tossed out John Kennedy but included Richard Nixon; we said no to Oprah Winfrey but gave Rosa Parks the nod; Paul Robeson is in, Mick Jagger's out. Ridiculous, you say? Don't blame us—it's the finely tuned BioGraph System that determined who's in and who's out.

There are more living people in this group than any other, and more than half these entries feature people who lived in the twentieth century. Many charted popular culture—fashion designer Coco Chanel and playboy Hugh Hefner, for example. We also pay homage to the American way of life—Coca-Cola, *USA Today,* suburban sprawl, disposable diapers, marching bands, soup cans, and *The Cat in the Hat.*

The reason so many contemporary movers and shakers are relegated to the back of the book is because the BioGraph System rewards a person's lasting influence. With the folks of our own century, it's simply impossible to gauge what their influence ultimately will be. They have had the misfortune of living at the end of the millennium. Time will determine their place in history, but not in time for this ranking.

That's why the last hundred people generated our most heated debates. Take President Kennedy, for example. He was enormously popu-

lar, even in death. But what was his lasting influence? Will he, a century from now, be considered the James Garfield of the twentieth century?

That's our bet.

Yet a folk hero like Michael Jordan makes the grade because there's no doubt he'll leave behind a tangible legacy. Jordan may hang up his Nikes, but the record book will reflect his achievements. He is the basketball player against whom all others are measured.

The 1997 death of Diana, princess of Wales, in a car accident in Paris generated an outpouring of affection and near-hysterical mourning. Does she belong on our list? Maybe the next millennium will show she was the one who sealed the fate of a dying monarchy or that her campaign against land mines ultimately forced their elimination. It's too early to tell. Look for the answers to that and other pressing questions in our sequel, scheduled for publication in the year 3000.

901 JOHN STEINBECK (1902–1968)
novelist of the little people

Steinbeck's masterpiece, *The Grapes of Wrath*, brought the plight of Dust Bowl migrants to the nation's consciousness. The Joad family leaves drought-stricken Oklahoma and strikes out for California to find work. But promised jobs don't materialize, family members suffer even crueler times, and except for Ma, they crumble. Steinbeck knew whereof he wrote: as a youth, he was a laborer in California's Salinas Valley; during the Depression he spent months interviewing families in government camps for displaced Okies. "What he cared about was writing itself," said biographer Jackson Benson. "He wrote because he loved to write, because he was addicted to it." As the Nobel Prize–winning Steinbeck saw it, "a writer out of loneliness is trying to communicate like a distant star sending signals." **3,039**

902 FRANCES PERKINS (1882–1965)
laborer for labor

When Franklin Roosevelt (37) was governor of New York, he appointed Perkins, a former social worker, as state industrial commissioner. She forged political connections that smoothed the path for social welfare bills. It was only fitting, then, that Roosevelt, as newly elected president, thought of Perkins for his labor secretary. She was the first woman appointed to a U.S. cabinet post, and she served eleven years. Labor leaders didn't put out the welcome mat. President William Green of the American Federation of Labor said his members could never accept Perkins as secretary of labor. But Fannie, as she was known, changed their minds. One of the staunchest New Dealers in the Roosevelt administration during the depths of the Depression, she promoted liberal labor legislation that established a minimum wage, a maximum work week, unemployment benefits, and limits on child labor. **3,029**

903 MICHAEL JORDAN (b. 1963)
his royal Airness

We're not going to get into an argument here about whether Jordan's the greatest athlete who ever lived (he wasn't much of a baseball player). He's simply the best basketball player. Even Isaac Newton (6) would be awed. With mouth wide open and tongue hanging out, the six-foot-six guard regularly defied gravity. Jordan and his Chicago Bulls dominated the National Basketball Association. One of the world's most recognizable faces, Jordan made money from endorsements for sneakers, hot dogs, hamburgers, cologne, and just about anything else. Although former Celtics star Larry Bird once said, "Maybe this guy is God disguised as Michael Jordan," his destiny was not always clear. Jordan was cut from the high school team his freshman year. He made a nice splash at the University of North Carolina but only went third in the 1984 NBA draft, behind Hakeem Olajuwon and Sam Bowie. Sam who? **3,023**

904 RICHARD M. NIXON (1913–1994)
first American president to resign

Writer Gore Vidal said Nixon was "too outsize an American figure" to be comprehended. As a boy, Nixon signed a letter to his mother, "Your good dog, RICHARD." As Ike's (374) running mate, he saved his political career by declaring his love for his dog Checkers on national TV. Defeated in bids for the White House and California governorship in the early 1960s, he snarled at reporters, "You won't have Richard Nixon to kick around anymore." Wrong. His five-year presidential record is marked by paradox. A free marketer, he imposed price controls. An anti-Communist, he opened ties to China, pursued détente with

Moscow, and ended the Vietnam War. Admired in Europe for his political acumen, he was driven from office in 1974 for covering up what he called a "two-bit burglary"—the Watergate scandal. If Tricky Dick had lived up to his nickname, he would have burned the incriminating tapes. **3,022**

905 REINHOLD NIEBUHR (1892–1971)
American politicians' favorite theologian

Millions who have never heard of him recite his most famous prayer: "God, give us the serenity to accept what cannot be changed, the courage to change what should be changed, and the wisdom to know the difference." In the 1930s he espoused pacifism and socialism. And though he dropped both causes to advocate resistance to Hitler (20) and Stalin (82), he helped found the liberal Americans for Democratic Action. But he scorned blind faith in human progress and preached a "Christian realism" that emphasized original sin. He was also an early opponent of the Vietnam War. His most lasting impact was on the political establishment, from George Kennan, who called him the "father of us all," to Arthur Schlesinger, Jr., who said "he cast a spell on my generation," to John Kennedy. A down-to-earth preacher, Niebuhr once broke a cabinet in his dining room while wrestling a parishioner. **2,969**

906 FRIEDRICH FROEBEL (1782–1852)
cultivator of kindergarten

German educator Froebel established a school for young children in Blankenburg in 1837. He emphasized coursework, gymnastics, and handicrafts including weaving, bookbinding, and gardening. Children played with balls, blocks, paper, and sewing cards. Pretty revolutionary in a society that thought children under seven too young for schooling. Froebel realized that play—children's natural activity—is key to learning. In *The Education of Man,* he wrote, "Play is the purest, the most spiritual, product of man at this stage, and is at once the prefiguration and imitation of the total human life." Froebel's mother died in his infancy, and his yearning for motherly love may have influenced his life's work. The Prussian government banned kindergarten as subversive in 1851—a jolt to Froebel, who died just months later. But thanks to the beneficence of a baroness, the program was spread throughout Europe and, eventually, the world. **2,950**

907 CÉSAR RITZ (1850–1918)
hotelier who personified elegance

Ritz quit his manager's job at London's Savoy Hotel in 1896 to open an elegant Parisian *auberge,* a home-away-from-home for the world's beautiful people. Ritz hired chef extraordinaire Auguste Escoffier (346) to attend to needs *gastronomique* and furnished 210 elegant rooms with enormous bathtubs, an unheard-of indulgence. His hotel was just so, well, ritzy. His name now shows up in dictionaries as a synonym for luxury. As *the* hotelier of the millennium, Ritz redefined *service* and fueled a rising consumer culture. "I know what guests want today, but what will they want tomorrow?" he mused. When the Allies stormed Paris during World War II, the hotel was personally liberated from German occupation by Ernest Hemingway (388). He sidled up to the bar that now bears his name, put down his gun, and ordered whiskey. "When I dream of an afterlife, the action always takes place in the Paris Ritz," Hemingway said. **2,948**

908 ERICH MARIA REMARQUE
(1898–1970) *antiwar novelist*

Remarque wrote *All Quiet on the Western Front,* the best-known depiction of World War I and the basis for the classic 1930 film. Remarque, who was drafted into the German army, culled memories of the camaraderie of soldiers amidst the horrors of everyday warfare to write his searing novel in 1929. The narrator is eighteen-year-old Paul Baumer, a foot soldier dreaming of a better life after the war. Baumer comes to understand the absurdity of the conflict yet realizes he is trapped in it. He dies at the front "almost glad," Remarque wrote, that "the end had come." The book infuriated German right-wingers, who bristled at the novel's indictment of capitalists, politicians, and the military. Leftists criticized Remarque for his apolitical stance, saying he should have demonstrated revolutionary sentiment. Remarque was safely in exile when Hitler (20) rose to power and the Nazis burned his book. **2,927**

909 GREGORY MARTIN (c.1540–1582)
English translator of the Catholic Bible

Catholic authorities discouraged lay people from reading the Scriptures but recognized that priests needed ammunition to counter Protestants versed in the Bible. In fact, when Martin's English Bible finally appeared, it was banned from alehouses and contained a warning that it should not be read by "husbandmen, artificers, apprentices, boys, girls, mistresses, maids." Martin, formerly an Oxford tutor, began his work in Reims in 1578. Translating two chapters a day, he completed the New Testament in 1582 but died before finishing the Old Testament, which was ultimately published in 1609. Martin's English version influenced the language selection in the 1611 King James Bible of the Anglican Church. Martin, who created such memorable images as the "fatted calf," was criticized for his reliance on Latin phraseology, but linguists believe his use of

Latin brought many new words into the English vocabulary. **2,911**

910 KARL BARTH (1886–1968)
cathedral of Christian thought

The Swiss scholar emphasized the "wholly otherness" of God that could never be captured in rationalism. "God is God and altogether different from all things human, even from human religion," declared the pipe-smoking aficionado of Mozart (52), mountain climbing, and mystery novels. The ultimate reality, he said, was neither science nor religion but two words, "Jesus Christ," because in Christ, God fastened himself to humanity forever. To be sure, we oversimplify his thirteen-thousand-page *Church Dogmatics,* which one admirer called a "veritable cathedral of Christian thought." Active in the Confessional Church, which opposed Nazism, Barth was bounced from the University of Bonn for refusing to take an oath of allegiance to Hitler (20). In his later years the theologian preached in the Basel prison as a "prisoner among prisoners." Alas, he had a blind spot, calling anticommunism "a greater evil than communism itself." **2,901**

911 WILLIAM JENNINGS BRYAN
(1860–1925) king of the also-rans

At age thirty-six Bryan electrified the Democratic National Convention with one of the most famous sound bites in American history, a dig at eastern bankers: "You shall not crucify mankind upon a cross of gold." Men wept; women screamed; the standing ovation lasted one hour. Nominated for president, Bryan ran on a populist platform, but his rural supporters' hero worship couldn't overcome Republican money. The Boy Orator lost—and lost again in 1900 and again in 1908. Though despised by liberals for siding with the prosecution in the Scopes trial of a schoolteacher accused of teaching evolution, Bryan was instrumental in the adoption of liberal reforms, from the popular election of senators to woman suffrage. Columnist H. L. Mencken mocked him as the leader of "anthropoid rabble," but poet Vachel Lindsay adored him as "that Heaven-born Bryan, that Homer Bryan, who sang from the West." **2,867**

912 NOAM CHOMSKY (b. 1928)
American linguist

Chomsky's theory of generative grammar, which states that the logic behind all the world's languages is wired into the human brain at birth, revolutionized his field. In essence, he is saying that children raised in the wild by wolves would develop their own language. Linguists refer to the publication of his *Syntactic Structures,* the book that lays down his arguments, as "the Event." Don't try reading it though; as one critic pointed out, for someone claiming that language is instinctive, his own use of it can get pretty convoluted. Chomsky gained even greater, if ephemeral, fame in the 1960s and 1970s as an éminence grise of the New Left, railing against the evil American empire and declaring that Presidents Kennedy, Johnson, Nixon (904), and Ford were all "guilty of racist murder on a scale undreamed of" by African tyrant Idi Amin. **2,856**

913 HANNAH ARENDT (1906–1975)
chronicler of evil

Arendt's 1951 book, *Origins of Totalitarianism,* made her famous. But she earns a place in this book for her controversial work, *Eichmann in Jerusalem.* In it, she chronicles Israel's 1961 trial of Adolf Eichmann, the middle-class bureaucrat who perfunctorily carried out Hitler's "final solution of the Jewish problem"—mass deportations and executions. Yet Arendt, who was Jewish, saw Eich-

mann not as a "monster" but as a symbol of "the banality of evil," the chilling phrase she coined to characterize everyone's potential for committing heinous acts in an atmosphere of normalcy. In 1933 the rising wave of Nazism prompted Arendt to flee her native Germany for Paris. She married, emigrated to the United States, and was soon recognized as an authority on anti-Semitism. Recent developments, however, have called her judgment into question. Arendt's letters to German philosopher Martin Heidegger (914) reveal their prewar affair and lingering attachment. Trouble is, Heidegger was a Nazi sympathizer. **2,839**

914 MARTIN HEIDEGGER (1889–1976)
evil genius

We are tempted to assess the German philosopher's influence and note, as an afterthought, the paradox of his support for Hitler (20) and lifelong friendship with the Jewish scholar of the Holocaust Hannah Arendt (913), whom he seduced when she was a teenager. But Heidegger's real importance is the warning he sends posterity to beware of intellectuals espousing higher forms of truth. He probed the nature of Being in obfuscatory language (Example: "Whatness, as the being of the essent, becomes that which is most beingful in an essent"), but the French savants Sartre, Marcuse, and company lapped up his existentialist drivel while Americans like self-help guru Werner Erhard made money from it. Alas, this lover of truth loved Hitler more, calling him "the German reality, present and future." After the war Arendt excused Heidegger's behavior as the "delusion of genius." **2,835**

915 FRANKLIN KAMENY (b. 1925)
activist who brought gays out of the closet

Kameny, an astronomer with a doctorate from Harvard, was fired in 1957 from his job with the

U.S. Army Map Service because he was homosexual. He tried to sue the government, but his case was thrown out. Even the Supreme Court refused to hear his appeal. Dejected, Kameny organized a chapter of Mattachine, a gay support group, in Washington, D.C. Instead of secret meetings to help members cope with their ostracism, however, Kameny's chapter went public. On July 4, 1964, he led a march on Philadelphia's Independence Hall. Borrowing from the civil rights movement, Kameny organized other public demonstrations and an exhaustive letter-writing campaign to government officials. His protests forced the American people to finally confront publicly the issue of government-sanctioned discrimination against homosexuals. Kameny claimed victory in 1975 when the federal government abandoned its ban on homosexuals in civil service jobs. **2,828**

916 FRANK GILBRETH (1868–1924)
original type A personality

Time is money; faster is better; it's cheaper by the dozen, et cetera, et cetera. Gilbreth made a career out of saving time and money. His studies eliminated unnecessary motion to increase industrial output. He was so consumed with efficiency that he lathered his face with two brushes to shave seventeen seconds off his morning ablutions. He tried using two razors, but the time saved was lost in the extra minutes it took to stop the bleeding. Working with his wife, Lillian, the "first lady of engineering" who taught at several universities, Gilbreth filmed a task to eliminate needless motions. For example, bricklayers who adopted his methods more than doubled their productivity. A generation after the death of this intellectual bedfellow of Frederick Taylor (414), two of Gilbreth's children memorialized his boisterous personality, eccentricities, and sometimes comical attempts to apply his theories to his household of twelve children in the bestseller *Cheaper by the Dozen.* **2,794**

917 WALTER HUNT (1796–1859)
pinhead

If this New Yorker's marketing and production skills had been half as good as his tinkering, Hunt sewing machines and Hunt fountain pens would be famous brands, and the Hunt repeating rifle would have won the West. He made early models of all those inventions only to see Singer, Parker, and Colt become rich and famous by building on his work. He invented the paper collar—a winning item when men could afford only one or two shirts—but died before it became popular. Hunt makes this list for an invention that was never bettered, the safety pin: a single loop of wire with a spring at one end and a clasp at the other. It took him only three hours to make the first pin. He obtained U.S. Patent No. 6281 for it on April 10, 1849, and then he sold the manufacturing rights for pin money: $400. **2,773**

918 JOSEPH GOEBBELS (1897–1945)
Nazi propagandist

As the ad exec in charge of the Hitler (20) account, Goebbels showed it was possible to sell anything, even garbage. He sank to the task with gusto, earning a niche in the evildoers' hall of infamy. His newspaper, *The Attack,* railed against Jews, Communists, and democrats, and as propaganda director, he legitimized Hitler in 1930 by whipping up votes that increased the Nazi Party's strength in the Reichstag from 12 delegates to 107. He had a doctorate in literature, which made him queasy about book burning, but he got over it. The clubfooted, cadaverous, dark-haired, squeaky-voiced Goebbels was no model Aryan type, and in the end he was self-delusional. Two days before Goebbels and his wife poisoned their six children and themselves in a Berlin bunker as the enemy closed in, he still believed he could negotiate an end to World War II. **2,761**

919 WILLIAM COBBETT (1763–1835)
porcupine with a pen

Cobbett liked to make sharp observations and toss pointed barbs in his *Porcupine's Gazette* newspaper. Nearly a century before muckrakers exposed social and political ills, Cobbett suggested reforms and stirred up trouble in print. He quit the British Army to avoid punishment for accusing his superiors of incompetence, and he took up journalism in America. But he ruined his welcome with articles denouncing just about everybody. He aired suggestions that George Washington (22) overdrew his salary and lent the excess at usurious rates. He said of James Madison (268), "his countenance has that sour aspect." With deportation for libel imminent, Cobbett went home to England to denounce Jews, German mercenaries, capitalists, and whatever government happened to be in power. Before Dickens (70), he railed against the crushing inhumanity of the Industrial Revolution. He supported his arguments with statistics, and his writings were so popular he was elected to the House of Commons. At last he had immunity to say what he wanted without fear of prosecution. **2,719**

920 GIROLAMO FRACASTORO (1478–1553)
medicinal poet

Venereal disease and verse? An unlikely pairing. But writer Fracastoro mated them seamlessly in his narrative poem, *Syphilis sive morbus Gallicus.* Translation: *Syphilis or the French Disease.* It presented a primitive germ theory three centuries before either Pasteur (26) or Koch (211). In thirteen hundred Latin verses filling three books,

physician Fracastoro told the mythological tale of Sifilo. Angry at Sifilo's licentiousness, the Sun God had zapped the shepherd with a disease that spawned an ulcer on his body. The poem mentions cures, including sap of the guaiacum tree and mercury. The books were blockbusters. Many say syphilis derived its name from the shepherd-character. Two years after Fracastoro's death, the Veronese erected a statue in his honor near the marble likenesses of Pliny and Catullus, two other literary luminaries, but of ancient times. **2,708**

921 SRI RAMANA MAHARISHI (1879–1950)
guru of all gurus

At the age of seventeen he realized that the self had no relationship to the body; self was unlimited, universal, and beyond space and time. He went to the holy city of Aranchala in southern India, threw away money and clothes (except a wrap for his loins), and never left. Word of his holiness spread, and the world flocked to him for spiritual advice. In 1911, his first European acolyte, F. H. Humphries, described Maharishi as "a sitting motionless corpse from which God was radiating terrifically." Maharishi taught: "If one realizes within the heart what one's true nature is, one will find that it is infinite wisdom, truth, and bliss, without beginning or end." As the leading Hindu saint of modern times, he did much to spread the notion that when it comes to religious truth, less is more. **2,697**

922 PAUL ROBESON (1898–1976)
America's deep voice of drama and dissent

As an actor, Robeson won acclaim in Eugene O'Neill's (426) *The Emperor Jones* and in Shakespeare's (5) *Othello.* His powerful bass voice brought him roles on the musical stage as well.

His rendition of the classic "Ol' Man River," from *Showboat,* made the song one with his name. As his career advanced, he also gained prominence for his recordings of black spirituals and working-class folk songs. The performing arts got Robeson on the rebound. This two-time all-American football player at Rutgers University graduated Phi Beta Kappa from Columbia University Law School in 1923. Seeing few job opportunities for black attorneys, he tried the stage and liked it. Robeson was also a concert singer, linguist, writer, and human rights activist. But his open admiration for Soviet Communism was condemned by the House Un-American Activities Committee, and he was blacklisted by Hollywood and Broadway producers. In death, his reputation as a performer and an advocate of social justice has widened like Ol' Man River at flood time. **2,680**

923 GROTE REBER (b. 1911)
charter of cosmic radio waves

Reber, an American electronics engineer, opened another door to the universe with his work in radio astronomy. He built the world's first radio telescope in his Illinois backyard in 1937. The bowl-shaped reflector, more than nine meters in diameter, sported an antenna. Neighbors must have rolled their eyes when Reber said this gizmo could "hear" extraterrestrial noises. But Reber knew something they didn't: Almost all objects in space transmit radio radiation, with pulsars, nebulas, and quasars topping the list. Reber found bursts of radio waves coming from constellations in the Milky Way. His telescope told him only the general direction of emissions. Later, sophisticated models interpreted the waves and identified the chemical composition of the pulsating body. Reber devoted the rest of his career to compiling a map of the sky, based on findings from more sensitive radio telescopes in Hawaii and Australia. **2,657**

924 JOHN PHILIP SOUSA (1854–1932)
the March King

Sousa raised the standards for performance and instrumentation in concert bands. He earned his royal title for composing 140 rousing, distinctly American military marches including "Semper Fidelis," the official march of the U.S. Marine Corps. But none of them electrifies like "Stars and Stripes Forever." He refused credit for his creativity: "All of my music, all of my melodies are not of my making; no matter how light, they came from a higher source." Legendary conductor Leopold Stokowski loved him, saying, "The music swept me off my feet. The rhythm of Sousa stirred me, for it was unique." Sousa enlisted as an apprentice in the Marine Corps band at age fourteen. Twelve years later he became its conductor and molded the band to world-class status. A good march, Sousa always maintained, "should make a man with a wooden leg step out." **2,611**

925 ANTONIO DE MENDOZA (1490–1552)
New World defender of the downtrodden

Mendoza, first viceroy of New Spain, wanted the Indians freed from slavery in 1542. But bondage continued another 178 years. As the Spanish king's personal representative in Mexico, Mendoza was an able bureaucrat who collected revenues honestly and presided over Indian affairs with compassion. He supported the king's New Laws in 1542 to limit royal land grants over the Indians but soon recognized they were unenforceable. Spanish landowners in Mexico had issued a collective howl, and the mother country buckled. Still, Mendoza got reduced hours for Indian mine workers and saw that free Indians got paid. "In the midst of all the fiery and unregulated spirit of a colony like Mexico, he sustained the dignity of his office unimpaired," wrote historian Brantz Mayer. "History must at least do him the justice to record the fact that his administration was tempered with mercy." **2,589**

926 JEAN-AUGUSTE-DOMINIQUE INGRES
(1780–1867) *grand old man of French painting*

Talk about hills and valleys—Ingres knew the landscape. He was a dominant figure in French painting for most of the nineteenth century and was the leading figure in the neoclassical school. Sure of his talents, he was often dismayed by critics' assessments. A student of Jacques-Louis David, Ingres continued his master's cool, carefully balanced style and won early acclaim. In 1806, however, his paintings were badly hung in a major exhibit, and critics panned them. In 1811 his *Jupiter and Thetis* got blasted by the Académie des Beaux-Arts. Three years after, the wondrous *Grande Odalisque*—the nude turbaned bather with the three extra vertebrae in her never-ending back—met the same reception. No wonder Ingres was worried about the reaction to his *Vow of Louis XIII* in 1824. But Parisians loved it. Charles X, no less, presented Ingres with the Cross of the Legion of Honor. Go figure. **2,576**

927 SAMUEL BECKETT (1906–1989)
leading dramatist of the theater of the absurd

This modern school of drama is all about alienation and noncommunication. Beckett's best-known achievement in this genre, the existential play *Waiting for Godot,* treats the hopelessness of the human condition with comic flair. In *Godot* the two heroes find themselves existing in the world while not knowing the purpose of that existence. They reason that they are there to wait for someone named Godot, not knowing if he will ever show or if he even exists. To the Irish-born Beckett, his heroes "seem to be falling to bits." Although Beckett often was identified with the powerless and feeble characters he created, he actually was tough, strong, and decisive. He won the Nobel Prize for literature in 1969, but shy and fiercely private, he shunned the award ceremonies in Stockholm. **2,565**

928 PETER BEHRENS (1868–1940)
master artist of the mundane

Modern consumers expect efficiency and good looks from the mass-produced products they buy. That makes every lamp, saucepan, and appliance the inspiration of an industrial designer. In the first wave of these designers, the German Behrens stands out. He was a mediocre artist dabbling in woodcuts, paintings, and ceramics when he was tapped in 1907 to be artistic adviser at Allgemeine Elektrizitäts-Gesellschaft, one of the world's largest manufacturing companies. He attracted top-notch students including Mies van der Rohe (364) and Le Corbusier (155). As a change from the curves and flourishes of art nouveau, Behrens displayed a simple, effective style with clear lines—like what we know today. One example: his electric kettle of 1908. But he's better known for his factory designs. Behrens built the company's factory complex and, later, its turbine assembly works with a glass wall. A little on the heavy side, but pleasing nonetheless. **2,563**

929 FEDERICO GARCÍA LORCA (1898–1936)
most popular modern poet of the Spanish-speaking world

Lorca's melancholy verse often dealt with death, love, lust, and violence. His greatest poem, the elegy *Lament for Ignacio Mejías,* commemorates a bullfighter fatally gored in 1934:

> At five in the afternoon.
> It was exactly five in the afternoon.
> A boy brought the white sheet
> at five in the afternoon.
> A frail of lime ready prepared
> at five in the afternoon.
> The rest was death, and death alone
> at five in the afternoon.

Lorca preferred to read his works at public gatherings before publishing them. "Verse is made to be recited," he declared. "In a book it is dead." His own death came at the hands of Nationalists during the Spanish Civil War. But they couldn't kill his poetry. His verses, Lorca once said, were "a conscious rocket of dark light let off among the dull and torpid." **2,521**

930 JANE CUNNINGHAM CROLY (1828–1901) *popularizer of women's clubs*

Croly was a well-known newspaper and magazine columnist when she tried to buy a ticket to hear Charles Dickens (70) speak at the New York Press Club. The club members laughed. She didn't get mad, she got even. In November 1868 she and her literary friends formed their own club, Sorosis. This previously unheard-of activity for respectable women was scorned by New York newspapers, which poked fun at the women in columns and cartoons. No matter. In a time when suffrage seemed radical, women's clubs provided their members with a less controversial way to involve themselves in public life. Croly's idea blossomed. Millions of women joined clubs that sprang up on the frontier, in farmlands, and in urban centers around the world. By 1900 most women's clubs were deeply involved in civic reform, fostering the kindergarten movement, creating thousands of parks, and funding public libraries. **2,499**

931 FRANÇOIS TRUFFAUT (1932–1984) *crest of the New Wave directors*

French directors who emerged after World War II dubbed themselves auteurs. They considered themselves—not the actors, writers, or producers—the creators of what appeared on the screen. Truffaut was in the forefront, making movies such as *Jules and Jim,* about the conflicts of a love triangle, and the autobiographical *400 Blows,* with its sympathetic treatment of adolescence. Except for a few deviations, like the sci-fi flick *Fahrenheit 451,* Truffaut's films are awash with gentleness, irony, and a youthful exuberance. "The characters in a film interest me more than the story," Truffaut said. "I enjoy unexpected details, things that prove nothing, things that show how vulnerable men are." Truffaut's love of film began in his troubled childhood. Neglected by his parents, he skipped school to take classes at the local cinema. "Movies acted on me like a drug," he said. "I felt a tremendous need to enter into the films." **2,471**

932 ROBERT PEEL (1788–1850) *law and order innovator*

Peel served as British prime minister for six turbulent years and was founder of England's Conservative Party. But we showcase him here for his stalwart contribution to the millennium: the Metropolitan Police Act of 1829. This law established the first disciplined police force for greater London, which became a model for crime-stoppers everywhere. Naturally these officers were dubbed "Bobby's boys," soon shortened to "bobbies." Over the years, they've earned a high level of public admiration for their no-nonsense, coolly polite, and civilized demeanor. And until recently they had to capture the bad guys without firepower, too. While Peel's crime-prevention policies were popular, his 1846 repeal of the Corn

Laws, which had restricted imports, led to his downfall. To political foe Benjamin Disraeli, Peel was "a burglar of others' intellect. There is no statesman who has committed political petty larceny on so great a scale."　**2,453**

933 STEPHEN BIKO (1946–1977)
martyr for the anti-apartheid cause

The founder of South Africa's Black Consciousness movement, Biko was jailed for illegal activities. Inside prison he and an accomplice ripped apart a paper outlining their plans and ate it—his "last supper." Biko's captors kept him naked in his cell for eighteen days, deprived him of food and water, beat him, and when he began foaming at the mouth, drove him seven hundred miles to another cell and left him to die. They later claimed he killed himself by banging his head against a wall. The murder galvanized opposition to apartheid, leading to American sanctions and hastening the fall of the white supremacist regime. Four months after Biko's death, his lover bore him a son, whom she named Hlumelo, "the shoot growing from a dead tree trunk."　**2,410**

934 MARCEL MARCEAU (b. 1923)
Frenchman who said everything by saying nothing

If a mime falls in a forest, does he make a sound? Not Marcel Marceau, whose performances, both live and cinematic, made the ancient practice of silent communication by body movements a staple of modern popular culture. At the age of five he fell in love with pantomime while watching a Charlie Chaplin (795) movie, and after World War II he studied with Étienne Decroux, a guru of French mimes. In 1947 the five-foot-nine Marceau invented Bip, the white-faced, mop-haired, rubber-bodied character who has become

synonymous with miming. Marceau was not an imitator, he was an actor-artist. And he has not been mum about his craft. "The actor mime vibrates like the strings of a harp," he said. "He is lyrical: his gesture seems to be invested with a poetic halo."　**2,379**

935 GEORGE MALLORY (1886–1924)
summit seeker

The English mountaineer was last seen heading into a cloud eight hundred feet below the summit of Mount Everest, and we like to think he got to the top. The most famous mountain climber of his generation was a literature teacher with courage, charm, and the wiry strength of those men who demonstrate fitness machines on television. His niche in history is secured by his existential quote about why he wanted to climb a mountain: "Because it is there." For most of the millennium, dying heroically was something done on battlefields. But modern war is impersonal, mechanical, and—let's face it—*outré*. Mallory and his followers—like Edmund Hillary and Tenzing Norkay, who conquered Everest in 1953—achieved glory by doing something dangerously unnecessary. Nowadays technology makes such feats easier. All Mallory had was a balky oxygen rig and a stiff upper lip.　**2,333**

936 HENRY CLAY (1777–1852)
America's Great Compromiser

One Georgia congressman refused to be introduced to Clay for fear of falling prey to the Kentucky politician's famous charm. Clay, like Lincoln, viewed preservation of the Union as the highest good. "Secession is treason," he declared. As the spirit of rebellion spread in the South, he sought to legislate compromise between slave and free states—a task political analyst George Will likened to lassoing a locomotive with cobwebs. But agreements he hammered out in 1820, 1833, and 1850 delayed the Civil War by a decade at least, saving the nation by giving the North time to grow strong enough to crush the Confederacy. Famed for his oratory, Clay stumbled once, forgetting his Shakespeare (5) and declaring, "A rose will smell the same, call it what you will." He prayed to God that if the South seceded, "I shall not survive to behold the heart-rending spectacle." His prayer was answered. **2,319**

937 HUGH HEFNER (b. 1926)
sexual revolutionary

He was a twentieth-century everyman; a child of prudish parents trapped in a loveless marriage and a dead-end job that had no moral purpose: writing ad copy. In 1953, with $10,000 in borrowed money and pictures of a naked Marilyn Monroe for his first issue, Hefner invented *Playboy* magazine, a glossy glorification of consumerism, good literature, and uninhibited sex. "It was like a mission—to publish a magazine that would thumb its nose at all the restrictions that had bound me," he told an interviewer in 1961. Hate them if you must, but Hefner's centerfolds and libidinous philosophy did much to loosen the grip of Judeo-Christian guilt on sexuality and legitimize our R-rated and X-rated popular culture. Beneath his celebrity Hefner was a boring, reclusive workaholic. And AIDS eventually made the world realize that sex can be deadly. **2,307**

938 PANCHO VILLA (1878–1923)
one mean revolutionary

As a youth, Doroteo Arango (his real name) became a fugitive and eventually a bandit after murdering the ranch owner who assaulted his sister. A natural leader and military strategist, Villa gathered a division of soldiers and joined rebel forces fighting the regimes of Porfirio Díaz and

Victoriano Huerta. When the United States threw its support to a revolutionary rival, the cruel and volatile Villa retaliated by killing Americans in a raid on Columbus, New Mexico, in 1916. President Woodrow Wilson dispatched an army expedition into Mexico but failed to capture this loose cannon. Years later Villa was living the life of a cattle baron in northern Mexico when vengeful peasants gunned him down. He soon became the stuff of legends and, nearly fifty years later, won Mexicans' recognition as a "Hero of the Revolution." **2,253**

939 IBN BATTUTAH (1304–1378)
traveling man

If they had frequent walker miles then, Ibn Batuta would have won a free trip anywhere in continental Asia. He wandered 75,000 miles around the medieval world, and his memoirs have been a source of knowledge of flyblown kingdoms from Castile to Canton, from Turkey to Timbuktu. Motivated by nothing more than restlessness, Ibn Battutah crisscrossed the Arab world, visited the Crimea's Christian settlements, which he hated—too much bell-ringing—spent eight years in the employ of the cruel Indian dictator Muhammad ibn Tughluq, decamped for Ceylon, Sumatra, and China, returned to the Middle East, and made a two-year trip to central Africa before settling in his native Tangier. After a life on the road, he wrote, there's no place like home. **2,169**

940 MATA HARI (1876–1917)
the spy who loved everyone

We doubt there's an ounce of truth to any of this, but like spies, we're not above passing on what we heard. One legend has it that when six French officers arrested Mata Hari, she greeted them at the door in the buff and tried to lure them en masse into her bed. Another story says the firing squad shot blank cartridges and that, like Elvis, Mata Hari lived to love again. We had to include exotic dancer Margaretha Geertruida Zelle Macleod because her story has sparked so many legends and her name is synonymous with espionage. She wasn't the best spy (after all, she got caught), but she's certainly the most famous. We'll never know whether she really spied for the Germans during World War I. Perhaps the French officers she seduced just wanted her silenced. But to the best of our knowledge, there were real bullets in the rifles. **2,144**

941 CHE GUEVARA (1928–1967)
guerrilla folk hero

Guevara's bearded image peers out from millions of T-shirts and posters. He was Fidel Castro's (466) right-hand man during the Cuban Revolution and later the organizer of guerrilla forces in Africa and South America. Born Ernesto Guevara de la Serna to a prosperous, left-leaning family in Argentina, he was plagued by asthma. Although Guevara earned a medical degree, he never practiced medicine and instead dedicated himself to violent struggle to free South American peasants from poverty. But his military blunders nearly destroyed Cuban revolutionary forces in 1953. Eventually Guevara grew disillusioned with Cuba's bureaucracy and left the country. "I leave behind the purest of my hopes as a builder," he wrote Castro. Two years later Guevara resurfaced as a guerrilla in Bolivia, where he failed to gain local Indians' support. His execution by government troops made him a cult hero. **2,143**

942 ANDRE MALRAUX (1901–1976)
highbrow Indiana Jones

A brilliant French writer, Malraux was also one of his century's most flamboyant adventurers. In 1923 he was jailed for trying to steal sculptures from a temple in the Cambodian jungle. As a young Marxist, he organized a revolutionary group in Indochina and fought in the Spanish Civil War, and as a Resistance fighter against the Germans, he was captured and forced to undergo a mock execution. He abandoned communism for Charles de Gaulle and served as France's minister of cultural affairs. His greatest novels, *Man's Fate* and *Man's Hope,* portray revolutionary struggles as tragic but noble battles against the absurdity of the universe. Malraux never talked about the absurdities of his own life—the death of his wife, the death of his two sons in a car accident—but in the sickness of old age he wrote of "seeing the warm face of death." **2,140**

943 MAXIMILIAN I (1459–1519)
Charlemagne wannabe

Maximilian, archduke of Austria, German king, and Holy Roman emperor, didn't lack titles. Nor did he lack military skill or diplomatic brilliance, with the result that he assured his family, the Habsburgs, a dominant position in Europe for four centuries. Alas, his achievements fell short of his romantic vision of himself as the Renaissance successor to Caesar and Charlemagne, the two great unifiers of Western Europe. He was a bit of a nut, believing himself to be the reincarnation of King Arthur and the descendant of Hercules and the ancient Egyptian god Osiris. He loved chivalry and tournaments and called himself the "last of the Knights." That said, he added vast territories to the Habsburg realm through marriage, military conquest, and treaty, including Burgundy, the Netherlands, Hungary, Bohemia, and the crown jewel—Spain and its empire. For which his successors doubtless said: Thanks a million, Maximilian! **2,137**

944 ROSA PARKS (b. 1913)
American refusenik

Jim Crow segregation was the law in the South. Rosa Parks was a black seamstress in Montgomery, Alabama. It was no contest. She was tired that afternoon of December 1, 1955, when she was ordered to surrender her bus seat to a white passenger, so she just said no—and the civil rights protest movement was born. Her arrest triggered a boycott against the bus company and the intervention of a young pastor named Martin Luther King, Jr. (56), who declared, "We have no alternative but to protest." The boycott led to sit-ins, freedom rides, voter registration drives, violent clashes, and the Voting Rights Act of 1965. In 1994, Parks was robbed and beaten by a black man in her home. "Many gains have been made," she said afterward through swollen lips. "But we still have a long way to go, and so many of our children are going astray." **2,133**

945 SIMON WIESENTHAL (b. 1908)
Nazi hunter

To measure his impact requires an act of the imagination: What future Holocausts has he prevented by keeping alive the memory of the Nazi horror? Founder of the Jewish Documentation Center in Vienna, Wiesenthal tracked down more than one thousand war criminals, including Adolf Eichmann, the chief executioner of European Jewry. Viewing the archdemon for the first time, he recalled, "I saw a frail, nondescript, shabby fellow. He looked like a bookkeeper who is afraid to ask for a raise." Wiesenthal could have emigrated to America and, with his brains, made a bundle, but he chased Nazis instead because "I have to do it. We must not forget." He was the doer; fellow concentration-camp survivor Elie Wiesel was the thinker. Wiesel didn't make our list, but we pay tribute here to the author of *And the World Remained Silent* and other novels that chronicle twentieth-century man's descent into evil. **2,129**

946 BENJAMIN LEE GUINNESS (1798–1868) *stout-hearted brewer*

The Guinness Book of Records notes that beer was around before this millennium, but the oldest brewer is Germany's Weihenstephan Brewery, founded in 1040, and the biggest is Anheuser-Busch, which averaged about 2.7 billion gallons annually in the 1990s. So why Guinness? Without doubt he's the world's most famous brewer, who made Irish stout an international favorite. In 1825 Guinness took over his father's small brewery and expanded it to become one of the largest in the world. He had his stout named the national drink of Ireland. His beers commanded such respect that in 1851 he was elected lord mayor of Dublin and later served in Parliament. Today dark, creamy Guinness Stout is sold in more than 120 countries. The book of superlatives that bears the Guinness name was first sold by the company in 1955 to resolve arguments started by blarney served up in pubs around the world. **2,122**

947 JOSEF PILSUDSKI (1867–1935)
liberator of Poland

Pilsudski was a master of the grand gesture. Imprisoned by Poland's Russian masters in 1900, he feigned insanity and escaped. Eight years later he and his confederates robbed a train and used the loot to start a militia. In 1918 he made a triumphal entry into Warsaw from a German jail and became Poland's first modern president. In 1923 he resigned, but three years later he marched on Warsaw and seized power again. Through it all he broke the Russian yoke, helped unite Poland, and showed how a small country caught between geopolitical giants can survive. "To be vanquished and not surrender—that is victory," he said. In a crisis he would imagine what his mother would want him to do. "As long as I can feel that I have done right in her eyes," he said, "I do not care if the whole world is against me."   **2,116**

948 MATTHEW ARNOLD (1822–1888)
gloomy poet, optimistic thinker

His disciplined verse presaged twentieth-century poets' pessimism. In "Dover Beach," he wrote, "the world, which seems to lie before us like a land of dreams, so various, so beautiful, so new, hath really neither joy, nor love, nor light." Who could blame him for being depressed? For thirty-five years, as a school inspector, Arnold checked ventilation and privies and administered tests to thousands of pupils and teachers each year. In one marathon day he gave oral exams in algebra, literature, the Bible, surveying, and grammar to 309 student teachers. The tedium eventually drove the poetry out of him, but his prose was fine. In *Culture and Anarchy* he called for intellectual excellence unfettered by politics and philistinism. He died of a heart attack a few days after jumping over a fence on a dare—a dumb stunt for a sixty-five-year-old man weighing 268 pounds.   **2,100**

949 TERESA OF ÁVILA (1515–1582)
religious reformer

She is one of the Catholic Church's most important saints and the first woman doctor of the church. Born to Castilian aristocracy, young Teresa ran away from home, pining for Christian martyrdom in Morocco. Then at age twenty she defied her father and entered a Carmelite convent. However, that life proved too comfortable for Teresa, who practiced mental prayer and favored solitude, hardship, and poverty. In 1562, despite societal and church opposition, she founded a new house called St. Joseph of Ávila, where nuns wore coarse brown habits and sandals, ate no meat, and performed manual labor. She established sixteen more convents and, for each, sought candidates of intelligence and good judgment. "God preserve us from stupid nuns!" she once exclaimed. The religious fervor she stirred extended beyond Spain and was a main impetus in the Counter-Reformation. Her writing, *Life and the Way of Perfection,* is among the greatest in mystical literature.   **2,038**

950 KAHLIL GIBRAN (1883–1931)
a prophet for a mass culture

The Lebanese Gibran's most famous book, *The Prophet,* turns up in every bookstore. That's because the Christian poet's philosophical bent, fusing Eastern and Western mysticism, appeals to so many. "While I was writing *The Prophet,*" Gibran said, "*The Prophet* was writing me." Consider these passages from this 1923 book: "Your daily life is your temple and your religion." Or "Work is love made visible." And "The soul is mightier than space, stronger than time, deeper than the sea, and higher than the stars." A gifted artist and linguist, it was in literature that Gibran made his mark. He wrote in both English and Arabic and dealt with themes of love, death, and nature. Deeply religious, he could be otherworldly, given to long, silent stretches that tuned out friends. "There are whole days at a time," Gibran said, "when I feel that I have just arrived from another planet."   **1,999**

951 KATHARINE HEPBURN (b. 1907)
Hollywood's leading leading lady

Director George Cukor described the ingenue Hepburn as a "boa constrictor on a fast," while

David Selznick declared, "Ye Gods, that horse face!" They cast her anyway, and her first film, *A Bill of Divorcement* in 1932, made her a star. She won an Academy Award for her next film, *Morning Glory.* Half a century later, she won an unparalleled fourth Oscar in *On Golden Pond.* We like Hepburn because she played them all— young heiress, savvy lawyer, passionate missionary, regal regent, and doddering old lady—in a career that spanned seven decades. While roles like the sophisticated Tracy Lord in *The Philadelphia Story* came naturally, the filming of John Huston's classic, *The African Queen,* with Humphrey Bogart, presented special challenges. When she was forced to climb into murky water in the Belgian Congo, the director had the prop men fire bullets into the water to scare the crocodiles away. **1,987**

952 CARY GRANT (1904–1986)
Hollywood idol

We almost rumbled over this one. What actor epitomized Hollywood in its heyday? John Wayne? Without a horse, he was nothing. Clark Gable? Frankly, my dear, we didn't give a damn. Paul Newman? Isn't he the salad dressing dude? We kept returning to Grant and his rags-to-riches story. Originally Archibald Leach, a British stilt walker in an acrobatic troupe, he moved to Hollywood in 1932 with a new name and a Pygmalion-like transformation into an elegant leading man. Grant's seventy-two movies include many of Hollywood's most memorable, like *The Philadelphia Story, Gunga Din, Bringing Up Baby, The Awful Truth,* and *Notorious.* Although romantic comedies were his specialty, he could carry dramas and Hitchcock thrillers. Nominated twice for an Oscar, he never won. Grant knew when to call it quits and made his last movie, *Walk Don't Run,* in 1966; he was given a special

oversight Oscar in 1970. He was debonair, witty, dangerously good-looking—and he always got the girl. **1,986**

953 JULIUS NYERERE (b. 1922)
independent Africa's elder statesman

Nyerere, president of Tanzania from its birth as Tanganyika in 1961 until his retirement in 1985, gets a mixed review. He banned opposition to his ruling Chama Cha Mapinduzi Party (the Party That Carries Things Around) and imposed Chinese-style socialism, policies that led to economic disaster, and prisons bursting with dissidents. Yet he was that rare bird, the honest politician. "I failed. Let's admit it," he said in his farewell speech. Africa loved him because he loved Africa, promoting African unity and Africa's cause in the world. And unlike so many other African leaders, he kept peace at home, lived simply, and gave up power voluntarily. "My success is building a nation out of this collection of tribes," he said. Returning to his village farm, he tilled the land himself, saying "It was great therapy to dirty your hands in some soil." **1,910**

954 DWIGHT L. MOODY (1837–1899)
American evangelist

We must pause to confess to a pro-Moody bias: One of the authors of this tome attended a boarding school founded by the bearded Bible thumper. The school's stern motto, coined by Moody himself, still rings in this alumnus's ears: "Eat your soup with a one-tined fork and don't complain." Moody was a key figure in the nineteenth-century evangelical movement, holding mass revivals in both America and Britain and establishing not only the Mt. Hermon School for Boys and the Northfield School for Girls in Massachusetts but also the Moody Bible Institute in Chicago. The former shoe salesman resembled an Old Testament prophet and sounded like one to the more than one million people who heard him speak. **1,907**

955 AMINA (1560–1610)
Nigerian warrior-queen

In one of the most male-dominated regions of a male-dominated world, men quaked at the mere mention of her name. Amina ruled the city of Zaria in West Africa and expanded it into the most powerful state of the Hausa people. Distant towns paid tribute to her; one sent forty eunuchs and ten thousand kola beans. But Amina didn't just sit around sipping an early version of Coke and chatting with a bunch of neutered attendants. Though she refused all suitors, legend has it that she took a different lover every night. A variation states that she had sex with a man in every city she subjugated—and then had him beheaded the next morning. After she died, her people sang this hymn to her memory: "Amina, daughter of Nikatau, a woman as capable as a man." **1,892**

956 LOUIS BRAILLE (1809–1852)
beacon for the blind

The Frenchman Braille went blind at age three. First an awl plunged into one of his eyes as he was playing in his father's harness shop. Then disease robbed him of sight in the other eye. At age fifteen, while attending the National Institute for Blind Children in Paris, Braille became intrigued by a system of tangible dots on paper developed by a French captain for night communications on the battlefield. Braille used it to create his own system, based on combinations of up to six raised dots, of printing and writing for the blind. While fellow students embraced Braille's code, it didn't catch on worldwide until 1932—eighty years after his death. To this day it serves as a major vehicle for the blind in gathering information. **1,874**

957 EDWARD LEAR (1812–1888)
nonsense poet

There was a scene painter named Lear
Who dabbled in poems quite queer;
His rhymes were all tricks
That we've dubbed limericks
His nonsense lived on through the years.

1,861

958 INGMAR BERGMAN (b. 1918)
cinema moralist

This Swedish screenwriter and director burst on the international scene in 1955 with his touching comedy *Smiles of a Summer Night.* He secured his place in film's hall of fame with the medieval morality drama *The Seventh Seal* in 1956; the psychological journey of an old man in *Wild Strawberries,* 1957; and the painful, intimate examination of family life in *Cries and Whispers,* 1972. Bergman's symbolic and complex films reveal the stark truth of human loneliness and torment. His themes and his trademark techniques—use of black and white film, frequent close-ups, and dream sequences—have profoundly influenced other filmmakers, including America's Woody Allen. Son of a Lutheran pastor, Bergman had a religious upbringing that surfaced in his preoccupation with right versus wrong. "For so many people, Bergman has been the man who showed the way to a cinema of the inner life," said critic David Thomson. **1,833**

959 JOHN VON NEUMANN (1903–1957)
gamesman and computer wizard

Nuclear physicist Edward Teller joked that IBM owed half its wealth to its star consultant, the Hungarian-born Von Neumann, a leading developer of computers after World War II. A machine he called *maniac*—mathematical analyzer, numerical integrator, and computer—solved the problems blocking production of the first hydrogen bomb. In 1944 Von Neumann and Oskar Morgenstern wrote *Theory of Games and Economic Behavior,* which used mathematics to predict how adversaries would react under varying circumstances. That helped create complex nuclear-deterrence strategies, and it may have been the wheelchair-using Von Neumann—not Henry Kissinger, as many viewers now believe—who was the model for *Dr. Strangelove* in Stanley Kubrick's movie about atomic Armageddon. Like a lot of geniuses, Von Neumann had a photographic memory, but he was no ivory tower pedant. He liked martinis, dirty jokes, and poker. At that game he was a consistent loser, proving that theories don't always work.   **1,825**

960 ADA BYRON LOVELACE (1815–1852)
the computer's programmer

"Her thoughts were theorems," runs a line in Lord Byron's (385) *Don Juan.* He was describing Ada, countess of Lovelace, his only legitimate child. Tutored and self-taught, the British Lovelace became a math whiz. "It is through mathematics alone, we can adequately express the great facts of the natural world," she declared. Lovelace was enthralled by Charles Babbage's (351) analytical engine, the first automatic digital computer, and the two became lifelong friends. In her translation of an Italian paper on Babbage's invention, Lovelace made the machine usable by adding directions for programming it to compute numbers. But it was, after all, just a tool, only capable of doing "whatever we know how to order it to perform," she said. Lovelace should have stopped there; instead, she and Babbage used his computer to create a horse-betting formula. It failed, leaving Lovelace deeply in debt.   **1,816**

961 ANDREW CARNEGIE (1835–1919)
steel-minded philanthropist

Critics say Carnegie built his fortune on the backs of workers and ruined competitors. That's likely so. We include him, however, for his philanthropic largesse and its benefits to the world. Son of a poor Scottish weaver, young Carnegie arrived in America and started working in a Pennsylvania factory. By age twenty-seven the ambitious Carnegie was a railroad manager making $50,000 a year, mainly through investments. In 1873 he began buying steel plants that later were merged into the Carnegie Steel Company, which by 1900 was producing a quarter of the nation's steel. He sold his empire to J. P. Morgan (124) for $492 million a year later, making Carnegie the world's richest man. Then he gave it all away. Requests flooded him. "The Lord has gotten tired of beggars," Carnegie said, "and He has sent them all to me." The result: libraries, research institutes, university endowments, and grants to struggling scientists like Marie Curie (75).   **1,803**

962 MARY PICKFORD (1892–1989)
doll turned dealmaker

Actress Pickford was "America's Sweetheart," heroine of 52 feature films and 141 shorts, nearly all of them silents. Pickford and husband Douglas Fairbanks were the golden couple of the world, and their Beverly Hills mansion, Pickfair, the haven for Tinseltown's elite. Off-camera, the Canadian-born Pickford was smart and tough. The two-time Academy Award–winner represents the birth of superstardom. She demanded—and got—top dollar for pictures. And to seize artistic control from the megastudios, she formed the distribution company United Artists in 1919, with Fairbanks, Charlie Chaplin (795), and D. W. Griffith (145). While moviegoers loved the curly-blond Pickford as the innocent in films such as *Pollyanna* and *Rebecca of*

Sunnybrook Farm, they rejected her attempts to branch out. That and the advent of talking pictures prompted Pickford to retire from filmmaking in 1933. Mistakenly, said biographer Eileen Whitfield, Pickford "went to her grave feeling that her work would not stand the test of time." **1,778**

963 ROGER BANNISTER (b. 1929)
the four-minute man

When statisticians started keeping track of race speeds in 1864, the record for running the mile was 4:56. Then runners got serious and shaved 55 seconds off the record by 1945. But sports aficionados believed it was physically impossible for man to break the four-minute barrier. Bannister, a medical student at Oxford, approached running scientifically, studying the physiological mechanics of the sport. Running against gusting winds on May 6, 1954, a nasty day in his native England, he won the race in 3:59.4. His feat was hailed on newspaper front pages around the world as a victory for the human race. Bannister received his medical degree, became a neurologist, then was knighted in 1975. He finishes our race in the millennium's top thousand because, by doing what couldn't be done, Bannister reminded us that our greatest struggles are within ourselves. **1,772**

964 JOHN L. LEWIS (1880–1969)
powerful voice of organized labor

Lewis wins praise for raising the standard of living of miners between the world wars, but blame for exerting dictatorial power over the United Mine Workers of America. The Iowa-born Lewis had forebears who were Welsh coal miners, and he, too, left school to work in a mine. But Lewis also was a leader. He rose through the ranks to seize the presidency of the UMW in 1920 and, during the Great Depression, unionized the rubber, auto, and steel indus-

tries as well. He became an important presence in national labor affairs and provoked President Roosevelt (37) and, later, President Truman (485) by launching crippling national strikes. Lewis was an imposing figure with his jutting chin, bushy eyebrows, and flair for the dramatic. "If ye be an anvil, lie very still," he often told followers. "If ye be a hammer, strike with all thy will." **1,751**

965 AARON COPLAND (1900–1990)
composer who made folk tunes classics

Son of a Russian-Jewish immigrant, Copland grew up in a drab Brooklyn neighborhood. Life changed after his sister taught him to play the piano. By age fifteen he wanted to become a composer. Copland learned harmony through a correspondence course until he could travel to Paris for study with musician and conductor Nadia Boulanger. He experimented with jazz rhythms in such works as *Music for the Theater,* then turned to leaner, more dissonant compositions. His complex *Piano Variations* is one of the most important works in contemporary piano literature. Copland is most famous for ballet scores like *Billy the Kid, Rodeo,* and *Appalachian Spring,* all based on folk themes. As a teacher at Harvard and the Tanglewood music festival, he exerted a strong influence on young American composers. Summing up his friend's legacy, critic and composer Virgil Thomson called Copland's life "a long, steady, indefatigable pastoral." **1,735**

966 SRINIVASA RAMANUJAN (1887–1920)
numbers theory guru

Just think: A fifteen-year-old boy living in the hinterlands of turn-of-the-century India comes across an out-of-date textbook in the local school and, without any other guidance, formulates theorems it took the finest minds of Europe centuries to develop and ideas that we are now only beginning to understand, including elements of so-called superstring theory. Ramanujan wrote plaintive letters to British mathematician Godfrey Harding who, recognizing his genius, invited him to England for a spot of tea and some tutoring. Hardy concluded that this son of an office clerk was a "thinker of profound and invincible originality," whose strange notions must be true because, "if they were not true, no one would have had the imagination to invent them." **1,721**

967 CHARLES DREW (1904–1950)
blood-bank pioneer

As America's foremost authority on blood preservation, Drew oversaw a project in 1941 to ship liquid plasma to Britain and was put in charge of the first American Red Cross blood bank the following year. His role in supplying dried plasma to American soldiers in World War II saved untold thousands of lives. Yet over his protests the military first excluded black donors, then segregated their blood. "No Negro blood accepted, but"—the *Chicago Defender,* a black newspaper, thundered—"when the Japanese bombed Pearl Harbor and maimed hundreds of American soldiers and sailors, it was blood collected by a Negro surgeon that saved their lives." In a horrible irony, Drew bled to death after an automobile accident in rural North Carolina. The myth persists that he was turned away from a white hospital; in fact, white doctors labored to save him. **1,703**

968 CAPTAIN KIDD (1645–1701)
the reluctant pirate

Cutlass in hand, Kidd roamed the seas under a flapping skull-and-crossbones flag, plundering merchant vessels and crying "Shiver me timbers." So much for the myth. In reality Kidd was a churchgoing family man, living in a Manhattan house with real pewter in the sideboard and a Turkish carpet on the parlor floor, when he was strong-armed by the British crown into pursuing pirates preying on the vessels of England's East India Company. He did his best but got sloppy and a little greedy, indulging in petty acts of quasi-piracy to secure enough loot to satisfy his near-mutinous crew. Once, in a rage, he bopped his gunner over the head with a wooden bucket, killing him. Hauled off to London, Kidd was convicted of murder and piracy and hanged. But to this day his ghost ship plies the misty coasts, guarding his buried pieces of eight. **1,691**

969 SCIOPONE RIVA-ROCCI (1863–1937)
sphygmomanometer man

Try saying that three times quickly, and you could end up with high blood pressure. But at least we've got the invention that can diagnose the problem. Often symptomless, high blood pressure afflicts sixty million Americans and is a chief contributor to deaths from stroke, heart failure, or other complications. Riva-Rocci, an Italian physician, invented the first accurate tool to diagnose hypertension by measuring the force of blood against artery walls. Eighteenth-century researchers devised cruder methods that required inserting a tube into a blood vessel to measure the pressure of the pumped blood. Then Samual Siegfried von Basch developed a sphygmomanometer (from the Greek word *sphygmos,* for "pulse") that was noninvasive but, unfortunately, inaccurate. In 1896 Riva-Rocci, building on Von Basch's work, fashioned an accurate arm cuff similar to the ones used today (minus the Velcro, of course). **1,677**

970 HARRY HOUDINI (1874–1926)
the great escaper

When Houdini boasted that he could break out of any jail, the warden of a Washington, D.C., prison locked him in an impenetrable cell. Twenty-one minutes later Houdini strolled into the warden's office after picking the locks of other cells and rearranging the prisoners. He escaped thousands of straitjackets, handcuffs, steamer trunks, water torture cells, and coffins. Born Ehrich Weiss in Budapest, he grew up in the United States and chose his stage name to honor the father of modern magic, Robert-Houdin. Houdini played vaudeville with his first sensational illusion, "Metamorphosis," in which he magically changed places with his assistant. He's the millennium's master of illusion. Part magician, part lock-picker, and part showman, Houdini died on Halloween from a burst appendix. He promised his wife he'd come back to haunt her, but repeated seances proved that Houdini ultimately failed to escape death. **1,602**

971 VIRGINIA APGAR (1909–1974)
baby's best friend

American anesthesiologist Apgar's system for evaluating the condition of a newborn right after birth has saved countless lives worldwide, including who knows how many baby boomers. As director of anesthesiology at Columbia-Presbyterian Medical Center in New York, she attended thousands of deliveries but found medical teams paid more attention to mothers than babies. "I kept wondering who was really responsible for the newborn," Apgar said. "Birth is the most hazardous time of life." So in 1952 she devised a way of gauging a newborn's well-being, and it became standard in delivery rooms and shifted the focus to the new arrival. The Apgar test evaluates breathing, heart rate, color, muscle tone, and reflexes at one minute and five minutes after birth. Each feature is scored from 0 to 2, making a total of 10 possible points. A low score of 0 to 3 signals the need for urgent medical care. **1,601**

972 COCO CHANEL (1883–1971)
arbiter of fashion

When the impatient Chanel dirtied her head in a gas heater explosion in her suite at the Paris Ritz in the 1920s, she hacked off her long dark hair so that it would be easier to shampoo. She appeared at the opera that evening with bobbed tresses, and a fashion earthquake rippled around the world. Such was the influence of Chanel, who revolutionized women's clothing. Her couture house dictated trends for much of the twentieth century. As fashion writer Enid Nemy noted, "She emancipated her sex from the tyrannies of fashion." Chanel simplified design, rejected whalebone stays and corsets, raised hemlines, and introduced jersey as a comfortable material for her signature suits. The force behind turtleneck sweaters, trench coats, costume jewelry, and bell-bottom pants, Chanel also made "the little black dress" an essential in women's closets. She earned a fortune with her perfume, Chanel No. 5. **1,600**

973 FRANCIS BARING (1740–1810)
founder of the world's first global investment bank

"There are six great powers," France's duc de Richelieu remarked in 1818, "England, France, Russia, Austria, Prussia, and the Baring brothers." The house of Baring financed European trade in the years leading up to the Industrial Revolution. It financed Britain's armies against George Washington (22) and Napoleon (16). It financed the Louisiana Purchase, which doubled the size of the United States. It financed the rail barons and industrialists of the booming American republic. It recovered from a lending fiasco in 1890 and subsequently financed Britain's imperialistic expansion. Then, 232 years after its founding, a twenty-eight-year-old trader in Singapore drove the bank under with a bad $1 billion bet on Japanese stocks. In his official portrait the eccentric Sir Francis is shown cupping his ear to display his deafness. Let's hope that, in the afterworld, he hasn't heard of his creation's ignominious end. **1,577**

974 RENÉ-THÉOPHILE-HYACINTHE LAËNNEC (1781–1826)
stethoscope inventor

The French Revolution and Napoleonic wars were busy times for French doctors such as Laënnec, who began working in hospitals when he was fourteen years old. He was best at treating tuberculosis and emphysema, which were diagnosed, in part, by the ancient art of auscultation—putting an ear to a patient's chest to hear the rhythms of the heart and lungs. Laënnec invented a better way—a simple hollow tube, twelve inches long, that he called the stethoscope, from the Greek word for chest, *stethos*. He got the idea in 1816 after watching two children amuse themselves on a Paris street by listening to the amplified sound of a stick tapping against a tube. He published his findings in 1819, and doctors all over the world were soon using stethoscopes. Laënnec probably used one on himself; he died of lung disease. **1,571**

975 JETHRO TULL (1674–1741)
farmer outstanding in his field

Rock fans may not know that the band Jethro Tull was named for an English farmer who created beautiful harmony with turnips and 'taters. In those days many farmers planted seeds haphazardly, the way a modern suburbanite throws grass seed on a lawn. Tull's 1731 book, *The New Horse-Houghing Husbandry*, synthesized his

lifetime of agricultural study and taught farmers how to maximize yields of grain, potatoes, beans, and turnips by sowing seeds deeply and aerating the soil between the furrows. Using Tull's methods, farmers needed less manure and didn't have to let land lie fallow year upon year. Some contemporaries complained that he hyped his claims. A good crop of wheat for thirteen years without using manure? Bull! said the critics. But Tull was right, and he had plenty of disciples, including the French philosopher Voltaire (36), who turned his own holdings into a Tullian model farm. **1,536**

976 SERGEY KOROLYOV (1907–1966)
space racer

The space age began on October 4, 1957, when a Soviet team led by Korolyov launched Sputnik, the first man-made satellite. He had been tinkering with rockets since the 1930s, even while he was in a special Soviet gulag that Stalin (82) reserved for valuable, politically suspect scientists. Stalin's successor, Nikita Khrushchev (619), pined for a space feat that would make America cringe, and Korolyov delivered. He sent the 184-pound Sputnik to an orbit 560 miles high. For the United States it was a technological Pearl Harbor. Korolyov followed by launching Laika, the first space dog, Yuri Gagarin (499), the first space man, and Valentina Tereshkova, the first space woman. Without such challenges the American space program that eventually surpassed the Russians'—complete with communications satellites, men on the moon, and space shuttles—might not have gotten off the ground until the twenty-first century. **1,521**

977 HENRY SHRAPNEL (1761–1824)
widow-maker

The duke of Wellington claimed that the Battle of Waterloo was won on the playing fields of Eton. His artillery commander, Sir George

Wood, gave the credit to Shrapnel, who invented the cannon shells filled with musket balls that mowed down Napoleon's (16) troops at the pivotal skirmish for the farmhouse at La Haye Sainte. Shrapnel was a career army officer who had spent his adulthood and thousands of pounds of his own money perfecting his shells; it was hard to get the delicate fuses to go off at the optimum moment. He finally got it right, and a grateful British government—after years of keeping his achievement a state secret—gave Shrapnel a £1,200 pension for life. Others built on his innovation and made shells, bombs, and hand grenades even more horrific, but shrapnel is still the universal name for the shards of deadly metal inside those weapons. **1,501**

978 ALFRED SLOAN, JR. (1875–1966)
trailblazer of modern corporate management

As head of General Motors in the 1920s, Sloan transformed a hodgepodge of fledgling car companies into America's biggest industrial enterprise. Under his leadership GM went from making one of every six cars sold in the country to one of every two. Sloan championed decentralization of operations, but centralization of administration. He preached the need for an "unending search for facts." Ironically, the first car he purchased as a young man lacked an engine. Attracted to its patent leather mud-guards and red leather seats, he forgot to look under the hood. He later sold the car, a Conrad, for one dollar to a man who, dissatisfied with its performance, dynamited it in a field in Newark, New Jersey. **1,490**

979 ALBERT LASKER (1880–1952)
capitalism's cheerleader

Lasker set the course of modern advertising. His Chicago agency, Lord & Thomas, made Kotex and Kleenex household names, sold America on Quaker Oats puffed cereals that were shot from guns, and hooked women on cigarettes by urging them to "reach for a Lucky instead of a sweet." With the help of a couple of geniuses who worked for him, Lasker transformed advertising from a business that merely placed ads to one that created them. From J. E. Kennedy he drew the inspiration that advertising was "salesmanship on paper," not just grand claims. From Claude C. Hopkins he gained the insight of viewing advertising as a science that requires careful analysis of both product and customer. Lasker also developed gimmicks like money-back guarantees, premiums, and coupons. "If the early twentieth century in advertising history can be described in a phrase," wrote scholar Stephen Fox, "it would be: The Age of Lasker." **1,472**

980 DANIEL HALE WILLIAMS (1856–1931)
first heart surgeon

In 1891 James Cornish was stabbed in a brawl. Ordinarily his treatment would have been opium, then a funeral. But in an era when surgery was primitive and it was tantamount to a death sentence if doctors cut into the chest cavity, Williams took the risk. After opening up Cornish's chest, Williams sutured the ruptured pericardium, the sac surrounding the heart. The operation was a success—and no infection followed either; Williams was scrupulous in sterilizing instruments and having his operating room scrubbed, then sprayed with carbolic acid. The son of multiracial parents, Williams founded Provident Hospital in Chicago, the first interracial hospital in the United States to provide training for black interns and nursing candidates excluded from white schools. He amassed honors throughout his life and died at age seventy-five. As it happened, Cornish outlived his surgeon by ten years. **1,461**

981 A. P. GIANNINI (1870–1949)
the people's banker

That is what this American son of Italian immigrants called himself, and that is what he was. The founder of the Bank of Italy in San Francisco, Giannini set up a stand on a pier after the earthquake of 1906 and offered to lend money to anybody who needed it, even as established banks held back. By the mid-1940s his two great innovations—extending credit to the masses and opening branch banks—had transformed his renamed Bank of America into the biggest bank in the world. For all Giannini's populist impulses, his creation came under attack by one of the most powerful writers of the day, John Steinbeck (901), who modeled the rapacious Bank of the West in his novel *Grapes of Wrath* after it, and by Congress, which outlawed interstate banking in the McFadden Act of 1927. **1,459**

982 JOHN PEMBERTON (1831–1888)
soda papa

Coca-Cola legend describes Pemberton as a southern gentleman pharmacist who concocted the world's most successful soft drink in a kettle in his backyard. However, Mark Pendergrast's unauthorized corporate biography asserts that the doctor was a morphine-using patent-medicine man who studied the properties of coca leaves to cure his own addiction. Whatever. The undisputed fact is that Pemberton invented the thick brown syrup that flavors the world's most successful soft drink. Before Pemberton's death Asa Candler bought the secret formula, created the signature logo, and masterminded the marketing. The soft drink industry took off, spawning dozens of Coke imitators, including the most formidable challenger, Pepsi-Cola. But Coke is still king. People in 195 countries drink an estimated forty thousand Cokes every second,
and Coke is one of the world's most recognizable products. Heck, it's one of the few universal words. **1,437**

983 MARION DONOVAN (fl.1950–1998)
parents' hero,
environmentalists' nemesis

How do you define an environmentalist? Someone whose kid was toilet-trained last week. In our heads we agree that the billions of disposable diapers that hit landfills annually can't possibly be good for the earth. But committed environmentalists though we are, in our hearts we loved throwing those stinky diapers into the garbage. Donovan was the genius behind the earliest disposable diapers. In 1950 manufacturers weren't interested in her "Boater," which she fashioned from cotton padding and covered with shower curtain material. She marketed it herself and made a fortune. About a decade later Procter & Gamble introduced its version of the disposable diaper, Pampers, but it took a harried New York housewife to come up with the original idea. **1,428**

984 MAHALIA JACKSON (1911–1972)
a joyful noise unto the Lord

Jackson was the queen of gospel music, an idiom she helped invent; one admirer said she bit into notes like a "terrier playing tug-o'-war with an old shoe." As a child in New Orleans, Jackson soaked up street music in the early years of jazz. Moving to Chicago at age sixteen, she was soon electrifying churches with her high-voltage performances. Some congregations objected to all the stomping and moaning, but she retorted by quoting Psalms 47:1: "Shout unto the Lord." A fundamentalist Christian, she refused all offers—as high as $25,000 a night in Las Vegas—to sing in nightclubs, despite her first husband's admonition to "stop wasting her voice hollering in churches." When she sang "He's Got the Whole World in His Hands," though, she had the whole world in hers. **1,400**

985 HENRY ROUS (1795–1877)
dictator of the turf

That was the nickname of the man who did more than anyone to bring honesty to professional horse racing, the most popular betting sport ever. Rous quit the Royal Navy after a frigate he commanded ran aground, and he became an officer of the London Jockey Club. His 1850 book, *Laws and Practice of Horse Racing,* railed against fixers, touts, sly bookmakers, and worst of all, freelance handicappers in cahoots with corrupt jockeys. In 1855 Rous was appointed honorary public handicapper, and the rules of racing in England and the odds at the best-attended course, Newmarket, were set under his supervision. His views "were invested with an official, almost divine, authority," racing historian Roger Longrigg wrote. Rous was so respected, he was allowed to bet on races whose odds he had set, and no one accused him of sharp practice. **1,376**

986 HENRY ROBERT (1837–1923)
order keeper

We offer, second, and approve a motion to recognize Robert as the most consulted authority on parliamentary procedure. Without such rules democratic assemblies would deteriorate into melees. Robert was a U.S. Army engineer and inveterate joiner who perceived a need for common procedures that would work for all kinds of organizations. The four-thousand-copy first edition of *Robert's Rules of Order,* published in 1876, sold out in three months, and its revised edition remains the bible of parliamentary procedure in much of the Western world. Most of the rules

are simple: One person speaks at a time. Others are arcane: "Privileged motions to recess take precedence over all subsidiary and incidental motions." The book made him famous, but he kept his job as an engineer in charge of river and harbor projects for the army, retiring in 1901 as a brigadier general. **1,370**

987 AL NEUHARTH (b. 1924)
newspaper innovator

Call it McPaper or Junk Food Journalism if you will, but Neuharth changed the direction of journalism when he launched the national-market *USA Today* in 1982. The newspaper's breezy style, reliance on computer graphics, and innovative use of color revived an outdated newspaper industry whose death had been regularly predicted since the advent of television. *USA Today* influenced other media. Even *The New York Times,* the great gray lady of journalism, beefed up its graphics and switched to color. The border between television news and entertainment blurred. Indeed, Neuharth created a newspaper for people who watched television. Like other highbrow journalists, columnist Jonathan Yardley of *The Washington Post* scoffed at McPaper: "Like parents who take their children to a different fast-food joint every night . . . USA Today gives its readers only what they want. No spinach, no bran, no liver." And don't forget the sour grapes. **1,352**

988 WALTER C. WINGFIELD (c.1833–1912)
tennis pro

The French *jeu de paume* was popular among priests in the Middle Ages to break up the monotony of monastic life. But when the monks started playing tennis instead of tending their flocks, *jeu de paume* was outlawed by Louis IX (613). We trace the roots of tennis to these monastic athletes but give credit for the modern game—complete with a standard court size, racket, and net—to Wingfield. A retired British army major, Wingfield invited some friends to a lawn party at his home in Wales to play his new-fangled game, Sphairistike (Greek for "ball-play-ing") in 1873. The guests were amused. Wingfield applied for a patent so he could market his hour-glass court, curved nets, and spoon-shaped rack-ets. He also wrote down twelve basic rules. The game was such a hit that four years later, in 1877, Britain played host to the first world tennis championship—at Wimbledon. **1,350**

989 FELA (1938–1997)
dissident with a saxophone

Fela was a cool jazzman in the Miles Davis mold until he visited the United States in 1969 and met the Black Panthers. He returned to Africa and invented what is now known as Afro-beat: music with insistent rhythms and searing lyrics in pidgin English. He became the most popular composer and performer of twentieth-century African music—and also the leading critic of his native Nigeria's repressive governments, a role he seized in 1977 after he and scores of political sup-porters were beaten and burned out of their compound in Lagos. In 1984, when Fela was jailed on a trumped-up charge of currency manipulation, he made Amnesty International's list of prisoners of conscience. In concert Fela wore only bikini briefs, and in a traditional cere-mony in 1978 he married twenty-seven dancing girls. All but eight left him, and he died after a long struggle with AIDS. **1,300**

990 JOSEPH BRAMAH (1748–1814)
inventor awash in ideas

An accident at age sixteen made him lame and unsuitable for work on his father's farm in England, so he was apprenticed to a carpenter

and began a life of tinkering that led to some of the millennium's most important inventions. In 1778 Bramah patented a water closet that ushered in the modern age of toilets. He perfected the hydraulic press in 1795, harnessing the laws of liquid motion to do the world's heavy lifting. He proposed the idea of propellers to move ships, a thought that became useful when steam-powered boats replaced sailing craft. He designed a lock with such precision he confidently promised £200 to the first person who could pick it. It took an American safecracker fifty-one hours to collect the bet, thirty-seven years after Bramah died. **1,286**

991 HUBERT BOOTH (1871–1955)
dust buster

Booth was a respected mechanical engineer when, in 1901, he saw a demonstration of a new railway car cleaning machine that used compressed air to blow dirt from one end of the car to another. Wrong approach, he thought, so he built the first successful dirt suction machine. At £350, the ini-tial vacuum cleaners, as he was the first to call them, were too expensive for the average family, but they couldn't be beat for big jobs like the 1902 cleanup of Westminster Abbey after the corona-tion of King Edward VII. The soon-to-be-ubiqui-tous smaller models that were based on Booth's prototype not only made the world's indoors cleaner, they stimulated women's liberation from household drudgery. In Booth's native England vacuum cleaners are called "Hoovers," after the more successfully marketed machines of an Amer-ican company. We think that sucks. **1,201**

992 EDMOND HOYLE (1672–1769)
absolute authority on games

This ace of a guy made it ungentlemanly to cheat at cards. As any four-year-old who desperately wants to win Go Fish knows, this is one of life's most difficult moral lessons. According to Hoyle, it's also one of the most important. A crackerjack card player in England, Hoyle earned a living by teaching whist, a forerunner of bridge. In 1742 his *Short Treatise on the Game of Whist* was published. It wasn't the first whist tutorial—an earlier one had advocated winning by any means necessary. Hoyle's play-by-the-rules approach, however, unequivocally established the polite way to play cards. Then he turned his attention to the rules of backgammon, chess, and other contests. Hoyle's rule books have been amended countless times to include later versions of card and board games. He's been dead for centuries, but Hoyle still has the last word on gamesmanship. **1,193**

993 ELLA FITZGERALD (1917–1996)
first lady of jazz

Fitzgerald's sixty-year career embraced big band songs, show tunes, bossa nova, and novelties like her first hit, "A-Tisket, A-Tasket." Originally a bebop singer, Fitzgerald outdid Louis Armstrong (322) in scat singing—improvising using sounds and syllables, as with an instrument. But her later jazz renditions, with her perfect intonation, clear diction, and nearly three-octave range, set her apart. Fitzgerald's triumphs were her American songbooks—comprehensive recordings of such composers as Ira and George Gershwin (857), Irving Berlin (469), and Cole Porter (900). Reared in a New York City orphanage, Fitzgerald was a teenage runaway when she won a Harlem talent show. She worked first with Chick Webb's band, then hooked up with impresario Norman Granz to tour Europe and Asia and perform at the New York Philharmonic. While some critics blasted her voice as girlish and shallow, fans and composers treasured her. "I never knew how good our songs were," Ira Gershwin said, "until I heard Ella Fizgerald sing them." **1,182**

994 WILLIAM LEVITT (1907–1994)
suburban sprawler

"Any damn fool can build homes. What counts is how many can you sell for how little," the father of suburbia once declared. Historians agree that Levitt was a genius in both areas, though for the longest time he refused to sell to blacks. After World War II Levitt's planned community on Long Island was a mecca for returning veterans and their baby boomers. En route to putting up about 140,000 boxlike homes, Levitt did for housing what Henry Ford (51) did for automobiles. He analyzed the construction and reduced the work to twenty-seven basic steps. Each worker was trained to repeat an assignment over and over again at different housing sites, beginning in Levittown, New York. Levitt ended up a multimillionaire who lived in a thirty-room mansion, but his "little boxes made of ticky-tacky," to quote one scornful folksong, were the prototypes for affordable housing that sparked the flight from urban centers and the development of suburbs. **1,167**

995 ELIJAH McCOY (1844–1929)
the original real McCoy

The Canadian-born son of fugitive slaves, McCoy became a mechanical engineer, but soon found that white employers didn't want his expertise. He finally got work on the Michigan Central Railroad as a fireman who oiled the engine, a duty that meant periodically stopping the train for lubrication. The same procedure applied to factory machines. Without a steady supply of oil, moving parts stuck together, friction resulted, and operations ground to a halt. To avoid these wasteful stoppages, McCoy invented the lubricating cup in 1872. Through a system of canals and connecting devices, it automatically oiled steam engines while they ran. Factories quickly adopted it. In 1892 McCoy developed a similar system for railroad locomotives. Thereafter buyers of heavy machinery would ask if the "McCoy system" were included. Invariably, salesmen would reply, "It's the real McCoy," a phrase that's come to mean "authentic." **1,143**

996 BERNARD CORNFELD (1927–1995)
the man who sold mutual funds to the American masses

The son of a Romanian immigrant, Cornfeld started peddling mutual funds—which spread investors' risk by putting their money in a basket of stocks—in the 1950s, just as the investment vehicles were catching on. Off he went to Paris, setting up Investors Overseas International and its huge Fund of Funds, and issuing the public this challenge: "Do you sincerely want to be rich?" He became almost as well known for jetting around the world from his French château accompanied by celebrities and bathing beauties as for his financial wizardry. Cornfeld fell afoul of American regulators, ultimately giving up his tottering empire to the soon-to-be-fugitive wheeler-dealer Robert Vesco. But for all Cornfeld's failure, it was he who pioneered the great American financial revolution that has since spread to the four corners of the globe. **1,122**

997 MARILYN MONROE (1926–1962)
original Candle in the Wind

Women imitated her, men fawned over her, playwright Arthur Miller and baseball slugger Joe DiMaggio married her, Andy Warhol (1,000) painted her, Norman Mailer wrote about her, and Elton John sang about her. Forget about her acting—Monroe makes the grade as the millennium's blond bombshell sex symbol. A charismatic presence on screen, Monroe starred in a few memorable films, like *Some Like It Hot* and *The Seven Year Itch*. It was only after her suicide in the nude at age thirty-six that Monroe achieved icon status, surpassed perhaps only by Elvis (352). For years after her death, DiMaggio had roses delivered regularly to her grave. When Elton John was asked to sing at the 1997 funeral of another of the century's fairy-tale characters, he chose to rework his elegy to the former Norma Jean Baker. "Candle in the Wind," à la Britain's Princess Diana, became the bestselling song ever. **1,050**

998 THEODORE SEUSS GEISEL (1904–1991)
author of zany children's books

Geisel, aka Dr. Seuss, makes our list for possessing the millennium's liveliest imagination. Since *The Cat in the Hat*'s 1957 publication, generations of children around the world have grown up with Geisel's rhyming absurdities. Publisher Bennett Cerf bet Geisel fifty dollars that he couldn't write a children's reader using just fifty words. Geisel won with the persistent Sam-I-Am in *Green Eggs and Ham*. Geisel published forty-seven books under his middle name (which incidentally rhymed with "voice," not "juice"). He imagined a power-hungry turtle named Yertle based on Hitler (20), a Christmas-hating Grinch who learns to love, the egg-hatching faithful elephant Horton, and a nameless naughty feline who wreaks havoc when children are home alone. Aside from his quirky half-human, half-beast characters, Geisel was a rhyming genius. Who else could have made millions from the line "I do not like green eggs and ham, I do not like them, Sam-I-Am"? **1,028**

999 GEORGE SANTAYANA (1863–1952)
profound thinker

Was it separation anxiety that infused the philosophy of this Spanish-American man of letters with such gloom and endowed him with what he called his "subconscious" homosexuality? Neglected by both parents as a child, he described in his autobiography his sense of disconnectedness: "I was brimming over with the sense of parting. I found myself, unwillingly and irreparably, separated from Spain, from England, from Europe, from my youth, and from my religion." Santayana was a materialist, for whom matter was the ultimate reality, and at times he seemed to embrace nihilism. "The brute necessity of believing something so long as life lasts does not justify any belief in particular," he wrote. Still, he drew lessons from history. To paraphrase his most famous epigram: Those who cannot remember the past are condemned to read this book. If necessary, go back to number 1 and start over. **1,004**

1,000 ANDY WARHOL (1928–1987)
fifteen-minute flash of hope for the rest of us

That's it, reader. You may not have made our list, and in all likelihood you're not going to be included in a *Who's Who* of the one thousand most important people of the century either, but don't despair. There's an easy solution. Under pop artist Warhol's scenario, everyone is in for a fleeting moment of fame. Remember Barney Clark? Donna Rice? Warhol, with his platinum wigs, dyed eyebrows, and flaming demeanor, got his own shot at immortality painting ordinary objects from his culture, including thirty-two Campbell's Soup cans, which sold for $100 each. After Warhol's death following gallbladder surgery, those signature soup cans were worth more than $10 million. All well and good, but there's no way Warhol would have made the cut here simply for that. We just loved his prediction, "In the future everybody will be world famous for fifteen minutes" . . . or perhaps 150 words. **1,000**

Ten Who Almost Made It

Here are some people we left out, and why they didn't make the grade.

LADY GODIVA (c.1040–1080)
She made a deal with her husband, the Earl of Mercia. He would lighten the tax burden on impoverished Coventry, England, if she would ride naked through town on a white horse. That makes her the patron saint of tax relief or the millennium's first exhibitionist. Either way, she deserves no more than a peep, here, among the also-rans.

AMERIGO VESPUCCI (1454–1512)
One of the unending debates of history is whether the Florentine writer, Vespucci, manufactured the story that he explored the New World in the decade after Columbus's discoveries. We say he hyped. German cartographer Martin Wald-seemüller said he didn't. In 1507 Waldseemüller published the first map that showed the Western Hemisphere to be separate from Asia and gave Vespucci credit for discovering the difference. He labeled the map "America," his translation of Amerigo. Having your name on two continents would be a thrill, but it's not enough to get you into the top thousand. Here's a thought: Maybe we should have included Waldseemüller?

POCAHONTAS (c.1595–1617)
The Native American princess came very close to making the list. Not for stopping Papa Powhatan from braining Virginia colonist John Smith, but for marrying Smith's pal John Rolfe. Some historians say their union helped the English preserve a toehold in America. But we decided it would have happened anyway, given the European settlers' superior firepower.

PYOTR ILICH TCHAIKOVSKY (1840–1893)
We took half of Chuck Berry's advice. We refused to roll over Beethoven (10), but we tell Tchaikovsky the news: He ranks below two dozen other music makers from Ludwig Van himself to Ella Fitzgerald (943). We dumped the Russian composer of lush symphonies and crowd-pleasers like *The Nutcracker* ballet score and the *1812 Overture,* because his unrelenting mélange of syrupy sweetness and bombast ends up being merely boring.

RONALD REAGAN (b. 1911)
We almost included the actor-turned-president for his portrayal of George Gipp, the dying football player in *Knute Rockne, All American.* What drama! His performance in the White House from 1981 to 1989 didn't measure up, except when he went to divided Berlin and said, "Mr. Gorbachev, tear down this wall." Gorbachev (237) did—or at least he didn't stop it from tumbling—and made the top thousand. Reagan's fans, accustomed to having their hero dismissed as a lightweight, are sure to say of our decision: "There you go again."

JOHN F. KENNEDY (1917–1963)

To prove our bipartisanship, we also exclude the man who said, "Ask not what your country can do for you, but what you can do for your country." Like millions around the world, we remember exactly what we were doing the moment we heard of his assassination on December 22, 1963: crying. But as those memories fade, what will be his legacy? A frat boy image and a three-year presidency cut short before it could achieve lasting influence.

OPRAH WINFREY (b. 1954)

At the end of the millennium, the richest black woman in America was more powerful than the president; when she spoke, people listened. She stopped eating beef, and cattlemen had a cow; she featured books on her talk show, and they hit the bestseller lists. We would have included her had her fame spread outside the United States or if she had invented the genre of talk television instead of being just a magical practitioner.

WILLIAM GATES (b. 1955)

As a scientist and technical innovator, the man who started Microsoft Corporation at age nineteen fails to equal the computer whizzes in this book. His achievement was in the field of salesmanship; his company's MS-DOS and Windows products captured the market for personal computer operating systems. That makes him a modern-day Jakob Fugger (493) or John D. Rockefeller (486): a mogul, but nothing more. Now that he is giving his zillions to charity, we'll consider him for a future edition.

CAL RIPKIN, JR. (b. 1960)

He broke Lou Gehrig's record by playing in 2,131 consecutive baseball games, making him the iron man of sports. Big deal. Millions of people had already accomplished his feat: showing up for work every day.

DIANA (1961–1997)

The beautiful princess who charmed the world died too soon for lasting influence. If her impossible dreams had come true—the abolition of land mines and the humanization of Britain's royal stuffed shirts—she would have ranked in the top thousand.

Some Interesting Facts

Where They Lived

We associated our top 1,000 people with fifty-nine countries, and it wasn't always easy to determine who came from where. Remember the old joke about why the Austrians are considered so clever? They have managed to convince the world that Beethoven (born in Germany) was an Austrian and that Hitler (born in Austria) was a German.

We say they were both Germans—and that Einstein, who emigrated to America when he was in his fifties, was, too. Many of the people born in the first one-third of the millennium, particularly those from the Islamic world, were assigned to the country where their birthplace is now located. An exception to that was our decision to assign three great Mongol leaders to Mongolia, though they weren't all born in what is now Mongolia. If nothing else, this proves that great people tend to move around.

Here's our list:

United States	267	Portugal	8	Afghanistan	2	Pakistan	1
Great Britain	173	Turkey	7	Israel	2	Byzantium	1
France	114	Denmark	6	Cuba	2	Tanzania	1
Germany	88	Sweden	6	Ethiopia	2	Nicaragua	1
Italy	75	Argentina	6	Nigeria	2	Tunisia	1
Russia	33	South Africa	6	Lebanon	1	Palestine	1
Netherlands	31	Ireland	5	Morocco	1	Arabia	1
Spain	27	Hungary	5	Peru	1	Chile	1
China	18	Czech/Slovakia	4	Cambodia	1	Iceland	1
Japan	17	Brazil	3	Haiti	1	Romania	1
India	13	Canada	3	Albania	1	Norway	1
Austria	12	Mexico	3	Zaire	1	Kenya	1
Poland	11	Egypt	3	Ghana	1	Bosnia	1
Switzerland	8	Venezuela	3	Australia	1	Iraq	1
Persia/Iran	8	Mongolia	3	Sudan	1		

When They Lived

We also thought it would be enlightening to track when the greats lived. To make things consistent, we've organized this list acording to date of birth (so anyone living on the cusp of a century change may fall within an earlier time) and further simplified things by looking at one-hundred-year blocks. Here's where they fall:

Century	Number
10th	7
11th	17
12th	29
13th	26
14th	22
15th	54
16th	71
17th	53
18th	168
19th	417
20th	136

How They Lived

How did our 1,000 achieve greatness? In looking at their occupations (for lack of a better word), we found that the top players of the millennium often played at many games, and that these games ran the gamut from choreographer to revolutionary.

What was most interesting to us as we compiled this list was that few people achieved greatness in only one area. Most excelled in many fields (some overlapping, some not), as a philosopher, lawyer, and mathematician; or revolutionary, leader, and soldier. You get the idea. Still, we tried to connect each person to a particular field. Because it's nearly impossible to categorize a person's life in one word, we've created general categories by *area* of interest. So painter, publisher, and dancer all fall in the category of Artist/Writer, etc., and likewise anthropologist, mathematician, and physician in Scientist/Inventor. At least in part, this list gives a different perspective on our choices for top 1,000—who, why, what. See what you think.

Selected Bibliography

Babe Didrickson Zaharias liked to lie about her age; some history books point to Elias Howe as the sewing machine's inventor; and Procter & Gamble's website credits one of its employees with designing disposable diapers. What's a researcher to do?

Prowl local libraries in search of information from literally thousands of books, magazine and newspaper articles, and, of course, the johnny-come-lately, the Internet. We weighed facts and made judgment calls. Sure, standard references like the *Columbia Encyclopedia, Encyclopaedia Britannica, Funk & Wagnalls,* and *World Book* were great. We couldn't have written this book without them. We even turned to our well-worn copy of *Britannica*'s eleventh edition, published in 1910. It was absolutely no use in flushing out entries on atomic warfare, rocket science, lasers, or pop art, but we liked its slant in long essays written by revered historians about the first nine-tenths of the millennium. But even the most up-to-date *Britannica* missed Zaharias's real birth date (1911—see Susan E. Cayleff, *Babe: The Life and Legend of Babe Didrickson Zaharias.* Urbana: University of Illinois Press, 1995) by three years and didn't even give a passing reference to Marion Donovan, the woman we decided invented the first crude version of a disposable diaper. (See *World of Invention: History's Most Significant Inventions and the People Behind Them.* Detroit: Gale Research Co., 1994.)

The Dictionary of National Biography, The Dictionary of American Biography, The Dictionary of Literary Biography, and *Current Biography* supplemented the old standards. *The New York Times* obituary index and its personal name index also provided information about people who lived in the last century and a half.

Still, we wanted to move beyond usual reference materials to pinpoint obscure inventions (like the phonograph record), credit important trends, and ensure cultural diversity. That's where books like the multivolume *Biographical Dictionary of Scientists* (David Abbott, ed., New York: Peter Bedrick Books, 1986) and the earlier series, *Dictionary of Scientific Biography* (Charles Coulston Gillispie, ed., New York: Charles Scribner's Sons, 1975) came in handy. So, too, did the myriad encylopedias that focused on specific countries and regions, including *Japan: An Illustrated Encyclopedia* (Tokyo: Kodansha, 1993); *The Cambridge Encyclopedia of China* (Brian Hook, ed., Cambridge: Cambridge University Press, 1991).

We discovered dictionaries and encyclopedias on almost every imaginable subject, from revered scientists (*Nobel Prize Winners*, Tyler Wasson, ed., New York: H.W. Wilson, 1987), to holy rollers (*Dictionary of Saints,* by John J. Delaney, Garden City, N.Y.: Doubleday, 1980), to nouvelle cuisine (*The Food Chronology*, by James Trager, New York: Henry Holt, 1995).

Books like *Notable American Women, 1607–1950: A Biographical Dictionary* (Edward T. James, ed., Cambridge, Mass.: Belknap Press of Harvard University, 1971), its companion volume, *Notable American Women: The Modern Period* (Barbara Sicherman and Carol Hurd Green, eds., Cambridge, Mass.: Belknap Press of Harvard University, 1980), and the *Great Lives in History* series (Frank N. Magill, ed., Pasadena, Calif.: Salem Press) were especially helpful in unearthing obscure facts about people omitted from standard encyclopedias or given only a paragraph. That's how, little by little, we made sure that our book represents a more diverse public than standard reference works on most library shelves.

During the two years spent on research and writing this book, the Internet emerged as an important tool for historians, as the National Archives, the Library of Congress, and virtually every important research facility in the English-speaking world began posting their catalogs and collections on home pages. Just as the printed book changed the course of research and study in the fifteenth century, the Internet is poised to reshape the discipline of historical research for the next millennium. Home pages for the National Inventors Hall of Fame, the National Women's Hall of Fame, and other organizations helped us in our search for the millennium's top dogs.

So, if we've whetted your appetite for these 1,000 superstars, there's plenty of reading material to supplement our facts. Some of it is slow going, like Christine de Pisan's rambling 1405 tome, *The Book of the City of Ladies* (reprinted, New York: Persea Books, 1982); others, like *The Guinness Book of World Records* (Mark C. Young, ed. Stamford, Conn.: Guinness Media, 1997) or *The Quotable Woman* (by Elaine Partnow, New York: Facts on File, 1982), are fun to skim.

It would be unwieldy to list our thousands of references, so we've left out most of the biographies we consulted during this two-year odyssey. Still, we wanted to give you a taste of some of the especially useful material we unearthed along the way.

Amberg, George. *From the New York Times Film Reviews, 1913–1970*. New York: Arno Press, 1971.

Ambrose, Stephen. *Undaunted Courage*. New York: Simon & Schuster, 1996.

Aveni, Gregory. *Empires of Time*. New York: Basic Books, 1989.

Bailleux, Nathalie, et al. *The Book of Chocolate*. Paris: Flammarion, 1995.

Barr, Roger. *The Importance of Malcolm X*. San Diego: Lucent Books, 1994.

Beasley, W. G. *The Rise of Modern Japan*. New York: St. Martin's Press, 1990.

Bissell, Richard. *You Can Always Tell a Harvard Man*. New York: McGraw-Hill, 1962.

Bliss, Michael. *The Discovery of Insulin*. Chicago: University of Chicago Press, 1982.

Boorstin, Daniel. *The Creators*. New York: Random House, 1992.

———. *The Discoverers*. New York: Random House, 1983.

Bratton, Fred Gladstone. *A History of the Bible*. Boston: Beacon Press, 1959.

Bromberger, Merry, and Serge Bromberger. *Jean Monnet and the United States of Europe*. New York: Coward-McCann, 1968.

Buchholz, Todd G. *New Ideas from Dead Economists*. New York: Penguin Books, 1989.

Cantor, Norman. *The Civilization of the Middle*

Ages. New York: HarperCollins, 1993.

Cardwell, Donald. *The Norton History of Technology.* New York: W.W. Norton, 1995.

Carman, W. Y. *A History of Firearms.* London: Routledge & Kegan Paul, 1955.

Carson, Rachel. *Silent Spring.* Boston: Houghton Mifflin, 1962.

Caruso, John Anthony. *The Liberators of Mexico.* New York: Pageant Press, 1954.

Christianson, Gale E. *Edwin Hubble: Mariner of the Nebulae.* New York: Farrar, Straus & Giroux, 1996.

Churchill, Winston. *A History of the English Speaking Peoples.* New York: Dodd Mead & Co., 1956.

Ciotti, Paul. "Revenge of the Nerds." *California* (July 1982), pp. 73–74, 128–134.

Clard, William H., and James H. S. Moynahan. *Famous Leaders of Industry.* Boston: L.C. Page, 1955.

Clark, William R. *Explorers of the World.* New York: Natural History Press, 1964.

Colacello, Bob. *Holy Terror: Andy Warhol Close Up.* New York: HarperCollins, 1990.

Coleman, Elizabeth Ann. *The Opulent Era: Fashions of Worth, Doucet and Pingat.* New York: Thames and Hudson, 1990.

Commager, Henry Steele, ed. *Documents of American History.* New York: Appleton-Century-Crofts, 1963.

Creighton, Donald. *A History of Canada.* Boston: Houghton Mifflin, 1958.

Cuddihy, John Murray. *The Ordeal of Civility.* New York: Basic Books, 1974.

Cunliffe, Marcus. *The American Heritage History of the Presidency.* New York: American Heritage, 1968.

Daniel, Glyn. *A Short History of Archaeology.* London: Thames and Hudson, 1981.

Danzig, Allison, and Joe Reichler. *The History of*

Baseball. Englewood Cliffs, N.J.: Prentice-Hall, 1959.

Day, Lance, and Ian McNeil, eds. *Biographical Dictionary of the History of Technology.* London: Routledge Reference, 1996.

de Pizan, Christine. *The Book of the City of Ladies.* New York: Persea Books, 1982.

Duffy, Maureen. *The Passionate Shepherdess: Aphra Behn 1640–89.* New York: Avon Books, 1977.

Durkin, Tish. "The UN-Candidate." *New York Times Magazine,* 20 October 1996, p. 48.

Einstein, Alfred. *A Short History of Music.* New York: Alfred Knopf, 1969.

Fadiman, Clifton, ed. *The Little, Brown Book of Anecdotes.* Boston: Little, Brown, 1985.

———. *The Lifetime Reading Plan.* New York: Harper & Row, 1960.

Fairbank, John King. *China: A New History.* Cambridge: Harvard University Press, 1992.

Farber, Eduard, ed. *Great Chemists.* New York: Interscience Publishers, 1961.

Feldman, Anthony, and Peter Ford. *Scientists and Inventors.* New York: Facts on File, 1979.

Ferguson, Donald. *A History of Musical Thought.* New York: Appleton-Century-Crofts, 1948.

FitzGerald, Edward, trans. *Rubaiyat of Omar Khayyam: The Astronomer Poet of Persia.* Mount Vernon, N.Y.: Golden Eagle Press, 1938.

Forbes, Malcolm, with Jeff Bloch. *Women Who Made a Difference.* New York: Simon & Schuster, 1990.

"Friendly Medicine." *Time,* 7 August 1989, p. 39.

Galas, Judith C. *Gay Rights.* San Diego: Lucent, 1996.

Garraty, John A., and Peter Gay. *The Columbia History of the World.* New York: Harper & Row, 1972.

Geneen, Harold, with Brent Bowers. *The Synergy Myth.* New York: St. Martin's Press, 1997.

Gilbert, Martin. *The First World War: A Complete*

History. New York: Henry Holt, 1994.

Gilbreth, Frank B., Jr., and Ernestine Gilbreth Carey. *Cheaper by the Dozen.* New York: Thomas Y. Crowell, 1948.

Gottlieb, Agnes Hooper. *Women Journalists and the Municipal Housekeeping Movement.* Ph.D. diss., University of Maryland, 1992.

Gottlieb, Sidney, ed. *Hitchcock on Hitchcock.* Berkeley: University of California Press, 1995.

Gillespie, Charles C. *Dictionary of Scientific Biography.* New York: Charles Scribner's Sons, 1973.

Gorn, Elliot. *The Manly Art: Bare-Knuckle Prize Fighting in America.* Ithaca: Cornell University Press, 1986.

Greenhouse, Linda. "Thurgood Marshall, Civil Rights Hero, Dies at 84." *New York Times,* 25 January 1991, p. 1.

Greenslade, S. L. *The Cambridge History of the Bible.* Cambridge: University Press, 1961.

Griffiths, Paul. *A Concise History of Avant-Garde Music.* New York: Oxford, 1978.

Grimm, Harold J. *The Reformation Era, 1500–1650.* New York: Macmillan, 1973.

Gussow, Mel. "Olivier Is Dead After 6-Decade Acting Career." *New York Times,* 12 July 1989, p. 1.

Gustaitis, Joseph. "E.R. Squibb: Pharmaceutical Pioneer." *American History* 26, no. 2 (May/June 1991), pp. 36–37.

Haber, Louis. *Black Pioneers of Science & Invention.* New York: Harcourt, Brace & World, 1970.

Harris, Ann Sutherland, and Linda Nochlin. *Women Artists: 1550–1950.* New York: Alfred A. Knopf, 1976.

Harris, Leon. *Merchant Princes: An Intimate History of Jewish Families Who Built Great Department Stores.* New York: Harper & Row, 1977.

Harrison, Barbara Grizzuti. "The First Weight Watcher." *McCall's* (September 1981), pp. 26–28, 142.

Hendrickson, Robert. *The Grand Emporiums: The Illustrated History of America's Great Department Stores.* New York: Stein and Day, 1979.

Hertsgaard, Mark. *A Day in the Life: The Music and Artistry of the Beatles.* New York: Delacorte, 1995.

Hibbert, Christopher. *The House of Medici.* New York: William Morrow, 1975.

Hickok, Ralph. *A Who's Who of Sports Champions.* Boston: Houghton Mifflin, 1995.

Higginson, William J. *The Haiku Handbook.* New York: McGraw-Hill, 1985.

Hochman, Gloria. *Heart Bypass: What Every Patient Must Know.* New York: St. Martin's Press, 1982.

Honour, Hugh. *Cabinet Makers and Furniture Designers.* New York: G.P. Putnam's Son, 1969.

"The Hotel Ritz: Paris' Resplendent Landmark on the Place Vendome." *Architectural Digest* 46 (September 1980), pp. 120–24, 174.

Howe, Russell Warren. *Mata Hari: The True Story.* New York: Dodd, Mead, 1986.

Hsia, C. T. *A History of Chinese Fiction: 1917–1957.* New Haven: Yale University Press, 1961.

Hubben, William. *Four Prophets of Our Destiny.* New York: Macmillan, 1954.

Janssen, Wallace F. "The Squad That Ate Poison." *FDA Consumer* (December 1981–January 1982), pp. 6–11.

Jeal, Tim. *The Boy-Man: The Life of Lord Baden-Powell.* New York: William Morrow, 1990.

Johansson, Warren, and William A. Percy. *Outing: Shattering the Conspiracy of Silence.* New York: Haworth, 1994.

"John H. Hammond Jr. Dies; Electronics Inventor Was 76." *New York Times*, 14 February 1965, p. 88.

Johnes, Raymond. *Japanese Art*. London: Spring Books, 1961.

Johnson, Paul. *Intellectuals*. New York: Harper & Row, 1988.

Johnson, Stephen L. *The History of Cardiac Surgery, 1896-1955*. Baltimore: Johns Hopkins, 1970.

Kalman, Laura. "Mr. Civil Rights." *New York Times*, 7 February 1993, sec. 7 (Book Review), p. 14.

Katz, Victor. *A History of Mathematics*. New York: HarperCollins, 1993.

Kaufman, Martin. *Homeopathy in America: The Rise and Fall of a Medical Heresy*. Baltimore: Johns Hopkins, 1971.

Keen, Benjamin, ed. *Latin American Civilization*. Boulder: Westview Press, 1986.

Kiry, Richard, Sidney Withington, Arthur Burr, and Frederick Gridley Kilgour. *Engineering in History*. New York: McGraw-Hill, 1956.

Kisselgoff, Anna. "Martha Graham Dies at 96; A Revolutionary in Dance." *New York Times*, 2 April 1991, p. 1.

Kleinknecht, William. *The New Ethnic Mobs*. New York: The Free Press, 1996.

Kluger, Richard. *Ashes to Ashes*. New York: Alfred A. Knopf, 1996.

Kobler, John. *Ardent Spirits: The Rise and Fall of Prohibition*. New York: G.P. Putnam's Sons, 1973.

Koegler, Horst. *The Concise Oxford Dictionary of Ballet*. London: Oxford, 1977.

Kotz, Samuel, and Norman Johnson, eds. *Encyclopedia of Statistical Sciences*. New York: John Wiley & Sons, 1985.

Krebs, Albin. "John Ford, the Movie Director Who Won 5 Oscars, Dies at 78." *New York Times*, 1 September 1973, p. 1.

Kroc, Ray. *Grinding It Out: The Making of McDonald's*. Chicago: Henry Regnery Company, 1977.

Kronenberger, Louis, ed. *Brief Lives: A Biographical Companion to the Arts*. Boston: Little, Brown, 1965.

Labaton, Stephen. "Thousands Fill Cathedral to Pay Tribute to Marshall." *New York Times*, 29 January 1991, p. 16.

"Langston Hughes, Writer, 65, Dead." *New York Times* 23 May 1967, p. 1.

Lash, Joseph P. *Eleanor and Franklin*. New York: Signet, 1971.

Leavitt, Judith Walzer. *Typhoid Mary: Captive to the Public Health*. Boston: Beacon Press, 1996.

Levy, Reuben. *An Introduction to Persian Literature*. New York: Columbia University Press, 1969.

Li, Dun J. *The Ageless Chinese*. New York: Charles Scribner's Sons, 1965.

Lives in Science: A Scientific American Book. New York: Simon & Schuster, 1957.

Lockie, Dr. Andrew, and Dr. Nicola Geddes. *Homeopathy: The Principles and Practice of Treatment*. London: Dorling Kindersley, 1995.

Lockwood, Luke Vincent. *Colonial Furniture in America: The Illustrated History of a Great Period of Craftsmanship*. New York: Castle, 1951.

Love, John F. *McDonald's: Behind the Arches*. New York: Bantam, 1995.

Lynch, Patrick, and John Viazey. *Guinness's Brewery in the Irish Economy, 1759-1876*. Cambridge: Cambridge University Press, 1960.

Mackey, Sandra. *The Iranians*. New York: Dutton, 1996.

Mann, Charles C., and Mark L. Plummer. *The Aspirin Wars: Money, Medicine, and 100 Years of Rampant Competition*. New York: Alfred A. Knopf, 1991.

Selected Bibliography

Mason, Penelope. *History of Japanese Art.* New York: Harry Abrams, 1993.

McGreal, Ian P., ed. *Great Thinkers of the Western World.* New York: HarperCollins, 1992.

McKenzie, A.E.E. *The Major Achievements of Science.* Cambridge: Cambridge University Press, 1960.

McNamara, Jo Ann Kay. *Sisters in Arms: Catholic Nuns Through Two Millennia.* Cambridge, Mass.: Harvard University Press, 1996.

McNaughton, William, ed. *Chinese Literature.* Rutland, Vt.: Charles E. Tuttle, 1974.

Messadie, Gerald. *Great Inventions Through History.* Edinburgh: Chambers, 1991.

Moquin, Wayne, with Charles Van Doren. *The American Way of Crime: A Documentary History.* New York: Praeger, 1976.

Morgan, Judith, and Neil Morgan. *Dr. Seuss & Mr. Geisel.* New York: Random House, 1995.

Morison, Samuel Eliot. *Admiral of the Ocean Sea.* Boston: Little, Brown, 1946.

———. *The Discovery of America: The Southern Voyages.* New York: Oxford University Press, 1974.

Nast, Thomas. *Thomas Nast's Christmas Drawings.* New York: Dover Publications, 1978.

Okker, Patricia. *Our Sister Editors: Sarah J. Hale and the Tradition of Nineteenth-Century American Women Editors.* Athens: University of Georgia, 1995.

O'Neill, Hugh B. *Companion to Chinese History.* New York: Facts on File, 1987.

Patota, Anne. "A First Day at Harvard." *Stamps,* 20 August 1986, pp. 22-23.

Peppard, Murray B. *Paths Through the Forest: A Biography of the Brothers Grimm.* New York: Holt, Rinehart and Winston, 1971.

Post, Edwin. *Truly Emily Post.* New York: Funk & Wagnalls, 1961.

Raeburn, Michael, and Alan Kendall, eds. *Heritage of Music.* New York: Oxford University Press, 1989.

Raven, Susan, and Alison Weir, *Women of Achievement: Thirty-five Centuries of History.* New York: Harmony, 1981.

Reid, T. R. *The Chip.* New York: Simon & Schuster, 1984.

Reyna, Ferdinando. *A Concise History of Ballet.* New York: Grosset & Dunlap, 1964.

Robertson, James A. *A History of Chile.* New York: Russell & Russell, 1964.

Robinson, Jackie. *I Never Had It Made.* New York: G.P. Putnam's Sons, 1972.

Rowse, A. L. *The Elizabethan Renaissance: The Life of Society.* New York: Charles Scribner's Sons, 1971.

Runciman, Steven. *A History of the Crusades.* London: Cambridge University Press, 1951.

Russell, Bertrand. *A History of Western Philosophy.* New York: Simon & Schuster, 1945.

Russell, Francis. *The Horizon Concise History of Germany.* New York: American Heritage, 1973.

Schwartz, Bernard. *The Roots of Freedom: A Constitutional History of England.* New York: Hill and Wang, 1967.

Shipp, Horace. *The Flemish Masters.* New York: Philosophical Library, 1954.

Shorter, Edward. *A History of Women's Bodies.* New York: Basic Books, 1982.

Smith, Adam. *An Inquiry into the Nature and Causes of the Wealth of Nations.* New York: Random House, 1937.

Smith, Vincent A. *The Oxford History of India.* Oxford: Oxford University Press, 1958.

Steinberg, S. H. *Five Hundred Years of Printing.* New York: Criterion Books, 1959.

Strasberg, Lee. *A Dream of Passion: The Development of the Method.* Boston: Little, Brown and Co., 1987.

Selected Bibliography

Swan, Peter C. *Chinese Painting*. New York: Universe Books, 1958.

Sykes, Percy. *History of Persia*. London: Macmillan, 1921.

Talbott, John H. *A Biographical History of Medicine*. New York: Grune & Strattor, 1970.

Taylor, Henry Osborn. *The Medieval Mind*. Cambridge: Harvard University Press, 1962.

Taylor, Stephen. *Shaka's Children: A History of the Zulu People*. London: HarperCollins, 1994.

Thomsen, Robert. *Bill W.* New York: Harper & Row, 1975.

Townes, Charles. "Harnessing Light." *Science 84* (November 1984), pp. 153–55.

Turner, Roland, and Stevin Goulden. *Great Engineers and Pioneers in Technology*. New York: St. Martin's Press, 1981.

Uglow, Jennifer, ed. *The International Dictionary of Women's Biography*. New York: Continuum, 1982.

Usher, Abbott Payson. *History of Mechanical Inventions*. Cambridge: Harvard University Press, 1954.

Walesa, Lech. *The Struggle and the Triumph: An Autobiography*. New York: Arcade, 1991.

Walker, Paul Robert. *The Italian Renaissance*. New York: Facts on File, 1995.

Watson, Robert. *The Great Psychologists*. Philadelphia: J.B. Lippincott, 1968.

Wechsberg, Joseph. *The Merchant Bankers*. Boston: Little, Brown, 1966.

Weisberger, Bernard A. "Doctor Wiley and His Poison Squad." *American Heritage* (February/March 1996), pp. 14–15.

White, Barbara Ehrlich. *Impressionists Side by Side*. New York: Alfred A. Knopf, 1996.

Whittaker, Edmund. *Schools and Streams of Economic Thought*. Chicago: Rand McNally, 1960.

Zimmerman, Leo M., and Ilza Veith. *Great Ideas in the History of Surgery*. New York: Dover, 1967.

Index

Index

Index

Index

Marie-Antoinette, Queen of France, **781,** 107, 212, 249
Marie de Médicis, 67
Marine Corps, U.S., 278
Marsh, George P., **376;** *Man and Nature,* 113
Marshall, George, **344,** 112
Marshall, John, **287,** 172
Marshall, Thurgood, **348**
Marsilius of Padua, **96;** *Defensor Pacis,* 28
Martí, José, **537**
Martie, Pietro, 36
Martin, Gregory, **909**
Marx, Karl, **14,** 7, 18, 39, 61, 165, 170, 195, 224; *Das Kapital,* 3–4, 6
Marxism, 5–6, 122, 125, 129–30, 224, 283
Mary I, Queen of England, 129, 141, 263
Mary Stuart, Queen of Scots, **610,** 10, 82
Masaccio, **159;** *Life of Saint Peter,* 48
mass production, 16, 125, 279
Mata Hari, **940**
mathematics, 8–9, 26, 34, 44, 45, 79, 100, 109, 147, 187, 214, 251, 258–59, 288, 289–90
Matisse, Henri, **269,** 218; *The Dance,* 80
Matsuo Basho, **218**
Mauchly, John, 23
Maudslay, Henry, **436**
Maugham, W. Somerset, 76
Maurin, Peter, 196
Maximilian I, Holy Roman emperor, **943**
Maxwell, James Clerk, **205,** 136, 248
Mazzini, Giuseppe, **892**
Mead, Margaret, **379,** 223; *Coming of Age in Samoa,* 114
Medici, Cosimo de', **851**
Medici, Giovanni de', 13
Medici, Lorenzo "the Magnificent" de', **228**
medicine and physiology, 17, 27, 33–34, 37–38, 64, 65, 67, 69, 71, 73–74, 75, 85, 86–87, 95, 131, 135, 136, 138–39, 148, 161, 162, 168, 169, 175, 192, 201, 205, 212, 213, 216, 219, 235, 236, 257, 259, 261, 264, 267, 277, 290, 291, 292, 293
Mehmed II the Conqueror, **173**
Meir, Golda, **894**

Meitner, Lise, **336**
Melville, Herman, **716,** 227; *Moby-Dick,* 216
Mendel, Gregor, **104,** 31, 38, 199
Mendeleyev, Dmitry, **253**
Mendelssohn, Felix, 128
Mendoza, Antonio de, **925**
Menelik II, **380**
mental illness, 192, 261
Mercator, Gerardus, **347**
Merici, Angela, **580**
Merton, Thomas, 77
Metternich, Prince, **179,** 86
Mexico, 45, 58, 85, 243, 278–79, 282
Meyer, Julius, 76
Michelangelo Buonarroti, **13,** 39, 48, 67, 69, 84, 97, 100; *David,* 5; *Pietà,* 5; Sistine Chapel, 5, 237–38
microbiology, 33
microscopes, 33
Middle Ages, 10, 23, 48–49, 51–52, 53, 102, 108, 161, 165, 174, 207
Mies van der Rohe, Ludwig, **364,** 279
Mi Fei, **295**
military, 6, 13–14, 18, 27, 35, 39, 45, 52, 54, 67, 68, 73, 82, 83, 94, 98, 100–101, 104, 108–9, 110, 111, 112, 118–19, 123, 126, 128, 140, 148, 153, 154, 155–56, 159, 166, 175, 179, 188, 190, 197, 199, 200, 202, 213, 222, 225, 233, 236, 239, 243, 247, 253, 255, 257, 260, 264, 268, 278, 282, 283, 290, 292–93
military marches, 278
Mill, James, 24
Mill, John Stuart, **81,** 207; "On Liberty," 24
Millardet, Pierre-Marie-Alexis, **643**
Miller, Henry, 269
Millet, Jean, 168
Milton, John, **53;** *Paradise Lost,* 3, 16, 54
mime, 281
Minamoto no Yoritomo, **598**
Ming dynasty, 18, 127–28, 222
Miranda, Francisco de, **588**
Mirandola, Pico della, 59
Mitsubishi, 153
Mitsui Takatoshi, **271,** 153
Mobutu Seso Seke, **734**
Moët & Chandon, 250
Molière, Jean-Baptiste Poquelin, **175;** *The Imaginary Invalid,* 52; *The Misanthrope,* 52; *Tartuffe,* 52

Moltke, Helmuth von, 35
Mondrian, Piet, **797,** 234
Monet, Claude, **196,** 115, 155, 188; *Impression: Sunrise, 1872,* 58
Mongol empire, 14–15, 18, 69, 100–101, 148, 154
Monier, Joseph, **440**
Monnet, Jean, **433**
Monroe, James, **708,** 208
Monroe, Marilyn, **997,** 282
Monroe Doctrine, 213–14
Montagu, John, **473**
Montaigne, Michel de, **432,** 142
Montesquieu, Charles-Louis, **106,** 42, 165; *Spirit of the Laws,* 33
Montessori, Maria, **650**
Monteverdi, Claudio, **231;** *Orfeo,* 70
Montezuma, 46
Moody, Dwight L., **954**
Moore, Henry, **895**
Moore, Marianne, 110
More, Thomas, **345,** 29; *Utopia,* 104
Morgan, John Pierpont, **435,** 121, 289
Morgan, Thomas Hunt, **124,** 31
Morison, Samuel Eliot, 2, 213
Morisot, Berthe, **625;** *Mother and Sister of the Artist,* 188
Mormons, 244–45
morphine, 250
Morris, William, **644;** *The Earthly Paradise,* 194
Morrison, Toni, **774;** *Beloved,* 232; *The Song of Solomon,* 232
Morse, Samuel, **329,** 91, 183
Morse code, 100
Morton, William, **701**
Moscow, 69, 73
Moscow Art Theater, 139
Moses, 40
Moses, Grandma, **664**
Mott, Lucretia, **240**
mountain climbing, 281
Mountbatten, Lord, 175
Mount Everest, 281
Mozart, Wolfgang Amadeus, **52,** 11, 65, 68, 82, 103, 107, 274; *Don Giovanni,* 16
Mughal empire, 27, 45
Murasaki Shikibu, **73;** *The Tale of the Genji,* 22
Museum of Modern Art, New York, 58, 109, 199, 234

Index

Your Chance for Fifteen Minutes of Fame

Okay, so you think we goofed.

Tell us whom we foolishly left out, and why. We may put your suggestion in a future book. If we do, we'll acknowledge your contribution; by signing this form, you'll give up rights to it and allow us to rewrite it as we see fit. We promise to respond promptly to all submissions.

Name of subject: _____ Years of birth/death: _____

In approximately 150 words, tell us why he or she is important. If possible, include an interesting anecdote and a telling quote by the subject, as well as commentary about him or her by somebody else. Use the space below or a separate sheet of paper.

Your name: _____ E-mail address: _____
Address: _____
_____

How would you like to be identified? _____

Telephone number: _____

Signature: _____ Date: _____

Please mail your response to: or e-mail it to:
1,000 Years, 1,000 People   Kabooks@aol.com
c/o Kodansha America   subject: 1,000 Years, 1,000 People
114 Fifth Avenue
New York, New York 10011